FOLLOW THE VULTURE

He Will Lead You to Death

FOLLOW THE VULTURE

He Will Lead You to Death

Stephen Francis Montagna

ARPress
ILLUMINATING IDEAS
EMPOWERING VOICES

ARPress
45 Dan Road Suite 5
Canton MA 02021

Hotline: 1(888) 821-0229
Fax: 1(508) 545-7580

Ordering Information:

Quantity sales. Special discounts are available on quantity purchases by corporations, associations, and others. For details, contact the publisher at the address above.

Printed in the United States of America.

ISBN-13:   Paperback   979-8-89389-251-2
                eBook   979-8-89389-252-9

Library of Congress Control Number: 2024906773

This novel is dictated to the brave young men and women who keep us with a democratic and free nation, thank you.

TABLE OF CONTENTS

PROLOGUE

Captain Robert Walker along with the rest of the elite group of specially trained and cared for troops that made up the soldiers known to the world as the Multinational Rapid Response Forces. Drove the heavy Humvees to the military base Camp Smith, stationed in Peekskill, New York State, as soon as they successfully attacked and killed the group of Afghanistan terrorists who attacked the main control center inside the Indian Point Nuclear Power Plant stationed on the shore of the Hudson River, in the sleepy little upstate town of Buchannan, New York.

The specialized soldiers were operating under the direct orders from their Commanding Officer, Colonel Bruce Leadbetter. Not to allow the hordes of news reporters who showed up at the nuclear power plant complex after their hard-hitting operation was a success against the terrorists that were hell bent on sending the nuclear furnace into a meltdown mode, thus destroying a huge section of New York State and City, to take pictures of his soldiers.

There were nineteen Afghan terrorists who invaded the United States from Afghanistan, armed with orders to attack and destroy the nuclear reactor at the power plant by Usama bin Laden. The cunning and extremely dangerous leader of the al-Qa'eda terrorist organization, wanted to destroy New York City, and to cause great embarrassment to the current President of the United States. The small group of Afghan terrorists successfully invaded the United States, along with the help of a young Saudi Arabian female agent named Laaha al-Jabali. She was being assisted by Captain Kenneth Carmichael, an Iranian operative who helped her get the small group of Afghan fighters safely into the United States.

So, the terrorists could carry out their orders for their leader, and destroy much of New York State with their attack against the nuclear power plant. Captain Carmichael was identified as a sleeper agent installed by Iran by the FBI, quickly after the opening attack on the nuclear-powered plant, and he was waiting to be aimed at his own target, after the Afghan fighters attacked the Indian Point Power Plant. But now he was discovered as a sleeper operative for Iran, he was under arrest and placed in jail in Miami, Florida. Along with Laaha al-Jabali, and they were waiting trial.

The exhausted and terribly bruised and battered young group of specialized American soldiers turned their military Humvees onto the massive Camp Smith military base, and they were directed to park their machines by a pair of barracks well separate from the rest of the usual barracks stationed on the expansive Army military base. Captain Robert Walker jumped out of his Humvee first, and he ordered the rest of the soldiers out of their machines, and with help coming from a Sergeant on loan to him from the Army Base, had his people enter the barrack with orders to shower and rest until the Captain found out what was next on the menu for them. He understood it would not be a long time before Colonel Bruce Leadbetter left the nuclear power plant complex, and made his way to Camp Smith. Once the Marine Colonel was back with his elite group of soldiers, Walker would allow him to take over their control, and tell the troopers what and where they were going next.

While the young Marine Captain was waiting for the rest of the one hundred and fifty five specially trained Special Forces soldiers involved in the latest anti terrorist operation to get out of the military vehicles, the soldiers the closest to Walker quickly gathered around him. Sergeant Dorothy Ramirez, Walker's girlfriend and future wife, as usual was the first one to get over to his side. When she reached him, she gave him a quick kiss and a smile that would have melted butter in the middle of a snowstorm. Then Lieutenant Frank Hall, better known to the rest of the specialized soldiers from the Unit as the Mutt, because he was blessed with a white mother and a black father, was the next soldier who joined Walker and Ramirez. Standing before the main doors of the borrowed barracks they were going to use while they were being held over on the new Army Base.

The Mutt started right off bragging to Captain Walker as he grinned at the military officer. "Hey Homes, we really took it to those last batch of stinking bad ass guys back there, man. I wanted to check on their dead fucking leader, because I bet the ranch he shit himself when we first came charging through the damn observation window like we did, and we attacked him and the rest of those lousy scumbags hold up in that damn control room of the power plant, man. I wanted to check it out, but the stinking FBI Agents wouldn't let me see if the stinking Afghan Colonel did shit his fucking pants when we were putting it to the damn terrorists, man. Then damn FBI pissants have no sense of humor, buddy."

"That's disgusting, what am I saying, you're always disgusting whenever you open your mouth, Mutt." Sergeant Ramirez complained at Walker's lifelong friend, as she shot him a smile that made her whole face shine.

"What the hell are you getting so pissed off at me for little sister? I was only saying it like it was back there girl. Remember, the fucking terrorists are the ones who attacked us, we didn't attack them first, sister. We only responded to what they were trying to do to us, and we came out on top over the situation, girl." The Mutt replied to Ramirez, as he returned her smile with one of his own.

The extremely tired and filthy Captain was about to say something at the Mutt when Buckethead, Sergeant Vincent Lambardo. A tree trunk size of a soldier who received his tag name in the Unit because his head was so large his helmet had to be specially made, and it almost resembled a bucket whenever it was resting on his noggin. No Neck, Sergeant Robert Abbott, an equally large sized massive soldier who received his name in the Unit, because his body was so large it looked like his head rested right on top of his shoulders. Along with the Ghost, Sergeant Walter Casper, who got his tag name with the Unit, because he was like a Ghost whenever he was out in the field hunting the enemy.

The Hunter, Sergeant Frank Whitcomb, who was every bit as dangerous in the field as the Ghost was, and the two soldiers were always picked for point duty. The point was the most dangerous position for any soldier carrying out a military operation, whenever the specialized soldiers were sent on a mission against the enemy of the United States or any of her allies. The four elite soldiers joined up with Walker, the Mutt, and Ramirez, as they then watched the other soldiers from their Unit dragging their asses on the ground while they were entering the barracks for showers and some much needed rest.

The soldiers did what they commonly referred to as banging sticks (Forearms) together as they greeted and congratulated each other on another job well done for the United States and her civilians. The soldiers were settling down when Blind Date, Sergeant Regina Raphael, who was on loan to the Rapid Response Force from France, along with Ice, Sergeant Diane Morrison, who received her Unit tag name, because she was as cold as ice whenever she was on a mission with the rest of the highly trained Unit, joined the other proud young soldiers standing in front of their borrowed barracks.

The Captain acknowledged the two pretty female fighters with a slight nod of his head. But the Mutt started to paw Blind Date's breasts through her shirt. She was his main squeeze since he lost his long time girlfriend, Sergeant Barbara Meyerhoff. When the soldiers were involved in Operation Sandstorm when they had to enter Iran, and they destroyed the nuclear warheads and missiles the Iranian government brought secretly from a rebel Russian Admiral. Ramirez got Walker's attention and once she had it, she shook her head over the way the Mutt was bothering the pretty young French warrior in front of the rest of the other elite soldiers.

He smiled at his lover, and then he tried to ignore what the Mutt was doing to the French warrior, but as hard as he tried not to pay attention to them. The Mutt made it impossible as he offered Walker and pulled one of Blind Date's breasts out of the front of her shirt.

"Hey man will you look at the nipples, pal. They're the kind you can dial a stinking phone with man, they're so large and sticking out, old buddy."

That was all Ice was able to take of this spectacle, and she walked up behind the Mutt and slapped him on the back of his head, as she complained at the ruff and tumble soldier.

"Hey dog man, will you leave that poor girl alone for a few moments and put her breast back in her shirt, stupid. Since when do you display someone who you're supposed to be in love with like this to the rest of the Unit, you asshole you." The angry Ice again slapped the Mutt on the back of his noggin, forcing him to say to her as he glared back hotly at her.

"Hey girl, if you keep swatting me in the bone dome like that, you're labile to scramble my stinking brains on me, baby sister. Whatsumatter with you all of a sudden, you don't like seeing another girl's tits being played with like this, little sister? Here, watch this and see if you like it any betta baby." The Mutt griped as he leaned his head over and he drew Blind Date's nipple in his mouth, and then he started to suck on it while making god awful noises while he was at it.

"Ohhhh baby, you do that so good to me." Blind Date purred back to her lover and soldier.

"Oh give me a break will you please girl. Blind Date, you're no better than the Mutt is lately you know, girl. Don't encourage him, or he'll try to do more to your body than he's doing now, baby girl." Ice snapped hotly at the pretty French fighter and again for the third time, she slapped the Mutt on the back of his head. Showing him she was still angry at him, and she wanted him to stop playing around with his girlfriend like he was doing.

"Owe dammit, there you go again hitting me in the stinking noggin like that, girl! If you keep it up, I'll bite you on the stinking tit, little sister." The Mutt mumbled hotly at Ice, allowing himself to get a little angry at her.

None of the other soldiers noticed the lone Humvee pull up to the barracks, and Colonel Bruce Leadbetter jumped out and he stomped his way over to the soldiers gathered in the front of the building. When the Colonel saw what the Mutt was doing to Blind Date, he growled at him.

"Hey stupid, if you don't leave that fucking woman's tits alone, I'm going to stitch your damn tongue to the end of her nipple. Then she can lead you around with her breast for the rest of the night, mister. Walker, how the hell come you're standing here with that dumb ass look plastered on your lousy puss, and you're allowing this damn sex show to be displayed to the rest of these so-called soldiers here, buster? How the fuck come you're not handling this crap, and how come you don't have the fricking Mutt on a damn leash, before he gets his fool ass in any further trouble, mister? And, how come you don't have these other flaming assholes who we call fucking elite soldiers inside their damn barracks, and have them settling in so they can rest up after this outstanding mission they just completed for their country, mister?

"How come you're still a fucking Captain in my beloved Marine Corps, Mr. Walker? Anyway, yes people, we did really well on this last operation. But we're still soldiers, and we cannot allow one of us to make a damn fool out of himself like the damn Mutt is doing, before the rest of the soldiers stationed on Camp Smith, people. Once we're back on our own base, I don't give a flying rat's fuck what the rest of you slobs do with yourselves and your stinking bodies, mister." The extremely angry Marine Colonel snarled at his second in command.

CHAPTER ONE

When Colonel Leadbetter barked at the soldier branded the Mutt, Lieutenant Frank Hall jumped away from Blind Date's fine firm body. Immediately, Sergeant Regina Raphael slid her breast back in her uniform blouse, and she turned a bright red, because she was caught by her Commanding Officer in a very compromising position. When she was dressed properly again, she glared harshly at the Mutt as she turned her back on him and the Colonel, and then she sort of tried to hide herself behind the broad back of Captain Walker, as he started to speak to the angry acting Marine Colonel.

"Colonel Leadbetter Sir, I'm damn glad you got over here as quickly as you did, sir. I wanted to know what you wanted me to do with the troops, sir. I have most of them hanging around in the barracks doing whatever the hell they wanna do, sir. Except for the few of the troopers you see standing here with me, sir. I ordered them to shower and get in clean uniforms this base has been kind enuf to offer for our use, sir. Sorry Colonel Leadbetter, but they're gonna be Army uniforms, and I know a good many of our troopers aren't gonna like being dressed in any Army fucking puke green uniforms, sir." The Captain reported to his Commanding Officer proudly, ignoring his bitch at what the Mutt was doing to his girlfriend while standing in front of the barracks they were using for the time being.

"You did real well with getting our people out of fucking sight of those damn news reporters running all over that damn nuclear complex, and any one of these swinging dicks or bouncing tits have a problem wearing the Army uniforms, you direct their asses to me, and I'll handle them for you, Captain. Look Walker, we done a helluva outstanding job stopping the damn terrorists from popping off that damn nuclear reactor, sir. Hell man, we even saved eight of the damn hostages while we were at it sir, and the computers informed us we wouldn't be able to save one of them dumb shits, sir. Once we find out what the hell General White wants us to do with our troops then we'll do it plain and simple, sir.

"His last orders were to keep you people out of the lime light with all the damn news reporters flooding the area and the nuclear complex. Walker, some of the stinking reporters even followed me over to this fucking base. They must have saw you people leaving the nuclear complex, and I guess they want to see if there's any story in it with your guys. We have to keep the troops inside the barracks until we see where we end up next."

The confused Captain cocked his head to the side and he looked at his Commanding Officer for a moment then he asked. "Colonel Leadbetter, you said we saved eight of the hostages, sir. I was under the impression we were able to save nine of the assholes in the operation, sir."

"Yeah Walker we did save nine of the dumb shits sir, but one of the dopey bastards up and died on us from the wounds he received when we first stormed the fucking control room, sir. Tough luck for this ass sir, but them are the breaks when you're running a no win mission, sir. Walker, once the troops showered and caught up on their rest, run them over to the mess and get them something to eat. I don't care when that happens, because I'll make preparations to have the mess hall held open for you guys all day and night if need be, sir. It's the least your country can offer to you and your pack of screaming eagles since the successful mission we just pulled off. Hell Walker, we taught them sonofabitches real good not to go messing around with the United States, sir." Colonel Leadbetter bragged as he rested his hand on Walker's shoulder.

The break in the Colonel and Walker's conversation gave the Mutt a chance to speak up, and he asked his Commanding Officer. "Say Colonel Leadbetter, do you have any idea when we might be getting the hell offa this puke ass Army Base, sir? These people give me the jerks, sir."

Colonel Leadbetter took his attention away from Walker and aimed a laser like glare at the Mutt, before snapping angrily at him. "What the hell do you know the damn fool can do something other than play around with a woman's fucking tits? Who would have ever think it's possible. As of this moment I have no fucking idea what we're doing from one minute to the next, mister. I don't know if the Chairman of the Joint Chief of Staff is going to call us down to Washington to pin some more chest salad (Medals) on our asses. Or if General White's going to keep us in the background, and allow the FBI to take the credit for the operation we just pulled off. So, I guess we'll be hanging around this damn base until we find out. I'll tell you this much though dog man, the moment I find out what we're doing, I'll inform Captain Walker and he'll inform the rest of you damn pissants about it, mister."

"Thank a lot sir, I wanna go home and enjoy some living in States, without having to go running all over this country taking out a bunch of puke terrorists who think they can hurt us, sir. This is the second mission we had on our own soil in the past few years, sir. So I wanna start enjoying some of the soil I protected sir." The Mutt grumbled at his Commander, not trying to hide the anger he was feeling about the missions the elite group of specially trained soldiers have been on lately.

The upset Colonel's glare at the Mutt sharpened as he stared in his eyes, and then he warned the extremely dangerous soldier in no uncertain terms. "You better watch how the fuck you're addressing me around here buster, before the terrorists end up the least of your damn problem you have to deal with, dog face. I'm getting sick and tired of this insubordination you keep aiming at my ass without my reacting against it, mister. It's about time you realize you're part of the armed services, and being such you better start respecting your Commanding Officers."

"Who the hell are you trying to intimidate Colonel Leadbetter? We just fucking pulled off an impossible operation against a mess of heavily armed shitball terrorists who could have easily erased New York State right offa the stinking face of the earth, sir. We ran that operation against the norm of military procedures sir, and now you're trying to tell me we're part of the normal armed forces, sir. Good luck with that bitch of yours Colonel Leadbetter Sir." The Mutt fired back at his commander without backing down an inch from him.

The rest of the Special Forces soldiers standing with the Colonel and the Mutt remained silent, because they wanted to see where this conversation was going between the two soldiers. They happened to agree with the Mutt's bitch at the Colonel, because they realized they were part of a special branch of the armed service. If they were going to be called on to do missions no other military branch of the service would be able to accomplish or would even try. They felt the regular regulations and other crap did not really apply to them. The elite soldiers further realized the other branches of the service even refused to acknowledge their Unit's very existence. Because they used extremely brutal and unconventional tactics outlawed by the normal Code of Military Conduct the other services were govern by.

Colonel Leadbetter continued to stare at the Mutt for several more long moments, before he was forced to shake his head, and then he let out his breath in a sigh and reply to the angry soldier. "Christ sake man, you have some set of balls on ya, soldier. Don't go choking on the damn things, mister. I guess you do have a good point there, even though I hate to admit it, Mutt. You show me a soldier who is ready for any mission he's sent out on, and I'll show you a soldier who'll surely fail inspection every fucking time, Lieutenant. Well, I think we have covered this subject well enough for the time being, mister." The wise Colonel decided to drop this part of his conversation with the always pain in the ass Mutt, and get on with what he felt was going to happen to his elite soldiers on Camp Smith.

"As far as I'm lead to believe Captain Walker, we're going to get stuck with hanging around this damn base until the heat from our latest mission dies down enough for us to get the hell out of here. Then we're supposed to be shipped back to Camp Lejeune, and we'll remain on our home base, to make certain none of these damn nosy ass reporters discovered we were part of this fucking mission, sir. Then we're scheduled to be sent on extended furloughs for who knows how long. But you have to keep in the back of your minds at all times that we still have two wars going on, and all furloughs can be rescinded without further explanation to you soldiers.

"And, you people can be ordered to report back to base any time while you're part of the armed services. Arrr… I'm wasting my fucking breath going over what I don't know much about myself, people. All I can tell you people for certain is to hang tight until we see what the damn Brass Pins (Commanders) have in store for us. Once they let us know what the hell's going on, we can react to it properly I guess."

"Man, Colonel Leadbetter Sir, I kinda agree with the stinking Mutt on his latest bitch, sir. We've been playing fucking soldier at Camp Lejeune for almost six months straight, sir. Then we were pulled up here and did our fucking act against another bunch of damn terrorists who invaded our country, and thought they were gonna hurt us again until we put the brakes to them, sir. Then we ended up missing the stinking holidays again sir, and now we find ourselves being held over for who know how the fuck long, until the damn bigwigs in Washington figure out what the frig they're gonna do with our stinking asses, sir. I, and I'm certain every other soldier involved with our Unit, wants to go the fuck home for a while and enjoy ourselves a little for crap sake, sir.

"If not, why the fuck don't the stinking top brass just send our damn asses to either Iraq or Afghanistan, and allow us to work out some of our fucking anger on those people for a change, sir? This last mission ended so quick we didn't even get to enjoy it or see who the hell we were taking out in there, sir. We're soldiers, and we need to be killing enemy combatants, or we should be allowed to go home and enjoy ourselves, until the next time our government has need of us somewhere in the stinking world, Colonel Leadbetter Sir." Captain Walker complained at the military officer as he held him in his angry stare.

The rest of the soldiers grumbled their agreement with Walker's last remarks to the Colonel.

Colonel Leadbetter moved his eyes from one soldier to the next, and in his heart he knew the troopers were correct with Walker's statements. But he also understood he did not have the power to send the troops home on leave. That order had to come from General John

White, the current Chairman of the Joint Chief's of Staff. Again he was forced to shake his head as he replied to the soldiers staring at him angrily, waiting for his reply.

Colonel Leadbetter drew in a breath and turned back to Captain Walker, and informed him in no uncertain terms. "Okay Walker, I have to make contact with General White, and inform him our latest mission was a complete success, and while I'm speaking with him I'll see if I can find out what he wants to do with you people, sir. Wait a minute mister and allow me to finish speaking before you interrupt and jump down my fucking throat, buster. While I'm speaking to the General, I'll see if he'll let you people go home on leave. That's the fucking best I can offer you Walker, and if he says ship you people down to Camp Lejeune, and keep you there until the rest of our troops come home from Iraq. Then that's what you people will do without complaints, period mister. We have to follow our fucking orders to the damn letter whether we like them or not, mister. It fucking comes with our damn oath, sir."

"I hear you Colonel Leadbetter, and I'm fine with it just as long as you breach the subject with the General about us wanting to go home for a while, it's great with me sir." The Captain remarked while wearing a smile.

"Okay Captain Walker now that we covered that bit of crap, get your people in the damn barracks and have them shower and rest, and then the troopers can go to the mess in pairs, if they want to get something to eat, or they can go to the mess as an invading fucking Army as one group for all I care, sir. Just make damn certain they have something to eat before the troops turn in for the night, sir. I'm going to look for an office with a damn phone to work out of, so I can make contact with the General and see what comes out of that fucking conversation, sir.

"If I know him, the General's probably more than likely chewing on the fucking rug in his damn office, waiting to find the outcome of our fucking operation against the damn terrorists who successfully attacked that damn nuclear complex, Captain Walker. Look, I'll be back to you people the moment I'm done speaking to the General, sir. Take care of your damn troops while I'm gone mister, and make damn sure they have something to eat before they turn in for the night, or it's your ass I'll hunt down, mister. I won't allow them to turn in without having something to eat, they need their strength back, mister."

"Will do Colonel." The grinning young Marine Captain replied with a snap in his tone, as he watched the Colonel head off for the nearest building on the base that looked like it had some offices and possible phones in it.

Colonel Leadbetter crossed a wide marching area and headed for a building he noticed a number of other soldiers coming in and out of. He figured this building had to be the base information center, and he knew he would be able to borrow an office and phone there. But before the quick marching Colonel reached the building, an Army jeep pulled up to his side, and a young Army MP jumped out of the jeep before the machine came to a full stop, and the MP sharply saluted the Colonel as he asked the other soldier.

"Excuse me for a moment Colonel Sir, but are you Colonel Bruce Leadbetter, Sir?"

"I am unless you have a summons on you, Sergeant." Colonel Leadbetter offered as he laughed at his own joke. Then he returned the Sergeant's salute with a half hearted one.

The MP Sergeant went on with his words without reacting to the Colonel's lame attempt to be funny. "Colonel Leadbetter Sir, I have an extremely upset Chairman of the Joint Chiefs of Staff on the horn, and he wants to speak with you immediately, sir. I'm operating under direct orders to take you to my office so he can speak to you sir, even if I have to place you under arrest while doing it, sir. Will the Colonel please get in the jeep sir, so I can get you over to my office, sir."

"Sure thing mister, I was searching for a phone to make contact with the General, Sergeant."

"Then I'm pleased I was able to intercept you before you disappeared into another office on me, sir. Then I might have never found you on the base, Colonel Leadbetter. If the Colonel pleases sir, be careful getting in the jeep, Colonel. I don't want anything happening to you sir…" The MP stopped speaking when he saw the angry look the Colonel gave him and he snapped to attention and saluted the upset Colonel, and he held the salute as Colonel Leadbetter snarled him.

"Now you look here sonny, I've been climbing in and out of fucking jeeps while you were still swimming around in your father's nuts, and you weren't even a twinkle in his eye yet, mister. So don't give me any of that watch your damn step lip shit, mister. Get in Sergeant and get me over to this damn office before the General comes up here himself, and he jumps on both of our asses, mister." Colonel Leadbetter growled at the Sergeant as he got in the passenger seat, and then he made the Sergeant get in the rear of the jeep.

When the Sergeant was in the rear of the machine, the MP driver took off and cut across the large grass field the Colonel just crossed, and he drove by a number of troop barracks and then across another but much smaller open field, and the jeep pulled up in front of the Camp Smith Brig and MP headquarters. The Colonel was the first one out of the machine and he waited for the Army Sergeant to get out and lead him to the office where the phone was.

The MP Sergeant caught up to the Marine Colonel and he offered him in a pleasant but commanding tone. "Colonel Leadbetter Sir, if you'll please follow me sir. I have an office set aside you can work out of sir, and you can speak to the General in private, sir."

Colonel Leadbetter followed the Sergeant in the building and when he entered the doors, three soldiers working at desks jumped to their feet and stood at full attention. The Colonel ignored them as he followed the Sergeant to a hallway, and then he barked over his shoulder at the other soldiers. "Carry on your duties people." Releasing the soldiers from their respect of him.

The Sergeant walked past two offices, and opened the door to a third room and stepped aside and allowed the Colonel to enter the room. When he was inside, the Sergeant closed the door and disappeared. Colonel Leadbetter saw the phone on the desk and the blinking light and he picked up the receiver and pressed the button down.

THE PENTAGON, WASHINGTON D.C. TWENTY TWO THIRTY THREE HOURS, JANUARY 29th, 2004

When General John White, the current Chairman of the Joint Chiefs of Staff heard the click on the phone, and he barked into the receiver angrily. "This better be Colonel Leadbetter on the other end of this damn phone, or I'm coming up there and I'll be taking hides when I do, mister."

"Good evening General White Sir, this is Colonel Leadbetter, sir. What can I do for you sir?"

"Fuck you and your damn good evening Colonel Leadbetter! What's so good about the damn evening, mister? It's about time I'm speaking with you, Colonel. How did the operation go up there, sir? Since there hasn't been a nuclear explosion in New York as yet Colonel, I'm taking it your mission was successful, Colonel Leadbetter." The overly excited and powerful General snarled hotly in the phone, and then he stopped speaking and waited for the Colonel's response as he tapped his fingers on his desk.

"Yes Sir General White Sir, it certainly was a successful operation General. My troops were able to drop the terrorists inside the damn control room of the nuclear power plant, sir. Also, General White, we were able to save eight of the hostages while we were at it sir and we stopped the terrorists before they were able to do any further damage to the building or the reactor sir…"

"That's an outstanding and stunning report you just offered me, Colonel Leadbetter. I can't believe we were able to save some of the damn hostages, sir. Hell sir, we saved half of them during the attack I see, sir. That's out fucking standing Colonel, just outstanding work from you and your damn troops, sir. You people done me justice on this one sir. Also Colonel Leadbetter, I was informed by an FBI Agent, Milton Rosborough, you were an active part of the assault team, sir. It seems you didn't make much of a friend out of this FBI Agent though, sir.

"Colonel Leadbetter, I'm not very fond of allowing one of my main Officers to be on the front line with the rest of my grunts in the field, mister. If I would've lost you on this damn operation, I would've lost one of my most important cogs for this Rapid Response Forces, sir. The next time mister, you'll stay out of the line of fire Colonel, or I'll shoot you myself, sir. What's with you and this damn FBI Agent anyhow, Colonel? The damn fool actually wanted me to stand you before a wall and have you shot, Colonel. He was screaming like a banshee at me about you and the hostages and how you were not interested with trying to save them before I was able to cut him off, sir."

"Yes Sir General White, he was a real pain in the ass during this entire situation, sir. The damn Agent kept busting my damn horns about the fucking hostages, and I kept telling him I couldn't be concerned with the hostages' lives while the damn terrorists had control over a nuclear reactor, General White. They and that damn reactor was my main concern, not the hostages, sir. I told the man to go through channels with a complaint he was threatening me with, evidently I see he did so, sir." Colonel Leadbetter replied to his Commanding Officer as he allowed a slight smile more of a sneer to cross his lips.

"That was your main concern during this operation Colonel Leadbetter. The reactor and the damn terrorists, sir. I'm damn glad I brushed him off when he called, Colonel. Err… Bruce, look, I'm going to be forced to get off the phone for a while, and report to the President over this mess and the conclusion of your successful operation, sir. I'm quite certain he's as upset as I was with the lack of information we were receiving from our people out in the field, sir. He's probably eating the rug in his office by now if I know him. I'm going to leave you and when I'm done give him oxygen at the White House with the President, I'll be back to you Colonel." General White offered his soldier as he tried to rush him off the phone.

"Errr… General White if you will for a moment longer, sir." The Colonel mumbled into the phone in a contrite tone of voice.

"Err… what Colonel Leadbetter? I told you I had to get off the damn phone and speak to the President of the United States who is waiting for a report from me." The General used the President's whole title to impress his Colonel, and see if that would force him to allow the General to get off the phone.

"Errr… you used the same phase about the President on me that I used on my troops, when I wanted to get away from them and report to you, sir. Anyway, General White, before I answered your call sir, I was meeting with my soldiers on the Camp Smith Base, sir. They were exhausted and beat up pretty bad sir, and they were jumping on my case about some leave time, sir. They complained they've been stuck on the base at Camp Lejeune for six months straight sir, and they were still pissed off about not being home for the holidays, General White. Now the soldiers were adding to their anger by being forced to wait at Camp Smith until I spoke with you sir, and I found out what you wanted me to do with these troopers, sir. I informed Captain Walker I'd bring up the fact of leave the first chance I got with you, General White Sir.

"I figured this was as good a time as any to breach this subject of leave for my troopers with you, General White Sir. I hope I didn't overstep my bounds on this request, sir." Colonel Leadbetter offered to the powerful and well liked General, and then he held his breath and waited for the General to get on him for bringing up such a minor detail to his attention.

"Well, I must say it was a good reason to delay me, Colonel Leadbetter. And, it was a good question to ask, especially at this time Colonel. But I'm afraid I can't answer that request sir, at least not until I can bring it up to the President's attention Colonel, and see what he wants to do with your soldiers, Colonel Leadbetter. If I had my way about it Colonel, I'd give them the damn leave time they want, and I'd give them the keys to my damn car for the job they just carried out for me, mister.

"But Colonel Leadbetter, I'd surely lock my daughter in her bedroom until this pack of nuts of yours was spread throughout the rest of the United States, and I felt it was safe for her to come out of her room again, Colonel. Arrr… I'll tell you what I'll do for you sir, when I'm meeting with the President, I'll try and bring up your troops and their leave request and see what he wants you to do with them, sir. He'll probably want to bring them down to Washington and stick a bunch of medals on their damn asses if I know him. But that's his decision to make and I'll try and convince him to get the kids out of the area all together, and once all the hubbub about this latest terrorists attack calms down some. Then he can bring the soldiers back to Washington and stick all the fucking medals he wants on their asses. That's the best I can offer you at this point, Colonel Leadbetter Sir. Will this do for you Colonel Sir?"

"That's the best I can ask for General White Sir, and I thank you for the kind words for my troops, sir. I'll make certain they hear what you think of them, sir. It'll do them a lot of good to know they're respected by their Commanding Officer, General White Sir. Every time we train these damn kids, we're dumping on them and making them feel they don't know what the hell they're doing, sir. Every once in a while, it's a great idea to throw them a damn bone, General White Sir." Colonel Leadbetter offered his Commanding Officer as his chest swelled with pride over the General's phrase of his troops.

"That's the fucking reason why I said it sir, even though my words were true as said, Colonel Leadbetter. Your troops did an outstanding job as usual, and it's about time they realize we appreciate everything they're doing for us and the country, Colonel Leadbetter. You give your troops a well done from me sir, and now let me get going before the President sends out his damn dogs on my ass, sir." With that said, General White simply hung up on his officer before he could continue with this conversation he did not want to be involved. He was hard pressed for time by his own Commander in Chief.

Colonel Leadbetter smiled over the way the powerful General ended their conversation, and then he leaned back in the borrow chair and placed his feet on the desk, as he tapped out a Marboro and lit it and inhaled the smoke, and then he blew it out over his head. He was thrilled to death with the latest accomplishment of his specialized soldiers on the last mission they had against another bunch of terrorists.

THE WHITE HOUSE, WASHINGTON D.C., JANURAY 29th, 2004.
TWENTY THREE FIFTEEN HOURS

General John White did not bother calling the President to inform him how the mission to kill the terrorists who invaded the Indian Point Nuclear Power Plant went down for his troops. He decided to go to the White House and report to the President in person. He had no doubt in his mind the President would be up, because he knew his Commander in Chief would not go to sleep until he knew how the troop's action turned out at the power plant. One thing he did do before leaving his office, he placed a call to his close friend, the CIA Director John Raincloud, and informed him he was heading for the White House. The CIA Director informed the General he would meet him at the White House, because he wanted to be involved with the Presidential briefing he was going to give to his boss.

The CIA Director was informed on how the American soldiers' action went at the nuclear power plant, but he was going to allow the General to brief the President on the operation so he could accept the well done for his troops. After all, it was his troops who placed their lives on the front end of the dime, to attack and kill the terrorists before they could cause the reactor to go through the meltdown mode and explode in New York State. So it was only fitting the General briefed the President, so he could take the bows for his elite troops which was justly deserved.

Both General White and the CIA Director reached the White House at the same time, and General White waited for the Director to linkup with him, and they followed the White House aide down the corridor leading to the Oval Office. The aide informed them the President was in the office waiting for their arrival, and he knocked on the door for the two men.

"Yes." Was offered from inside the office from the exhausted sounding American President.

The White House aide opened the door and then he stepped aside and allowed the two powerful men to enter the office. When the General entered the office, he noticed the President's permanent National Security Council members. The President of the United States, Albert Cole, the Vice President, Mary Hirshfield, the Secretary of State, Maria Hernandez, the Secretary of Defense Harold B. Clifford, along with the NSA National Security Advisor William (Billy) Blaylocke, along with a host of other Presidential and Cabinet aides and a number of secretaries and military advisors were already seated in the room, with the Chairman of the Joint Chiefs of Staff, General John White and the CIA Director, John Raincloud filling out the rest of the membership of the special council.

The Chairman took the lead and walked in the office nodding politely to the seated President who in turn nodded back at the powerful military officer. Everyone at the meeting remained silent and seated until the General and CIA Director were likewise seated on the only open seating left in the room, one of the two couches. When the General was comfortable, the President could not wait a moment longer and he snapped hotly at the military officer.

"Well General White, how the hell did it go with your soldiers in New York with the Indian Point Nuclear Reactor nightmare, sir? Evidently it went well for us sir, because I have no reports stating a nuclear explosion happened. So I'm forced to believe the terrorists didn't explode the damn thing sir, and your soldiers were able to talk the terrorists out of the place, sir. Or the terrorists extended the deadline, and the situation is still on going, General. Or you have employed the soldiers General White Sir, and they were able to get inside the control room, and they were able to end this extremely dangerous situation, General White Sir. Which of the three is it General? I can't take this pressure any longer, General."

"With all due respect sir, it's the latter of the three scenarios you just offered that has worked out quite well for us, Mr. President Sir. Our troops have successfully engaged and killed all the terrorists who invaded the Indian Point Nuclear Power Plant complex, sir. Although this is good news Mr. President, it doesn't end there I'm afraid, sir. Our soldiers were not only able to stop the terrorist's actions sir, but they have successfully saved eight of the fifteen hostages held in the room by the damn terrorist's sir…" The General had to stop speaking, because the other members attending the meeting, started to clap over this news, even the President was excited on how the operation went.

When the clapping ended, the General gave the President all the particular of the fast and hard hitting operation his specialized soldiers engaged in. He informed the President what was currently going on at the nuclear reactor complex, and what the New York police department,

State Troopers, and FBI were doing to secure the complex, and turn it over to the security guards who usually guarded the complex against attack.

The General's briefing lasted an hour and a half, and when the President noticed his people were starting to nod off because it was getting late, he decided to call the meeting to an end. With a sudden clap of his hands, the President let everyone know he was done with the meeting in his usual matter. The members stood and they happily congratulated the General on his soldier's mission against the terrorists. Then one by one, the members started to file out of the Oval Office, and soon General White and the CIA Director Raincloud were the only ones remaining with the exhausted President.

The President thought the General wanted a few words with him, so he remained seated as the others quickly left the room. When everyone was gone, the President offered. "General White, I'm pleased you decided to remain for a minute, I wanted to have a few words with you in private, sir. General, the most important thing I wanted to say to you sir was, I can't believe your Special Forces soldiers were able to get at the terrorists and kill them, before they were able to destroy the reactor. That was outstanding work by your…"

General White went to a full attention stance before the President, and then he offered as he dared to interrupt the leader of the United States' words. "With all due respect Mr. President Sir, but it's funny you should bring up my soldiers in this conversation, sir. Because that's why I decided to remain after you concluded the meeting sir…"

"Is that so General White?" President Albert Cole replied while he interrupted the military officer before adding to his words. "Why is that General White Sir? I hope you're not going to tell me some of your soldiers were wounded or maybe even killed in this operation, General. That's the only thing we didn't go over during the meeting with the other members of the council, sir. I also have to apologize to you for not asking you if any of your fine soldiers were wounded in this latest operation, General White Sir."

"I thank you for the concern you're displaying for my soldiers, Mr. President Sir. But no, that's not the reason I brought my troopers up to your attention, Mr. President Sir. But since this subject was brought up by you sir, none of my soldiers were killed in this operation, and only two of them were slightly wounded on the mission, sir. Even Colonel Bruce Leadbetter, the Commanding Officer of these specialized soldiers was involved in this operation, and he was on the front line with the invading troops, Mr. President Sir. I read him the riot act about his placing his life on the line with the rest of his troops, sir. I informed him he was more valuable to these soldiers by remaining behind where he'd be safe, in case the attacking soldiers ran into trouble, and he had to get the backup troops on the move to support the troops in the field, sir." The General stopped speaking to allow the President to reply to this last information.

"General White, I can't believe none of your soldiers were wounded in this extremely operation, sir. That's outstanding work sir, just outstanding sir. I'm pleased you were able to talk me into supporting these elite and highly trained specialized soldiers, sir. That was the best move of my Administration General White, and I owe you all the success of these soldiers and how they made me look in this mess, just outstanding General White Sir." The excited American Leader offered as he smiled the General.

When he stopped smiling, he noticed his General was telling him why he wanted to speak to him about his specialized soldiers, and none of them were seriously wounded in the exchange with the terrorists in New York State. The President sat back in his overstuffed chair, and he made a steeple of his fingers after he rested his elbows on the arms of the chair. He looked at his Chairman of the Joint Chiefs of Staff over the tips of his fingers as he said while keeping the General locked up in his pleasant gaze. "Excuse me General White, but I'm a little confused, sir. If you didn't remain behind at the conclusion of our briefing to inform me none of your soldiers were wounded or killed on this mission. Why the devil did you want to remain and speak to me privately over these soldiers of yours, sir?"

General White shifted his weight on his feet as he tried to formulate his words to the American Leader. After he gathered his thoughts, he replied.

"Mr. President Sir…" The General started to offer, but he was again interrupted by his Commander in Chief, who almost snapped at him in an angry tone of voice as he corrected the well respected General.

"Please General White, with all we have just gone through, and all I own you and these troops of yours, there's no need for us to stand on ridged formalities here, sir. Al with suffice for the rest of this meeting with you General, and that goes for you as well, Director Raincloud Sir."

Both General John White and Director John Raincloud nodded politely in reply to the President's last order, and then the General started to speak to the American Leader again.

"Mr. President, the reason I brought my soldiers up to your attention at this time sir, is for the following reason sir. When I made contact with Colonel Leadbetter, and after he reported on everything that took place at the Indian Point Nuclear Power Plant, sir. He brought up the fact his soldiers had been held on Camp Lejeune for the past six months without any leave time, sir. Then we forced these soldiers to miss the Christmas Holidays home when we got word a band of terrorists were heading for the United States, and we know where they surfaced for their mission against us, sir. Mr. President Sir, my Colonel brought up the fact his soldiers were interested in getting some leave time, sir. I agreed with my Colonel's request for leave for the soldiers. But I also informed him the leave wasn't up to me it was up to you Mr. President Sir." The wise General stopped speaking and he just sort of grinned back at the American Leader.

"Ahhh… I see the madness that's behind your wanting to speak with me after the meeting, General White. I have to admit General, I happen to agree with this requested leave for the troops from your Colonel Leadbetter, sir. I'm sorry and slightly disappointed in myself that I didn't think of granting some leave time for your elite troops, sir. But with all that was happening in New York with that damn power plant sir, I'm quite certain you can understand why I didn't give this very much thought, General White Sir." Now it was the President's turn to give the Chairman of the Joint Chiefs of Staff a sort of half ass smile, as he grinned at his military officer for a moment.

General White smiled and then added. "Mr. Presi… Excuse me Al; we have to discuss what we're going to do about my troops cooling their heels off at Camp Smith, sir. Al, I believe they deserve some time off for the jobs they have been accomplishing for us, sir. But I'll keep the soldiers on a twenty four hour standby alert status while they're on leave, sir. This is so if the wars in Afghanistan or Iraq heats up, I can have these soldiers back on their home base in that short a time sir, and they'll be ready to go wherever we may need them that quickly as well, Al."

"That's great John." The President decided to address the General with his first name as he went on with his words to the officer. "John, I feel we have to allow these soldiers to go home on leave, for the reason you have brought up to my attention, for the jobs they have been doing sir. They saved the United States a number of major disasters over the years, and we have to reward them justly, sir. It was so hard for me to sign the orders keeping them locked up on base for the Christmas Holidays. Errr… Speaking about rewarding them for a job well done sir, I want to pull them down here to Washington so we can pin some medals on them, sir. Heaven knows they earned them General White. How do you feel about that offer before we allow them to go home on an extended leave, sir? I might as well tell you General, I've been doing a helluva lot of thinking about these well trained specialized soldiers of yours, sir.

"The thoughts I've been having about these brave soldiers, General White. I believe I feel they'll serve us with staying here in the States, no matter what's happening in those ongoing two wars, sir. John, we know bin Laden's going to keep trying to attack us at home, sir. Having these soldiers to pit against any terrorists bin Laden decides to send to the States, has been making me sleep a helluva lot better at night I don't mind telling you, sir. It's a good branch of the service we have developed, General. I've also been thinking of branding them with a new label, maybe a Homeland Defense Rapid Response Force, or something along that term, and then cutting orders no future President could overturn keeping these soldiers in the States for our protection, sir." The President decided to take a quick breath, and this allowed his General to get his two cents in the conversation with the American Leader.

"Errr... Al, I believe that's a good idea sir. I like having th4ese soldiers working in the States myself, sir. I too have been toying around with making a new Unit of soldiers up sir, for a defense against any possible terrorist attack here in the United States, sir. Using these specialized troops we have so well trained has entered my mind, but I felt they were also a great asset to employ against any such actions overseas in case one of our allies gets hit. Or in actions such as when we had them invade Iran to locate and destroy their nuclear aims, and when we sent these elite troops to Libya to destroy those twin chemical development plants they constructed in their desert. We know there are many more missions like these few I just mentioned, coming up in the near future against us, Al. Also keeping in mind Iran is again working on developing their own breed of nuclear weapons, and the delivery systems to get them to target, sir.

CHAPTER TWO

"Mr. President, I don't know if it's so wise an idea to keep these tried and tested troops aimed at a sort of National Homeland Defense Unit, sir. So far sir, we have to be able to respond to any such threats overseas like those few cropping up on us at this time, Mr. President Sir." General John White offered to his Commander in Chief this time around confidently, as he flashed a quick smile at him and then he relaxed a little.

The concerned American Leader was paying close attention to everything his military officer was telling him, and he took a few moments to sort through what he heard coming from his military leader. After thinking about it a little further, the President offered his General. "General White, is it possible for us to train these elite soldiers in a sort of Homeland Defense Mode, and yet continue with their specialized training to hit any of these other concerns you're bring to my attention today, sir? Kind of giving the soldier's a double duty so to say, General White Sir. We both know damn well that we need a rapid response force for any overseas operations, but having one also operating here in the United States, I don't mind telling you sits very well with me, General White Sir."

"Anything is possible I'd imagine at this point, Al. But if I'm forced to double dip with these highly trained soldiers then I'm going to be forced to ask you for permission to increase the size of these specialized soldiers, sir. So I can split these Special Forces up for this double duty we're speaking about, Mr. President Sir."

"Jesus Christ Almighty General White, here you go already, asking me to increase the size of these specialized soldiers of yours, sir. I don't mind telling you sir, I'm sinking nearly as much of the taxpayer's money into the special training of these soldiers as I'm allotting to the Home Port Defense budget, sir. How the hell many of these soldiers do you have in this Unit already, sir?" The President snapped at his military office as he held him in his harsh glare.

"Mr. President, we have a total of one hundred and fifty five male and female soldiers in the Multi National Rapid Response Force, and fifteen of the soldiers come from a number of other nations who donated some of their best trained soldiers to the Unit, sir." General White went back to addressing the President with his proper title again, because of the tone the conversation was taking and he wanted to respect him completely.

"A hundred and fifty five soldiers General and you want to increase it to what size? If we try and use these same soldiers on a double front duty, sir?" The President asked his military officer.

"I'd like to increase the size of the force to around two hundred and fifty specialized soldiers if it's at all possible at this time, Mr. President Sir." The Chairman of the Joint Chiefs of Staff offered cautiously to the American Leader this time.

"You want to increase the size of the force by over thirty five percent, General White? At what cost to the taxpayers would this increase cost us, sir?" The President demanded to know.

"I'd say the price increase would be in the vicinity of about another four to five billion dollars of the force per year as it stands at the moment, Mr. President Sir."

"Good God Almighty will you please, General White! You're throwing these numbers around like you're asking your father for your damn allowance for the week, sir. Gees General." The President moaned as he shook his head at the General, and then he took a deep breath and held it as he thought about what his military officer and he was speaking about. When he was done sorting out his thoughts he spoke again.

"General White, we're both exhausted and we're trying to make extremely important decisions that neither one of us are in the proper frame of mind to think about, sir. So I suggest we place this conversation on the back burner for the time being, and we'll revisit this conversation at some future date when we're both rested and we can speak proper over this subject, sir. Since we happen to agree for the need of this Rapid Response Force to exist sir and to be operating overseas and here in the States, at least half the battle is solved already, sir. Besides General White, I believe we have become a little sidetracked here, sir. If I remember right General, we were originally speaking about giving your soldiers some leave time, sir.

"By the way General White, have you noticed the time it's getting to be, sir. It's after four in the morning, and if we don't end this conversation soon, the First Lady is going to come in here and she'll skin us both alive. Quite frankly General White, I'm surprised she hasn't come here to see what the devil we're doing in the office so early, sir. She's been keeping a close eye on me with my damn cigars lately, sir." The President offered with a pleasant smile.

"I hear you Al, she's been checking me out I have to inform you sir, and twice since you tried to stop smoking the damn things, she warned me against allowing you to smoke a cigar with me in the office, sir. I believed she used the phase of threatening to shoot me, if I allow you to smoke another cigar with me, Mr. President Sir." General White offered to the American Leader as he slightly nodded at him.

"Yes General White, and I believe she has also warned Director Raincloud as well if I'm not mistaken, sir." The President offered as he turned his eyes on the forgotten man sitting in on their meeting, and he smiled at the Director and then nodded to the man.

CIA Director John Raincloud smiled back at the President politely as he replied. "You're right Mr. President Sir, she also warned me about allowing you to smoke your cigars sir, and she further warned me in much the same way she warned the General, Mr. President Sir. She warned me she was thinking about searching anyone coming into your office, sir. A word to the wise and the cautious Mr. President, I don't think she was speaking with a forked tongue, and she's labile to start searching everyone coming into your office at that, sir."

"Yes Director Raincloud, I believe you have a good point and warning there, sir. So we're going to have to be a helluva lot more careful where we enjoy one of my cigars together, gentlemen." The

President felt better after bringing the Director into the conversation, because he was feeling bad he was only speaking with the General, and he was ignoring the Director while they were speaking. "I believe we were speaking about sending your troops home for some leave time sir, and I was thinking about bringing them here to Washington, to honor them before allowing them to go home for a while sir."

"Yes sir, we certainly were Mr. President, but bringing the soldier here to Washington to honor them is completely out of the question at this time sir." The General offered and he was immediately cut off by the President as he asked him with some concern in his tone.

"What is that General White Sir? Knowing you and how you care about these specialized soldiers of yours, sir, I'd think you'd be jumping all over bringing them to here Washington to honor these brave young kids of ours, sir. I don't understand your logic in not wanting to bring the troops here so we can introduce them to the press and allow the United States, and the rest of the world know what these kids have accomplished for their country, sir.

"It'd sure help me quite well with the press at the same time, after the way the horde of reporters have been constantly dogging my can in their damn papers every chance they get to jump on me or my Administration, sir. Saying I'm not doing enough to protect the citizens of our country from further terrorist attack like the Nine, One, One, attack they hit us with, General White. I feel we should allow the civilians know how close another band of damn terrorists have come to nearly destroying all of New York, sir. It'll be a way for me to shut some of my critics up for a damn change, General White Sir." The President stopped speaking, and he held his military officer in his gaze.

"I understand where you're coming from Al, and I agree with you this successful action would take a lot of the heat off your shoulders, if we were to announce our diligence to the latest terrorist attack had been foiled, sir. But Mr. President, on the other hand there are a few reasons I wouldn't care to bring these soldiers into the limelight, sir." General White offered to the President and smiled. Knowing it was getting real late now, and he was hoping the President would let it go at that, and not force him to get involved in a long winded explanation, as to why he did not want to bring his elite troops before the news reporters.

The President cocked his head to the side and he kind of stared back at his military officer for a few moments. Then he drew in his breath and asked the General.

"Christ sake John, I could sure use a little help with the damn news reporters, along with the Democratic side of the Isle of Congress, and your soldiers could provide that help I desperately need, sir. I'm at a total loss as to why you won't allow me to use them, if the soldiers could make me look good for a change in the papers, sir? Do you mind explaining this reluctance on your part to help me out here, General White Sir?"

"Very well Mr. President, I'll inform you as to why I don't want my soldiers marched out before the damn press, sir." The General offered in a pleasant tone, while respecting the American Leader by addressing him. "Mr. President Sir, the first and foremost reason why I don't want any of my specialized troops to meet the press sir, is because I want to keep their identities a secret for as long as possible, sir. Al, as long as my troops are working while hiding their identity from the rest of the world, they'll be able to complete any mission we send them out on, sir. We're aware many of our enemy are constantly monitoring our news broadcasts sir, and if we go and march these elite soldiers before the world. Our enemy will create a file on these soldiers, and then they'll keep their eyes glued on them and possibly take them out here in the States, much like the Iraqi Colonel killed a number of my people a few months ago, sir.

"Furthermore Mr. President Sir, if any of my specialized troops are known to our damn enemy. We'd be forced to send these same soldiers in their country, our enemy would immediately know they're there and they'll hunt them down and kill them, even before our soldiers try and start any mission we sent them out on against a possible hostile nation, Mr. President Sir.

"Also Mr. President, another reason for my not wanting my elite soldiers to be known to the public sir, is because if we have another need of them here in the United States. When any reporters who are constantly monitoring our military bases in search of a damn story. Notice we're moving some of these highly trained soldiers around, they'll begin to follow them to the ends of the earth for a damn story, sir. Thus compromising the operation and hindering these specialized troops from doing what they were trained for, stopping another possible terrorist attack aimed against us here in the States, sir.

"Mr. President, we moved these soldiers off the Indian Point Nuclear Power Plant property under the QT for the same exact reasons I just explained to you, sir. And, we have allowed the FBI Agents to take all the bows for the successful action where we stopped a devastating terrorist attack against our country, sir. So if we were to countermand the subterfuge we played out against the damn reporters over this latest incident sir, and we now try to convince them our soldiers were the ones who stopped this latest terrorist attack. Knowing the damn reporters and how they hate all Republicans, sir. They'd immediately adopt the idea you were trying to add something to the credit of your Administration, by stopping a terrorist attack and trying to now make them believe our soldiers were the ones who stopped it. After it was announced the FBI Agents were the ones who ran the successful operation against the terrorist cell, sir.

"Besides Mr. President, it's normal operating procedures for the FBI to handle any and all possible terrorist attacks within the borders of the United States, sir. So this was one of the other reasons I decided in advance to allow the FBI to take the damn credit for stopping the latest terrorist attack to help avoid problems with that office, sir."

"Well General White, I must say you made a good argument for keeping your soldiers out of the limelight sir, and I'm forced to agree with you on that decision I see, sir. But I do find myself being forced to ask you another question though, sir. General White Sir, how do your soldiers feel about giving the credit for their successful operation to the FBI, sir? I know if I was one of them kids and I just accomplished what they did, I'd sure as hell want to tell the entire world what we accomplished, General." The President remarked as he stared at his military officer while waiting for his reply.

"My soldiers don't care a lick for any personal gains or medals and recognition, for doing what they were trained to do, Mr. President.

Even though I know they'd surely like the pat on the back from every civilian in the United States once in a while, sir. They'll do whatever the hell I order them without complaints, sir. Besides sir, my soldiers believe a pat on the back is only twelve inches away from a kick in the ass, sir. We train these kids to believe this so they're never disappointed, sir. They understand if their faces ended up on a news broadcast, they'd immediately be dropped from the elite Unit they're serving. That's another reason they aren't looking for any personal recognition for following their orders, sir." General White finished replying to the President's last question of him and smiled.

"Arrrr… General White, I don't know what to think about these troops of yours, sir." The President bitched as he waved his hand before his face, showing the military officer he was going to allow him to handle his troops in any fashion he saw fit. And, he will use the FBI as his vehicle to make him look good to the public, as the American Leader asked his soldier while continuing to stare him square in the eyes.

"John, where were we when we kind of got a little sidetracked, and we left the subject we were originally discussing, before talking about the FBI, sir? I lost where we were in this conversation General White." The President moaned as he shot his military officer a quick smile again.

"Mr. President, we were discussing the possibility of some leave time for my soldiers, sir." The General replied, and then nodded at the man.

"Yes, quite right General White. Well John, I don't have a problem with sending the troops home for a vacation, sir. Heaven knows the soldiers earned it, General. Where are your troops stationed at this moment, sir? I know you already mentioned the military base you moved the soldiers to, but quite frankly sir I forgotten it General."

"Mr. President, I have my troops cooling their heels off at Camp Smith sir, which is a military base about seven miles south from the Indian Point Nuclear Power Plant facility, sir. I was planning to keep the soldiers stationed there until I can make further arrangement to have the troops transported back to their main base at Camp Lejeune in Jacksonville, North Carolina under the cover of night, sir. Once I'm able to get the troops back to their main base, I figure I'll release them on leave from that point, sir. As I mentioned Mr. President, the troops will be allowed to go on leave, but they'll be under strict orders of a twenty four hour standby and call back situation, sir. That means that's the amount of time needed to have the troopers ordered back to their main base, in case another possible terrorist attack was inevitable, or these specialized troops were needed somewhere else on the face of the earth, Mr. President Sir.

"Furthermore Mr. President, I'm planning to maintain the troops stationed on the Camp Smith complex for a few weeks, to allow all the damn hubbub of this latest terrorist attack to die down a little, sir. Then I'll start moving the troops down to Camp Lejeune to release them on leave, sir. Since you already agreed over the need for these troopers to be sent home on leave, Mr. President Sir, I want to start them for home the first moment I feel it'll be alright to get the soldiers moving out of the base, sir."

The American Leader drew in a deep breath, and then let it out slowly. He was trying to force his mind to continue working. He wanted nothing more then to place his head down on his pillow and sleeping for a week. The news his soldiers stopped the terrorist attack on the nuclear power plant drained him of all his strength. He lifted his burning eyes and stared at his General for a few moments, while thinking of what he was going to say to him as he offered.

"General White, I believe I'm going to leave what you intend to do with these troops in your hands, sir. Whatever you want to do with or for them has my stamp of approval on it, sir. I don't know how else to honor them for what they have accomplished on this operation, sir. As you stated sir, when possible, start these soldiers for home sir. But before you let them go, make certain you give them a well done from me personally, sir. General, I can make a call to the base and thank them for myself if you feel this might help, sir?"

"Mr. President, I don't believe that'll be necessary, sir. No offense but I believe my soldiers would be much more interested in knowing when they were going home on leave, rather than speaking with you sir. As you ordered sir, I'll handle the troops, and once this attack is forgotten. If you'd want, we can have these soldiers come up to

Washington and you can do anything you want for them, sir. I don't want to have them hanging around New York State for too long a time, sir. I believe the longer they're up there sir, the better possibility of some nosy ass reporter locating them, and putting two and two together, and then we find ourselves in one helluva shit storm with trying to explain why these specialized soldiers were suddenly stationed in New York in the first place, Mr. President Sir." General White offered the concerned President, as he tried to stifle a yawn, because he too was thoroughly exhausted and in need of sleep.

"Yes General White, get it done, because I'm all done in and I'm going to bed, sir." With that said the exhausted President stood and he walked out of the Oval Office, leaving the aide to handle the General now.

CAMP SMITH MILITARY BASE, NEW YORK. JANUARY 30th, 2004. ZERO SIX HUNDRED HOURS EST

General John White returned to his office at the Pentagon from his latest meeting with the President, and he immediately placed a call to Colonel Bruce Leadbetter, the Commander of the Marine Base. Before he placed the call, he took a few moments stopping by the lunchroom and getting a cup of strong coffee and a cheese Danish. Even thought he did not sleep a wink last night, he wanted to allow the Marine Colonel to get as much sleep as possible, before he disturbed him. He sat at his desk and sipped his coffee, it felt so good going down and he took another swallow. He put his Danish on the desk and looked up the contact number for Camp Smith, and once he had it he dialed the number. As the phone rang, he took another sip of his coffee, but he almost chocked on it when the phone was answered for him so quickly.

"Yes sir, this is Sergeant William Johnson sir, and I'm the desk Sergeant stationed at Camp Smith for the day duty, sir. Who is this and how may I direct your call for you, sir?" The young Army Sergeant had no idea it was the very powerful and well respected Chairman of the Joint Chiefs of Staff on the other end of the line.

"Yes Sergeant, this is General John White, and I'm requesting to speak to Colonel Bruce Leadbetter, who is sharing the comforts of your Base at the moment, mister. Is it possible for you to transfer my call to this Marine Colonel? I'm certain you know who I'm speaking about Sergeant. And, I'm as certain he and the soldiers with him are being treated well, and there's to be no acknowledgement of these soldiers ever being stationed on that base, mister." The General growled at the Sergeant to get him moving on his request to speak to the Colonel.

"Good morning General White Sir, it's a pleasure to be speaking with you sir. Yes Sir General White, I know this Colonel and I'll transfer your call over to his barracks at once for you sir. Also General White Sir, everyone stationed on Base has been already briefed about these invisible soldiers, and the word is, what soldiers, sir? General White Sir, your soldiers are being treated like visiting Officers to the Base sir, well sir. Sir, hold the line while I transfer your call to the Colonel's barracks for you, General." The Sergeant nearly barked in the phone as he went to an attention.

The powerful Army General smiled, because he knew this Sergeant nearly had the shit scared out of him over the fact he was speaking to the Chairman on the horn. He took this time to take a quick bit from his Danish, and then wash it down with another sip of coffee, while he continued to wait for the Colonel to answer his call.

In no time, the Colonel's voice came in over the phone and the General had to swallow his coffee before he replied to his officer. "Ahh Colonel Leadbetter, excuse me for a second will you sir. Yes Colonel, I'm sorry for waking you this morning, sir. I'm quite certain you're still exhausted from the operation yesterday, sir. I wanted to inform you I just finished meeting with the President, sir." General White wanted to inform the Colonel he did not sleep last night.

"Colonel Leadbetter, it's been decided to allow your specialized troops including yourself, to head home on an extended leave the first moment it's possible for you to start the soldiers on their way home, sir. Colonel Leadbetter, you'll place your soldiers on a twenty four hour stand by call back to Base order, before you allow the asses to head home, sir. We have to keep the troops on the full alert status, just in case there's another situation like the one they have just conducted successfully, sir." General White was speaking in a sort of a code to the Colonel, because he was aware he was not on a secured line, and he did not know if any news reporters were able to listen in on their communications.

"Colonel Leadbetter, I trust you do understand the reason for this order being issued to you, and also the need to keep certain people from discovering this troop movement, sir."

"Yes Sir General White, I read my orders loud and clear sir." Colonel Leadbetter replied to his commanding officer, knowing the reason for the coded call.

"Very well then Colonel, now we understand each other, sir. I want your troops to continue with their temporary training of the Army soldiers on Camp Smith for another week, sir." General White knew he was lying to the Colonel, but he knew what he was telling him. "And, once they finished with this special training program, sir. You're to then ship your troops down to Camp Lejeune and keep them there for another week, and then you may release them on leave as you will, sir. The leave will remain in effect for the next twelve months sir, unless we have special need for these troops on a call back order situation, Colonel. At the end of the year leave, we'll pull the pain in the asses in for some quick refresher training programs, to keep them operating at their peak of their operating perfection, sir.

"This new training will last for one month's time sir, and if things are still without trouble in the world, we'll release the soldiers on another leave for thirty days at a time. In this way the soldiers will be forced to maintain constant communication with their command post while they're on leave, sir. These soldiers are exhausted and they need their down time, starting today sir. Feed them then rest them and keep them down until the end of the week. Then you're ordered to ship them to their home base, sir. Are you reading your orders as issued, Colonel Leadbetter?" General White snorted at his officer because he was getting even more tired as he continued to speak to the Colonel on the phone, and he wanted to cut the conversation short with the Colonel, finish off his coffee and Danish, and then head home to catch up on his sleep now.

"I read you loud and clear General White Sir, so don't worry about our soldiers, sir. I'll take care of them and have them home in two week's time as ordered, sir. I hear in your voice you sound exhausted General, and you informed me you were with the President all night, sir. So why don't you head on home and sleep and I'll carry out your orders as received, General." Colonel Leadbetter offered to his Commanding Officer, because he like the exhausted General and he also wanted to end this conversation, so he could get at his troops and inform them they're going home on leave.

"You can say that again Colonel Leadbetter. Last night had to be one of the longest nights I ever spent in my entire life, sir. All I kept seeing in my mind's eye was New York City going up in a nuclear cloud, and the bodies piling up, sir. I thank God for those Screaming Eagles of ours, Colonel. Oh, by the way Colonel Leadbetter, the President wants you to give the troops a well done for him, sir. Give the troops a well done for me as well sir. Errr… Colonel, I believe I'm going to take your advice and finish off my coffee, and then I'm heading home to rest for the day. You have my private cell phone number, Colonel. Use it if you dare sir. If you wake me, you might find yourself counting Polar bears at the North Pole if you catch my drift, Colonel." General White warned his military office with a slight laugh.

"You got it General White I assure you I won't bother you unless it's a national emergency, sir." Colonel Leadbetter replied to his Commanding Officer with the same smirk in his tone.

"I'm glad you understand me sir. I'll speak to you tomorrow morning if I'm still alive sir. Sorry I woke you this morning Colonel, but I wanted to speak to you before I left my office for the rest of the day, Colonel Leadbetter. If you have to speak to me call, especially if it has anything to do with that damn attack on the nuclear reactor complex. I'll speak to you later Colonel." The General mumbled exhaustedly to the Colonel as he broke off the connection.

Colonel Leadbetter did not reply because he knew the General was trying to cut off their conversation so he could go home and rest. When he was off the phone, he leaned back in the chair, and placed his feet on top of the desk as he lit up a Marlboro cigarette, and then inhaled the smoke deep into his lungs. He smiled as he read the sign written on the edge of the borrow desk, 'thank you for not smoking'. The Colonel flipped his ashes on the floor as a response to the sign, and then he continued enjoying the smoke in the office as he waited for his day to begin.

The Sergeant, who brought the Colonel to the office was sort of standing guard duty outside and he smelt the smoke from the cigarette and he smiled as he shook his head. But the smile left his lips when a Lieutenant came rushing down the hallway when he smelt the smoke, and he stopped in front of the Sergeant and barked.

"Sergeant Johnson, is someone smoking inside that room, mister? And if so, why haven't you placed the offender under arrest, mister. Get in there and drag his ass out by his heels, Sergeant!"

"No disrespect intended Lieutenant, but no way in hell am I going to place a full bird Colonel under arrest for smoking, sir. Especially after what the Rug Rank (military slang for any officer high enough in rank to have a rug in his office) and his specialized soldiers done at the nuclear plant mess, Lieutenant." The Sergeant fired back at the Lieutenant as he released his salute because he had his cap on.

"You mean that Special Forces Colonel is inside that room mister, and he's the one smoking in there, Sergeant Johnson?" The Lieutenant asked his three stripers (Sergeant) as he backed down from his angry stance and orders to the Sergeant.

"Damn right it's that Colonel, Lieutenant. So if you want to bust the man for smoking, I suggest you do it yourself sir. There's no way in hell I'm going to do it for you, Lieutenant."

"No thank you mister, I'm not going in there and try to dump on a full bird myself, mister. You continue to stand guard duty on this office, Sergeant. I'll stop anyone from coming down this hallway and bitching about the smoke. I'm getting out of here before that damn Colonel comes out of there looking to cook someone's balls for bothering him." The Lieutenant offered as he backed away from the door to the office, and then he turned on his heels and took off with the Sergeant calling after him.

"You chicken shit you, Lieutenant Sir." The Sergeant said with a laugh to the Lieutenant.

"Damn right I am when it comes to a Colonel on base, Sergeant." The Lieutenant retorted as he laughed himself, and then he turned the corner of the hallway in a rush.

Colonel Leadbetter heard the conversation between the Lieutenant and his Sergeant and smiled, knowing no one was going to bust his horns for smoking in the building. He finished off his smoke then looked at his watch, it was Zero Seven Ten Hundred hours and he could not believe he spoken to the General for an hour. He field stripped the cigarette and stuffed the filter in his pocket, and then he kicked the ashes around on the floor until it was hard to see them, and he went for the door. When he grabbed the doorknob and started to turn it, the Sergeant stationed outside went to attention in the hallway and waited for the Colonel to appear.

When he opened the door, he came face to face with Sergeant Johnson, and he smiled at the three striper as he offered him. "Hey Sarge, I hope I didn't get you in too much fucking trouble with the damn hot shot Lieutenant, mister? I heard him busting your horns, mister."

The Sergeant saluted the Colonel because he was in his full uniform and replied. "No way Colonel Leadbetter Sir, he's a cool dude, but your smoke got to him sir. He's probably half way across the base by now, Colonel. I trust everything when well with your call from General White, Colonel? It's not everyday we get a call to the base from the Chairman of the joint Chief of Staff himself, Colonel Leadbetter Sir."

"I guess so Sergeant it looks like it is going to be one helluva fucking day today, cold as a witch's tit but sunny, mister."

"I heard does the Colonel want me to take him back to the soldier's barracks, sir?"

"Naw, I think I'm going to allow the soldiers to sleep until they wake up on their own accord today, Sarge. They had one bad ass day yesterday, and they fucking deserve the extra sleep. I believe I'd like to head to your mess and get myself something to eat, and then I'm going to turn in for the day myself, Sergeant. I didn't have the heart to inform the General I didn't sleep last night either, son. But it didn't affect me the same way it did him. I'm a helluva lot younger than he is, and in better shape, Sergeant. Have you eaten yet this morning, Sarge?"

"Not yet Colonel Leadbetter Sir. I was putting it off until you were where you were heading on this morning, Colonel Leadbetter Sir." The Sergeant replied pleasantly to the officer.

"Fine, then allow me to buy you breakfast, Sergeant." Colonel Leadbetter offered as he slapped the Sergeant on his back, and he allowed the strip to lead him to the mess.

The two soldiers ate with the Sergeant asking the Colonel a flood of questions about the action against the terrorists at the power plant, and when they finished. Colonel Leadbetter allowed the Sergeant to bring him to the Officer's Bachelor Barracks so he could catch up on his sleep.

CAMP SMITH, UPSTATE NEW YORK, THE BACHELOR'S BARRACKS JANURAY 31st, 2004. ZERO SEVEN HUNDRED HOURS

Colonel Leadbetter slept until seven a.m. the following morning, and when he stirred he was shocked at the time. He jumped out of bed, dressed, and went hunting his soldiers down. He headed to what the Army soldiers branded as the beast barracks, and he found a few of his elite troopers in the barracks. He asked one of the soldiers where Captain Walker was, and the soldier reported he was at the mess hall. He left the barracks and went to the mess, entering it he spotted his soldiers in the back of the mess eating. He headed to them.

The Mutt, Lieutenant Frank Hall was on the alert and noticed the Colonel enter, and brought him up to Walker's attention. "Hey Homes, whatisface is here, and looks like he hunting us."

"So what's the big fucking deal about the stinking Colonel coming over to talk with us, dog man? It's about friggin time he showed up. I didn't see hide nor hair of the lousy prick all day yesterday, and I was wondering if he was still hanging around on this Army puke base, man. Anyway dog man, after what we pulled off two days ago, our shit don't stink around here anymore, man. Sit back and relax and let's see what the hell the stinking Colonel has on his damn mind, man. Maybe he found out when the frig we're getting offa this lousy puke Army base, buddy." Captain Robert Walker snapped at his lifelong friend, and then he watched as the Colonel headed for his table.

The young Captain kept a close eye on him until the Colonel ended up standing by his table, and he looked down at Wacko, Sergeant Salvatore Tomassi. Who immediately stood up and he took off for another table in the mess hall with his food tray, giving the angry looking Colonel his seat next to Captain Walker.

He sat down and he breathed out, and then he looked at Walker, and the Captain asked him. "Say Colonel, are you gonna get yourself something to eat today, sir?"

"Yeah, but first we have to talk some, mister. My first question to you is, how the fuck are the troops doing, Captain? Did they get enough rest, did they eat and is everything going well with them, mister? No problems and their minor wounds are being looked after by the Army Medics, Captain? I don't want anyone hurt waiting until we get back to our home base before looking after their damn injuries, mister. I know how our people are, and they don't like reporting to any other Doctor for medical treatment but our own medical staff, sir. If they don't want to see one of the Army Doctors then let Blood Clot (Sergeant Richard Burmbach) pull the duty and look after their wounds until we get back to Lejeune, Walker." Colonel Leadbetter informed his officer as he held him in his gaze.

"Colonel Leadbetter, any soldiers wounded during the last mission are being well looked after, sir. I have two soldiers slightly wounded, one of them was hit in the hand and he..."

"Don't tell me Walker, it has to be that missing link No Neck who got hit in the hand."

"How the hell didja know Neck was wounded in the operation, Colonel Leadbetter Sir?"

"That one is always getting wounded on any mission we go out on Walker. For Christ sake mister, when the hell are you going to start training that one to get out of the way of a damn incoming round, mister? Neck is dumber than a bail of fucking hair Walker, and it's up to you to start taking him under your damn wing, and showing him how the hell to dodge rounds fired at his damn ass, Captain." Colonel Leadbetter complained at the Captain as he cast a lazar like glare at the massive soldier who was wounded in the operation.

When the Neck saw the Colonel glaring at him, he put his head down and stared eating again. The Colonel noticed his bandaged hand and he shook his head at him.

"Not for nuthin Colonel Leadbetter, but the man's so fricking large he's an easy fucking target for any enemy to take some pot shots at, sir. That's why he's always getting tagged sir."

"If that's a fact Captain Walker then I want you to carve a hundred pounds off the dumb sod. Maybe if he was smaller, he wouldn't be such an easy target to hit, sir. Look at the flaming asshole sitting there he can't even fit in one chair, mister. Do something with him Walker."

"Colonel Leadbetter, he's all muscle, where the hell can I carve any weight or size from his lard ass, sir?" Walker complained at his Commanding Officer with a sort of smirk on his lips.

"Cut his damn head off, that should remove at least a hundred pounds of dumb from the fool, mister." The Colonel fired back at Walker as he returned his smirk with one of his own.

"Look Colonel, I'm certain you didn't sit by me to dump on one of my soldiers, sir. What's on your mind Colonel? Do you have any idea when we're getting the hell offa this stinking dump and back to our own base, sir? I have a mess of my people busting my horn because they wanna go home and cop some serious down time, sir." Captain Walker bitched at the Colonel.

"I'm making certain our troops are being taken care of properly, Walker. Yes Captain, I had a long and rather fruitful conversation with General White yesterday, sir. But I decided to take the rest of the fricking day off to catch up on some of my fucking sleep, Walker. And, I gave you people the rest of yesterday off for you people to lick your damn wounds, or anything else you people might want to lick around here, mister. General White has informed me you people will be remaining on this base until next Thursday, that's March 4th, on

Thursday at Zero, Seven, Thirty Hundred Hours, you people will leave for Camp Lejeune, sir. Walker, you'll remain stuck on home base for a week, to make certain no fricking reporters discovered our part in this damn operation, sir. Once this week passes, your entire force will be sent home for what the General has referred to as a year long leave and down time, sir.

"There are a number of other parts to his order I have to inform you about, mister. Your fucking troops will be placed on a twenty four hour alert and stand by status all the time while your troops are on leave, and after the year you'll go on ready alert. Where you and your pack of misfits will be ordered every once in a while, back to base for refresher training courses to keep you people sharp as ever. Arrr… this is all bullshit and bad manners, Captain. Who the fuck knows what the hell the damn future will hold for us, sir. You keep in mind your people will be home within the next two weeks at the latest, and that's that Captain Walker."

"That's fantastic Colonel Leadbetter Sir, Raz and me are looking forward to getting home and being with our son for a little while for a change, sir. Hell Colonel, Robert Jr. is heading for five years old, and we rarely been with him lately, sir. With all the stinking missions we've been sent out on lately, we're afraid he's not gonna even know us when we get the fuck home and spend some quality time with him again, Colonel. Besides sir, Raz is starting to hint around she wants another stinking kid, and she's also been thinking about dropping out of the Unit, sir. We're starting to get up there in age sir, and we're not as young as we once were, and she's been really thinking of even moving out of the Florida Keys. She told me she might want to move up to Clearwater in Florida, or maybe even so far up as North Carolina for a change of pace, because we're spending so much stinking time in that damn state because we're on base so muc…"

"That's bullshit and bad manners Walker. What the fuck are you two assholes talking about, mister? How can you and Raz even think of dumping out of the damn Unit, mister? These soldiers are your brothers and sisters, your blood, your damn family. These people are your friends, your birthright. What the hell will you two do without these damn wingnuts hanging around you all the time, mister? You both know as well as I and the rest of these Screaming Eagles, the only way out of the fucking Unit, is when you're old enough to pump rust instead of iron. Or you're carried out either feet or tits up, mister. So stop trying to give me a damn snow job here, buster. I'm sorry to hear you might leave the Keys though Captain, I always wanted to get down there myself and try some of the outstanding fishing there, mister.

"But moving to North Carolina might not be so bad an idea either, Captain. If you're concerned with being with your kid more then it might be wise on your part to move to that state, and settle down there for a change, mister. Dammit, you know Walker, there's not enough aspirin in the damn world for the fucking headache you give me all the damn time, mister." Colonel Leadbetter complained as he rubbed his temples for a moment, and then he let out his breath as he looked from Walker and glanced at Sergeant Dorothy Ramirez.

CHAPTER THREE

"Colonel Leadbetter, Walker is only telling you what I've been saying to him for the past few years now, sir. I'm really tired of running all over the world and stopping some nuts from destroying another country or wanting to take over the world, or slaughtering their innocent civilians for sport, sir. I want to settle down and raise a family of my own with the man I love, sir. Like Robert just said to you sir, we're starting to get older, and soon I won't be able to have any more kids. So I want another child before my biological clock runs out of time on me, Colonel Leadbetter." Sergeant Ramirez complained at her Commanding Officer as she placed a look on her face that showed him, she was not fooling around, or she was not going to be talked out of what she wanted to do so easily.

But even before Colonel Leadbetter was able to reply to Sergeant Ramirez's bitch, the Mutt who was sitting directly across the table from the Colonel, Walker, and Ramirez, piped up and offered to the concerned female soldier.

"Hey Raz, how the hell many times do I gotta tell ya, baby. If the big slob over there can get the stinking job done for ya good and proper like, take a quick ride on my tune bus to slow town, and I'll knock ya up real good, baby."

Colonel Leadbetter shot a glare at the Mutt for interrupting him that would have made the strongest of men back down and hunt a place to hide. Then he barked at the soldier. "You open your fucking mouth again mister, and I'll put my damn foot so far up your stinking ass that you'll be wearing my fucking toes as your damn teeth, buster. The only thing you have working in your favor is your willingness to humiliate yourself, every fucking time you open that damn mouth of yours, and you show the rest of the world just how dumb you truly are…"

"Hey Colonel, are you done with this sappy hallmark moment, I hate this sentimental clap crap, sir." The Mutt snapped back at the Colonel, not displaying any fear of him whatsoever.

The Colonel stared at the Mutt for a long moment, what he wanted to do with the man was, he wanted to take him apart one bone at a time. Finally, he broke eye contact while mumbling at the soldier. "You're the type of guy who'll bring a stinking tear to a glass eye, buster."

"Say Colonel Leadbetter, the Mutt's so desperate he's been rubbing himself around the couch like a damn cat does, sir." Baby Tee, Sergeant Teri Dorland offered to her Commanding Officer, not wanting to miss a chance to dump on any male soldier of the Unit.

"Hey Colonel, you can't blame the Mutt for his stupid remarks, sir. He once sat in front of a slot machine for over an hour while hitting the coin return, and thinking he was breaking even with the darn thing, sir." Ice, Sergeant Diane Morrison called out, and then she turned and slapped sticks (Forearms) with Mother Flanagan, Sergeant Richard Flanagan, who got his tag name because whenever a new soldier joined the group, Mother was usually saddled with him or her, until the new soldier knew what they were doing with the elite Unit. The rest of the soldiers at the table broke out with a series of 'oorahs', which was the Unit's word for anything good or bad happening to them.

"Good God Captain Walker, I don't know why the hell I waste my damn time with trying to talk any sense to these so called soldiers of yours, mister. I should've know better by now, and save my damn breath for all the damn good my words mean to this group of stinking tickies, sir. One of these damn days I'll finally be rid of the lot of you pack of nuts, and then I can start training a group of real soldiers around here for a change, dammit." The Colonel grumbled as he smiled at the elite group of soldiers having a little fun with him, because they were so pleased with the success of their last operation.

The Mutt was in such a good mood he was not going to let it go so easily, and he popped off at the angry Colonel again. "Hey Colonel Leadbetter Sir, I have some scruples you know sir."

Now the Colonel was getting into the ribbing and he fired back at the Mutt with a smirk on his lips. "Well mister if you have any fucking scruples then it's a sure bet they belong to someone else, buster. You don't even have a damn conscious, buster."

"Whoa, that one almost hurt you know, Colonel Leadbetter Sir. That wasn't a very fair slug you just fired off at me, sir."

Now the Colonel sharpened his stare on the Mutt as he snapped at the young soldier. "You want fair, fair is when you go down to a damn park and ride rides, and eat some damn cotton candy and step in some fucking monkey shit, buster. That's the only place on earth you're going to find fair, buster."

Walker noticed the Colonel was starting to get upset for some reason, and he decided to get the back involved with the conversation and get it off the Mutt's case, before it got out of hand between the two soldiers as he offered to the military officer. "Say Colonel, I didn't think we were gonna save any of the stinking hostages on the fucking operation over at the Indian Point Nuclear Power Plant, sir."

"Neither did I mister, and according to the combat computers and statistics, we shouldn't have been able to save one of the dumb shits, Captain. You people really looked good on this mission." Colonel Leadbetter offered proudly to the group of soldiers as he turned his attention to Captain Walker. Happy they were speaking like soldiers, and stopped the fooling around.

But the Mutt being the Mutt could not leave it alone and he got right back on the Colonel's backside by saying. "Hey Colonel, you know what they say about statistics, sir."

"No, I don't know what the fuck they say about statistics, wise ass. Suppose you enlighten me with what you have on your lousy mind, if you have a mind that is, mister. What do they say about them dog man?" The Colonel growled at the Mutt as he allowed his shoulders to hunch up while he waited for these words of wisdom to come out of Lieutenant Frank Hall's mouth.

"Colonel Leadbetter Sir, statistics are like a stinking bikini in that, what they reveal is very interesting, but what they conceal, is vital sir." The Mutt put on one of the larges smiles he had as he looked at the Colonel.

The Colonel could only stare angrily at the grinning soldier for the moment, even though the Mutt's words were said to obviously get under his skin. He had to agree with them nevertheless. All the military officer could do was smile at the Mutt this time.

"I didn't see that one coming from the stinking Mutt, sir. Hey Colonel, you have to admit sir, that one was pretty good sir." The Ghost, Sergeant Walter Casper offered to Leadbetter as he got into the conversation. Casper was branded the Ghost, mainly because of his last name, and the way he moved in the bush when he was hunting enemy. He was also one of the Unit's regular point men, and he was considered one of the most dangerous of the elite soldiers.

The Mutt went to say something to the Ghost, but he was cut off by the Colonel who growled at him. "If you say another fucking smart remark buster, I'm going to shoot you in the fucking forehead, and then I'm going to fuck the hole, mister. I'm trying to have a serious conversation with the Captain here, and all you stinking jack rabbits are screwing around with me. Knock it off so I can finish up with Walker, and then get away from you flaming asshole and start hanging around with some normal soldiers for a change."

Captain Walker gave the Mutt the look to knock it off, and he backed down so he could see where the Colonel was going with this conversation. Colonel Leadbetter noticed the look and when the Mutt was quiet, he began speaking to his Captain because he wanted to inform him of what was going to be happening to his people.

"Walker, once your people are released from Lejeune for the start of their leaves, hopefully you'll have a full year off to grow another kid if you want to, mister. Personally, I think one more Walker roaming around the United States is more than enough. Perhaps if we're lucky, Raz will have a girl, and maybe the United States will be safe from the Walkers. I suggest you use this time off for rest, because you can never tell if you or these other Screaming Eagles will be called back to Base for another mission at any time, sir. I'll do my best to keep Command off your backsides until you have the full year off while I'm at it, mister. But while you people are on leave, I want you jerks to keep up with your strength training and endurance exercises. I don't want any damn fat bodies or out of shape soldiers showing up on my beloved Base, if and when you people are ordered back here for any reason, mister.

"Also, Walker, like I warned you before, you people are placed on a twenty four hour call back order situation, sir. When you're on leave, you're to maintain a constant communication with your soldiers and with me, no matter where I might be stationed while you people are on leave. You're the head cheese mister, so it's up to you to make certain none of these flaming assholes get in trouble with the law, or with their wives and husbands, and they maintain themselves in a good fighting condition, mister. Over this year of down time Captain, if any of these damn jack rabbits get out of shape and they're forcibly released from our Unit, it's not going to make you look too good before me and the rest of Command, mister."

The Colonel stopped speaking to Walker and he turned to Sergeant Ramirez, who he had great respect for, as he did for Walker. The Colonel did not deceive himself in the least, and he believed all the women fighters of his elite group were just as great a fighter as any male soldiers, and Ramirez was one of the best between the male and female fighters he had command over.

Sergeant Dorothy Ramirez stared back into the glaring eyes of the Colonel, fearing he was going to get on her ass, and she waited for his onslaught against her to begin. But he never did attack her, instead he offered to her in a calm and almost polite tone of voice.

"Sergeant Ramirez, if you do decide to have another child, you'll do it during this year off, that way you can have this child and have a few months to get your damn shape and stamina back, before you're called back to base for any added training or the likes or another operation, Ma'am. One thing you have to keep in the back of your mind at all times, and this goes for any other female soldiers of our Unit, young lady. If you're pregnant and the force gets called back to base for another operation or special training program, I'll be forced to hold you back like the last time when you were pregnant, and the troops went to Iraq to get that damn Iraqi Colonel, and drag his slimy ass back here to stand trial for his part in the attempted assassination of our Boss.

"So you better weigh this threat very carefully before you allow Walker to crawl between your legs and pop off inside you and make you with child again, young lady. I'll not send a female soldier out on a mission if she's with child under any circumstances, period dammit. You'll be lucky if I don't bounce you out of the damn service all together for getting pregnant in the first place, Sergeant. Yeah, I know so don't bring it up to my attention, honey. You're getting older and your biological clock is ticking off the time for you to have another kid safely.

"But you have to also understand, we all are getting older and soon the thought of another kid is either going to be just that, a damn thought. Or if you wait any longer and get pregnant, it'll most likely force you out of the service all together, honey." The Colonel stopped speaking and then he looked deeply into Ramirez eyes, in an attempt to see if he was making any sense to her. To his surprise, he saw tears building up in her beautiful blue eyes, and she was biting a trembling lower lip, in an attempt to hold back her tears.

He forced his attention away from Sergeant Ramirez's face, because he understood why she was on the verge of tears, and he did not want to witness them if she cried. He hated stealing the youth from these young soldiers, but he had to protect the United States, and he needed these kids to do it with. The Colonel turned back to Walker and saw in his eyes he was concerned over Ramirez's condition, so he offered to his military officer.

"Say Walker, if we're going to pull a year off from active duty. Then I'm going to make damn certain I come down to the Keys at least once on our down time, and try out some of the damn fishing down there, before you two people move off the damn Island. From what I hear about the fishing there, it's great mister. I can find a place to rent on the Island while I'm down there…"

The Colonel's words were cut off as Ramirez said to her Commander. "Oh no you won't Colonel Leadbetter! If you come down to Marathon to visit us and do some fishing, you'll stay with us and you'll like it, sir.

I'll not have you staying on the Island in some damn hotel room, sir. I'd love for you to come down and pay us a visit sir. You can finally meet little Robert, and have some real fun fishing and diving for lobsters with us, sir. The Mutt and Blind Date have a home about a half a mile away from us, and they like to fish and dive as well, sir. So we can really make a great vacation for you, Colonel.

"Please allow us to show you a good time for once sir, and you take a good vacation for yourself this time, sir. And please Colonel Leadbetter, bring your wife and kids with you, and allow them to enjoy some of the sun, sir. But I suggest you come down to the Island during the winter, sir. The temperature on the Island rarely goes below sixty all winter long, and the big game bill fish are in around March. That way we can get you out of the cold of the north, sir."

The Colonel turned back to Sergeant Ramirez and he was pleased she did not cry as he shot her one of his best smiled, and then he offered her. "Thanks for the invite Raz, and I think I'll do just that honey. I'd like to spend some time with my soldiers when we're not in a training secession, or we're on some other operation and getting shot at, dammit. And, I'd love to stay at your home, and I'll be bringing my wife and kids with me. I thank you for the invitation and I'll take full advantage of it I assure you, Sergeant. The only thing that might make me hesitate a bit is being down there with that war wacky bastard, the dog man. I don't know how you people ever put up with him. He's nothing but trouble Sergeant."

"But he's one helluva soldier to rely on sir, and that's why we put up with his crazy antics all the time, sir. Besides Colonel Leadbetter, you can never tell if any of the other soldiers from the force might come down to the Island while you're visiting with us, sir." Sergeant Ramirez added in an excited tone of voice as she flashed one of her great smiles that would melt butter on the table. She was always asking the Colonel to come down to the Island to spend some time with them. She was thrilled to death he was finally talking about going to take them up on their offer for him to come down to the Island and spend some time with them. She wanted to show little Robert off to the Colonel, and also show him how big he was growing, and to also show him their home and the water in their back yard. She liked the Colonel, and she felt he was one of the best trainers in the entire Marine Corps.

Colonel Leadbetter noticed the mess was thinning out and he looked at his watch, and he was shocked at the time. It was ten thirty and he wanted to get a few of his book keeping chores completed, and then head back to the Indian Point Power Plant and see how things were shaping up there after their hard hitting action there against the terrorists. He was certain the FBI would have removed the dead terrorists and hostages from the all but destroyed control room of the complex by this time. He was going back dress in civilian clothes, and he was the only soldier from his force who would be allowed off the military base at Camp Smith for any reason.

The Colonel did not want to draw any attention to himself by wearing his military uniform to the site, not with the horde of reporters he knew was still going to be flooding the site in search of what truly had happened there. As long as the Marine Colonel was still in the area, he would be allowed back on the nuclear power plant complex site to examine the area.

He wanted to return to the complex and examine the actions of his soldiers, and try to discover any area where his soldiers could have been more efficient in their attack against the Afghan terrorists who attacked the place. He understood if he went over what was classified as the crime scene long enough, he was certain to find a few things where his soldiers could have been a little better with their actions. Or the soldiers could have conducted themselves a lot wiser to get the job done more professionally, and possibly save a few more hostage lives. Finally, he turned his attention back to Walker who was speaking with the Ghost and he said.

"Okay Captain, it's getting kind of late morning and I have a number of other items I have to take care of sir, and then I'm heading back to the fucking nuclear complex, and see what's going on over there, mister. You're in command of this bunch of damn snowflakes while we're guests at this military installation, and remember mister we're guests on this military Base. Anyone who screws up or embarrasses themselves or me in any way, shape, or form while sharing this damn

Base. I'll deal with them personally with deadly force, but not before I take it out on your ass first, mister. This Base will remain in the same god damn shape we found it in when we first entered the damn installation! You'll keep a tight leash especially on the dog man, or I'll skin the both of you alive, Captain Walker. Well people, I guess we have covered about everything I wanted to speak to you people about, so I'll leave and take care of my business. You people have the complete run of the Base while we're here.

"I was informed there's a movie complex, and phones are available to you people, but no reference to this action is to be discussed with anyone, even ourselves. As far as we're concerned, this action never took place, and we don't know shit from shinola about it, people. Any of you see anything even resembling a stinking news reporter, you're to double time it away from them quick as shit through a goose, or if you're cornered, act as dumb as the Neck is, and confuse the crap out of them…"

The elite young soldiers looked at the massive man, and then they laughed at him while interrupting the angry Colonel's words.

The huge Neck looked back at the laughing soldiers and grumbled at them. "What?"

The Neck's foolish response made the other soldiers laugh all the more, and it caused the Colonel to add to his angry words as he offered. "There, that's what I mean, and that's exactly how I want you fucking people to respond to any damn reporter trying to interview you people. The look from him is exactly the look I want you people to wear, if a damn reporter questions you about what you people are doing here in New York. Or if you people know anything about what took place over at the damn nuclear complex. This is extremely important for you people to carry out these last orders as if they're law to you people, because they are dammit. No one speaks to any damn news reporters under any circumstances, dammit."

With that said, Colonel Leadbetter stood, and then he looked at the rest of his soldiers one last time as a further warning for them to remain on their toes. Then he turned on his heels and he practically stomped his way out of the mess hall at a good clip of speed. When he was gone from the building, some of the soldiers let their breath out relieved the Colonel did not find much to get on them about.

Of course, the Mutt was the first soldier to have something to say to the other troopers. "Is it only me here, or did anyone else get turned on by the Colonel's words to us, people?"

Immediately, Baby Tee who received her unit's tag name because her breasts were small got on the Mutt's ass by snapping at him. "Well what do you people know about this shit? Who ever knew masturbation could make a person so damn witty as the Mutt is today?"

"That's right bitch, get on my stinking ass again. Who the hell lit the fricking fuse on your tampon, honey? Hey Baby, why don't you go back to the damn barracks and grow yourself some tits for us to play with, honey? You need them girl." The Mutt fired at her rather nastily.

"Hey man lay offa her, she gives good headache, Homes." Boot Camp, Sergeant Fred Moorehouse offered as he got in the conversation and grinned at Baby then they slapped sticks.

"Hey Mutt, if you open your filthy mouth once more, I'll shove you head so far up your ass you'll be talking out of your armpit, man. Can't you be serious at least once in your wasted life, man? This shit the stinking Colonel just dumped on our asses was real important man, and here you are still screwing around again, man. We hafta keep a low profile while we're stuck on this puke Army Base. We have almost an entire week here and then we head for our own Base, and another stinking week stuck there, and then we're home for a year off, people. I don't know about the rest of you guys, but I'm looking forward to getting home for that long. So let's stop the clowning around and get serious. No more screwing up until we're gone from this damn dump. We have a short time here so watch your Ps and Qs people." Walker complained more at the Mutt than the other soldiers in the mess.

"Amen to that, Robert." Sergeant Dorothy Ramirez added, pleased they were finally going home for a full year off.

The Mutt, Lieutenant Frank Hall turned to Sergeant Ramirez and he offered, because he knew Walker was getting pissed off at him for screwing around with him in a serious tone. "Hey Raz, are you really sincere about having another ankle biter, baby?"

Ramirez smiled at her dear friend and replied. "I sure am honey."

"Well Raz, I've been thinking about you lately and…" The Mutt started to say, but he was cut off by Sergeant Ramirez as she said with a woman's sweet viciousness. "I wish you really wouldn't think about me, Mutt. Hell buster, I might catch something the Doctors can't cure while hanging around in that filthy mind of yours, mister."

The Mutt cocked his head to the side as he tried to figure out the slug Ramirez just fired off at him, and while he was thinking about it. He started to scratch himself on the side of his face which prompted another soldier from the elite group of specialized soldiers to get on his case when she saw her chance to get on him.

"Damn, will you look at the stinking Mutt scratching himself? I once had a pet dog that did that same thing all the time, man. We hadda put him down because he scratched himself until he bleed." Ice, Sergeant Diane Morrison called out, and then she turned and slapped sticks with Siberia, Sergeant Taras Zarugnaya, who was on loan from Russia to the Multi National Rapid Response Force. The special Unit attached to the JSOC, or the United States Joint Special Operations Command that worked out of the Pentagon, under the direct command of General John White, the Chairman of the Joint Chiefs of Staff.

"Hey man, I'm not gonna stay here and be the stinking brunt of all these slobs jokes at my expense, Homes." The Mutt complained, and then he looked at Blind Date, Sergeant Regina Raphael and grumbled at her. "C'mon baby, let's go and find ourselves someplace where we can be alone for a little while, honey. Hey guys, if you come back to the stinking barracks and hear the water running in the head, stay the hell out of it. Because we're gonna be doing the stinking nasty in there man."

The Mutt waited for Blind Date to get ready to leave the other soldiers. The pretty French female soldier smiled pleasantly at the other soldiers remaining in the mess, and then she looped her arm in the Mutt's and he rested his hand on her rearend, and they both walked out of the mess while speaking together. Some Army soldiers watched the two leave, and they wondered why one soldier was resting his hand on a female soldier's bottom, and some of them got upset over it as they glared at the two soldiers.

Captain Walker watched the two soldiers leave and he smiled, but he was also concerned if the Mutt and Blind Date used the showers for their little fun and games. They might get caught by the barracks fire watch soldier and get in trouble. He turned to Buckethead and growled at the large soldier. "Hey big guy, get over to our temporary barracks and stand fucking guard, so those two don't get into any stinking trouble, buddy. We're not on our Base, and if the fire watch trooper catch them two in there going at it, they just might get Court Marshaled. Then we'll all find ourselves in Dutch with the stinking Colonel again, man."

"Sure thing Walker, I'm off." Buckethead, Sergeant Vincent Lambardo replied as he stood and prepared to leave the mess. He shoved his chair under the table when Ice called out to him.

"Bucket, I think I'm going to go back to the barracks with you, honey. I'm really exhausted and I need to catch up on some of my rest." Ice stood and she also shoved her chair under the table and then headed for the large soldier who was waiting for her to catch up to him.

Blood Clot, Sergeant Richard Brumbach laughed as he threw a sharp barb at the pretty and hurting from being wounded female fighter from the group. "Yeah baby, you're gonna catch up on your rest going back to the barracks with that guy. I though you were in love with me?"

"Yes I am, but if you remember right Sergeant, when you were working on my wound, I warned you not to fall in love with me, because I'd only end up cheating on you, Blood Clot." Ice fired back at Blood Clot, and then she licked the tip of her index finger and she turned her hip towards him, and she lightly touched the finger to her backside, and she made a hissing sound like her rearend was hot and ready for some serious action.

"You did at that honey, and if you remember right I told you it was okay if you cheated on me when I was working on ya, baby." Blood Clot replied in a crisp tone, more than happy Ice was getting over the terrible wound she received when they went into Iraq to capture the missing Iraqi Colonel. He was the ring leader of the Iraqi terrorist cell who tried to assassinate the American President as he was boarding Air Force One, the Special Agents branded Eagle's Nest. Blood Clot watched Ice and Buckethead until they were out of the mess hall, and he found himself thinking Ice was showing no signs of the terrible wound to her body. He liked Ice a lot, but he was not that interested in her romantically though. He was the Unit Medic, and he could not allow himself to get personally involved with any of the female soldiers from the elite Unit. Or he would be dishonoring his profession.

Captain Walker watched Ice leave the building, and then he looked at Blood Clot and when the medic saw him looking at him, he nodded and quickly informed the Captain.

"Yeah Walker, she looks great buddy, and there's no signs the damn wound is hampering her ability to be a complete soldier in any way, shape, or form, man. She's a helluva special woman and soldier, and I hope the stinking Bucket and her hits it off and they become an item, man. The both of them deserve a stinking break, Captain."

"Yeah, she's a damn good soldier Clot, I'm glad you did such a good job fixing her up, man. If you didn't get to her as fast as you did, we probably woulda lost her, or at least lost her to the force, man. Nevertheless, Blood Clot, I want you to keep a close eye on her man, and if you see her hurting, or slowing down any on us. I want you to pull her out of the Unit that fast man. I don't want Colonel Leadbetter seeing her dogging it and getting on her purdy ass, before we can hide her from him if she's having any problems with the damn wound, man." Walker warned the Unit Medic as he held him in his glare.

"No problem Walker, I really love keeping my eyes glued on that lovely little dish, buddy. I only wish all my stinking assignments were as cool as keeping my eyes on the Ice lady, man." Blood Clot offered with a huge grin on his lips as he smiled back at his Commanding Officer.

"Yeah, I didn't think you'd mind that last order, buster. Keep an eye on her and if you see something going wrong with her, pull her out of active duty and you don't need my fucking permission to do so, buster. I'm glad we pulled a year off though, that should give her enough time to heal up fully, and when we're forced to report back to Base. She should be good to go on any mission we might pull." Walker offered, showing real concern for the young female fighter as he nodded his head.

"I read you Captain, that year off should make her come back at one hundred percent and as good as new, and then we won't hafta worry about the lady after that, man. We have the uther soldiers wounded on the same mission coming back, and Stainless, Sergeant Alan Langworth should be reporting back to the Unit any day now, sir. I heard some scuttlebutt he was about good to go again, sir. In fact Walker, I heard he even tried to get back to the Unit before we left Camp Lejeune to come up to New York for this last fucking mission, sir. But Colonel Leadbetter ordered him to stay outta it because he wasn't certain he was fully up to snuff again, man. That wound to his throat almost done him in man. I didn't think we were ever going to get him back to the Unit, Captain." Blood Clot reported to Walker, feeling he should know about the condition of the wounded soldier who was well liked by the rest of the soldiers in the unit.

"Shit Blood Clot, I didn't know Stainless requested to be returned to the Unit. I'm telling you mister; anytime you get any fucking reports on our wounded brothers and sisters. I want know about it immediately, dammit. If I knew Stainless wanted to report back for active duty buddy, I woulda pulled him in and found something for him to do, so he woulda felt he was still part of the damn Unit, man. Dammit to hell and back again, I woulda put him in the damn FBI Mobile Command Center, and had him work there and kept him out of harm's way, until we iced the lousy terrorists on the nuclear complex, man." Captain Walker snapped at the Unit Medic, showing him he was really pissed off about Blood Clot holding this information from him until now, as he openly glared at him.

"You got it Walker, hey man, I'm sorry but I thought the Colonel woulda informed you about Stainless' request to return to the Unit, or I woulda informed you about it man." Blood Clot replied as he watched the rest of the group of Special Forces soldiers stand up as one, and then they assembled around Walker as they waited for the Captain to leave the mess hall.

"Yeah, he shoulda fucking informed me about Stainless man, I hate when he keeps any information about our stinking people from me, Clot. I'm gonna have a little chitchat about that with him when I see the Colonel later on today I can tell you, man. Okay people let's head back to the stinking barracks and get the hell outta sight for a little while. I don't know about the rest of you shitbirds, but I could sure use some more sleep for myself." Walker grumbled as he looked at and the soldiers left the building.

"Hey man, what about the uther soldiers who might be using the barracks for a little tête-à-tête, man? Maybe we should give them a little more time to be together, Walker? They both need a little loving, man." Six Pack remarked to the Captain.

"Tough shit, if they ain't finished playing with each uther by now. Then they're gonna have an audience in a few moments." Walker replied as he led the rest of the soldiers out of the mess.

SATURDAY, FEBRUARY 7th, 2004. CAMP LEJEUNE, JACKSONVILLE NORTH CAROLINA. ZERO TEN TWENTY ONE HUNDRED HOURS

Captain Robert Walker was the first soldier off the nine civilian buses General John White ordered, to transport the elite soldiers back to their home Military Base. The week at Camp Smith was used by the soldiers to get all the rest they needed. But as the soldiers piled out of the parked buses, they were bristling with energy and excitement. Most of their energy was from the rest they enjoyed while at the other Military Base, but it also stemmed from being back on their home Base. The last hour and a half on the bus, many of the soldiers started to get a bit antsy, because they were cooped up on the buses since Zero One Ten Hundred Hours.

The soldiers left Camp Smith early because the Chairman of the Joint Chiefs of Staff wanted to make their leaving the base unobvious to anyone who might be watching the large Army Base in search of a news story. That was the reason for the civilian buses to transport the soldiers down to their Base stationed in North Carolina. The General was still trying to keep his soldiers out of the limelight, and now they were out of New York, he was feeling a lot better about maintaining the secrecy of having his soldiers involved in the operation to kill the terrorist cell who took over the control room of the Indian Point Nuclear Power Plant Facility a week ago.

So far, everything about the attack on the nuclear power plant complex went off the way the General wanted it to go, with no mention or connection to his soldiers. The FBI was in the newspapers every day and taking all the bows for the successful operation, and even the Agent in Charge, Agent Milton Rosborough was seen in every newspaper of the United States, grinning from ear to ear. While he explained to the public how his Agents stopped the terrorists in the control room, and how they stopped the attack on the nuclear plant in its tracks. General White smiled every time he saw the FBI Agent smiling so proudly in the newspapers.

President Albert Cole was pleased to all get out on how well the operation was being handled by his Chairman, even though he could not understand how the General or his soldiers were able to take allowing the FBI to assume all the credit for what they were able to accomplish with the terrorists inside the plant complex. The President and General were both relieved none of the usual reporters were able to put two and two together, and they realize the FBI did not have the assists needed to mount such an attack against a group of well dug in terrorists, and kill them and not have any of their Agents killed during the attack.

The American President still intended to call up to Washington the elite troops from the Special Forces who were involved in securing the nuclear power producing complex, and give them a fist full of medals once this nightmare was put in the past, and he could then pull the group of specialized soldiers up to the White House without causing so much interest from the local news reporters.

They had many discussions about his troops, and the President relented and he allowed the Chairman to expand his soldiers by only forty-five extra troopers. This would place the Multi National Rapid Response force up to manpower of two hundred soldiers. The reason for the increase was because he ordered the General to take fifty of his best soldiers from the group, and train them in urban response to a terrorist attack within the bounders of the United States. That would still give the military officer a working force of one hundred and fifty other soldiers he could use in any response they needed anywhere else throughout the world.

The Chairman of the Joint Chiefs of Staff was elated with the addition of forty-five soldiers for his strike force, and the promised monies from the President to expand his force, and he left the Oval Office walking on cloud nine. Even though he wanted an additional one hundred soldiers, he happily accepted the forty-five extra troopers, and he headed for his office at the Pentagon so he could order Colonel Bruce Leadbetter. The Commandant of Camp Lejeune for the Special Forces group, to start picking through the 201 files of all soldiers in the Armed Forces, in search for the added elite and best of the best soldiers.

General White entered his office like a bull in a China shop and he rushed by his secretary, and he went into his office and plopped down in front of his desk after almost throwing his briefcase at the extra chair in the room. The briefcase hit the chair and tumbled onto the floor and he left it lying there. He just got comfortable when his secretary came in the room, she was carrying a cup of coffee and she set it down on his desk.

When she placed the cup of coffee down, she went over and picked up the General's briefcase and rested it on the chair. He saw her pick up his case and mumbled at her.

"Mary, you're a real doll, I needed the coffee, the President's driving me nuts lately, honey."

"How did it go with the President, John?" Mary asked as she smiled at her exhausted boss.

"Great, this is great Mary. He's allowing me to increase the size of my specialized troops by another forty-five soldiers. I'm planning to call Colonel Leadbetter and have him start hunting down these new soldiers." He offered as he carefully sipped his coffee and relaxed a little.

"General, I thought the Colonel was on leave for a year along with the rest of the soldiers?"

"C'mon Mary, do you really think for one moment that I'm going to allow Colonel Leadbetter to disappear for a full year on me, honey? No way in hell Mary, yes I'll allow him a thirty day leave, but his ass is going to be stuck back on that Military Base until he's so old he can pump rust instead of weighs. I need him stationed down there because we know sure as hell we're going to be hit somewhere in the States by another group of terrorists in the near future. I had a number of private meetings with CIA Director John Raincloud over this very subject, and he feels in five years we'll suffer some kind of a nuclear release within the borders of the United States. Before you ask me young lady, I asked him if he was referring to a dirty bomb and he replied no. He stated the nuclear release is going to be an active nuclear weapon, and it was going to destroy one of the major capital cities of the United States, honey.

"That's why I want Colonel Leadbetter chained to that damn Base in North Carolina, honey. Because when we're hit again by another group of terrorists, we're going to react with all the damn assets we have available to use here in the States and abroad, Mary." The General offered as he suddenly let his breath out in a rush, and then sipped his coffee again.

"General White, this chills me to my very soul that you're referring to a nuclear device being released against one of our major cities like it's no big deal to you sir. Which city was Director Raincloud referring to when he made that statement to you, sir?"

"Where else would he think the attack would come at, Mary. It'll happen in the greatest city in the entire world, New York City, young lady. If the damn terrorists release a nuclear weapon in that city, it'd severely destroy the economy of the United States for a number of years at the least. Not to mention the uncountable number of deaths such a damn release would cause in that city, Mary." He mumbled as he slowly shook his head in response of reflecting on the vast number of deaths a release of a nuclear weapon would cause New York City, and the rest of the United States at the same time.

"Then why the devil are you wasting time speaking to me, General White? You should be speaking to Colonel Leadbetter, and stop this from happening to us, sir." Mary mumbled as she dabbed at her tearing eyes with the sleeve of her blouse, because she was so scared over what she and the General was speaking about, that she was actually crying now.

"Calm down a little will ya honey, we're not speaking about this nuclear weapon being detonated sometime this week, young lady. The Director believes we're at least five years away from any such possible attack aimed against us. By the time these assholes have the capabilities of detonating a nuclear weapon anywhere in the United States. I promise you that we'll have at least ten different ways of detecting the damn thing before it explodes. But this is the reason I'm not releasing our Colonel Leadbetter on any extended leave time, Mary. We'll be well prepared for any such attack before it happens here in the States, young lady." He offered with a warming smile as he stared at his pretty secretary.

"General White, I don't understand how you can possibly be so calm with speaking about a nuclear device being detonated here in the United States, sir? The mere thought any terrorist cell could get their filthy hands on an active nuclear weapon scares me to no end, General. I can't believe what I'm hearing from your lips, like we're speaking about no big thing here, sir. Where the hell would any terrorists get their hands on an active nuclear device, sir? Would they get a complete and active weapon from the Soviet Union, General White?"

"Mary there's no way Russia who is no longer the Soviet Union, would ever allow an active nuclear weapon to fall into the hands of a terrorist group. They understand full well that if we're hit with a nuclear device, and we discover it was in the possession of Russia. The entire weight of the United States would come to bear on their necks, and why would they possibly risk a nuclear exchange with us, when they don't stand a chance in hell of taking over the damn world, honey? No Mary, we know the nuclear weapon the terrorists will get their damn hands on, will come from Iran!

"One thing I'll tell you young lady, Russia and China will do everything in their power to assist Iran with their development of nuclear weapons, and the missiles to get these weapons to their target.

And they will try and stop us at ever twist and turn in our quest of stopping the Iranians on this want for their development of their own stockpile of weapons of mass destruction, young lady."

64

CHAPTER FOUR

"Both Russia and China would be dancing in the damn streets if we were hit by a nuclear device, and it was Iran doing their dirty work for them for Pete's sake. The two of them would immediately cry they had nothing to do with the nuclear attack against us, honey. Then they'd sit on the sidelines and watch us destroy Iran in a nuclear response, and they'd try to get in Iran and take over their oil reserves, before anyone left in Iran came to the front to run the country again.

"That's what this crap is all about with Russia and China not backing us with our attempt to stop Iran from developing their own breed of nuclear weapons and the missiles to get their warheads to target. Because Russia and China both knows damn well once the nut running that nation develops nuclear weapons, he'll use them against Israel or the United States. They'd hit Israel first, and then threaten us if we come to Israel's aide. They'd also hit our interests throughout the Middle East without the slightest hesitation. The Iranians at least twenty years away from being able to hit the United States with any long range missile system fired from Iranian soil. But we'll have the THAD Missile Defense Systems on line within two years, and a year later we'll have them stationed on a number of our nuclear powered submarines we removed from the active nuclear response force.

"These once nuclear armed submarines will be equipped with the THAD Defense Missiles, and we can park the damn subs right off the coast of Iran and any missile, whether it's heading for the nation of Israel or the United States or for any of our other allies in the region. We'll intercept that missile before it could achieve orbit. But the damn Iranian command structure still doesn't understand if they release a nuclear weapon against any other nation of the world. We'll destroy them from our own soil. We'll burn Iran into a nuclear ash heap if they resort to the use of nuclear weapons anywhere on the face of the earth. They don't understand Russia and or China would also respond with a nuclear strike on Iranian soil, if the Iranian fired off one of their own nuclear tipped missiles at any other nation of the world.

"Could you imagine it Mary, if Russia or China was able to take over the oil fields of Iran? Hell woman, they'd end up with all the oil either nation would need until we're able to develop alternate means for generating a power source to replace our dependency on oil. Russia and or China would become nations of great power and wealth, not that they aren't already young lady. Then they'd have countless other smaller nations depending on them for their oil and energy needs, and we'd again be faced with a mess of Communist nations trying to take over the damn world again, young lady. Mary, if Russia ever got their damn hands on Iran's oil reserves, the Russians would be placed in a position where they'd be able to challenge, and even take over Europe, and we'd be nearly powerless to try and stop them while they move against Europe…"

"And, they'd try and attack us in the States, General White Sir." Mary interrupted as she trembled with the thought of what he was telling her.

"No, not really Mary, I seriously doubt Russia would ever outright attack us because of our capability to respond with our own nuclear weapons. They'd never go through all this trouble, just so we could wipe each other off the face of the earth. But it wouldn't stop them from supporting any terrorist groups who'd attack us on every level, and soon the terrorists would be able to weaken us to the point where Russia might openly consider to dare challenge us. Arrr… all I know is it'd be a helluva mess if Russia or China got their damn hands on the Iranian oil fields. The CIA Director and myself, believe that's why China and Russia are supporting Iran's quest to develop their own breed of nuclear weapons, because they understand Iran would use them without hesitation anywhere in the Middle East, and their use of these damn weapons of mass destruction will in return, force us to destroy Iran as an active nation.

"Then Russia and or China will get in there and take over Iran before we can stop them from doing so, honey. It'll be one helluva mess to clean up, if these damn events ever came to past as I told them, young lady. That's why we're trying to talk Iran into allowing the International Atomic Energy Agency Representatives to visit these suspected nuclear developing sites spread throughout their miserable country, and have them conform to the conditions of that agency. If we can get these Representatives in there, Iran will not be able to follow through with their quest to produce their own breed of nuclear weapons."

"Are we having any luck having Iran meet with the Representatives of that Agency, General?" Mary asked with much concern lacing her tone as she stared into the eyes of the military officer.

"About as much luck as I'm having with picking the winning six numbers for the damn lottery. We're getting nowhere with the Iranian's, not with Russia and China refusing to go along with the other members of the Security Council to instigate severe sanctions leveled against the nation of Iran. Nether Russia or China will ever support any sanctions level against Iran, until it's too damn late, and Iran went on with their nuclear development of weapons of mass destruction and aim them against the free nations of the world. Russia and China say they want to give Iran the right to develop their own nuclear energy, but in the back of their minds they know damn well Iran's in the hunt to develop nuclear weapons, and once they have them, they'll use the damn things as sure as I'm sitting here, young lady. And, then Russia and China will get on the damn bandwagon along with the rest of us to disarm Iran once they have the damn things.

"Those two nations understand full well that once Iran has developed their own nuclear weapon, the world will have to step in and do something about them in a fast hurry. Most likely by a military intervention, and once Russian and Chinese troops are in Iran, they won't leave the nation, and they'll jump after the oil fields, and claim them for themselves, honey. The only thing that'll get their troops the hell out of Iran once they join us on attacking Iran will be by engaging their troops with soldiers from our forces. Let me tell you honey, no matter how much the other nations of the world who assist us on the future invasion of Iran, none of them want to engage Russian or Chinese troops for fear of starting World War Three.

"Thus Russia or China, or the combination of the both of them, will be in command of the selected oil fields they want in Iran, and that's what's in the back of their damn minds, young lady." The General stopped speaking and stared at his pretty secretary to see if she wanted to ask him any further questions. When Mary saw him looking at her, she drew in her breath and said with quivering lips and tears building in her eyes.

"General White, I can't believe some of the things you're telling me sir. I always believed Russia and China were our friends, especially with Russia giving up their Communist beliefs."

"Allow me to tell you something else you might not understand or be aware of, Mary. If you believe the present leadership of Russia wouldn't jump on our throats the first chance they got then I have a bridge to sell ya in Brooklyn. Russia is our friends while they're looking us in the eyes, but behind the scenes they're still praying something terrible will happen to us to weaken us enough, and then they'd try to move in on us, honey. They were hoping against hope we'd get bogged down in Afghanistan like they did, when Russia's military invaded that damn country. China and Russia are flooding military supplies and weapons to a number of South American nations, and with that asshole in Venezuela dumping on our Boss every chance the jackass gets.

"The Russians and Chinese love the crap out of this shit, and they're supporting the living shit out of this scumbag, hoping the fool can organize enough South American nations to the ways this nut believes. If the ass can turn enough of the other South American nations to his leftist beliefs and against our country, then Russia and China will move in and the next thing you know, young lady. We'll be facing the same situation we're facing when Ronald Reagan was President, and most of the Central American nations were fighting with the insurgents, and the slaughter of the innocent was going on full force down there. I believe the Central and South American nations are more of a threat than the terrorists, and it's only a matter of time before the terrorists realize this, and they start causing their own kind of problems down there on the world.

"Look Mary, we dodged a helluva bullet when the guy I don't remember his name right now, was planning to run again President Fox, in his attempt to win the Presidency of Mexico and President Fox didn't win. We know Felipe Calderon is running against the leftist candidate will win the Mexican elections, but we believe he'll win by the skin on his teeth. But if Felipe Calderon lost the election for President over Mexico, Mexico would be one helluva mess, and the other guy would've done what Castro and this other nut Chavez did, when they first came to power over Cuba and Venezuela. This other guy who'd be the new President of Mexico would've taken over the American factories that moved down there from the United States, for the cheaper labor force. He would've thrown out our citizens and just taken over the damn companies, without offering any monetary returned to the displaced owners.

"Then both countries, the United States and Mexico would be forced to resort to military actions, and we would've been destined to destroy Mexico, and then a number of other South and Central American nations would be spitting hell at us, and the disgruntle nations would be leaning more towards Russia and China, like Cuba did in the past. We'd be forced to deal with the illegal immigrants in this country surely to be rioting, once we went after Mexico with our military forces. Then we'll be forced to deal with the legal Mexican American citizens who'd be torn between the United States and their mother nation.

"The Venezuelan nut job President Hugo Chavez, has taken over national ownership of the oil producing factories along with the phone company. He's also threatening to take over the damn steel producing company that's owned and being ran by nationals of Argentina. If the nut does that crap then it's sure as hell going to cause a shooting war between those two countries, and you know we'll be forced to back Argentina, and so would the United Kingdom, if that nation decided to engage this nut running Venezuela.

"We know the reason the Venezuelan President is going after Argentina, is because Argentina is friendly with the United States, and the nut is trying to develop his own Communist style situation in Central and South America. The ass thinks he's going to be able to lead the other nations if they turn their back on us, and they lean towards Russia and China for future military and monetary aide and development. We know China has already signed a trade pact with Venezuela for their oil needs, making China the future main user of the heavy Venezuela crude and in this pact, China agreed to supply Venezuela with modern anti-aircraft missile defense systems. China has agreed to this sale though they understood we were dead set against it, which shows us where and what China is trying to do in South America. They want a strong hand, and a number of military bases in those ass backwards countries, and this would hurt us dearly.

"I'm telling you right off the shoulder Mary, Russia and China know what the hell they're doing down there, and it's only a matter of time before this shit comes around and bites us on the damn ass, if we don't start worrying about what's happening there now. We have a total of nine South and Central American nations on the verge of electing Presidents to their country that are anti America, leftists, and pro Communist followers. We know for a fact three of these damn nations will turn. Arrr… this is a subject that'll have to be addressed in the coming years, right now the al-Qa'eda terrorist organization is the main threat we have to deal with, young lady."

"General White, I believe we should leave this conversation, and you should speak to Colonel Leadbetter, sir. I'm stunned about what you have just told me, and I have to compose myself so I can get back to work, sir." Mary offered as she dabbed at her eyes, and then she got out of her chair and headed for the door to give the General privacy to speak to his military officer stationed at Camp Lejeune, North Carolina. She wanted to go to the bathroom and have herself a good cry, because she realized more of America's children will soon be engaged in fighting others who wished to hurt the United States, and she was already grieving for them.

General John White watched his secretary leave his office and he felt sorry for her, because she was so sensitive. When she was out of the room, he reached for the phone and dialed the Colonel's private number at Camp Lejeune.

CAMP LEJEUNE, JACKSONVILLE, NORTH CAROLINA. SATURDAY, FEBRUARY 7th, 2004. ZERO, ELEVEN FORTY FIVE HUNDRED HOURS

Colonel Bruce Leadbetter made his way to his office shortly after he and the rest of his troops returned to their home base. He ordered his soldiers to settle in on the Base while he checked on what was happening in the rest of the world. He wanted to see if he received any new orders or requests, while he was stationed in New York along with his specialized soldiers. He entered his office and hung his cap on the hook and then he went to his desk and saw the inbox was full to overflowing with reports. He shook his head as he sat down and took a deep breath, and then he reached for the first report lying on his desk.

He took the paper and then leaned back in his chair and started reading the report, when his phone rang. Giving out with a disgusted sigh he moaned at the wall. "It starts again I see dammit, I wonder who this one is for crap sake? These damn people don't give me a damn chance to breathe, before they start busting my fucking horns again, dammit."

He picked up the phone and growled in it. "Colonel Leadbetter here!"

"Good Morning Colonel Leadbetter, this is General White sir."

When he heard the General's voice, he sat forward and replied to the Commander. "Good morning General White Sir, what's up sir? It's good hearing from you so soon sir."

"I have some good news for you for a change Colonel. It seems the President gave me permission to increase the size of your Rapid Response Force by another forty five soldiers, sir. I trust now you know this, you'll start pulling the soldiers we need from the other services at our disposal, sir? Also Colonel, I think I'm going to reduce the time the soldiers have to remain stationed on Base. We might as well allow the troops to go home as soon as possible, and you'll look after this for me, Colonel. They're to have a six month leave with no reporting back to Base, but they're to maintain constant communications with their radios with Command, in case we have emergency need of them, sir. I'm sorry Colonel, but you're ordered to remain on Base until you located the new soldiers needed to fill out the rest of the Unit sir, and once you interviewed them, you can take a thirty day leave for yourself, sir.

"Then you'll start training these new soldiers when you return to Base, Colonel Leadbetter. One other thing Colonel, once you finish with their first training session, inform Captain Walker of the new soldiers, and see if he wants to link up with them and see if he wants any of them in his group. I'm going to use Captain Walker as the leader of the soldiers we'll maintain here in the States in case there's a possibility of another terrorist attack aimed against us on our soil, sir." The General took a quick breath which allowed the Colonel to reply to his words.

"This is great news sir we could sure use the new recruits to bolster our forces, sir. The way we're taxing our troopers with operations one after the other, was beginning to take a heavy toll on my soldiers, sir. When we had them here for the refresher training classes, they were moving like shit warmed over, General White. I almost had to threaten them with my rifle to get their asses in gear, sir. Also General White, after I have the new soldiers picked for the Unit, I'll ship their 201 files down to Captain Walker on his damn Island in the Florida Keys, sir. That way he can review them, and if he sees anyone he wants to include in his Unit, he can take the soldiers and check them out, sir." Colonel Leadbetter offered to his Commanding Officer.

"That's a good idea Colonel Leadbetter, that way if Captain Walker wants any of the new recruits, he can have them visit the Island and he can check them out first hand, sir. So he won't be forced to head up to Camp Lejeune to review these new soldiers and see if he likes any of them, sir. Errr… let me see Colonel, today's Saturday, and even though the soldiers were ordered to remain on Base for a full week. None of the damn reporters are giving a hint they suspect our soldiers were involved in the operation that went down at the Indian Point Nuclear Plant, sir. So I don't believe it's really necessary to keep the soldiers cooped up on the damn Base for the full week as was ordered, sir.

"Tell you what Colonel Leadbetter, any soldier from the Response Force who have their own cars on Base, or have their own transportation, can go on leave Sunday morning. All others will be forced to wait until you can setup their transportation back home, Colonel. But I'd like to have all the soldiers on their way home by Wednesday of next week, on the eleventh of February if it's at all possible, Colonel Leadbetter Sir."

"I'll try my best to get our soldier's home by the eleventh of February as ordered, General White Sir. I'll inform Captain Walker of the change in orders sir, and I'll allow him to get the soldiers who have transportation on the road by tomorrow morning, General."Colonel Leadbetter offered as he smiled while hanging onto the phone, pleased at what he was hearing.

"Good Colonel, I knew you'd handle this crap in your usual attention to detail, sir. Look Bruce, I'm sorry I'm going to cut this conversation short on ya sir. But Mary's upset and being it's close to lunch, I'm going to take her to the cafeteria and buy her lunch. Then I'm going to send her home for the rest of the day, sir. I hate it when she gets so upset because of the damn work we have to do to protect our country, sir. She's still hurting because she lost three close friends in the terrorist attack on this fucking building (The Pentagon). But she's being a real trooper about it though, and she never brings it up to me, Colonel." General White offered to the other military officer while showing genuine concern for his secretary and her feelings, and the work she does for him and his office and country.

Colonel Bruce Leadbetter knew the powerful Chairman of the Joint Chiefs of Staff was speaking about his secretary, because he met her on numerous occasions when he was ordered to report to the General's office at the Pentagon for a special briefing or report. He liked the young lady because she was always so helpful when he was visiting Washington. He did not blame the Chairman for worrying about her, because if she was his secretary, he would likewise be trying to protect her just as much, as he replied to his Commanding Officer over the phone.

"General White, I'd be honored if you allow me to buy Mary and you lunch, sir. I can give you my credit card number and you can charge it to me, sir. That's how much I respect your secretary, General." Colonel Leadbetter offered seriously to the General this time.

"That's real nice of you Colonel, but I assure you it's not necessary sir. I'll be the one who's going to spoil my secretary if you don't mind, sir. Well Colonel, let me get off of this damn thing and start looking after my secretary for a change, and you worry about your soldiers, sir." The General replied as he broke off the communication, and then he got up from his desk and looked for his cover and popped it on his head. Then he walked out to Mary's office and saw her sitting at her desk, and offered to her his hand as he smiled at her.

"C'mon young lady, we're going out to lunch and it's on me honey. And, I'm telling you after we eat lunch you're going home for the rest of the day, and I'll not take any lip from you."

"But General White, I have so much work I have to catch up on today already sir, and if I lose a half a day because you ordered me to take some time off, sir. I'll be swamped tomorrow sir."

"I just told you I wasn't going take any lip from you over this order, young lady. So if you find yourself falling a little behind on your work load tomorrow, Mary. Then you're to call down to the damn secretary pool and ask for a temp to help you catch up on your work, honey. It's that simple young lady. C'mon, I'm hungry as hell, we're going to eat and then you're going home for the rest of the day with no if, ands, or buts about it I'm telling you." General White put his offer more in a form of an order than an offer to his pretty secretary as he smiled back at her and waited for her to get ready to head down to the cafeteria.

"Well General White, since you're putting it that way sir. I don't see I have any other choice but to follow your orders, sir." She offered as she took the file she was working on and stuffed it in her lock box, and then she stood and straightened out her dress, picked up her pocketbook and waited for the military officer to lead her out of the office with her own smile.

"You don't have any choice in the matter young lady, and let me warn you in advance, if I see you hanging around anywhere else in this damn building for the rest of the day. I'll call security and have you driven home, and then I'll post two guards outside your home so you stay there, young lady." He remarked with a grin on his lips as he opened the door for her.

"You're really serious about my taking off the rest of the day I see, General White." She purred at the powerful and well liked military officer as she walked out of the office before him.

"I'm as serious as a heart attack about this order honey." When he said the words to Mary, he wanted to bit the end of his tongue off, because that was how he was bumped up to the Chairman of the Joint Chiefs of Staff. It happened when Mary's previous boss, General William Weidenbacher died in his sleep of a heart attack almost six years ago. He looked in her eyes and was relieved because he could tell she did not link his foolish comment to the General death, as he followed her out of the office.

CAMP LEJEUNE, JACKSONVILLE, NORTH CAROLINA. TWELVE HUNDRED AND FIFTEEN HOURS

Colonel Bruce Leadbetter smiled for two reasons as he hung up the phone with General White. He was extremely pleased he was going to get another forty five elite troopers to add to his specialized group of soldiers, but he was ecstatic over the fact he was going to be able to send the rest of his specialized troops on leave earlier than it was planned for. He leaned back in his chair, and then he bellowed out in a booming voice at his assistant working in the outer office. "Sergeant Kirkpatrick, get your damn can in here on the double quick mister! You have some work to carry out for my ass toot sweet, Sergeant."

Instantly, the stunned and concerned Sergeant came charging in the Colonel's office and he immediately snapped to attention and saluted the seated Colonel. Then he waited for his Commanding Officer to dump on him for something he did not know he done wrong, and the Colonel was informed about his infraction by someone on the base.

Colonel Leadbetter put a grin on his lips because he caused such fear in this young man as he grumbled at his three striper. "Relax will ya Sergeant, you ain't in any fucking trouble here, mister. But judging by the look on your damn puss, you're guilty of something and I'll find out about it sooner or later mister…"

"Me sir, no way sir, I never do anything wrong, Colonel Sir." Sergeant Kirkpatrick offered his Commanding Officer as he pointed at his chest with his finger and grinned himself.

"Yeah sure mister, no one ever does anything wrong around here for crap sake, but I'm the one who always gets called on the fucking carpet for these wrongs you guys never do. Sergeant, I want you to run over to Walker's barracks and inform the Captain I want to see him ten minute ago, mister. I have some news for the pain in the ass, and the sooner he hears about it, the better he's going to feel about it. Get going and get him back here A-SAP." He barked at the Sergeant.

"Yes Sir Colonel Leadbetter, right away sir." The Sergeant replied as he turned on his heels and shot out of the office like he was shooting sparks out of his ass, pleased the Colonel was not angry at him. He ran across the grinder, the training and marching field as he headed for Captain Walker's barracks on the other side of the opened field. Even before he reached the barracks, the Sergeant spotted some of the soldiers hanging around on the outside of the building, and they were enjoying a cigarette and talking amongst themselves.

The Ghost, Sergeant Walter Casper, the Hunter, Sergeant Frank Whitcomb, and the massive soldier branded Buckethead, Sergeant Vincent Lambardo, were outside the barracks standing on the grass enjoying a smoke, and they noticed the Colonel's henchman heading for them and Buckethead grumbled at the man when he was within ear shot. "Here comes the scumbag who does the Colonel's dirty work for him."

Sergeant John Kirkpatrick shot a nasty look at the large man as he headed in the barracks.

Buckethead was angry enough at the Sergeant that he actually flipped his cigarette at him as he disappeared back in the barracks. This action caused the Ghost to grumble. "Hey big guy, you know what Walker said about that guy, he's cool so you betta get offa his stinking ass a little if you know what's good for ya, man."

When the Sergeant entered the barracks, the soldiers who spotted him stopped speaking. Sergeant Kirkpatrick looked around the barracks and picked up Walker sitting on his bunk, and he was speaking to the Mutt, Lieutenant Frank Hall. All the elite soldiers in this Unit had to be of the rank of at least Sergeant, or better. He headed right for Captain Walker.

The alert Mutt noticed the Sergeant come into the barrack out of the corner of his eye, and he warned Walker about his presence by hissing at him. "Here comes that fucking scumbag Sergeant again, man. He's so far up the damn Colonel's stinking ass he can tell what the fuck had for breakfast, man. I wanna put a fricking cap in his damn ass for him man."

Walker turned and looked where the Mutt motioned to with his chin, and spotted the Sergeant coming at them and snapped at the Mutt. "Hey dog man, I gave the order to everyone to stay offa the Sarge's ass, and that goes for you too as well, man. He went to the friggin wall for you when that uther Army Colonel wanted to cook your stinking ass with a shit load of bad paper, for setting the bar on fire back in Egypt, man."

"I don't care what he mighta done for me or your damn orders either man. I hate the guy so stinking much I can taste it and nuthin you say can change that fact, Homes." The Mutt fired off at Walker as he glared at him, and he held the glare until the out of breath Sergeant was standing right by Walker's bunk.

"I'll speak to you later about this shit, mister." Walker warned his lifelong friend, and he turned his attention to the Sergeant and growled. "What the fuck's up with you now, mister?"

The Sergeant went to attention, but he refrained from saluting the Captain, because he was not in uniform as he replied. "Captain Walker Sir, Colonel Leadbetter sent me here to order you to report to his office as he put it, ten minutes ago sir. He wasn't pissed off any Captain."

"Thank God for that much I guess. Do you have any idea why the Colonel wants my ass in his fucking office, mister?" He asked the Sergeant, and then he held his breath as he noticed Ramirez come walking out of the shower area, and all she had was a towel wrapped around the lower half of her body. He watched and when Ramirez saw the Sergeant speaking with him, she headed for them at a fast pace. The Captain knew what was coming from the scared soldier.

Sergeant Kirkpatrick turned to the direction Walker was staring in, and he spotted Ramirez heading for them and knew what was coming with his presence in the barracks. Neither man spoke until the female Sergeant was standing by their side she was already near tears.

"Calm down Raz, you're already upset and you don't even know what this shit's all about."

"C'mon Walker, you know damn well every time the Sergeant comes in our barracks, we're always sent out on another mission, Robert. I thought we were going home for a year furlough. I swear Bobby, if this shit's about another god darn mission so soon, I'm resigning from the service and I'm going home, with or without you this time, mister." Ramirez warned Walker in no uncertain terms.

"You betta back off some honey, I really hate it when you get so fucking upset before you even know what the fuck's going on, baby. Sergeant Kirkpatrick has just informed me I have to head over to the friggin Colonel's office, but he also stated the stinking Colonel wasn't upset, honey. So I doubt this shit's about another stinking mission, baby. It probably has something to do with what I'm gonna have our people doing while they're cooling their damn heels off on the stinking Base, while we're waiting to be sent home on leave, honey." Captain Walker offered to Sergeant Ramirez as he looked up at her and smiled.

Sergeant John Kirkpatrick was enjoying staring at Sergeant Ramirez's exquisite breasts as she stood by the two men like she did not even realize she was topless.

Sergeant Ramirez complained to her lover. "I know I might be overacting a little here Bobby, but you know as well as I do, most of the times the Colonel sends for you. We always get stuck with another mission, and some of us don't come home again, Robert."

"C'mon and give me a stinking break here will ya Raz. I gotta get dressed and head over to the Colonel's office and see what his fucking problem is. Hummmm… I suggest you get something on before the Sergeant comes in his damn pants, baby." He warned his lover as he cast his eyes towards Ramirez's breasts, and then he smiled again.

"Look Bobby, I'd ball the crap out of the damn Sergeant if this isn't another mission. I want to go home and be with our son and have some fun on the Island, Robert." Ramirez nearly yelled at Walker because she was so frustrated, and she did not want another mission.

Sergeant Kirkpatrick grinned over Ramirez's remark as he continued to enjoy the view she was offering him. The Captain shook his head as he stood and started getting into his uniform. In seconds he was following the Sergeant over to the Colonel's office. The Sergeant stopped at the door and he allowed Walker to slam his hand on the door, and they waited for the Colonel's response, they did not have to wait long before they heard.

"Who the fuck's in the fucking hallway trying to kick my damn door down on me, for Christ sake? Get your slimy ass in here on the fucking double quick, so I can slam you around like you're slamming my door. That better be you Walker or I'm sending out the damn MP's for your sagging ass, mister. Get in here dammit." The Colonel roared at Walker from inside his office as he closed the report he was working on, and then he sat back in his chair.

The Sergeant opened the door for the Captain, but he was wise enough to remain standing in the hallway and he allowed Walker to enter the room by himself. When the Captain was in the office, the Sergeant closed the door and smiled as he headed for his office to finish up what he was working on, when the Colonel interrupted him moments ago.

When the Colonel laid his eyes on Walker, he growled at him. "Take a fucking seat mister. I have a change in your fricking orders, Captain." The angry sounding Colonel waited until Walker was comfortable in the chair, and then he asked him. "You want a cold bud mister?"

"Yeah sure why not, Colonel Leadbetter." Captain Robert Walker replied with a grin plastered on his lips, now knowing what the wise

Colonel wanted to speak to him about was not over another emergency mission his troops had to handle. He too was concerned if it was another operation, he wanted to speak to him about.

"You know where the stinking beers are in my office, you drank enough of them on me, mister. If you're waiting for me to get you one then you're going to die of fucking thirst and old age first, mister." He growled at Walker as he made a quick motion with the end of his chin towards the small ice box resting in his office.

He got himself an ice cold beer and popped the top and took a slug before he returned to his seat, once he was comfortable again he asked the Colonel. "Say sir, you mentioned something about a change in my orders, sir? What are these changes sir?"

"Yeah, I did at that mister, and it seems the General doesn't want you and the rest of your rift raft hanging around this military base for as long as was previously ordered, mister. I can't say I blame him in the least. Having your pack of Screaming Eagles hanging around the Base is bringing down the rest of the soldiers stationed on this installation, mister. Arrr… fuck that shit Captain Walker, the General decided to get everyone home by Wednesday of next week, sir. He also stated any soldiers who have their own transportation set up or on the Base, will be free to leave beginning tomorrow morning, mister. I have Sergeant Kirkpatrick already working on printing up your damn leave papers for the troop's sir, and he'll be finished with them by the end of the damn work day, sir. He's going to start working on setting up the needed aircraft transportation for the other soldiers who have to be flown home on leave.

"Also Walker, General White allowed our forces to be increased by another forty five soldiers, and he's offering you first pick of the new cream of the crap soldiers, sir. It seems the General's going to place your ass in Command of the Rapid Response Force we're going to maintain in the borders of the United States, Captain. Before you allow that last bit of information to go to your stinking head mister, I'm telling you buster. If the shit gets hot anywhere on the earth, I'll pull your Unit in, and stick another Unit in to protect the United States from any possible attacks, sir.

"Walker, the frigging reason I warn you of this, is because if the shit gets hot I want my best Unit involved in any damn operation we're sent out on, mister. So it seems your Unit's going to get stuck pulling double duty from this point on, mister. Captain, make no fucking mistake about it sir, we're going to be hit again here in the States, but we'll be chasing these flaming asshole terrorists all over the fricking globe. We have them running everywhere at it is already, and we're going to keep them on the damn run until we finally get our hands on their head cheese, and we hang him high and dry by his buster browns. I'm not going to rest until we have their leader in our custody, and I'm going to be the one who'll pull the fucking leaver, and send his sagging ass on its way to Paradise, and on that day I'm going to get blind stinking drunk, man." The Colonel grumbled as he flashed a quick smile at the Captain.

"I'll tell you this Colonel, I'm gonna be sitting right by your side, and I'm gonna be as drunk as you are when we hang that lousy sonofabitch, sir. That's the fucking day I'm living for sir." Walker replied as he fired off a smile of his own at his Commanding Officer.

"Amen to that Walker, and I'll be damn proud to bend an elbow with you on that day, sir. Anyway Walker, you have to find out who the hell in your group has their own transportation setup, and get them on their way home, sir. I don't know how you're going to keep a lid on the rest of the soldiers who'll have to stay on Base until we setup their transportation, but that's your problem to deal with, mister. It comes with your position in the service mister. What about these new soldiers we're going to draft in the near future, sir? How do you want to handle them sir?" He asked as he stared into Walker's eyes while waiting for his reply.

"I don't know Colonel Leadbetter I guess I can come up to our Base when you pick out the new soldiers, sir. Then I can give them the first over and pick out the ones I'll add to my Unit, sir. I don't see any other way to handle it, Colonel Leadbetter Sir." The Captain grumbled at the Colonel, pissed off he will be forced to return to Base to check out the new FnG's (Soldier's slang for Fucking new Guys) when they arrived.

"I see by the look in your eye you're pissed off because you think you have to report back to Base to check out these new soldiers, Captain. You're dead wrong there Walker, I thought about this and I can ship their 201 files down to you while you're on Marathon, and then you can go over them there at your leisure. Then, when the new pukes go on their first fucking liberty, you can invite them down and give them the once over on your Island, it's that easy mister. Look Walker, it's a proven point you and your war wacky bastards and bitches have done a helluva job sir, and I'm trying to make it a little easier on you people, buddy. So anything I can do for you, just let me know and I'll try my best to get some this shit off your damn shoulders, Captain." Colonel Leadbetter offered to his officer as he flashed a quick smile at him.

"Thanks Colonel, I can sure use a little bit of help sir. If I knew being a stinking Officer was such a drag, I woulda stayed a stinking Gunny and kept my damn mouth shut, sir. I like what you offered me though, and I wanna do it the way you just suggested, sir. Is there anything else you wanna share with me Colonel, I kinda wanna get back to my people and start cutting the ones I can, loose sir?" The Captain asked his Commanding Officer while trying to keep the excitement of leaving the Base earlier under his control. Right now, he wanted to get back to his barracks and inform the rest of his troopers, and then have some fun with them before a good many of them left the Base before the others.

"I know what you have on that evil fucking mind of yours, mister. Yeah Walker, I guess that's it for the time being buster, go back to your pack of criminals and have one of your damn fun nights, mister." Colonel Leadbetter growled at Walker, wondering if he was going to be stupid enough to run one of his so called fun nights this close to getting released on leave. The practice was highly illegal, and if the soldiers were caught while engaging the women of the outfit in sex, they would be dumped out of the service.

"Thanks a lot Colonel I wanna get the ones that can leave on their way home, sir." Walker announced as he nearly jumped out of his chair, and he tried to leave the office.

"Hold on a second there mister, when Sergeant Kirkpatrick's done writing up the damn furlough orders for the soldiers who can cut out tomorrow morning. I'll have him run the paperwork over to your barracks for you, sir. Any of your shits want to get out of here early, all they have to do is report to my Sergeant, and he'll complete their damn paperwork and then they can leave the Base and find their own way home. The soldiers who live too far from Base are going to get stuck waiting until my Sergeant can arrange their damn transportation home, mister. Well Captain, that's all I have for you, you're dismissed sir."

Walker was about out of the office by the time the Colonel finished speaking with him. He smiled as he shook his head, proud of the troops under his command. The Captain ran across the grinder, and then he took the four steps leading into his barracks two at a time. He charged down the sleeping quarters and headed for his bunk, because he knew most of the soldiers who had their way home. He grabbed the list of soldiers and went to the center of the barracks and bellowed out to his troop in a commanding tone.

"People, people, people, I got some fucking news for you pack of shitbirds so gather round." The Captain waited a few seconds until the excited soldiers were gathered around him, and then he announced. "Okay people, I just finished speaking to the stinking Colonel, and he has a change of orders for us. Anyone who has their own fucking transportation home on Base, or any other way to get home by themselves, can leave the Base tomorrow morning right after fucking mess, if you wanna leave that is. We might as well allow the stinking government to feed us one last time, before we cut out for home people…"

CHAPTER FIVE

A roar broke out from the other troops, and Walker cast a quick look at Sergeant Ramirez, and he could see she was ecstatic over this latest news, and she was smiling a smile that melted his heart and he returned her smile, and then he gave her a quick wink of his eye.

"Okay people, you know who you guys are who can leave the stinking Base early, and when you get your damn leave papers from the stinking Colonel's Sergeant, you can bug the fuck outta town toot sweet. The rest of us are gonna be stuck cooling our heels on base until Wednesday, that's the earliest Sergeant Kirkpatrick can arrange for our transportation the fuck home. The Colonel didn't give me any orders for you people while we're stuck on this Base. So the only thing I can gather by that is, we're not pulling any stinking work duty until we're released from base. I guess he's giving us that much of a frigging break, so if you don't get caught screwing up while we're stuck on the base, we'll all be home soon and having a fucking blast in civilian life.

"You people know the friggin routine, and anyone who wants to come down to Marathon and hang with Raz and me, are more than welcome to do so. But everyone has to remember we're on call twenty fours a day while on furlough, which means you all have to check in with the stinking Colonel once a week, or he'll be out head hunting ya…"

"Hey Walker, how bout we have a fun night before we lose half the guys from the stinking Unit, man?" Roach, Sergeant David Burgwald called out from in the middle of the excited group of soldiers. Instantly, his call for a fun night was picked up by the rest of the excited soldiers. Even the women of the group were excited over the offer.

"We gotta skip that kinda shit people, Leadbetter warned me about trying to pull off a party. I don't know about the rest of you people, but I don't wanna do anything that might cause me to get stuck staying on this stinking Base any longer than I have to be here, people." Walker offered to the other soldiers.

"Man, what a fucking buzz killer you're turning out to be lately, Road Kill. (Road Kill was Walker's Unit's tag name) I guess when you made brass you lost your stinking balls and sense of humor, man." Wacko, Sergeant Salvatore Tomassi dared to call out while standing in the middle of the group of elite soldiers.

The instantly upset Captain glared angrily at Wacko who got his Unit name because he always acted wacko whenever he smoked some pot. The look was more than enough of a reprimand for the dangerous soldier, and he put his head down and looked at the floor. Knowing he overstepped his bounds of friendship with the Captain.

The soldiers agreed with Walker about skipping a fun night party with the women from the Unit. The soldiers were more interested in getting home than anything else. It took a few moments for the soldiers to calm down enough to break up the group, and the soldiers able to leave the Base tomorrow morning, got down to packing their stuff. The Captain smiled when he noticed many of the soldiers going to remain on Base until Wednesday, pitched in and they helped out the soldiers leaving the Base early. It made him realize no matter what, his soldiers would stick together tighter than two coats of paint, and this made he believe he was standing with the greatest men and women, soldiers the world had to offer.

Sergeant Ramirez laid her hand on Walker's shoulder, and this broke his thoughts as he turned to see who wanted him. When he saw his girlfriend smiling at him, he returned her smile, but that was not enough for Ramirez. She looped her arms around his neck and pulled his head to her lips. She kissed him like she never kissed him before in her life. It was loaded with passion and love, and it made him weak in his knees. When the kiss ended, she whispered in his ear. "Hey soldier, what say we go and visit the showers for a little while? I want to make love to my favorite man and soldier, and I'm not waiting until we get home either, mister."

The Captain did the only thing he could think of doing, he smiled with love in his eyes, but Ramirez's eyes clouded over with concern. Then she cried to her lover barely over a whisper. "Bobby, I'm sorry for the way I was acting before, honey. I was being such a child, but I was worried about us going out on another mission so soon. I wanted to go home and enjoy little Robert, you and our home for while. Can you forgive me for being so foolish, Robert?"

"Forgive what for Pete's sake? Look girl, I fell in love with you for the way you are, baby. You being you is exactly what caused me to fall in love with you in the first place, and I wouldn't have you any other way, honey. But I'll tell you this much though baby, once we're back home we're getting married, baby sister. We were supposed to get married before we were pulled up for this last mission, and we never got around to tying the knot. But this time we'll do the deed I promise you, baby. I'm not going to let you get away from me so easily again I tell ya, baby." Walker announced as he pulled Ramirez's body close to his, and he gave her a breath robbing hug and a kiss on the end of her nose.

She wrapped her arms around his neck and kissed him back as she offered. "Walker, Bobby, I love you so much, and if anything, ever happened to you, I'll never forgive you. C'mon my soldier and lover, I want to make love to you." She released her hold on her soldier, and she led him hand in hand towards the shower area of the barracks.

The Mutt, who was with his girlfriend Blind Date, Sergeant Regina Raphael, saw the two heading for the showers and he knew what they were up to, and he called out in a booming voice at them. "Yeah sure Walker, you just fucking voted down a fun night for the rest of us assholes stuck in this stinking barracks, but you two are gonna have you own stinking fun night in the damn showers, man. This shit sucks the big one I tell you pal, we can't have a damn party, but you two can party out anytime you want one, man."

The Captain didn't miss a step as he called back over his shoulder at his lifelong friend. "Hey dog man, what the hell can I tell ya buddy. Rank has its fucking privilege. Besides man, what the fuck are you complaining about anyway man. You got your own squeeze with ya all the time as well, stupid. So if you want some fun and games, try tickling the pretty lady you're with and see what happens next, you asshole you."

After they finished making love in the showers, the two soldiers made themselves busy helping the other soldiers going home early. The next day was a somber one as half of the elite group of soldiers left for home. For the rest of the week it was a drag, with each soldier thinking about going home and nothing else. The soldiers ate, ran through a number of minor exercises to have something to do while others read, or they called home to warn their loved ones they would soon be home with them. Monday morning was a stressful one for the soldiers, because they were getting excited about going home in two days. The tensions ended when Sergeant Kirkpatrick entered Walker's barracks, and handed the Captain the airplane tickets he made up for the soldiers on Base.

Tuesday was used by the soldiers packing their personal belongings and turning in their weapons and other military equipment. This day was spent by the soldiers walking like they were walking on eggs, because none of them wanted to make mistakes that might force them to be held back on the Base from heading home. Their last supper on Base was a blast, the cooks made steaks and one beer apiece for the soldiers was handed out. Even Colonel Leadbetter made certain he spent the last night on the installation with his troopers. The jokes, ribbing and general good mood of his soldiers spread among the other soldiers stationed on Base, and they even joined in on the bantering going on between the elite troopers.

Wednesday came with Walker not having to wake the other soldiers, most of them did not sleep a wink, and when the barracks lights came on. Many of them were out of their bunks and were waiting for Walker to lead them over to the waiting buses that would bring them out to the airport, so they could get on their planes and head home.

WEDNESDAY, FEBRUARY 11th, 2004. ZERO SIX HUNDRED HOURS

The buses carrying the remaining soldiers from Camp Lejeune pulled up to the terminal and they piled off the buses. They assembled around the buses, and Sergeant John Kirkpatrick started to call out the soldiers' names and handed them their tickets, and informed them what gate they had to head for. Ramirez, Walker, the Mutt, Blind Date, Buckethead, No Neck, Ice, Baby Tee, the Ghost and the Hunter got on the same plane. The extra soldiers were coming down to Walker's place to spend time on Marathon to enjoy some fishing, diving, and hitting Key Weird (Key West) to enjoy the craziness of the tiny Island. Then the Ghost and Hunter were going to be heading home to get reacquainted with their families and friends. The other soldiers did not have a family to go home to, so they were going to stay with Walker and the Mutt until they threw them out of their homes.

The trip from North Carolina down to Miami took over six hours, and the troopers split up there and headed for their own homes. The soldiers with Walker and the Mutt were forced to hang around the terminal for an hour, before they boarded the plane that would take them down to Marathon. Even though it was in the higher sixties in Miami, it was in the upper seventies on Marathon, and the soldiers realized they were overdressed for this temperature. As they waited outside the Marathon terminal for their cabs to arrive to take them home, they shed their heavier outerwear. By the time the cabs arrived, the soldiers were standing in their tee shirts, and they stuffed their other clothes in the duffle bags resting by their feet.

The trip to the two homes took less than ten minutes, and because the Mutt and Blind Date's home was before Walker's and Ramirez's place. The soldiers staying with them piled out of the cabs. Buckethead, the Hunter, and Baby Tee got out with the Mutt and Blind Date, and they headed for the home, while the other cabs headed for Walker's place.

Walker and Ramirez were grinning from ear to ear as they set their eyes on their home, and Ramirez started to cry when she noticed the lady taking care of Robert Jr. and her son was waiting for them outside the home. She could not believe how large and tall her son had grown since the last time she set eyes on him. Robert Jr. was four years old, and he broke away from the babysitter and wildly charged her when he spotted his mother coming at him. The child actually jumped and Ramirez caught him in the air and she hugged and smothered his with a flood of kisses and tears.

Captain Walker rested his hand lightly on his son's back under his shirt, so it was a skin to skin contact. When the child had enough of his mother fussing over him and kissing his face, he started to struggle out of her arms and she was forced to place him on the ground, and the child immediately jumped at his father. Walker picked up his son and he raised him high over head, and he spun the child around in the air and the youngster laughed with glee. The other soldiers left the other two enjoying their son, and they headed in Walker's home so they could change into cooler clothes and start to relax.

Sergeant Dorothy Ramirez kissed the babysitter on the cheek, and then she thanked her over and over for taking such good care of her son. Then they all walked into the home, and there were glasses of ice cold lemonade sitting on the table, and the home was cool to almost cold. The Sergeant looked around the first floor of her home, and she was pleased the babysitter took care of their home as well while they were gone.

The babysitter took a back seat to all the activity by the soldiers, and once she was certain everything was okay, she made her excuses and left. Ramirez was holding onto Robert Jr. hand for dear life, as she checked out the rest of her home. Walker grabbed one of the glasses of lemonade and slugged it down. Ice came down from upstairs and she was wearing a blue bathing suit, at least Walker though it was a bathing suit. The thing was so small it barely covered Ice's outstanding treasures. He smiled at her because she looked hot, but his eyes did notice the ugly scare on her body from the wound, but he was pleased she was able to get over it, and what it done to her body. Of course, the massive No Neck was right on Ice's heels and he was following her around like a puppy dog in heat while desperately trying to get her to notice him.

Walker noticed the Neck trying to get Ice's attention and he smiled, knowing the two were starting to play patty cake with each other, and he was happy for them. The two other soldiers headed outside and they walked over to the dock, and sat down and hung their feet in the water. The Ghost came down from upstairs next, and he was dressed in a bathing suit. Walker saw the physical condition of the Ghost, and again he smiled as the Ghost bitched at him.

"I see the two stinking love birds are outside already man, you got any beer buddy?"

"Try the damn fridge man. Where the hell do you think I would have the beer, buddy?" The Captain snapped at the extremely dangerous soldier.

The Ghost walked to the kitchen refrigerator and took an ice cold bud out, as he asked over his shoulder. "Hey buddy you want one of these little babies, man?"

"Does Hoody Doody have wooden balls, buddy?" He replied and took the offered beer and took a slug after opening it, and then he asked the Ghost. "What are you up to man?"

"I'm gonna go outside and rain on the stinking Neck's parade, man. If he thinks he's gonna get some while I'm still dry as a popcorn fart, he has another stinking think coming Walker."

"Man, that's colder than the other side of the pillow, Ghost. If he can tap Ice, what the hell's it to you, man? But if you're going out there, you betta bring a stinking beer out for the other two pukes out there, man." He fired back at the Ghost, already knowing the soldiers were letting down their guards, and they were looking to bust each others horn again.

"Hey Walker, you got any stinking fishing poles in this dump, man? I might as well try my luck doing some fishing while I'm out there. By the way oh fearless leader of mine, what the hell are we gonna do for a little bit of excitement around this place, man? You know it's not gonna take long for us to become bored if you know what I mean, Homes." The Ghost grumbled at Walker as he stared at him and waited for his reply.

"Yeah buddy, there's plenty of fricking fishing poles and tackle stacked up in the stinking garage, but I ain't got any stinking bait to go with the poles, man. And, to answer your last question buddy, I figure we'll kill off the rest of the week chilling a bit at my place, and then Sunday night we'll all head over to the bar Dockside, and see if the Rocket man's hanging around there, and what bands are playing at the bar for the night." He replied as he took a second slug from his beer and he stared at the Ghost.

"Sounds like a fucking plan to me man. Looking forward to tying one on big time buddy, it's been a while since the last time we took over Dockside and had some fun for ourselves man."

"What the hell are you gonna do for a play toy while you're down here Ghost? From the looks of it buddy, it seems the Neck has laid claim to Ice's little can on ya, pal. So you and the Hunter are gonna be the only ones without a date on Sunday night man. You know the Neck has claimed Ice, and unless I miss my guess, Buckethead has Baby Tee sewed up also. So you two guys are gonna find yourselves sitting on your thumbs spinning when we go out Sunday man."

"Don't worry about us Walker, once the Hunter and I hit the stinking bar, we'll find someone to occupy our time with, Homes. The last time we were at the bar, we had the local hens following us all over the fricking place man. So the way I look at it, it hasta be the same stinking way again man." The Ghost boasted proudly as he allowed a huge grin to cross his lips now.

"I hope you're right buddy, but I gotta warn ya man. I don't want you or the Hunter hitting on any of the local chicks with any other guys, or they're married, man. I don't want any trouble, at least not on our first night out on the Island. I have no intention of sitting in a stinking bird cage (jail) overnight, and you know if you two get in trouble, me and the rest of the guys will be there with you two puds." Walker warned the Ghost as he sharpened his stare on the dangerous soldier and he held him locked in his glare for the moment.

"Like I already told ya man, I'm not gonna start stinking trouble at the damn bar man. But I think you should speak to the Mutt though. Because if anyone is gonna make any trouble for us, it's surely him buddy." The Ghost offered to Walker with a huge grin on his lips.

"Mutt's my fucking problem to deal with man, and I'll handle him as I always do pal." Walker replied to the man.

"Yeah, anyway Walker, I'm gonna get me a damn pole and try my luck at fishing man."

"Be my guest man." Walker grumbled as he decided to go and check on his kid and Ramirez.

TORBAT-e-HEYDARIYEH, IRAN. FEBUARY 11th, 2004 AT ZERO TEN HUNDRED HOURS IRANIAN TIME

At the Iranian town of Torbat-e-Heydariyeh situated seventy fives from the Afghanistan border. A secret meeting was being conducted by Abdol Karim Kalantari, a General in the QUDS, which was a deadly trained terrorist group who carried out all of Iran's terrorist activities aboard. The Iranian General was responsible for the training of many other Islamic terrorist groups including Hamas and Hezbollah. The well feared and powerful Iranian General was sitting with a number of his fellow leaders of the group, and they were going over their latest plans to attack and harm the United States. In their attempt to drive the America soldiers out of Iraq, so Iran could march in and take over the country and their vast oil fields. The General was known by his fellow fighters as the Vulture, and it was believed if you were to follow the Vulture, he would lead you to their dead enemy.

The Iranian General was surrounded by Major Sayeh Rahimi, who was as ruthless a killer as one could be, along with the Iranian Colonel Nasser Makaeem Taleqani, a master explosive expert along with Captain Jahangeer Keshavaz, who was another man trained in the explosive field. Major Ghassan Abidal al-Zubedi trained other Iranian warriors on the art of the Special Forces, and he was seated with Major Hamidoz al-Layluz, who was trained in special tactics with soldiers. Captain Saeed Mahebian who was responsible for the special drugging and training of the suicide attackers, sat with Captain Morteza Dastjeedi. Colonel Amir Jolaipour, a weapons expert as was Captain Farhad Nobakht. The remaining Iranian soldiers were the bombers who transported the deadly weapons under their control into Iraq, and they were used to kill American soldiers trying to bring peace to that war torn country.

The first bomber was Major Feresheteh Mansouri, a young and pretty female Persian fighter. The second bomber as they liked to be referred to as was Sergeant Bassam Abu Fallahi, and he was sitting with the last woman of the soon to be terrorist group, Sergeant Azamalaie Shirazi. The last of the bombers was Major Gholamhossein Mahajerani, and he was the reason for this meeting to be convened. Because the Major was working with the explosive experts developing the specialized IED's or Improvised Explosive Devices that was taking so many American soldier's lives in Iraq. He requested the meeting take place with the Vulture, because his workers developed a new type weapon the Major was assured by the producers would kill the newly delivered and heavily armored plated Humvees to Iraq.

The Vulture, General Abdol Karim Kalantari sat at the head of the room wearing his usual angry and disgusted looking scowl, as he stared directly at his Major, while they waited for everyone to be seated for the meeting. The moment everyone was comfortable, General Kalantari growled at Major Mohajerani in a savage tone.

"Well Major Mohajerani, now that you have dragged me out to this cursed town of lowly pigs, what was so important that you demanded these Officers to attend this foul meeting, sir?"

"General Kalantari, I needed to speak with you over a new weapon my people were able to develop, that'll easily destroy the newly designed American heavier armored plated vehicles they are delivering to the worthless nation of Iraq, for the protection of their cursed soldiers sir…"

"If this is true as you state Major then this is good news, and you were wise to request a special meeting with our command structure take place. What is this new weapon you speak of Major? We have to maintain constant pressure on the hated American troops operating in Iraq, and soon the milkless fools who call themselves Democrats in America, will cry to the other fools who do not believe in the war in Iraq. This is the only chance we have of taking power in Iraq, if we drive the hated Americans out of that worthless country of dog eaters.

Once we own Iraq, we'll set up special training camps, and when our people are properly trained, we'll follow the evil American soldiers back to their foul country. Then we'll destroy more building, and kill more lowly infidels, until we're successful with driving all American troops out of every Arab nation in the world, Major. Once again, I ask you of this new weapon, Major?"

"General Kalantari, the new weapon is classified as an EFP or Explosive Formed Penetrators. We have tried out one of the weapons last week, and although it missed its target, when the weapon was fired at one of the new armored American Humvees riding in a convoy in Iraq. The weapon did go right through the trunk of a parked car, and it continued through that vehicle through the rear of the car, and the warhead continued through the back and then the front seat, and it lodged in the engine block. The warhead would've penetrated the best armored vehicles the worthless American are employing against us, sir." The Iranian Major reported to his leader.

"That is interesting to hear Major, but you have still failed to inform me what and how this new weapon operates. I'm waiting for this part of your report to come forth from your foolish lips to my ears, Major. I warn you Major, my patience does have its limits and I suggest you don't reach that point foolishly." The Vulture snarled at his Major as he held him in a lazar like stare, while waiting for his to explain further to him.

"I'm sorry for my failure to explain this new weapon's operation to your understanding, General Kalantari. This weapon is a simple and rather cheap device to aim and operate. It's merely a twelve inch wide chunk of heavy duty oil pipe we cut to two feet long, with a sealed back end to the pipe. Then we pack it full with high explosive and cap the other end of the pipe with a thick curved copper plate, and the weapon is fired by means of a common garage door opener. Or it can be fired by means of a telephone call to the weapon that triggers the firing mechanism held inside the weapon, sir. Once the weapon is fired, the copper lid becomes more curved until it takes the shape of a nose cone traveling at supersonic speed, and the chards penetrate anything the weapon is aimed at and comes in contact with, sir.

"The deadly warhead of this weapon is more than capable of penetrating up to four inches of heavy armor plating that's not reactive. The weapon weighs no more than seventy pounds depending on the size of the pipe employed, and it can easily be hidden in a mere pile of rubble lying alongside the foul road. Or it could even be placed in a common pile of garbage, and the weapon can also be buried in the sands to hide it completely from discovery from any of the new bomb detection devices the cursed American soldiers are employing, in an effort to find our hidden weapons before we're able to employ the weapon against the lowly dogs, sir."

"This is fantastic information Major it's the answer to our problem that has been sent to us by Allah's great wisdom, to eliminate the lowly infidels and jackals from the lands of Arab nations, Major Mohajerani. How many of these faithful weapons have we been able to infiltrate into the hated lands of the great dog eaters, sir?" The Vulture demanded to know from his lesser officer, as he continued to stare at him like he was going to order his death any minute.

"General Kalantari, we have been able to deliver to our comrades in arms inside Iraq fifty of these new weapons, and the fools are still trying to master the aiming and firing of these weapons. But my workers are working diligently with the worthless dog eating nation, and soon we shall be flooding the foul lands of Iraq with hundreds of these new weapons, and we're praying to the Almighty Allah these weapons will force the hated Americans to abandon their loathsome and misbegotten efforts inside Iraq, sir. Once the lowly Khawajis, the outsiders, the infidels of America and the United Kingdom are driven out of Iraq, our forces will follow their departure into Iraq, and we'll slaughter the foul Kafir, the non-believers of the Sunni sect. Then we'll go after and destroy the equally as foul believing Kurds of Iraq, sir.

"Once we have destroyed these miserable forces trying to rip the worthless nation of Iraq apart, we'll own Iraq, and soon if Ansh Allah, if God wills it so. We'll be in complete control of the entire Middle East, and the cursed oil fields that dot the great sands of the Arabs. Of course General Kalantari, I'm only speaking after we've been able to destroy Saudi Arabia first, sir. The hated American and foul puppet government that is trying to persuade other good Arab nations from backing us on our quest to rid the sacred Arab lands of all foul infidels, who are polluting this world with their evil presence, General Kalantari Sir."

"This is outstanding news for my foul ears to absorb, Major Mohajerani. If all you have stated before me comes to past. Then you'll end up being one of my most important cogs in our future conquest over Iraq and the United States soldiers. But on the other hand Major, if all you have stated here today does not come to past. Then you shall die the slow and agonizing death of a thousand cuts. But your death will not be so forthcoming for you to enjoy Major. First you shall endure the pleasure of watching your entire family be put to the sword before your foolish eyes if you have dared to lie to me about this new weapon.

"But my wrath will not end there, I shall order the graves of your ancestors opened, and their bones will be spread out upon the roads of Iran, and our military trucks will grind their foul bones to the dust they were made from, and all traces of you and your entire family heritage will be erased from the face of the earth, as if you have never existed in the lands of Allah. I trust I am making myself perfectly clear on my wants and needs of this new weapon, Major? And, the deployment of this weapon to our fellow Persian and Arab brothers and sisters, who are waging a sacred war with the lowly infidels from the lands of the great Satan, Major Mohajerani."

"You made it clear to me how our forces operating in Iraq, so desperately have need of this new weapons, General Kalantari Sir. I'll order the mast production of this weapon and the rapid deployment of the weapon into Iraq, to our forces struggling there against the infidels, sir. Yes General Kalantari Sir, it shall be as I stated, sir. This weapon with be the instrument that'll break the fighting spirit of the cursed American infidels, and it'll also force them out of Iraq completely, sir." Major Mohajerani boated to the Iranian General known to him as the Vulture.

"It better be the way you just boasted to me or you will not enjoy your short future on this earth, Major Mohajerani. Because you understand the fate that awaits your success, or your unholy failure to my orders and demands, Major. You'll enjoy the death of the lowly and despised jackal, if you fail me and your country on this mission, or any other mission I order you to travel upon for our sakes and for the sake of our Religion. Also Major, I have further ideas for my Persian brothers and sisters gathered before me. In the years to come, I know our President of Iran will dispatch us to the shores of the great Satan, to attack the foul infidel's inside their own cursed lands. Now that Usama bin Laden has shown and proven to we Persians it's possible to attack the foul land of Satan successfully. We shall do likewise, and will cause further civilian death and destruction to the United States.

"As bin Laden believes, thus do I believe. There is no difference between America's soldiers and their worthless civilians who pollute the lands of Allah. Although we believe Satan is in control of the United States that does not mean the land once we have destroyed the lowly infidels of that land, is not salvageable and usable to our needs. Once we have taken over the cursed lands of the United States, we'll purge the Satan from the foul lands, and then we'll convert anyone who we shall allow to live in that land, to the sacred beliefs of Ali and Allah and the Islam faith. Bah Major, this is mere talk, and I don't waste my time with idle talk. I rely on actions, and faithful followers will do my bidding, or you'll all suffer the same foul fate I have offered to Major Mohajerani here.

"I believe we covered all of what I had on my mind, and what the Major has offered my fellow faithful Persian brothers and sisters. I order all of you to return to your troops, and order your soldiers to continue with their faithful war against the lowly American infidels who invaded the Arab lands in Iraq, and elsewhere in the Middle East." The Vulture snarled at his warriors gathered at the meeting as he stood, and then he left the room in haste, not requesting to speak to any of them further. This was common for the Iranian General known as the Vulture, because he was exercising his complete control and dominance over his subordinates, and he was furthering his command over them at the same time.

Every Iranian Officer who remained seated in the room was quiet until the Vulture was gone from the room, and then their conversations started in mere low whispers and quick glances. Over fear the ruthless and extremely deadly Vulture was waiting outside the room to hear what they had to say about his last orders. The rest of the Iranian officers filed out of the room once they understood their orders and they wanted to be well away from the frightening and powerful Iranian General, and then they headed back to their prospective military units to get their soldiers working on the Vulture's orders. None of the Iranian soldiers wanted to risk the great wrath of the man they feared and called the Vulture.

The terrorist leader known as the Vulture, rushed to a private room in the building they were using for their meeting, and he reported in with the President of Iran, to inform him of what his soldier was able to develop to continue their war against the American forces occupying the Arab lands of Iraq. Every thought locked in the Vulture's hate filled mind of late, was directed to the task of attacking the American soldiers operating in Iraq. He was constantly begging his Iranian President to allow him to send his Persian fighters to the land of Satan itself, to strike at the very heart of the evil land from within its own borders.

His unfettered anger and hatred of the United States and all she stood for knew no bounds, and he wanted to strike at America from anywhere or however he could. Another force driving the Iranian General on with his mounting anger, was the fear that bin Laden was going to hit the United States again, and he wanted to hit the hated Americans before bin Laden aimed his sights at the United States for another time, and caused serious problems to his future plans to attack the United States.

Right now the extremely dangerous Vulture understood all too well, if he was successful and attacked the United States at the same time. The blame for the attack would surely be leveled on bin Laden's shoulders. That would leave him and his forces free to hit the United States again and again, until the foolish Americans were finally able to discover Iran and himself, were the ones who were behind the latest terrorist attacks aimed at their cursed and foul country.

The Iranian General felt by the time the Americans were able to discover it was his nation behind the attacks against them. The United States would be so weakened by his efforts they would be almost powerless, or the American troops would be stretched so thin they would never be able to mount a retaliatory military response against his country. But again, the Iranian President continued to refuse his request to place one of his terrorist cells operating within the borders of the United States. The Iranian Leader merely ordered his fearful terrorist to remain in the borders of Iran, and to continue with his attacks against the American forces killing their brothers and sisters in Iraq and Afghanistan.

This order from his Iranian President served to further the Persian General's anger towards the United States, and now against his own President. He was chomping at the bit to engage the American forces with the forces Iran was massing for attack inside Iraq, once the American invaders were forced out of that country. With the defensive missiles Iran was currently developing and also secretly buying from Russia and China, along with their secret nuclear weapons research and development program. The Vulture believed Iran would be able to fight America to at least a stand still. And, that would place Iran on the winning side, because the Iranian forces will be fighting closer to their military support structure, and the American forces would be forced to have their military supplies shipped across the oceans for their use, and this would place them at the serious disadvantage with any war against his country.

The Vulture leaned back in the chair and forced himself to relax, and place these troubling thoughts out of his mind. Because he understood sooner or later, his President would finally send him and a good number of his Persian fighters to the United States, to begin their opening attacks against that country from within its own borders. Then his lifelong dream of destroying the United States would start in earnest. The Vulture removed a pack of American made cigarettes from his pocket, and he tapped out a Marboro cigarette and placed it between his lips, after that he removed the sold gold cigarette lighter and lit it. He drew the smoke deep into his lungs and he held his breath and the smoke trapped in his lungs.

The Vulture had no qualms about smoking the American made cigarette, because he enjoyed smoking so much, and he felt in the near future he would be in the land that made the evil things, and he would be able to get an endless supply of the well liked cigarettes. The cigarette helped him to relax a little easier and he closed his eyes, and then the Vulture dreamed of himself leading his faithful Persian fighters against the hated American forces in their own country. He closed his eyes and allowed a slight smile to slowly cross his lips, over the pleasing thought as he took another drag from the cigarette.

THE ISLAND OF MARATHON IN THE FLORIDA KEYS. FEBRUARY 15th, 2004. SUNDAY

This was the first Sunday since the elite group of specialized soldiers returned to the tiny Island of Marathon in the Florida Keys, and as promised. The soldiers were looking forward to tonight when they would head for the local bar known as Dockside. The soldiers knew once they showed up at the bar, they would take it over, and Walker and Ramirez were looking forward to letting down their hair and having a good time for the night. He checked in with the Rocket man, and he informed Walker there was going to be three different bands at the bar on this night.

Rocket man was a well liked local on the Island, and he knew much about the interesting history of the Island, and he was as old as dirt. But he sang great, and he was involved in pushing many local kids forming up bands, and he was getting them work at local bars across the Island. What started out as the battle of the bands at Dockside, turned into a few selected bands that would play for most of the night and entertain the drinkers who showed up for a night out on the Island. Dockside was a great bar, because you could actually dock your boat at the bar, get good cooked food, and meet many of the locals from the Island, and it was also the place to be on a weekend night as well.

It was nine thirty a.m. on Sunday, and the soldiers staying at Walker's home were excited about tonight. Their energy level was up, and No Neck and Ice were out of the home and took a walk around Treasure Island on Marathon. There were seventeen homes in this section, and one was bigger than the other. There was an empty lot and the two walked out to the ocean and stared at the water and the many pleasure boats dotting the calm and crystal clear water. The day was beautiful, sunny with a slight breeze, and the temperature was supposed to climb into the upper seventies to the low eighties for the day, with no hint of rain.

Sergeant Dorothy Ramirez was filled with added energy, because she was home and enjoying her son and Walker. She made breakfast for her lover and her son. The Ghost joined them for breakfast, and he asked Walker were the other two soldiers from their Unit were at. Walker grumbled they must have gone for a walk.

The Ghost finished off his breakfast, and then he went outside and picked up the pole and went fishing. He brought bait the other day and shoved in Walker's freezer. He loved fishing and he was going to make the most of it while visiting with Walker and Ramirez, before he went home to his family for a while. He sat on the dock and pitched the line in the canal. Yesterday he caught three mangrove snappers about two to three pounds each and he wanted to catch a few more. A boat started coming down the canal and it forced him to pull in his line, or the prop from the motor would have cut his line.

While Walker was seated at the kitchen table the phone rang, but he made no attempt to answer it. Ramirez was at the sink cleaning the dishes and she was nearer to the phone, so she answered it. It was the Rocket man and he asked Ramirez if he could speak to Walker. She told him to hang on and she brought the phone to Walker and told him who wanted to speak to him. He grabbed the phone and smiled as he said into the receiver.

"Hey man, what the fuck's happening with you today, good buddy?"

"Walker, I wanted to warn you there's going to be a professional country and western singer at the bar tonight, and he's supposed to do a few songs for us, man." The Rocket replied.

"That's great the stinking bar must be making money hand over fist to be able to afford to pay a professional singer now, buddy." Walker mumbled back at his friend over the phone this time.

"It's not that way man, the dude's here fishing and I happened to bump into him at the fishing docks and we started talking. I told him about the bar and he thought that was great and he would meet me there tonight. I joked to him I sang for drinks at the bar, and he offered to do a few of his songs to help me out with my drinking, man. He's a real cool dude and a big time singer, man. I wanted to tell you about him so you can tell the other soldiers about the singer, man. It looks like it's going to be a great night. I also told many of my friends, so the bar should be over packed and really hoping tonight, man." Rocket informed Walker over the phone.

CHAPTER SIX

"Great man, I like country singing and I'll tell the others about the dude, man." Walker replied as he hung up the phone on his friend because he hated speaking on the thing. He laid the receiver down on the table and looked out the window and saw the Ghost trying to pull in a fish he caught and he smiled. But his thoughts were interrupted by Ramirez as she asked him if he wanted anything else to eat.

He turned to face her and saw her smiling so lovingly and he returned her smile as he replied he was full. But he never did tell her about the country singer who was going to be at the bar tonight. The reason he did not was because he knew Ramirez loved country singing, so he was going to use this as a surprise when they showed up at the bar.

He could not be happier, because he was home with his future wife and their son, and a few of their closest friends and fellow soldiers. He thought what more could he ask for in life than what he was presently surrounded with. Ramirez walked to the kitchen table and she straddled his legs and sat down on his lap and smiled in his face. Automatically, his hands went for her breasts and he stared playing with them. She purred and he lifted the front of her bathing suit and drew her nipple in his mouth. She held his head to her breast and wiggled her chest in his face. He was starting to get aroused and the way she was sitting on his lap, she could feel him and this turned her on all the more. She stood still straddling his legs and hitched the bottom of her bathing suit to the side, while he worked himself out of his bathing suit. When he was out she sat down after guiding him home, and started to make love facing him.

Just as they were really getting into the act of loving each other, the Ghost charged in the kitchen holding a large fish and asked Walker. "Hey buddy, what the hell do you call this damn thing I just caught man? I never saw a stinking fish like this one, man." When he asked Walker the question, he realized what the two were doing and he added. "Hey man, you two are worse than a pair of dogs in fucking heat, man. Have you two no shame?" The Ghost asked as he moved so he could better see them doing the dirty, and the two of them did not miss a beat with their lovemaking.

"Hey Raz, can you move your right leg a little so I can see what's going on in there baby."

She did not look back at the Ghost as she moved her leg a little as he requested.

"That's it baby, now I can see what you two are doing and I was right, you two don't have shame." The Ghost said as he moved a little closer to the two so he could get a better look now.

Walker was thrusting his hips up and rubbing both of her breasts and he growled at the Ghost. "I thought you were fucking fishing buster. Get the fuck outta here and leave us alone will ya."

"I was fishing man, but I didn't catch anything like you caught, buddy. Besides, this is a helluva lot better than any fucking fishing, man." The Ghost replied as he pulled a chair out from under the kitchen table and he sat and made himself comfortable, as he continued to watch the two of them make love to each other.

"What's better than fucking fishing, man?" The massive No Neck asked as he and Ice came walking into the kitchen, and the two of them saw what was going on in the room.

"Hey man, watching Walker making love to Raz is much better than fucking fishing, pal." The Ghost replied as he turned and smiled at the two other soldiers, and then he went back to watching the two still going at it.

Ice moved a little deeper into the kitchen and she moved to the Ghost's side and looked at what he was watching, and then she said. "Gees Ghost, you have one helluva ringside seat here, buster. You can see him sinking his whole thing into Raz. Is there another seat around here I can use, I want to watch some of this myself. Will you look at the two of them going at it please? I never knew it was so exciting to watch two people while they were making love to each other like this, Ghost. This is crazy."

Neither Walker nor Ramirez stopped what they were doing, and before he came, he pulled out of Ramirez and started jerking himself off as he growled at Ice. "Hey baby, if you liked watching us making love, you're gonna get a real bang outta this shit, little sister." Just as he finished his words, he came between Ramirez's legs and it sprayed all over her.

"Oh man, that was fucking nasty buster. Exciting yes, but nevertheless it was nasty, Walker." Ice cried out, but she did not take her eyes off of what he was doing to his girlfriend.

Ramirez kissed Walker as she also came, and then she hugged his head close to her chest again. When she was finished, she got off his lap and complained at her soldier and lover. "Gees Robert, you made one helluva mess on the front of my bathing suit, mister." She took a towel and wiped the mess from her. All the while she was cleaning herself, she was topless and unashamed about it.

"Man Raz, you got some nice tits there girl." Neck mumbled at her as he enjoyed the view.

Ice turned to the big man and complained as she pulled open the front of her bathing suit and flashed the Neck and the Ghost as she complained at them. "What do you think of my boobs?"

Even Walker looked at her as the Neck replied. "You got some great tits as well baby."

"You're lucky mister." Ice snapped at him as she wiggled her chest at everyone in the room.

"Hey people, it looks like I hafta find myself a chick at the stinking bar tonight, so I can have someone to stick their boobs in the front of the rest of you guy's faces. Don't get me wrong guys, I love seeing the boobs being stuck in my face this morning. But I feel kinda left out, because I don't have a lady to play with. Man Ice, you're looking fucking real good, and after that little sex show Walker and Raz just gave us, I think you better put your puppies away before I make a damn fool of myself. I'm horny enough to take my pen in hand, baby."

"Oh you poor thing you." Ice said as she walked over to the Ghost and she stuck her breasts in his face and wiggled her chest, slapping him on both sides of his face with them.

"That's it girl, beat me to death with those little puppies of yours, girl." The Ghost offered as he made the best of having Ice's breasts shoved in his face, as he licked at the hard nipples now.

Walker smiled over Ice's actions with the Ghost, now he was certain she was over the terrible wound she received in one of their operations when she was wounded in the shoulder, and the wound was serious and it almost drove her out of the service.

Ramirez straightened out her bathing suit, and it was none too soon, because when she was dressed, the Mutt, Blind Date, Buckethead, Baby Tee, and the Hunter walked into the home, and they got right on Ice for popping her breasts out in front of the Ghost. Everyone was in great moods, and it was carrying over to each of them.

Ramirez served everyone a cold Bud and the conversations flowed. The soldiers were making so much noise Robert Jr. came in the kitchen because he was afraid he was missing something. His mother picked him up and her son wrapped his legs around her waist and she ended up carrying him around while speaking to the other soldiers in the kitchen.

Buckethead was hungry and he went to the refrigerator and searched it for something to eat, causing the Hunter to bitch at Walker. "It looks like the walking garbage can is looking for some food. Maybe I'll head out and pick up some burgers, and we can cook out and chill until tonight when we head out to the stinking bar, man. Say Walker, can I use your car man?"

"Yeah sure, any time man." Walker replied as he went fishing in his bathing suit pocket for his car keys, and once he found them he tossed them to the Ghost who caught them in the air, and then he turned and headed out of the room. Buckethead followed the Ghost because he wanted to see if he needed to pick up some other stuff to eat while they were out.

Ramirez fed her son while the soldiers went out back. She was waiting for the babysitter to arrive and take care of Robert Jr. for the night out she was planning with the other soldiers. Walker and the other soldiers set up the cook out and prepared for the burgers. Baby Tee and Ice went to the dock and they stared at the water, they saw a number of boats on the water. The two sat on the edge of the dock and dangled their feet in the water and spoke together. Neck, and the Hunter stayed with Walker and the Hunter commented about Ice.

"Walker, Ice looks great man. I'm glad she toughed it out and she stayed with the stinking Unit and us man. She's a damn good soldier, and she has earned her damn dog tags, buddy."

"You can say that again my friend, but there was no way in hell I was gonna allow her to scrub outta the Unit because she was wounded carrying out a mission along with the rest of us pukes, Homes. It's not that easy to get into our Unit and it's twice as hard to get out of our Unit, friend." He replied as he looked at the two female soldiers sitting on his dock and he grinned at them. All three elite soldiers were now looking at the two women, but their concentration was interrupted by the Ghost and Buckethead, as they came charging around the home with their arms full of beer and burgers.

Buckethead put his packages on the table and tore into them. He pulled a tray of raw chop meat out and chucked six burger patties on the fire. The Ghost took his place as the cook and he started flipping the burgers as Buckethead took another packages of chop meat out, and he dumped more burgers on the fire as the Ghost bitched at him. "Holy shit man, how the hell many of the damn things are you going to eat, big man?"

"Hey man there's eight of us here and I figured the stinking chicks would only eat one of the damn things, and we'll eat at least two apiece. Don't worry about it man, if there's any of the damn things left over, I'll clean them up for us." The massive man replied as he watched the Ghost flip the burgers again.

"Yeah, I bet you will, you walking garbage can." The Ghost growled at the large man, and then added. "Hey Bucket, dig out some of the stinking hot dogs, I want one of them buddy."

"How many should I take out Ghost?" Bucket asked the extremely dangerous soldiers.

"What the hell do you care, you told me you'll neaten up anything left over, man. Just dig out some of them I'm sure they'll go sooner or later man. We can leave them and graze on them until we're ready to head out for the bar later on tonight, buddy. But I'm not gonna eat too much today, I wanna leave some room for the suds tonight, man. I intend to tie one on." The Ghost announced proudly loud enough for everyone to hear his words as he grinned at Bucket.

The rest of the day went by at a snail's pace as usual, whenever someone was looking to go out and have some fun at night. The twenty seven year old babysitter came over and she was taking care of Robert Jr. and she put him to sleep at seven p.m. Then the babysitter sat with the soldiers as they talked about the upcoming night, and some of their exploits while in the service of their country. Many of the stories were so colorful it made the babysitter laugh, while others chilled her to her very soul.

Walker and Ramirez disappeared upstairs to get dressed for the night's festivities, the other soldiers were going the way they were dressed. Everyone was sitting in the kitchen when Ramirez came walking downstairs, and her appearance nearly made the soldiers choke. She was dressed in a skirt that barely covered her private parts, and her blouse was one of the halter tops so small, the fabric of the blouse was having trouble keeping her breasts inside the blouse. She smiled, because the effect of the way she was dressed was exactly what she was looking for from the other soldiers. She was proud of her shape, and she was not afraid to show it off, and tonight she was going to be the center of attention if she had anything to do with it.

Ice stared at Ramirez for a few moments until she said. "Hey girl, in an outfit like that, there's going to be no doubt about your fine shape, or what you're wearing under there, lady."

"That's what I want to say with this outfit, honey. Tonight, I'll going to drive Robert out of his ever loving mind with want and desire for me, and when I have him right where I want him. I'm going to make love to him like I never made love to him before in our lives, honey." She offered with an evil grin as she turned her hips to the side, and she licked the tip of her finger and then touched it to her rearend, and she made a hissing sound with her mouth, and then grinned sexily at the soldiers gathered in the kitchen.

"I have some bad news for you girl, Walker isn't the only one you're going to drive wild on this night dressed like that, little lady. Any man at that stinking bar tonight in his right mind, and some of the women as well, are going to be drooling all over you tonight looking like that, girl." Baby Tee offered this time while getting on Ramirez a little herself now.

"What's your point girl?" She asked the young female soldier with a grin on her lips.

"I think the point she's trying to make Raz, is you look hot enough to eat right where you're standing, pretty girl. And, I'd like to be the first one to offer you my kind lovemaking abilities, and make a fine meal outta ya right off while I'm at it, girl. Here, allow me to clean a place for you to sit down honey." The Mutt offered as he rapidly rubbed his hands over his mouth, and then he licked his lips at her.

"Hey dog man I'm afraid you already have someone who claimed that place for sitting on your ugly puss, old buddy." Ramirez retorted happily to the Mutt as she smiled pleasantly at the soldier. She could not hide the love she felt for the extremely dangerous soldier, he was Walker's best and closest friend, and she was really happy because of that fact.

"Well girl, like I said, I have no one with me, so allow me to make you the same offer that the stinking Mutt has just offered you, lady." The Ghost now offered to Sergeant Ramirez, as he took a step towards her.

"And what offer is that Ghost?" Walker asked as he now came walking down the steps from upstairs, and he looked at the well-liked soldier.

"Nothing man, it was nothing buddy. I was just popping off a little, that's all Walker." The Ghost said as he stepped back and started to speak to his partner in crime, the Hunter.

"You missed it Robert. The Mutt offered for me to sit on his face because of the way I'm dressed, but I pointed out he was with Blind Date now. So Walter offered to do what the Mutt wanted to do to my body, because he doesn't have someone to play with on the Island yet, honey." She offered as she put on a wide smile and aimed it at her lover.

He took a look at the way she was dressed, and then he mumbled at her. "Do you have a permit for the way you're dress, honey? Well baby, after getting an eye full of you, I can blame the poor man, baby. Tell ya what, if the stinking Ghost can't score with any hens from the bar tonight, maybe you can take care of the both of us when we get back home, baby. It's been quite a while since the last time we played patty cake with some of the uthers from the group, and you seem like one guy won't be enough for you tonight, baby."

"Walker please, Cathy's here and I don't want her to get the wrong impression about us." She complained at her soldier, and then she turned her attention to the babysitter and offered with concern in her tone. "Cathy, Robert was just being a wiseguy we never do anything like that. We don't swing honey. Isn't that right Robert dear?" She asked as she turned her attention on Walker, and she gave him the look that warned him he better agree with her, or he was not going to get any tonight, or for a long time to come either.

He placed a ridicules look on his face as he corrected himself before the stunned looking young baby sitter. "Say Cathy, I was only busting my lady's horns a little, that's all. We don't do anything like that honey."

"Why not, it's nothing new on the Island, Mr. Walker. I have a few friends who do that kind of stuff you know. Now don't get me wrong, I don't do that kind of thing, and I'm happily married, Mr. Walker." She offered in her defense after seeing the look that crossed over Walker's face as he stared at her now.

"Hey honey, where do these friends of yours live? Even though Walker and Raz won't admit they're into swinging, me and my lady are." The Mutt remarked as he grinned at her.

"Knock it off wiseguy, or you and I are going to have a private little conversation, dog man." Ramirez snapped at the Mutt, and then she gave him the same look she just aimed at Walker a few moments before. It was enough to cut the Mutt off and end his words to the babysitter.

Everyone in the kitchen laugh as the talk about swinging ended, and Baby Tee and Ice said they were going to use one of Ramirez's bathrooms to freshen up a little, so they could join in on some of the fun time for later tonight. The soldiers watched the two pretty girls head upstairs, and then Ramirez asked the others if they wanted to start off the night early by having a beer, before they left for the bar. She passed out the beers, and the babysitter had one which concerned her a little, but when she never asked for another, Ramirez felt much better about leaving her with her son for the night.

The soldiers decided not to head out for the bar until around eight, because that's when the bands started to play. Being Walker's home was less than five minutes away from the bar eight o'clock was a good time to head out for the place. The soldiers were on their second beers when the female soldiers came downstairs. They not only fixed their faces, but they altered their clothes because they did not want to be outshined by Ramirez, and the way she was dressed. Ice cut the sleeves off her blouse, and now she had one lower button buttoned, and she tied the rest of the shirt in a knot which exposed her great midriff, she rolled up her dress until it was almost as short as Ramirez's. It was easy for the male soldiers to realize Ice had removed her bra, because of the way she cut off the sleeves of the blouse. They could easily see the sides of her outstanding breasts.

Baby Tee was also dressed to kill for the upcoming night's festivities, she was dressed in a sort of halter top blouse, and she had it tied around her neck and her breasts seemed like they were fighting the soft fabric in there want to be free of the restricting cloth. The effect was perfect on the two pretty women, and because they were not committed like Ramirez and Blind Date were, all four male soldiers closed in on them. Because of the smallness of Baby Tee's breasts, it was easy to see everything she had if you stood by her side and looked under her arms into her blouse.

Walker looked at his watch and saw it was a quarter to eight and he announced in a booming voice. "Okay people, enuf fooling around and finish off your stinking beers. It's almost time for us to head out for the damn bar. When you people drain your beers we'll leave for some fun and games for the night. Cathy, you have Robert Jr. and the house to watch. No more drinking from you until we get back home and relieve you of your duty with my son. I'm driving, so you pukes who wanna hitch a stinking ride with us, betta be ready to head out when I wanna leave. Or you'll find yourselves having to walk over to the stinking bar."

"I'm gonna drive my car tonight man, so the rest of you stinking pukes hafta go along with me." The Mutt announced as he placed a wide, shit eating grin on his lips this time.

"In your dreams you're driving our car tonight, mister. You can't even drive a stick up a dog's ass. You already had too much to drink, and if you think I'm going to allow you to drive in your present condition, you're sadly mistaken, mista. I'm driving the car, and if you don't like it, you can always walk over to the bar tonight." Blind Date hissed at the Mutt as she put out her hand, and then she wiggled her fingers and waited for the Mutt to turn the keys over to her.

The Mutt stared at the pretty French female soldier he was dating, and he made no attempt to give up the car keys to her. He hesitated because he did not want to look pussy whipped in front of the rest of the soldiers, so all he did was stare back at his lover with a dumb look on his face.

"Forget about the stupid look mista, and give me the keys to the car. Don't keep me waiting too long, or I'm going to get angry and I'll take the keys away from you by force if I have to, mista." Blind Date warned the Mutt as she placed her hands on her hips and her angry stare sharpened as she continued to glare at him.

The other specialized soldiers smiled at the foolish looking Mutt as they grumbled "whoa" at him, and then they waited for the Mutt to respond to Blind Date's last threat she just leveled against him. They all knew he was going to give into the pretty and young female soldier, and give her the keys so she could drive the car for them, and the Mutt was only being stubborn and stupid for the time being until he finally did the right thing and gave her the keys.

"Don't make me get you in a head lock and beat the crap out of you in front of the rest of our people, and then have to take the keys from your broken and battered body while it's lying out cold on the floor, mista. I'm waiting Mutt, give me the car keys!" Blind Date growled at the Mutt as she turned more directly at him, and she removed her hands from her hips now and took a more threatening stance against him.

"Hey girl, you're really serious about this shit aren't you? You're gonna really try and beat me over the stinking head for my damn car keys, aren't ya, honey?" The Mutt mumbled at her as he stared back at his girlfriend again.

"Damn right I am Mutt. I didn't go through a military action and survive it, only to get hurt driving with a drunk driver, mista. You better give me those damn car keys right now if you know what's good for you, buster."

"Who the hell lit the fuse on your tampon, baby? Okay, you win and you can drive the damn car if it'll make you feel any betta, honey. Tonight, when we get back home we go a little one on one on the stinking mats, and we'll see who'll come out on top once I pin your purdy little ass to the damn mats. When I'm on top of ya, you gotta take care of me with your stinking mouth, honey. That's the only way you're gonna get me offa the top of you tonight, baby." The Mutt smirked happily at his lover as he gave her a quick wink of the eye, and then he slowly ran his tongue over his lips as a further warning to her and then grinned at her.

"C'mon Mutt we have company will ya please, and I don't think she really needs to hear any of that filthy talk that's usually coming from your disgusting mouth and mind, dog man." Sergeant Dorothy Ramirez bitched at the soldier, but before he could respond to her angry words. Blind Date fired back at him because she was so caught up in their conversation that she was not going to let it go that easily now.

"You really think you're going to get on top over me, huh wiseguy. It's going to be the other way around and when I get you pinned on the mats, I'm going to straddle your face and make you take care of me for a change with your mouth, Mista Wiseguy. When was the last time you did me that way anyway mista? All I do any longer is work you over with my mouth, and it's about time you return the favor to me once in a while you know, mista."

Ramirez turned to Cathy thoroughly embarrassed by the way the two soldiers were bantering around with each other, and she was surprised to see her smiling and staring at the both of them as she announced to the younger lady. "Honey, I'm going to get all of these crude soldiers out of my home, so you don't have to hear any more of their filthy jaw jacking. We'll be home at two or three in the morning."

DOCKSIDE BAR ON MARATHIN IN THE FLORIDA KEYS
SUNDAY, FEBRUARY 15th, 2004. EIGHT OH FIVE P.M.

Captain Robert Walker parked his car across the street from the bar in the designated parking area for the place, and Blind Date had to drive about a half a block further down the road, because the other parking places were full. As he got out of the car, he could already hear Rocket man introducing the first band to play for the night. They waited for the other soldiers to linkup back up with them, and then the soldiers entered the bar together. The girls headed right for the bar to get the drinks for the soldiers, as Walker and the others took over the back area of the bar for the rest of the night.

As usual, Walker and the Mutt sat with their backs against the wall, and they had a great view of the entire bar from their position. The ever on alert Marine Captain remembered his training, when he sat with his back against the wall, he had a much better field of vision, and a better line of fire also. The Mutt scanned the bar and saw five women who did not seem like they were with anyone, so he knew the Hunter and Ghost should be able to find someone to go home with tonight. He drew Walker's attention to a young and good looking blonde on the dance floor and she was dancing by herself, but she knew what she was doing alright.

Walker looked at the blonde then he mumbled at the Mutt, because of the way the blonde's breasts were bouncing. "Hey man, she's not making milk she's making fucking butter, man."

"She sure as hell is man, but at least the uther guys stand a pretty good chance of picking someone up tonight, man." The Mutt shut up when the women came over to their tables carrying beers and wine for the group. Already, the women were drawing attention from the men in the bar, and even some of the women were looking at them as they sat down with the others.

Rocket man was with the band singing, and when he noticed Walker and the others come in the bar, he left his friends and headed for Walker. When Rocket man reached the table, Walker stood and they shook hands and hugged each other as the Rocket offered. "Hey Walker, I'm glad you made it tonight, I have someone I want you to meet, man. He's the dude I was telling you about on the phone." Rocket man stopped talking and he turned and looked until he saw the guy he wanted, and then he waved him over with his hand.

A guy sitting at the bar got out of the seat and headed for the Rocket. When he reached them, Rocket offered to Walker. "Hey Robert Walker, this guy is Toby, we all call him Tee K, man. He's going to be doing a number of his top songs for us tonight, once this band finishes up their gig and they get off the stage…"

"Isn't your last name Keith, and aren't you a popular country and western singer, Tee K?" The suddenly excited Sergeant Ramirez asked as she stood and she could not hide the glitter in her eyes, as she smiled at him and then waited for him to reply to her question.

"I'm afraid you have me there young lady, but please don't let my name get out Ma'am, or I'll be flooded with people hanging onto me all night long, Ma'am. I'm here trying to get some fishing in, and to relax a little. I just finished my last tour and I'm taking a few months off."

"You don't have to worry about me letting your name out Tee K. I want to keep you all to myself tonight. I have every CD you ever made, and I love your singing, Tee K. Are you really going to sing for us tonight? I'd really love that." Ramirez asked the country western singer as she continued to grin at him now.

"Yes, but I'm going to wait until everyone's good and drunk first, so they might not recognize me so easily. But I'll tell you what. If you want, I can come over to your place tomorrow and sign the CDs you have of mine, young lady." Tee K offered to Ramirez as he flashed a great smile of his own at her.

"Hey man, if you're gonna do that for my girl, I'll tell ya what man. If you sign her CDs, I'll take you out on my boat for a day of some serious fishing, man. We can have a real blast and you can stay over with us for a few days if you wanna hide from the other pukes on this stinking Island, man." Walker offered as he released the singer's hand and he nodded at him.

"I'd love that sir, and we can jam one night for what you're offering me, young lady." Tee K offered as he turned and he faced Ramirez again. He hated to stay at the small motel room he was using to hide out in on the Island.

"Really, I can't believe you might be staying with us, let alone sing a few songs for us one night, Tee K." Ramirez replied as she stared at the singer with star struck eyes.

"I'm sorry Ma'am, but I don't know your name or the names of the others with you, Ma'am."

"I guess that's my fault buddy." Walker offered as he introduced Tee K to the other soldiers, and once the singer found out the people he was speaking to were part of the elite Special Forces Unit he heard so much about lately, it was his turned to be awed by them. Being a part of the country singing profession, the singers were very patriotic and proud of any soldiers fighting for their country. Tee K started to go on and on with his admiration of the soldiers, almost to the point where he was starting to bore them. The Mutt cut Tee K off as he offered in a matter of fact voice to the singer.

"Hey man there's only two defining forces that ever offered to die for you, Homes. Jesus Christ and the American soldier. One died for your stinking sins, the other died for your damn freedom, Dude."

"Wow, that's deep soldier, I never heard it stated quite like that, and so eloquently at that might I add, sir." Tee K replied as he now stared with admiration at the Mutt.

The band was really starting to get into the songs, and this caused the soldiers to look at what was going on on the dance floor. Guys and dolls were dancing and the Ghost and Hunter spotted a few women sitting alone, or dancing with each other. The Ghost locked onto a pretty little brown haired girl, and he stood and announced. "Hey people excuse me for a few minutes, but I think I see something I might like to spend the night with. I'm going out there and asking that little hen for a stinking dance. C'mon Hunter, there's another pretty little bitch out there looking for someone to dance with also, man."

Tee K watched the soldiers head for the dance floor. He turned red because the soldiers were cursing so much in front of the women. He was a good man who respected women, he did not drink much and never smoked pot, but all that was going to change on this night.

Walker saw the look on the singer's face and he realized he was never with people like his, and he smiled as he sort of felt sorry for what the singer was going to go through. He watched the Mutt dancing with Blind Date, and they looked great. The Mutt was an excellent dancer and he was really making the best of it, he was all over the dance floor and many of the other dancers were giving him the room to work it.

The Ghost hooked up with the brown haired girl, and they were off the dance floor and sharing a drink at the bar. He found out her name was Linda, and they were laughing and joking together, and the Ghost had his hand resting protectively on her back and Walker knew it would not be long before he had his hands all over her fine body. The Hunter was busy dancing with the blonde that Walker and the Mutt locked their eyes on as they first entered the bar.

The drinks flowed all night long and the Ghost brought Linda over to the table and she was speaking with the other soldiers. She was friendly and hitting it off with the Ghost. But the Hunter came back to the table alone, and he looked dejected which forced Walker to laugh and ask him. "Whatsumatter man, it's not so easy picking up a hen I see, buddy."

"Arrr… man, she's like Venus Dalmio, she's beautifully but she's not all there man. We were getting along real good until she told me she was into girls, and she liked Baby Tee, man." The Ghost complained as he shot a quick smile at Tee, and she grinned back at him.

Ice noticed the Mutt and Blind Date coming back to the table and she warned Walker. "Hey Walker, here comes your twin brother from another mother, the king of slime square, mister."

The Mutt sat and noticed Walker looking at him and he griped at his lifelong friend. "Hey man, what the fuck you looking at me like that for, man? I didn't fucking do nuthin wrong yet you know, buddy. I've been friendly with everyone at the stinking bar, man. But I gotta warn ya buddy, the night's still young and I sure one of these pukes is gonna get on my dick nerve."

"I see you're still holding a stinking grudge against the English language, buddy." Walker fired back at his lifelong friend as he grinned at him again.

The Mutt ignored Walker's snappy words as he got on the Hunter's case and said. "Hey Hunter, I see you didn't do too well with that stinking chick you were aiming yourself at man. She looks severely fuckable to me man. You should keep at her and see where it goes man. Tell you what, if you can't land her yourself, I'll give her a try and then I'll dump her off on you."

Blind Date got angry at the Mutt for offering to get the girl for the Hunter and she snapped angrily at him. "You think so mista you go anywhere near that girl and you'll be looking for a new girlfriend come morning time, mista. You belong to me and I won't share you with her."

"Arrr… she had a voice that sounded like broken plumbing, man. It was grating on my stinking dick nerve, buddy." The Hunter replied in a flat tone as he did not look at the Mutt.

"Yeah, but I bet her pussy's tighter than two coats of frigging paint, man." The Mutt retorted while trying to keep the conversation going about the other girl.

Walker cast a quick glance at the country singer, and noticed he turned a little red over Mutt's comment about the girl now dancing with another girl from the bar. He again realized it was going to be a long night for the poor guy the longer he hung around with them. He turned to Ramirez and she knew what was bothering her lover.

Ice took offense to the Mutt's crude words about the young girl, and she snapped hotly at him. "Hey Mutt, that was really disgusting you know, if I click my heels together will you disappear for the rest of the night?"

"Ha fucking ha little sister, that was funny, real fucking funny girl. Keep it up Ice, and you might make comedian of the stinking year, baby sister. Hey, who's the new breast of fresh air at the stinking table, man? She didn't come in with us, where did she come from, people. Hey baby, what's your sign and who the hell are you, girl?" The Mutt asked as he looked at the pretty girl sitting with the Ghost.

"My sign to you is 'Do not enter' mister." Linda growled at the Mutt, not liking him already.

"Hey girl, that was a good one, I didn't see that one coming, honey. What's your name baby?"

"Linda." The lady replied to the Mutt as she held him in an angry stare down. "Linda wouldn't you like to know buster." Linda added in a hot tone of voice to the Mutt, refusing to back down an inch to the most insulting soldier covered with sweat from dancing.

"Hey Mutt, it looks like you gotta ask one of those guys who have ESPN, if you wanna know the rest of her name, man. I don't know, but before you came back to the table, we were getting to know her pretty well, and now she seems angry at the stinking world since you sat down with us, man." The massive No Neck offered, and he did not realize he made a mistake and meant to say ESP when he was speaking to the Mutt.

Even Buckethead turned and looked at the Neck, wondering if he knew what he just said. But the Neck was unaware of his comment, so everyone decided to let it go.

The Hunter noticed a new girl walk into the bar and he drew the Ghost's attention to her with a quick movement of his chin and he announced. "Hey pal, I see a serious burner over there and I'm gonna try my luck and see how I make out with her, man. I wanna be with someone tonight, and she looks real good man. You coming with, lady?"

The Ghost looked at Linda and she smiled, but she let him know she was not going out on the dance floor again. She told the Ghost she wanted to finish off her drink first.

"Linda, do you mind if I help my buddy out with this new girl he just spotted? He'll never land a girl for himself if I don't help him any, baby. He's kinda stupid when he tries to pick up a chick at a bar." The Ghost offered to his new friend, and then he waited for her reply.

"You can help him if you want to Walter. I'm going to stay behind and get to know the rest of your friends here a little better." Linda did not tell the Ghost, but she recognized the country singer and she wanted to stay near and get to know him and see what he was up to tonight.

"Thanks for being so understanding about this, honey. I'll be right back and I'll buy you another drink, and then we can get to know each uther a little betta, baby." The Ghost offered, and then he was off like a shot with his closest friend.

Ice watched the Unit's two-point men circle the unsuspecting girl, and she mumbled at the other soldiers. "Well, there goes frick and frack, and I feel sorry for the poor girl they have just leveled their evil eyes on. She doesn't stand a chance in hell with those two tonight."

The Mutt did not offer anything, he merely stood and pulled Blind Date up to her feet and announced to her. "C'mon baby, I wanna do some more dancing." The Mutt led Blind Date back onto the dance floor, and started dancing.

"Well, it looks like we just lost Adam and Evil as well. Look at them two dancing. I never realized the Mutt was such a good dancer." Ice said as she looked at Walker.

"Hey Ice, you're getting good with the stinking barbs lately, baby sister. You keep it up and we might hafta change your Unit name on ya." Walker warned her with a smile of his own.

"No thank you I like the nickname I have if you don't mind, Captain." Ice replied with a woman's sweet viciousness, as she stared at her Commanding Officer now.

Walker looked at Tee K and then he asked him as he sipped on his beer. "Hey Tee K, how long you gonna be staying on the stinking Island, man? I gotta know this shit, that way I know when to set up our fishing trip I promised ya, man."

"I'm on the Island until Tuesday night, and then I'm going home and start some work on a few new songs I have been meaning to work on, since I first thought of them sir."

"That's cool then we'll plan on going out tomorrow morning I guess at around nine. I need to stretch out my motors a little anyhow, man." Captain Walker replied as he took another pull from his beer.

"That'd be great with me sir. Say Walker, what kind of boat do you run anyway, sir?"

"I got a thirty three foot World Cat Tournament Edition center console with an eleven foot six beam. She's powered by twin Honda four stroke two hundred fifty horse power fuel injected outboards. It's purely set up as a fishing boat with the center console, but it has an inboard head and shower and a small cabin that can accommodate two people comfortable. I got a tuna tower with dual control stations, and she's an outstanding off shore fishing platform, and I can hit up fifty knots with her engines flat out. Hell man, I can do doughnuts in ten foot seas, and no one gets sick on her, she's so stable and smooth sailing in the roughest weather conditions. I have a tuna door and a ton of fishing and tackle stations and two live wells on her. I love the boat, I never found another boat that can take the water like she can, and once I take you out on her you'll want the World Cat also man." Walker proudly boasted about his boat.

CHAPTER SEVEN

"What's the name of your boat if you don't mind my asking, Walker?" Tee K was having a problem calling the soldier by Walker, but he heard everyone else refer to him that way, so he was only following suite. The Captain did not seem to mind being called by his last name.

"Whiskey Lullaby and she's a helluva deep sea fishing boat, Tee K. Like I told ya man, I can take her out in almost any weather conditions." Again, he bragged about his World Cat boat to the country western singer, as he finished off his third beer since entering the bar.

"Are you certain we're going to be able to get out that early tomorrow, Walker? Some of your friends are getting a little drunk I see." Tee K offered as he looked at the Neck and Buckethead.

Walker looked at the two soldiers Tee K was looking at, and then he added. "Don't worry about it man, all the soldiers won't be going out fishing with us. Just the Mutt and his lady will be going, and myself, and Raz. I'm not too worried about drinking too much either, because Raz can run the boat betta than I can Captain her. She never gets polluted and she'll pour me and you in the boat and take us out. When she's the Captain, I do the rigging of the rods and she hunts down the stinking fish for us. The last I heard, the bill fish are in and I wanna try and catch a sail fish, man. I catch and release them, I never kill a bill fish. Even when I Charter out, if the party want a bill fish, I won't allow them to kill one, it's only catch and release with me, man."

"That's great I'm looking forward to going out fishing tomorrow…" Tee K's words were cut off in mid sentence when the Rocket man got in front of the mike and announced there was a special guest singer who wanted to try his luck with some country songs for everyone at the bar.

Walker smiled at Tee K and then he grumbled at him in a pleasant tone. "Hey man, it looks like you're up next my friend. Are you really gonna try and sing some, sir?"

"I'll try my best Walker." Tee K smirked at the Special Forces soldier, and then he got up and headed for the mike. After speaking to the band that was his back up as he sung, Tee K took the mike and belted out a few songs.

Ramirez left the table and made her way to the platform and she ended up standing two feet away from Tee K, and she stared at him as he sang three songs. When he started to sing, many people at the bar immediately recognized him mainly by his songs. She cursed herself for not having a camera with her, but she was beaming from ear to ear because Tee K was staring at her all the while he sang, and she felt he was singing to her which made her proud.

When he finished, he looked for the soldiers, Ramirez was the only one who watched him sing, so Toby walked over to her and asked where the rest of her friends were at. She smiled as she replied they must have gone out to the cars, she knew what they were doing and she asked Tee K if he wanted to go out with the rest of the guys.

He followed her to the cars and spotted the few soldiers standing in front of Walker's car, and they looked like they were looking over the golf course. Ramirez led Tee K over to the group and the Mutt offered him the cooking joint.

"What's this sir?" He asked as he looked at the joint but he did not take it from the Mutt.

"It's a fucking joint asshole, if you wanna hang round with us, you gotta do what we do."

"Oh, I never did any of that stuff in my life sir." He offered politely as he refused the joint.

"Oh man, he's a fucking pussy I thought he was with all this no sir and yes Ma'am crap he keeps popping off with man." The Mutt griped as he took the joint back and a hit from it.

Tee K almost fell over because the female soldier he was introduced to as Baby Tee, had Buckethead's dick out of his pants and she was playing with it with her hand. Even though he was thirty three years old, he never witnessed someone doing a live sexual act.

Walker laughed when he noticed what the singer was looking at, as the bottle of rye reached him and he took a good slug from it, and then he passed it on to Tee K to see if he drank any hard stuff. He took the bottle and hit it good and strong. The bottle made the rounds and by the time it reached Tee K a second time, he took another strong pull from it. The Mutt saw him stagger a bit and he offered him a second joint the Ghost just rolled for them. This time he took the joint and took a hard pull from it. Instantly he started choking on the harsh smoke.

"Now you're flying with both fucking wings, man." The Mutt grumbled as he took the joint back and then passed it on to the Hunter. The Ghost had his hand stuffed down Linda's blouse, and Linda was watching what Baby Tee was doing to the soldier she knew as Buckethead.

Baby Tee was feeling the booze and pot, and she was now on her knees and had Buckethead's member in her mouth, and she was working over his shaft good and proper.

Tee K was feeling the booze and grass, and he was now leaning against the front of Walker's car for extra support, but he too was staring at what Baby Tee was doing to the massive soldier. Some of the other people at the bar started to leave, and Walker looked at his watch and saw it was ten minutes past eleven, and he knew the bands stopped playing at eleven, or the neighbors closest to the bar would start complaining to the police. Knowing the singing was over and being he offered to take him out fishing tomorrow, he decided to end the night and asked the others gathered by the front of his car.

"Hey guys, it's getting fucking late and if we're going out fishing tomorrow, what say we go back to my place and call it an early end to the night. Hey Tee K, you can come over and spend the night at my place, that way you won't hafta worry about getting over early, and we can leave the dock when we're ready to shove off." Walker offered to the singer as he smirked at him.

"Oh please stay at our place for the night Toby. I'd really love that you know sir." She offered as she looked like a young groupie as she grinned at Tee K and then waited for him to reply.

"I guess that would be fine then Ma'am. I want to go fishing tomorrow morning Ma'am."

"Then it settled man, you dumping off at our place for the night, pal. C'mon people let's get the hell outta here. Hey Baby, either get off his stinking knob or finish him off good and proper girl, we wanna leave for home honey." He complained at the pretty and smallish female soldier as he and everyone else watched her working over Buckethead's member like a pro.

Baby Tee did not miss a stroke as she moved one hand off of Buckethead's shaft, and she shot the bird at Walker as she continued working over Buckethead's member with her mouth.

"Hey girl, is that your IQ or the number of white parents you got?" The Mutt fired off at her.

Baby Tee pulled off Buckethead's shaft and she was about to bitch at the Mutt when Buckethead suddenly erupted, spraying himself all over her lips and face. Baby Tee pulled back and snapped at Bucket. "Man, you're disgusting, you sprayed all over my damn blouse you big pig you. Do any of the people have a rag or napkin I can use to clean myself up with please?"

Ramirez laughed as she offered her a napkin she took from the bar, and the soldiers watched as she cleaned herself up. Tee K was so high he even enjoyed the sex show, and when Buckethead came, he could not help it and he said as he watched the act finish. "Holy shit," because he felt the soldier almost drowned the poor petite female soldier with a flood of cum.

"Hey Walker, I think we're corrupting this square peg a little, man. Look at the prick, he's really fucked up, smoking grass and enjoying watching a sex act, and we got him cursing also, man. If the singing prick isn't more careful, we're gonna hafta draft his stinking ass into the damn Unit, buddy." The Mutt bitched as he watched Tee K staring at what Baby Tee was doing to Bucket's member and cleaning herself.

Baby Tee was trying to clean him up with the napkin, but he had come so much the napkin was soaked and it was falling apart in her hands. The ride to Walker's place was short, and Ramirez showed Tee K where he was going to sleep for the night. She gave him the extra room and he felt he just fallen asleep when he heard someone rummaging around in the kitchen.

Tee K looked at his watch and saw it was seven ten a.m. on Monday, and he got up and went out of the room. When Ramirez saw him she placed a smile on her lips as she announced. "The coffee's hot, so help yourself please. I'm making a bunch of sandwiches for our fishing trip today, Toby. From the looks of it, it's going to be a great day to be out on the water, sir."

She was making so much noise everyone else in the house woke and they stumbled out or their rooms. Buckethead and Baby Tee were planning to hang around the house, and the Ghost and Linda who stayed the night with him, were going down to Key Weird for the day.

As she poured a cup of coffee for her lover the phone ran, it was the Mutt and he was asking when they were heading out on for fishing. She handed the phone to Walker and he bitched at his lifelong friend. "Hey man, we're up and it seems we're waiting for you to get your ass over here, and then we're heading out, pal. When you coming over man? We're already late to head out, so I wanna shove off as soon as possible, man."

"Walker, me and Regina are heading for your place now, buddy. But no one else is in good enuf shape to make the stinking fishing trip with us, man. They're all still wasted from last night, man." The Mutt offered to Walker over the phone.

"Fine, I only wanted you and your lady to come out with us I'll drop the World Cat in the water. Raz is making a stack of stinking sandwiches, you bring the beer." Walker replied as he hung up and he said to Tee K. "Hey man, you wanna give me a stinking hand with the boat? I gotta get her offa the lift, and then start the motors. The others are on their way over."

It took the group forty five minutes to get out to the known fishing lanes. Ramirez was handling the World Cat like a pro, and Walker was busy setting up the tackle for fishing. Once the lines were baited, he had three lines out and two teasers out on the outriggers. Blind Date watched the Mutt playing with the line, trying to entice a bill fish to strike his bait. After fifteen minutes of trolling, Blind Date had enough and she took her top off and leaned against the tuna tower. Tee K was controlling the second pole, and when he noticed Blind Date take her //top off, he could not help it and he found himself trying to look at her lightly swaying breasts. Ramirez looked behind herself to see how the guys were making out with their fishing, and when she noticed Blind Date standing topless, she also removed her top as she continued to control the World Cat Catamaran.

After two hours of fishing, Walker's line snapped out and his reel started stripping off line by the yard. He called out over his shoulder to Ramirez. "Fish on."

Ramirez looked behind her again and when she saw Walker was fighting the fish, she placed the boat in idle for the moment as she yelled back at him from the helm. "Keep her head up or she'll dive on ya and you'll work like hell to get her back up, baby. You have to get her to jump once, and then she can't dive on ya any longer once her sacks are filled with air, honey."

"I know what the fuck I'm doing here baby. You just be ready to back down on the damn fish if she starts to strip more line on me, she's got about two hundred yards out already, baby."

"You got it Walker, Mutt, Tee K, get your lines in so they won't tangle with Robert's." Ramirez yelled, and then she made certain they did what she ordered them. Then she yelled at Blind Date. "Regina, pull in the outriggers for me so they don't get tangled up with Walker's line." She noticed the fish was tracking to the portside of the boat, so she started a wide slow turn to the starboard side. She wanted to keep the fish tracking off the stern. Everyone on board the boat was excited now as Walker fought the fish.

Blind Date had the gaff hook locked in her hands, and she was holding it like she held her weapon. Ramirez laughed as she watched Blind Date, she looked so good standing there without her top on with the hook in her hands, even though they we're not going to bring the fish on board the Cat or hurt it in any way.

After about twenty-five minutes of fighting the fish, it broke the water and it looked like it was actually dancing on the surface of the water on her tail. It was a large sail fish and Ramirez figured was at least eight foot, and weighing between one hundred to one hundred and twenty five pounds. She was dancing on the water about two hundred and fifty yards off the stern of the World Cat. The vivid colors of the fish were captivating, and Ramirez yelled at Blind Date.

"Regina put down the damn gaff hook and grab the camera and take a couple pictures of the fish before we release it, will you please honey!"

Regina jumped into action as Ramirez yelled at her, and she replaced the hook and took the camera from under the seat locker of the World Cat, and she started to get a number of fine pictures of the jumping fish shaking its head violently, as it tried to shake the hook from her mouth free and escape.

Walker was sweating heavily and his arms were killing him, because of the fight the fish was putting up against him. He let go of the rod with one hand and tried to swipe at the sweat running in his eyes. The Mutt saw Walker was getting beat out so he offered.

"Pass me the damn pole, I'll take over and play with the fish for a while. When I get tired, I'll pass the rod over to Tee K and let him have a go at it with the stinking fish for a while, man."

A number of other boats came in close to their World Cat, and the passengers watched the fish jumping and splashing across the surface of the water. But they pulled away when Ramirez waved them away from their boat. She knew the other guys on the boats wanted to take a look at her and Blind Date, because they were still topless, as much as they wanted to see the fish.

The Mutt fought the fish for an hour and the fish still did not show any signs of giving up the fight just yet. The Mutt's arms were killing him, but he did not want to give up his fight with the fish. So he did not ask Tee K to relieve him yet. But he committed a mistake and allowed the fish to get its head down, and it started stripping out line again. Ramirez saw the fish go down and she threw the twin engines of the World Cat in reverse, and started to back down on the fish, so the Mutt could pull in line without having the fish break it as she yelled at the struggling Mutt.

"C'mon dog man you let the damn fish get her head down. You're tired so why don't you let Tee K fight the fish for a little while, before you lose it or the damn pole on us, stupid."

"I'm alright you keep backing down on the damn fish until I can get her head up again."

"Judging by the way the fish is fighting you, dog man. I don't believe it's a female fish any longer, buddy. It has to be a male to put up a fight like this. Pass the pole over to Tee K for a while, and be careful about passing the pole to him. I don't want the fish to pull it out of your hands. I'd rather lose the fish than the pole and reel, Mutt." She bellowed at the Mutt as she continued to back down the boat on the fish.

"I'll give the pole up when I get his head up again, honey. I'm dying for a stinking beer and a break myself, baby. Will you get the hell outta my way, the stinking fish is heading to the starboard side of the boat, and you're getting in my way, dammit." The Mutt yelled at Blind Date who was getting in his way as she tried to get a few more pictures of the fish.

"But I want to get some better pictures of the fish dancing out there, honey." Blind Date complained at the Mutt.

"Just keep your puppy's the hell outta my stinking way will ya please baby."

Tee K was having a blast watching the soldiers fight the fish, and the two women on the boat running around topless. But when he heard the Mutt was going to give him a turn with the fish, he really got excited and he moved a little closer to the Mutt and the fishing pole.

"Stop backing up Raz, I got his stinking head up again and he's dancing on the water. I won't let him get the best of me again I can tell you that much, baby." The Mutt barked at Ramirez.

She set the boat in idle again and then she watched the fish as it was not going so wild, and many of the outstanding colors on the fish was starting to fade, and she realized the fish was starting to get exhausted and it would not be long before they could get the fish to the side of the World Cat so they could release it.

Ramirez looked at Tee K and saw he was dying to get his turn with the fighting bill fish, and she knew the fish was starting to tire with her fight with the Mutt. She wanted him to work the fish for a while and pull it to the side of the World Cat. She drew in her breath and barked at the Mutt. "C'mon dog man, you're exhausted already, why the hell don't you give the damn pole over to Tee K for a little while, and let him have a turn with the damn fish, stupid."

"Yeah yeah, will you cut me some damn slack not flack. I'm gonna give him the damn pole when I turn the fish again, honey. Hey Tee K, get on my left side and be ready to take the damn pole. Once you have it I'll get out of the fighting chair and you can jump in. There's plenty of fight left in this sucka, and it's a real blast playing with the fish. Remember man, when I hand you the rod, you gotta keep the line tight until you're in the chair. If you allow the line to go slack on ya, the damn fish will snap the line on ya ass. Then you'll find yourself holding onto a pole like you hold onto your dick, man. Hey Regina, can you get me a stinking beer, I'm so thirsty I'll bit the end of the damn bottle off with my teeth, girl."

"You got it baby, when you give him the poll, you'll have a beer in hand, lover." Regina said as she was almost jumping in place while watching the fish continuing to jump on the water.

"Hey baby you betta stop jumping around like that or you're gonna hurt yourself, girl. And, if you don't hurt yourself, you're gonna end up giving me a kink in my neck, because I'm trying to keep up with your bouncing tits with my eyes, baby sister." The Mutt complained at Regina.

He wiggled his rearend until he was barely sitting in the fighting chair, and then he pushed off holding the fishing line tight and he moved out of Tee K's way. Once he was sitting in the chair, the Mutt moved the pole across his chest and shoved it in Tee K's hand. He did not let go of the pole until he was certain Tee K had the pole with both hands. The Mutt forced the tip of the pole up to keep tension on the line. When he let go, Tee K plastered a smile on his lips as he felt the full weight of the fish, and the fight he still had left. He took the beer from Regina and kissed her and took a pull of the beer.

Ramirez called out in an excited voice while standing at the helm, and the World Cat boat was sitting dead still in the calm flat water. "How the hell does it feel Tee K? Is the fish still fighting you, or do you think it's about giving up the fight and come in so we can release him before he hurts himself more?"

"He's no where near ready to give it up yet, Dorothy." He called back to her over his shoulder.

"Keep working him because he looks like he's tiring quite a bit on ya." Ramirez replied as she watched the singer work the fish pretty well. She smiled when she saw the fish turn and start coming towards the boat, and she warned him. "When the fish notices the boat, he's labile run on you again Tee K. Be aware of thc possibility."

"I know that, this isn't the first bill fish I landed, Ma'am." He called back to Ramirez as he continued to struggle with the fish. Everyone on board the World Cat boat were hanging back and allowing the singer land the fish.

After another fifteen minutes of fighting the fish, Tee K was able to get the exhausted fish up to the portside of the boat. Ramirez left the helm and she went to the fish and allowed the line to drag over her hand, the first knot came up and she ordered Tee K to continue reeling in the fish, when the second knot was touched by her, she announced to the exhausted singer. "Fish caught. You caught yourself a hundred and ten pound sail fish, mister." This was because if they were in a tournament for bill fish, the fish would not be acknowledged as caught until the Captain of the boat touched the second knot on the line.

When she touched the second knot of the line, she reached back and removed her long nose pliers from her back pocket, and then she tried to dislodge the hook from the exhausted fish. Try as she might, she could not get the hook out because there was still enough fight in the fish, and it was shaking its head away from her hand. Walker was helping her by holding onto the bill of the fish. She ordered Tee K to keep tension on the line as she continued to work on the fish. She was being extremely careful not to allow the fish to pull his bill out of

Walker's hand and spear her hands with its bill, because she knew there was enough bacteria on the bill to cause her a bad infection. Not taking into account the damage the fish could do to her hand if it was able to spear her. She saw the fish staring at her with its huge eye.

Since she could not get the hook out of the fish's mouth safely without getting hurt or hurting the fish more, she carefully slid her cutting pliers down the line until the cutting edge was resting against the loop in the hook. She cut the line and watched as the exhausted fish turned and then it started headed down to the deep when Walker released the bill, and she knew the fish was going to survive its battle. She wanted to grab the bill and drag the fish in the water to get oxygen back in the fish, but it broke away from them before she could get it.

Once she cut the line free of the hook, she straightened up and turned Tee K and smiled as she announced. "Well mister, you just caught yourself a bill fish, and that means we can fly the flag of a caught bill fish as we go to back port. Congratulations, how do you feel Tee K?"

"I'm about as exhausted as the fish was, Ma'am." He replied, but he could not help himself as he stared at Ramirez's breasts as they swayed gently with the motion of the boat.

Walker saw the poor guy staring at Ramirez and he smiled as he said to his lady. "Hey Raz, before you run the flag up the riggers, how's bout you allowing Tee K to hold it and we take some pictures of him with the pole sitting in the fighting chair?"

"What a wonderful idea and keep sake for him to have of our fishing trip, Robert. I'll get the flag for him while Regina can take the picture." She replied as she ran for the flag, she removed it from under the console of the boat and unfurled the small flag as she walked back to Tee K as he propped himself in the fighting chair, and he was grinning from ear to ear.

Ramirez straightened him up in the chair and she made him hold the heavy fishing pole in his left hand, and she stuffed one edge of the flag in his left hand, and then she stretched the flag out across his chest and made him hold that end with his other hand. When he was positioned properly with the pole and flag, she stepped back and allowed Blind Date to take three pictures of the proud looking singer grinning at her.

But Walker was not going to allow the singer off the hook that easily, as he moved to Ramirez's side and whispered. "Hey honey, you know you and Blind Date are driving the poor slob fucking crazy having your purdy tits sticking out, baby."

"I noticed Robert, do you want us to put our tops back on, honey?" She asked her lover.

"Hell no, what a helluva question to ask me, after as long as you've known me, baby? When the hell have you ever heard me tell you to put your top back on, honey?" Walker fired at his girlfriend as he shot her a quick and leering smile, and a quick wink of his eye.

"Uh oh, I think you have something evil locked up in the back of your filthy little mind of yours again, mister." She replied as she returned Walker's evil smile with one of her own.

"I sure do, I wanna take a picture of the jerk. But, here's what I want you to do. I want you and Blind Date standing on either side of the asshole and when I say smile, I want you girls to stick your tits in his stinking face and keep them there until I take two pictures of the prick…"

"Bobby, why are you calling him so many bad names for, don't you like the guy honey?" She asked as she allowed a huge smile to cross her lips over Walker's plan.

"Yeah I think he's a cool dude, just force of habit until I get to know him a little betta I guess. Well what do you think of my stinking plan, baby? We might as well send him home with a great memory of us, sister."

"I love it Bobby, but I don't know what his wife's going to say about us sticking our tits in his face for the picture, Robert. It could get him in some serious trouble with her you know." She warned her lover, but she still wanted to do what he offered.

"Fuck her if she can take a stinking joke, baby. When you girls are standing by his stinking side, I want the both of you holding poles in your hands to add to the picture, honey." He added as he placed a smile on his lips as he continued to stare at her.

"Okay honey, you got it Robert, you tell me when you want to take a picture of us, baby and we'll do the rest for ya."

"You'll know when I wanna do it easy enuf, baby. I'll take the camera from Blind Date and you call her over to you and then you guys stand in the picture with the flaming asshole, honey."

She smiled at Walker, and then she watched his every move. When he felt the time was right, because Tee K was enjoying a cold beer, he grumbled. "Hey pal, I wanna take a few pictures of you for the boat, man."

"Sure thing sir, I'd really like that, Walker." He replied as he straightened up in the fighting chair again, and then he placed a smile on his lips as he waited for Walker to take the camera from Blind Date and take the pictures of him.

When he had the camera set up he said to Ramirez with a snap in his voice. "C'mon girl, I want the Captain of the boat to get in the picture with the little dude." He waited until Ramirez picked up a loose pole and she sexily walked over to his right, and she called out to Blind Date. "C'mon Regina, I want you to get in the picture with me also, honey."

When Blind Date had a pole in her hands and she was standing on the right side of the singer sitting so proudly in the fighting chair. Ramirez made a quick hand motion and Regina realized what she wanted to do to the poor man, and she nodded back at her.

Now both Blind Date and Ramirez waited for Walker's signal, and when he told everyone to smile for the camera. Both girls moved a little closer to Tee K until their breasts were actually squashed up against his red as a beet face. While the two girls were trying to smother him with their breasts, Walker took three pictures of the lucky stiff seated in the chair. The Mutt was laughing his backside off at the singer, because he had such a shocked look locked on his puss now as he tried to look at both girls at the same time.

The girls were not finished with the singer as they continued to rub their breasts in his face, and Walker took another couple of pictures as he dropped his pole, and he tried to look at the girls a little better. When he removed the camera from his face, the two girls stopped attacking the poor singer and they straightened up.

When he was able to get his breathing back under control, he announced to everyone on the boat. "Well you guys, I must say that was one of the most interesting pictures I ever had taken of me in all my life."

"Yeah, and I'm gonna make certain you go home with a number of copies of them, man." Walker offered proudly to him as he grinned at the still red in the face singer.

"Ahhh… I believe my wife will skin me alive if she ever sees any those pictures you just took of me, Mr. Walker."

"Fuck that 'Mister' shit will ya, its Bobby or Robert, man. You're now one of us my friend."

Ramirez smiled now that Walker just called the singer one of them as she informed him. "Hey Toby, when we get back to the dock I'll fill out the form for you so if you want to get a cast of the fish. It's the only way to register the fish as caught, until you had the permit to allow you to take a sail fish to the dock. We never kill any the bill fish we catch, we always catch and release them Tee K. That way there'll always be more for other people to catch and release."

The small group of fishermen stayed out on the water for the rest of the day, and they were luck enough to hook on to another two sail fish, but the fish broke off the line before they were able to get them anywhere near the World Cat. They also caught two large Groupers, and several Yellow Tails legally to keep once they stopped fishing for bill fish. By the time Ramirez decided to call it a day, everyone on board the Whiskey Lullaby was thoroughly exhausted. It took them two hours to return to port, and Walker took the time to wash down the boat with fresh water, as the others removed the gear and anything else they might have brought on board her. By the time he lifted the boat out of the water everything was cleaned up and properly put away.

Ramirez made supper for everyone, and before he left for his apartment, he sang ten songs for the group. He also signed all the CD's she had of him, and then he bid everyone good-bye. But not before promising he was going to return to the Island of Marathon on the 17th of April of 2005, and he wanted to make a date to go out fishing with the soldiers again. In the back of his mind, he wanted to make it a yearly thing of it, and always around April he took some time off from his busy schedule of singing, to enjoy himself a little.

Walker was all for it, and Ramirez marked down the date he was planning to return to the Island on her calendar, because she was already looking forward to his returning to the Island again.

CHAPTER EIGHT

IRAN, WEDNESDAY, JANUARY 9th 2005

At another meeting being held between the Vulture, the Iranian General Abdol Karim Kalantari and the rest of his Persian fighters, Major Gholamhossein Mohajerani was reporting on the progress he enjoyed over distributing the newly developed and deadly EFP's, or Explosive Formed Penetrators to their forces operating within the borders of Iraq. They were attacking the American soldiers who were desperately trying to bring some form of law and order to the troubled lands of that country. The Iranian Major was beaming with pride as he made the report to his leader. The EFP's were doing terrible damage to the American vehicles they were aimed at, and he was proudly explaining their success to the fearsome General.

General Kalantari was all smiles over the trouble he was giving the American troops occupying Iraq. He was more than please at what the Democrats were saying about their Republican President, and when they took over control of Congress and the House of Representatives. They were going to force the American President to pull all the troops out of Iraq no matter what they leave that country in.

The Vulture was ecstatic over this threat, because he knew once the American troops were out of Iraq, his President was going to order his troops to march and invade Iraq, and they could then start the slaughter of the Sunni and Kurds, and any Shitte fool who would not back Iran in its quest to take over Iraq and their oil vast fields. The Vulture understood once they had complete control over Iraq, Saudi Arabia was the next one on their hit list.

The Persian General understood full well his President would order his troops to follow the retreating American soldier's back to their cursed country, and start attacking the United States with countless terrorist actions within their own borders. The Vulture was dying to begin his attack on the United States from their borders. He wanted to show them they were dealing with Iran, and the Iranians knew how to fight, not like the Afghanistan and worthless Iraqi soldiers who buckled so quickly and easily under America's military might.

The Vulture knew the Democrats of the United States were out to embarrass their Republican President, even if it meant an immediate pull out in Iraq, no matter the consequences to the Iraqi country or the rest of the Middle East. He also understood if the Democrats were able to throw out the Republicans from their law making houses. The Democrats would do everything in their power to weaken the United States' military power, thus opening them up to more terrorist attacks within their own country.

That was the reason why Usama bin Laden's attack against the United States worked out so well for him and his attackers. Because a weaken American President was in power, and he was more concerned with saving his own feathers, than he was with protecting the American civilians and country. And, now it was the turn of the Democrats to weaken this Republican President so severely, so they could return to power over their country.

The Vulture marveled over the foolishness of the leaders of the United States, because they were guilty of the same sins the Arab nations were guilty of committing against themselves. He understood if he could organize all the foolish Arab nations under one flag and belief, the Arab nations would be undefeatable as a military force in the world. Just as if the American people organized together and put aside all their petty fears and ambitions. They would surely have been able to defeat al-Qa'eda in Afghanistan, and al-Qa-eda in Iraq. But the

American law makers were more interested in doing what was good for their foul parties, rather than what was good for their nation and civilians as a whole.

He smiled over his thoughts, because he understood it was only a matter of time before the United States became a second class country, and they no longer controlled the vast money and military might that made that country such a powerful force in the flow of world events. He was counting on this fact, and he was going to do everything in his power to bring this dream to become real. The Vulture knew within six years, Iran would have their own nuclear weapons they could use to hold most of the entire Middle East hostage to their demands and wants, and with the Democrats pulling their military might out of the Middle East.

The Americans would never be able to reestablish those military bases on any Arab soil throughout the Middle East. Not after Iran became so powerful militarily with the new breed of intercept missiles they were developing for their arsenal, and they would then be able to cut off the world's flow of oil at a mere snap of their fingers.

The Vulture's daydreaming was interrupted by Major Gholamhossein Mahajerani, as he suddenly cleared his throat because he noticed the General was not paying much attention to his words any longer. The General had to shake his head to bring his mind back to reality, and he could make the decisions that would control what they were speaking about.

"Yes, yes Major Mohajerani, excuse me, my mind had wandered a bit on me I fear. A thousand pardons I beg of you, it's taking our foolish leaders too long a time to allow us to begin our Holy Jihad against the Satan of the United States. I have so longed for the honorable day when we can finally begin our revenge against the cursed lowly infidels who had invaded, and they have occupied any Arab lands of the world, Major." The Vulture offered as he flashed one of his extremely rare smiled at the Iranian Major he was speaking with.

"Yes General Kalantari that'll be a great day indeed for Iran, sir. Do you have any idea when our leaders might allow our wrath to fall down upon the head of America, sir?" The crafty and wise Iranian Major asked the leader of his group with much concern lacing his tone.

"I have no idea when we'll be allowed to release our Holy Jihad against the hated American fools, Major. But I do know we'll be sent to Cuba for a number of months, while we're waiting for our orders to begin our attack against the hated United States. It has to be soon, because I understand our leaders want to being our attacks against the United States in late 2006, or the beginning of 2007. That is because I was informed we have to begin our attacks against the worthless United States, to place even more pressure of the foolish leadership of America.

"The more mayhem we can create for the foul fools, the more the Republican leaders will be driven from their offices, and the foolish Democrats will again be in power over the American lands. We want this we need this event to take place, because once the Democrats are back in power over the United States. Then we'll be free to take over Iraq once they remove their cursed soldiers from the foul Iraqi soil. We'll then be free to attack Iraq, because we understand the American Democrats are afraid to engage in war with the Middle East nations.

"We Persians scare the worthless Democrats, and this fear will make them extremely foolish, and they'll remain within their foul borders to not make themselves look weak before their foolish civilians. As you're aware Major Mohajerani, once we own Iraq, we'll be free to attack Saudi Arabia, Jordan, and Syria at our leisure. But we'll also be attacking the United States, in that way we will keep their military forces locked at home, in their stupid attempt to stop us from attack them, Major. Bah, sometimes I believe our leaders are as weak as the foolish Democrats of America are, because we should have already started our attacks on the land of Satan." The Vulture complained at his lesser officer.

"I guess we'll be forced to be patient my General. But at least we are becoming more active in our fight against the hated American occupiers of the worthless nation of Iraq. Our efforts are beginning to bear fruit, General Kalantari. The fools who we're supplying these new weapons to are beginning to kill American soldiers, sir. Already, there are many American leaders in the United States complaining they should pull all their worthless military forces out of Iraq, because of the puppet government the loathsome Americans have installed in Iraq, are so powerless to get control over the lawlessness we are causing inside that foul country, sir.

"Soon, the few cries will be picked up by more and more of the foolish American leaders, and the worthless public will also start to cry to bring their useless soldiers back home, sir. General Kalantari, we have another ally working for us within the United States, sir. They are doing much more harm to their soldier's moral than all our attacks on the foolish American soldiers, sir. We're even supplying this ally with even…"

"Who is this new ally you speak of Major? I'm unaware we have any help in America, sir."

"General Kalantari, it is the foolish American newspapers and reporters I speak of, sir. Their news reporters never show what good the efforts of their soldiers are bringing forth in Iraq. All they want to show the American public is the death of their cursed soldiers, and they lead their foolish civilians to believe this is all that is happening within Iraq, sir. The reporters are trying to make their worthless civilians believe everything wrong with Iraq, is the fault of their foolish Republican President and his policies. The misleading reporters are hounding their cursed President in much the same manner that we're hunting down and killing their infidel soldiers inside Iraq, sir." Major Mohajerani offered the Vulture, and he fell silent to allow his words to be thought over by the Iranian General.

The Vulture smiled over his Major's words, because he knew about what the narrow minded news reporters were doing to the leadership in their own country. He was greatly pleased his government ordered the complete shutdown of all newspapers within their country, and the government did not allow any reports to be displayed on the TV, unless those reports were cleared by the government officials first. In his heart he understood if the Iranian public knew what was truly going on within their own country, and all the trouble and unrest they were causing the world, the youth of his country would be rioting in the streets of their capital and other major cities, and demanding a purge of their government.

The feared General knew it was only a matter of time before Iran and the United States went to war with each other, and he could only hope their defenses were completed before the hated American soldiers came for their country in the Middle East. He understood his government was begging to be attacked by the United States, and his leaders believed foolishly they would be able to defeat the powerful American troops once they come for them. But he did not suffer from the same delusions as his government did.

Because he knew no matter how powerful Iran grew militarily, their troops would never be able to defeat the American warriors in a protracted war. Yes, they could carry out a guerrilla war against the American soldiers, and do the same thing that was taking place in Iraq. But it would not stop the destruction of their country in the war. He was forced to shake his head to bring his mind back to the conversation he was having with his soon to be terrorists.

"Errr… a thousand pardons for my allowing my foolish mind to wander on me for a second time, Major Mohajerani. It's just that there is so much taking place that I'm finding it nearly impossible to keep my mind on this never ending cursed conversation. Yes Major, your words ring with the sound of truth in them. The American reporters are relentlessly going after their foolish American leadership, because they did not like the political party in office.

"And, it's true we're embarrassing the worthless American soldiers occupying Iraq with our supplying many new weapons for the foul dog eaters of that cursed country, to employ against the American soldiers occupying their country. All this is taking place like we have deemed it to take place, and yet the American soldiers remain stationed in Iraq, and stopping our future plans for that miserable country. I guess we have to be patience and wait for Allah to wave his mighty Hand of Fate before Him, and then we'll know what we shall do next in our attempt to force the hated American soldiers out of Iraq, and then we can start our own takeover of that miserable country of camel eaters and lowly jackals.

"In Allah's great Hand rests the future fate of that loathsome nation of Saudi Arabia, and their misbegotten beliefs in the false Sunni religion. I cannot wait until we purge that evil land of their Kafis,

(Non-believers) and then we convert the worthless fools who we shall allow to live to Shiite, the true Islamic beliefs, Major. Bah, I grow tired of all these threats and dreams for the future of the Middle East. The time for wagging one's tongue has long past, and now it's time for us to take action against the cursed infidels of the world. I'm completely exhausted and I want to be alone with my troubling thoughts. All of you know what is expected of you, carry out the orders you're currently operating under, and if there is change in your orders, I shall inform you of them well in advance. Be gone with the lot of you."

With that said, the Vulture leaned forward and rested his head in his hands, and then he closed his eyes as he rubbed his temples and then let out an exhausted sigh. Everyone at the meeting took this action as their dismissal, and they stood quietly left the Iranian General's office. Each left the Vulture's side breathing a sigh of relieve, because at some times of visiting the always angry Iranian General, could cost the ones summon before him their lives, if they committed some infraction against his orders. They all understood the Vulture was a man who did not know the meaning or mercy or understanding. It was his way, or the death of a thousand cuts. There was not one member of his council who had not witnessed the death of someone who had failed on a mission he was sent out on by the Iranian General.

When General Kalantari was certain everyone was out of his office, he suppressed the button on his intercom and then he barked into the machine. "Fereshteh, my mind is troubled and I am afraid I'm in serious need to relax. Bring me a drink of American Rye, woman." The Vulture released the button and then he leaned back in his chair and he waited for his secretary to bring his requested drink before him.

There was a light tap on the door which forced the Vulture to sit forward in his chair as he snapped at the closed door. "Enter woman." When his eyes beheld his secretary, a smile instantly crossed his lips. Because Fereshteh entered the Vulture's office naked except for a pair of thigh high black nylons, and she was carrying his favorite drink in her hands like it was the greatest treasure on the face of the earth. The Vulture offered her. "Fereshteh, you certainly do understand how to get me out of my black moods, young woman. Come here to me and release the pressure I'm suffering under."

With that said General Kalantari unzipped his pants and he removed himself, and then waited for his secretary to finally come towards him.

MARATHON ISLAND, THE FLORIDA KEYS. THURSDAY, MARCH 10th, 2005

The American soldier branded the Ghost, Sergeant Walter Casper, along with the Hunter, Sergeant Frank Whitcomb, was planning to leave the Island on this day and go home and spend some time with their families. It was a sad day for the American soldiers, because they were having so much fun with each other on the tiny Island. The two specialized soldiers leaving were packed up and waiting for Walker to bring them over to the small airport on the Island.

Sergeant Dorothy Ramirez, Blind Date, Sergeant Regina Raphael and Ice, Sergeant Diane Morrison, were hanging all over the two soldiers because they were leaving. The three women were crying because that was how close these elite soldiers were to each other. Baby Tee, Sergeant Teri Dorland, and Ice, were planning to leave the Island also, but they intended to stay until the country and western singer returned to the Island, so they could see him again before they headed home to visit their families.

Tee K was keeping in constant contact with Captain Robert Walker and his future wife, Sergeant Dorothy Ramirez. He liked the two soldiers he spent some time with last year, and he was looking forward to seeing them again. He informed Walker he was still planning to visit the Island on April 17th, of 2005 and he was looking forward to going out fishing with the soldiers.

Walker pulled the car out of the garage and waited for the two soldiers to get in, so he could run them over to the airport. Baby Tee was going along with Walker, and it took them five minutes to pull up to the airport, and the soldiers got out and Walker and Baby Tee waited for them to unload the trunk, and then they escorted them to the terminal. The soldiers went to the American Eagle counter, and the Hunter and Ghost dumped their luggage on the platform and produced their tickets. The lady checked their tickets and informed them the plane was going to be taking off in the hour. The Ghost nodded and smiled at the lady, and then he and the Hunter brought their carry on over to the X-ray machine and dumped it on the conveyor belt. Instantly, the luggage disappeared into the machine as the soldiers walked through the metal detector gate.

The Hunter set off the machine because he forgot to remove his keys from his pocket. Once they were cleared, Walker and Baby Tee walked through the detector, and they headed to the window and saw the American Eagle aircraft resting on the tarmac. The security guards knew the group was soldiers, so they allowed Walker and Tee to join the other two soldiers in the gate area. It was a somber wait, with none of them engaging in conversation as they watched the workers refueling their plane. The Captain tried to have the two soldiers wait to leave until after Tee K's upcoming visit, but they already made plans with their families, and they did not want to put it off any longer. They spend a little more than a year with Walker and the other soldiers staying on the small Island.

When the announcement the boarding of American Eagle Flight One, One, Seven came, the two specialized soldiers stood and hugged Walker and Baby Tee, and then they walked out the glass door and quickly ran crossed the tarmac. It was a twenty seven passenger plane, and Walker and Baby Tee watched until the two soldiers disappeared in the plane. It was then Baby Tee hugged Walker and she allowed herself to shed a tear for the two departing soldiers. He smiled as he hugged the pretty woman in his arms. He allowed Baby Tee to get it out of her system before they returned to his home, then he announced.

"C'mon honey, we gotta get back to my place before the others think we took off with the Ghost and Hunter." He released his hold on her and then he led her out of the terminal.

The two headed back to Walker's place, and by the time they got there, the other soldiers were back to their old selves. Buckethead was by the dock and he was trying to fish, so Baby Tee headed for the massive man and settled down and watched him fishing.

Sergeant Ramirez went over to Walker's side and asked him barely over a whisper. "How did it go with our two friends Robert, did our point men get off alright Bobby?

"Yeah, the two stinking turds got off okay I guess, baby. Baby Tee took it hard \over their leaving though, harder than I ever figured. What the hell are we gonna do now honey?" He asked her as he hugged Ramirez close to him for a moment.

"You don't want to take the rest of our friends out fishing on the boat, do you Robert?"

"Naw, it's too late for any good fishing, and besides I'm not in the mood to go out with the boat. Do you wanna just cook supper for the rest of these stinking pukes? That way we'll stay together for the rest of the day. Honey, I've been thinking, maybe we should plan to head over to Dockside on Sunday night, it seems we have to breathe a little life back into these pukes, honey." He grumbled as he smiled at his lady as he waited for her reply.

"Oh I'd love that Bobby it's been a few weeks since the last time we went out together. I could sure use a little breath pumped into me as well, honey." She replied to her lover.

Sunday did not come too soon for the specialized soldiers on Marathon, and by noontime they were looking forward to heading out for Dockside. Sergeant Ramirez set up the babysitter and when she arrived, Walker asked his lady if she wanted to eat supper at Dockside. She jumped all over the offer, and Buckethead and Baby Tee was going to go along with them. Walker called the Mutt and informed him he was taking Ramirez and the others out to Dockside early, and they were going to eat supper there. He was not very thrilled over eating supper at Dockside, but he did ask the soldiers with him if they wanted to eat out, and then he replied they were coming. By the time they linked up and headed for Dockside, it was after five in the afternoon, and the bar was already showing the first signs of coming alive.

The Mutt smiled when he sat at their usual table when he noticed a new sign the bar put it. It read, "Men, no shirt, no service, Women, no shirt, free beer." He drew the other soldier's attention to the sign, and they shared a laugh over it. But as usual, Baby Tee had to push the issue by whipping her shirt off. She did get her free beer, but she also received a stiff warning from the bartender not to take her shirt off again, or she would be asked to leave.

They ate hamburgers and French Fries and drank sodas with their meal. It did not seem like the soldiers were very interested in getting drunk for the night, they were out more to have a good time. Walker was warned by Colonel Leadbetter he was interviewing the new soldiers he picked out from the other branches of the services to fill their ranks. The Colonel also informed the Captain he was going to send five new soldiers down to the Island, so he could check them out himself. He assured the Captain these five new soldiers were the best of the ones he pick out. He asked the Colonel when the new guys were coming down to the Island and he replied they should be arriving at the end of April.

The concerned Captain had a quick discussion with the Colonel about what was happening in Afghanistan and Iraq. Lately, the insurgents were doing some heavy pushing of their own, and they were starting to hit the troop supply columns with some new type of weapons the military branded EFP's or Explosive Formed Penetrators, and the new weapons were defeating the best armor on most of their Humvees and light armored vehicles. He warned Walker the Taliban were starting to pick it up in Afghanistan, and for the first time in quite a while, the Taliban resorted to employing suicide bombers against the NATO forces, who had assumed most of the protection of that country for the past few months.

The Captain took in everything the wise Colonel informed him about on the two wars, but he never heard the Colonel warn him they might be pulled up for some active duty. Although he was upset about the wars getting hot, he was also pleased his troops were not being activated.

He forced the Colonel's words out of his mind, because he was out to have a good time tonight, and not worry about what the military was doing for the rest of the day. There were a few women who did not seem to be attached to anyone hanging around the bar, but everyone with Walker was already paired up. But it did not stop the men from looking though.

One of the waitresses came over to their table and Walker asked if the Rocket man was going to be at the bar tonight. She informed him he was not scheduled to be there tonight. But she told him Rocket's son was going to be running the show tonight for him, and they had two different bands going to play. He hid the fact he was disappointed the Rocket was not going to be there as he ordered his first beer of the day.

Sergeant Ramirez heard what Walker asked the waitress, and she moved a little closer to him and when he looked at her, she smiled. Even though they had a good time, it was not the same without Rocket man running the act, and the elite soldiers left the place after ten p.m.

For the rest of March, it was kind of boring for the specialized soldiers relaxing on the Island, not many fish were biting because April started the bill fish coming in, and then the true fun of fishing stated on the Islands of the Keys. April 2nd, Tee K placed a call to Walker, and informed him he was planning to hit the Island on April 15th, and he was going stay until the twentieth, before having to leave to start another tour scheduled to begin on June 20th. Walker offered him his place to stay while he was visiting the Island, and Tee K accepted the offer, but he told Walker he was going to be paying for all the food and beers they drank while he was visiting the Island and enjoying his hospitality.

Even though he did not like the offer he accepted it, because he felt it was the only way the singer was going to stay at his place for the visit. When he was off the phone with the singer, he told Ramirez that Tee K was going to be staying at their place for five days. She could not, nor did she even try to hide her excitement he was going to be staying at their place.

FRIDAY, APRIL 15th, 2005.

Although the soldiers staying on the Island wanted to go to the Marathon Airport to greet the country singer when he landed, both Walker and Ramirez were the only ones who went to pick him up. Walker was concerned over the scene the other soldiers might create at the small airport. The country singer came off the unmarked chartered airplane and smiled instantly when he spotted the two elite soldiers waiting for him. He headed right for the soldiers and shook hands with Walker and kissed Ramirez on the cheek, and then he followed them to their car.

Walker jumped in the car and drove back to his place, when they pulled up the other soldiers were hanging around in front waiting for them to return. When the singer got out of the car, he shook hands with everyone, and then he was lead to the back where the soldiers had the cookers going. A cold beer was shoved in his hand and he took a pull from it. When everyone was comfortable, everything got back to normal. Ramirez brought Tee K's luggage to the spare room he was going to use for his stay with them.

The three women soldiers were dressed in bathing suits barely covering their treasures. But within the hour, all three women were walking around topless like it was nothing to them while the guys ate, drank, and enjoyed what the girls were showing them. The surprised singer could not believe the three beautiful women were so comfortable the way they were walking around in front of him and the other men.

The day and night was beautiful, and the next day Baby Tee and Ramirez took Tee K around the small Island, and they enjoyed some of the many things the Island had to offer anyone visiting the Island. They walked out to Pigeon Key using the old seven mile bridge, and Ramirez showed him where they filmed the movie True Lies. The group stopped and watched some people fishing off the old bridge, and they even looked over the edge and were able to actually see fish as they went after the bait, the water was so crystal clear. The singer was amazed at the vast schools of large tarpons that were fighting the strong current of the water, as they waited for bait fish to come floating by them.

Ramirez spotted and then pointed out two bull sharks shadowing the school of tarpons, waiting their chance to attack and feed off the large fish. There were a number of boats anchored up near, under or between the old and new seven mile bridge, and the fishermen were trying to land one of the tarpons for sport, because you could not eat tarpons.

It was a great day to enjoy, and on their way home, they all stop at one of the local fish and tackle places and brought a ton of hooks, lures, and bait for their upcoming fishing trip. Tee K did not want to lose any of Walker's equipment, and he had Ramirez also stop at Publics, and there he brought a ton of food, snacks, beers and sodas for the boat. Once they had everything they needed, the singer wanted to pick up they headed for home.

The fishing trip went off great for the group, even though they were not able to latch onto a bill fish this time. But they did catch three good size keeper grouper, and a number of yellow tail snappers. That night they shared a shrimp boil and cooked grouper, and then they settled back and listened to Tee K sing his best songs for them. The next few days went by with the soldiers enjoying the singer's presence, and when he left after promising he would be back on the Island of Marathon sometime in May of next year. He said he would call them a few weeks before he was scheduled to return to Marathon. This time he wanted to come to the Island when the dolphin (Maui Maui) was starting to run, so he could try his hand at catching some of them. When he left Walker and Ramirez's place it was almost as bad for the remaining soldiers as when the Hunter and Ghost left the group a few weeks before.

CHAPTER NINE

FRIDAY, APRIL 29th, 2007

Captain Robert Walker was in the back yard trying his hand at catching a fish from the dock, and Sergeant Dorothy Ramirez was sitting on the dock enjoying the sun and watching him play with a fish he could not hook. Suddenly, five men walked around the house and one of them called out. "Hello, I'm looking for a Captain Robert Walker, does he live here please?"

Ramirez looked to where she heard the voice and she saw the five men standing there, but Walker did not pay attention to the guys. Buckethead and Baby Tee were in Walker's home, and they were sharing their last few days together by playing a little patty cake in the bedroom.

The Sergeant replied to the strangers. "Yes, you have the right place. Can I help you please?"

The five men walked over to the two people on the dock, and the one who called out began to speak for the others. "Yes Ma'am, we were ordered to report to a Captain Walker, Ma'am."

Now Walker had to pay attention to the new guys and he snarled at them for interrupting his day and enjoyment. "Yeah man, I'm fucking Captain Walker. Who the fuck are ya and what the hell do you want here with us, buster?"

The speaker went to an attention stance even though the Marine Captain was not dressed in his military uniform, and he replied.

"Captain Walker Sir, we were ordered to report to you by Colonel Bruce Leadbetter, sir. I guess we're supposed to be part of your Unit now, sir."

"I know who the hell sent you stinking people down here to get in my face, buster. ID yourselves immediately to me." Walker snapped angrily at the man as he put down his fishing pole, and then he turned to look at the men now.

"Yes Sir Captain Walker Sir, I'm Sergeant William Glennallen, sir. I've been in the service for seven years, and I'm a weapon's expert and I come with a tag name of High Spade, sir. My ex Unit of the Rangers branded me with the tag because I'm black I guess, sir. The man standing to my left is Sergeant Carl Youngblood sir, and he knows his way around any explosive devices we may come across, sir. He's highly trained in the inner workings of most of the IED's, or the Improvised Explosive Devices they're employing against us in Iraq against our forces, sir.

"He's also well trained with the newer weapons currently being employed by our enemy in Iraq, sir. The more sophisticated EFP's or the Explosive Formed Penetrators being masses produced in Iran, and they're being smuggled into Iraq by the sneaky bastards, sir. He comes with a tag name of Sleeper, and he was in the Rangers with me, Captain. He was branded that because if he's not on a mission sir, he's usually sleeping or zoning out sir.

"The next man standing in line is Sergeant Steven Stingold sir, and he was a member of the Green Berets, and he's a damn good SATCOM (Satellite Communications) soldier, sir. He can repair most things that might go wrong with any unit we're employing on a mission we're out on, sir. He's damn good with a weapon, Captain. He comes with the tag name of Mule, that's because he eats anything and everything sir, and once he makes up his mind, he rarely changes it sir." The Sergeant's remarks about the Mule made Walker smile as he listened to the Sergeant go on with identifying the other soldiers with him to Walker and Ramirez.

"Captain Walker Sir, the next man in line is Sergeant Edward London sir, and he was a member of SEAL Team Six Operations for over nine years, Captain. He can be inserted by any means to a target, and once he's on the ground, he's extremely deadly, sir. He's a weapons expert and he can double as a sniper if need be. Captain Walker, he comes with a tag name of Small Change, he was branded that because every time we go out to the bar, he only takes chump change with him so he doesn't get too drunk while out, sir." This time Sergeant Glennallen stopped speaking and he laughed at his own remarks, making Ramirez laugh with him.

The Captain held a straight and dead pan face as he cast a wiry eye at the soldier the Sergeant was speaking about. Then he looked at the remaining soldier and Sergeant Glennallen started to speak again when he saw the Captain's sudden harsh look.

"Errr… Captain Walker Sir, the last man standing in line is Sergeant Michael Nettestad, sir. He's a Marine and has been for six years, sir. He was attached to the One Hundred and Forty Third Force Recon Unit of the Third Marine Division, sir. He's a heavy weapons expert and he can also double as an artillery and tube (Mortar) man if needed, sir. He comes along with a tag name sir, its Sweat Stain I'm afraid, Captain Walker Sir.

"From what I was told about this man, the Unit originally branded him Road Kill because of his strong body odor, sir. But then it was discovered the tag name was already being used, sir." The Sergeant gave Walker a quick smile, knowing his nickname was Road Kill for the same reason, and then he went on with his words. "When the Captain works with the man in the field sir, you'll understand the reason for his tag name, sir. I had the pleasure of working with the man on one mission, and he's damn good sir. But I'm afraid the name is the right one for him."

"Well Sergeant Glennallen, I'm pleased you people come along with tag names and rates of Sergeants, mister. Because you know damn well no one in the Special Forces can be under the rank of Sergeant, mister. So that saves us some stinking time around welcoming you people into our Unit, man. You turds were sent here for me to see you people, and to evaluate and see if I'd accept you people into our Unit the way you come. From what I see of you turds so far, you'll do just fine for our needs. We're the best damn Unit in our line of work, and you people will live up to our standards, or I'll dump your stinking asses outta the Unit faster than a beer keg disappears at a stinking Frat House party, pal. You guys are obviously that good a soldiers, but you're gonna hafta be twice that good or you'll get washed out of this outfit, buddy.

"You guys will have the pleasure of meeting the rest of the guys from our Unit when we hafta report back to Camp Lejeune for some special tune up work in the future, until then I guess you people are on your fucking own. Do you guys hafta report back to Colonel Leadbetter or your old Units until we have need of you people or what? Has anyone told you what was up next for you people, once you were accepted into our group of the best, Sergeant Glennallen?"

"Yes Sir Captain Walker, we have been ordered by the Colonel to report to you today sir, and then we were ordered to stay on the Island until Monday to get better acquainted with you and the few soldiers staying on the Island along with you, Captain Walker. We have flight tickets back to Camp Lejeune, and we're to report to Colonel Leadbetter on that date, sir. It seems he wants to run us through some minor operations and exercises he dreamed up, I guess to make certain we meet his expectations Captain, and once he accepts us into the Unit. We're supposed to be sent home on some kind of extended leave, until called up for any special exercises or other needs, Captain Walker Sir." When the Sergeant finished speaking, he went silent as he looked at the other soldiers, Walker and Ramirez.

"Hey pal, let's get something straight right off the damn bat, man. I don't like to be saluted, especially when we're out in the fucking field, mister. Here's another thing for you new people to keep in the back of your stinking minds as long as you're connected with our specialized Unit. I came up through the damn ranks, so can the 'sir' shit when speaking to me. The only time you people have to salute or add the sir when addressing my ass, is when we're on a military base, or there's other brass hanging around, you got it people? We're all family here so relax and enjoy the fricking sun and fun until you hafta report back to Colonel Leadbetter. By the way Sergeant, you seem to be battle tried, have you seen any fucking action in either Iraq or Afghanistan, buddy? If you did Sergeant, I'd like to know what the shit's going on over there, mister?" Walker snapped at the new Sergeant standing before him.

"Yes Sir Captain Walker, I done two tours of duty in Iraq, working with the Hunter Company, and we were working in the Najaf region of Iraq for my two tour, sir. It was the worst mission I was ever set out on, we had a downed flyer and we were ordered to get out and see if we could rescue a possible alive flyer in the fucking war zone, sir. We pulled the entire company into the rescue operation, and we entered the damn city from three different points. But we were unaware the insurgents had setup on the remains of the flyer, and they were waiting for us to come after his body, sir. The combatants massed over a couple of hundred of their fighters in the area of the body, and they were well organized and heavily armed, sir.

"The combatants took over a number of abandoned buildings and homes, and they had a damn good fucking ambush setup against us, and we walked right into the mess like we were marching into the fires of hell, sir. The First Squad entered the Holy City of Najaf from the south, and when the soldiers were on the main street, the gates of hell flung open and the damn insurgents attacked us with heavy machine gun fire and a flood of fucking RPG's (Rocket Propelled Grenades) sir. Well Captain Walker Sir, from the moment First Squad came under enemy fire sir, the Second and Third Squad opened fire as support and backup of the First Squad, sir.

"It was a helluva mess with lead flying heavy from both sides, but when we moved in our armor, we were able get a damn handle on the fucking situation, sir. We called for some air assets, and this action turned the battle in our favor when the attack aircraft arrived on scene, sir. Don't get me wrong Captain, for at least an hour and a half, it was real touch and go for us sir, with the outcome of the battle seriously in doubt for either side.

"Captain Walker, the fighting was so heavy we were forced to pick and choose our targets, because there was a flood of easily recognized none military combatants trying to flee the damn area of combat, sir. I saw men and women carrying children in their hands and I knew the kids were dead, but the parents still tried to save their lives, sir. Hell Captain, at one fucking point I had a bloody and battered Iraqi father carrying the body of his baby child in his arms, and he approached me and asked for help with the severely injured child.

"I could see the child was still breathing but I didn't know how, because half of her head was blown away, and I was torn between helping the man and his child, and standing my post of support, sir. I chose to stand my post and I scooted the devastated man away from my position, sir. I had to actually aim my weapon at the old man to force him away from my position, sir. Well, he gave up trying to get me to help his dying child, but before he left my position, he laid his child on the body of a dead female caught up in the fire fight. He didn't leave the area until he folded the dead woman's hand over his dead child, and then he walked away like he was dead of soul and spirit. That action really tore my nuts up sir.

"But I didn't have the fucking luxury of thoughts of pity for the poor old dude, sir. Because there was heavy weapons fire coming from a large building, and First and Second Squads were organized and making a frontal attack on the building. My Squad was ordered out of position of support, and we bolstered the right side of the attack on the civilian buildings in question, sir. Captain Walker Sir, for me to try and tell you what I was witnessing good enough for you to understand the horror and death visiting this damn village, would only serve to minimize the terrible death and destruction happening there, sir. Words couldn't explain it for you sir, you would've had been there to understand it fully, sir. Anyway Captain, we put on a major push for these two buildings, the rest of the fighting in our area of responsibility stopped, and these two buildings were the last hot spots in the entire Hoggie town, sir.

"We hit the first building from four sides and for fifteen minutes, the enemy fire from the building was holding us at bay pretty much, sir. It was heavy, but we beaten back the fucking enemy's fire power, and then we entered the building in force. What we found inside was a scene right out of the pits of hell, sir. There were bodies of the dead piled up two and three high in the center of the main room. I figured there were at least a couple hundred dead Iraqi insurgents and innocent civilians piled up in this damn room, sir. It must have been some kind of collection point for the enemy troops, and I felt they were intending to burn the building and bodies to keep our enemy killed numbers down, sir. But the dead weren't the only ones in this room, sir. The enemy moved in a number of people, many were civilians so badly wounded, and it seemed they just left these people in there to die slowly and in much pain, sir.

"The room was strewn about with countless empty and half empty AK-47 magazines, hand grenades, fire bombs, and other weapons the enemy combatants could use against us, sir. Hell sir, when the battle was over sir, we loaded five of our armor vehicles up with all sorts of weapons, and we moved the crap out in a field and destroyed the crap with explosives and fire. We even found bomb making supplies, artillery projectiles, and mortar round and tubes, plus a horde of RPG's and rounds for other weapons, sir.

"But this was only half the horror I witnessed on this day, sir. To show you how fanatical these people we were engaging were sir, when we entered the building. There was this one guy lying on the floor and the moment he spotted me, he began to point to the ugly and terrible wound he received in his chest, sir. It was obvious he was raked by a fifty (Fifty Caliber machine gun) and his chest was ripped apart, sir. But here's the strange thing about his reactions during this fucking mess, sir. He was begging me to lend him some medical attention, sir. But I couldn't take the time to begin first aide on the downed man sir. Because we were still engaging active Iraqi fighters inside the damn building and holding out on us sir. The only thing I could think of doing for the poor man, was down smile at him as I prepared to move a little deeper into the damn building to lend extra support to my people, sir.

"When I smiled at the lousy scumbag, he smiled back at me and then he went reaching for a pistol with his good hand lying at his side. The crazy sonofabitch was going to still try and kill me while he was slowly dying before my eyes sir, and all the while the prick was still reaching for his weapon, he was continuing to smile at me, Captain Walker Sir."

"Gees, the asshole, what the fuck do you do about his threat against you, Sergeant?" Walker asked as he stared back at the young man, proud of what he was telling him.

"I'll tell ya what I did to the rotten bastard sir. I emptied my damn clip in his fucking face, sir. I made certain he wasn't going to lift another damn weapon against another American soldier ever again, sir." The Sergeant replied in an angry voice, and then he was going to speak further until he was cut off by another soldier.

Buckethead roared at Walker as he and Baby Tee came out of their home. Baby Tee was topless and when she noticed the five men speaking with Walker and Ramirez, she forced Buckethead to put her down, he was carrying her. The two soldiers walked over to Walker with Baby Tee making no attempt to cover her breasts. When Bucket was by Walker's side, he pointed at the new men with his chin and asked. "Who's this shit man?"

"These are the FNGs (Fucking New Guys) Colonel Leadbetter picked to full out the Unit, big man. Sergeant, this man is Sergeant Vincent Lambardo and his tag is Buckethead. I'm certain you can understand how he got his tag with the Unit by just looking at him." Walker grumbled as he slapped Bucket on the back of his head, and then he grinned at him.

The five new soldiers laughed over Walker's remark and his actions as they allowed themselves to relax for the first time since showing up on Walker's property.

"The chick with him is Sergeant Teri Dorland, and her tag name is Baby Tee for the obvious reason, people." Walker looked at Tee's breasts and again the new soldiers laughed with Walker, and then he added. "And, the other lady standing here is Sergeant Dorothy Ramirez, and she's my future wife, guys."

"It's nothing like keeping it all in the family, Captain Walker." Sergeant Glennallen offered over the fact he was dating one of the female soldiers from the elite group of soldiers.

"Hey man, you missed your true calling in fucking life, fella. You shoulda been a fucking comedian, buster." The suddenly angry looking Buckethead snapped at the grinning Sergeant.

"Back off him big man, these guys don't know you or your wrapped sense of fucking humor yet, buddy." Walker fired back at the massive man standing by his right side.

The Captain turned his attention back to the five new soldiers and offered them. "You people got some place to stay on the stinking

Island? If you don't have anything setup, Raz will be glad to help you people out with getting some rooms on the Island. But if you people don't mind sleeping on the floor, you guys can always stay with us until you gotta leave the place and report back to base. That way we can get to know each other a helluva lot betta, guys. I'd prefer you people stayed with us while you're on the damn Island."

Sergeant William Glennallen turned and looked at each of the other soldiers he brought to the Island. They sort of shrugged at him and the Sergeant turned and faced Walker and offered him. "Well Captain Walker Sir, it looks like you got yourself some company for yourself, sir. Where do you want us to stow our gear, sir?"

"You can run it to the house and drop it in the living room, and we'll talk more when you get back. While you people are inside, you might as well get out of your damn uniforms and get comfortable. Then come out and enjoy a cold one with the rest of us. I'll call the Mutt and have him come over with the other grunts he has staying at his place, and you can meet the rest of the guys hanging on the Island. Maybe we can get some fishing in while you people are on the Island. I'm pleased you people decided to stay with us, that way it won't cost you anything while you're visiting on the Island. Everything here is rather expensive." Walker offered as he turned away from the new men and he picked up his fishing pole and went back to fishing.

The new guys ran into the home while following Ramirez. Buckethead grumbled at Walker. "Hey man, I like the new pukes already they seem to have the guts to make it in our Unit."

"Yeah, they're the cream of the crap I guess buddy, but it's too early to decide if they'll work out well with the Unit, man. C'mon, I wanna try and catch a stinking fish here man." Walker bitched as he pulled back on the pole, but he could not set the hook on the fish.

Ramirez left the new soldiers changing and she rushed back to Walker's side and said. "Robert, they seem like good people and soldiers, I like them already Bobby."

"Yeah, shake hands with the big guy, he likes them as well, honey. Me, I'm taking the wait and see attitude if you don't mind, baby." Walker snapped at Ramirez as he again tried to catch the fish constantly stripping his bait from the hook.

When the five new guys came out of his home and gathered on the dock, Walker's fishing was over for the day and he pulled in his line and dropped the pole in the holder and went to the cooler and took out a beer. The soldiers spent the rest of the day getting to know each other. It was interesting when they met the Mutt and the other soldiers from his place. For the next two days, Walker pumped all the information he could gather from the new soldiers, because he was interested where he was going to place them in the Unit when they began their exercises. The concerned Captain did not care a lick what the soldiers did in their old Units. He was going to place them where he felt they would do the best for the Units involved in the Multi National Rapid Response Force he was basically in command of.

Monday came and Walker brought the new soldiers over to the airport and once they were gone, he was happy to have his home free of the new guys. Now, the problem of losing Ice, Sergeant Diane Morrison, and Baby Tee, Sergeant Teri Dorland, had to be dealt with by the remaining soldiers still staying at Walker's place. No Neck and Buckethead had no family alive, so they were planning to stay with Walker and the Mutt until they had to report back to base for special training or new mission. Even Walker was feeling down when the two female warriors packed up and prepared to leave the Island on the next morning.

Buckethead and the Neck were the saddest because they were getting involved with the two women soldiers. They moped around Walker's place all day, and when the women were ready to leave, they acted like they were losing their best friends. Walker, Ramirez, the Mutt, and Blind Date accompanied the massive Neck and Buckethead to the airport to see the women off.

Ice was as heart broken over leaving because she was beginning to love the Neck, and she cared for Walker as well. She loved him because he did not scrub her out of the Unit when she was wounded in one of their operations. She understood the Captain placed her on light duty with the Unit until she was at one hundred percent. She would never forget what he and other soldiers did for her, protecting her whenever Colonel Leadbetter came around. Then how they helped her get her strength back, caring for her like they were her family.

With the women waiting for the plane to allow boarding, Ice kissed Neck like he was never kissed before, and then she walked over to Walker and hugged him for dear life as she whispered in his ear. "Robert, I love you for taking care of me when I was hurt, sir. I own you my still being in the Unit. Both you and Raz were great dealing with me." Ice kissed Walker on the lips.

"What kinda crap are you trying to dump down on my stinking ass now, young lady? I didn't do nuthin fucking special for your baby sister, you did it for yourself honey. You're too good a fighter for me to lose you from the outfit, and besides you worked your lovely little ass off getting back to perfect, little sister. So it should be me thanking you for toughing it out for the Unit, honey. I'm damn glad to have you in the Unit, baby."

"Boy Walker, you won't cut anyone any slack will you sir? I was trying to thank you for putting up with me, sir. I was so scared you were going to force me out of the Unit when I was hurt a few years ago, sir. Even Colonel Leadbetter put up with me, and that makes you soldiers my real family for the rest of my life, Robert." Ice cried as she swiped at a tear she felt was betraying her by running down her cheek.

"C'mon baby, you did it all on your own, all we did was support you like we would any wounded soldier from the outfit when you needed a little extra help every now and then, baby sister. You're a soldiers and I didn't do nuthin more for you that I woulda done for any uther stinking soldier from the damn Unit, baby. But let me tell you this sister, if I believed for one moment you wouldn't come back from the wound, I woulda dumped your lovely little ass out of the Unit so fast your damn drawers woulda had trouble keeping up with your purdy little ass, baby sister." Walker snapped at Ice while trying to act like he was getting angry with her, but Ice was easily able to see through the front he was putting up, and she smiled a smile that would have melted butter on the kitchen table. Then she lovingly ran a finger slowly down the side of his face and she smiled up at him.

The Neck saw Ice was having a hard time leaving them, and he moved up to her and looped his branch like arm over Ice's slender shoulder, and she immediately melted into the warming protection his powerful arm offered her. She looked into the Neck's steel blue eyes and smiled and he gave her a hug to his body as he returned the smile.

The unnaturally large Buckethead was not having much trouble with Baby Tee, because they did not get as close as the other two soldiers were. Baby Tee was excited about going home to be with her brother and sister. She lost both parents in a car crash some years back, but she was over the loss if it was possible to get over losing of ones parents. She was waiting not so patiently for Ice to finish up speaking with Walker and the other soldiers, and when Ice moved away from Walker's side, she moved in and kissed Walker and Ramirez goodbye. Then she swung her duffle bag over her shoulder and pushed Ice away from the Neck. The plane was allowing boarding and the women walked through the glass sliding doors and walked across the landing strip and entered the plane, without turning and looking back at the other soldiers.

Ramirez replaced Baby Tee by Walker's side and she held onto his hand as they both watched the plane close and the engines idle up to take off speed. Then the plane moved onto the tarmac and drifted towards the far end of the field, and its engines went to full take off power again. The roar coming from the engines was deafening, and then the plane shot down the crumbling runway and slowly lifted in the air. The small group of soldiers remained inside the building until they could no longer see the plane. Then they headed for the cars and started for their home while the Mutt, Blind Date, and the Neck headed for his home.

When they got home, Ramirez went in the place and Walker and Buckethead walked to the back dock area. The sun was starting to go down, and the bait fish were coming in the canal in hordes to hide from the larger night hunters. The Captain looked down the canal and spotted three pleasure boats still out fishing, and he wished he was on the water with his World Cat. Little by little, he was starting to enjoy going out fishing in the crystal clean waters of the Keys. He was also starting to like not running all over the world in search of another batch of flaming assholes who wanted to do nothing in their wasted lives but harm some of the United States interests abroad, or inside his country.

He and Ramirez have been doing a lot of talking about not returning to the Unit and settling down and enjoying life with their son for a change. The longer he was not called back for some special training, the more he was enjoying being free and living on the tiny Island. He was even toying around with getting himself a second charter boat, and making some real money with chartering his boats out for a living to the people who visit the Island. Even though he was in the Carpenters Union, he did not want to go back to that kind of work either.

Buckethead broke Walker's concentration by resting his heavy hand down on his shoulder, and pointing out of the canal. He picked up what drew Buckethead's interest it was a beat up old lobster fishing boat coming in from its day of checking out the traps for their catch. For the way the night was shaping up it was going to be a beautiful one, and he was planning to make love to his lady under the star filled sky.

TEHRAN, IRAN. THE IMPERIAL PALACE, WEDNESDAY, JULY 27th, 2005

The Iranian terrorist known as the Vulture, General Abdol Karim Kalanteri was summoned to appear before the President of Iran for a secret meeting. The Vulture was early for the meeting and he was forced to cool his heels in the outer office, until the Iranian President sent for him. He did not want to be late and after sitting in the outer office for nearly an hour, General Kalantari was finally sent for. Once he entered the large office, the Vulture noticed the President and Prime Minister of Iran sitting in the office. He crossed the rather large room but he did not sit right down, instead he went to full attention and he saluted the President.

President Mahestan Hassanzadeh totally ignored the well feared Iranian General as he finished his conversation with Prime Minister, Khosrow Khosrashahi. Once he was done speaking with the Minister, the Iranian President finally turned his attention to the still saluting Persian General, and he snapped at him angrily.

"Allahu Akhbar General Kalantari Sir, I'm quite certain you're more than a little interested in knowing the reason why I decided to sent for you today, sir?" The Iranian President suddenly leaned back in his overstuffed chair, and then he stared at the feared General.

"Allahu Akhbar President Hassanzadeh. Yes sir, I must admit the thought has crossed my mind, sir." The Persian General replied politely as he smiled back at his respected leader.

"Yes General Kalantari, the war in Iraq is slowly turning in our favor, and the foolish American leaders are starting to turn on their foul President, and soon they'll be at each other's cursed throats over that unending war. I believe it's time for you to start making preparations of heading out for Cuba, so you can begin getting your group of terrorists into the United States, so they can begin their attacks in the heart of the great Satan. I have advance word Usama bin Laden is planning to try another faithful attack with his freedom fighters against the hated Americans in the near future, and before he acts against them, I want your terrorist cell safely inside the borders of the worthless United States.

"I trust you have the way you'll get your freedom fighters into Cuba, and you have been in contact with the worthless Cubans who are more than willing to assist you on your faithful mission, sir? I know the foul fool who is still in command of that miserable country is ill, and soon he'll be entering the hospital, sir." The Iranian President stopped speaking at this time in order to allow his General to reply to some of his questions of him now.

"Yes Sir my President, I've been in constant contact with our Cuban brothers who are willing to assist me with getting my Persian fighters inside the United States safely, sir. I've been waiting much too long a period of time for my summons before you my President, and for your permission to begin my opening attacks on the great evil, sir. I have my fighters foaming at the mouth over their want to attack the hated United States at a moment's notice. I have been keeping a close eye on what was happening in that wasteful nation of Iraq, and I was well aware our new weapons were starting to cause the hated American soldiers many dead, sir. But I must admit I had no idea bin Laden was planning another attack against the United States, sir. Do you have any idea what he is planning this time, and when it is scheduled to begin." The Iranian General stopped speaking and he waited for his President's reply to his last question.

"I have no idea when he plans to begin his attacks against the Americans, General Kalantari. But I'm with the knowledge he plans to use planes again on the great fools. From what I was lead to believe about his next mission, Usama plans to knock down a number of planes coming to the United States foul lands from the United Kingdom. I believe he'll be as successful with this next attack, just as he was with the attack on America's great phallic symbols he has destroyed in his last attack on the great evil of the United States, General Kalantari Sir."

"Then it's absolutely imperative I get my Persian fighters into the United States as soon as possible, sir. Like you have stated my President, I want my fighters safely in the United States borders, before Usama attacks the lands of Satan. Because once he attacks the United States again, the cursed American military will close all avenues into and out of their foul borders, and they'll remain safe until the worthless American public feel safe within their borders again, sir. I fear this time it'll take many years before the great American fools relax their lowly defenses enough for us to begin successfully getting our people into their cursed land again, sir. It'll not be a long time before the hated Americans start to get control of their border with Mexico, and when they close that avenue into their foul and worthless lands, we'll be forced to be extremely inventive of finding other successful ways into the United States.

"I have been keeping a close eye on that cursed situation, and more and more of the worthless America's civilians are starting to demand their government does something with the illegal aliens constantly crossing the Mexican border into the United States. In their search of a better living, or to transfer the drugs Usama bin Laden is shipping into Mexico for transport into the hated United States, sir. Usama is hell bent on destroying the United States one way or the other my President. Either by destroying their foul cities, or killing the civilians by flooding the United States with heroin, he'll kill Americans sir…"

"By the Almighty hand of Allah General Kalantari, I'm not here to discuss what bin Laden is up to in the future with the evil American fools. I summoned you before me to hear what you're going to do, now I gave you permission to begin you opening attacks on the great land of Satan, sir." President Hassanzadeh nearly roared at his powerful General as he suddenly interrupted his words on him, as he openly glared right into the fearsome General eyes as he waited for his reply.

General Kalantari was momentarily taken aback by the ferocity of his President's angry words aimed at him, especially because the Iranian Leader yelled at him before the Prime Minister of Iran. But the wise and crafty Iranian General quickly regrouped himself and he got composer over his rampaging anger and rage, and he offered to his President in a calm tone of voice.

"President Hassanzadeh Sir, I can have my people heading for Cuba by the end of this week at the latest, sir. Once we're inside Cuba, we'll blend ourselves with the local population for a few months, until we're certain the foul American intelligence systems are not aware of any of our movements inside that cursed country of dog eaters, sir. Once we're certain we have made it into Cuba unobserved, we'll start making our plans to invade the United States, with the help of our Cuban brothers and sisters and after that. I'll deploy my people and attack the selected target we discussed and settled upon a number of months ago, sir.

"We'll enter the cursed United States by the so called Cuban Railroad, or we can simply buy a worthless pleasure boat of our own and then sail it right into the Florida Keys, land there and sink the boat. Then we can make our way to Miami and hit the target we have our sights leveled upon, sir. Before you ask of me my President, I'm planning to begin my attack on America at the end of April, or the beginning of May of next year at the…"

"You're that confident you'll have no unforeseen problem hitting this target we have selected, General Kalantari Sir?" Prime Minister Khosrashahi asked as he interrupted the General's words in an extremely nasty tone of voice, as he spoke for the first time.

"Prime Minister Khosrashahi, I have no fear in my heart whatsoever of not succeeding on my faithful mission for Allah and my President, Sir. I'm so confident over the future success of my mission I'm willing to stake the lives on myself, and every one of my Persian fighters on it, sir. If I fail on my mission, I will die, and I'll take as many of the cursed Americans I can take with me, sir." General Kalantari so proudly boasted to the seated Prime Minister of Iran.

"The lives of your worthless followers and yourself are not the only lives you'll take with you to the foul grave, if you fail me on this mission General Kalantari. If you dare to fail me on this mission, every one of the members of your lowly family will follow you into the lands of hell, sir. But my revenge against you will not stop there I assure you. I shall order all the graves of your long departed ancestors violated, and their bones will be spread out upon the roads of Iran, and the vehicles will grind their bones into the dust they were made from, sir. Your entire bloodline will cease to exist in this world, so I warn you General Kalantari, you better not fail on the mission I'll send you out on, sir." Iranian President Hassanzadeh suddenly snarled at the General as he cut off the Prime Minister in the conversation he was having with his officer.

"I hear and I shall obey your orders so help me Allah, and I'll not fail on my mission for my President. May Allah take my eyes and my foul breath, if I don't carry out my mission to its faithful conclusion. We have to lay claim to the Prophet Muhammad's mantle, and the only way we can lay claim to that, is by destroying all the hated infidels and non-believers of the world. And, we have to start by eliminating all the cursed Sunni's of Iraq and Saudi Arabia, and also the Zionists of Israel. Once we established the true Shiite religion in all the Middle East, then we can spread the true word of Islam to the rest of the world, President Hassanzadeh Sir."

"More words, I'm growing sick and tired of hearing words and constant threats bantered about by anyone and everyone I speak of. I assure you sir I live only by my actions, General Kalantari Sir. I issued you the order to begin your plans to attack the hated United States, and I expect to see actions and no further words from you, General. Leave my side and assemble your foul fighters. I shall expect to be notified that your fighters for Allah are inside Cuba by Sunday of this week at the latest, as you have just suggested to me, sir." President Hassanzadeh suddenly snarled savagely at his powerful General, as he interrupted him again in this conversation, and then he merely dismissed the dangerous Iranian Military Officer with a crude flick of his hand, and an ugly glare and sneer on his face.

"Your wish is my command my President. It shall be as you ordered, sir. By Allah's will and command, my fighters and I will be in Cuba by Sunday morning of this coming week, President Hassanzadeh Sir." General Kalantari offered as he bowed towards his President, and then he brought his fingers up to his mouth, he then touched his chest with them and moved them out before his chest as he held his bow towards both the Iranian President and the Prime Minister.

"Very well General Kalantari Sir, I expect to hear from you on Sunday. You may leave my office so I can have further words with my Prime Minister, sir. I wish you all the success Allah shall bestow upon your foul head and your mission, General. But I caution you again over any failure for this mission, General. You better remember my threat against you and your family maybe this will give you the resolve to see this mission to its successful conclusion, sir." The Iranian President warned his General as he held him in his harsh glare, until the dangerous Vulture finally backed out of his office, and he was again alone with his Prime Minister.

Once the Vulture was out of sight of his Persian President, he slapped at the air before him, because he was so angry his unwise leader resorted to threatening him over his mission. He felt was it not enough for his President to understand he and his fighters were endeavoring upon an extremely dangerous mission, and there was a good chance he and his fighters might die on this faithful mission? The Vulture could not understand why his President was threatening to take any possible failure out on the rest of his family and his ancestors. This angered him to no end, and the Vulture headed for a meeting with the rest of his fighters. But he was going to take out his anger on them, since he could not really reply the way he wanted to his leader of Iran.

The Iranian Officer left the palace in a huff and he headed for his military jeep, he started it up and jammed the transmission in gear, popped the clutch and the vehicle jumped out into the flow of traffic. Any civilian cars on the road immediately got out of the way of the speeding military vehicle. The Vulture was heading directly for the airport, so he could board a plane and then head for the small Iranian town of Torbat-e-Heydariyeh near the border of Afghanistan and Iran.

CHAPTER TEN

THE IRANIAN VILLAGE OF TORBAT-e-HEYDARIYEH

It took the Iranian Military Officer the Vulture, General Abdol Karim Kalantari over seven hours to reach the out of the way Iranian village of Torbat-e-Heydariyeh by plane. The wise Persian Officer chose this village to assembly his fighters, because it was out of the normal flight paths of the known American spy satellites. The village was so secluded and meaningless to any military needs or target that it was the perfect place for the General to assemble his fighters and soon to be terrorists. The village was also the place where the Iranian's were assembling the IED's and EFP's being employed by their resistance warriors working against the American forces operating in Iraq, and now Afghanistan. It was also the exact place where the General understood he could get his fighters out of Iran and heading for Cuba, undetected by any American intelligence systems.

There was a civilian vehicle waiting for the feared and respected Iranian General as his plane lightly touched down on the makeshift runway of hard packed sand. The Persian Military Officer got out of the small aircraft and he climbed into the waiting car and he just nodded towards his fighter Captain Jahangeer Keshavaz, and the Captain smiled back at the General as he pulled away from the parked plane. Even though the small village was so well secluded, he was not taking anything for granted, and he wanted to get out of sight as quickly as possible.

He never knew if and when the cursed American military might divert one of their hated spy satellites, in their attempt to observe this part of the vast Iranian desert. He only started breathing normally once he was far enough away from the aircraft not to be connected to it any longer. The civilian car headed straight for the Vulture's private headquarters setup in a certain part of the lightly populated village. It took them fifteen minutes to reach his headquarters, and for the entire drive, the Vulture did not speak one word to his Captain. He was preoccupied with formulating what he was going to say to the rest of his fighters when he met with them, over what his President had to tell them.

The car pulled in front of his headquarters and he was out of the vehicle a moment before it came to a full stop. There was not one civilian from the village out in the open, this was because they were warned in advance he was coming to the village, and none of the civilian wanted to dare risk being seen by the always angry General for fear of their lives. General Kalantari stomped his way into the only large building in the entire small village, and he barked over his shoulder at his stunned Captain. "Captain Keshavaz, I trust you have everyone assembled in the cursed meeting room for me to address, and the fools are waiting my arrival. If not, I shall open your foul back with the bite of the lash, and then I shall order salt to be poured into every cursed wound I opened on your worthless body, Captain."

"General Kalantari Sir, everyone is assembled in the meeting room, and they're waiting to hear your words, sir." The Captain replied to the back of the Vulture, and he was not certain if the Vulture heard his words as he followed him into the building.

General Kalantari allowed the rest of his fighters to wait for his appearance, as he charged into his office, and he ripped opened a drawer and removed a number of files. He tucked the papers under his arm as he checked his answering machine, to see if his orders might have been changed on him. After going through the messages and not hearing one from his President, he turned and left his office and headed for the meeting room, and the other fighters waiting there for him.

He entered the meeting room without acknowledging anyone, and he went to his chair and dumped the papers under his arm out on the desk. The Vulture then took his seat as he tossed his Kaffiyeh headdress on the desk next to his papers. He took a second to draw in a huge gulp of air in an attempt to calm down his angry mood, but it did not help as he looked from one staring face to the other seated in the room. When his eyes finally landed on the one man he was looking for from the group, he smiled slightly at his favorite fighter and second on command, Colonel Hestmotallah Khatami. Who he was certain one day, he would surely become his Capiph, his successor in his war aimed against the hated United States.

The Vulture began by addressing the Colonel directly. "As Allah is my witness to all things that happen on the face of the earth, Colonel Khatami, I have just come from a private meeting with our President, and he has ordered me to start all of you to head out for Cuba as soon as possible. So we could begin our private Islamic Jihad or Holy War aimed against the cursed and hated Americans on their foul lands of the United States. He wants all our fighters in Cuba by no later than on Sunday of this week. And, the reason he has pushed up our orders, is because our wise President has advance word that Usama bin Laden is again going to attack the hated lands of the great Satan, and he wants us set in place before he begins his next attacks aimed against the United States. But I have my own special want and desire to have all of you installed inside the land of Satan, before he attacks them again.

"I want to hit the loathsome Americans before he does, so I can have the foul infidels point their accusing fingers at bin Laden and his followers, for the crime we shall commit against the fools of that worthless land in the near future. I shall use this great deception in hopes of having some of our Persian fighters survive our upcoming attack on the cursed and lowly American infidels. I have no intention of sending my fighters out on a suicide mission, and lose every one of my faithful people in just one attack against the hated American dog eaters. I want to try and keep everyone alive, so we could continue our assault on the unsuspecting horde of lowly infidels who live in the great land of Satan."

The Colonel was smiling at his Commander like he was a bazaar merchant, because it seemed like he was addressing him as he addressed the others through him at the meeting. This action had elevated him to be the next in Command of the fighters, if anything happened to the General.

The Colonel's constant smiling caused the Vulture to lose his concentration for the brief moment, and he had to stop speaking for a second to rethink what he was saying to the rest of his fighters or warriors. In his mind, he was constantly referring to his group of fighters as just that, because if he did not think of them as fighters, he would have to think of them as what they truly were. Terrorists, who were soon going to be slaughtering countless innocent civilians of another land, and he would never allow himself to dare think of his fighters or himself as being terrorists. The Vulture was trying to deceive himself into believing he was doing Allah's faithful work on the earth, by riding it of all the lowly Kafirs, the none-believers. His every thought was he was doing this to please Allah.

Finally, the feared Iranian General added to his words for his fighters at the meeting, while still directing his words at the Colonel. "Colonel Khatami, I order you to get the fighter's flight tickets from here to Ankara, Turkey. Since Turkey is a foul member of the worthless NATO Alliance, most of the countries involved in that cursed and worthless organization allow other members to visit their foul countries at will. Once we're in Turkey, we'll get flights to Venezuela. Since the fool in command of that country of dog eaters is friendly with Cuba, we will use his foul country to get us to Cuba. Once we're inside Cuba, we'll buy a fishing boat and cross the Florida Straits, and we'll enter the United States from the Florida Keys. From the Keys, we'll work our way up the coastline until we end up in Miami and hit our intended target.

"Once we have successfully destroyed our target in that cursed country, we'll then return to the Florida Keys, and then we'll get ourselves back to the filthy Island of Cuba. So we can live to attack the United States again in the future. These are my plans, but I only want you my faithful brother to concern yourself with getting us the flight tickets we need from our country to Turkey. Once we're in Turkey, it'll be an easy matter for us to get air flights to the worthless land of Venezuela, and then we can make it to Cuba, Colonel Khatami."

The Iranian Officer known to his group of Persian fighters as the Vulture, stopped speaking at this point, and he stared at the man he picked to replace him when he was no longer forced to be an active member of a terrorist cell operating in the field. When Colonel Khatami read the look from the fearsome Vulture, and he realized he wanted these orders carried out instantly. The Colonel rose to his feet and he bowed slightly to his leader, and then he turned on his heels and left the meeting room to carry out his orders from the deadly Vulture. The Colonel had no ill feelings of leaving the meeting first, not after the powerful General made it perfectly clear to him and the other fighters gathered at the meeting, that he was going to be the next in command of the terrorist cell when the General finally decided to retired from active duty, or if he was felled in battle for his country.

From what the Vulture informed him of, the crafty Colonel knew they were working with time restraints aimed against them, and the Persian fighters had to be in Cuba by Sunday of this week at the latest, or they would face the unfettered wrath of their dangerous President. He also knew where he had to go, and he rushed for the small airport that served the village they were using for their meetings and protection from the American spy satellites. He wanted to get the air flight tickets and then return to the meeting if it was still going on. If not, he would visit the General in his private office, and hand him the tickets he purchased for them personally.

When the Iranian Colonel was out of the room, the Vulture started to speak to the remaining members of his terrorist group. While clearing his throat, he began his words anew. "I order the rest of my faithful fighters for Allah's just cause, to leave this cursed room when I'm finished addressing you fools, and you'll gather up everything you might need for our successful operation against the great land of the Satan. Don't be a group of fools and try to carry any weapons on board the foul plane. I assure each one of you fools, the weapons we shall need for our mission will be supplied by our Cuban brothers and sisters.

"I've been in constant contact with those foul and hated fools, and I have informed the ones who have been selected by their lowly and near death Cuban President to assist us, because we'll be in desperate need of weapons when we enter their miserable country of worthless people. I was informed anything and everything we might need or desire for the success of our operation will be placed at our disposal. I have spoken to our President, and I asked him what will the future fate of Cuba going to be, once we have finally mastered complete control over the entire Middle East, and driven the hated American soldiers out of the entire region.

"Our wise and all seeing President has informed me he'll allow Cuba to live in peace in our future world, but the fate of the worthless nation of Venezuela will be another matter to be dealt with. Our President believes the fool running that foul country is too unstable to be left in command of that worthless nation. Besides, that country has oil to be sold to the highest bidder for their below grade crude. Since our President plans to control all the oil from the Middle East, our leader also plans to control any oil reserves from South America.

"That way we'll be able to bend the unshakable will of the yellow devils from China and Japan to our will, and force the fools to join us on our sacred Jihad we shall wage against the United States and the United Kingdom. Since they're trying to become the nation who consumes the most oil of the world, we'll use our supply of oil to them to control the yellow devils until we have no further need of them. Once we're done with China, we'll merely cut their oil flow off, and all the great gains they accomplished in the world will come to a grinding halt on them.

"Before any of you foul fools ask of me, we will continue to maintain our peaceful relations with Russia, because we'll need that cursed country of lowly mongrels to be on our side. So they can help defend us against China once we cut their oil supplies off from that miserable country. Although Russia is a fangless Bear, the country is still in control of their nuclear weapons, and our alliance with Russia will inform the Chinese not to thread upon our soil.

"Unless they want to tangle with hated Russia as well as all Arab nations we'll bring under the Iranian flag, and our true religion. We understand the United States will threaten our country with military intervention, once we make our move against Iraq, and Saudi Arabia. So the knowledge we're still friendly with the loathsome Russian nation, this will help to keep the United States' military at bay, until it's too late for them to be able to be a true threat against our future plans for the Middle East, or our country my fellow Persian brothers and sisters.

"Besides my faithful warriors, by the time my thoughts come to reality, we'll be able to produce our own breed of nuclear warheads, along with the long range missiles we'll need to get our warheads to their selected targets throughout the rest of the world. We'll soon be as much of a threat to the world peace as Russia is to the world, and once we command our own stockpile of nuclear weapons. The hated United States will be completely helpless to invade our country like they have with the useless Saudi Arabia, Iraq, and Kuwait nations.

"We'll own the entire Middle East Region, and any other Arab country we'll allow to live, will owe their full allegiance solely to Iran and our great and wise leadership. But the mission presently at hand is to attack the worthless United States from within their own foul borders. We have to make the civilians of that cursed country afraid to come out of their foul homes, and the only way to accomplish that great feat is to attack, and then to continue to attack them within their own country with terrorist attacks like we threaten.

"These devastating attacks will be designed to force the hated American leadership to pull their cursed and hated military troops out of all Arab lands of the Middle East and elsewhere, in an effort to protect their civilians in their own cursed and foul borders. Once their lowly troops are out of Iraq, we'll move in quickly and then take over that worthless country, and then we'll merely use it for our own wants and needs. Once we have destroyed all the lowly Sunni and Kurds from that country of waste. Then we shall go after Saudi Arabia who'll no longer enjoy the protection of the American military protecting their foul lands from attacks by our faithful followers. Then we'll go after Kuwait at our own leisure, and any and all other Arab nations we want to draw into our influence and control."

The dangerous and respected Iranian General stopped speaking for a moment to catch his breath, and to better formulate his next thoughts. What he was doing was killing off time until Colonel Khatami returned with his fighter's flight tickets. In the back of the Vulture's cunning mind, he wanted his Colonel and second in command to dismiss the rest of his fighters to cement his standing with the rest of them.

The Vulture was of the mind that once he finished this last mission for his President, he was going to request to become a more active member of the government of Iran. He was dreaming of the illusion of one day being place in command of Iraq, once they have successfully taken over that entire country. Once he was the President of Iraq, the rest of the world would be forced to respect and acknowledged his presence in the future flow of world events. Never again would he ever be thought of as a lowly and foul terrorist by anyone every again, as long as he lived.

The Iranian Military Officer wanted to be recognized as a legitimate world leader, and he would do anything in his power to forward his dreams of being a world leader. This was one of the reasons and his driving force for his hatred of the United States, for America's power over the rest of the world, had to be admired or hated with every thought in ones body. The United States was so powerful, so well respected that almost anything the cursed Americans did in the world, always seemed to end up coming out in their favor. So many nations were deeply depend upon the Americans for their very survival, even with the power of oil cut backs Iran controlled, did very little to harm the great respect and need by these other nations to the United States.

The Vulture wanted to command some of this unending power commanded by the United States. His need to be respected was confusing his thoughts of duty to his country. He was thinking of commanding the nation of Iraq more than he was thinking, and planning his mission for his President. Someone at the meeting suddenly cleared his throat, and this noise forced the General's mind to return to the conversation with the rest of his terrorist cell. The Vulture had to shake his head slightly, in an effort to force his mind back to the conversation at hand.

He looked at the Persian fighter who just cleared his throat, and then the Vulture offered. "Major al-Zubedu, do you have something else on your foul mind that you might want to share with the rest of us fools at the meeting, sir? If you do, I'm certain everyone here would be most interested in hearing what you have to offer, Major."

Major al-Zubedu drew in his breath, because he did not know if the General singled him out of the group because he was angry at him. He knew if the General got angry at anyone, that one person could find himself being assigned to a suicide mission. Sweating, the young Major offered to the Vulture cautiously. "General Kalantari Sir, I just wanted to know from you if we should leave the meeting now, and then go and gather everything we'll need to leave Iran, sir."

The Persian General held the Major locked in his harsh glare for a long moment, because he knew very well what his terrible stare was doing to the man, and he was enjoying the ultimate power he held over every one of his fighters gathered at the meeting. Suddenly, the powerful General suddenly allowed a slight smile to slowly cross his lips, as he replied to the Iranian Military Officer this time.

"Yes Major Zubedu, I believe that shall be a most wise move on every one of these fool's part. Because I have to gather everything up I shall need to take along with me as well. I was hoping the foolish Colonel would have returned with the flight tickets, before I released you from this meeting. To carry out what has to be looked after by all you fools before we have to leave Iran, to begin our opening attacks against the great land of Satan in the United States. But it looks like it's going to take the Colonel a lot longer time than I had figured on. Yes, by all means, everyone should leave the meeting, and when the Colonel finally returns to my office. I shall have him bring each and all of you your air flight tickets, and the exact time we shall be leaving Iran for the cursed land of Turkey.

"But I shall inform all of you, we'll all be in Turkey by this same time tomorrow, and then we'll be arriving in the nation of Venezuela by the next day. Then we'll enter the loathsome country of Cuba by Saturday, Sunday at the latest. So I can then report back to our great President we were successful with following out his orders to me and the rest of you as well. Be gone with you now and look after what has to be looked after, because once our sacred mission begins, we'll not look behind ourselves for any reason whatsoever. The mission we'll be on will be the only true reason why we shall draw in another breath for the Almighty Allah, and our President on his great earth."

With that said, the extremely dangerous Vulture glared angrily at every Persian fighter gathered in the room, and he continued to glare at them until each and every one of them rose, and then they quickly left the room so as to carry out his last orders to them. Even though he did not tell the other fighters, he was already packed for his mission, and he had been ever since his President first spoke to him over the possible upcoming mission. Once everyone was gone from the room, the Vulture leaned back in his chair and he allowed himself to relax for the first time since his meeting with the Iranian President took place. But his relaxation was cut short by Colonel Heshomtallah Khatami, and he was rather excited because he held locked in his hands the flight tickets for all their Persian fighters.

General Kalantari let his breath out in a rush and an exhausted sign as he sat forward in his chair, and he grinned at the concerned looking Colonel as he snatched the airline tickets from his outstretched hand. The Vulture fished out his ticket from the stack, and he also removed the Colonel's ticket from the many also, and then he handed the Colonel back the rest of the tickets as he offered him in a very calm tone of voice this time. "Colonel Khatami Sir, I'm pleased you possessed the smarts to have the both of us seated together on the foul flight to Turkey. Because there is much of our upcoming operation I wish to speak over with you during the flight to that foul and cursed country, sir.

"I'm going to use you to control a number of our faithful fighters, while I control the rest of the fools, Colonel. Our mission must meet with absolute success, if we plan to be important cogs in the future Iranian government our President intends to cast over the entire of the Middle East. I for one am tired of placing my foul life on the line, while others make a name for themselves off our great successes, Colonel. Once this latest mission we have been sent out on has been completed successfully, I intend to take my rightful place in the future of Iran, and I shall also remember all those people who have served me faithfully on my own rise to power over Iran and all her peoples, Colonel Khatami.

"I assure you Colonel Khatami there is a place set aside for you in the command I shall setup, once I'm finally recognized for my great efforts for our President and the Almighty Allah. You shall be important to me as I am to our President. There shall be many other future missions we shall run against the cursed and hated American fools. But you Colonel Khatami, I shall keep you out of the death zone on all future operations we shall run against any other nation in the world, sir. The reason I offer this to you is solely because over the many years I have come to know and work with you, sir. You have become one of my main Military Officers I can truly and always rely on sir, and know all my orders to you will be carried out in the manner you have received them faithfully, Colonel Khatami Sir.

"This is extremely important to me, and as I just stated. I remember all those who served me well in our countless endeavors, Colonel. Now you have another mission to carry out for me Colonel, I order you to bring the tickets you hold in your foul hand to those fools whose names are printed upon them. Once you have accomplished this, you shall return to your private living quarters and pack your belongings for our upcoming mission, sir. As I warned the other fools, you shall not carry a weapon on your person for this trip. We'll receive the weapons we'll need at our final destination, and then we shall open our attack on the loathsome land of Satan. Be gone with you now Colonel Khatami, so I might be alone with my thoughts, sir." The Vulture moaned at his second in command, and then he watched him quickly leave the room and again he leaned back in his chair and let out an exhausted sigh.

MASHHAD INTERNATIONAL AIRPORT, IRAN. THURSDAY, JULY 28th, 2005. 9:30 A.M. IRANIAN TIME

All the future terrorists' working with General Abdol Karim Kalatari, cautiously arrived at the International Airport stationed in the much larger Iranian town of Mashhad at the same time, which was about twenty five miles from the General's town of Torbat-e-Heydariyeh. The soon to be attackers acted like they did not know each other as they lingered around the terminal until the announcement to board Flight One, Seven, Seven, was made over the intercom of the airport. The only man anywhere near the Vulture, was Colonel Heshmotallah Khatami, but he was acting like he did not know the extremely dangerous Persian General.

The fifteen other Persian terrorists were spread out in the waiting area of the airport, and some of them were sipping the bitter tea they enjoyed so much to kill off some of the time they had to labor through. Some of the male fighters paired up with the women of the group, and they were acting like lovers waiting to go on vacation at the terminal. The General smiled over this fact, because he was pleased some of his fighters showed the wherewithal to act so carefree over their intended mission and present situation.

General Kalantari was keeping a close eye on his fighters as they milled about the large waiting area of the airport, because he wanted to make certain no one dared to challenge them as they waited for their flight to take off. The Vulture was the only one of the group who carried papers identifying him as working for the feared QUD, and his papers would automatically cover anyone within Iran he wanted to offer this extended protection to. The General was prepared to come to his fighter's aide if they were challenged by the Iranian Secret Police, he successfully picked out from the maddening crowd of civilians waiting inside the terminal.

Finally, the announcement came over the loud speaker stating Flight One, Seven, Seven was ready to begin boarding the aircraft, and there was a rush by a number of people as they headed for the boarding gate. The Vulture held back and watched his people get their tickets checked in, and then go down the tunnel and enter the waiting plane. The Iranian General was the next to last person who walked onto the aircraft, and he headed for the first class section. Colonel Heshmotallah Khatami was the only other terrorist who was going to be allowed to fly in the first class section of the plane with the General.

The rest of the Persian fighters were seated spread throughout the coach section of the aircraft. The Iranian Military Officer ended up sitting in the plane for fifteen minutes, before it was backed away from the terminal loading area. Then the aircraft went under its own power towards the far end of the main runway of the airport. There it sat for another three minutes as it rapidly built up its full take off power, and then in less than a heartbeat the huge plane shot up in the bright morning sky.

It seemed to the overtired Iranian General he just got comfortable and finished his drink, when the Captain of the aircraft announced they were starting their decent for landing at Ankara, in Turkey. The Iranian Flight Captain also gave a complete weather forecast for the people in his plane. Then the fasten seat belt sign lit up and the young stewardesses immediately started to clean up the glasses and food trays, and then also locking the drop down trays back in place in preparation for their landing. When everything was done, the stewardesses took their seats and strapped themselves in for the landing.

The thoroughly bored General looked at the Colonel for a long second, because he was acting like he did not know the man seated at his side, and he gave him a slight nod and a quick smile, and then he looked out the window again.

The landing was smooth and when the plane was at the Turkey Terminal, all first class passengers stood and were let off the plane first. The terminal was nothing short of sheer mayhem, with people getting off a number of planes, and assembling at the luggage area to wait for their stuff. The screaming, cursing and shoving was irritating to the General and at one point, he actually shoved another young Arab who happened to step on his foot by accident.

The thoroughly exhausted and upset Iranian General headed for one of the massive concrete support columns of the airport, once he had his two pieces of luggage in hand. There he waited for the rest of his fighters/terrorists to gather around him, so he could direct them as where to go next inside the busy airport. Their flight to Venezuela was scheduled to take off within two hours, and the terrorist cell was scheduled to be landing in that country at six a.m. sharp the following morning on Friday.

But there was a full twenty four hour layover in Venezuela, before they could finally board their flight for the country of Cuba. But the Vulture was still going to be landing in Cuba on Saturday afternoon at exactly two p.m. This would give him enough time to locate their apartments, and to also scout out the rest of the Capital of Cuba for a full night, before he had to make contact with his President back in Iran.

By the time the rest of his people had their luggage and assembled around their commander, it was almost a full hour they wasted. The commander of the terrorists looked at his watch and then he barked at his people. "We have over an hour to wait until our flight into that cursed nation of Venezuela takes off, and then we'll be forced to sleep in that country of lowly dog eaters. I believe we'll be better serves if we took this time to get ourselves something substantial to eat and drink. The Almighty Allah only knows what we might be forced to eat while trapped in Venezuela. Knowing how the fool running that lowly country is of late, we might be eating his own people for all we will know. Look, there is a good Arab restaurant over there we shall eat in that place. I want three seated to a table, and make it seem each person at the table does not know the others seated near them.

"I have a feeling there are many hated American undercover agents working in this foul terminal, and I don't want you people to draw any special attention to yourselves while we wait for our flight to the other foul country. We'll be having enough trouble getting into Cuba, without drawing any of Satan's spies eyes drawn upon ourselves and our actions. Break up and head for the restaurant and take tables well away from each other. Colonel Khatami and Major Fereshyeh Mansouri will be seated with me in the foul foreign restaurant. I feel I need a woman seated at my table in case there are any American spies operating inside this foul terminal.

"I believe if there is a woman with us, the watchers would be more inclined to consider we're on vacation, and they'll aim their worthless jackal eyes on someone else who might be in this cursed terminal waiting for another flight. Leave my side you fool's and enter the worthless restaurant and seek out your foul tables and order food. I want to be at the loading Gate fifteen minutes before we have to report to the foul plane headed for the worthless country of Venezuela, and we can check in and wait at the Gate to board the foul plane."

The Vulture stopped speaking and he gave the look to the other fighters gathered within hearing his words to leave his side. The two other fighters remained near the column, and once the other fighters were gone, they both closed in on the General and he hissed angrily at them.

"We shall wait here until all the foul fools are inside the cursed eatery. Once they're inside, we'll then enter and take a table well away from the other fools. I want you two to keep your eyes opened, and if you believe you see anyone looking like they're keeping their eyes on any of our fighters, I want to know about it immediately. We have to remember we're in a country even though it is an Arab country, these worthless fools allow the hated Americans to dictate their foul rules to them. Turkey is our enemy, and we have to remain on full alert all the while we're forced to remain within this cursed country. Ahhh… there goes the last of our foolish fighters into this foul eating place. We can now go in ourselves to eat."

The Persian General snarled as he shoved his weight off the column with his powerful shoulders, and then he bent down and picked up his two pieces of luggage and carried them into the restaurant with him. This was the only time they were going to be saddled with their luggage, when they board the plane for Venezuela, their luggage was to remain on board the aircraft and the same plane will be bringing them out to Cuba the next day.

General Abdol Karim Kalantari and the two Persian fighters with him entered the restaurant and they looked around the nearly overcrowded eatery in search of a free table, and where the rest of the fighters were seated in the place. He smiled over the way his other people had spread out inside the restaurant. It was Major Mansouri who spotted an empty table near the front of the place, and she immediately pointed it out to the General. The Vulture nodded and all three of them headed for the empty table and when they were seated, a waitress immediately came over to the table to see what they might want to drink or eat.

All the soon to be terrorists ate, and within half an hour they were done and they paid for their meals and started assembling around the boarding gate for their flight to Venezuela. General Abdol Karim Kalantari stood with Colonel Heshmotallah Khatami and Major Fereshteh Mansouri, and they waited for the rest of their Persian fighters to board the waiting plane. This time the female Major was scheduled to sit with the General and other Major on board the plane in first class. This was because the General wanted the overseas flight to look as normal as possible, and he felt if he was flying with a female and another man in his company, the accusing eye of any spy would be much more likely to overlook the three of them as possible terrorists.

The flight to Venezuela was as uneventful as was General Kalantari's flight from Iran to Turkey hours before. The plane picked up a good tail wind, and it landed fifteen minutes ahead of schedule in the South American nation at five forty five a.m. In this country, the Vulture was not so concerned with gathering his Iranian fighters around him, and the fifteen member attack team walked around the capital city of Caracas like they had no fears in the world. Even before General Kalantari's fighters left Iran for Turkey, the Iranian President was in contact with the President of Venezuela, and the Iranian leader informed the leader of Venezuela he was sending a terrorist team to his nation, and they were only using his country as a quick layover spot for their trip to Cuba.

The Venezuelan leader was pleased to do anything in his power to help assist Iran with their future attack against the United States. But the Venezuelan President was not so trusting as he led on to believe the Iranian Operatives, and the moment General Kalantari and his small terrorist cell landed in his country, the highly unpredictable Venezuelan President had the group of Persian terrorists trailed and held under constant surveillance by his so called secret police, all the while the terrorists were visiting his country.

During his stay in Venezuela, General Kalantari was on constant alert, and a number of times he picked out the Venezuelan police assigned to keep an eye on him and the rest of his people. Once he spotted them, he knew the Venezuelan President did not trust him or his people, and he also vowed to himself he would register a stern complaint with his President, once he made contact with him again. The Vulture also alerted the rest of his group of terrorists they were being trailed by Venezuelan secret police officers, and he further warned them not to do anything wrong while visiting the South American country that would cause what he believed was the secret police to stop, or even possibly detain them while they were stuck waiting in the country.

General Abdol Karim Kalantari allowed his fighters to visit one of the many strip bars in the Venezuelan capital, and he himself enjoyed the young and naked South American women dancing on the stage before them, and walking around the tables of the bar totally naked. The Vulture was amazed at the number of young women who approached him and a number of his other fighters, and the women offered their sexual treasures to them for cash.

Before General Kalantari left his home country of Iran, he took with him two million American dollars in cash to support his fighters while they were in transit to attack the United States. The crafty Iranian General transferred another five million American dollars to an Arab bank operating in Miami, Florida, and he was intending to use this sum of money to support him and his fighters while they were within the borders of the United States, and to also get him and the rest of the terrorists with him who survived their attack on their selected target. Out of the United States safely once they had completed their mission, and they had to get out of the country before they were discovered by the police authorities.

General Abdol Karim Kalantari also had access to other monies inside the United States through a number of Arab Embassies and Mosques, where their followers were sympatric to what Iran was trying to do in the Middle East. He was going to be well funded on this operation, and he was pleased with the American cash he had at his disposal. The General enjoyed an extended list of other Persians and Arab help he could rely on to assist him, while in the United States if anything went wrong with his mission. Or he needed help with getting his surviving fighters out of the country safely. He was operating under the direct orders of his President of Iran as he was the only Persian warrior his President was concerned with getting out of the United States alive, once they had completed their mission.

The Iranian President informed his General all the other fighters under his command were expendable and the Iranian Leader gave his

General a short list of people and places he could make his way to, and these people would assist with getting him alone out of the United States.

The Vulture was pleased with these orders, because he felt his leader was not sending him out on a suicide mission, that he wanted him to come back to Iran alive. This knowledge gave him the mood that made it much easier for him to control and order his group of terrorists around confidently.

The food, drinks, and horde of naked young women dancing before him and the rest of his young and excited Persian fighters seemed to revitalize everyone of the Iranian fighters, and to his surprise. Even the few women fighters seemed to be enjoying all the attention from the naked women their Arab brothers were receiving from them. But the wise and well tested General did not allow his guard down all together, especially when he picked out at least four of what he believed were Venezuelan secret police roaming around inside the bar, and these four men were obviously keeping a close eye on him and the rest of his fighters.

The General leaned closer to Colonel Khatami at his table, and he whispered about the four police officers keeping a close eye on them inside the bar. But he was hit by another surprise when the Colonel informed him he was already aware of the people in the bar watching them. He smiled at his Colonel, pleased because he was keeping his eyes opened for any possible trouble while they were visiting the country of Venezuela. It only served to strengthen his convictions that the young Colonel was the only logical pick to replace him, once he was no longer a field operative for his government. The Vulture also vowed to himself if he was going to be given safe passage out of the United States, once their mission was completed successfully. He was also going to do everything in his power to try and get the young Colonel out of America safely with him once he left.

CHAPTER ELEVEN

After realizing the Colonel was on the alert, General Kalantari leaned back in his chair and he allowed himself to relax a little. Again he smiled as he watched a beautiful young Spanish woman he figured was no more than nineteen years of age, strip to the sound of the blaring music, and then she started dancing wildly on the stage with two other women. The heavy smoke in the bar was suffocating, and the extremely blaring music was giving him a pounding headache. But the Vulture was determined to allow his fighters to enjoy the last possible days of their lives to the best of their abilities. He did not even get upset when Major Ghassan Abidal al-Zebedi was suddenly pulled up to his feet by a young and pretty naked woman, and then he was lead to some private rooms that were in the back of the bar.

General Kalantari gave each of his Persian fighter's one thousand American dollars to spend any way they deemed fit, while they were stuck on layover in Venezuela. He knew what the two young people would be doing in the back room of the filthy bar, and it did not concern him in the least, as long as his foolish Major came back to the table, and he was not harmed by anyone else in the overcrowded bar. He was well aware some times, visitors to these types of bars were brought out to the back, and then they were beaten and robbed of their cash and other valuables.

For a fleeting moment, the Vulture thought about sending two of his male fighters out, to make certain his foolish Major was not harmed by the young woman, or anyone else who might be working with her in the bar. But he decided the unwise Major was a well trained military officer, and he was more than capable of protecting himself under any threatening circumstances. But another reason why he did not send any of the other fighters out to keep an eye on the Major was because he felt if he was stupid enough to get beaten and robbed. He understood if he sent any of the other fighters out to protect him, it would only end up in an all out brawl where he could lose more of his fighters to death, or jail, and place his mission in jeopardy.

It was after about fifteen minutes since the Major left the other terrorists with the young woman, and the General started tapping his fingers on the table over the concern his actions were causing him in the bar. After another ten minutes he was getting noticeably upset, and it forced Colonel Khatami to lean over and ask the Vulture. "General Kalantari, is there a problem sir? You seem rather upset suddenly sir."

"Yes Colonel Khatami Sir, I am upset at that. It's because of this fool of a Major we have in our group. He left the table with that lowly cursed female whore, and I'm becoming extremely concerned over the amount of time it's taking the great fool to come back here to us." The General snarled at he looked in the direction the Major and the woman disappeared into.

As the Colonel looked in the direction the Persian General looked in, he spotted the Major coming out from the back room, and he was grinning from ear to ear and staggering slightly. He was still in the presence of the woman hanging all over the side of him, and they both were heading for their table. The Colonel smiled as he shook his head slightly because the young woman was topless, and the Major was pawing her exposed breasts with both his hands. With his chin he drew the Vulture's attention towards the back area of the bar, as he announced to the General at the same time. "General Kalantari Sir, I see the great fool is coming back to us, and he seems to be still in good health, sir. But I'm afraid he's still in the presence of the foul young woman of this miserable country, sir."

The Vulture looked to the back of the bar and then he let his breath out in a rush, when he noticed his Major coming back to them. He was angrier at himself more than he was at the Major, because he would have been able to avoid all the stress his actions caused him, by simply refusing him to go along with the evil woman. He was guilty of a moment's weakness to allow his officer to spend time with this strange woman, and he vowed he would never display such weakness again for any of his fighters or for his enemy as well. He continued to stare at the young Major until he was standing right by the table, and then the Vulture snarled at him.

"Major al-Zubedi, you'll tell this foul woman to go and find someone else to be with, and then you'll take your seat with us and never leave this table again, until we leave this ill-begotten establishment. You're lucky I don't order your foul back to be opened by the lash, fool."

"Oh my lover, you did not tell me you were a Major in our military when we were making love in the back room. If you would have told me you were with our military, the price would have been far less for you." The young and pretty Spanish woman said to the Major in very heavily accented English. She spoke in English because the two men were speaking English also.

The Major turned to the young lady, but before he was able to say anything to her, the fuming Vulture snarled at her this time in an extremely threatening tone of voice. "Young and foul whore from this land, if you don't take your cursed and filthy hands away from my soldier's body, it'll not be he who'll have his back opened with the sting of the lash, it'll be you who shall have the pleasure of feeling what the lash can do to your body, witch. Leave us so I might speak further with my Major in private, evil and cursed woman!"

The young Spanish woman stiffened up, because in Venezuela the only soldiers who spoke to the civilians in this matter, were the special killer units who handled any civilian unrest in the country. Instantly, the woman turned a bright red as she bowed towards the angry looking Iranian General, and then she backed away from the table surrounded by the obvious soldiers, even though everyone there was dressed in civilian clothes. Then the young woman quickly disappeared into the maddening crowd of the bar, and then the first chance she got, she even left the bar altogether, for fear this angry man might order her to disappear for no other reason than she shared sex with the one the obvious leader was calling his Major.

Major Ghassab Abidal al-Zubedi was drunk enough and satisfied with his lovemaking to the lovely looking South American woman that this mood gave him the courage not to be so fearful of the angry Iranian

General. Proudly while trying to walk as straight as he could back to his seat at the large table. But General Kalantari kept the slightly staggering Major locked up in his angry and harsh stare, until he was seated at the table again. Once the Persian Major was seated and he finally glanced back at the General, the Vulture snapped at his military officer.

"Well Major al-Zubedi, I trust you have enjoyed your fun with that evil foul and lowly whore from this filthy god cursed country of miserable dog eaters, sir?"

Major al-Zubedi stifled a belch as he replied in a slurred voice to his angry looking Commander of the group of Persian terrorists. "Yes Sir General Kalantari, it was pleasurable sir. She has done something our women would never dare think of doing for their men, sir." The Major looked at Major Mansouri because she was sitting at the left hand side of the General, and she was the only one he was able to see while looking at the Vulture. He actually gave her a lingering leer as well.

"Be still with that foul mouth of yours, Major al-Zubedi. Is it not bad enough you have just insulted Allah and your religious beliefs, by sharing yourself with that filthy whore of this lowly establishment? Now you have to compound your cursed sins by bragging about them before these true and faithful followers of Allah. I shall speak further to you about this evil crime, once we finished our mission and we're back in our own country again, Major. Until then you'll not share what Allah has blessed you with another woman, unless she is Iranian, you foul fool you. I have a good mind to have a bag of hot ash tied to your foul and evil face for your evil sins, Major. You're lower than the regurgitated filth that comes from the loathsome Vultures of our lands. Your mother must have mated with a scorpion."

The Major's slight smile left his lips once he realized the fuming General was truly angry at him. Still being held in the Vulture's angry and harsh stare, the drunken Iranian Major put his head down and he looked at his hands as he rested them on the surface of the table he was seated at. Reality quickly set in and the Persian Major now worried if the Vulture might inform the Sheika's and allow them to punish him for the sins he committed in this foul country. Now his hands were shaking with fright for his life.

Once the Vulture received the proper and contrite reaction he was looking for from his foolish and drunken Major, he got off his back and he turned to look at a pair of young Spanish women who just walked out on the large dance stage, and they were now in the process of removing their clothes to the beat of the extremely loud music.

The Persian women of the group did not seem to mind all the nudity they were witnessing for the sake of the male members of the terrorist group.

General Kalantari was pleased he ordered his fighters to speak only English while they were trapped in Venezuela while waiting for their flight to Cuba to arrive. He was well aware many people in this country spoke English and besides, he wanted his people to also get used to speaking English every change they received for when they made it into the United States. He did not want them slipping and speaking their native tongue of Farsi. Since the foolish Major went with the young woman, he knew he was correct by ordering his people to speak English ever since they left their own lands.

General Abdol Karim Kalantari looked at his watch when he noticed Major Mansouri cover her mouth as she yawned, and he was stunned it was so late. It was three thirty on Saturday morning, and their flight was scheduled to leave for Cuba at ten thirty, and it was a fifty five minute flight from Venezuela to Cuba. He did not want his people getting off the plane in Cuba and walking around like zombies, so he drew in his breath and barked at them. "Everyone, it's later than I though and we have to get some rest before we leave for Cuba later today. Finish up with you drinks and anything else you might want to do in this cursed establishment, and then we're heading for our foul hotel and rest a little. We have to be at the airport by nine a.m."

The Vulture watched his fighters finish their last drinks and he paid their bill as each of his fighters stood and they waited for the others. They left the bar as a group and walked the five blocks to their apartments. Colonel Katami and Major Mansouri was going to share a room with the General, and the rest of the Persian fighters were going to pair up and take their rooms in the hotel. On their way to the hotel, the General kept taking glances behind them, and he noticed the four South American males walking and acting like they were not following them. He smiled over their poor attempt to follow his people, knowing if he wanted to kill these four people, he could do it easily, because they were not able to hide themselves properly.

The Vulture, Colonel, and the Major entered their apartment and Major Mansouri announced she was going to take a quick shower. While she was showering, the Vulture sent the Colonel out of the room on a mission to make certain the rest of his people were settled in their rooms, and not out trying to pick up more whores for them to enjoy from this country. Just as soon as the Colonel was out of his room, the Vulture quickly undressed and he entered the bathroom while the Major was showering. He walked over to the tub and pulled the shower curtain aside, and then he got into the shower with the female Major.

The Iranian Commander did not offer any explanation why he invaded the Major's shower, and she did not ask why he was with her. The powerful General was standing behind her as she continued to lather up her body with the soap, and he reached around her and started to play with her soap covered breasts, while rubbing his rock hard manhood against her rearend. Suddenly, the General shoved her forward and she ended up leaning over. He then roughly grabbed her left leg and lifted it up in his hand, and he entered her from behind.

Major Mansouri had to place both her hands up against the wall of the shower stall to help stead herself, as the powerful General shoved himself in and out of her without displaying any concern over her enjoyment of the act. He was so excited he increased his pace, and this action caused the female Major to moan, because of what the Vulture was doing to her body. All the time he was making love to the pretty Major, he continued to roll her soap covered breasts in his hands. The soap made her breasts slippery, and it increased the pleasure for the both of them to enjoy. Finally, he came and then he leaned his full weight up against her body, and he pushed himself deeper inside her. When he was done, he pulled out of her and he sat down on the edge of the tub as he struggled to try and get his breathing under control, and he smiled contently at the female Major.

Major Mansouri turned around while standing in the tub and the water beating directly on her back, and she rested her hands lightly on her hips. This action made her breasts stick out further and also point up as she moaned at the Iranian General with a sort of smirk on her lips. "Well General Kalantari, that was rather interesting I must admit, sir. To what do I own this suddenly interest you're displaying toward me? For as long as I have known you sir, I have never known you to cheat on your wife. Not that I mind what you have done so with me sir. For years I have dreamed about what it might be like to make love with you, sir. Now I have experienced it, I hope we shall do it again and again, sir." Now Major Mansouri laughed as she looked down at the grinning leader of her group of terrorists, while making no attempt whatsoever at covering her nakedness to his steady glaze, as she continued to smile down at him.

The Iranian Warrior could do nothing but merely smile back at the extremely beautiful and young Persian woman with the outstanding shape he had just made love to in the shower.

"I'm afraid I didn't hear your reply to me my General and leader. Now that we have made love once, I hope we shall repeat the process again, sir?" Major Mansouri continued to smile at the exhausted military officer, as she waited for his reply.

General Kalantrai stood up in the shower again as he quickly closed in on the female Major, and he pulled her naked and wet body close to his, and he planted an extremely passionate kiss on her lips, and again he slid his hand between them and cupped her breast.

Major Mansouri pulled her lips away from the General's and she turned her cheek to his lips, or he would have tried to continue to kiss her as she offered calmly to him with a smile on her lips. "I see by the passion you're showering me with, this is the answer to my question if we shall make love to each other again, my wonderful General. Hummmmm… I see you're ready to repeat what you have done to my body again so soon, my General." Major Mansouri said as her hand searched between them until she found his manhood, and she was thrilled to death that he was rock hard and ready to go again.

This time she leaned against the shower wall while facing the excited General, and she leaned way back to give him easy access to her womanhood. He dove into her and this time he took his time making love to the young and beautiful female Persian Major. It had been over six months since the last time he made love to his wife, and he was now making up his time for his abstinence from making love to any woman in the world.

Major Mansouri moaned to the rhythm of his love making motions, and when he could no longer control himself, he came inside her. But it was good he ended it when he did, because as soon as he finished making love to the Major, Colonel Khatami came back in the large apartment, and he immediately started to search for the leader of the terrorist group.

Colonel Khatami crossed the apartment and stopped at the bathroom door, and he heard the shower water running and he smiled. It was no leap of faith to realize what was happening in the bathroom, and he was pleased the General was enjoying himself. He stepped away from the door and walked over to the second bed in the room, and he yanked the blankets back and lay down on the bed, and then he snapped the TV on.

Major Mansouri did not allow the General to dry himself off instead she took the towel and wiped down his hard body, taking special care around his manhood. When she dried him in this area, she leaned forward and drew his soft member in her mouth. She knew what she was doing she was trying to get him ready for a third time. But after about five minutes of working him over with her mouth, she gave up because he was not responding to her manipulations.

Standing straight before him, Major Mansouri complained with a pleasant smile crossing her lips. "Well my General, I see not only you are calling it a day. I'm afraid your wonderful friend here has also called it a day for himself, sir. It looks like I've done my duty for tonight, but I shall wait for you to please me the next time we make love together, my General." With that said she placed her hands on her hips and wiggled her them slightly at the grinning Iranian General, as she waited for him to play with her offered breasts.

"Ahhhh… my insatiable young sister of the vast desert sands, I'm afraid I'm not quite up to satisfying you any further on this foul night. But I assure you once we're on the foul Island of Cuba, there'll be countless days and nights when I shall please you in ways you have never dared to believe possible, young woman. Come my little one, I believe the foolish Colonel has returned to the room."

"Yes my General, I heard him return while we were making love moments ago, sir."

"I must speak with him Major, I don't want his imagination running wild tonight, woman."

"To the burning sands of the desert to what he might think he knows of what we were doing in the bathroom. If he's upset with what we shared together then his anger is only because he's upset with me because it was not he I chose to make love to on this day, my great General." Major Mansouri complained at her leader as she smiled at him.

"Be that as it may, I have to speak to the Colonel for a few moments." He replied as he stood and then he only wrapped a towel around himself and left the bathroom.

When he was out of the bathroom, he immediately noticed the Major lying down on the one large bed watching TV. The Vulture nodded at the Colonel and asked him. "How are the rest of our foolish fighters, Colonel? Are they in their cursed rooms, and is the pack of fools going to rest? I want to head for this miserable country's airport by nine o'clock in the morning, and I don't want any one of them walking around like they are half dead, Colonel. Even though we're in a country already at odds with our sworn enemy, does not meant the great Satan does not have their foul and cursed Operatives working inside this miserable country of infidels. If they see our people walking around like they're half dead and drawing attention to themselves, because of the way they're walking. The foul American Operatives (CIA) will take special notice of them and they might watch us even when we get into Cuba, Colonel."

"General Kalantari, you don't mean to inform me the hated Americans might have their infidel Operatives working in Cuba, sir? I thought once we're in Cuba, we'd be safe from the cursed American ever prying eyes, sir. I would've thought the Cuba police and their worthless

Operatives would search out and captured any American Operatives working within their foul country, sir." The Colonel grumbled at the General as he sat up and stared at his leader.

"Come on Colonel Khatami and think about it for a moment will you. If the cursed loathsome American government has their Special Operatives working within our country like we know they do. Then what makes you believe they would not have their foul cursed Operatives working within the loathsome borders of Cuba, sir? The United States CIA Operatives are as countless and like the lowly locusts in the fields, they're everywhere ones looks throughout the entire world, Colonel. They hide under every lowly rock, behind every foul tree, and they also hide in any place where they could possibly hide their foul and worthless bodies within. Even though we shall be hiding within a cursed country that is sympatric to our just cause, and they even hate the foul and lowly Americans as much as we do, Colonel Khatami.

"We'll have to keep our wits about ourselves at all times until we're moved out of the Cuban Capital of Havana, and we're moved deeper into the foul country, so we could hide much easier and safely work on our attack plans in Cuba, Colonel Kalantari. But even when we're far away from any main cities of Cuba, we'll still have to keep our ears on the constant alert and our eyes opened. One can never be certain if the small village we shall be using for our purposed in Cuba will ever be visited by someone working for the hated Americans." The General gave a look at the Colonel like he should have known while they were in Cuba. They still had to be on the lookout for any possible American Agents working in that country.

The extremely cautious and concerned Persian Colonel was ready to reply to the General's last remarks, when Major Mansouri walked out of the bathroom and like the General before her. She also had a towel wrapped around the lower half of her body. She walked across the room topless like she was fully dressed, and she did not display the slightest concern the two Persian men stopped speaking, and they were now openly staring at her breasts as they gently swayed as she walked around the room before the two men.

Colonel Khatami got off of the bed so he could get a better look at the topless Persian Major as she started to comb her long wet hair in the mirror. The General and Colonel smiled as they both enjoyed the lovely view she was giving them. But the grins quickly left their lips when she asked the General while looking at him through the mirror.

"General Abdol Karim Kalantari, what are the sleeping arrangements to be now there are three of us sharing this one room together sir, and there are only two beds in the room sir?"

The General looked at the two beds, and he returned to look at the Major in the mirror, as he asked her in a sort of sarcastic tone of voice. "What do you suggest they be Major?"

"Well the two of you could always share one of the beds and that will allow me to have the other bed to myself I guess, General." Major Mansouri wiggled her chest at the General in the mirror as she grinned at him again.

"That'll be the god cursed day I ever share my miserable bed with another man, foul and evil thinking young woman who has just insulted the both of us." The Vulture snarled back at her, angry over her suggestion.

"Then I ask you again General Kalantari, what do you suggest the sleeping arrangements should be, sir?" She knew what she wanted and what she was doing to the Iranian General. But she wanted him to suggest before the Colonel for her to share his bed for the rest of the night.

He shifted his weight from one foot to the other, because he wanted the pretty female Major to spend the night with him. But he was concerned if he should make such a rude offer to the Persian woman. Because as bad as his life was in Iran, he tried to respect a woman, even though he about raped the Persian woman in the shower moments ago. So the Vulture continued to hesitate with his response to the young female Major still looking at him in the mirror, while she was obviously waiting for his reply to her.

"Huh, I see a lowly camel has stolen the foul tongue from you, General Abdol Kalantari."Major Mansouri dared to take a joking tone with the usually upset and fearsome Iranian General, because she now felt she shared their lovemaking. They were no longer on a professional standings with each other any longer, as she then continued with her words aimed at the Iranian Military Officer, who was now staring back at her reflection in the mirror.

"General Kalantari, why do you not come out with what is truly on your evil mind, and you tell me to share your foul bed with you for the rest of this night, sir? It's easy to say sir, all you have to do is tell me Major Mansouri, you'll share my bed with me, and Colonel Khatami will have the other bed to himself. That is unless you don't want my company in your foul bed, General?" Major Mansouri grumbled as she turned her body so she could look directly at the suddenly shy looking General, and then she stared at him while she waited for his reply.

"Yes Major Mansouri that would be the simplest solution to this dilemma we're faced with inside this foul room. But I was not certain how you would've reacted to such a suggestion from me, woman." The usually confident Iranian General mumbled at the female.

"I guess you'll never know the answer to that question unless you ask me first, my General?" Major Mansouri replied in a playful tone this time at the Iranian Military Officer.

"Yes, I see you are most correct with your cursed words aimed at me, Major. Very well then foul woman, you shall share my bed and the Colonel will have the other bed to himself." The Iranian Commander replied as he looked at his reflection in the mirror. He was still having a hard time because he shaved off his beard, and he ordered his other male members of his terrorist group, to do likewise, before they left Iran on their latest mission for his country. He believed it was a serious sin for any Persian man who believed in Islam, to shave his beard at any time in his life, and he had such a full beard before he was ordered by his President to shave it off. It was still bothering him over the loss. He shook his head as he diverted his eyes from his face and he looked at the beautiful young female Persian woman, and he was surprised to see her smiling at him with her eyes shining and displaying her want to share his bed with him.

"Huh evil and lowly woman born from the armpit of the devil himself, I see the lust clouding your foul eyes, and I can hear the evil thoughts you're entertaining in your filthy mind, woman. I see you agreed with my decision for you to share my bed, woman." He tried to sound and look like he was angry with the young woman, but his eyes betrayed him and he could not act like he was angry at her after what they have just shared together.

"General Kalantari, I'll not dare to try and hide the fact that I want to share your bed on what is left of this night sir, and for many nights to come I'm afraid, my General. I'd be betraying my true love for Allah, if I dared to lie to you over this want of mine, sir. Shall we go to bed now my General, I'm exhausted sir?" Major Mansouri asked as she whipped off the towel from her body, and she now stood before the General and Colonel at the same time, totally naked and smiling from ear to ear at the both of them.

The Vulture stepped aside and Major Mansouri walked over to the second bed and she pulled the covers from it, and then she lied on the bed and motioned for the General to come join her. Major Mansouri did not care the stunned Iranian Colonel was watching her as she crossed the room and got in bed, and she beckoned the General to join her. He did the only thing he could think of doing, he sat down on his edge of the bed and stared at the other two who were now laying on the other bed together. He figured if they were going to engage in lovemaking in front of him, he might as well sit back and enjoy the show they were going to give him.

Major Mansouri noticed the Colonel making himself comfortable and she brought him to the General's attention, as he amused himself by playing with the Major's breasts. He turned and saw the Colonel staring at what he was doing, and he barked at the young military officer.

"Colonel Khatami, I'm quite certain you don't intend to amuse yourself by watching the Major and myself enjoy each others pleasures tonight. If you will turn off the foul light, and if you're done watching the TV, turn that foul thing off. We have to get up early morning to make certain the other foul fighters are prepared to leave this filthy nation when it's time for our flight, sir." He actually glared harshly at the staring Colonel until he turned off the light, and then the TV.

Colonel Heshmotallah Khatami was able to fall asleep to the sounds of the General making love to the young and pretty and Persian Major in the bed right next to his. Try as he might, the nosy Colonel was unable to watch the two clearly, so he slowly drifted off to sleep.

General Abdol Karim Kalantari took his time making love to the Major, and when they were done they fell asleep wrapped up in each others arms. It seemed to the Vulture he had just fallen asleep when the telephone rang by the side of his bed. It was the man taking care of the front desk of the hotel, and he was informing him it was seven thirty a.m. That was the time the General asked for a wakeup call to be placed to him from the desk, and he cursed as he forced himself out of bed, and then he headed for the bathroom. After relieving himself, he took a hot soaking shower. When he was done, he came out of the bathroom and was surprised to see his other two soldiers up and functioning. The Persian Colonel was dressed, but Major Mansouri was waiting for the General to come out of the bath so she could take a quick shower. She was sitting on the edge of the bed with the towel wrapped around her exquisite body.

When she disappeared in the bathroom, Colonel Khatami moved closer to the General and asked him barely over a whisper. "General Kalantari Sir, please forgive my next question sir, but it's a question I must ask of you, sir. How is the female Major in bed sir?"

"By the sacred grey beard of the great Prophet Muhammad Himself, only you could survive such a foul and cursed question of me, Colonel Khatami. If any other worthless fool had dared to ask me such a foul question, he would've found his bones being bleached in the always angry Eye of Allah. (The Sun) Yes Colonel, I must admit I have made love to many women of the world in my long and sinful and foul life. But Major Mansouri has a special way to make a man feel like he is the King of the world.

"I have never been so satisfied in my entire life, like I am with the few times I have made love to this wicked witch of the hot flowing sands of the vast deserts of our country, sir. May Allah forgive me please, but I cannot wait until we make love to each other again, Colonel Khatami. For the first time in my life, I'm truly happy with myself, and the soldiers I chosen to surround myself with, sir." General Kalantari allowed a large smile to cross his lips as his eyes tinkled as he sneered at his Colonel.

"I wondered what it might be like to mate with that wild one myself, General. For the past three years since she joined our group of fighters. I dreamed of making love to that wild cat, General. You're twice blessed by Allah's mercy to have parted her foul legs for your manhood, my General." Colonel Khatami suddenly announced, pleased his wise General and leader was able to enjoy himself a little.

"It was well worth your foul dreams Colonel Khatami, I'm sorry you may never get the chance to enjoy her fine sexual treasures yourself. Because after last night's lovemaking, when I return to Iran I'm going to leave my wife, and then I shall ask the Major to share my life forever." The General offered his Colonel, but he had no idea the Major had come out of the bathroom, and she overheard the Vulture's proud boast to the Persian Officer.

She dropped back in the bathroom, because she did not want the General to know she overheard his words, and she also had to stop herself, because she was crying happily over his last words.

General Abdol Karim Kalantari saw the Colonel look behind him and he turned, but he did not see the female Major, so he turned back to the other officer and ordered. "Colonel Khatami, I believe it'd be a good idea on your part to check on our other fighters. I want you to make certain they're up, and the fools are preparing to leave this cursed land of ugly people, sir. I'll make certain the Major is prepared to leave by the time you return to this foul room, sir."

Colonel Heshmotallah Khatami jumped to his feet and saluted his Commanding Officer. He then turned on his heels and walked out of the room to carry out his last orders.

Once he was out of the room, the General called out to the female Major without turning to look at the bathroom. "Major Mansouri, it's getting late, and I do want to have a little breakfast before we have to leave this foul and miserable country. I'm ordering you to make haste while preparing yourself for our flight to Cuba, young woman. I cannot wait to leave this miserable country of lowly dog eaters. I even detest the smell of this country and their people. There is nothing I like of this land of fools."

"I'm ready to leave this country this moment, my General." Major Mansouri replied as she stepped out of the shadows. She was dressed in the civilian clothes she brought with her for the trip. None of the Persian fighters had any of their military uniforms with them.

General Kalantari turned to face her and he nearly choked, because of the lovely vision of the Major. She was dressed in a tight fitting black skirt that ended at least five inches above her knees, and the nylons she wore accented her long and slender legs perfectly. Her blouse was as white as the driven snow, and the buttons of the blouse ended just below her outstanding breasts. Her dark brown hair was combed to the side of her head, and her long hair flowed freely down her back on the right side of her body.

Major Mansouri walked over to the Vulture and she kissed him on the side of his cheek and smiled. She was trying to reassure herself he was her lover now. He smiled pleasantly as he offered to the Persian woman. "Come Major Mansouri, as surely as I'd dearly like to make love to you again, we don't have the luxury of time for such foolishness. We have to be prepared to leave this foul and miserable country within a few hours, and I want to make certain we have everything we're taking with us to Cuba, with us woman."

"Okay General Katantari, but it's your loss I fear, sir. I'm all packed and ready to leave sir."

"I am also Major Mansouri, shall we leave and get ourselves something to eat? I'm starved."

The two Persian Military Officers left their room and when they walked into the hallway, the Vulture smiled when he noticed the Colonel had the rest of his fighters out of their room, and they were already assembled in the hallway of the fourth floor of the hotel. Now, all they had to do was to sit and wait for Colonel Khatami to return to their room and get his belongings, and then they could leave for the nearest restaurant and eat their breakfast, and then head for the airport to catch their flight to Cuba.

The moment the group of Persian terrorists left the hotel. General Kalantari picked up the three Venezuelan police officers trying to act like they were not following them again. The General shook his head over the fact the police officers were so sloppy with their assignment of following them that they were so easily detected by him. The Vulture drew Colonel Khatami and Major Mansouri's attention to the three new South American police officers standing about a half a block away from them, and they were busy looking into a small pottery shop like they were truly interested in what they were selling, and the two smiled back at the General.

The group of Persian terrorists crossed the busy street, and then they entered a foul smelling restaurant and ordered their breakfast. They ate quickly, paid for their food, and then they went out of the eatery and hailed three cabs. Once in the vehicles, General Kalantari ordered his driver to take them to the airport. The other two cabs followed the one in the lead.

It took fifteen minutes for the cabs to get the terrorists to the airport, because the narrow streets of the capital city of Venezuela were maddening. The fighters piled out of the cabs and allowed the General to lead the way for the rest of them. It was ten minutes to nine in the morning, and they had arrived at the time the fearsome Iranian General wanted to be there. The terrorists entered the terminal and headed for their boarding Gate, and there they handed the tickets to the attendant and they piled their luggage on the revolving conveyer belt. None of the Persians were taking any carryon luggage on the plane with them.

Once they were cleared for their flight, the Iranian soldiers entered the waiting area and they took over seats near each other, but not sitting directly with each other though. The General was surrounded by Colonel Khatami on his right, and Major Mansouri on his left. They were the only ones of the group sitting with each other while waiting for their flights to leave the airport. They were scheduled to board Flight Three, Two, Seven at exactly ten thirty, and then they would be landing in Cuba at around eleven twenty five, barring any possible in flight delays or any other problems with the flight.

While General Abdol Karim Kalantari waited for the call to board his flight, he snuggled into his seat because he was bored to death with waiting. He closed his eyes and rested while thinking. A smile slowly crossed his lips as he remembered speaking to his President, and referring to the suicide bombers he was releasing against the American occupation forces stationed in Iraq as mere ordinance. The Iranian President could not hide the disgust he held for the dangerous General over his lackluster concern for the brave fighters of Iran taking their own lives, in an effort to kill American soldiers. The Vulture told his President when they employed their suicide bombers, it was one of those rare moments of clarity raging in their storm of violence they were waging against the hated American soldiers that swirled through this inchoate movement they were involved in.

The Iranian General shifted his weight in the hard plastic chair as he struggled to get comfortable, as he continued to allow his mind to wander over what he was attempting to do for his country. He knew better than to refer to his fighters as Arabs, because Iran was not a land of Arabs. It was the land of Persians, with their own beliefs of Islamic religion and language. General Kalantari remembered when his father told him before he died in their war with Iraq when Persia's name was changed to Iran, which meant the land of the Arians. It was during World War Two when Iran backed Nazi Germany with their war against the world. This change was still fueling Iran's hatred of Israel, and all the Jewish peoples of the world. Old habits and beliefs suffered an extremely slow and tortuous death in the great land and sands of Iran.

The more General Kalantari allowed his troubled mind to wander over his most disturbing thoughts, the more they turned to dreams of grandeur for the powerful Iranian General. Now he was remembering the rich history of Persia, and the many times the ancient ones engaged in wars with neighbors of the Middle East. The one man in the history of Iran who General Kalantari respected and nearly worshiped the most, was Cyeus the Great. In General Klanatari's mind, he was the greatest leader Persia ever had to respect and follow, or will ever have. He did more for Persia to bring his country out of the stone ages than any other leader for his country. He was a great warrior, but a far better politician, and he led the Persian forces to conquer most of Iraq, and Iraq would have never became a separate nation if Cyeus was not killed in battle in the long ago past of Iran.

The next leader of Persia was a worthless fool, and he was easily defeated in battle by Alexander the Great's overwhelming forces, and thus Persia was absorbed into Alexander's ever expanding Kingdom. The only thing General Kalantari disagreed with Cyeus the Greats reign, was he was a leader who displayed tolerance for the lands he had conquered. Instead of taking over those foul lands he conquered, he offered true friendship to those people, and he allowed them to remain in control of their own countries.

CHAPTER TWELVE

When the Vulture was placed in control of Iraq once the American troops were forced out of Iraq, he would live up to his name, and the phrase the Iranian's had attached to that name. Follow the Vulture, and he would truly lead you to death. The cursed and worthless Iraqi people not Shiite, would be put to the sword of justice deadly edge. The General was planning to kill all the Sunni and Kurds of Iraq, and he would also kill any Shiite followers not pure and true to their Islamic faith and allegiance to Iran. In his mind, he even toyed with renaming Iraq to Persia, because he hated being known as coming from the land of the Arians.

He even entertained the thoughts once he was placed in control of Iraq and all the weapons in that land, with the Almighty Allah's help and guidance, he would turn those weapons against Iran itself. And, if he was successful with his plans, he could very well be in command of both Iraq and Persia if all his dreams came to be a reality. A sudden chill forced him to hug himself in his attempt to warm his body as he waited for his flight to leave.

Major Mansouri was keeping a close eye on her daydreaming leader, because she could feel the troubling thoughts he was dreaming about. She could only guess what he was thinking about in his sleep. At one point she almost woke him because he was squirming all around in his chair. She turned in her chair to see him better, and just when she was going to wake him, the loud speaker bellowed out that Flight Three, Two, Seven, was now boarding.

General Abdol Karim Katantari's eyes flipped open and he found himself staring into the eyes of Major Mansouri, and she was smiling at him. The Vulture shook his head in an attempt to wake himself up as he asked his Major. "Have I been sleeping long woman?"

"No General, you slept for a half an hour sir. It's time for us to board our plane for Cuba, sir. I'm afraid they have just called for us sir." Major Mansouri offered pleasantly to him.

"This is good to hear, but Colonel Khatami and you and I shall wait until the other of our fighters board the god cursed plane first, woman. Yes, I know we're supposed to board first because we're sitting in the first class section of the aircraft. But I care not one grain of worthless sand for what we are supposed to do. We'll do as I order, and that'll be that woman." The Vulture growled at the Major.

"Your wish is my command, General Kalantari Sir. I don't believe they'll penalize us any, if we board the plane after all the other great fools have boarded the plane first, sir."

Iranian General Abdol Karim Kalantari ignored the female Major's reply as he kept a close eye on the rest of his Persian fighters, as the last one of them walked down the walkway for the waiting plane. Then Colonel Khatami, Major Mansouri, and General Kalantrai made their way for the aircraft. There were a large number of second class and coach persons still boarding the aircraft, but when the three Persians reached the opened door, they were directed towards the front of the plane, once the stewardess read their boarding passes.

The flight to Cuba was smooth as silk, but it was heavily cloudy leaving Venezuela, and with landing in Cuba. As soon as the plane touched down in Cuba, the three Persians in first class stood, and they headed for the door. They wanted to be the first ones off the plane this time.

General Abdol Karim Kalantari was correct with wanting to get off the aircraft first, because when he stepped off the aircraft, two Cuban people dressed in military uniforms approached him, and one of them asked and then he identified himself to the foreign General.

"General Kalantari Sir? Please allow me to introduce myself to you, sir. My name is Colonel Felix Gonzales of the First Infantry Brigade of

Havana, General. Allow me to offer how great it is you and your fellow Arab fighters have come to Cuba for our common cause and hatred for the United States, sir." Colonel Gonzales said as he offered his hand to the Persian Officer, not realizing he called the Persian soldiers Arabs.

General Kalantari stared at the Cuban Colonel for a long second as he took his hand to shake it, and he grumbled at the man. "Colonel Gonzales Sir, first off sir, we are not Arab fighters, sir. We're Persian Warriors, sir. There is a big difference my Colonel and fellow brother."

"Please forgive my error General Kalantari, I was informed of this, but I must have forgotten my warning, sir. I assure you, it'll not happen a second time, sir. Are the rest of your Persian fighters on board this aircraft, or are they spread out on other flights visiting our country, sir." The Cuban Military Officer asked, even though he was well aware all the Persian terrorists were bunched up on this one plane. He was warned in advance of this from his commanding officer after the Venezuelan police informed the Cuban Officer the Persians boarded their plane to Cuba.

"All my Warriors are on board this one cursed aircraft, Colonel Gonzales. May I suggest you get my people off this airport as soon as possible, sir. We know the foul and hated Americans have many of their undercover Operatives working within your great and honorable country, sir. I'd like to keep our presence within your great country a secret, so any of these worthless American Operatives don't take it upon themselves to start trailing us everywhere we go in Cuba, while we are here sir." General Kalantrai snapped at the Cuban Officer, informing him that Iran was well aware Cuba was not secured within their country.

A flash of anger crossed over the Cuban Colonel's eyes, as he stared harshly at the Iranian General for a brief moment. Then he got control of his anger and offered the Iranian in a calm and polite tone of voice. "Yes General Kalantari, what you offered is quite true, sir. As you're aware of sir, we're in a constant state of war with the hated United States, and the Cuban traitors who had fled our country for the safety of the United States. And, these hated traitors to our country are constantly causing trouble for our El-Presidente every chance they muster, sir. The worthless traitors are begging the American government to intercede on their behalf to overthrow our El-Presidente, and then install one of the traitors to rule over Cuba, sir. The filthy cochones will one day pay dearly for their filthy crimes against our country and our Presidente, sir."

"Yes Colonel Gonzales, it seems both our countries are dealing with foul traitors, and these traitors are doing the same thing, begging the cursed Americans to attack our two countries and destroy them. Just so the foul and loathsome traitors can take over our countries, and then lead our two great nations into becoming puppet governments for the United States, sir."

There conversation was cut short as the rest of General Kalantari's Persian fighters started to gather around the two men speaking together. As General Kalantari was worried, Colonel Gonzalas became concerned some possible American Operatives working within his country, might take an active interest in his people. With a quick movement of his hand, a number of civilian trucks pulled up to them, and the Persian fighters quickly climbed in the vehicles. General Kalantari was the only Persian Officer who got in the civilian car along with the Cuban Colonel. Within seconds, the Iranian terrorist cell was whisked off the tarmac of the badly neglected Havana International Airport.

As they drove along the main road to the heart of the capital city, Colonel Gonzales continued to speak with the Iranian Military Officer. "General Kalantari, I'm sorry and I must apologize to you and the rest of your Persian Warriors that our Presidente was not here to welcome you into our country, sir. We discussed the possibility of him greeting you when you and your fighters first arrived in Cuba. But we felt if our Presidente showed up at the airport to greet you upon your arrival. Every American Operative monitoring our activities in Cuba would've been alerted to your honorable presence in our country. General Kalantari, our aged Presidente's health is suffering terribly of late, and he's no longer a young man, and if he had chosen to meet you upon your arrival in Cuba, we felt it might be too taxing on his failing health and body, sir.

"Nevertheless, General Kalantari, we're taking you and the rest of your arr... err... Persian fighters through Havana, and we'll be traveling to an old Soviet built military base that hasn't been used by us since the old days when the Soviet military were as thick as flees on our tiny Island, sir. I ordered a certain part of the base cleaned up for you, and it'll be livable by the time we arrive there, sir. But I must also warn you in advance that your office will be the only building that'll have air-conditioning. The Army barracks has no such luxuries sir…"

"Nor will my faithful Persian Warriors have any worthless need of those kinds of foolish luxuries, Colonel Gonzales Sir." General Kalantari snapped at the Cuban Military Officer as he stared back at the man for the moment.

"I understand what you're offering, General Kalantari Sir. The only reason why I was informing you where we're going was for me to reassure you we're doing everything within our power to keep your presence here in Cuba a secret from the ever pressing and loathsome American eyes, sir. We not only have to worry about their Secret Operatives working in Cuba, sir. But we have to be on the alert for their constant flyovers of their damn spy satellites and other spying equipment, sir. Or from their manned and unmanned aircraft that are always spying on our every move, sir. This is another reason why we're moving your Persian fighters out to this old abandoned military base, because we're well aware the god dom Americans have also classified this once military base as abandoned, and they rarely if ever observe it with their spy equipment any longer, sir."

"This is good to hear coming from your lips, Colonel Gonzales. The security of my fighters was the foremost question troubling my mind, since I was ordered to visit your country by my President, Colonel. I don't need any cursed American fools to know I entered your country with fourteen of my best Persian fighters, sir. It wouldn't be a far jump of the imagination what our reason for being in Cuba is to the hated Americans, if they ever discover we're within your great country, Colonel." General Kalantari offered politely to the concerned looking young Cuban Military Officer, as he flashed a quick and mind easing smile at the man this time.

"I'm pleased I was able to set your mind at easy, General Kalantari Sir. By the way General, I stationed eight of my Officers on this once abandoned military base, sir. Their main purpose for sharing this base with you and your soldiers is solely to make certain you have everything you and your fighters might possibly need for your brief stay in my country, General Kalantari. Anything you might need or want for yourself or any of your other fighters, all you have to do is let Colonel Rodrigo Perez know, and if he cannot supply it for you, he'll be in touch with me, and I'll acquire anything you have need or want of sir…"

"I take it you'll not be staying on this abandoned military base with the rest of my fighters, Colonel Gonzales?"

"No General Katantari, I'll be reporting to my Presidente on your progress, sir. But I shall be visiting the military base and you once a week, for every week you shall remain in my country, Genera Kalantari Sir. I do have other duties I must also attend to for my Presidente, sir."

"I understand Colonel Gonzales, because I too am a soldier in my country's service, sir. And, I know and understand the extra duties we Officers have resting upon our shoulders, and we have to look after for our leaders, sir." General Kalantari offered in the politest tone he could muster. The Iranian General was trying to sound so understand and caring for the Cuban soldiers. But the Persian Military Officer made up his mind he did not like this Cuban Officer, and he wanted to leave Cuba soon as possible. He was wondering if he could trust this Cuban Colonel and his people he was going to have sharing this military base with his fighters.

The Vulture did not deceive himself in the least, because he knew if these leaders from Venezuela or Cuba decided to get on the side of the United States, all they had to do was turn him and his fighters in to the Americans. The wise and cautious Iranian General did not like to have to rely on anyone else whenever he was out on a mission for his country and leader. It was too easy for one of them to betray him and his fighters to the Americans, and his life would end that quickly. The Vulture's attention was brought back to the conversation when the young Cuban Officer started speaking to him as the civilian car just left the outskirts of the capital city of Havana.

"General Kalantari, the people I'm leaving on the military base to look after your fighters, will be responsible for anything you or they need, sir. You can ask them for anything and they'll acquire it for you, down to women for you and your fighters to enjoy while you're visiting our country, General. Also General Kalantari, you'll also find a vast array of weapons and explosive devices I placed at your disposal stored on this old Soviet Base, sir. You can have your fighters get used to our equipment so they know how to use it when the proper time comes. Of course, you understand these weapons and explosive devices I'm offering you and your fine soldiers, was collected from many other countries of the world, sir. Our wise Presidente does not need our country to be discovered supplying these weapons to your fighters for the lack of a better word to use here, General.

"Err… terrorists' I believe is a much more fitting word to employ in this conversation, sir. We have many weapons collected from the old Soviet Union, other weapons from different South American nations, sir. We even have a number of Chinese weapons to supply you and your soldiers to train with, General Kalantari. I'm sorry for this caution sir, but just as your nation is doing, we're being forced to take the same type of precautions here, sir. We're aware your wise leader has sent you to Cuba, and then to the United States with no way for you and the rest of your fighters being traced back to your nation of Iran, sir. Presidente Castro has informed me if your own country is not willing to let the world know where these new terrorists are coming from. Then why should we allow the god dom Americans to believe Cuba was an active partner in this latest attack aimed against them, sir?"

"Yes Colonel Gonzales, I understand the reason for these extremely wise precautions our two nations are taking over this latest operation, sir. I have no problem with what you're offering to me here today, Colonel. It's better to be safe than sorry for overlooking any problems before they become problems to my operation." The Iranian Commander offered as he tried his best to hide his mounting anger and mistrust he was suffering over this Cuban Military Officer, speaking to him so smugly and as if he had known him for many years.

"I'm thankful for your kind understanding in this matter, General Kalantari Sir. It's making my job all that much easier for me to accomplish for you, your fighters, and your President and my Presidente at the same time, sir." Colonel Felix Gonzales offered as he nodded slightly at the Iranian Officer, and then he smiled at him for the brief moment.

Both officers fell silent, because they felt they had nothing further to offer the other at this time. So they sort of settled back and enjoyed the ride out to the old base.

It took another hour for the small caravan of vehicles to reach their destination of the old abandoned Soviet Military Base. General Kalantari understood why this secluded base was chosen to house his Iranian fighters while they were stationed in Cuba. It was obviously constructed in the middle of nowhere in the country, and from the looks of the buildings dotting the once massive military base, not one of them seemed safe to house soldiers in. The buildings seemed to be standing out of force of habit. Some rows of buildings were actually caved in on themselves, and it seemed like not one window was left intact throughout the entire base. Weeds even grew between the countless cracks in the concrete, and the grass where the buildings were constructed was waist high to a grown man. It was obvious to the Iranian Operative that none of the Cuban soldiers stayed on this base in many years from its dilapidated condition.

With the severe poverty the Cuban people were suffering through on the tiny Island of Cuba for countless years, with housing being much of the problem facing them. The Vulture could not understand why any of the fools did not move onto this base and make the buildings livable for them to share. If the buildings were properly looked after, they would be good structures to live and raise a family in.

As the civilian vehicles entered the once large and well looked after old Russian military base, the caravan of machines continued on until it was obvious to the Iranian General they were heading for one certain section of the old Soviet Base. General Abdol Karim Kalantari could not hide the smile crossing his face as the vehicles pulled up to about twenty Army barracks that looked like they were just constructed. Here and there he saw clear evidence the supposed abandoned military base was everything but abandoned. This large section of the base was in absolutely perfect condition, no weeds were seen anywhere, and the grass was cut and well maintained properly, and new military vehicles, tanks, and a number of armored vehicles were parked in well hidden cover. The Vulture knew immediately why no civilians were allowed to use this base as their own living quarters.

He now understood the military vehicles were parked on this base in case they were needed to help support the troops protecting the capital city from any civilian unrest in the future. There were also two large storage buildings that had their doors flung wide opened, and the Iranian General could easily see many stacks of ammunition and heavy weapons stored inside the buildings in new condition. The Persian Officer looked at three other large storage structures on the base, and he could only guess what was stored inside those building.

Colonel Felix Gonzales smiled, because he read the amazed look plastered on the Iranian General's face, and he now knew he did not have to explain anything further to the foreign military officer. The Cuban Officer suddenly reached out and he rested his hand lightly on the foreign General's shoulder, in an attempt to get his attention for the moment. The instant the Iranian turned to look at the Cuban Officer, Colonel Gonzales immediately pointed towards another section of the base, and the General noticed a number of Cuban soldiers hard at work doing a number of exercises for their Commander. In a smug and confident tone of voice, Colonel Gonzales offered to the Iranian.

"You see General Kalantari, just as you believed when we first entered this thought to be abandoned military base. There was not one building safe to live in. We created this illusion for the benefit of our god dom American watchers to our Island. We knew if we allowed the hated Americans to see what was truly taking place on this dom base, they would keep it under their constant surveillance, and we would've been forced to move our support vehicles and soldiers much further away from our capital city, sir. It's a true sin and a crime for us not to be able to use our own country in the manner we deem fit and necessary, sir.

"Even though the dom Americans never invaded our country in force, we understand if we show any improvement in our military condition, this improvement would force the Americans to attack us, sir. Thus we're forced to carry out such wise masquerades as these in order for us to strengthen our military might without any interference from the dom Americans, and all the dom traitors who hide in that miserable country, and they constantly try to get the foolish and unwise Americans fight their battles for them while they remain safe in their country."

"Yes Sir Colonel Gonzales Sir, I understand completely what you're telling me, sir. We too have our own traitors we have to deal with who hide inside the United States, and these cursed traitors are always trying to destroy what we're trying to accomplish within the very borders of our own country, and throughout the Middle East as well Colonel Gonzales Sir." General Kalantari moaned in an angry tone of voice as he sympathized with the young Cuban Colonel for the present moment.

"True, true, perhaps it's time for us to get out of the dom vehicle and see where you and the rest of your soldiers will be staying while you're visiting my country, General Kalantari Sir." Colonel Felix Gonzales suggested to the Iranian Military Officer as their vehicle came to a complete stop right before a building that looked more like a command center than a barracks. The two officers got out of the car and they quickly entered the building. It was actually cold inside the structure, and Colonel Gonzales began showing the Iranian around the building he was going to be using all the while he and the rest of his fighters remained inside Cuba.

Colonel Gonzales showed General Kalantari around the office and his private sleeping quarters that had its own air-conditioner unit in the large room, along with a small television and a well stocked bar and refrigerator, along with his own bathroom inside the room with a shower and bath. It was living quarters like he was used to enjoying in his country of Iran.

The Cuban Colonel showed the foreign Persian General how easy it was to see the rest of the well cared for section of the base from out the window of his new office. From the window, the Iranian General was able to see the rest of his fighters getting out of the other vehicles, and they were now milling about near the parked machines. A number of Cuban soldiers came over and it seemed they were trying to speak to some of his fighters, and the cunning General smiled, because of the way his people were already getting along with their Cuban brothers. A phone inside the office suddenly rang and Colonel Gonzales informed the Iranian the call was for him, because he knew who was calling.

General Abdol Karim Kalantari looked at the grinning Cuban colonel with questioning eyes, as if they were asking how he knew who was on the other end of the line, and how this call was for him. The Iranian knew there were few people aware he was in Cuba, and he was confused someone was already trying to get in contact with him so soon from entering Cuba. It was the warmest time of the year to be visiting Cuba, and the heat almost robbed the Iranian of his breath. If it was not for the air-conditioning in the room, the Vulture would be melting.

Colonel Gonzales noticed the Iranian was suffering from the heat he was so used to, and the Cuban wondered why if this man came from the land of vast deserts and high temperatures. The heat could be affecting him so severely as it obviously was. He had no idea the powerful Iranian Officer spent most of his time in air-conditioning in his land, and he was rarely used as a field operative. And, when he was placed on a mission, it was usually to another country where the weather was not so oppressive as it was in Cuba. The Cuban Officer picked up the confused look locked in the Persian Officer's eyes, and he understood he could not understand who might be calling him in Cuba so soon. So Colonel Gonzales picked up the phone receiver and he passed it over to the hesitant General.

General Kalantari answered the phone as if the devil himself was on the other end, and to his surprise, he was correct with his troubling thoughts. Because when he answered the phone, Presidente Fidel Castro began to speak to him. "I trust I am speaking to General Abdol Karim Kalantari?"

When Presidente Castro began to speak in poor English to the Persian, General Kalantari immediately recognized who he was speaking to, and he actually went to a form of attention, as he replied to the voice on the other end of the line. "Yes Sir Presidente Castro Sir."

"This is good General Kalantari. First I must tell you how pleased I am to have you and the rest of your brave warriors visiting my country. Since we share a common cause and enemy and you are going to be attacking our enemy for us, I assure you General Kalantari Sir. I and my soldiers will assist you and your soldiers in any and every possible way on your mission, sir." Presidente Castro suddenly stopped speaking and the Persian Officer heard him draw in his breath as if he was in some kind of pain.

Now the Iranian knew Castro was in very poor health, and he now found himself wondering if the old man was going to die by the time he finished his sacred mission inside the United States.

The well aged Cuban President began speaking again. "General Kalantari, I shall be speaking directly to your President in the next few days, and I will be complimenting him on his warrior's professionalism. I read the reports filed on your fine soldiers. How well you have respected our fellow Latin American friends in Venezuela and now here in Cuba, sir. I am quite certain he will be most pleased over his people's respecting other nations you are visiting, sir. General Kalantari Sir, this is all I have to say and I must be going now, sir. I have many other matters that concern Cuba and her people I must look after at this time, sir." With that said, the powerful Cuban Leader immediately broke off the communication as abruptly as he called.

When General Kalantari heard the dial tone, he pulled the receiver away and set it in its cradle. When the Persian Officer finished speaking to his Presidente, Colonel Gonzales offered to the General in a respectful tone of voice. "General Kalantari Sir, I cannot tell you what a great honor our Presidente just leveled upon your person, sir. To speak directly to our leader is something to be most proud of sir. Yes General it was a great honor indeed sir."

The Vulture could not hide the matter of fact look in his eyes as he turned to the Cuban Colonel and he tried a smile. Although the Cuban Officer thought of it as an honor to be speaking to Presidente Castro, he had no such feelings about it. True, when Castro spoke to his Persian President, it was going to bring him great face in Iran. But speaking to Castro was not such a great thrill to the Iranian Military Officer. Without saying another word to the Cuban soldier, General Kalantari turned and he walked back to the window to see what the rest of his Persian fighters were up to. He did not like being separated from his people for long.

When the Persian Officer looked out of the window, he was pleased at what greeted his eyes. His fighters were being mobbed by the Cuban soldiers on the base, and they were looking at a number of weapons the Cubans brought out for their inspection. With a deep sigh of relief, he turned to the Cuban soldier and offered him calmly.

"Colonel Gonzales, it's good my soldiers are getting along so well with your soldiers stationed on this base, sir. I see many good things happening in the near future for the both of our countries, sir. Soon, very soon we'll start bringing the United States and her foul people down to their cursed foul knees, and proving to them once and for all they are not as all powerful as they might believe they are in the matters that concern the rest of the world, sir. I plan to give my people the rest of the day off for them to get better acquainted with your soldiers and their present surroundings, sir. But I assure you Colonel Gonzales Sir, tomorrow, and tomorrow's tomorrow will be vastly different for my foolish fighters while they are on this military installation, sir. I shall start their training for our attack against the United States.

"I shall be working them from sun light to sun down, and I'll be running countless different training schedules in the middle of the night, sir. General Gonzales, by the time we set off for our attack against the cursed United States, my soldiers will know what they're doing, and they'll be able to carry out their operation with their eyes shut, and even wounded sir. I'll have them so well trained by the time we finally attack the lowly infidels in their worthless country, even if we are discovered and only one or two of my warriors are able to escape capture or their deaths. That one or two of my soldiers will still be able to complete our sacred mission as ordered by my leader, sir." The Persian General offered extremely proudly to the Cuban Officer as he flashed him a quick smile now.

"That is an extremely proud boast you offer to me, General Kalantari Sir. I hope your soldiers will be able to live up to what you believe they'll be able to accomplish against our common enemy and cause, sir. We have been suffering under the oppressive thumb of the United States and these endless stifling sanctions they have self imposed upon the good people of Cuba for long enough. Just to please the lowly traitors who have fled Cuba for the safety of the United States and they are in the government's ear to harm Cuba in their favor.

"What America chooses to call Cuban Exiles, are nothing more than traitors to my country, General. If they wanted to change the rule of Cuba, the fools would've remained in our country and do what Castro has accomplished, that caused him to come to power over my country, sir. These traitors want to create a change, but they don't want to risk their blood to cause that change to happen, General Kalantari Sir." The obviously upset Cuban Officer said as he almost spit his words out of his mouth, because he had that much disgust for the Cubans who chose to run and hide in the United States, instead of fighting for their beliefs and country.

For the most part, General Abdol Karim Kalantari ignored the Cuban Colonel's rant about his people as he continued to watch what his soldiers were doing with the Cuban soldiers.

Colonel Gonzales offered the Persian General calmly. "General Kalantari, I'd like to take a moment or two to introduce you to the other Officers I shall be leaving on this military base to help assist your soldiers with their training with the weapons and explosive devices we made available for your use in attacking the United States. I believe this is necessary before I leave this military base. Shall we go out so I can accomplish this for you sir. Because I have orders to return to Havana and report personally to my Presidente on how well it's going on the base, sir?" Colonel Gonzales actually stepped aside and he waved his hand out before him, as he waited for the Iranian to leave the office he would be using while he was on the Cuban military base.

General Abdol Kairm Kalantari moved away from the window and walked out of the office before the Cuban soldier. But when Colonel Gonzales came out of the building, he suddenly bellowed out in a commanding tone of voice at his Cuban soldiers manning the base.

"My Special Operations Officers will assemble before me immediately." Once he made this order, the Cuban Officer placed his hands on his hips as he waited for his soldiers to quickly form a sharp line before him and the Iranian General. When his specialized soldiers were standing in good formation and at full attention before him, Colonel Gonzales turned to the Iranian and said to him.

"General Kalantari, the first man who stands on line is Colonel Rodrigo Perez, sir. He'll be in strict command of the other Cuban soldiers I'll leave stationed on this military base, sir. Any complaints you might have, or any special needs you or your warriors might also have, will be addressed to him, sir."

General Kalantari nodded slightly at the proud looking young Cuban Officer, and the officer instantly returned the nod just as slightly to him with a quick smile.

"General Kalantari, the next soldier in the line is Major Johan Rodriguez, and he's my explosive expert, and he'll show your proud soldiers how to use the explosives we'll make available to you and your soldiers correctly, sir. And, the next soldier in the line is Major Javier Santana, and he's also an explosive expert. He'll be assisting Major Rodriguez with the ongoing training of your soldiers' with these items of war.

"The next soldier in the line is Captain Ramon Aurlia sir, and he's a weapons expert with countless foreign weapons, and he'll be assisted by Captain Orlando Martinez, who is also an expert with many foreign weapons you'll be employing in your attack against the dom United States, sir. Both of these Captains have been highly trained by the Soviet experts with these special weapons sir, and they know how to handle all forms of the weapons your soldiers will be using for this upcoming attack against our hated enemies, sir.

"The next men in the line are Lieutenants Jorge Sanchez, and Esteban Navarro, and these two soldiers are experts who have been well trained in the countless ways of attacking a protected target, such as the one you and your soldiers leveled your eyes on, General Kalantari Sir." The extremely proud and young Cuban Officer suddenly smiled at the Iranian Officer.

General Abdol Karim Kalantari went to a full attention himself, and then he sharply saluted the group of assembled Cuban soldiers standing before him. Out of the corner of his eye, the sharp Persian General easily spotted the rest of his soldiers doing the same thing. They were all now standing at full attention, and they were likewise saluting and paying honor to the group of young Cuban soldiers standing on formation before the two officers.

Colonel Felix Gonzales saw the respect the Iranian soldiers were offering his soldiers in formation, and he bellowed out at his gathered troopers. "Attention on the line, hand salute, soldiers." Even Colonel Gonzales sharply saluted the foreign soldiers presently respecting his troopers and himself, and he was very proud of them.

Once General Kalantari finished with his and the Cuban troops, Colonel Gonzales made his apologies and he quickly left the Iranian's side, so he could report to his President in Havana on how well things went with the Persian soldiers hiding inside their country.

The moment the Cuban Colonel left his side, General Abdol Karim Kalantari dismissed his soldiers, and then turned on his heels and entered the building he was using as his headquarters, as long as he was trapped on the small Island of Cuba. The General rushed across the room and plopped down in the chair and lifted the phone receiver. As soon as he heard the dial tone, he placed a call to the private number he was given by his President. The phone rang five times before it was answered by someone he felt was out of breath. When he heard the other voice he said in the phone. "This is the Vulture and I wish to speak to Sand Dune, sir."

The person on the other end of the phone realized it was the powerful Persian General on the other end of the phone, and he immediately ordered the Vulture to remain on the line while he got Sand Dune for him.

In moments, a new voice filled the receiver, but the General realized he was not speaking to the President of Iran. The Vulture drew in his breath, and he offered in a calm tone of voice to the new speaker. "Yes Sand Dune, this is the Vulture, and I wanted to report I have successfully arrived at my destination as was ordered, sir. I have my fellow Vultures working on how to pick a carcass clean, sir." General Kalantari was speaking in code because he was not on a secured line, and besides he was not certain who he was speaking with, even though he believed he was speaking to the Prime Minister of Iran, and he was going to remain polite until he found out if it was truly him.

"This is good for me to hear Vulture. The Scorpion (General Kalantari knew the Scorpion was the code name for his President) was becoming concerned if you were going to arrive at your destination without problems, sir." Sand Dune replied to the General on the phone.

Now General Kalantari realized it was the Prime Minister by the way he pronounced his name, and he relaxed as he continued with his report to the man. "Yes Sand Dune, everything is as was stated to you before I arrived at my destination. Our fellow brothers and sisters are doing everything in their power to make us as comfortable as possible, and they made all the equipment we need in our search for oil a successful one at that, sir. I have no complaints about how we're being treated, sir. It seems our new brothers are just as interested in searching for oil as we are, and they cannot wait until we set out on our faithful mission for this project, sir."

"Again, I'm most pleased so far how our project is taking good shape for our investment, sir. I cannot tell you how forward the Scorpion is looking to when you start your mission to search for oil where we believe it rests. He's extremely worried the other company (Meaning Usama bin Laden) might begin their own search for oil where we intend to look for it before we do, sir. It's an absolute must that we find oil where we're looking for it, so we can break the reliance of our fellow brothers and sisters of their dependence upon the ones they rely so heavily on for their needs, sir.

"All nations should be free to do whatever they want without having to rely on any other nation for their needs, sir. I shall inform the Scorpion of your great successes so far, sir. It'll set his mind at ease, and then we can start our other projects we have resting on the table, sir. I expect to hear from you at the end of each week, and you will report on your progress at that time, sir." With that said, the Persian Prime Minister broke off the connection, and then he started to report to the Iranian President of everything General Kalantari just reported to him.

ON BOARD THE T-AGOS-7 INDOMITABLE, A STALWART CLASS SURVEILLANCE SHIP OPERATING OFF OF THE NORTHERN COAST OF CUBA

On board the Indomitable, was a United States Naval vessel of two hundred and twenty two foot ship operated by what was commonly referred to as civilian contractors, who were CIA Agents constantly monitoring any new activities being carried out on the tiny Island of Cuba, twenty four hours a day, every day of the year. The reason for this ship to be stationed in the area of Cuba was reported as assisting the American Coast Guard with their drug enforcement efforts. The ship was able to monitor all radio, telephone or microwave communications coming off and entering Cuba was hard at work on this day. Agent Carl Johnson was monitoring his station when he suddenly picked up the call originating from inside Cuba, and it was going out directly to Iran. He immediately called the Agent in Command over to his side, and together they both listened in on the conversation while also taping it at the same time.

"The AIC (Agent in Command) leaned back and laughed as he announced to the concerned agent monitoring the call. "Agent Johnson, it seems the old man who is the President of that damn Island, has successfully talked a fool from Iran to search his damn Island for any possible hidden oil reserves. What is this, the fifth time he was able to talk some asshole into looking for oil on his stinking Island? Whoever said Castro was slipping, doesn't understand the man in the least. If Castro can talk the Iranians into wasting their money and time looking for oil on that Island that isn't there then he's still a very sharp man."

Agent Johnson joined his Commander in his laugh, and then he asked him how he wanted to log this communication. The AIC ordered him to mark it down as a level nine communication, which was the least interested communication they could mark it as.

WEDNESDAY, AUGUST 10th, 2005. THE ISLAND OF MARATHON IN THE FLORIDA KEYS

Captain Robert Walker was taking care of his World Cat boat, the last time he used it was a week ago, and he was washing the salt water spray that hit his boat because of the increased wind of the past few days. Nothing was running in the way of fish at this time of the year, and when he and the other soldiers staying on the Island went fishing, they had to fish in one hundred and ten feet of water to catch two just legal groupers. The fish moved away from the shallow waters while following the cooler waters of the deep. He was kind of excited, because in five days lobster season was scheduled to start, and he would go out once a week to catch enough lobsters to have a good meal. Even though he was allowed to take twenty four lobsters a day per boat, he rarely caught that many of the so called Florida critters.

He hated when the local islanders went out every day, and they caught twenty four lobsters, ringed them which meant the fishermen took only the tails of the lobsters, and then froze them. He knew one guy on the Island who would stuff over two hundred and fifty lobster tails stored in the freezer, and he would keep them while still going out and catching more of them. The dude always told Walker he would eat the frozen tails when lobster season closed. But one day he was at this guys place when he was cleaning out his freezer, just before the start of another lobster season, and he watched this guy actually throw away over one hundred and seventy lobster tails to make room for this season's catch in the freezer.

This really pissed Captain Robert Walker off so bad he actually broke off his friendship with the other dude. He could not see wasting so many lobster tails. He believed why take more than you could possibly eat in one night, because lobster season lasted so long on the tiny Island. The only time he took more than one night's supply of lobsters from the waters, was when he was expecting company, and he wanted to make an impression on his visiting friends.

Lobster season caused such a wild flurry of activity on the Island, but he had a self imposed law he would never go out during the co called mini lobster season period. The reason for this was because of the flood of the nuts from the main land and across the nation, came down to the Island for the two day event. The waters off most of the Keys were filled with a bunch of crazy ass amateurs who crashed their boats into each other or damaged their boats. Or countless fights broke out at the fuel docks, or between the visitors who tried to land on private property in their search for lobsters to catch.

The day after mini season, the local newspaper was always filled with many arrests from people taking shorts or lobsters that were too small to harvest, or they were females loaded down with eggs, to fights and other infractions of the law on the Island. These two days was the only time in his life he did not like being on the small Island of Marathon.

For the rest of the day, he checked out his gear especially made for catching lobsters. He went over the side of his boat with a hooker rig, that's an airline supply so he could stay down longer than any free divers. He laughed whenever he saw someone go over the side to check out a certain coral head, and only come up with one or two lobsters. Because they were free diving with no air supply. He always waited for the boat to move off the coral head, and then he would dive it with his air supply and come up with usually between four and six more legal size lobsters the other guy missed because he had to come up for air.

Once he had his gear checked out properly and his air tanks filled for the opening of lobster season, he started loading the gear on board the 32 feet World Cat. He also loaded the boat with twenty four bottles of drinking water and a ton of snacks for when they were out on the water diving for the critters. Colonel Bruce Leadbetter warned

Walker he was coming down to the Island, and this was going to be the Colonel's first visit to the Island and his place. So he was looking forward to showing off before his Commanding Officer, and he had enough lobsters on hand to make the Colonel sick of eating them, before he left the Island to return to their home military base of Camp Lejeune in North Carolina.

Sergeant Dorothy Ramirez was doing everything she could to help Walker prepare the boat for the Colonel's visit. She loved having company and she was planning a shrimp boil to share with their Commanding Officer, and the rest of the soldiers staying on the Island. The soldier branded Neck was staying at their place, and Buckethead was sharing the Mutt's and Blind Date's home with them. But they were planning to visit Key West, or Key Weird as the soldiers always called the place. These two soldiers did not want to be anywhere near Marathon as long as their Commander was visiting the Island.

The two massive men were making pests of themselves since their love interests left the Island to visit their family. They always wanted to go to the Dockside bar and drink for the night, but Walker and Ramirez were not going to the bar as much. They were kind of staying more at home and enjoying their young son and teaching him how to swim, and then dive from the boat.

The usually always angry Colonel Bruce Leadbetter stayed on the Island for the full weekend and he had a real blast while staying there. He even enjoyed the one visit down to the local watering hole named Dockside on the Island. Once the younger Marine Colonel was finally gone from the Island, both Buckethead Sergeant Vincent Lambardo, and the equally as large No Neck, Sergeant Robert Abbott returned to the Island and their fellow soldiers.

Captain Walker was getting used to having No Neck hanging around the home, because he was a real help to him while there. Neck worked on the home with Walker, and he even helped him with anything he had to do to the boat. He also paid his fair share for food, but Walker would not allow him to pay anything towards the electric or the water for the place.

The latest lobster season was not as good as the ones before, so Walker started turning his attention towards looking forward to the start of stone crab season, which was still a month after lobster season began. This was much easier for him to trap, because everyone living on the Island was allowed five crab traps apiece, so with Neck staying at his place he was able to set out twenty crab traps. Five for himself, five for his son, and another five for Ramirez, and the last five he was allowed, because Neck staying at his home and he was taking full advantage of his stay. Twice a week he and Neck would go out with the boat and check on their crab traps. It was a good crab season this year, and they never came in without at least fifteen to twenty pounds of crab legs every time out.

The days were passing quickly and Walker and the rest of his elite soldiers were called for a second time up to Camp Lejeune, to run a number of specialized training exercises and classes on the latest tactics on how to deal with a terrorist situation. This time they spent a full month at the military base until Colonel Leadbetter felt the elite soldiers understood the new actions they would employ the next time they went up against another terrorist cell working within the United States borders. The specialized soldiers were also able to play around with a number of new weapons being developed to counter any terrorist actions anywhere in the world.

Once the elite group of soldiers was again released from their latest training program, they returned to their perspective homes. At least Buckethead got to see Baby Tee, Sergeant Teri Dorland again over the month they were stationed at Camp Lejeune, and they really got a chance to rekindle their sort of budding relationship over. But when Neck got to see Ice, Sergeant Diane Morrison, they became a close item. Neck even offered the pretty and young female soldier a ring, and he stated his intentions of being with her for the rest of his life.

He was in a great mood, because Ice promised him she would return to the Island of Marathon, and she would spend the upcoming Christmas Holidays with him and the other soldiers still staying on the Island. The days for the soldiers living on Marathon was great, and they relaxed and built up their strength and healed all their slight nicks and cuts they received during their last training exercises.

Captain Walker finally started the charter business he was always threatening to begin, and he was using Neck as his First Mate, who was working out fine and they were beginning to make some serious money with renting out his boat to some of the many visitors to Marathon Island.

He was charging seven hundred and fifty dollars for a full day of fishing, and four hundred and fifty dollars for a half day of fishing. He was taking on three and sometimes four charters a week during the busy season for the Island. Only three times while chartering out his boat, he was skunked coming in with no fish, and he gave the guys who chartered his boat a break, and offered them a free fishing trip the next time they came back down to the Island for another visit, and some fishing again.

The wars in both Afghanistan and Iraq were starting to heat up again, and he was keeping a close eye on what was happening in those two troublesome countries, because he actually longed to be part of those actions. He was getting angry as hell when the news was released that Iran was arming the numbers of different insurgents operating in Iraq with new weapons that were starting to take a heavy toll on his fellow soldiers in the field.

He could not understand why nothing was being done about Iran, and her attempts to develop nuclear weapons. He laughed when he heard the Iranian President stating their nuclear program was for civilian use only, to generate electricity for Iran. Anyone with one brain cell working knew Iran was secretly developing a nuclear weapons program in the Middle East. He was fuming Iran was sticking their nose in the battle for Iraq. He felt if the Iranians were arming the insurgents, the United States should declare war on Iran and give them a bloody nose.

Sergeant Dorothy Ramirez realized Walker was getting upset with the latest news about the two wars, and she decided to bother him by walking around the home topless. It worked and it got him out of his doldrums and he was interested in her and also chasing her all around the home wanting to make love to her.

THE ISLAND OF CUBA, SUNDAY SEPTEMBER 11th, 2005

General Abdol Karim Kalantari enjoyed two full months working with his Persian fighters, and the soldiers from Cuba assisting them. The new weapons his soldiers were going to be working with were easily adopted by his Persian fighters, and they became very skilled with them. The different explosive devices were giving the Persian General's terrorists some fits to work through though. Their firing mechanism was far different than what his soldiers were used to working with in the past, and even the explosive was different to work with, and they had to learn and understand the full power of the explosive. Then understand how to shape the charge, and also confine it so the true power of the new explosive would be fully released against their intended target.

General Kalantari was spending a large part of his time working with his explosive team, most mornings were used with the explosive men, and the afternoons were spent with his entire strike force. He would run them through a number of different scenarios on how to attack their target no matter how well protected, and the security the Americans would be surrounding their target with. The Persian General was trying to cover his bases with his target. He was trying to take into consideration any defenses the Americans would use against them during their attack.

Colonel Heshmotallah Khatami was proving to be the General's most important cog to the terrorist cell. Anytime he was working with his explosive teams, the Colonel would take the rest of his people and run them through the different ways to kill their enemy. And, when the Colonel was not working with his fighters, he was speaking to the Cuban soldiers, always pumping their minds for any new ways of attacking an enemy. Any new information he would gleam from the Cuban fighters, he would instantly employ with his group of soldiers.

After another long and exhausting day working with his Persian fighters, General Kalantari entered his office and sat at his desk, and then he leaned back in the chair and swung his feet on the surface of his desk, and let his breath out in an exhausted sigh. Just as he closed his eyes and rubbed them with his fingers, than did Colonel Khatami came walking into the office and quickly informed the tired General he wanted to have a few words with him in private.

Not trying to hide his anger at being disturbed by the excited acting Colonel, General Kalantari sat forward after removing his feet from the top of the desk, and he snapped at his Colonel. "Well Colonel Khatami, now you disturbed me in the only time I have taken to rest for a little while, what do you have on your mind sir? I'm planning to work on a night time attack against our intended target, in case we're forced to do our work in the dark, sir."

"A thousand pardons for disturbing you at this time General Kalantari Sir, but I wanted to inform you our Cuban brothers informed me they're going to be bringing in a bunch of their foul whores from Havana for the night, sir. Our fighters are exhausted and they're looking for some relief from the back breaking exercises you're constantly running them through both day and night sir…"

"Their foul backs would be breaking a whole lot worse but not from the work I'm putting the fools through, Colonel. They'd be broken by the stacks or rocks I'll order to be piled upon their cursed worthless backs if they fail this mission, Colonel Khatami. Don't tell me you dared to enter my office and disturbed me in this manner, to beg me to allow the worthless fools out there to have the night off. So they could engage in their decadent ways of sharing what Allah has given them to bring forth the new generations of faithful Islamic fighters for His cause, General Khatami Sir. I guess I'm supposed to decide if I shall allow my good and Allah fearing soldiers to have some fun with this cursed country's loathsome whores who roam the nights, sir.

"Bah, after all the time I've known you Colonel, and I helped guide you along to replace me as the new leader for our terrorist team. You dare come to me with this foul of requests in the behalf of these cursed fools we're training to attack the hated United States, sir." The instantly angry looking Persian General suddenly snapped savagely at his Colonel, and he then turned and looked at him dead in the eyes for a long and strained moment, while waiting for his reply.

Colonel Khatami did not reply to the General's words, because he understood the Vulture was agreeing with taking a night off for his tired fighters to enjoy themselves, but he could not allow this without complaining first about it. Slowly, the Colonel allowed a slight smile to slowly cross his lips as he continued to stare back at his Commanding Officer.

General Kalantari noticed the slight smile and it softened his heart, and he finally nodded at his second in command as he offered him in a calm voice. "Ahhhh, I see you know me better than I know myself I guess, Colonel Khatami. After thinking about this cursed request you have just placed before me, I believe I have no choice but to allow this sinful night to take place, Colonel. Yes, by all means, I shall allow our foolish fighters to have this night off for this crime they intend to commit against Allah's sacred words.

"But I shall not allow this to pass that easily I assure you, I'm ordering you to inform our foolish warriors not to allow themselves to get drunk on this foul night. Because tomorrow morning we'll be working on our assignment in earnest, and any fool who cannot carry out their duties properly, will rule the foul day they mothers ever gave birth to the great fools. Be off with you now Colonel, and inform the worthless fools they have this night off to rest properly sir, but tomorrow morning is work as usual, sir. I shall be running the training exercises for myself tomorrow, and may Allah help the worthless ones once I'm through with the great fools tomorrow, Colonel Khatami Sir."

General Abdol Karim Katantari had all he could do to hide the smile from crossing his lips. Because he was going to take full advantage of this night off by sharing it with Major Fereshiteh Mansouri, because it had been at least a full week since the last time they were alone together.

Reading his Commander's light mood, Colonel Khatami allowed the smile to grow larger, because he knew the General was going to give the okay for the fighters to share time with the Cuban women the Spanish soldiers were going to allow on the base for a night of drinking and sexual fun. With a nod of his head, he placed his hands on his hips as he waited for the Vulture to finally give the permission for the Persian soldiers to enjoy themselves on this night.

The Persian Commander turned his chair so he could look directly at his excited Colonel standing to the side of him, and he let down his guard. The General drew in a gulp of air and announced to his second in command. "Well Colonel Khatami, for the love of Allah I don't understand why you're still standing here and continuing to waste my time, sir. You should be outside informing our foolish brothers and sisters of their night off. One thing I must ask you before you leave my office though, Colonel Khatami. What are you going to do with our female fighters while the foolish male soldiers are enjoying this night of debauchery you and they have planned? I'll not stand for our female fighters to be insulted by what you fools have planned sir. I must warn you Colonel, if I see one of our female fighters getting upset tonight, I shall place an immediate stop to this night of sin and crime you requested, sir."

"General Kalantari, the women fighters will not be insulted by the activities of this night, sir. I have plans to allow the women fighters to sleep in a free barracks for the night, sir. I spoke to our Cuban brothers, and they informed me a barracks two buildings from where we're staying, has no soldiers inside them. I'll place the women warriors in that building, sir." Colonel Khatami offered to his Commanding Officer proudly and with a smile on his lips.

"Very well then Colonel, you're free to leave and make your plans for this sinful night, fool. I'll busy myself with work I planned to look after when we finished our exercise tomorrow. I guess I shall look at this night off for me to get ahead of my paperwork. Paperwork is the curse of the Commanding Officer, but everything we do has to be documented for our wise leaders back in our country, sir." General Kalantari grumbled as he cast his eyes towards the surface of his desk that was covered with opened files.

Colonel Heshmotallah Khatami straightened his back and then he grinned widely towards his Commanding Officer, and he replied at the same time. "Yes General Kalantari Sir, what you stated is absolutely correct, sir. Paperwork is the true curse for us proud soldiers, sir. But I have a rather interesting idea if you'll allow me to offer it to you, sir."

General Kalantari cocked his head to the side as he held his officer in his questioning stare, and then he asked him in a calm tone. "Colonel Khatami, you successfully aroused my interest with your foul words, sir. What is this foul idea that has entered that foul and cursed mind of yours, sir? Knowing you the way I do, I'm quite certain it has to do something with sex. I promise you Colonel Khatami, if you try to talk me into visiting your foul barracks and these filthy Cuban whores from this loathsome country. You'll fail miserable with this worthless attempt at corrupting my will.

"You and the rest of our foolish fighters will be committing a terrible crime against Allah's will, and I'll not be a partner in this foul crime with you great fools. Because I assure you Colonel, I have no intention of sharing what Allah has given me to share with good Persian women of our country, with any foreign whores of this filthy nation, sir." The Persian General stopped speaking and then he angrily stared back at his Colonel, while waiting to hear what he had to offer him now.

"General Kalantari, I assure you that was the furthest thing from my mind, sir. I know you're a true follower of the Islamic beliefs. On the contrary General, I was going to suggest if you're planning to work on these reports, sir. Perhaps I might be allowed to order Major Mansouri to come over to your office and help assist you with this foul paperwork resting heavily upon your mind, sir. She's very good with paperwork, General Kalantari Sir."

Now, General Kalantari allowed himself to laugh aloud over his wise Colonel's last suggestion. He was beginning to fear his officer knew him a little too well. The Vulture planned to order Major Mansouri to come to his office as soon as the Colonel left the room. Now he did not have to insult the female Major by ordering her to come to his office for the night. The foolish Colonel was going to do it for him, and he would have just as much fun with a true Persian female fighter on this night, as the rest of his soldiers were going to enjoy. Letting out his breath rapidly, he replied to his Colonel's suggestion.

"Yes Colonel Khatami, perhaps it'd be a wise idea at that to order Major Mansouri to help me with this foul paperwork. It'll also serve to keep her away from the barracks you fools are going to be sharing with our other female soldiers. I know beyond a shadow of a doubt if the Major knew what the male soldiers were planning on this foul night. She'd be standing outside the barracks, and she'd kill these foreign

Cuban whores before they were able to enter your barracks, sir." The Vulture warned his next in command, while making a rather lame excuse for wanting the female Major to assist him.

Again the Persian Colonel laughed at his Commanding Officer, but this time he was joined in his laughter by the General, as they both knew what he was trying to do for himself on this night. When the Vulture stopped laughing, he said to his Colonel who was still enjoying himself at the General's expense. "Heshmotallah, I believe you should go out and attend to your foul and worthless troops, before the foolish Cuban brothers bring these cursed whores over to your barracks, and our faithful women fighters happen to see them arriving. Make haste before there is some trouble between our women and male soldiers, Colonel Khatami."

Colonel Khatami did not reply to his Commanding Officer, this time he snapped to attention and saluted the seated Commander. Then the Persian Colonel turned on his heels and he walked out of the General's private office and he headed right for his gathered soldiers. There were a number of Cuban soldiers also standing with his troopers, and they were waiting to see how the officer made out with the General, and their request for a night off and some fun. The moment he reached the other soldiers he said to them. "We have off tonight for any further exercises, and it's also alright for our Cuban brothers to bring their women to our barracks."

The three young Cuban soldiers mixed in with the Persian fighters, broke out into huge grins, because they were using the Persian soldiers as their own excuse to bring the seven prostitutes onto the military base, so they could also enjoy their treasures for the night.

When the powerful Iranian Officer finished speaking to the lesser soldiers, he started to search the area for his group of women soldiers. He spotted the three women standing well away from the male soldiers, and he headed directly for them in a rush. He could easily tell the women knew something was up as he walked towards them at a fast pace. He smiled at them as he announced in a commanding tone. "Major Mansouri, Major Rahimi, and Sergeant Shirazi, we don't have to work on any night time exercises on this foul night. General Kalantari has chosen to give all of us but you Major Mansouri, off because of the way we have been carrying out our exercises. Our wise General believes we were entitled to a night off to relax a little. Major Mansouri, the General wants you to assist him with a mound of paperwork he's going to be working on for the rest of this night.

"By the way Major Mansouri, even though we have the night off tonight, I'm planning to work with the male soldiers on some special conditions we might face when we start on our faithful mission in the United States. In an attempt for these special workups, I'm ordering the two other women to Barracks Four, and you women will sleep there for the night so we male warriors do not disturb you with our further activities. Major Mansouri, when you're finished working with the General, you'll report to Barracks Four for the rest of the night, woman. That is all I have to order the three of you women." With that said, the young Colonel turned and he headed back for the still gathered male soldiers.

The three women smirked as Major Mansouri complained to the other women fighters. "Huh, what do you think of the great fool and his foul words? He must really think of us as fools to believe the line of lies he just spouted off to us. Like none of us know the great fools are going to sneak a bunch of Cuban whores into the barracks to satisfy their foul cursed lust. I hope Allah will give them all infections in their sex organs, for the sins they'll commit tonight."

"But what about you Major Mansouri?" Major Sayeh Rahimi asked as she stared at her sister soldiers, and then she went on with her words. "You're going to get stuck working on this night with the General while we get to rest tonight. I don't think that's very fair for you my sister."

"Oh brother, give me a break will you please, and you think the foolish male soldiers think of us women as fools, Major Mansouri. I cannot believe Major Rahimi doesn't understand why our Commanding Officer ordered you to assist him with this so called extra paperwork." Sergeant Azamalair Shirazi laughed as she looked at Major Mansouri who joined her in the laugh.

Major Rahimi stared at the two other women warriors, and then it struck her what they were talking about, and she put her hand to her lips and she mumbled. "Oh, may Allah forgive me for being so foolish, my sisters. I didn't know you and the General was sharing the bed together, Major Mansouri. Now I understand what you two will be doing tonight, my sister." Now, Major Rahimi joined her other two sisters in their laughter, as all three of them looked at the laughing and shoving male soldiers of their group now. The women could not believe the grown men were acting like a bunch of young school children, who were going to their first sex education class of their lives.

The women kept glancing at their male counterparts until they started to drift towards their barracks. Then Major Mansouri announced to her two sisters. "Well there the fools go, Allah's gift to women. They believe they're so important to the matters that concern the earth and our country. May Allah affect them all with the foul plague that affects all sinners to His great laws of the land! I guess it's time I report to our Commanding Officer as ordered, and see what he has on his foul mind for my body, my sisters."

All three women laughed, and then Major Mansouri started walking towards the General's office. She made certain she wiggled her rearend back at the two other women terrorists from her group as she sashayed her way towards the General's office. Major Rahimi called out to the other Major as she walked away from them. "You go girl, don't leave enough of the great fool left to feed the foul scavengers of our vast desert sands, my sister. It'll teach him to use our temples of Allah for them to satisfy their evil and foul lust with. One day our fellow Persian brothers will look at us as more than just something to satisfy the foul lusts with. One day we'll finally become equal with the great fools, my sister."

Sergeant Shirazi rested her hand lightly on Rahimi's shoulder, and she applied slight pressure as she turned her fellow female fighter, and then they both headed her towards their temporary barracks for the night as she complained to her bitterly. "Come on my faithful sister, we'll never be equal with the lowly males of our country no matter how much progress Iran makes in the future. But we have to look at the brighter side of this situation, my faithful desert sister. At least we'll be spared and not be forced to watch the filthy and lowly pigs as they defile the evil Cuban women of this foul and hot beyond endurance country of lowly pigs, my sister. It could've been a whole lot worse for us to endure though, we might have been forced to share our usual barracks with the lowly jackals, while the fools satisfy themselves with these filthy pigs they'll be sneaking onto the military base tonight."

"You have that right my sister of the hot burning sands of the desert. I don't feel I would've been able to survive this ugly night, if I was forced to watch such a disgusting spectacle as what these evil sinful male soldiers are planning for tonight. They are such filthy pigs whenever it comes down to sharing a bed with a true and respectable Persian woman, my little sister."

Major Mansouri walked up to the door of the General's private office like she owned the world, and she tapped on the closed door lightly. As she stood on the porch and waited to be summoned into the room by her Commanding Officer, she ran her hands slowly through her long, jet black hair as she tried to fix it a little for the General's pleasure. Even though she was still dressed in the same clothes she wore all day, she was not worried about it. Because she knew the Persian Officer enjoyed a bathroom in his private office, and she was planning to bath when she entered the room. She smiled, because she knew she was not going to need a change of clothes for this night of pleasure and enjoyment with her Commander. Because she was not planning to be wearing any clothes once she closed the General's door behind her, and they were together for the entire night.

After the fun night for his soldiers, true to his word, General Kalantari began to put his troops through their paces. The night he spent with the Major invigorated him, and the Vulture made it a twice a week thing, with the Major satisfying all his needs sexually. The days turned into weeks, and then the weeks turned into months, and still the Vulture was not pleased with his soldier's progress for their upcoming attack against the United States. News of how the war was going for the Americans in both Afghanistan and Iraq, only served to increase the anger that was the driving force pushing the Vulture on with his want and desire to harm the United States.

Even though the Iranian and Iraq soldiers were employing the new IED's or Improvised Explosive Devices and the more successful and far more deadlier and sophisticated EFP's or Explosive Formed Penetrators, the American President persisted with keeping his troops operating inside the two Arab countries.

General Abdol Karim Kalantari was becoming angry with his forces assisting their Shiite brothers and sisters operating inside Iraq. Because they could not assemble enough of the EFP's and trap a large enough force of American soldiers to kill, to force the foul civilians and Democratic leaders back in the United States to demand an early end to the war raging inside Iraq. The Vulture was depending on forcing the American occupying forces out of Iraq, so he could move into that country and begin training masses of attackers who would follow the American soldiers back to their foul cursed country, and create the death in the United States they were causing inside Iraq.

The latest news reaching General Kalantari while he was stationed in Cuba, caused him to take his anger out on the rest of his Persian soldiers. For some reason, they were the only ones the fuming Vulture could take his anger out on. The dangerous and well feared Persian General stayed on his soldiers, always pushing them to better master the weapons and explosive devices the Cuban government was making available for their use for their upcoming operation in the United States. In the next two weeks, the Vulture was going to use a certain section of Cuba that closely resembled the selected target area they picked out in the United States for their opening attack against them. The Iranian Commander was going to run a full size attack on the facility and see if his soldiers would be able to carry out their orders successfully.

If they were able to complete a successful attack against their future target, the Vulture was then going to split up his Persian soldiers into two man attack units, and see if just two of his well trained fighters would be able to get into the facility they wanted to attack, and destroy it as easily as a fourteen man attacking unit could.

The Vulture was not trying to fool himself in the least, because he knew how the hated American's were, and they would do their best to try and protect the target they had selected for destruction with their attack. In the back of his sharp mind, he was almost certain some of his soldiers would be discovered, and then he and the rest of his troops would be forced to attack their target in a piecemeal type of attack on the facility. The Persian General had to prove to himself if the main body of his Persian attackers were discovered by some of the cursed American security officers. Then the smaller units of his attackers would still be able to carry out their attack, and he would still succeed with the complete destruction of his assigned mission.

The well trained Cuban soldier's ordered by Colonel Felix Gonzales to assist the group of Persian fighters, were doing everything in their power to try and help assist his Iranian fighters to better understand the proper way to attack the supposed facility they were going after in the United States. The Cuban soldiers were going to be acting as the American security defenders of the facility, and his Persian fighters were going to try and breach their security ring of the complex, and see how the attacking Iranians made out with an attack against the installation and defenders. This was the only way for the Vulture to judge if his terrorists were really ready to attack such a critical target as the one they have selected for destruction within the United States.

Energy at the thought to be abandoned Cuban military base was high, as the group of Persian and Cuban soldiers prepared for the next simulated attack against the supposed facility that closely resembled their main target in the United States. The Vulture's Persian fighters expertly prepared the explosive devices without the explosive end to the weapon, and they loaded their weapons with blank rounds, as did the Cuban soldiers working with them.

This was going to be a good test for the Persian General to witness, and see how well his soldiers were shaping up, and he could not wait for the simulated attack to begin. The Cubans were as excited as their Persian counterparts, because they were bored just hanging around the large military installation for so long, without anything more constructive to do with themselves.

CHAPTER FOURTEEN

General Abdol Karim Kalantari was standing in the opened jeep he was using for his personal staff vehicle on the base, as he watched the large number of Cuban soldiers quickly taking up their defensive positions to protect the one main target surrounded by a number of other easier targets also resting in the area of their present responsibility. The young Persian General was thoroughly amazed the Cuban soldiers were easily able to make this area look so much like their intended target site in the United States. Once the Cuban troops assumed their positions properly on the site, the Iranian Officer turned to his second in command and then he growled at him.

"Colonel Khatami Sir, everything we wanted to try our soldiers on is at this site, sir. Our Cuban brothers have done a masterful job making this place look so much like our target in the cursed United States, sir. I'm going to allow you to lead our Persian fighters on this first supposed attack, so I can observe how well or poorly they'll do with attacking this assigned target. I shall warn you and you can warn the other fools under your direct command, Colonel.

"If the foul fools fail on this attack, there'll be no more allowing the worthless Cuban whores to visit our base for their personal pleasures. If they want to sin again while breath remains in their foul bodies, they better attack this cursed target successfully, Colonel Khatami. If they do this I shall give every one of the fools three days off from further training and exercises, and they'll also have their filthy Cuban whores to play with, Colonel. Be gone with you now and prepare your fighters wisely for the attack, I'm waiting for it to begin Colonel Khatami Sir."

The Iranian Colonel snapped to a full attention as he proudly saluted his Commanding Officer, and then he took off without replying to his last words to him, as he headed for where his Persian fighters were gathered for the moment and waiting for him to address them.

Colonel Khatami walked up to his soldiers and ordered them to separate into two person assault teams, for the pending attack on the makeshift installation. This was so if some of his people were spotted by their enemy and supposedly killed by the Cuban defenders of the base. He was hoping to get at least a few of them to their target successfully, and destroy the target as was ordered by him and the General in full command of the Persian so called freedom fighters.

General Abdol Karim Kalantari was allowing his Colonel to run the attack scenario, as he watched his freedom fighters move out with some amusement, as was ordered by his Colonel. The Persian soldiers were clumsy at best as they began their attack on the intended target.

Colonel Heshmotallah Khatami took Major Fereshteh Mansouri as his partner in the opening attack, because he knew the Vulture was having his pleasure with the pretty female fighter. He believed if he was working with her, he was placing himself in a good light with his Commanding Officer at the same time. The wise Colonel held back the female Major as he allowed five of the seven other assault teams attack the fence protecting the Cuban base they were using for this attack. It was close to the real target as was humanly capable to duplicate, and the Cubans had accomplished a masterful job at copying their target in the United States.

Colonel Khatami cut his way through the heavy metal cyclone fence in the sixth different area of the installation, to allow him and the female Major to enter the Cuban complex. The two soldiers hid in a shallow drainage ditch circling the entire large military base, as he watched one hit team move out from their cover behind a parked military truck. The attackers quickly scrambled over to a neatly stacked row of empty fifty five gallon drums.

The moment Sergeant Bassam Abu Fallahi and Colonel Amir Jolaipour reached the drums, six Cuban defenders circled where his Persian fighters took up their new positions. Six more Cuban fighters came at his Iranian fighters from another direction, and they fired their blanks at the now trapped Persian fighters, killing the both of them.

The Iranian Colonel shook his head in anger at the easy of how his attack team was naturalized by the Cuban defenders. But he also smiled, because he understood the Cuban soldiers were expecting his freedom fighters to attack the installation, and they did in the only real area they could possibly attack the area. But he also understood the American defenders would not know they were going to hit them, and he felt if any of his seven assault teams succeeded in this attack. They would surely enjoy greater success with their attack against the Americans.

Suddenly, the Iranian Colonel heard someone yell out in a commanding tone in Spanish, and then he heard the sound of automatic weapons fire going off, and he understood another of his assault teams was discovered by the base defenders, and they were naturalized by the Cuban defending soldiers. Now Colonel Khatami was getting angry over the ease at how his fighters were being discovered by the Cuban defenders, but his anger caused him not to notice the four Cuban soldiers who detected him and the female Major still hiding in the shallow drainage ditch. They were now quickly moving out to circle, and then trap the two Persian attackers.

More weapons fire to the Colonel left side, and it caused him to look in that direction, and it was at this point he noticed the two Cuban soldiers skillfully working their way towards them. The Persian Officer ordered the Major to move out as he set himself up to protect her forward progress. He wanted her to make it to the target before they were both killed by the Cuban defenders. But as the Major moved out, she ran into the other two Cuban defenders also skillfully working their way towards them from the right side. The Cuban soldiers fired at the female soldier, splattering her with small, stinging white paint balls, signifying her death as the other two Cuban defenders peppered the Persian Colonel with paint balls.

Now, the irate foreign Colonel was fit to be tied, because he felt he did not truly get onto the installation, and he was of no real assistance to any of his fellow attackers, before he was successfully eliminated from the exercise by the Cuban defenders.

There were still two other Persian assault teams still active on the opening exercise, but the moment the Vulture saw his Colonel and Major get stopped by the Cuban defenders, he leaned down and pressed the horn button on his parked jeep. The noise signaled the end of the exercise as he angrily jumped out of the jeep, and then he walked towards the extremely upset looking Colonel as he lit up a Marboro cigarette, and he then drew in a large lung full of the harsh smoke.

The female Major sort of hid behind the Colonel as the Vulture continued walking towards them. He stared at his Commanding Officer, and to his surprise when the Vulture walked up to him, he tapped out an extra cigarette and offered it to him as he allowed a smile to quickly cross his lips. The Vulture even lit the cigarette for the exhausted Persian Colonel, as he waited for the rest of his freedom fighters to quickly assemble with the rest of the soldiers standing before the Vulture, and they were looking like they were in deep trouble.

General Abdol Karim Kalantari found the proper name to brand and address his soldiers other than calling them terrorists. He decided to label them freedom fighters for their sacred cause aimed against the United States, so they could not be classified as any enemy combatants or terrorists. If they were taken prisoners by the American soldiers in that country, and this would assure them of a legal defense, if they were captured by the Americans during their attack against the United States. He did not want his soldiers ending up being held at the Guantanamo Bay facility for the rest of their lives, like his fellow Arab brothers and sisters were being held on the Island of Cuba at the American installation. Ever since the United States took the Muslim terrorist captive during the American invasion of Afghanistan so many years back.

Once his Persian fighters were assembled before him, General Kalantari began to address the group, but he leveled his words mostly at his second in command, who he placed in command of the other fighters for this exercise. "Colonel Khatami, this exercise was a complete and utter disaster. If this was a true attack we aimed against the cursed American installation we intend to destroy in that foul country. I'd be forced to declare our assault teams have been killed long before they were successfully able to attack their cursed target, sir.

"Although I'm truly upset over the poor actions of my foolish freedom fighters, I'm not the least bit surprised by the outcome of our opening attack aimed against this cursed installation and its Cuban defenders. After all Colonel Khatami, our Cuban brothers in arms were well aware of our pending attack planned against their installation, which forced them to be on an even greater alert status than the cursed American defenders would be, when we finally open our attack against them in their own country, sir.

"I thank my extremely helpful Cuban brothers and sisters for their kind and much needed assistance in this opening exercise." The Vulture nodded slightly towards Colonel Rodrigo Perez, who instantly returned the slight nod, and then the Persian General went on with his words to the rest of his fighters staring back at him.

"Colonel Khatami, I decided to spend the rest of this week on this base, and we shall run a number of further simulated attacks on our target, until all the foolish fighters are able to successfully attack and destroy our intended target, sir. This was the reason why I had our freedom fighters transferred over to this new military base on a Monday. I knew in my heart the first attack would fail miserably, and this would allow me to keep our foolish fighters here for the rest of the week, Colonel. I warn my Persian brothers and sisters, by the end of this week we'll have succeeded in destroying our target at least once during the exercises. But it shall not be the last time we'll visit this military base. For a full month before we move to the United States, we shall be staying on this new base, and we'll carry out both day and nighttime attacks against our intended target, until we're able to destroy it in our foul sleep, Colonel Khatami Sir.

"The only bright side to this worthless exercise I can see is where we have completed one exercise, and every one of our faithful warriors did at least make it onto the cursed installation. Before the great fools were captured by our Cuban brothers, and that says something for our upcoming operation planned against the United States. I cannot wait until I see how the loathsome American fools react to another such attack upon their cursed soil, and we'll make certain it looks like Usama bin Laden and his terrorist organization was the one who was truly behind the latest attack aimed against them once again at the same time, sir. That way the American's revenge will fall upon his sacred head and all his foolish followers, and the Americans will not level their god cursed foul eyes upon us or our own country. It is very good we have someone else who'll be blamed for our faithful actions aimed against the loathsome and hated American dog eaters, sir.

"It'll also help strengthen our President's power and position in our own country, and it'll further cause more Arab fools to come flocking to our side in our never ending war planned against the United States. When Iran becomes the true seat of power in all the Middle East, we'll then attack the other Arab nations of the Middle East, and we'll force the great fools to follow our leader's commands, or they'll die for their failures to do so once we defeated their country's and we take over their lands. Soon, Iran will be in complete control of the other foul and useless Arab nations of the world, and we'll force the rest of the world to bend their foul cursed knees to our country, or their machinery will grind to a stop from the lack of the oil we'll control by then. By the time our dreams are fully realized, the world's oil will be commanded by our great leaders. We'll then pick and choose what other foul nations we'll give oil to, and the others will slowly dry up and become the new deserts of the world.

"Bah, I again find myself repeating the foul and boring words of our leaders, and I'm not a man of many worthless words. I'm a man of actions, and that is what we're going to do against the hated United States. Alright my Persian fighters for Allah and our Cuban brothers, we have accomplished all of what I have set out to accomplish on this day. I'm giving you fools the rest of the day off, tomorrow morning we shall try to attack this installation again. We'll complete two exercises tomorrow, and then maybe one at night. Colonel Gonzales Sir…"

"Yes General Kalantari, I'm here, sir." The Cuban Officer announced as he moved forward so the Persian Commander could see him easier. The Cuban Officer did not care who was blamed for the upcoming attack on the United States, because he did not like

Usama bin Laden, or any of these Persian fighters for that matter. The Cuban Officer felt any attacks on America should be leveled at their military personnel only. He did not particularly like when well trained soldiers attacked defenseless civilians of any country, and these Persian terrorists were only attacking the civilians of the countries they attack.

"Colonel Rodrigo Perez Sir, since I chose to give my freedom fighters the rest of the day off, sir. I was wondering if you might be able to locate some of your Cuban women from the other night, so they can help my soldiers relax from this exhausting exercise, sir. I'm quite certain they could use another night like the last one they shared with the fine women of your proud country, sir. I decided to allow them to commit their further sins against Allah once again, Colonel Gonzales Sir." General Kalantari offered as he shot a quick smile at the young Cuban soldier, and he nodded towards him.

A wide grin crossed the Cuban Officer's lips as he offered the Persian General confidently. "General Kalantari Sir, it'll be a simple matter for me to get in contact with the lady who brought the other women to our old base the other day, sir. I'm certain the women will arrive on this base long before darkness falls, sir. Believe it or not General Kalantari Sir, I was going to make this very suggestion to you a little later on today, sir. Some of my soldiers have been asking me to allow the women to visit them again, sir. I cannot blame my soldiers in the least for their desires, because this extra work for my soldiers they're doing for your Persian warriors, have my soldiers spending many lonely nights away from their wives and lovers and loved ones sir, and it's only right they find other ways to relieve themselves, General Kalantari Sir."

General Abdol Karim Kalantari could not hide the smile that crossed his lips, because he was looking forward to spending another wonderful night alone with his Major Fereshyeh Mansouri, himself. He enjoyed watching her working with Colonel Khatami on this last exercise. Her uniform was so tight it clearly showed off her outstanding and exquisite shape, and this sort of turned him on while he stared at her actions with lust locked in his eyes. The powerful Iranian Commander made up his mind the last time they were together that he was going to have an accident befall his foul and hateful wife living in Iran. Then he would be free to ask the young and very pretty female Major Mansouri to spend the rest of her life with him.

She was ten years younger than his wife of fifteen years, and the pretty Major looked well after her outstanding shape, and she knew how to bring great pleasures to her lover at the same time. She was a true pleasure to look at, especially when she was standing naked before him like the other night. The General's sort of daydreaming was suddenly interrupted by the Cuban Colonel who cleared his throat loudly, when he noticed the Iranian Commander was not paying any further attention to his words at this time.

General Abdol Karim Kalantari had to shake his head to bring himself back to the conversation with the Cuban soldier. He looked at the Cuban Officer smiling at him as he waited for further words from the powerful and well respected Persian General. When his head cleared, the Vulture offered to Colonel Perez. "My Cuban Brother Colonel from this country, I'm pleased you'll be able to get your lady friends to visit my soldiers, sir. It's important I look after the health and welfare of my freedom fighters, Colonel. I'm certain if any of my young female fighters are interested in any of your fine Cuban soldiers, sir. They'll make their feelings well known to them, Colonel. I'm sorry it's not so easy for me to look after my female fighter's health as it is for the male soldiers, sir. But that is Allah's concern and not my sir.

"Errr… I guess I shall be spending the rest of my foul night looking after my never ending pile paperwork once again, Colonel Perez Sir. I also have to make contact with my Commander back in my country within the next few days, and I need my paperwork up to date when I finally speak to my concerned President, Colonel Perez Sir. I'm quite certain they're becoming more than concerned with my progress in training my faithful soldiers to the best possible standards to carry out their mission successfully, sir."

General Kalantari looked at the many faces of his concerned Persian fighters, and he stopped moving his head when his eyes found the female Major Mansouri, standing within the rest of the group of his warriors. She was smiling at him because she knew what the General was going to say to her next. So did Colonel Khatami and Colonel Perez know what the Vulture was going to say to the pretty female fighter he was presently staring at.

"Errr… Major Mansouri, you shall again assist me with my paperwork on this foul and endless night, woman. I have a backlog of paperwork I must complete before I speak to our President in Iran. I shall allow you to miss the first morning exercise, because we'll be working well into the night to finish my work for our President, woman. The rest of my fighters will be free to amuse themselves in any matter they may chose on this most foul of nights. But I warn all of you, I don't wish to be disturbed for any reason while I'm working later on this night. If a problem arises and you cannot work it out between yourselves. Then you shall address your foul cursed problem to Colonel Khatami, and he'll settle it for you foul fools.

"Major Mansouri, I'll expect you to arrive at my temporary headquarters after we have eaten our supper. Colonel Perez Sir, I'll be reporting our accomplishments to Colonel Gonzales, and the report I shall be offering him will work out well for you and the rest of your proud soldiers, sir. The only way my Persian fighters will be ready for this upcoming attack against the United States, will be because of the outstanding assistance you and your fine young soldiers are offering us, Colonel. I think it's necessary for your Commanding Officer to know with you and your soldier's outstanding help, my operation shall be a successful one against the United States, Colonel Perez Sir. I shall also be informing my President of your assistance to my soldiers, and I'm certain he'll report this fact to your President, sir. It's good when one General reports on the help another soldier offers to his Commanding Officer."

Now it was Colonel Rodrigo Perez's turn to smile over the fine compliments the Persian Commander offered him and his Cuban soldiers. The Colonel was aware there was a promotion in the future for him, if his assistance aided in the successful attack on the United States by these Persian fighters. The Cuban Officer also understood Colonel Felix Gonzales was scheduled to be lifted to the rank of General in the Cuban Army, once this mission was completed, and he was looking forward to getting a raise in rank himself. The Cuban Colonel again nodded to the proud looking Persian Officer as he accepted his compliments for him and his soldiers, and now he was looking forward to when the Iranian General reported to his leaders on how well his operation was shaping up for him and his soldiers, because it will be the first step in his raise in rank.

The rest of the Cuban soldiers were pleased with the Persian General's words aimed at them. Even though they were not looking for any raises in rank, they were looking forward to much better living conditions for themselves, and for their families and loved ones, because of their help to these Persian fighters training in their country. The military of Cuba was still the forgotten peoples of the Island under Castro's iron fisted rule. Sometimes the soldiers went months without pay, and the only reason they did not revolt against Castro, was because they were getting better food from their government, and that was more than a lot of other people living on the Island were getting under Castro's extremely suppressive rule. Many Cuban soldiers were aware of Castro's failing health, and secretly there were many troops praying for death to overtake the old and outdated leader of their tiny Island.

There was little paperwork accomplished by the Vulture and the female Persian Major for the night. Their night was filled with mingled bodies and sweat and lovemaking. They enjoyed each others treasures long into this night, and true to his word. The General allowed the Major to sleep in while he organized another attempted assault on the Cuban installation being defended by the Island's soldiers, and this second assault was as much of a disaster as the first assault was. Not one of his six assault teams were able to get anywhere near enough to their intended target to do any real damage to it, before they were discovered by the Cuban defenders.

This time General Abdol Karim Kalantari held Colonel Heshmoallah Khatami out of the assault exercise, because with the Major not engaging in the exercise, it left the Colonel without a partner for his assault team. The Vulture was angry over the ease his Persian attackers were again discovered and defeated by the Cuban soldiers, and this time he laced into his fighters.

The Vulture's uncontrolled anger was aimed at his Colonel and second in command, as he screamed and threatened him in particular, and he including the rest of his fighters in his anger. "Colonel Khatami, if you cannot get better control of your cursed foul assault teams, I'll have you replaced and sent back to Iran in disgrace, and I shall allow our President to melt out your punishment for your failures to this operation and my command. I cannot believe I'm depending so heavily on you to make this attack a successful one, and yet you cannot even get your worthless and foolish fighters anywhere near the intended target. Before your foul fools are captured or killed by the Cuban defenders of this base, Colonel Khatami.

"Why in the Almighty Allah's great name should I continue to rely upon your worthless skills, when those worthless skills do not get any of your lazy and foolish fighters onto the base we intend to attack, Colonel Khatami? I can allow any of these foul fools to lead the other warriors in the assault, if I don't want it to be successful. I warn you Colonel Khatami, my patience is wearing thin with you, and you know what your foul fate will be, if I send you back to Iran because you were unable to carry out your assigned orders successfully. I wouldn't want to suffer what our great President will have done to your worthless body for your failures to him and to this operation, sir."

The Vulture stopped speaking as he allowed his eyes to wander over the many faces of his other Persian fighters, and then he went on with his assault against them. "And the rest of you cursed fools are no better than the foul Colonel is to this operation. I warn all of you gathered before my burning and displeased eyes that the same foul fate awaits each and every one of you fools. If you people cannot carry out your orders successfully, I'll send the lot of you back to Iran in total disgrace, and I'll allow our wise President to punish you as he sees fit. While I have everyone of you replaced with soldiers who'll succeed on our faithful mission.

"All I complain to the Colonel about is not all his fault either. If you foolish fighters were the great soldiers I was lead to believe you are. Then this cursed target we seek to destroy on this military installation would have been successfully destroyed, and we'd be seated by the fire and laughing over the ease at which we have destroyed our target in the hated United States. I shall not accept another failure of attack on this foul complex I warn you fools. The next exercise will be successful or heads will roll I assure you fools. I shall give you two hours to rest and think about the next exercise, and figure out how you people will accomplish the assault successfully. Get out of my sight before I forget myself and order the heads of you fools be taken by our Cuban brothers. Colonel Khatami, I wish further words with you."

The fuming Persian General rested his hands on his hips and he stared as his fighters rapidly disappeared from his angry glare, and when he was finally alone with his Colonel and second in command, he began speaking in a much calmer tone of voice. Even of the Cuban soldiers who gathered to watch the Iranian General get on his troops, also disappeared from the officer's sight fast as they could get away.

General Kalantari moved until he was standing by his Colonel's side, and he rested his hand lightly on his should as he offered. "Of course you know my angry words I aimed at you, was more for the benefit of the worthless fools we're trying to shape into a great assault teams, my old friend. By no means am I angry at you Heshmotallah. I know we're trying to hit a target the cursed defenders are aware we're come for it, and this knowledge is making it impossible for us to attack the installation successfully, Colonel Khatami. But this is the only way I can get my foul and useless fighters used to attacking a target like the one we'll soon be going after in the United States. We have to get them some kind of experience attacking such a target as the one we have selected, and this is the only way I can think of getting them the needed experience, sir.

"You'll give the pack of worthless fools two hours of rest, and then you'll begin the next exercise, Colonel. This time you'll have Major Mansouri as your partner in the exercise. Hopefully, with all seven assault teams attacking at the same time, some of you might be able to breach the security of the complex and destroy the target. We have to have at least one successful assault before we return to our old base on this god forsaken Island of fools, sir."

Colonel Khatami smiled at his Commanding Officer now he understood the dangerous Vulture was not upset with him, and the threat to be sent back to Iran in disgrace was just that, a threat issued for the other Persian fighter's benefit, as he replied to the General's last words. "General Kalantari Sir, I shall allow our worthless fighters to rest for the two hour's you have offered them sir, and then I shall go over a new way to attack this foul base we aim our eyes upon, and I shall hope and pray to Allah for success with the next attack we employ against these cursed defenders, sir. We might be late for the next exercise to begin, because I intend to lay the law out to our worthless fighters, and if they fail me again on this next attack, I shall be the one who'll punish them, not you General Kalantari Sir."

"That's all I wanted to hear coming from your lips, Colonel Khatami Sir. For you to offer me you're taking over the command of our foolish fighters, sir. That is the way it has to be sir, if you plan to replace me in the future when I'm moved into Iraq, and you take over Command of our attackers, Colonel Sir. We have as many months as we need for us to be prepared to attack the installation that lies within the United States successfully, Colonel Khatami Sir. But I do understand the patience of our President in Iran does have a limit to it, sir. If we reach that end of his patience before we attack the loathsome Americans in their country. We might be pulled off this operation and be replaced by other Persian fighters, and our President will be the one to punish us all for our failure to his orders, sir." The Vulture gave his Colonel the look that informed him he better start working their fighters correctly for this operation.

"I understand what you're saying General Kalantari, and I assure you sir when we enter the United States to destroy our faithful target, our freedom fighters will be well prepared to carry out that attack successfully, sir. I shall swear a sacred oath to both Allah and yourself that we will be successful in our attack against the hated United States, General Kalantari Sir." The Colonel suddenly looked deeply into the eyes of his Commanding Officer, and they were displaying nothing but sheer confidence over the words he just spoke to the General.

"I can expect no less from you and the rest of our freedom fighters, Colonel Khatami Sir. Now Colonel, I suggest you leave my side and start to attend to your troublesome and foolish soldiers, sir. I have a number of other things I must attend to immediately, before we start our second exercise for the foul day, sir. I have to also speak to the pest of the Colonel Perez before the start of the next exercise, Colonel

Khatami Sir. I want to make absolutely certain he has his worthless soldiers ready for when we begin our attack against the fools, sir. I also have to warn the Major she'll be part of the assault teams this time sir."

"Yes Sir General Kalantari, I understand what you're offering me, sir. There is much you have to look after before the start of the next exercise, sir." The Colonel replied as he snapped to attention and he sharply saluted his Commanding Officer before turning on his heels, and then quickly heading off to where the other fighters went when the Persian Commander ordered the Colonel to remain behind so he could speak privately with him for a few moments.

When the Colonel was out of his sight, General Kalantari started to search the base while looking for Colonel Rodrigo Perez. Spotting the young and good looking Cuban Colonel who seemed busy speaking with a number of his own soldiers, the Iranian Commander headed for him. Walking up behind the Cuban Colonel, General Kalantari offered to him in a polite tone of voice this time. "Errr… Colonel Perez Sir, if you have a little time to spare for me, sir. I'd like to speak privately with you for a moment or two, Colonel?"

"One moment please, General Kalantari Sir. Okay Major Rodriguez Sir, you have you orders and I suggest you get the rest of our soldiers well prepared for the next exercise, sir."

Without a reply, the Cuban Major moved off to carry out his orders as the Cuban Colonel turned to the Persian General and he sharply saluted the foreign military officer. Instantly, General Kalantari returned the salute as he started to speak just as quickly to the Colonel.

"Colonel Perez Sir, I know you must feel I'm being harsh with my foolish fighters, sir. But it is necessary sir. I have to have them ready to attack when the proper time comes, sir…"

"General Kalantari Sir, you don't have to offer me any explanations on how you treat your soldiers, sir. I have enough problems trying to controlling my soldiers, without my having to worry about yours, and how you're treating them sir. What is it you wish to speak to me over sir? I'm afraid I'm rather busy at the present moment, General Kalantari Sir." Colonel Perez offered as he let out his breath and then stared at the Persian soldier.

"Colonel Perez Sir, I was thinking about asking you if you could see a way to have your soldiers not being so alert when my fighters next attack your installation, sir. I'm in fear if my fighters continue to be spotted and destroyed so easily by your defenders, sir. They might lose their confidence about the attack, and it'd cause our attack to fail once we're in the United States, sir. But after thinking about it further sir, I shall not make that request of your fine soldiers, sir. I want your soldiers to be well prepared for our attack against them when it comes, that way if we are successful against your proud defenders. We'll most assuredly be successful with our attack in the United States, sir. Besides Colonel Perez, how could I possibly ask your soldiers not to be what they were trained for, sir?" General Kalantari stopped speaking and he now found himself staring back at the Cuban Military Officer for the moment.

"General Kalantari Sir, I'm pleased you didn't ask me to have my soldiers allow your fighters to attack them successfully, even though you're concerned with their confidence, sir. But what kind of confidence would you be instilling in them if we weren't to be what we were trained for General? A lack of confidence is better than to have a false confidence installed in your fighters, sir." The Cuban Officer replied with a sort of snap in his tone.

"Yes Colonel Perez Sir, it is as you have just offered and it's far better to have their confidence shaken, than to give them a false feeling of success in an assault, if they were unable to accomplish what they were ordered to do on their own, sir. You're a wise Military Officer and again I thank you for all your much needed assistance in the training of my worthless soldiers, Colonel Perez Sir." The Persian Officer replied to him.

"Very well then General Kalantari Sir, is that all you wanted to speak to me about, sir? Because if it is General, I have my own soldiers I have to look after, General Kalantari Sir." Colonel Perez offered while still carrying the sharp tone of voice addressing the foreign officer.

"That is all I had to speak to you of sir. And, much like yourself I too must look after my soldiers to make certain they're well prepared for the next assault, Colonel Perez Sir." General Kalantari replied in the same sharp tone the Cuban Officer was addressing him.

Colonel Perez again saluted General Kalantari, and then he watched the Persian Commander turn and leave his side. Once he was gone, Colonel Perez called Major Javier Santana to his side, and he started speaking to him in private, giving him new orders for the next exercise.

General Abdol Karim Kalantari rushed back to his temporary headquarters, he was angry for daring to breach the subject of having the Cuban defenders going light on his Persian attackers. The moment he entered his office, his anger left his being once he laid his eyes on Major Mansouri. The pretty female Major was watching her lover speaking with the Cuban Officer, and from her position she could tell her lover was in a heated discussion with the Cuban. She watched General Kalantari until he left the Cuban Officer and started heading for his office. The Major took off her clothes and she met the General standing by the door completely naked. He smiled as he gently cupped one of her breasts, and then he informed her she was going to be part of the next exercise, and he also ordered her to dress quickly for the mission.

Major Fereshteh Mansouri put on a hurt and disappointed look on her face as she turned, allowing the Persian General to see all of her outstanding treasures as she quickly dressed in the same uniform she worn the day before. It was cold because the uniform was slightly damp from her sweat from their first exercise of yesterday. Major Mansouri was sorry she did not take the time to carry a second and clean uniform into his private quarters when she stayed the night with him. She was already uncomfortable and their next exercise had not even started yet.

The Iranian General code named the Vulture, assumed his position on the back of his jeep as he watched his Persian troops move out on their third assault on the Cuban complex made up to look almost exactly like their intended target in the United States. This time his seven assault teams set out in good formation, and they again attacked the heavy cyclone fence that ran around the entire installation. The assault teams hit the fence in seven different areas, and once they entered the base, the attackers quickly spread out to make their way to their target.

General Abdol Karin Kalantari noticed something was slightly different with the way the Cuban defenders assisting his freedom fighters in their training, were going about their business of protecting the base on this exercise. The Cuban soldiers were kind of staying close together, and they were not paying much attention to his Persian fighters as they made their way towards them and the target. Suddenly, the Vulture found himself smiling as he noticed Colonel Perez must have ordered his defenders to allow the invaders to get a little closer to the target, before they reacted to their presence on the base. The General looked at two of his assault teams he was able to pick out as they cautiously made their way further onto the base, and he saw they had also picked up the forward progress they were making, and this seemed to give them new energy to attack the target and with more confidence.

Try as he might, General Kalantari could not pick up the lead team of Colonel Heshmoallah Khatami and Major Fereshteh Mansouri, as they skillfully made up their assault team and the both of them headed for their target under cover of the actions of the other six assault teams. Of course, General Kalantari had no way of knowing his wise and crafty Colonel issued orders to the other six assault teams to run interference for him and the female Major, as they went after the target. One way or the other, the Persian Colonel was going to make certain at least one of his terrorist attack teams made it all the way to the target, and successfully destroyed it on this latest training exercise, or he was going to take some heads of his soldiers for himself, because he was that upset with his Persian attackers.

General Abdol Karim Kalantari allowed himself to relax a little as he enjoyed the way his assault teams were attacking the base during this exercise. Even though he knew the Cuban Colonel was giving his fighters a better than even chance of succeeding on this latest attack, he was nevertheless going to allow it to continue until he witnessed how the latest exercise worked out for his fighters.

Colonel Khatami and Major Mansouri were using the drainage ditch to protect themselves, until the Colonel noticed there were no Cuban defenders anywhere near where he was attacking the target from. Silently, the overly concerned Colonel tapped the Major on her foot, and once he had her attention, he pointed towards a large stack of lumber piled about fifty yards away from the target area. But just as she was about to move out, three Cuban defenders suddenly went running by the stack of lumber, and they quickly crossed over a large open area, and then they continued heading for a number of parked military vehicles. Immediately, the sound of automatic weapons fire was heard as the Cuban defenders engaged one of the Persian assault teams they discovered attacking the base.

Again, Colonel Khatami tapped the Major lightly on the leg, and he again pointed towards the lumber stack. The Major instantly darted out from her hiding place, and she ran over to the stack of wood. Once she was there, she instantly assumed a protective stance, and then she waited for the Colonel to join her there. In less than a heartbeat, he was kneeling by her side, and he was now pointing towards a large number of wood boxes stacked at about ten feet away from their target. The Major jumped up and then ran for her next cover, but this time he followed right behind her. When the two Persian invaders to the installation were so near their intended target, the Colonel in command of the explosive devices, pulled the fuse pin to the explosive, and then he tossed the simulated satchel charge onto the target and with a loud but harmless explosion. The bomb would have easily destroyed the target along with a large section of the surrounding area at the same time if this was a true attack.

Shouts of encouragement and phrase by the Persian attackers were joined by curses coming from a number of the Cuban defenders who were highly upset over the fact the Persian attackers were successful in their attack on a target they were assigned to protect by their commander.

General Abdol Karim Kalantari immediately jumped out of the back of his jeep, and he entered the Cuban installation as the three Persian assault teams not detected and killed by the Cuban defenders, came out of their hiding places to join up with the other freedom fighters and the Colonel and Major who successfully destroyed their target. Many of the Cuban defenders also came out of their hiding places and they joined the attackers, so they could hear from their Commanding Officers on how they done with the latest exercise.

By the time the Persian General made his way to his Colonel and Major, the rest of his fighters were gathered around the two officers, and they were congratulating the two on their successful attack on their target. His fighters immediately made a path for the angry looking General to use as he walked towards his two officer's, and by the time he reached them, Colonel Perez was already standing by their side, and he was speaking to them in a calm tone.

CHAPTER FIFTEEN

General Kalantari offered his hand to the Colonel he picked to replace him when he was called to Tehran to be placed in command of the conquered land of Iraq, when Iran took over the rebel country of Arabs as he offered. "Ahhh… You see Colonel Khatami Sir if you motivate our foolish fighters properly, there is nothing in this worthless world they cannot accomplish for you, sir. That was a good exercise you completed Colonel, and since we proven to ourselves and the world we could attack any target we're sent out to destroy no matter how well protected it is, or even if the cursed defenders were aware we were coming for the target. I shall expect the same success in any future exercise we engage in, before we make it to the United States and attack our assigned target, Colonel Khatami Sir."

The now extremely proud Persian General stopped speaking to his Colonel for a moment, and then he looked at the Cuban Colonel standing with his other military officer. He walked up to the Cuban and then looped his arm over the Cuban's shoulder, and sort of guided him away from the rest of the attackers and defenders, so he could speak privately with his counterpart. When the two officers were far enough away from the mixed group of Cuban and Iranian soldiers from both sides, so as no one else was able to hear their words. The wise Persian General offered kindly to the concerned Cuban Colonel.

"Colonel Perez, I thank you for allowing my fumbling soldiers to make a successful attack against your defenders during this latest exercise, sir. I understand it must have been one of the hardest things for you to order your fine soldiers, to allow my worthless soldiers to be successful on this attack against them, sir. But as you can see the effect of this attack has on my fighters, sir. I shall be beholding to you for enabling my worthless soldiers to enjoy this slight victory over your outstanding warriors, sir. Even though I fully understand it was by your orders that my foolish soldiers were finally able to defeat your defending soldiers on this latest attack, Colonel Perez Sir."

Colonel Rodrigo Perez returned the General's smile as he offered to the other military officer in a rush of words. "General Kalantari Sir, it was an order that almost cost my life I hate to offer you, sir. My soldiers did not want to be made to look like they were unable to defend any position assigned to their responsibility of protection, sir. I had to promise my soldiers women, and an endless flow of good Cuban rum to enjoy sir, to help set the mood for the night for them, sir. I must offer sir I hope my soldiers did not make it that obvious they were lagging behind slightly to allow your soldiers to accomplish their mission, sir. I also warned them if they made it too obvious, their night of expected sexual pleasures was going to be nothing like they were expecting it to be, General Kalantari Sir."

"Quite on the contrary Colonel Perez, your fine soldiers have acted out their part in this drama rather convincingly, sir. If it was not for the position that I enjoyed as I observed the exercise and my worthless soldiers as they attacked the installation and your troops, sir. I would have never been able to detect the difference in the way your proud defenders were protecting their installation, Colonel. I must offer you Colonel Perez that I am well pleased you shall allow the women back on the military base for your soldier's special enjoyment on this night, sir. But also Colonel Perez, you must allow me to pay for the rum your soldiers' will enjoy on this night of enjoyment and sex, sir. It is the least I can offer to you for your outstanding assistance and your proud soldiers on this exercise, sir." General Kalantari offered as he went fishing in his pocket and removed a stack of American cash, and he started peeling off a number of hundred dollar bills, and then offered them to the Cuban Officer.

Colonel Perez was stunned because this was the first time he witnessed so many American hundred dollar bills in one place in his entire life. Of course, he was going to pocket many of the American bills for himself, and only use what he had to, to pay for the women and booze for his soldiers and himself. The grinning Cuban Colonel took the bills from the General, and quickly stuffed them in his pocket before any of his soldiers saw the transfer of cash between the two officers.

General Kalantari smiled, because he realized the Cuban Officer was going to keep much of the American money, and he half expected him to so. The wise Persian General was actually bribing the Cuban Officer for future needs and wants he might need of him while he was preparing the rest of his soldiers for their mission. He understood he was going to need this Cuban Officer in the future, and the American cash had just bonded the Cuban soldier to his needs for the rest of the time he and his terrorists were on the Island of Cuba. Now, there was nothing the General felt he could not ask of the Cuban, and not receive it.

Colonel Rodrigo Perez nodded towards the grinning foreign General as if he was reading his mind. The Cuban did not care the Persian man knew he was going to keep most of the money for his own needs. After suffering for so long under Castro's iron fisted and oppressive rule, and going without a raise in pay for many years while he was in the service. The Cuban soldier felt he was entitled to keep any money he was able to make on the side, no matter how he made it. Now he understood this Persian Officer was going to be so free with the money he offered him, he decided to milk the foreign invader for all he could get from him.

Colonel Perez decided if he made enough money off this ugly person who had invaded his country with a horde of ugly terrorists, he might share some of it with other selected officers under his command. In this way he could cement their loyalty to him for the rest of their lives.

A voice suddenly called out the General's name, and the Vulture turned to see who was trying to speak to him. A wide smile instantly crossed his dry lips as he found himself staring at the Major as she left the group of Persian and Cuban soldiers, and she was walking directly towards him and the Cuban Colonel.

Colonel Perez also smiled as he offered the Persian in a sneer, displaying he was aware the female warrior was more than just another soldier to the officer. "General Kalantari, it seems your female Officer wishes to speak with you in private, sir. So I shall take my leave of you and look after my own soldiers, sir. There is much I must prepare for the night's festivities, sir. I trust you shall allow your soldiers to join mine in this upcoming night of enjoyment, General?"

"Yes, of course Colonel Perez, from the looks of it I myself might be busy, sir. If you know what I mean Colonel." General Kalantari cast a look at the female officer about near him, and the look caused the Colonel to reply to him.

THURSDAY, MARCH 9th, 2006. THE ISLAND OF MARATHON IN THE FLORIDA KEYS

Captain Robert Walker was at the back of his home trying to teach his son how to swim. It was a beautiful day in the Florida Keys, and Sergeant Dorothy Ramirez was making the two men in her life lunch. The other soldiers staying with the Captain and Sergeant were off doing their own thing on the surrounding Islands of the Keys. The Mutt, Lieutenant Frank Hall was with his girlfriend Blind Date, Sergeant Regina Raphael, and Buckethead, Sergeant Vincent Lambardo was with No Neck, Sergeant Robert Abbott, and the two were at the bar known as the Hurricane, and they were trying to pick up some local ladies to have a little fun with.

Ramirez was cooking hamburgers out back, and she was keeping an eye on Walker and their son. She had the portable phone resting on the table and it rang and made her jump. Lately, the Sergeant was getting more than edgy, because she was worried the service was going to call the elite soldiers in for a special operation, and she was dreading the call from their commanding officer. Because every time the soldiers went on another mission, someone never came home. Any chance she got, she tried to talk Walker out of staying in the service, especially with the wars in Afghanistan and Iraq heating up. His charter company was doing great, and the Neck worked out perfectly for a First Mate for the World Cat. They were making money hand over foot, and she was enjoying being home with their son and her lover on their Island.

When the phone rang a second and third time, she froze in place and all she could do was stare at the phone as she tried to will it to stop ringing. Again she jumped when Walker charged up to the table and he picked up the phone as he bitched at her. "Hey baby what the hell's wrong with ya huh? Why didn't you answer the damn thing, honey?"

Robert Jr. followed his father to the table and hugged his mother's legs, as he watched his father answer the phone. He was hungry and he lost interest in leaning how to swim, and he wanted to see why his father was acting so upset at his mother.

Walker kept his eyes glued on Ramirez's scared face, because she was as white as a ghost as he answered the phone. "Yeah this is Walker, who the hell is this, god dammit?"

"Captain Walker, its Tee K and I wanted to confirm our fishing trip for April, sir. What's wrong with you, you seem awful upset Robert? Are you certain you still want to do this fishing trip we were planning for so long, sir?" The polite country western singer asked his friend with concern lacing his tone.

"Hey Tee K, how the hell are they hanging man? Sure I wanna do the fishing thing with ya man. I was hoping you'd get in contact with me soon, so we can set it up man. When the hell you coming to the Island, man? And yeah, I'm kinda upset at that old buddy. It's Raz, she's been driving me crazy lately with this constant fear we're gonna get called in for some active duty crap, buddy. I can't wait until she lets it go man." He complained in the phone as he looked at Ramirez again, to make certain she was over her fear. She tried to smile at Walker to get him off her rearend.

"I can understand how she must feel Robert. It must be driving her nuts with the fear she has of being called up for active duty at anytime, sir. Anyway Robert, I was planning to be on the Island of Marathon from April 22nd, right on through to April 30th my friend. I have a few minor commitments I have to attend to, and I was hoping to set the date for our fishing trip on say Friday, April 27th. But this time we're not going to use your boat, Robert…"

"What the hell do you mean by that load of crap, buddy? Who the hell's boat are we gonna use if we're not gonna use mine, man? Look pal, I've been looking forward to this stinking fishing trip for the past year buddy, and now you wanna screw it up on us, man?" He growled as he interrupted his friend on the phone.

"Robert, this time I want to rent a boat and have another Captain and Mate do all the work for us while we get some serious fishing in, sir. The last two times we went fishing, you were so busy rigging the poles and doing everything else for the boat, you never got a chance to get any fishing in. It wasn't fair for either you or your lovely girlfriend, you two worked your tails off all the while, and I was the only one who enjoyed the fishing, sir. This time the trip is on me Robert. Please allow me to show you two a good time for a change. I warn you Robert, if you don't agree to do this, I'll tell Dorothy and I'll let her get on your back until you agree with me."

"Okay man, just don't go and start threatening to beat me over the head with Raz, man. I'm having enuf stinking trouble with her ass trying to talk me out of the service as it is, man. Yeah sure why the hell not, you can run the next fishing trip if you really wanna, man. Do you want me to reserve a boat for us, or are you gonna handle it on your own, man? I know most of the uther Captains on the Island." He asked the singer as he looked at Ramirez, and noticed she was happy he was speaking to Tee K again.

"I have my PR person working on getting us a boat when I get to the Island, Robert. That was how sure I was of renting a boat and taking you guys out fishing for a change, my friend. I want to repay you for all the fun you have shown me already, Robert."

"Cool fucking deal man, I don't mind sitting back for a stinking change and having some other poor slob do all the god damn work for us, man. Are you bringing anyone along with you for this fishing trip, man?" The surprised Marine Captain asked, worried he was going to be forced to leave his other soldiers behind, if the singer was going to be bringing any of his own friends along on their next fishing trip.

"No Robert, just myself, but my wife and three daughters will be with me for the time I'm on the island, she really wants to meet you guys, but she doesn't want to fish. She's not into it like I am Robert. Besides, I know you have the other soldiers you'll want to bring on the boat, and it wouldn't be fair to have you leave the other guys behind because I wanted to bring some people on the fishing trip. No Robert, this is going to be our private time together, sir." Tee K replied happily as he looked at one of his people, and had him start calling Marathon and have him reserve them a charter boat for their fishing trip with the elite soldiers he loved being around, and listening to their terrifying stories of military actions they were involved in over the years.

"That's great Tee K, I wasn't looking forward to leaving some of my people behind standing on the dock while we went out fishing with some strangers I don't know from fucking Adam. I'll get the stinking beer and sandwiches for the trip, man. I betta pick up some wine for the girls, I know Raz don't like drinking beer on the boat, it makes her wanna pee and she don't like using the head on the boats, man." He offered with a quick smirk as he smiled at Ramirez who was hanging on his every word, while he was on the phone with the country singer.

"That won't be necessary Robert. I'll have my people set everything up, food and all for us, Captain." He replied in a calm tone as he cut Walker off and smiled pleased he was going to get the chance to repay Walker for his past fishing trips. They had so much fun while on those trips that he was looking forward to getting back on the ocean with the soldiers living on Marathon Island. Lately, he was thinking about buying a home on the Island, that way he could disappear to Marathon anytime he was not on tour, and enjoy himself a little on the water.

"Okay man, but I ain't too usta having someone else doing this shit for me, buddy. But if this is gonna make your day for ya man then knock your fucking socks off pal." Walker snapped at his friend on the phone, because he did not like someone else doing some thing for him and his friends. He always liked being in complete control of everything he did.

"Then it's time you allowed someone to do something for you for a change, Robert. Look Bob, I have to go, I have people wanting to speak with me, and besides, I want to make certain my people reserve a good boat for us when I get to Marathon Island, Robert. I'll speak to you a week before I head out for the Island, and I'll let you know when I'll be arriving by then. Make certain you tell your lovely girlfriend I said hey to her, Robert. I'll be back to you the first moment I get, I can't tell you how much I'm looking forward to seeing you people again, and getting back on the water for a day or two Robert." With that said he broke off the conversation and hung up and started speaking to his people.

The pleased Captain smiled as he hung up the receiver, and then he look at Ramirez who was almost jumping up and down in place, as she waited for him to finish speaking with the country singer.

He did not say anything to Ramirez about his conversation with Tee K which prompted her to complain at him angrily. "Okay mister, I guess you're going to force me to ask you what Toby had to say, buster. What do I have to do to find out what he said, big shot? I hate when you do this shit like this, Walker!"

"A blowjob would do just fine if you really wanna know what he said, baby." He replied with a big grin plastered on his lips as she stared at Ramirez.

"In your dreams you'll get a blow job, tell me what he said or else, mister. If you don't tell me what he said, a blowjob is going to be the least of your problems you'll be looking for, buster." She snapped at her lover, she was that excited to know when Tee K was coming back to the Island. She was dying to hear him sing again, especially if he did it in her home like he did the last time he was on the Island.

"Calm down a little, will ya. I was just busting your stinking horns on ya, that's all girl. What happened to your sense of humor anyway, baby?" He said as he allowed a quick smile as he realized how upset his girlfriend was, and he was having a blast making her wait to find out what they spoke of.

"Okay Walker, you had your little fun and games with me. Tell me what he said and when is he coming back to the Island? I'll tell you this honey, if I like what you tell me, you just might get your blowjob, mister." She offered as she smiled at her soldier, and then she sexily ran her tongue slowly over her lips to drive her point home to him.

"You got yourself a stinking deal there, baby. He's coming back to the Island on Sunday, April 22nd, and we're planning to go fishing on the 27th. But the asshole wants to rent a stinking boat and take us out fishing for a change, baby. I guess he wants to spoil us a little honey, to repay us for taking him out fishing twice. I like the prick after all girl, this is the first time anyone wanted to pamper us for a stinking change, honey." He offered as he flashed a smile of victory, feeling this information should make her happy, and he would end up with a hell of a blowjob for his trouble.

She could not hide the smile on her lips as she stared at her soldier with love flashing wildly in her eyes. Remembering her offer she ushered Robert Jr. to his room, she told him he could watch TV for a while, or he could take a nap. Once Robert Jr. was settled in and comfortable, she returned to the kitchen and laughed when she saw the condition he was in. In anticipation of his blowjob, he was naked from the waist down and he was as hard as a rock, and he was grinning from ear to ear.

"Huh, I see you're going to hold me to my offer, mister. Well, you're not going to get anything until you tell me everything Toby told you on the phone, buster. I can't wait until he returns to the Island, and we can have some time to spend with him. Did he say if he was going to be staying at our place while he's on the Island, Robert?" She asked while allowing extra excitement to enter her tone of voice as she stared at her soldier and waited not so patiently for him to reply to her last question.

"I dunno for sure baby, he didn't say. But if he's gonna rent a stinking boat and take us on it, I'd be forced to believe he and his wife are gonna be staying at one of the local hotel rooms on the Island, honey." He replied as he shook his hips and made his member sway slightly with the movement, in an attempt to get Ramirez's attention to his desires.

"Stop wiggling that damn thing in my face like that, I see it and you'll get what you want when, but only when I know everything Toby said to you on the phone, buster." She snapped at Walker, displaying she was starting to get more than upset with him over his constant stalling on what he and the country singer spoke about on the phone.

"C'mon Raz, if you make me tell you everything he said to me right now. I'm gonna lose my damn hardon, honey." He offered while trying to get her to carry out her offer to him.

"Don't go worrying about that little problem there, mister. If you tell me everything and you lose your hardon, I'll get you back in the mood easy enough, I promise you lover." She offered with a purr as she licked her lips in a sexy move again, and she smiled at him and she flipped her shirt off her shoulders, to drive her point home to her lover and soldier.

"You got it honey." Walker moaned again, and then he went over everything he spoke about with the country and western singer on the phone before.

After he was done telling her everything they spoke about and his words excited her more than she was, she slowly walked through the kitchen and got on her knees and drew his member in her mouth and started to work him over. With her excitement over the singer coming back to the Island, along with the love she had for her soldier, her act was better and she put her full effort into it. Within seconds, she had him wiggling all over the place as he tried to lean against the wall as Ramirez worked him over. In no time she had him pop off, but she did not stop working on him until his member went soft between her lips.

When she was done, she stood and took the dish towel and wiped the side of her face and lips off. Some of his cum had dribbled onto her breasts and she had to wipe that off as she smiled at him and he was still grinning at her as he offered.

"Man that was great baby, remind me to thank the stinking singer when he comes down to the Island for it, honey. If you're gonna do blowjobs like that when he's on the damn Island, maybe I'll try and talk the dude into moving onto the Island for good. That way I can use him to excite you, and I can cash in on the profits later on when he leaves." Walker offered to his girlfriend as he allowed a huge smile to cross his lips.

"I don't think I need him to turn me mister. All I need is you and my love for you, stupid. But I wouldn't mind if he moved to the Island, I could listen to him sing all day, Bobby." She was not kidding with her last statement, ever since they linked up with the singer, she made certain she had every CD he ever made. She was also listening to them anytime she had the stereo on. Walker did not mind the singer's songs, because he was that good. But he got on her ass any time he walked in the home and heard the country songs being played on the stereo.

Ramirez smiled at Walker as she started cleaning up the kitchen, but she remained topless while she worked. As always, the Mutt, Lieutenant Frank Hall walked into the home without knocking, and he went right for the coffee pot and poured himself a cup.

"Nice of you to show up like this man, one day you're gonna give me advance warning before you pop up, dog man." He complained at his lifelong friend with a smirk on his lips.

"Why, are you afraid I might walk in on you two people doing something I'm not supposed to see all a sudden, good buddy." The Mutt complained, and then he looked at Ramirez who did nothing to cover her breasts as she smiled at him.

"Hmmmm… from the look on Raz's face, she musta did you good and proper, and I fucking missed it buddy." The Mutt offered as he continued to stare at Ramirez.

"You sure did and she was really into it man. It was the best blowjob she ever gave me, Homes." He announced as he looked from the Mutt to Ramirez.

"Gees… Walker, why don't you go off and announce what we just had to the rest of the world, buster? And you dog man, you're no better that he is mister. Stop looking at my damn tits and look me in the eyes for once will you please! I don't think you even realize the color of my eyes any longer, mister." Ramirez snapped at the Mutt who was making no bones about his staring at her breasts.

"He girl, my name isn't a dick so keep it outta your mouth when you're angry like this, sister. Well what the hell's bugging your purdy little ass anyway, girl? Since when don't you like me looking at your fantastic boobs, little sister? It never bothered you before just because you're angry at the big slob don't take it out on my ass honey. Hell girl, if I wanted to argue with someone, I woulda stayed home and started a fight with Regina. She wasn't in too gooda mood anyway, so I left and came here for a cup of coffee, and to see what you guys are to today. Hey man, are you going fishing later Walker?" The Mutt complained as he shifted his eyes from Ramirez and looked at Walker. He was holding on a cat and he was petting it while he spoke to Ramirez, and though this was strange because the Mutt rarely took anything in as a pet.

Her face turned a bright red over the ugly remark the Mutt fired off at her about his name. But she chose to let it go because she was angry when she started speaking to him.

The Captain noticed the look and he knew why she turned red as he snapped at the Mutt. He was also angry over the crude remark, but since Ramirez chose to let it go, so was he until he got a change to speak to the Mutt privately over it. "No, not this late in the stinking day, dog man. To go out fishing this late, all we're gonna catch is bait, man. Besides, Raz and I were talking, it seems Tee K's coming back to the stinking Island next month, and he wants to take us out on a private chartered fishing boat, buddy. You betta keep Friday, April 27th opened for the day, that's when we're going out with the fuck, man." Walker warned the Mutt who got his tag name because he had a white mother and a black father. Then Walker growled at his friend. "Hey stupid, what's with the fricking cat, man?"

"It's a female cat buddy, and it's the only female I have held in my arms that did not slap my stinking face right away, man. And, that's no problem there with keeping that day open, my boss will give me the day off easy enuf if I ask him man. We're getting slow at the place anyhow man." The Mutt replied, he was working at the only factory on the Island, and they constructed the prefab rafters for buildings on all the Key Islands.

"Is your lady gonna come with us dog man?" Walker asked his friend as he laughed over the Mutt's statement over the cat he was scratching her head with his fingers.

"I doubt it man, I don't think she'll be able to pull the day off, man. When I slow down, her company usually gets pretty busy." The Mutt replied as he took a sip of his coffee.

"That means I'm going to be the only woman on the boat." Sergeant Dorothy Ramirez offered as she smiled at both men hanging around in her kitchen.

"Why, you worried about that little sister? C'mon honey, I saw you in action baby, and there's only gonna be five of us guys on the stinking boat. So you shouldn't have any problem wit taking care of all of us at the same time, girl." The Mutt smirked as he smiled at Ramirez, and then he waited for her reply to her taking care of the guys on the boat.

"Hey look stupid, I'm not going to spend my time on the boat with taking care of you so called men you know. If I'm going out fishing and I don't have to drive the boat or rig the fishing poles. Then I'm going to get some fishing in, dog man." She snapped hotly as she put on an angry look on her face as she stared at the Mutt, further driving the point home that she was not going to be a sexual play toy on the boat for all of them.

"Gees Raz, you're in some shitty ass mood today I see, little sister. Since when aren't you up for some fun and games while we're on a boat and the water, baby?" The Mutt complained at the angry Ramirez, and then he tried a quick smile on her.

"Look, I'll play around with you slobs before and after the fishing trip if it calls for it. But while I'm on the boat, I'm going to be doing some serious fishing, dog man." She warned the Mutt as she put her hands on her hips and stared at him hotly.

"Hey little sister you got it, no cha cha while we're fishing this time, honey. But before and after, I guess you're fair game, right girl?" The Mutt offered with a crude smirk as he finished his coffee, and then he set the cup down in the kitchen sink.

"We'll have to see about that mister, I don't know how Toby might act if we start fooling around in front of him like that, dog man." Ramirez fired back at the Mutt as she shot a hot smile at him as well.

"Hey girl what the hell is this shit all about? Since when do we care what someone else might thing about us fooling around on the boat, little sister? If he don't like what he's seeing, he can go to hell in a hand bag for all I care, baby. He don't hafta come out with us if he might not like how we act out there, sister." The Mutt complained angrily at her this time around.

"Hey stupid, you have to remember he's the one paying for the boat and this stinking fishing trip this time, mister." Ramirez complained this time at her very dear friend and fellow soldier.

"Yeah so what, we can fix that little bit of bullshit easy enuf, little sister. We can go out on your boat and if he don't like what we're doing, he can swim his ass back to the Island and do whatever with the rest of his stinking life, girl."

"Hang on a minute dog man, if you think for one moment I'm going to miss out on a free fishing trip where someone else does all of the work for us, you're sadly mistaken buster. If you can't control yourself for one day of fishing then you can stay behind and go to work, mister." She complained again, this time she was actually getting angry at the Mutt as she placed her hands on her hips, and stared at him while waiting to hear his next words.

The Mutt knew he better leave this conversation before it got out of hand, and Ramirez really got angry with him. He had seen Ramirez's famous Spanish temper go off, and he was not looking forward to seeing her explode on him again as he grumbled. "Hey little sister, lately you're not being a bowl of cherries to be around. I guess I'll make Regina take care of me before she goes off to work, so I don't get so horny on the boat, girl." The Mutt flashed a smile.

"Now you listen to me buster, I have known you for over ten years, and I never seen you not horny, stupid. You're horny after you make love to someone. I want you and Walker to remain civil while we're on the boat with Toby. If either of you two fools embarrass me in any way, shape, or form while we're fishing with him, you two better start thinking about going out and finding yourselves some overripe tomatoes to make love with. Because that'll be all you birds will be making love to for a full month, or longer. This fishing trip is important to me, do you two heroes without a clue read me loud and clear on this one." She snapped hotly at the two soldiers as she held them in her angry glared as she waited for their reply to her angry words.

Walker gave a sideways glance at his lifelong friend, and then they broke out in laughter as he replied to his girlfriend. "Hey Raz, we'll be on our best behavior while we're out on the boat with your new boyfriend, honey. We'll go out to do fishing and that's all, and if you feel like partying while we're out, you give me the signal and I'll take it from there, baby."

"My new boyfriend huh buster, that remark just cost you a night of severe lovemaking mister. I'm going to hold you two clowns to your word of being cool while we're fishing with Toby. I warn the both of you again, embarrass me just once while we're out there, and you'll pay dearly for it. Mutt, I'll tell Regina and she'll cut you off like I'll cut Walker off from lovemaking, so don't go and mess around while we're with Toby, please." Again she stared angrily at them.

"Yeah yeah, it looks like you won this round I guess, little sister. But the next time we go out on your stinking boat, it is fun and games with everyone on the boat, honey." The Mutt offered, hoping to get a commitment from her to give them a good time if they were cool on this fishing trip with the singer.

"Let me tell you two fool's something right here and now. Be good while we're on this fishing trip with Toby, and the next time we go out. I'll give the both of you slugs a day on the water to remember for the rest of your worthless lives." She offered with a huge smile on her lips and a twinkle in her eyes that warned them they were in for it. Only if they could control themselves while on this fishing trip with the country western singer coming to the Island next month to be with them.

"You got yourself a stinking deal little sister." The Mutt replied as he scratched himself between the legs, and he stared at Ramirez that gave her the same warning she was giving them.

THURSDAY, MARCH 9th, 2006. ON THE ISLAND OF CUBA

The Persian General Abdol Karim Kalantari, better known to his group of freedom fighters as the Vulture, stared at his soldiers as they ran another attack scenario on the makeshift target the Cuban soldiers constructed for their exercises and training. For the past two months he had his fighters stationed on the second military base in Cuba, and they were working both day and night running countless different attack scenarios on their target in the United States. The Iranian General smiled over the professionalism his fighters were displaying, as they attacked the base and supposedly killed many Cuban soldiers assisting their steady progress. At least two and sometimes even up to five of his teams made it successfully to the target and destroyed it.

This was what the Persian Officer wanted from his warriors, to destroy the target every time they assaulted it. The work the Cuban soldiers were doing was making his soldiers perfect in the past seventeen attacks on the supposed target.

After the last attack of the makeshift target, General Kalantari blew his whistle and his soldiers gathered where he was standing. When the soldiers were around him, he announced. "My soldiers for Allah's cause to rid the world of the Satan and all his evil followers, you have grown into a perfect fighting unit, and this ability you have accomplished will make it possible for us to carry out our mission faithfully for Allah in the United States. I believe you have developed to where any practice attacks would be useless for further development. I believe we are ready to carry out our mission in the United States.

"Ahhh… my faithful Children of the Almighty Allah, soon you will be back in our beloved Iran and the sands of her vast deserts, and once there you will be treated as the true heroes you are to the cause of Allah and our government against the great land of Satan, the United States. I would like to take a moment before I dismiss you, to thank our Cuban brothers for their outstanding help with my training of you fighters to be the best we could shape you into. Colonel Perez, if you would not mind sir, I would like to speak to you sir?" General Kalantari bellowed as he looked for the young Cuban Military Officer standing in the formation of other soldiers, and once he picked him out he continued.

"Colonel Perez, again and for the last time I might add, I wish to thank you and your proud soldiers for the help they have offered to me and my worthless fighters, sir. Without your help, I would have never been able to get my soldiers into the shape they needed to be in, to successfully attack our target in the United States, sir. For this help you have offered us sir, I will forever be in your debt. My soldiers are so well trained because of this assistance, and I believe there is not a target in the world I can aim them at that they would not be able to destroy, sir. I am proud of my freedom fighters, and it is due to you help and guidance, Colonel Perez. I shall inform my President of this assistance, and I am certain he will inform your President, and you shall be rewarded by both Presidents, Colonel Perez Sir." General Kalantari nodded towards the beaming Cuban Military Officer, and then the Vulture went back to addressing his own soldiers again.

"My Faithful Soldiers of Allah, I shall give you the rest of this day and night off, to commit any sins against Allah you fool's may deem necessary to commit. But I warn you, you better be prepared to move to our next base in Cuba, and then we will be boarding a pleasure boat and heading for the god cursed United States within the next two days. Any fool who engages in sin on this day, and he finds himself unable to muster for to the military base better commit suicide, because you do not want me to get my hands on your bodies if you are unable to report for our move. Be gone from my sight before I resend this order and find something for you to do, so I can save your worthless souls from the sins you shall commit in your lives." The angry looking General stopped speaking and he glared at his gathered soldiers.

None of the Iranian soldiers had to be told twice by their commanding officer to move off, they disappeared from the Vulture's sight as the soldiers headed for their barracks.

The General smiled as he watched his soldiers get out of his gaze, and rush to their assigned barracks. He rested his hands on his hips as he turned to where his soldiers stood, and he was surprised to see the Cuban Colonel still standing to his left. He was able to read his eyes and they informed him the Cuban wished to speak to him privately.

The exhausted Iranian Officer let his breath out in a sigh and acknowledged the Cuban Officer, who once he looked at him, he moved closer to the Vulture's side, and now he was positive he wanted to speak with him. The Vulture drew in his breath and asked the Cuban Officer. "Yes Colonel Perez, it seems you have something troubling your mind you wish to speak of, sir? I am exhausted as you can plainly understand, and I have a lot to prepare to get my soldiers to the coast of Cuba, so we could then head for the United States. I offer this to inform you I do not have much time to offer you for this conversation you desire with me, Colonel Perez. What is it you wish to speak to me about, sir?" The Vulture could not hide the sharp tone he was addressing the Cuban with.

Colonel Perez chose to overlook the way the Persian was addressing him for the moment as he replied. "General Abdol Karim Kalantari Sir, I understand how exhausted you are sir, and I know you have much you have to look after to get your fighters to the coast, sir. I know of this because it falls upon my shoulders to get your fighters out to the coast of Cuba, so you can get on the boat and head for the United States, sir. That is what I wish to speak to you about, General Kalantari Sir." The Cuban Officer replied to the Persian with the same snap in his tone. He was not going to allow the Iranian to bark at him and get away with it. Not after all the effort he and his soldiers wasted on these Persian fighters, helping them train while they were on his Island. The Cuban Officer could not wait to be rid of the foreign fighters.

"Well Colonel Perez, it seems I must listen to your words even though I am in no mood to get involved in a protracted conversation with you, sir. What is it you wish to discuss with me sir?" General Kalantari barked at the Cuban, not even attempting to cover the disgust in his tone this time, because he was being forced to speak with this man.

CHAPTER SIXTEEN

Ignoring the way the Persian General addressed him again, the Cuban offered. "General Kalantari Sir, I must inform you we have everything set for you and your fighters. I have the pleasure boat you shall use to get your fighters to the United States safely, and a list of people living in the United States that will be available to assist your soldiers further, once they are in the United States. But their help will consist of getting your fighters to Miami, and the rest will be up to you and your warriors to carry out, General Kalantari Sir. Once you are in Miami you and your people will be on your own from that point forward, sir. By the way General Kalantari, I made certain preparations to get your surviving soldiers out of the United States, once you have completely your mission against our common enemy, sir.

"Before you leave for the United States, I shall give you a way to get in contact with a fellow Cuban living in the United States for the past seven years, and he's beyond reproach and loyal to our cause. He has been given a large sum of American money, and has agreed to supply you with a boat to make your way back to my country, and once you return to my Island. We'll get you back to your country of Iran safely, General Kalantari Sir."

"I thank you for all these arrangements Colonel Perez Sir, and I'm sorry for the way I spoke to you, sir. You deserve my full respect whenever we speak. But as I stated sir, I'm tired and perhaps you'll see your way to overlook the way I obviously insulted you, sir. I'm planning to head for the United States on Sunday. That way it'll give me time I need for me to set my people in position, and then take out our target, Colonel. I'm thinking about getting some of my…"

"I'm sorry to offer General Kalantari Sir. But I'm going to be forced to correct some of the orders to your fighter's sir, and stop you from leaving Cuba at the time you stated, General Kalantari Sir." Colonel Perez said with a snap in his tone as he interrupted the Iranian.

General Kalantari cocked his head to the side as he stared at the Cuban, and then he grumbled harshly at the officer. "Why is that Colonel Perez? I was planning to head for the United States just as quickly as possible. You heard the orders I gave my fighters. If you had a problem with my orders, why did you not interrupt me when I was giving the orders to my soldiers, sir?"

"Because General Kalantari Sir, I'd never dare to think of correcting you while you were speaking to your soldiers, sir. I believe that might serve to undermine your command over them, General. Besides General Kalantari, I'd become upset if another other Officer dared to counterman any of my orders if I was speaking to my troops, and issuing them new orders to follow, sir. I was taught to hold my tongue until the proper time in which to speak of any problems facing me, sir."

"I thank you again for that consideration Colonel Perez." General Kalantari offered the Cuban Colonel's words, and then he waited for him to continue with his explanation of why the Cuban was demanding he change the orders to his warriors.

With a slight nod, the Cuban Officer acknowledged the General thanking him for not interrupting his orders as he when on with his words to the Persian. "General Kalantari Sir, I'm in fear we'll be forced to put off your operation to the United States until Thursday night, April the 26th, sir. That's the only night next month when there is no moon scheduled out, sir. That way you'll be able to head for the United States under the cover of total darkness all the way, sir. Also General Kalantari Sir, we need at least that much time to setup the pleasure boat that'll carry you and the rest of your fighters to the United States, sir. We want you to head for America under the cover of darkness, that way it'd be much harder for the United States Coast Guard ships constantly on the prowl for any boats trying to smuggle Cuban refugees or drugs into the hated United States, sir.

"We don't want the American Coast Guard to pick up your boat and stop and board you, sir. This is the time we usually schedule our drug shipments to the United States, General Kalantari Sir. We found on these moonless nights, the Coast Guard ships stay much closer to their shoreline, sir. Once you're in the United States territorial waters, you should not be bothered by the Coast Guard ships, because the boat we procured for your use is registered with the Coast Guard, and it's supposed to be in Miami for minor repairs to the boat, sir. When you come in to dock your boat at Marathon in the Keys sir, if the Coast Guard spot your boat on the water, they'll run your numbers and see it was sent to Miami for its timely maintenance, sir.

"We tried to think of everything to make it possible for you and your Persian fighters to make it to the United States unmolested by the hated protectors of that dom country, General Kalantari Sir. So if you leave the coast of Cuba at ten thirty on Thursday night as I suggested sir, you should be landing on the small Island of Marathon at nine thirty a.m. It's the busiest time of the day for anyone living on the miserable Island, sir. We decided the people of the Island would be more worried and concerned about their work day start, than looking into what you and your fighters are doing on the Island, General Kalantari.

"Besides General, the Coast Guard ships wouldn't be looking for illegal business happening against them at this time of the day, sir. No one is fool enough to dare run drugs or aliens into the United States at this particular time. It'd be too easy to spot this illegal activity, and be intercepted by the United States protectors, sir. The Coast Guard is usually looking for most of their troublemakers in the dead of night, and your boat will be well within the Florida Straits at the time most drug smugglers are doing what they do, sir. That is why we come to the conclusion it'd be much wiser on your part, if you'd head out of Cuba at ten thirty at night on Thursday, April 26th sir. I don't aim to tell you how to run your operation General Kalantari Sir.

"But I do believe we Cubans have more experience in dealing with the United States and their protectors on the water than you do sir." The Cuban stopped speaking to see if the Persian had anything he wanted to ask of him. The Cuban could see the puzzled look etched in the Iranian's eyes, and he did not want him to be confused by what he was saying.

"Allow me to tell you a little information Colonel Perez Sir. If the hated American Coast Guard ships dare to intercept my boat as we head for the hated United States. The foul fools will be in for the fight of their worthless lives I assure you. I shall allow no one to stop me before my Persian fighters are safely in the evil United States, sir. I'll give orders to my fighters to attack any boat that challenges me, while we're on the water sir." The Persian announced in an angry tone of voice to the Cuban Officer.

"That'd be an extremely foolish mistake to commit on your part, to dare try against them General Kalantari Sir…"

"And why is that Colonel Perez?" The Persian snapped at the Cuban.

"Because General Kalantari Sir, the American Coast Guard ships are equipped with heavy machine guns, even in the smaller and fast moving speed boats employed in their drug running intercept operations, sir. Also General Kalantari Sir, the larger interceptor Coast Guard ships has cannons that can blast your boat out of the water, sir. I'd caution you on your conduct if you're intercepted by any Coast Guard ships, sir. They're prepared for any trouble they might get into while they're out on patrol of the Ocean.

"The boat we have procured for you will be equipped with a number of fishing poles, fishing gear and bait. I suggest if you're challenged by the Coast Guard, you allow your boat to be boarded and inspected by them. As I offered sir, your boat will be registered with the Americans, and hopefully if you're challenged by them, you'll be in the United States territorial waters, and this will help stop you from being inspected closely by the Coast Guard, General. If you're stopped in their waters, the Coast Guard will be looking for illegally caught fish, and to make certain your boat passes their safety inspection, and not carrying illegal drugs or aliens on board the boat. I shall be providing you with a legal fishing license, and all the proper paperwork that'll make you legal to all their dom laws, sir.

"Also General Kalantari Sir, you'll be traveling the waters with only two weapons on board the boat sir, and these weapons are there for your protection against possible Pirates, or to kill a shark if you capture one on your fishing trip, sir. So any attempt of your fighters engaging the dom Americans on the water, would be totally out of the question for you and your Persian fighters, General. The number of fighters you'll have on board your boat might cause the Coast Guard some concern, and that's why we procured a fifty five foot boat for your use, sir. A boat of that size will allow you to carry as many passengers as you'll have on board the boat, at the time of any possible intercept by the Coast Guard, sir.

"General Kalantari, we made certain if your boat is boarded by America's coastal defenders, it will pass their inspections and rules, sir. We have enough life vests stored on board and more than needed fire extinguishers and flares, sir. We tried to think of everything to get you safely to the shores of the United States, sir. This is why I must insist you wait until the time I have suggested to you sir, for you and your fighters to set out for America and begin your operation against the lowly mongrels, General Kalantari Sir."

"Colonel Perez, I don't see I have much choice in the matter, sir. Everything you suggested is wise precautions, and I shall adhere to all you offered me, Colonel. Colonel Perez, again I find myself thanking you for your diligence to my orders and mission, sir. If it wasn't for your wisdom, I'm certain I would've committed many mistakes on my mission, sir. Mistakes that would've alerted the hated Americans, and they would've stopped my operation before my fighters attacked their ordered target. Again, I offer my President along with your leader will be informed of the assistance you showered upon my foolish head, sir." General Kalantari nodded towards the concerned Cuban as he added a smile at the young officer.

"I thank you for that kind offer General Kalantari Sir, and I hope when I'm sent on a mission against our common enemy. You sir will be looking over my shoulder, and your wisdom will stop me from making mistakes that would cause my mission to fail, sir." The craft Cuban offered to the smug looking Persian.

"You're wise with the words offered me, Colonel Perez. If I didn't know better, I'd swear to the Almighty Allah I was speaking to a faithful Persian fighter, sir. You honor your country and family name properly, Colonel. It's a great pleasure to be working with such a proud warrior as yourself, sir. Colonel, I'd be proud to assist you on any mission you might be sent on to hurt our common enemy anywhere in the world, sir." General Kalantari was trying his best to be overly nice and complementary to the Cuban Officer, but like the foreign soldier, General Kalantari could not wait until he no longer had to deal with these people that in his mind he felt were filthy, and they worshiped a false God.

"You're likewise offering me much phrase for my carrying out my orders from my Presidente, General Kalantari Sir. I shall be looking forward to having you being my guiding light, if I and the soldiers under my command are ordered to attack our enemy throughout the world, sir. I must admit General Kalantari Sir I'm quite envious of your being able to attack the United States within her own country, sir. I cannot tell you how long I wanted to attack the dom country helping to destroy my country from their shores, sir. What with the stifling sanctions the United States has installed upon our shoulders, because we follow a Presidente who'll not bend a knee and bow head to the all powerful United States, sir.

"Furthermore, General Kalantari, the United States allows our godless traitors to populate their country, and they treat these dom fools like they're the conquering heroes for Cuba! The United States spreads the polluted cheeks of their arse wide, for these cowards who were afraid to stand and fight for their convictions against Presidente Fidel Castro and his soldiers, and yet the Americans continue to turn their hateful backs on the true heroes to Cuba, Fidel Castro and those proud soldiers who follow his words and guidance to power, sir. I cannot wait until I get a chance to pay the American people back for these terrible insults they have heaped upon our shoulders, General Kalantari Sir." Colonel Perez offered as he took a quick breath, and this break allowed the Persian to offer him his wisdom.

"Colonel Perez, I see we both harbor the same ill will towards the hated Americans and their worthless land of sin and lust. We in Iran had their sanctions leveled against our civilians, and for the same reasons Cuba is being punished by the United States. Because we wouldn't bow our heads towards the great Satan, and allow them to dictate their evil wills and wants on the proud peoples of my land, sir. I'll tell you this much Colonel Perez, the bomb I shall toss at the hated ones, will be tossed in your honor, sir. That way you'll be attacking them through my hand, sir." The General remarked as he smiled at the Cuban.

"I thank you kindly for that proud offer sir, because it shall bring me great peace of mind in my sleep, General Kalantari Sir. Because I continue to live so I can bring some of Cuba's revenge against the country that punishes Cuba's proud and loyal people, for the sake of a horde of traitors who have fled Cuba's shore, rather than stand and fight for her sake, General Kalantari Sir." Colonel Perez nodded slightly at the Persian.

ON THE TINY ISLAND OF MARATHON IN THE FLORIDA KEYS. FRIDAY, APRIL 7th, 2006

Captain Robert Walker and his girlfriend, Sergeant Dorothy Ramirez was busy preparing for the arrival of the country singer they knew as Tee K, to arrive on the Island of Marathon within two weeks. Ramirez was walking on cloud nine since the month turned to April. This was because she was looking so forward to being with the country singer staying at their home again. Their son was at school and since he started school, it gave the two lovers more time to be alone with each other.

Sergeant Ramirez was so excited she was walking around the house topless and constantly teasing Walker in any way she could get at him. She was cleaning the house while he put his stuff he had hanging around the house away. The war in Iraq was getting angry again, and with Iran supplying more deadly EFP's, the Explosive Formed Penetrators, along with an endless supply of the less dangerous IED's or Improvised Explosive Devices, more and more Senators were turning up the heat against Iran and their own President.

The American Leader sent two nuclear powered Aircraft Carrier Task Forces into the Persian Gulf, as a show of force aimed against Iran. But it did little to stem the constant flow of these deadly weapons to the Shiite insurgents working their evil inside Iraq. The American President stirred up many angry Senators further, demanding he remove the American troops from Iraq, and allow the unstable Iraqi government to fend for themselves for a change, by offering to place more boots (Troops) on the ground in Iraq.

Nevertheless, the President was staying the course he originally set out on, and he was going to send the extra troops into Iraq to get a handle on some of the violence the insurgents were carrying out against the innocent civilians and police of the country.

The Marine Captain had no problem sending extra troops to Iraq, because he felt there were not enough soldiers on the ground to turn the corner, and stop the internal violence happening in Iraq. Besides, he liked the American President, because he felt this man was going to do what he said he was going to do, and that was that. He felt if there was a Democratic President in place, we would still be discussing the savage terrorist attack on the Twin Towers and the Pentagon. At least this guy destroyed the safe havens bin Laden enjoyed in the nation of Afghanistan. He further believed if the President said something, he better do it, and this one was doing everything he said he was going to do, even if it bent the noses of Republican Senators out of shape at the same time. That was all he expected from the leader of his country, to do whatever he said he was going to do and then carry it out, even if it was wrong or unfavorable.

Captain Walker was also excited with the country singer coming back to the Island, and he was constantly bothering Ramirez every chance he got by grabbing her breasts, or chasing her around the house when she entered the room he was working in. She ran from him laughing all the way. It was a great day for the both of them, and Walker told her he was going to take her and their son out to eat tonight. The Mutt, Lieutenant Frank Hall and his girlfriend Blind Date, Sergeant Regina Raphael were going out with them to supper, and that also added to Ramirez's excitement and her great mood for the day.

She loved to eat out, and being the Mutt and Blind Date were coming with them, she knew this night was going to be nothing but all fun and games for them. But she knew it was not going to be a long night out either, because Walker had a paid charter scheduled for tomorrow morning, and that meant he was going to have to be up by five a.m. to get the boat and fishing tackle ready for the charter. No Neck was going to be his mate on the charter as usual, and they were going to make five hundred dollars free and clear tomorrow from the one charter, and she was pleased with this because their mortgage payment was due in the next few days.

Robert Jr. came home from school and she put a shirt on and made him something to nibble on, to hold him over until they went out tonight. The Mutt and Blind Date came over as their child came home, and Walker offered the Mutt a cold beer. Ramirez hugged Regina and asked if she wanted a drink, but she waved it off. She did not want to ruin her appetite or get high drinking on an empty stomach. She looked tired because her job was busy this time of the year, and she was putting in a lot of overtime to catch up on the work.

The Mutt and Walker went outside to enjoy their beers and speak together, and they left the women in the home, knowing they wanted to talk also. Walker wanted to tell the Mutt what they were going to do when the country singer came back to the Island.

"Hey Mutt, you know Raz was dead serious about us behaving when this pain in the stinking ass singer gets down here, man. I hate not being myself though out on the water, buddy. But it evidently means a shit load to Raz, so we better be on our best behavior when he's down here, man." He kind of warned his lifelong friend as he stared him in his eyes.

"Arrr… It's only gonna be for a stinking week man, and besides buddy, we only have to be good when the fucking prick is around us, man. If he's not around, we can be ourselves and bug the shit outta the girls, man. I don't see us having a problem wit the stinking dude while he's down here, or wit the girls either for that matter. I got the warning from Regina last night, so I guess Raz musta spoke to her about the frigging dude, man. Besides Homes, I'm kinda looking forward going fishing with the lousy prick, Walker. The last time he was on the stinking

Island, we had some fun with the stinking dude." The Mutt offered as he took a pull on his beer and smiled at the concerned looking Walker, as he waited for his reply.

"Yeah, he was kinda fun to be around at that man, and Raz really likes the way the little prick sings. I guess he's okay and we'll hafta be civil with the prick while he's on the Island. Are you sure Regina can't come with us on the fishing trip, buddy? I'd love to have her come along. It's a shame she's so fricking busy at stinking work, man. She's a blast to be around, and she sets off Raz, and when Raz is set off, she's hot as hell man."

"I know man, and I'd love to have her on the boat wit us, Homes. But she can't make it man, she asked her boss if she could have the day off, but he gripped at her they were too far behind in their work to give anyone a day off. Hell man, he even wanted her to work on Saturday man, but she told him no way because the dude was gonna be on the Island, buddy. I kinda feel shitty she won't be able to come on the boat myself, Walker." The Mutt replied as he looked at Walker's home, and he saw the girls speaking to each other on the patio in the backyard.

"Yeah, that sucks the big one buddy. I know we woulda had a helluva lot more fun if she came with us, man." Walker moaned as he followed the Mutt's eyes and saw he was looking at the girls, and he added to his words. "But the next time the lousy dude's down here man, and the next time I don't give a shit if Raz likes it or not, man. If we're on the boat, it's gonna be fun and games as usual old buddy, and I don't give a shit who's on the fucking boat with us, pal. I don't like being forced to be someone I'm not man. It goes against my stinking grain, dog man." Walker bitched as he finished off his beer and threw the crushed can in the trash bucket he had resting on the dock for recycling.

He and the Mutt looked down the dock towards the open Ocean, and they were able to see a number of small boats coming in from their day of fishing and fun on the water. The Mutt complained at Walker as he took the last pull from his beer. "Hey man, we shoulda went out fucking fishing with the girls today, and had some stinking fun with them. We're wasting away waiting for this little prick to come down to the Island, man."

"How could we have done that shit man? If you remember right man, your girl had to work today buddy, and Raz was dead set on cleaning up the place for the fuck coming down to the stinking Island, man. I woulda ended up in a fighting with her sure as shit hits the fucking fan, if I suggested we went out fishing today, man. I've been chasing her all over the place as it is, and I couldn't get her interested in making love, man. She was only interested in cleaning up the dump for the stinking dude coming down here, man. We can't go out tomorrow because I got a stinking charter, and I'm waiting for that big marmaluke to get home so I can make sure he's okay to be out on the water with tomorrow.

"He's gonna be my stinking mate for the damn charter, and I don't need the damn Neck throwing up all over the back of the damn boat or on the uther slobs on the boat, because he drank too fucking much today, buster." He was bitching about No Neck, Sergeant Robert Abbott, and the Mutt knew it as he replied.

"Don't worry about the big jerk, he's with Buckethead and they're trying to pick up some hens at the Hurricane bar, man. Bucket called me about an hour ago, and he said they weren't drinking much, and they were having some fun with a pair of chicks interested in them, man. I think they should be home well before we head out for supper tonight, buddy. If not, we can stop by the Hurricane and see what the fuck they're up to man, and if they're drinking you can put the kibosh to it, and send the big sweat warrior home man."

"They betta not be still drinking if they know what's good for them, man. The stinking Neck knows I don't like him drinking the day before we go out on a damn charter, dog man." Walker moaned at his friend with anger lacing this tone.

Ramirez and Blind Date came out of the home and they were holding Robert Jr.'s hands, and all three headed for the two soldiers standing on the dock. When Ramirez reached Walker she offered in a pleasant tone. "Hey big man, what say we head out and do a little shopping before we stop for supper, honey? I want to pick up a few things and have them in the home when Toby gets here, Walker. I have to make certain we have enough toilet paper and some other things like that, honey. Besides, we have to load up the freezer in case he and his wife eat with us a couple of times while they're visiting the Island, Robert." Ramirez shot a quick smile at her lover.

"Man honey, I wish you'd show me some of the stinking concern you're showing for this little fucking pissant when I'm home, baby. I feel like you don't care if I was around the house or not today, girl. You hurt my feeling you know girl. I tried to get you to make love to me a coupla times today, and you weren't hearing out of that ear I guess, baby." He griped at his lover as he wasted a quick smile on her.

"Ahhhh…you poor baby, don't start with me mister, I didn't mean to hurt your itty bitty feeling. But to tell you the truth Robert, it would've been better if you weren't home today, my lover. With the constant pestering you were doing all day, I didn't get as much done as I wanted to. But I'll make up for it tomorrow while you're out on the charter, mister. Regina said she'd come over after work and help me clean a little."

"Hell honey, you really know how to make a guy feel unwanted around here you know girl."

"Look Walker, you know how important this visit from Toby and his wife and their girls is to me, and once he leaves the Island I'll make it up to you in any way you chose, for all I'm putting you through, mister. Right now, I need to do whatever I have to to impress this man and his lovely wife and their children, lover." She replied to Walker's grumble as she gave him one of her sexiest smiles and a slight wiggle of her hip, as Regina took Robert Jr. from her and she led him to the edge of the dock, so he could see the water and countless little fish hanging around at the edge looking for something to eat.

"Well little sister, since you put it that way, you got yourself a stinking deal, baby. You do what you gotta do and I'll put up with it until this schmuch is gone from the stinking Island, honey." He mumbled with a huge smile on his lips as he looked Ramirez in the eye.

"Boy, you guy's are so easy, a little wiggle of the hips and a hot smile and I can have my way with you I see." She retorted as she wiggled her hips at Walker who was taking it all in.

"What the hell can I tell ya baby, I'm easy girl." He replied to his lady with a grin.

"Shall we leave and get that bit of shopping done?" She more or less asked her lover.

"Yeah sure, why the hell not girl, I wanna get out early myself and check on the big guy, and make certain he's not still drinking at the stinking bar anyway, lady."

With that said the five picked up and headed in the house. Ramirez locked the backdoor and then she followed the rest of them out of the house and she then locked the front door. Walker stared the car and everyone got in and they headed out for their night of some fun and food.

THE ISLAND OF CUBA. SUNDAY, APRIL 9th, 2006

General Abdol Karim Kalantari was doing his best to get his soldiers comfortable at their new location on the northern coast of Cuba at the City of Matanzas, over forty miles east of the capital city of Havana. Where General Kalantari's soldiers were stationed, was the military base that provided the security for the west side of the cove where the city was constructed. The city of Matanzas was a fine resort town where hordes of foreigners flocked to enjoy the sun, warm water, and the beautiful sands of the beach. It was a nude beach, and from where he stood, he could see young women walking on the beach naked as the day they were born. But today the Persian General was excited, and he was having trouble hiding his excitement from his soldiers.

Although his soldiers were on this new base for two weeks, today Colonel Felix Gonzales was scheduled to arrive on the base, and he made it known he wanted to speak with the Iranian Officer. Adding to the General's excitement was the fact today, the pleasure boat they were to use to get the Iranian soldiers to the United States was supposed to arrive at the base. The Vulture was dying to get acquainted with the boat, and to make certain he knew how to run it properly and to get familiar with the charts of the coastline of the Florida Keys, and the path he would take to get safely to the United States.

The General's excitement was infecting with the rest of his soldiers. The Iranian fighters were doing everything in their power to look busy on the Cuban base. Of course, the Iranian males were trying to watch the European women as they strolled along the waterline naked. But when a few women started to play volleyball on the beach, all the activity on the military base stopped, and the soldiers stationed there, even the Cuban soldiers stopped what they were doing, and they stared at the naked women jumping and bouncing all over on the beach. Even some of the female Persian fighters stopped what they were doing, and they also watched the young naked women enjoying themselves on the sand.

A seaplane circled the base and the resort opposite the military base, and then it landed in the calm and flat water, and it carefully coasted up to the shore of the base. Colonel Rodrigo Perez left his position and he rushed to greet the passenger of the small plane. The plane's door flipped opened and Colonel Felix Gonzales wiggled his body out of the craft, and the two Colonels hugged, and then Colonel Gonzales started walking towards the base. The Cuban soldiers were standing in formation at attention, and when the respected Colonel walked before them, the soldiers immediately saluted their Commanding Officer.

The Persian soldiers were mustered at the far end of the Cuban formation, and they were being led by General Kalantari standing at attention and when Colonel Gonzales walked up to him, the Vulture snapped off a sharp salute to the powerful Cuban Officer. Colonel Gonzales smiled at the foreign General as he returned his salute as briskly, and then he stepped forward and kissed the Iranian on both cheeks, as he offered him in a friendly tone.

"Ahhh… General Kalantari Sir, I cannot tell you how much of a pleasure it is for me to lay eyes upon my fellow brother and soldier again, sir. It has been too long since the last time we spoke together General. There is much I have to speak over with you sir, and I want to inform you that your pleasure boat will be arriving at this military installation within the next hour or so, sir. Shall we get out of this burning sun and speak in the air-conditioning of your private quarters, General?" Colonel Gonzales again flashed a quick smile at the Iranian Officer as he waited for his reply.

"Yes Colonel Gonzales Sir, it has been much too long since the last time we spoke together, sir. I believe I would prefer to carry out our conversation in the luxury of the air-conditioning of my private quarters, Colonel Gonzales Sir." He offered to the Cuban Colonel.

"Very well General Kalantari Sir, Colonel Perez front and center, sir." The Cuban Officer barked over his shoulder, and he waited for the Colonel to join him and the Persian.

"Yes Sir Colonel Gonzales." The second Colonel snapped as he left his formation, and rushed to the other Colonel's side, to find out his next orders from his Commanding Officer.

When Colonel Perez reached Colonel Gonzales' side, the commander barked at his second in command. "Colonel Perez, you'll dismiss your soldiers after ordering them back to their duties, and then you'll accompany General Kalantari and myself to the General's private quarters. I want you to be part of this conversation, Colonel. Dismiss your people sir."

"Yes Sir Colonel Gonzales Sir, Major Rodriguez, you'll dismiss your soldiers after you give them orders to follow, sir. I don't want the soldiers hanging around the base without anything to do, sir." Colonel Perez snarled at his second in command, and then he waited for his orders to be carried out by the Major and his soldiers.

When the Cuban Colonel's orders were issued, General Kalantari went in action, and he snarled at his second in command while barking over his shoulder, and not bothering to look at his Colonel. "Colonel Khatami Sir, you'll dismiss our soldiers after you assigned responsibilities to them, sir. I don't want our soldiers wasting their worthless time watching the cursed civilians enjoying themselves at that cursed resort across the bay, sir. We're soldiers and we have certain duties to perform, and if I spot any foolish soldiers wasting their foul time watching those lowly people, they'll wish their mothers have never met their fathers when I finish with them, sir. Carry out your orders as received, Major Khatami Sir."

"Yes General Kalantari Sir." Then the Persian Major barked at his soldiers and then waited for them to disperse and carry out the orders he issued them.

Colonel Gonzales leaned closer to General Kalantari and whispered so only he could hear his words. He was impressed at how well the Persian General controlled his soldiers as he offered. "General Kalantari Sir, you must keep in your mind while you're visiting my country, sir. Those civilians you seem so upset with are one of Cuba's mainstays in our surviving the stifling sanctions America imposed against my country for forty four years, sir. We're beholding to the foreigners who come to Cuba in droves to enjoy our sun and beaches. For their sake, and for the sake of Cuba, my soldiers join your warriors against our enemy ninety miles from my coast, sir."

General Kalantari allowed a smirk to cross his lips as he looked the Cuban Colonel dead in the eyes before he replied to the Spanish Officer. "Yes Colonel Gonzales Sir, I understand what you are offering me sir, and I appreciate what these visitors to your fine country mean to the economy of Cuba, sir. That's another reason why I don't want my soldiers wasting their cursed time watching these foolish people running around in the nude, sir. I don't want my soldiers to insult any visitors to your country."

Colonel Felix Gonzales found himself staring at the Persian as intensely, and then he cocked his head to the side as he replied. "You're correct General Kalantari Sir I never looked at it in that light, sir. I believe I shall take an example from your logic, and I'll order it's forbidden for my soldiers to be staring at the naked foreign females on the beaches, sir. I shall enforce my order by adding if any Cuban soldier is found guilty of staring and making any visitors to our country uncomfortable, will be stood up before the wall and shot, sir."

General Kalantari was shocked by the harshness of the Cuban Officer's orders as he said in reply. "Colonel Gonzales Sir, that is a heavy punishment for a soldier found guilty of merely looking at a naked woman, sir. Punish him yes, but to kill him over such a minor infraction I believe is an extremely harsh reprisal for the minor offense, sir."

"That might be so in your country General Kalantari Sir. But one example will serve wonders for my future orders to my soldiers, sir. Besides General Kalantari Sir, I believe you should leave the discipline of my soldiers to me, and I shall do likewise and leave the discipline and training of your soldiers to you, sir. You must remember you and your warriors are visitors to my country sir, you're not here as an advisor to the training programs of my soldiers, sir. Bah, this heat is making me short tempered General Kalantari Sir. I believe it's time for us to get out of this heat and speak like civilized soldiers in your private quarters, sir."

"Yes Sir Colonel Gonzales, I stand before you corrected which is right, sir. How you treat and train your soldiers is your business sir, and I shall keep my nose out of your business, Colonel." General Kalantari bowed slightly towards the Cuban, and then he added. "I believe your last order Colonel is a most wise order at that, sir. I'm exhausted and hot, and I'd like to enjoy the luxury of the air-conditioning of my quarters while we speak further, sir."

"Very well General Kalantari Sir, Colonel Perez Sir, you and the Major will attend us, sir."

"Yes Sir Colonel Gonzales Sir." The second Colonel offered to his Commanding Officer.

The soldiers left the others as they ran off to carry out their orders. The moment the officers entered the General's quarters, they removed their covers (hats) and loosened the top two buttons of their uniforms and then they relaxed together. Colonel Gonzales took the General's usual chair behind his desk without asking, and he popped his feet up on top of the desk, while Colonel Perez followed his orders without being told by his Commander.

Colonel Rodrigo Perez walked over to a locked cabinet that General Abdol Karim Kalantari did not have keys for and once it was opened, he removed a bottle of rum and poured three drinks. Colonel Felix Gonzales picked up his glass and saluted the Persian Officer, and then he belted down the harsh tasting liquid. The other officers followed suit and downed their drinks with General Kalantari displaying a horrible look, as the drink assaulted his body. "Now we're comfortable General Kalantari Sir, there's much I have to go over with you, and little time to accomplish it, sir. First General, I have the boat you shall use to infiltrate the United States coming here shortly, and it's being operated by one of my best Navel Officers, sir. His name is Lieutenant Miguel Castillo, and he has been sailing boats like this one most of his life, sir.

He shall acquaint you with the proper operation and the electronics of the craft, sir. The boat we chose for your use will be equipped with an automatic helm, and once your course is set into the machine, all you'll have to do is sit back and allow the dom boat basically drive itself to your final destination in the United States, sir.

"The system will keep your boat in deep water all the way to the United States, that way you'll not have to worry about running aground in the shallows, and be discovered by the American Coast Guard, General Kalantari Sir. Also General, the boat will be equipped with fishing poles and tackle sir, and I suggest the moment it begins to get light, you have some of your soldiers drop lines in the water, to make it seem your boat is out fishing for sport. After all General Kalantari Sir, a boat on the water fishing is less likely to be challenged by the coastal defenders, sir." Colonel Gonzales took a moment so he could take a drag from his cigar, and this break in his conversation gave the Persian terrorist a chance to respond to his last words.

"Colonel Gonzales Sir, I like everything you set up for my soldiers, sir. I shall be looking forward to meeting Lieutenant Castillo, sir. I'm certain he'll be an excellent teacher for my needs, sir. But I must add for your information Colonel, I don't come without experience on the water sir, and I have some knowledge operating of a water craft, sir. Colonel, Iran is bordered by the Persian Gulf, and there is great fishing in the Gulf, and I spent many great days with my children fishing the waters, sir." General Kalantari gave the Cuban Colonel a proud victory smile as he stared at him for the moment.

"This is good to know General Kalantari Sir, because any possible experience you might have, will make it much easier for my Lieutenant to show you how this boat and electronics works, sir. I'm pleased to understand you have some minor experience on the water, General Kalantari. I'm having the dom boat dock at the northern end of the base, that way a boat of this size will not arouse the fools enjoying the beauty that Cuba has to offer our visitors from aboard, sir. We don't need any of the god dom civilians becoming too interested and trying to see what we're up to with a civilian pleasure craft being docked on a military base, sir. Before you ask General Kalantari Sir, we have this possible situation covered as well, sir.

"We're planning to release a matter of fact information statement that a visiting Cuban General from the interior of Cuba is visiting our base for inspection purposes, and he's an avid fisherman, and that's the reason for the boat being docked on our military base, sir. I assure you General Kalantari, we tried to cover all possible bases when it comes down to your future operation within the United States, sir." Again the sharp Cuban Colonel stopped speaking as he took another drag from his cigar.

CHAPTER SEVENTEEN

The Cuban offered the Persian a cigar sarcastically, because he knew the foreign General refused every cigar offered him, and he was enjoying the insult he aimed at the Persian fool, without him being aware he was trying to insult him. The Colonel smiled as he and Colonel Perez purposely blew the smoke from their cigars at the Iranian Officer, and he noticed the Persian was turning green from the foul smoke. Even though he was in command of helping the terrorists with their future attack against the United States, the Cuban Officer was having a hard time hiding his sheer and outright dislike for the Iranian soldiers in his country. He could not wait until he was rid of the fools and he could get back to his regular duties.

General Kalantari was seated across from the Cuban Officer in a thick halo of cigar smoke, and he was trying to speak to the Cuban while also trying to hold his breath, because of the breath robbing and terrible smelling smoke. When another thick cloud of cigar smoke headed at his face, he could not help himself, and he finally growled under his breath at the smug looking Cuban soldier. "Why you filthy Ebn el Metanaka, (Son of a bitch) Elif air ab tizak! (A thousand Dicks in your ass!) When the proper time comes, I shall seek my revenge against you and your worthless ancestors for this terrible insult you are forcing in my face. Waj ab zibik (An infection in your dick) foul one whose mother has mated with a lowly scorpion. How dare you force me to breathe that filthy smoke in! My revenge against you will be complete for this foul insult."

Cuban Colonel Felix Gonzales noticed the harsh look locked in the angry and pitch black eyes of the fuming Persian soldier, and the foreign officer also seemed like he was no longer paying attention to his words. The Cuban soldier cleared his throat in an attempt to get the Iranian Officer's thoughts back to their conversation and mission.

General Kalantari nearly jumped because of the sound, and he shook his head and focused his attention on the Cuban soldier who was now leaning closer to him, and looking into the angry Persian's eyes while holding his cigar in his hand.

"I'm terribly sorry General Kalantari Sir, but you seemed to have been off somewhere else in your mind and you were no longer paying attention to my words, sir. What I have to say to you is extremely important, and I must be blessed with your complete attention during this entire conversation, General." Colonel Felix Gonzales grumbled as he sat back in his chair and placed the smug look on his face, and he purposely took another drag from his cigar, and this time he blew the smoke over his head towards the ceiling. But it still chocked the Persian Officer, and again he tried to hold his breath and talk.

The cunning Vulture placed a weak smile on his lips as he replied to the Cuban in a soft tone of voice. "Yes Sir Colonel Gonzales Sir, I'm sorry for allowing my mind to wander a bit in this conversation, sir. I was guilty of thinking about my mission to the hated United States, more than what we were discussing here, Colonel. I can assure you it'll not happen again while we're speaking together and in your country, Colonel."

Colonel Gonzales took another drag from his cigar and purposely blew the smoke in the direction of the Persian, before subbing it out in the astray. Again, the Cuban smiled, enjoying the victory he had over this foreigner. But before he was able to say another word to the man, Major Javier Santana came in the office and announced to his Commander. "General Gonzales Sir, the civilian boat has just docked at its station, and Lieutenant Castillo is already securing the boat safely to the dock, sir."

"Ahhh… it's about time he has got that dom boat here, Major." Colonel Gonzales turned his attention to General Kalantari and offered. "General, I'd like to see what this boat looks like, and I'm certain you're as interested in viewing it as I am, sir. Shall we go down to the dock and see what my Lieutenant has brought for us, sir?"

"By all means shall we go Colonel Gonzales Sir. I want to see what this boat looks like." General Kalantari replied as he rose from his chair, and waited for the Cuban Commander to lead the way for him. As Colonel Gonzales left the room, Major Rodriguez and Colonel Perez followed him, leaving the Persian and Major Santana to bring up the rear. General Kalantari took it for what it was worth from the Cuban Colonel, an insult by forcing him to follow the three officers out of the room, and again he cursed the man.

Once outside the Colonel's office, Major Santana peeled off the group and went to carry out his regular duties on the base. He did not want to be involved with the boat or the Persian soldiers, because he did not like the foreign soldiers hanging around on Cuban soil. He was worried if the Americans discovered these Iranian fighters in Cuba, they might attack his Island like they attacked Afghanistan in search of terrorists against their country.

The four officers headed for the dock and they noticed the Lieutenant still busy working on the boat. Colonel Gonzales increased his pace heading for his officer. The Colonel marched up to the Lieutenant and he stopped what he was doing and snapped off a fine salute to the Army Colonel, who returned the salute as quickly. He walked onto the dock and started looking at the boat, and then he said. "Lieutenant Castillo Sir, what type of boat is this thing sir?"

"Colonel Gonzales Sir, it's a forty two foot Black Fin watercraft that's legally registered in the United States, sir. It's powered by a pair of five hundred and six cubic inch diesel engines, sir. It is equipped with two three hundred gallon fuel tanks, and a pair of one hundred and fifty gallon reserve tanks, sir. This much fuel is more than enough to get the watercraft to the shores of the Florida Keys, and it gives the Captain of the boat enough fuel to turn course and flee, in case any American Coast Guard ships happen to challenge the operator of the boat, Colonel. As you can see sir, we have a number of fishing poles stored on board the boat, and there's plenty of tackle stored on board her as well, Colonel Gonzales Sir." Again, the Naval Officer saluted his Commanding Officer, and then he waited for his reply.

"This is good Lieutenant Castillo, you have taken care of everything I wanted you to look after for this operation, sir. Outstanding work

Lieutenant Castillo. By the way Lieutenant, this man standing by my side is General Abdol Karim Kalantari, and he's here to learn more about this watercraft, sir. Then he shall employ it against our enemy from across the water, sir. I believe you already know Colonel Perez and Major Rodriguez, sir? Because is it not a fact you're married to Major Rodriguez's sister, Lieutenant Castillo Sir?"

"Yes I am and proud of it as well Colonel Gonzales Sir." The pleased Cuban Lieutenant replied as he also nodded towards his brother-in-law, and then he allowed a quick smile to cross his lips.

"Then I need not be forced to introduce you to my other Officers, sir. Lieutenant Castillo Sir, you know you were given to me to teach our Persian brother how this boat and all its electronics operate properly, sir. Before I allow General Kalantari to sail off in this dom boat, I want to make certain he knows how everything on board her works, sir." Colonel Gonzales nearly snapped at the Naval Officer as he held him in his harsh glare while waiting his reply.

"Yes Sir Colonel Gonzales, I was briefed before I left port with the boat, sir. I understand everything expected of me when it comes to the Persian fighters, sir. When do you want me to begin my training of our fellow brother in arms, Colonel Gonzales Sir?" The Lieutenant offered as he went to full attention before the other officer.

Colonel Gonzales turned to the Vulture standing by his side and asked him. "General Kalantari Sir, are you prepared to begin your training with the watercraft, sir?"

"Yes I am Colonel Gonzales Sir, but before I start with my training I wish to speak to my Colonel, and make certain he knows what I want my soldiers doing while I'm out on the water, Lieutenant." The Vulture replied as he stared at the young Cuban Officer.

"Very well Vul… err… General Kalantari you look after your troops and I shall speak with my Lieutenant further, sir. When you're done speaking to your next in command sir, you shall return to the dock and my Officer will take you out on your first training period with the boat, sir." Colonel Gonzales knew of the Persian's nickname, and he almost slipped by addressing him with it before he caught himself, and he might have insulted the foreigner with the slip of his tongue.

General Kalantari nodded at the Cuban Officer, and then he turned on his heels and headed for his soldiers beginning to muster before Colonel Khatami. The Vulture walked up to his second in command and placed his hand on his shoulder as he informed his officer. "Colonel Khatami Sir, you'll run our soldiers through their daily exercises and then order them to look after their weapons. I might make an inspection of their weapons and anyone whose weapon is not clean and in proper working order, will wish his mother never met his father. I shall be busy for a number of hours, and I'm leaving you're in command of our troops, sir. Have them eat, and if I'm not back by that time, have them police up their area and go over our target with them again, sir. I want our soldiers to know our target and be able to see it in their cursed sleep, sir."

Colonel Khatami went to a full attention stance and saluted his Commanding Officer as he replied in a confident tone. "General Kalantari Sir, you need not worry about our soldiers in your absence, sir. I'll look after them and I shall go over our target with them until it pours from their worthless ears, sir. You worry about your mission and I'll look after the soldiers, sir."

"I thank you for taking this much off my shoulders, Colonel Khatami Sir. I knew I chose the proper Officer to replace me when I'm picked to join the elite running our country, sir. I'll report to you once I completely my trip in this cursed boat they brought here for our use, sir. I see in the future we shall accomplish our mission as ordered for our country, and we'll return to the lands of our ancestors as conquering heroes for our cause, and be justly rewarded by Allah and our President, Colonel." The Vulture replied to his next in command, and then he turned and headed back for the dock without further words to his Colonel.

Colonel Khatami watched as his Commander rapidly walked away from his position, and then he turned his attention towards his soldiers standing in a sloppy formation, waiting while he spoke to their Commander. When he noticed the formation he bellowed at his soldiers. "What in the name of Allah do you cursed soldiers call what you're standing? We're faithful soldiers for Allah, and He must be embarrassed by this formation you adopted before me, fools. Sharpen those lines before I make each of you worthless fools work into the middle of the cursed night, for this failure to your proper duties."

General Kalantari rushed to the Cuban Colonel who dismissed the other two Army Officers who accompanied them to the dock, and now Colonel Gonzales was sitting on the back of the boat smoking another of his hated cigars. He was speaking calmly with the young Naval Lieutenant. General Kalantari stopped at the side of the boat and waited, because he did not know what to do next, and he did not want to overstep his bounds with the hated Cuban Officer in command of his soldiers, all the why his soldiers were in Cuba.

Colonel Gonzales stopped speaking to his Lieutenant when he noticed the foreign General standing by the boat, and he turned to the Persian Officer and snapped at him. "General Kalantari, I don't believe you'll not learn the workings of this boat by standing on the dock like a Cuban wife bidding her husband good-bye as he heads off for a hard day of fishing, sir. You may come aboard and my Lieutenant will be pleased to begin your training on this boat."

"Yes, of course Colonel Gonzales Sir, you're correct, sir. I need to be on board your boat to learn how to operate it properly, sir." The Vulture replied while trying to hide the anger rapidly building up within him, over the way the Cuban Officer insulted his intelligence in front of the Naval Officer who would soon be training him on the boat.

Carefully, the fuming Persian Commander and soon to be terrorist, climbed on board the boat and saluted the Cuban Colonel and his Lieutenant. Neither of the officers returned the salute as Colonel Gonzales offered the foreign General a drink of warm rum. He refrained from offering the Persian one of his cigars.

Colonel Gonzales waved his hand and he drew the Persian's attention to a second fighting chair planted in the deck of the boat, and the General moved over and seated himself in the wood and steel chair. The moment he was comfortable, the Cuban Lieutenant began speaking to him rather than his Commanding Officer. "General Kalantari Sir, Colonel Gonzales informed me he went over much of the boat's operation with you already, sir. He has further informed me he explained how the automatic helm worked, but I shall show you how it works, and how to get it working again if you run into any trouble with the machine while you are out on the water, sir. The automatic helm will be the most important item on the entire boat besides your soldiers, sir.

"If anything happens to it and you cannot get it working properly again, I'd say your mission is in serious danger, sir. The shallow waters surrounding most of the Florida Key chain are extremely traitorous at best, sir. They have claimed even the best trained Captains at one time or another. They ended up running aground on a reef and the American Coast Guard had to come to their aide, sir. For someone who is not very familiar with the waters and hidden reefs dotting the dangerous waters would be nothing short of lunacy to try and continue your approach of the Keys, if your automatic helm becomes disabled, General Kalantari Sir."

"That's a good point you offer, Lieutenant Castillo Sir. I thank you for this information sir. What shall I do if I discover the automatic helm has somehow become disabled, sir?" General Kalantari asked with concern lacing his tone as he smiled at the young man, already liking this soldier much better than he liked the Cuban Colonel.

"General Kalantari Sir, I anticipated about every possible problem you might suffer with your automatic helm while you're sailing for the United States, sir. I decided to take a second boat out the same time you and your fighters leave Cuba for your training on the boat, sir. I shall be on the water when you leave for the United States, sir. I'll shadow your boat in this second boat and if you run into trouble with your watercraft, all you have to do is get on channel seventeen on your radio, and announce you saw a whale with calf.

"If I hear this repot from you sir, I'll immediately close in on your boat and board and try and correct any problems with your helm, sir. If I can correct it, you'll continue on with your mission sir. If not, I'll take your soldiers on board my boat, and I'll leave one of my crew members on your boat, and he'll return it to Cuba where we shall correct the situation for your mission, sir." The Lieutenant returned the Persian's smile as he stopped speaking to see if the foreign officer had any questions about the helm.

General Kalantari noticeably let out his breath before the two Cuban Officers as he replied to the Lieutenant. "Errr… Lieutenant Castillo Sir, I don't mind to inform you that you took much fear from my foolish shoulders, by informing me you'll be on the water with me and my freedom fighters, and you'll shadow my watercraft with your own, sir. I'm very fearful of something happening to the cursed boat that I cannot correct, and it stops me from completing my mission for my country, Lieutenant Castillo Sir."

"That is another reason why I decided to shadow your boat until you're well on your way for the United States, General Kalantari Sir, and you're back in safer waters to travel upon sir. But another thing I must warn you of General, even though the automatic helm will be guiding your watercraft while you are out on the water sir, you must also maintain a constant watch of your depth finder sir, and if you see your boat heading for shadow waters, you must immediately take command of the helm of the boat and you must move the boat out to deeper waters, and once you're back in deep waters. You can then allow the automatic helm take back control of the boat again, sir.General Kalantari Sir, have you had any experience with the cruise control device of a civilian car, sir?"

"Yes, I am familiar with that type of device Lieutenant Castillo Sir. Why do you ask me of such a foolish question, sir? Even my worthless wife in Iran is familiar with the operation of a cruise control system of a car, sir." General Kalantari replied, a little confused by the Lieutenant's last question.

"I asked you this question General Kalantari Sir, so you can better understand how the automatic helm works, sir. You see General the automatic helm works much in the same way as does the cruise control device of a normal car, sir. By this I mean you can take control of the helm at any time you deem necessary, and once you placed your needed corrections on the boat, all you have to do is let go of the helm and it'll be controlled by the automatic helm again, General Kalantari Sir." The Cuban Lieutenant smiled at the Persian.

"I understand much better now Lieutenant, and I thank you for explaining this to me sir."

"I thank you for your attention in this matter, General Kalantari Sir. Shall we get started sir? Colonel Gonzales is going to be accompanying us on our first sailing trip, so he can witness how well you do commanding the boat, General." The Lieutenant offered as he also smiled at the smug looking Cuban Colonel enjoying his fine cigar.

"Yes, by all means Lieutenant Castillo, Sir. Shall we begin." The Vulture replied to the young man as he smiled at him again.

Even before they cast off the boat, the young Cuban Lieutenant showed the Persian Officer the proper way to moor the boat to the dock, and to also cast her off. He had the Iranian General try his hand at trying to shove off and then carefully guiding the boat a few yards from the dock, and then had him turn back and try and dock the boat properly. The first two times he tried to dock, he slammed into the dock, but the third time he tried, he lightly bumped into the peer and the Lieutenant watched as he secured the boat to the dock. Once the Lieutenant felt comfortable with the way the General commanded the boat, he took him on the water and into the Grand Bahamas Banks area where they entered the main shipping lanes, and then he allowed him to run the boat. The Lieutenant went over many things that could go wrong with the boat, and he had the General try to correct them.

The Lieutenant had to show the Persian Commander how to work through any possible problems he was suffering through. He shut down the automatic helm and went over some of the problems he could encounter with the device, while he and his Iranian fighters were heading for the coast of the United States. Most of the time, the Persian Officer was extremely sloppy and he showed he did not have much experience with commanding a boat, especially when the water turned a little rough on them.

After nearly five hours of being bounced around in the growing rough waters, the Cuban Lieutenant finally announced to the other officers he was going to have the Persian General head the boat back to their home port. Colonel Gonzales smiled at the Lieutenant because the Persian soldier seemed so out of sorts with trying to run the boat properly, but he allowed the Lieutenant to leave him to maintain control of the helm. All the way back to their home port, the concerned and attentive Cuban Lieutenant tried to show the Persian General the right way to hit a wave, so the boat took it much better. But the General was having so much trouble with trying to master the bow of the boat, and head it into the waves properly.

For some reason the Persian General wanted to take the wave with the side of the boat, which showered them with a heavy spray of salt water, and then bounced the boat around more roughly in the water than he headed right into the wave with the bow of the boat to take the water better. By the time the military base came back in view, the General was beginning to finally master the proper way to meet a wave and also control of the boat at the same time. Twice while they were out, he actually got a little sick to his stomach, and once he even heaved over the side of the boat, because of the rough waters of the Grand Bahamas Bank and the bouncing back and forth in the boat. Once they got closer to Cuba's coast, the waters calmed down, but a new problem suddenly faced the General at this point.

General Kalantari found himself being forced to give way to a number of smaller fishing boats almost constantly cutting across his beam, and once he actually tapped one of the smaller boats which immediately brought a flood of curses aimed at him, and a dead fish flung at his boat from the extremely angry Cuban Captain of the other fishing boat. The two officers laughed at the Persian because he did not know how to respond.

Lieutenant Castillo allowed General Kalantari who was thoroughly exhausted, to dock the boat at the peer. He offered him no help or advice, and the Lieutenant was surprised at how well the Persian docked up to the peer, and then he tied off the boat by himself correctly.

Once they were on dry land, General Kalantari let out his breath as he said to the grinning Colonel. "Sir, I believe I shall allow myself to have a glass of your rum sir.

ON THE TINY ISLAND OF MARATHON IN THE FLORIDA KEYS. SUNDAY, APRIL 22nd, 2006

Captain Robert Walker, along with Sergeant Dorothy Ramirez and Lieutenant Frank Hall and his girlfriend, Sergeant Regina Raphael, were waiting at the Marathon Airport for Tee K's plane to land. It was nine thirty a.m. and Ramirez had the three other soldiers out of the house since seven a.m., and they were waiting for the country singer to arrive on the Island. Toby's private plane was not scheduled to arrive until ten a.m., but the time did not matter to her in the least. She wanted to be at the airport when he and his family arrived on the Island.

No Neck, Sergeant Robert Abbott, and Buckethead, Sergeant Vincent Lambardo was waiting at Walker's place for them to return with the singer and his family. Ramirez ordered the two to remain at her place, because she feared the massive men might scare Toby's wife and daughters by their mere presence, they were so large. The two soldiers did not mind remaining behind, because they were not thrilled having this guy coming to their Island and interrupting their usual way of life and fun.

The Mutt was in a pissy mood, this was because Regina had him dress in long pants and a collar shirt, and this was the first time he was dressed like this on the Island since the last time the soldiers were placed on extended leave from the military service. The Mutt was in leather shoes and socks rather than his usual sandals, and this was bugging the devil out of him. All the while he was dressing, he bitched at his lady maybe he should be in a suit and tie, and when she agreed with his gripe, he snapped at her angrily. "No way in hell and I gonna be dressed in a stinking suit for this lousy dude, lady. The only time I'm gonna be dressed in a suit is when I'm laid out to be buried, girl."

Regina and Ramirez ignored their boyfriend's lousy moods as they watched and grew more excited with each plane that landed on the narrow runway. From where they were standing in the small airport terminal, they had a clear vision of the only runway of the airport. Regina was getting as excited as Ramirez was now, even though she did not really like country music.

Walker wanted to go outside and grab a smoke, but Ramirez refused to allow him out of her sight for fear of him and the Mutt taking off on them, and not returning until after Toby was at their home. She warned Walker if he tried to take off on her, she would skin him alive.

The Mutt leaned over to Walker and whispered to him. "What the fuck are we doing standing here like a pair of flaming assholes waiting for some stinking royalty to arrive, man? Let me tell you Walker, if you can't eat it, drink it, fuck it, or fire it. I'm not interested in it, and believe me, man. I'm not the least bit interested in this fucking pissant coming here and fucking things up between us and our girls, man. I thought Malice in Wonderland over there was more grown up than she's acting here, man. Since when does Raz get this excited over some stinking stiff dick just because he can sing a little, man? You betta have a stinking talk with your lady and bring her back down to earth, before she goes soaring off with the clouds, man."

"You love showing off that fucking fifth grade education of yours, man. If you're so damn hot at Raz then bitch to her about standing here like a set of twinkies, buddy. I'm not gonna lose my stinking dick because you can't hack a little discomfort for your lady, man. But I like the Malice in Wonderland thing though, and I'm gonna tell her what you called her, man." He warned his extremely uncomfortable looking friend as they looked at the two girls to see if they were listening to their gripes.

"Hey man be fucking cool, I don't want her that pissed at my stinking ass, man." He complained at Walker as he tried his best to get relaxed while they continued to wait for this dude to arrive on their Island, so they could go home and get comfortable again.

Ramirez looked over her shoulder at the two soldiers standing behind her. She was listening to them complain since they arrived at the airport, and she felt she had to say something to calm them down a little, and she snapped at Walker in a hot tone. "Hey boys, if I had a dick, this is where I'd tell you to suck it. You better not embarrass me when Toby and his family arrive, or the two of you birds will pay dearly for your mistakes. Be still and shut up, dammit!"

Regina also leaned her head back and she bitched at the Mutt. "Yeah!" And that was all she said to her lover, but it was enough to calm him down, and the Mutt fired back at his lady. "Hey girl, you're being very naughty girl, go to my room."

"If you don't behave yourself a little better, you'll go to your room, and you'll go to it all by yourself, and you'll also be sleeping in your room by yourself for a full week if you keep all this complaining, mista. Now do as Raz just told you and be still and quiet or else, mista. Neither one of us ladies are joking with you two he men" Regina snapped angrily at the Mutt as she replied to the little zinger he just aimed at her.

The Mutt coughed and grumbled at Walker. "Hey man, it's so fucking dry in this damn place I think I'm gonna cough up a stinking hair ball. I need this shit like I need an infection in my scrotum, man. I wanna get the hell outta here right now buddy."

"Didn't I just tell you two birds to cut out the stinking bitching and clowning around?" Ramirez snapped as she again turned her head and glared at the two elite soldiers who just smiled back at her. Then the Mutt made like he was masturbating when Ramirez turned her head to look back out the viewing window of the terminal.

"Hey stupid…" Walker started to complaint, but he was cut off by the Mutt who said with a straight face. "C'mon man, you don't gotta try and butter me up any, buddy."

Walker laughed at his friend as he finished with his though. "I'd like to see you do that shit to Raz's face and live to talk about it, man. You know what she'd do to your body if she ever caught that last action of yours, man. Talk about being skinned a fucking live man. Sheesh."

"Fuck you man…" Now it was Walker's turn to interrupt the Mutt's response as he added. "Always with the big words stupid. Say that to Raz and see what happens to you and then…"

"I'm not going to tell you two fools again, dammit. I told you two birds to knock it off or else, so knock it off will you please." She warned them again in an extremely nasty tone, and she did not bother to turn and face the two men this time.

"Ahhhh… Raz, you're just a stinking breast of fresh air today you know girl."

She turned and glared at the Mutt who shot her a wide grin for fear he might have pushed her a bit too far with his constant complaining since they arrived at the airport. But before she could respond to the Mutt's last words, Regina bitched at him this time. "You get your backside over here by my side and stop your complaining, or I'm going to put the shock paddles on you again, mista. We told you two birds enough, and it's enough already. It's a nice day so why don't you two try and enjoy it a little will you please."

"Nicely said sister." Ramirez said as she and Regina slapped hands together, and then the both of them shot another warning glared at the two men standing behind them.

The Mutt moved up until he was standing by Regina's left side, and he smiled at her as he offered. "Yeah baby, it is a beautiful day out at that honey. The stinking birds are out in force, and the bees are trying to have sex with them, honey."

Regina looked at the Mutt and shook her head, but she refused to laugh at his last comment.

It was starting to get late and Ramirez was getting more and more excited as it neared ten in the morning, and she started to get up on her toes as she tried to locate Toby's plane in the sky. Walker remained standing behind her and he smiled as he caught her actions, and he also looked at the Mutt and thought now he knew who wore the pants in his family, as the Mutt stopped his complaining and stood by his girlfriend's side and was quiet for a change.

Finally, she noticed a small leer jet lining itself up to land on the runway of the airport, and when she noticed the large blue strip painted on both sides of the private plane, she announced to the other three people with her. "There's his plane, the one coming in from the West. I see the blue strip painted on it. Robert, remember Toby's going to be with his wife and children, and I want you to be at your best and behave yourself and watch your mouth, mister."

"Yeah yeah baby, I won't fricking embarrass your ass before your new boyfriend, honey."

"Again with the new boyfriend shit I see Mr. Walker. If you're not more careful, I might make love to him right before your eyes Mister Wiseguy, and then we'll see if you have any more smart ass remarks to bug me with." Ramirez snapped back at Walker.

"Oh good, and can I sell tickets to the event if you do him good and proper on the floor in front of us, Raz? I gotta make myself some money somehow around here little sister, and a hot sex show from you would net me big time, girl." The Mutt offered while getting his two cents in the conversation going on between Walker and Ramirez.

"Oh no, another Jerk Benny heard from I see. You would sell tickets to my making love to anyone, mister. Behave yourself Mr. Mutt before you get me angry. Can't you stand there and be good for once in your life, mister?" She warned him hotly this time.

The four Tier One no fail soldiers stopped speaking and Ramirez moved over to the pair of wide glass doors that allowed the people from the plane to enter the terminal, and she waited at the opening until she saw a beautiful young lady followed by three little girls. One was so young she was being carried by a child care worker. Two men followed them off the private plane, and then a third man walked off the plane and she immediately recognized him as the country singer, and she announced to the others. "There he is and I want everyone on their best behavior from now on. The woman from the plane has to be his wife, so I don't want any cursing and telling dirty jokes in front of her." She added to her warning against the Mutt and Walker by glaring harshly at each of them for a quick moment.

"Yeah yeah I read ya loud and clear Raz. Man, are you being a hard nose for this stinking dude, little sister." The Mutt complained at her, but she ignored his words as she continued to stare at Toby as he escorted his wife and children to the airport terminal, and they were followed by everyone else riding on the plane with them.

Walker made his way to the Mutt's side and the dog man bitched at him as he leaned over and spoke so only he could hear his words. "Man, I hope this stinking dude's worth all the fucking hubbub Raz is making us jump through for his stinking ass, Walker."

"Relax, this shit will be over before you know it man. You grab the wife's luggage and I'll carry the singer's crap. We'll lug it over to the damn car and then we'll dump them in it, and drive the lousy prick and the rest of his entourage to wherever the hell he's gonna be staying while they're on the Island, and then we'll be rid of the lousy dude, man." He warned the Mutt as they moved forward and grabbed the luggage after shaking hands with everyone they were introduced to. He rushed everyone who could fit in his car to it, and shoved the luggage in the back of his SUV and everyone piled into the car. It was crowded but yet still comfortable and Walker barked at the singer. "Where to Tee K?"

"We have a number of rooms reserved at the Marathon Hilton Robert, and they're expecting us today, my friend." He replied as he looked around his daughter sitting on his lap in order to see Walker's face in the rear view mirror of the car as he spoke to him.

"That's fine with me, hang on and I'll get you there safe and sound man." He put the car in gear and pulled into the flow of traffic, but he did not go three blocks before a police car pulled up behind him with his lights and siren screaming and scaring the girls in the car.

The Mutt, who was riding in the front passenger's seat with Walker, leaned over and mumbled at him as he continued to drive the car like the cop was not riding behind him. "Hey man this one could amount to our first non alcoholic arrest, buddy. What the hell did you do to upset the stinking cop this much, man? I looked in the rear view mirror and this cop looks like he's really pissed off at you, man. Are you gonna stop or what for the lousy prick, pal?"

"I didn't do nuthin to bug his stinking ass man, and that's why I'm not pulling over for the prick, buddy. I think he's staying behind us because the uther cars have him hemmed in behind us, pal. But if he doesn't pass us soon, I'm gonna hafta pull over and see what the prick wants from us man." Walker replied as he continued to drive the car.

As he said the words, the police car suddenly pulled out from behind him, and then it went shooting down the road at a high rate of speed, and Ramirez breathed out a sigh of relief. She was scared he might have cut the police officer off and he took exception over it.

The Mutt continued speaking to Walker just above a whisper as he drove the car over the Vaca Cut Bridge and then headed for the Hilton hotel. "Hey Walker, I gotta talk to ya, man. I think I'm having a little trouble lately and I don't know what to do about it man."

Walker turned serious because anytime the Mutt started speaking like he was serious he paid attention as he asked his friend. "What's your problem man? You know you can come to me with any problems and I'll help you through them man."

"Thanks a shit load man, this one is really getting to me. Lately, I think I'm becoming allergic to women." The Mutt offered to Walker with a straight face and sharp look in his eyes.

"Are you fucking with me buster? If you are, I'll rip you a new asshole for this one, buddy." He warned his friend while trying to keep his voice low so no one heard his anger.

"No way in hell man, I'm being as serious as a heart attack with ya, buddy." The Mutt replied as he continued to keep a straight face and looked at Walker.

"Okay man, what the hell do you mean you think you're becoming allergic to women?" He growled while keeping his tone serious.

"Lately Walker, anytime I walk passed by a woman, I always seem to break out with a hardon man." The Mutt could not take it any longer and he broke out with a large grin.

Captain Walker took his eyes off the road and glared at his friend as he growled barely over a strained whisper at him. "When we get these damn people to where they're going, I'm gonna have a little chitchat with you in private, buster. I hope you have your hospitalization paid up buddy? You're gonna need it by the time I'm done with your butt, wiseass. You know we're supposed to be cool when we're with these damn people, you little prick you. I hate when you do this damn shit to me man."

Ramirez was trying to listen to the Mutt and Walker's conversation, to make certain there was not something wrong with either of them, and when she heard what the Mutt said to Walker, she reached up and swatted the Mutt on the back of the head.

The Mutt rubbed the side of his head and then he turned around and when he saw the terrible look she was giving him, he turned back around and hunched his shoulders up. Now he knew he was going to hear an ear full from her when they returned home later on.

The Captain was steaming at the Mutt as he pulled the car in the parking lot of the hotel, and everyone quickly piled out. As Ramirez passed the Mutt, she gave him a swift kick in his leg, and the Mutt moved a little further away from her and tried to hide behind Walker, who wanted nothing to do with him as everyone walked into the hotel lobby. Walker looked at his friend, and then he snarled at him when they were alone outside the place.

"Hey man, don't go and fucking try and hide behind my stinking ass, buster. You hadta keep pushing it for all it was worth, and now you got Raz pissed off at ya stinking ass, man." He smirked as he removed the luggage, but someone from the hotel came rushing out of the building and took over this chore for him. So he and the Mutt entered the hotel lobby area and headed for the others standing by the main desk.

CHAPTER EIGHTEEN

The Mutt, Lieutenant Frank Hall stayed well away from Sergeant Dorothy Ramirez, and now he was trying to hide behind Blind Date Sergeant Regina Raphael. When the room keys were given out to the singer and his group, Toby spoke with Walker before heading for his room.

"Say Robert, how about we go out for supper once we're settled in the rooms? I'd like to take everyone to Annette's and have a good meal and pay for it, and after we eat maybe we can head to Dockside for some drinks and relaxing. That's why I made certain I came to the Island on a Sunday, Robert. I wanted to see the Rocket and maybe have a little fun at the bar he's always hanging around at, sir." He offered with questioning eyes as he stared at Walker for the moment.

"Yeah sure why the hell not buddy. Once you're comfortable and you wanna head out for the night, just give me a call and we'll meet you at Annette's restaurant. Then we'll head over to Dockside for some real fun, man. Hell man, I sure could use tying one on myself Tee K. Raz was driving me absolutely crazy with you coming back to the damn Island for the last three weeks man. She had me up since three this morning to get her over to the damn airport to pick you people up, buddy." Walker complained as he glanced back at Ramirez and noticed she was busy speaking to his wife, Brenda.

"That's fine Robert and I'll call you after we're all settled in." Toby put out his hand and Walker shook it, and he then turned and said to Ramirez in a pleasant tone. "C'mon honey, we gotta leave these people and give them some time to get settled in their rooms, baby. We're going out for supper tonight when he's is ready to go, honey."

Ramirez moved over to Walker's side and she leaned against his rock hard body and took his hand in hers and held on to it for dear life. She was so pleased at how well it went for the first time they met Toby's wife and daughters. She was afraid Walker or the Mutt was going to curse in front of them, or tell one of their off color jokes and embarrass her and his wife. But it never happened. The two soldiers were perfect gentlemen all the while they were with the others from his entourage.

Walker and the others left the hotel and headed back for their homes. He dropped the Mutt and Regina off at their place and then headed home. Ramirez was so excited she was playing with Walker's member as he drove the car home. When they pulled into their driveway, both Neck Sergeant Robert Abbott and Buckethead, Sergeant Vincent Lombardo was standing outside waiting for them to return home. He got out of the car first and the two men immediately closed in on him. Ramirez walked around the car and then she joined the three soldiers and they headed for the backyard.

Walker proudly announced to the other three soldiers they were going out for supper with the visitors to the Island, which prompted Buckethead to complain at the Captain. "Hey man, I hate to burst your stinking bubble like this man. But Neck and me set up some dates with two hens we met on the stinking Island a few months ago, man. And, if you think for one moment we're gonna give up some hot dates like these two hens are, just to sit down with some stinking singer, and I hate that fucking country shit and his wife and kids, you got another fucking think coming to ya, man. We been after these two fine looking chicks for the past three months now, and we wore them down enuf and they finally agreed to go out with us tonight, man. You gotta let us miss this one, you gotta buddy."

Ramirez did not want to admit it, but she was pleased the two large soldiers wanted to go out on their own with their dates, instead of hanging around with them and the others tonight. She knew she could control Walker and the Mutt easy enough, but these two were not afraid of anything, and she could not use the threat of cutting off sex to control them. So she saw a way out of leaving them behind without insulting them, as she calmly offered to the massive Buckethead doing all the talking for the both of them.

"Gees Vinny, don't tell me you've been able to talk that pretty little blonde chick into going out with you tonight, mister? Does she know what she's getting herself in for by going out on a date with you, buster? From what I remember of her, she's gorgeous and you're lucky if you're going out with her tonight. I don't know the girl Neck has his evil eyes leveled on though, big man." She smiled at the massive man.

"You mean you don't mind we're not gonna be tagging along with you two birds and the others Dingoes' tonight, little sister? I thought you were going to skin us alive over our not wanting to hang with you guys tonight." Buckethead replied as he placed a huge grin on his lips.

"Not in the least Vinny, if you have a date set up, I won't stand in your way to enjoy yourselves tonight, sweetheart." She purred as she stared at the big man to make certain he did not see through what she was trying to do on him.

"Gee thanks a helluva lot for understanding us like this, Raz. You see stupid, I told you this gal would understand what we were up to tonight, and she wouldn't beat the hell out of us for not wanting to go out with them tonight. She's the coolest chick I fucking know around here, man." Buckethead complained as he turned and looked at the equally as large Neck, who was already grinning from ear to ear in anticipation of their upcoming dates.

Walker smiled, because he knew why Ramirez was being so understanding with the other two soldiers. Usually, if she set up something and wanted everyone with her for the night, the only way anyone would get out of it was by dying. He saw the two men breathing easier after Ramirez said it was okay for them to go out on their dates with the girls.

The meal was great, and the two female soldiers enjoyed speaking to Brenda and getting to know her a little better. Toby left his daughters at the hotel with their babysitter for day, so the night was theirs to enjoy any way they wanted. Once they finished eating the group headed to the Dockside bar to finish off their night of enjoyment. Walker, the Mutt and Toby drank beers from red plastic cups in honor of one of the singer's songs, while the girls enjoyed cool glasses of wine, and the two bands busy playing for the patrons crowding the bar. Walker introduced Rocket man to Tee K's wife when he came strolling over to their table, but she already knew the man but did not bother to inform Walker of the fact though.

Rocket man said hello to Brenda and he immediately tried to get Toby to belt out a few songs with the band entertaining the patrons of the bar, but the singer did not want to leave his wife and friends. Rocket man kind of shrugged and then he turned and headed off for the stage. Once he was there he took over the mike and started singing one of Jimmy Buffets terribly boring songs, and in the middle of it Rocket stopped singing, and he bellowed out for all at the bar to hear. "Hey girls, show me your tits."

Four other women at the bar immediately flashed Rocket man and band then he started singing again. Ramirez kept an eye glued on Brenda, and when she watched the other women flash the band members, Brenda turned red and she looked away from the other women. Ramirez smile slightly when Toby leaned over and whispered something in his wife's ear, and that seemed to settle her down and she acted like she was enjoying herself again.

Ramirez was pleased to see how much Toby loved and respected his wife, and now she was sorry she ever allowed them to come down to Dockside. Toby was embarrassed for his wife, because he did not warn her in advance of the call Rocket man usually yelled out every now and then, to liven up the place a little and any women visiting the bar. Soon, everyone seemed to have forgotten about the flashing thing and they started speaking about their upcoming fishing trip. When Toby noticed the band stop playing, he motioned Rocket over to his table, and then he whispered for him to stop the band from wrapping up their instruments. Toby stood and announced to the others he was going to sing a special song for his wife, and he headed for the stage and exhausted band members.

Rocket was pleased Toby was going to sing for bar and he started telling everyone about the special treat they were going to enjoy, and when he made it to the stage, Rocket man moved away from the mike and picked up his guitar and began to prepare to play as he sang his song.

Toby smiled lovingly at his wife while he was on the stage, and he sang her favorite song and when he was done, he returned to their table and he kissed her tenderly on her forehead.

Walker knew he was making up to his wife for the other women for embarrassing her by flashing at Rocket man and his band.

Ramirez was exhausted from her exciting day, and when she yawned, Walker took notice and he offered to the people seated at his table. "Well guys, I think I had it for the stinking day. I believe I'm heading home with my pretty lady here and turning in for the night. You know what they say, tomorrow's another day. Do you have any plans for tomorrow, Tee K?"

"I believe my lady has something scheduled for us to do as a family, Robert. But once we're done with our business, I'll let you know and maybe we can do something a little later on if you and your lady wants to." He offered as he looked at Ramirez to see if she agreed.

Again, Ramirez got excited by the thought of spending even more time with Toby and his lovely wife, but her excitement quickly faded and her exhaustion took over her body and she slumped a little. She was standing with Walker, but leaning against him because she feared she might fall asleep while standing on her feet.

Walker felt Ramirez leaning on his side and he knew she was done for the night, and he continued speaking to Tee K. "That'd be real cool with me man, but I gotta go before I lose my lady, and I'll be forced to carry her to the car and pour her into bed tonight, my friend. I'll call you later on in the day man, and if you're not home then you call me when you get back, and we'll see where it goes from there I guess, man."

"Yes Robert, I noticed your lady having some trouble keeping her eyes opened. I guess you better get her home before you lose her at that. My lady looks like she has had it as well. I'll call you when we finish with what we have planned for tomorrow, and then we'll go from there. It has been real great seeing you people again, and I'm looking forward to spending more time with you and your friends, Robert. By the way, I've been meaning to ask you if you and your soldiers had anything to do with what happened at the Indian Point Nuclear Power Plant up there in New York State, sir." He put out his hand and the two men shook hands.

"I'm afraid I don't know what you're talking about, friend. Something happened to one of our nuclear power plants? I'll have to look into it and see what I can find out about it. But I can tell you this much about it, none of my stinking people were involved in anything like what you're asking, friend." He put a look on his face that informed Toby he did not want to talk about it.

The Mutt stepped up to get Tee K off the subject of the attack against the power plant with Walker, and he put out his hand and shook with the singer. Then everyone started to leave the bar. The group left as a whole, but they broke up outside the bar and headed for their cars.

As usual, the Mutt was bringing up the rear for Walker, and Regina was still revved up and looking to party further. The Mutt went to his car after telling Walker he would call him in the morning. It was the Mutt's turn to pay for their night out and he did before they left the bar over Toby and his wife's objections. The Mutt and Walker left with Tee K warning them the next time out was on him, and he was not going to take any arguments from them.

Walker drove home even though he was as high as a kite, but Ramirez was also feeling pretty good from the wine she drank and besides, she was too tired to drive home. He pulled up to the house and helped her out of the car and led her to the house. The babysitter opened the door and Walker gave her thirty dollars for the night's work, and she left as he was now almost carrying the exhausted Ramirez in his arms. He dropped her softly on the couch and checked on Robert Jr. and found him sleeping comfortably. He then returned to their living room and started undressing his lady and when she was naked, he started playing with her breasts. In no time and as tired as she was, her motor was running on full forward and they made love right on the floor. When they were finished, Walker remained lying on the floor with Ramirez resting her head on his outstretched arm, and he had his last cigarette for the night.

They were looking outside the sliding glass doors at the star filled sky and loving the sight, especially when a cloud crossed over the three quarter moon, and it caused the moon to take on an eerie sight. He could not help it and found himself remembering the story of Sleepy Hollow and the headless horseman. He always thought of that story whenever he saw the sky like it was on this night. He stifled a yawn and Ramirez asked him in almost a purr. "A penny for your thoughts, lover?"

"Huh? Oh, I was kinda thinking about Tee K and his wife, honey. I like them baby, and I'm happy we made friends with them. I think they're good people, honey."

"Me too Bobby, and they are good people. You're not jealous I made such a fuss about them returning to the Island today, are you Bobby?" She asked him in a serious tone.

"C'mon will ya, no way in hell am I upset with you, baby. I love it when you make such a thing out of our friends paying us a visit on the Island. Besides honey, that's the way you are, and I wouldn't change one thing about you, lover." He offered as he closed his arm and brought his lady's head close to his chest and he hugged and kissed her lightly on the forehead.

"Mmmmmm…I love it when you're like this Bobby. I wish our friends could see you when you're like this, instead of barking all the time because you're in command of them, my love. I can't believe you're so strong, and yet so loving and caring and soft a man, mister." She purred in a dreamy voice as she kissed her lover on his arm and then hugged his arm to her chest. They ended up sleeping on the floor for the rest of the night, and Ramirez got up the following morning when she heard her son stirring, and she got him up and prepared him for school. Before she when after her son, she covered her naked and still sleeping soldier, so their son did not see him like that. She smiled, because she knew neither Walker nor herself ever tried to hide their bodies from their son. She wanted him to be comfortable with his own body, and the only way she knew how to make him so, was to show him his parents were comfortable with their bodies and each other.

When she got their son off to school, she undressed and snuggled back up to Walker's warm body on the floor, and she went back to sleep. He had no charters setup for this day, so he had it off and she decided she was going to spend the entire day with her man. They slept on the floor until nine thirty when Walker was woken by a noise from the kitchen, and he got up to see what was going on. He noticed Ramirez was still lying on the floor, so he knew it was not her fooling around in the kitchen, and his defensive senses were on full alert, and he was ready to act against anyone who was foolish enough to enter his home uninvited.

Walker entered the kitchen like he was going to kill the world, and when he noticed the Mutt helping himself to a cup of coffee, he relaxed and bitched angrily at him. "What the fuck are you doing man? Don't you sleep any more, you fucking asshole you? You scared the living shit outta my stinking ass, buster. I should hop you in the ass for waking me, bubby."

"Sorrrrry man, but you know how much I hate those moments of death you people call sleeping. Besides, Regina had to shove off for work and I was bored to death. So I came here to see what you people were doing. You betta get something on before you hurt yourself, man." He replied as he made notice Walker was naked and looking for trouble at the same time, which placed him at a severe disadvantage.

"Fuck you you asshole you, pour me a cup of lifer's juice. How come you ain't out working yourself, buster?" He snarled at the Mutt as he took the coffee and took a sip as he continued to glare at his friend. He did not mind in the least the Mutt would walk into their home anytime he pleased. If he did, he would have never showed the Mutt where the emergency key was to their front door. Besides, the Mutt had his own key to his place, and he had a key to the Mutt's.

"I told you before we were kinda slow down at the stinking shop, so I decided to take the fucking week off. So I can be with you guys and the pissant we were out with last night, Homes. Are we maybe going out fishing today, good buddy? I need something to do man." The Mutt asked as he flashed a quick smile at Walker.

"I don't think so buddy, I believe Raz has something she wants to look after today, and she made mention she wanted to spend some down time with me, man. Besides, it's too late to go out and have any luck fishing. I might clean up the tackle room and garage though buddy. You wanna maybe lend me a hand with the work? I could sure use some help if you don't mind, man? The both places are a fucking mess because of the all the stinking charters I've been having lately, buddy." He asked as he took another sip of coffee, and he lit up his first cigarette.

"Sure thing, I ain't got nuthin special to do today. I'll help you with the clean up in the…" The Mutt offered, but his words were cut off in mid-sentence by a sleepy sounding Ramirez, as she came stumbling into the kitchen to see who Walker was talking with so early in the morning.

"Mutt's helping you with what Bobby?" She asked as she rubbed her eyes with both hands.

"Man girl, you look hot enuf to eat even in the stinking morning while you're still half asleep, little sister. I love looking at your Casabas, girl." The Mutt offered as he drank in the lovely nakedness of his friend's girlfriend.

"I see you're horny as usually dog man. Why don't you bug Regina as much as you've been bugging me lately, stupid? I'm sure she'll love all the attention. Your game is getting a little lame if you ask me, mister." She grumbled in an exhausted voice at the Mutt as she took a deep breath to try and wake herself up some, but it did not help though.

"I was trying to get some loving this morning lady, but she did not want to have anything to do with me, girl. She was so busy getting ready for work I couldn't even get a hand full from her this morning, little sister. To be truthful with you girl, she told me to come over here and get some from you. I hope you wanna play around a little today, I wanna play with your Dos Chichies, girlfriend. I'm horny as hell baby." The Mutt said with a grin as he reached between his legs and began to rub himself.

"Well you're not going to get any loving here either, mister. It looks like you're shot down twice today, buster. Will you stop playing with yourself it's disgusting to see so early in the morning, mister. Is there any coffee left? I can sure use a cup to wake up a little." She asked as she crossed the room without thinking of her nakedness, and she checked the pot. There was enough coffee left for her to have a cup, so she poured it and added sugar and cream.

The Mutt reached out and gently cupped one of Ramirez's breasts and he began to roll it around in his sweaty hand. This caused her to bitch at him. "Tough luck dog man, you couldn't get my motor running this morning no matter what you try on me, mister. Stop that will ya please stupid! I'm not your personal sex toy you know, dog face."

"Man Raz, you're getting to be no fun any longer, girl." He moaned back at her.

"Huh and where have I heard that gripe before, dog man? You better change your tune if you ever expect to have any fun, buster." She fired right back at him.

"You heard it coming from me a few weeks ago when I was trying to get you to take care of us guys when we go on the boat when this prick got back to our Island, little sister." The Mutt responded to her bitch by reminding her of his past gripe at her.

"Well buster, it didn't work then and it's sure as hell not going to work today either, mister. I'm not up yet, and you're hitting on me like a dog in heat, buster. I'll tell you this much mister, the soldiers of our Unit branded you with the right tag name. I just told you to stop playing with my boob, didn't I mister? You better stop or I'm going to pop you in the eye with my fist, buster." She snapped as she leaned against the counter top and stared angrily at the grinning Mutt. But her angry look had no affect on the Mutt as he continued playing with her breast.

The Mutt gave her a quick once over and complimented again. "Man Raz, you look hot as always sister. I wish you'd tell Regina how you look so hot in the morning, girl. She's been slipping a little lately, and I find myself having to start her motor running before we have a little fun and games together, girl. Are you sure you don't wanna fool around some this morning, girl? I can sure use it and Walker won't care if we screw around you know."

"Flattery isn't going to help you out either mister. And stop drooling all over me like that mister, you're dripping your damn salvia in my coffee, stupid. Don't you have something you can do today besides looking at my body, mister? I thought you were supposed to help Bobby doing something in the garage dog man. Gees, you won't stop today will ya buster?" She growled at the Mutt as she pulled away from him now.

"Not when there's still a chance of me ripping off a piece of trim this morning, baby." He said as he moved over to get in front of Ramirez again.

"A piece of trim is it now buster? You wait until I tell Regina what you just said to me, buster. I believe after that, the only piece of trim you're going to be enjoying is when you trim the tree for Christmas, stupid." She complained as she set her cup down on the counter, and slapped the Mutt's hand away from her breast and she glared at the man until he backed off of her, and finished his coffee as he left her alone now.

"God dammit lady, why the hell are you beating me over the stinking head like this by threatening to tell Regina on me, girl? She knows when I screw up even before I know it lately, baby girl. You know if she gets pissed off at me, I'm only gonna turn up the heat on you until she makes love to me again, little sister." He grinned at Ramirez, because he knew she was not really angry at him, and she was only trying to bust his horns like he was trying to do to her on this fine morning.

"I guess you have a point at that mister. If Regina cuts you off then there's not going to be a woman on this entire Island who'll be safe until she gives in and makes love to you again, buster. Get over there with your partner in crime, at least Walker's behaving himself this morning, dog face." She griped as she made a motion with her hand for the Mutt to move away from her, and go and stand by his friend.

"Don't bet on it lady, I was kinda getting turned on watching the Mutt playing with your tits, honey." Walker warned Ramirez as he smirked at her.

"Oh brother give me a break please, don't tell me you were thinking of me taking care of you two fools this morning, Walker? I don't know if I'm in the right mood for that kind of action today, mister. Hell guys, you have to allow me to wake up before you want me to make love to the two of you. Besides, I have some things I want to do before I can even thing about playing some fun and game with the two of you birds. Walker, you told me last night you were going to clean the garage today. Are you going to work on it or what? If you do, I'll make lunch for you, and I'll serve it topless to you two, buster. We need to clean it up and today is as good a day to do it as any other, mister." She complained at the two grinning men.

"Yeah, I'm still gonna clean the damn garage, lady." He griped back at his love.

"Good, take this other pain in the ass with you and you can get the job done in half the time, Bobby. If the Mutt helps you cleaning the garage, I'll serve you two lunch and we'll see what happens after we eat. That's if you two birds might still interested in some fun and games a little later on, lover." Ramirez offered as she wiggled her chest and this caused her breasts to sway slightly before them and she smiled.

"Hey girl you got a stinking deal there. Is the garage all you wanted cleaned today, Raz? Hell girl, for some fun and games I'll clean the whole fucking place for you, little sister." The Mutt offered in an excited voice as he grinned at her and he continued to look at her slightly swaying breasts.

"Boy, you guys are so easy to get you to do what we ladies need done around the house. All I have to do is wiggle my tits a little and you two fools would be willing to kill for me. And, you guys think you fools rule the world do ya? In your wildest dreams you do. Now get out there and start work before I really get angry at you two birds." She tried to make herself look angry at them, but she failed miserably.

"Yeah, but do you mind if I get dressed before you send me off to work, lady?" Walker asked as he drew Ramirez's attention to his nakedness, and then he smiled at his lady again.

"If you have to, go ahead and when you're dressed, take this walking hormone with eyes out to the garage with you, so I can get dressed and get what I have to get done before Robert Jr. comes home from school, and I won't be able to get anything done then, Bobby." She replied as she stepped aside and allowed her lover to walk passed her. But she swatted Walker on his behind, and it sounded more like a gunshot going off than a slap, and it caused him to yell.

"Yeeeeoooowwww that hurt like hell girl. I bet it left a mark. I'm gonna get even with you for that one, sister." He complained as he rubbed the spot Ramirez smack him on.

"Oh you poor baby, did I hurt your itty bitty rump, mister? C'mere and I'll rub it for you."

"I got something right here you can rub alright if you want something to rub, little sister." He snapped at Ramirez as he continued to rub his backside.

"You're being awful nasty this morning you know Robert. Stop being such a cry baby and get dressed and get going with cleaning up the garage will you please, lover." She offered without giving him any sympathy whatsoever.

The Mutt laughed as Walker headed for the stairs and he remarked to Ramirez with a smirk. "Hey girl, if you wanna swat me on the rump like that, I promise not to cry out like the big jerk did, honey." He turned his backside towards Ramirez to give her an easy shot at it.

"I'm not going to smack you on the ass mister. You're labile to enjoy it too much buster." Ramirez smirked at him as she left the kitchen and went to get dressed upstairs.

The Mutt watched Ramirez leave and he shrugged, not knowing what to do next so he hung around the kitchen. Walker came downstairs and headed for the kitchen and he cast a glance at the Mutt and snapped at him. "Hey stupid, if you're hungry I think there's an opened can of stinking beer in the fridge you can drink, man."

He watched his friend finish off the beer, and then he announced. "C'mon screwball, let's get the damn garage cleaned before Raz comes down and really gets on our asses about it again. She's not in a good mood as I believe you can tell man?"

"Man, I never saw her in such a pissy mood as the one she's in today, man. You betta tickle her bottom so she lightens up a little on us man, or we're gonna hafta bury her ass standing up, buddy." The Mutt fired at Walker as he followed him out of the house.

"Funny, let's get to work friend." He led the Mutt to his garage and they began to tackle the clean up of the area. Walker did not realize how much of a mess the garage was in until he started to clean it. He misplaced tackle that belonged in his tackle room. He also found an old reel he wanted to repair on his desk covered with tools and wood.

It took the two of them three hours to get everything put back in its proper place. It was just after one in the afternoon when they were about finished, and true to her words. Ramirez strolled in the garage topless, and she was carrying two hamburgers a piece for the men. She set the tray on an overturned pail and stepped back and watched the two chow down the burgers like they haven't eaten in a week, and she smiled.

Once they ate, they did not attack Ramirez. Instead, Walker was so into cleaning he walked into the tackle room and almost fell over. It was in worse shape than his garage. The Mutt followed him in and moaned at his best friend.

"Holy shit man, what the hell happened in here Dude? Did we suffer a fucking earthquake I wasn't aware of buddy? What a fucking mess this place is in man? How the hell can you find anything hiding in here man? Shit and I thought my place was in a mess."

"I can't and that's why we're gonna do something about it right now, man." Walker replied in a snap as he got right to working on the cluttered room.

"Hey man, I wanna play around with Raz's Casabas first. Look at her standing behind us with her tits sticking out like that man." The Mutt complained as he cupped one of Ramirez's breasts.

"If you don't get your damn hands offa her stinking boobs buddy, I'm gonna cut your hands off on ya, and then I'm gonna stick them up your ass for you. C'mon buddy, we got some work to do here man." He growled at the Mutt, and then he glared at his friend until he left his girlfriend alone, and he started to help him cleaning up the mess.

By the time they finished cleaning the tackle room, neither one of them were very interested in any fun and games with Ramirez, as they entered the kitchen and got a cold beer. She also forgot about playing around with the guys, because she was so wrapped up in her own cleaning and looking after Robert Jr. since he came home from school. The next few days passed at a rapid pace for everyone, with the elite soldiers going out twice with the singer and his wife for supper, and also hitting the Dockside bar again.

CHAPTER NINETEEN

This was the day before Captain Robert Walker and the rest of his elite group of specialized soldiers on the Island was scheduled to go out on their fishing trip with the country singer, and he was looking for something to do to help pass this day away. He was so worked up with anticipation he attacked his boat. He worked on it even though they were not using his World Cat for their fishing trip tomorrow. He broke out the can of PB Blaster and rubbed down all the aluminum rails and tuna tower on the Cat, he also covered the hinges and locks on any doors, helping to protect them from pitting. Next he checked his tackle stored on the boat, and replenished items he was low on. He pulled out his fishing rods and reels on the World Cat and cleaned them down, and checked the line and replaced the line on two reels.

Once he was satisfied with the rods, he stowed the gear back in the boat. He next checked his electronic to make certain they were in proper working order. He used the radio and contacted a boat on the water to make sure it was working correctly. He busied himself cleaning the two live wells on the World Cat, and checked the well pumps and four bilge pumps, and then he checked and cleaned out the two fish storage wells in the main deck of the World Cat. They had fish scales from the last time he went fishing, and cursed himself for not cleaning them out properly.

He dropped the twin Honda two hundred twenty five horse power four stroke motors in the water, and ran them for a few moments. Then he lifted the motors out of the water and ran clean, fresh water in the lower ends to wash out the salt water, so they did not pit up on him. Then he checked out the life jackets and the rest of his survivor gear he had to have stored on board the World Cat for safety needs. Once he finished this, he checked on the four fire extinguishers to make certain they were fully charged and ready for use.

There was a good reason for his doing this house cleaning on his World Cat. He was planning to take Toby and his wife with Ramirez, the Mutt, and his girlfriend out to do a little diving, and some lazy fishing the next day after they went on the private charter the country singer reserved for their use. The Captain was thinking of a way to pay the singer back by taking them on a relaxing day on the water.

He was in a great mood, and he loved to clean his World Cat. His boat was the next love of his life after Dorothy Ramirez and their son. He climbed up the tuna tower and checked out the electronics of the second helm control center of the boat. Once he was finished, he leaned back on the protection rail and glanced towards the end of the canal and out to the open Ocean. It seemed like he could see forever on this morning, and he picked up a number of small boats obviously working over a weed line they discovered in the water, and he smiled as he watched the boats trolling along the weed line in search of bait fish, trying to use the weeds to hide from the larger game fish trailing them. He knew once the Captains found the bait fish, the game fish could not be too far off and they would start hitting their lines.

His pleasant thoughts were interrupted by Ramirez who came out of their home carrying two cups of coffee. She climbed on board the sleek World Cat and offered him a cup while she sipped her own. He looped his arm around her and enjoyed the coffee with his girlfriend.

"Boy Walker, you have the boat looking great, honey. What's up with you lover?" She asked as she looked down the canal to the open waters beyond.

"I think I'm gonna invite Tee K and his wife out diving with us, and maybe do some light fishing on Saturday morning, so we can sorta relax and maybe get to know them a little betta, baby. You know

Friday's fishing is gonna be everything but relaxing honey, and I wanna speak with them before they leave the stinking Island again, honey." He offered as he gave her tug, pulling her body closer to his.

"I think I'd really love that Bobby. I thank you for being so considerate with them, Robert." She purred as she looked over the work he done on the boat.

"Arrrr, it's no big deal baby, besides, I hafta stretch out the motors some anyway, lady. It's been over two weeks since the last time I used the engines." He replied while still trying to keep the mirror of his masculinity up in front of his girlfriend.

Ramirez went into a dream state and Walker gave her her space while she was daydreaming. But when she spoke, he was surprised. "Bobby I've been doing a lot of thinking lately, honey. I remember we were supposed to get married when we returned to the Island nearly two years ago, baby. But we've been so busy with everyone else's problems and wants, we never got around to getting married, mister. I think it might be a good idea to, you know, before Robert Jr. is old enough and he starts asking us those hard questions we can't answer." She stopped speaking and looked him dead in his eyes like she was wanted him to finish her thought. Then she rested her head against his, fearing she started a conversation her soldier did not want to deal with.

He was surprised because his lady never brought up this subject before now. He wanted to marry her, but for some reason he never got around to it. But since she brought up the subject, he decided to see what she truly had on her mind. He was getting a little worried that soon they were going to be called up for active duty, what with the way the Iraqi war was heating up again, and he wanted to be married before they were.

"You know lady I think that'd be a good idea." He offered to his girlfriend.

She pushed away from her lover, even though she did not realize it, tears were streaming down her cheeks as she looked at him with so much love locked in her eyes. She pulled his head close to hers and said barely over a whisper. "You really mean that my love?"

"C'mon lady, you know me betta than that, baby. I'd never hurt you that way, of course I mean it, honey. I want to marry you yesterday, baby." Captain Robert Walker replied tenderly as he kissed her on the tip of her nose, and then he smiled into her tear clouded eyes.

"Oh God, I can't believe this Robert. When are we going to do it Bobby? Ramirez asked as she was almost dancing on her tip toes and hugged him to her chest.

"Hell girl, if I had my way about it sister, I'd marry you tomorrow morning at the latest, honey." He proudly announced to Ramirez as he flashed her one of his best smiles.

"You really mean it this time, don't you Robert? You're not just saying you want to marry me. I can't tell you how many times I wanted to bring this subject up to you while we were on the Island on leave, Robert. But I could never find the right time and place to bring it up to your attention before now, honey. When do you want to tie the knot with me, my lover and soldier?" Ramirez asked him as she tried to keep her rapidly mounting excitement under control during their conversation.

"Like I just said baby, tomorrow morning wouldn't be soon enuf for my likes, baby girl. But you know we're going fishing with that stinking singing pissant tomorrow, so tomorrow is out I guess. I don't know lady, how soon can we get a priest and church and get her done right, girl?" He asked with concern, hoping she would tell him not to worry about the preparations. She would set everything up for them.

"I can't believe this Robert you want a priest and church to get married in. Robert, you made me the happiest girl in the ever loving world. We have a lot to setup for Robert, but I can get Regina to help me with all the particulars, honey. She's going to be my Maid of Honor, and she'd die if I didn't ask her for our wedding. We can get everything setup in a week or two. Hell, we can have Robert Jr. be the ring bearer. Oh God how I love you, mister!" She purred as she pulled his head to hers and she kissed him like he was never kissed before by her.

"Hey baby, I know where I can rent a stinking tux on the Island, and I'm gonna drag the stinking Mutt along with me for some soul support. He's gonna be my Best Man, and he's gonna need a damn tux too I guess, baby." He offered her as he pulled away from the breath robbing bear hug she had him locked up in.

"We have to go to the jewelry store and pick our rings. I want a matching pair so the world will know you belong to me, and I to you, Robert." She said as she let go of him now.

"I don't think so young lady." He replied as he smiled at his lady again.

"What do you mean by that remark, mister? Don't tell me you're changing your mind about marrying me already, Bobby." She questioned him as she got upset and found herself glaring at her lover now.

He let out his breath and snapped at his lover. "Give me a stinking break will ya honey. I didn't mean that. What I mean was I was trying to say you know I lost my mother and father in a car accident some ten years ago..."

"Yes, and I'm sorry about that Bobby. I would've loved to have met your parents, Robert."

"That's okay baby, they're with us all the time anyway, doll. Well honey, one of the things I got when they died was their wedding rings. I was wondering if you wouldn't mind getting married with them instead of us buying our own rings, honey. I'm hoping it'll keep their memory alive between us, and also with our son." He offered in a calm and tender voice.

"Oh, I'd love to get married with your parent's rings, Bobby. Where are they Robert? I haven't seen them since we got together. I want to see them please." Ramirez offered, feeling better now she knew what he was trying to tell her. She was touched by the lovely thought of them getting married with his parent's rings that she could not help it and she started to cry as she stared at her lover.

"I have them sitting in the top drawer of my desk. Wait and I'll get them so you can see them honey." He took off like a shot and rushed to his desk and removed a box, and then rushed back to her side and handed her the small box and waited for her to open it.

Her hands were shaking so much she had trouble opening the box, but when it opened she cried as she let out her breath. "Oh Robert, they're so beautiful, they're a matching set honey. Robert, I'd be honored to get married with your parent's rings my lover and soldier."

"No baby, it's me who is honored if we get married with my parent's rings, honey."

"Then we're both going to be honored, because I won't get married unless we use these rings after seeing them, Robert." She said as she shifted her eyes from the set of rings, and then she stared in her lover's eyes.

"Thanks honey, this means a helluva lot to me. You're being real cool about this baby. I always wanted to get married with my parent's rings. Well honey, it looks like we got this much settled between us. Are you gonna handle the rest of the stuff for the marriage deal, or do you want me to help ya with some of the stuff, honey?" He asked with caution and he started shifting his weight on his feet. He was dreading she was going to ask him to help her with the preparations for wedding.

"I know how you are when it comes to this kind of thing Robert, and if you think I'm going to ask you to help me with the stuff we have to setup for the wedding, you're sadly mistaken, mister. I hate to say this Robert, but I believe you'd be more of a hindrance than a help to me. You're safe and I'll have Regina help me with everything I have to look after, honey. All you and the Mutt have to worry about is getting your tuxes, mister. You know something Robert I was just hit by another thought. Wouldn't it be fantastic if Toby and his wife could be part of the wedding? I'd really love to have him standing by your side as we get married, honey." She purred happily as she did whenever she tried to get him to do something he did not want to do, and she was pulling out all the stops on him.

"C'mon and get a grip on yourself will ya, baby. Why the hell would he and his wife ever wanna be part of our stinking wedding for, sister? Yeah, he's a friend I guess okay, but I don't believe he's that much of a stinking friend that he and his wife would wanna do that much for us, honey. Look baby, after we're finally married, you can write him a stinking letter and invite him down to the Island for a quick visit, and we can have a little celebration with him and his wife if you wanna do it that way. No baby, I think it'd be much betta if we leave them out of this deal, and then we invite the people we want to come to our wedding." He offered with concern in his voice, hoping she would agree with him.

"Yes I guess you're right about this one, my lover. And yes, we have enough of our friends to invite to our wedding, without trying to include them in on it, honey. But I'll do what you suggested and I'll drop them a line afterwards, and I'll invite them back to the Island for a private little party with us. Err… I think we better not tell them we're planning to get married while they're on the Island though, honey. They might want to be invited and that might place us in a very uncomfortable position where we'd have to invite them, Robert."

"I can't argue with you there honey. You're swift and you know what you'll have to do with them, if word of our wedding came out. But I think you're acting smart with this decision you made, honey. You know if we told them we were getting married, they'd wanna be part of it just because they're trying to become close friends with us and we with them, baby. I think its much betta this way, and we'll tell them later on about us, honey. They might get mad at us, but I'd rather that then make them feel like we invited them for a stinking present or some fucking money, honey." Captain Walker shot her a warm smile.

Sergeant Ramirez nodded yes in response to his last words.

ON THE ISLAND OF CUBA, APRIL 26th, 2006. ALSO AT SIX THIRTY A.M.

General Abdol Karim Kalantari who was also known as the extremely dangerous and the perfect killing machine the Vulture, was screaming at his Persian fighters as they prepared for their last day on the Island of Cuba. Over the past week, the powerful Persian General became rather astute with running and caring for the boat they were going to use to get the group of terrorists into the United States. The Vulture was getting so comfortable with the operation of the boat that he was thinking about getting one for his private use when he returned to Iran, once they completed their mission to attack the United States.

General Kalantari kept a close eye on his soldiers as they properly stowed their gear on the boat, so it would be impossible for anyone searching the craft to find their equipment. He was standing on the dock watching his terrorists run all over the craft. Standing to his left was Colonel Felix Gonzales, who made certain he was on the military base before the Persian Officer and the rest of his soldiers left for their attack against America. Also standing on the dock with the Persian Commander was Lieutenant Miguel Castillo, who done a masterful job familiarizing the Iranian with the workings and electronics on board the rather large pleasure craft.

Lieutenant Castillo was standing by a large box he seemed to be actually guarding with his life, while it rested on the planks of the dock. The ever alert Vulture took close notice the Cuban soldiers assisting his troops with their tasks, were giving the wooden crate a wide birth. Now, he was giving the crate a lot of attention, in hopes of finding out if it was meant for him, or it was just a crate they had stored on the dock.

Colonel Gonzales leaned a little forward and he offered to the Persian Commander. "General Kalantari Sir, I believe between your soldiers and mine, they seem to have everything in hand with preparing the craft for sea duty, sir. It's early and I have not eaten as yet this morning, sir. What do you say to us having breakfast at the mess on the base together, sir? There, I shall give you your last minute instruction on how you shall guide your boat to the dom American coast, sir. Besides General Kalantari it's getting hot, and I want to get into the air-conditioning of the mess hall before it gets too warm today, sir."

"Yes Colonel Gonzales that seems like a good suggestion, because I too am hungry this morning Colonel, and I'm feeling the heat of the day already as well, sir. It's like you have just mentioned, sir. My lesser Officers seem to have everything moving along well for my mission. So I don't see any further necessity for my standing here watching them carry out their duty, and suffering with being uncomfortable any longer, Colonel. Shall we head to your mess and get something to eat for ourselves, and we can speak of any further instruction you might have for my worthless soldiers and myself, sir?" General Kalantari offered in a polite tone of voice to the Cuban Colonel, as he slightly nodded towards him.

"Please General Kalantari Sir, if you'd be so kind as to follow me, sir." Both officers from different military groups were trying their best to be polite with each other. Because they both understood soon, they shall not be forced to deal with the other.

"Yes Sir Colonel Gonzales, by all means sir." The Persian General replied just as kindly.

The two officers headed for the mess after placing their next in command caring for their troops. They walked in silence with each of them thinking about the upcoming mission.

The Cuban base was a beehive of activity. Military trucks dart in between soldiers hustling around to carry out their duties. More Cuban soldiers were exercising, or otherwise finding ways to look busy. There was a pair of armed military helicopters, up and patrolling not only the military base, but the civilian resort three miles away from the special base.

The Cuban Colonel and Persian General entered the mess hall like they owned the place, and they took over a large table for themselves. Any Cuban soldier within ear shot of the two officers, nervously got up and they quickly moved away from the higher ranking soldiers, to give them the privacy they needed to speak to one another. Instantly, a Cuban Private rushed over to the table and asked the Colonel what they wanted to eat.

Colonel Gonzales ordered breakfast for them, and when the Private left them, he began speaking to the Persian in private. "General Kalantari as you had already been informed sir. I have a number of Cuban sympathizers who entered the god dom United States during the last boat lift from my country to America, sir. They have been warned in advance of your soldiers entering the United States and how, and they have been instructed to assist your fighters in any manner possible, to assure you success on your mission sir. I have four sympathizers standing by on the Island of Marathon where you shall be docking your boat, sir. They're operating under my direct orders to help supply you and your proud soldiers with any vehicles needed to get your warriors up to the Miami area and your intended target, sir.

"These sympathizers are ordered to protect you and your Persian fighters on the Island until you leave for the mainland of the United States, sir. They're scheduled to linkup with you at the peer you shall dock the boat at, sir. But there has been a slight change in their orders though, sir. Originally the sympathizers were supposed to arm your soldiers with weapons for the operation, sir. But I decided they should not be operating on the Island and moving weapons around with them, sir. I was concerned about them being stopped by the local Deputies, and if they were found with weapons on their person, or inside their vehicles, it might place your entire mission in jeopardy, sir. This is the only change to the original plans we have discussed since you first entered my country, General Kalantari Sir."

"That was obviously a wise decision on your part, Colonel Gonzales. But that does create a rather interesting problem for myself and the rest of my freedom fighters, sir? If your four sympathizers no longer plan to arm my soldiers when we reach the Island of Marathon, where the devil am I supposed to locate the weapons and explosives I need for my operation's success, sir?" General Kalantari snapped at the Cuban soldier. He was angry there was a change in his orders so near where his terrorist cell was scheduled to go into operation, and he was unable to hide his mounting displeasure in his tone over this change in his orders.

"General Kalantari Sir, I can hear the anger lacing your voice at this time, and I fully understand why you're suddenly so upset, sir. I can assure you sir, it's unnecessary for you to be upset over the change in your original plan, sir. Be assured General Kalantari Sir, everything has been worked out to my complete satisfaction on how your Persian soldiers will get the weapons and explosives they shall need for this successful mission, sir." Colonel Gonzales offered in a smug tone of voice to the concerned Persian Officer.

"I'm pleased you're obviously satisfied with this minor change to my original orders, Colonel Gonzales. But I'm not very pleased until I discover how you intend to arm my soldiers in the field. I don't mind informing you Colonel, I'm greatly displeased to have my plans change so near to instigating them. Colonel, any possible changes to an operation so close to its beginning, usually spells terribly disaster for the soldiers involved in the mission." The Persian Commander said his words to the Colonel with a sharp snap in them.

"Yes General Kalantari Sir, I appreciate your concern to the change in your orders, sir. And, I understand your concern to have this change placed against you so near to the beginning of your mission, sir. But I assure you General Kalantari, the change to your plan is no concern, and you'll be pleased by the time you leave my Island, after understanding the changes, sir. Ahhh… here comes our breakfast, so I suggest you relax and enjoy your meal, sir. Once we have eaten, I shall bring you to the boat, and then show you how we corrected the change to your orders, sir."

The two officers stopped speaking the instant the Private approached their table carrying their meals. The Private placed the trays before each officer. All the while they ate, the officers engaged in talk but once Colonel Gonzales was done with his meal, he stood and announced to the Persian. "General Kalantari Sir, you may finish your meal sir, but I'm going to return to the dock and check on our soldier's progress, sir. I want to make certain they're looking after everything that has to be prepared for your trip to the United States, sir." The Cuban Officer allowed a smirk to cross his lips as he watched the Iranian try to stuff the rest of his meal into his mouth rapidly. The Persian General began to stand as he continued to shovel his food in his mouth, and then he wiped his hands and joined the Cuban.

As they headed for the dock and activity, the Colonel smiled because the General was still chewing his food. That was why he ate so fast, because he wanted to push the Persian and keep any pressure going for as long as possible. By the time they reached the dock and boat, the General finished chewing and he was trying to speak to the Cuban Commander, but the Colonel was more interested in what was going on at the dock than speaking to the Persian again.

Colonel Gonzales walked up to Lieutenant Castillo and gave him a sort of sarcastic smile, and the Naval Officer gave him a quick nod, and then he turned his attention to the soldiers still assisting the Persian troops with stowing their gear on board the boat. A large number of bottled water was being passed by one of his soldiers to one of the Iranian fighters on the boat, and the Persian quickly ran the bottles inside the cabin.

While they were standing on the dock, twice the two officers had to move out of the way of the other soldiers moving equipment around the dock, or they passed it to the Iranian's on the boat. It was almost sheer mayhem on the dock with officers screaming at soldiers, and the lesser soldiers scurrying off to carry out their latest orders. A number of civilians visiting the resort directly across the inlet from the military base, stopped enjoying themselves and they began to watch what the soldiers were doing in haste on the dock and boat.

Colonel Gonzales brought a pretty young woman who was topless up to the Persian's attention, and she stopped playing and was resting her hands on her hips in reply to his stare. General Kalantari stared at the stunningly beautiful young woman until she lost all interest in what the other soldiers were doing on the base, and she turned her back on him and went back to playing a game of volley ball with a number of her friends.

With all the frantic activity going on along the length of the wooden dock, General Kalantari had another chance to look around himself. He was looking for that one crate he was most interested in, before he and the Cuban went off for their morning breakfast. When he finally located it, he noticed it was moved further away from the boat, and now he felt the crate was not scheduled to go with him to the United States. Now the Persian Officer started to search what he could see of the boat and the dock area. He was looking for any possible weapons he could use during his mission. Try as he might, he could not locate any, so he figured they would somehow be armed once they entered the United States.

The Iranian General's concentration was interrupted when a Cuban soldier accidently bumped into him with a piece of equipment. The soldier immediately apologized to the General, and he moved out of his way so the other soldier could get by with the item he was carrying.

"I see if we're not more careful General Kalantari Sir, we might end up with getting ourselves hurt by standing here like this, sir." Colonel Felix Gonzales remarked in a sarcastic tone while still taking full advantage of every possibility of trying to get on the Iranian Officer's nerves.

General Kalantari was forced to turn his body to see the Cuban's eyes, and what he saw etched in them angered him to all ends. It was easy for him to recognize the smug look from the Cuban and he resented it. The Vulture was having trouble trying to keep his rampaging rage for this Cuban Officer under check. What he wanted to do was draw a sword against him, and force the Colonel to suffer the slow and painful death of a thousand cuts from the sword's edge.

Now it was Colonel Gonzales' turn to read the anger locked in the foreign General's blazing eyes, but he did not return anger for anger, or evil for evil. Instead, he allowed a grin to cross his lips as he continued to hold the Persian fool in his glaze. In his mind he felt he won a complete victory over this foreign invader to his Island Paradise. No matter the orders from his President, the Cuban Colonel could not hide his dislike for these Persian invaders, and he was no longer trying to act like he liked them.

General Kalantari was the first one to break the stare down as he turned his head and watched what his people were doing on the boat again. But under his breath he was raging as he called the Cuban Officer every foul word in his book. He found himself hating this man more than he hated the people living in the land he was going to attack.

The Persian's body was actually shaking from the anger raging in his body. Suddenly, he found someone he could vent this anger against. Sergeant Azamalaie Shirazi took a box from the Cuban helper and she dropped it. When the box hit the deck of the boat, it split open and its contents spilled out on the deck. Even though it was items he did not need for their operation, it was only fishing tackle, he roared at the female warrior.

"By the sacred gray beard of the great and all seeing Prophet Muhammad, Sergeant Shirazi, what the devil is wrong with your foul mind, you worthless woman I am forced to rely upon. How dare you allow yourself to destroy items we need for a successful mission, woman who has feasted upon sour mother's milk. How I have allowed myself to be talked into taking worthless women on such an important an operation as the one we are preparing for. I should have had my head examined before I agreed to allow any god cursed women to come on my mission.

"The Almighty Allah is too merciful, but you will find the exact opposite with me, woman. By the ten Prophets of Islam, I should have your foul body stripped naked, and then open your god cursed back with the bite of the lash, kelbeh. (Bitch) Ebn el Matanaka, (Son of a Bitch) Sergeant Shirazi, you'll pick up the god cursed items and you'll get them back in that box and have them stored properly on board the boat, before I act out against you, and I order a bag of hot ash tied to your worthless face as punishment for your failure.

"Defiled and lowly one, if you're not more careful about yourself and your actions. I shall leave your worthless being on this foul Island as a gift for our Cuban brothers to enjoy at their leisure. Once they're finished with your god cursed body, they'll ship what is left of you back to our country where our President will melt out your final punishment and fate for you to suffer, woman. Move like you have a purpose woman, or I shall carry out my threat against your worthless body, female. I have no room in my cell for anyone who is as clumsy as you are, woman who has been born from the arse of the filthy camel." General Kalantari was so angered by the Cuban's actions carried out against him. He was leaning over the dock and boat at the same time as he continued to roar at the female fighter.

General Kalantari turned his attention to Sergeant Bassam Abu Fallahi, the other soldier who was not an officer in his cell, and he barked. "Sergeant Fallahi, you'll lend the foolish lazy woman a hand and clean up all that is lying on the cursed deck of the foul boat and get it back inside its box. Or I shall order your back opened with the lash as well, Sergeant!"

The Vulture was so angry he was glaring at any of his warriors he laid eyes on. Just with his harsh glare, forced all the Persian soldiers to work harder, or find a way to get out of his sight. The female fighters were feeling his anger the most.

Colonel Gonzales was enjoying the fit of unprofessional rage he placed the Persian Commander in, and he was further enjoying how the Iranian General was taking his anger out on the rest of his soldiers. The Cuban found what he was looking for, the one weakness in the Iranian's strength, and now he believed he was a weak commander. The Cuban Officer was trained no matter what happened to him in his personal or military life, he was not to take any anger out on his troops for a poor cause. He was informed it was a sign of a weak commander, and it would lead to the loss of respect from the rest of his soldiers, if he ever committed what the Iranian Commander was currently doing to his troops.

Slowly, General Kalantari's rage began to subside, and he was finally able to get control of his actions. Even though he knew what he had done to his soldiers, especially his female warriors, no way was he going to apologize to them. Especially in front of the Cuban Colonel, or his hated troops. Besides, the Vulture always felt he was well beyond the need to apologize for anything he committed in his life. He was of the mind everything revolved around him now.

Colonel Gonzales noticed the Persian Officer calming down some and he decided to get off of him. He was worried about pushing him too far, and receiving a complaint from his President to President Castro, and then he gets pulled on the carpet for the disrespect he was aiming at the Iranian General. With a sigh of sheer disgust, the Cuban Officer moved a little nearer to the General, and he offered him in a much more pleasant tone.

"General Kalantari Sir, I believe while we were enjoying our breakfast sir, you asked me a rather important question of how I was going to arm your proud fighters for your mission once your warriors were safely in the United States, sir." Colonel Gonzales grinned at the Iranian, because he was trying to repair what he destroyed between them.

"Yes, I certainly did Colonel Gonzales Sir. That question is still weighing rather heavy on my mind, Colonel." General Kalantari replied hotly, not trying to hide the anger flowing within his veins, as he openly glared at the Cuban Officer.

"General Kalantari Sir, allow me to set your mind at easy, sir. General, if you wouldn't mind following me to a new position, sir. I shall be most pleased to display how we'll arm your warriors before you leave my country, sir." Colonel Gonzales replied confidently as he waved his arm out before his body, and he aimed the Iranian towards his Naval Lieutenant who was sort of standing by the side of the crate lying on the dock. The Cuban Officer completely ignored the tone in the hated Iranian's voice he was addressing him with in front of his soldiers, who seemed like they were taking an exception to his disrespect of their commander that the Colonel was taking against it himself.

General Kalantari did not respond as he walked out before the Cuban and headed in the direction he was aimed in. They covered the fifteen feet separating them from the Lieutenant, and when they were standing besides him, Colonel Gonzales ordered. "Lieutenant Castillo, I give you permission to display the weapons we have acquired for the General and his soldier's use in their soon to be operation in the United States, sir."

Instantly, Lieutenant Castillo snapped to full attention, and then he quickly ripped off a rather sharp salute as he replied to his commander. "Yes Sir Colonel Gonzales Sir, immediately sir."

With that said, he turned and went to work opening the crate for the two officers. It took him a few seconds to remove the lid of the crate, and then he reached in and pulled what looked like a heavy burlap cover from the weapons hidden below it.

General Kalantari leaned forward so he could look at the weapons neatly stacked inside the large crate. Although the weapons looked rather familiar to him, they were different in the construction than the ones he was used to working with. The Vulture turned back to the grinning Cuban Officer and asked him in a concerned tone of voice. All his anger had drained from his body once he saw the weapons.

"Colonel Gonzales, though I am very familiar with the make of these weapons you off me, these are nothing like the ones I'm used to working with, sir. They're smaller, barely a little larger than a normal cursed pistol, sir."

"Ahhhh General Kalantari, I see you do have the eye for weapons, sir. Yes General Kalantari, this is the German made MP-5 Heckler and Koch, 9 mm MP5K-PDW, or the Personal Defense Weapon, but it's not a new design at all, sir. This weapon has been in service for a number of years by many nations of the world. But it's basically used by anyone who wants to better conceal a weapon, and yet maintain a powerful response if the user is challenged by his enemy in the field, sir. This weapon has been specially designed as a compact weapon carried by drivers of vehicles, to protect their ward with a great return rate of fire, sir. It's also being carried by aircraft crew members both military and civilian in nature, or it's sometimes used when a full size automatic weapon is not appropriate for their assignment, and an automatic pistol is not enough fire power for the situation, sir.

"This weapon can be concealed inside soft luggage or inside a simple shoulder carrying case, or it can also be hidden on the body of the user by employing the holster, or the specially designed swing harness that allows the weapon to be carried under the arm, and with a swing of the shoulder. The weapon is instantly moved into the correct firing position for the user. General Kalantari, the MP-5K-PDW is similar to the normal MP-5K sub-machine gun sir, but this weapon comes equipped with a fold down stock to better afford the user a full size heavy assault weapon, or the stock can be folded to give the weapon the size of a pistol, but with a return firing rate of murderous killing power, sir."

Colonel Gonzales took a quick breath in his explanation now that he had the Persian's full attention again, and then he went on with his words. "General Kalantari, the stock of this weapon is able to be completely removed from the weapon to allow it to be concealed upon the body of the user much easier, sir. The weapon is as accurate as the original MP-5K assault weapon designed by the Germany company Heckler and Koch developers, and it comes with the fifteen, or thirty round magazine for the weapon, sir. All controls for this specialized weapon are ambidextrous, and the firing mechanism permits a selective firing rate at automatic, or firing one round at a time, and we included the optional three round burst mechanism for the weapons we supplied for you and the rest of your warriors, sir. I believe this weapon will meet with your approval and your needs in the field, General Kalantari? We have tried to locate the perfect weapon for your operation, and after much consideration, we believe we have supplied you with the perfect weapon, General."

The Vulture was only half paying attention to the Cuban as he spoke. The rest of his attention was placed on the crated weapons as he reached in the box and removed one and examined it. The stock of the weapon was folded down, and though it was out of the way to enable him to fire the weapon correctly. The Persian fighter realized he was going to remove the folding stock from the weapon for better firing and concealment purposes. He was impressed by the weapon, and the decision of the Cuban's part to choose this weapon for his use on the mission.

General Kalantari forgot about the anger he was once holding for Colonel Gonzales as he tried the action on the weapon. The bolt slid with ease and slammed home soundly. If he had a loaded clip in the weapon, he would have just armed it. Everything about this weapon was to the General's likes as he shifted the weapon from one hand to the other. He held it at arm's length to see if he would be able to fire it with one hand. Even though he wasn't firing it, General Kalantari realized the weapon would be able to be fired accurate with one hand.

The pleased Persian Officer placed the weapon back inside the crate, and he turned his attention to Colonel Gonzales and said to the Cuban. "Colonel Gonzales, I cannot tell you how much I appreciate the needed assistance you and the fine soldiers under your command offered my people, sir. These weapons are a perfect choice for my operation, sir. I shall be successful with my mission sir. I shall inform my President of this much needed help, and I'm certain he'll take it on himself to reward you properly for this assistance."

General Kalantari reached out his hand and waited for the Cuban to shake it. When the Cuban grasped his hand, the Vulture added. "Colonel Gonzales, when I return to my country after I concluded my mission successfully in the United States, I shall send personally for you, and you'll be invited to take an extended vacation in my country, sir. That way my President will be able to properly thank you for this assistance you have offered me, sir."

Colonel Gonzales smiled at the Persian warrior and offered. "We shall see about that offer General Kalantari, we shall see sir. I believe you should concern yourself with the boat and your soldiers, sir. Vacations are something we dare dream about when we have nothing else troubling our mind, sir. General Kalantari, if you'll excuse me for a few moments, I have to check in with my Commander and inform him of the progress of your soldiers, sir." Colonel Gonzales nodded towards the Persian Officer, and turned on his heels and headed for his own private quarters on the base. As the Colonel left the dock, all of his soldiers saluted him.

General Kalantari watched the Cuban leave, and when he was gone from the dock, he turned his attention to the Naval Officer standing by the crate of weapons. The Vulture asked him with concern lacing his tone. "Errr… Lieutenant Castillo, when do we load the weapons on the boat sir? Also Lieutenant, I believe I'd like to use one of the harnesses to allow my weapon to hang under my arm, sir. Are any of the harnesses included with the shipment of weapons, sir?"

"General Kalantari Sir, there is one of these harnesses included for each of the weapons stored inside the crate and for each of your proud soldiers, sir. General, there is also a holster included for each of the weapons as well. I wasn't sure which holders for the weapons your soldiers might want to employ for the carrying of the weapons for their operation, sir. So I took it upon myself to include one each of the items, sir. I hope I've done correct to include one each of the items for you needs, General Kalantari Sir."

"Lieutenant Castillo, you have done more for me than you can ever imagine possible, sir. I thank you for your diligence to your orders, sir. I shall make note of this assistance to my President, and I'm certain he'll speak to your President and your Commander. Lieutenant, allow me to suggest I see a raise in your rank as Officer in your future, sir." General Kalantari nodded at the young Naval Officer he was so pleased with him.

"General Kalantari Sir, I thank you for your kind words, sir. I shall have the weapons loaded on board the boat for your needs, sir. Lieutenant Sanchez, Lieutenant Navarro, you'll pass this crate over to the Persians stationed on board the boat, and they're ordered to stow the weapons inside the cabin until it leaves the dock, sir. I want you Officers to protect the crate with your lives until General Kalantari relieves you of these latest orders." Lieutenant Castillo moved away from the crate for the first time since it was delivered to the dock, and he watched as the two Army Lieutenants followed his order without hesitation.

Once the wood crate was stored away properly on the boat, Lieutenant Castillo made his excuses to the Vulture, and then he turned on his heels and quickly left the dock area of the military base.

CHAPTER TWENTY

Captain Robert Walker along with Sergeant Dorothy Ramirez, gathered the items they were going to need for their scheduled fishing date with the country western singer on the following morning. The Captain and the ones going fishing tomorrow with him were going to gather at the Seven Mile Marina at five a.m. They were going to meet Toby there, and the fishing charter was not scheduled to leave the dock until seven a.m. sharp. But the female Captain of the boat informed the singer when his people reserved the boat she wanted everyone to be waiting at the dock by six a.m. at the latest.

This was no surprise to Walker, because every time he had a charter scheduled, he always told everyone to make sure they were at his boat two hours before they were scheduled to shove off for the fishing trip. He handled the last minute details at that time, and it allowed the Captains to do a last minute check of their gear and people, to make certain they had everything they were going to need stored on board the boat before they shoved off.

Even though Walker was going on the private charter, he wanted to take his favorite fishing rods and tackle on the other boat with him. He knew the female Captain of the charter boat was going to be upset with this decision, but he was certain she would understand and offer the professional consideration given by one Captain of a boat to another. Either way, he did not care because he was going to use his fishing rod and gear no matter what.

Ramirez was busy with her packing for the fishing trip. She made certain she took two bottles of number thirty sun blocker, and she made sure she had enough sun glasses for everyone going on the boat. She remembered being told by Walker many times she never wanted to be caught on the water without sun glasses, or she would pay for it that night when her eyes would swell and hurt like crazy. It's called flash burn to the fishermen, the same as what you received if you were to watch an electric welder without the protective glasses on. She packed a number of snacks to enjoy on the water, because she knew everyone would get hungry, and the sandwiches the Captain supplied, was never enough to keep them satisfied for the entire trip. She even added a few extra bottles of water just in case.

She also included a book to read, in case the fish were not biting, and she did not want to be bored on the boat. Once she had the items packed in her survival bag, she went to her room and picked out the bathing suit she was going to wear under her clothes. Even though they were going to be fishing, she was going to pay attention to her tan while they were out. When she was done with her preparations, she went out to the tackle room to see what Walker was doing out there and to make certain he did not need a hand at what he was doing.

Walker had so much extra tackle piled up on the work table that it looked like he was going to be the Captain of the charter, and this caused Ramirez to laugh as she remarked. "Gees Walker, who is going to be in command of this charter, mister? You have enough tackle to supply six fishermen on board the boat. I wish you'd remember the Captain of the boat is going to supply the tackle and rods we need for this charter. C'mon will you please Bobby, and allow someone else to worry about catching fish for us for a change."

"Whatdaya think, I'm taking too much crap with me, honey?" Walker asked his lover.

"Too much stuff, hell Walker, like I told you, you have enough tackle for six fishermen."

Walker cocked his head to the side and he placed a smile or smirk on his lips as he looked at his girlfriend. Then he looked at the pile of tackle he had stacked on the table by the door and realized he was packing the tackle for the charter as if he was running it. He released his breath and he went to the stack and removed six of his best lures, and placed them in the carrying sleeve. Then he started to replace the tackle on the hangers on the wall in the tackle room.

He felt rather foolish with the amount of stuff he was planning to take on the fishing trip with him, and knew if she did not come in when she did, he would have continued to add to the pile until he was satisfied he had enough tackle to catch any fish in the Ocean. When he came out of the tackle room carrying his one pole and gear, he spotted where Ramirez placed the items she was going to take with her on board the boat. He smiled as he laid his stuff with hers, now he felt he was ready for anything on the fishing boat.

THURSDAY, APRIL 26th, 2006, AT ELEVEN THIRTY EIGHT IN THE MORNING ON THE ISLAND OF CUBA

An extremely angry General Abdol Karim Kalantari was busy watching everything his soldiers were doing while preparing for their operation in the United States to begin. Everything possible to be done by his freedom fighters was being carried out by the excited Persian soldiers, and now his soldiers were just trying to look like they were busy before their Commanding Officer. The Vulture smiled at them when he realized what they were up to, and he checked his watch and realized none of his freedom fighters had breakfast, and yet none of them dared to complain about it to him. The dangerous terrorist leader called out in a booming tone to his soldiers, but he was actually addressing his second in command.

"Colonel Heshmotallah Khatami, it's heading for lunch and none of our soldiers have taken time to eat, sir. We have accomplished everything we could to be prepared for the beginning of our operation. I believe it'd be a wise idea if you took charge of our fighters, and lead them to the mess so they can eat before we leave, sir. You shall allow our warriors an hour to enjoy their meal and rest once this time is up you'll lead them in exercises. I want them ready to begin their mission for Allah and our President on time, and not suffering from boredom, sir.

"You'll exercise them for two full hours, and then they'll be allowed to shower and rest until supper mess, Colonel. Once we finished supper, our soldiers will be allowed to rest until two hours before it's finally time for us to begin our mission for the Prophet Muhammad. I don't want our people falling asleep while we're heading for the hated United States, Colonel. I want everyone on their best alert for our trip to America, in this way, if we're challenged by the cursed Coast Guard. We'll be ready to defend ourselves against any possible attack from them waged against us, sir. Everyone on board this foul boat will be armed at all times while we're on the cursed water Colonel Khatami, and the fools will be ready to defend our boat against anyone who dares to try and challenge us, sir."

Colonel Khatami snapped to attention and he ripped off a sharp salute to his Commander as he replied to his orders. "Yes Sir General Kalantari, I understand my orders and I shall follow them out faithfully, sir. Soldiers of the Forth Brigade of QUD Forces, you'll line up on the dock in formation, and sound off names and rank, so I know everyone is present. Once I have completed the roll call, we'll head to the mess and eat. You fools heard our Commander's orders, and I expect them to be carried out without my need to repeat them to you fools. We shall be starting our mission for Allah in a few hours, and I expect every one of you fools to be ready, willing, and able to carry out orders as received. Anyone found not up to peak performance for this operation, I shall deal with your foul selves personally. I warn you, you'll rule the day you were born if you embarrass me before our Commander. Form up your lines before me!"

Colonel Khatami stood with his hands resting on his hips while glaring at his troopers as they quickly scurried out of the boat and assembled before him at an arm's distance between each soldier, and an arm's distance between each of the four lines of Persian soldiers. The Colonel waited until each soldier called out their name and rank for Colonel Nasser Makaeem Taleqani, as he checked off each name as it was called out to him on his list. Once the roll call was completed, Colonel Taleqani turned to Colonel Khatami and announced. "Colonel, all soldiers are present and accounted for sir."

"Good Colonel Taleqani Sir, you shall lead them to the mess and allow them to eat their lunch, sir." Colonel Khatami returned the other Colonel's salute, and then he watched the formation of mixed male and female soldiers turn as one and all head over to the Cuban mess.

General Kalantari remained standing on the dock by the boat, but he allowed his second in command to take control of the soldiers, and when they left the dock in formation, he moved to his Colonel's side and offered. "Colonel Khatami, I'm pleased by the way our soldiers are prepared for our mission against the United States, sir. With the weapons we have available for our use and the enthusiasm our soldiers are displaying for this operation, I see no way for us to fail sir. Think about it Colonel Khatami, in the next few days we shall deliver a lethal and devastating blow against our enemy in the hated land of Satan, sir. A blow that'll make the Nine, One, One, attack from bin Laden against the fools look like it was a training mission sir.

"I'm proud our President has placed me in command of this operation, Colonel Khatami. Our leader in Iran will know of the efforts you have been instrumental in to ensure the success of our mission, sir. I know once we return to our country in victory, our leader will raise us to our proper standing in the military, and the civilian leadership of our lands, sir. It'll be a great day for us to experience when we bring the mighty United States down to their cursed knees before Allah's feet. Again the American television will display for the world to enjoy, their civilians killed and injured in our attack, sir. But the best part of our mission will be when bin Laden and his freedom fighters are blamed for our attack on the United States, sir. Colonel Khatami Sir, allow me to inform you why our great leader wants this belief to take place, sir."

General Kalantari stopped speaking to draw in a breath, and then he went on with his words for the lesser officer. "Colonel Khatami, the reason our cunning President's wants to blame bin Laden and his warriors for this attack against the United States, is because after all the cursed hubbub has calmed down in that foul country. Our President is going to step up and he'll offer to the United States to act as a go between the United States and the forces of the al-Qa'eda terrorist organization. This is so our President can get America's worthless eyes and mind off of our nuclear weapons research and development program inside our country, sir.

"Our President wants to get a number of nuclear weapons in our stockpile, so we have enough weapons on hand to stop the United States, or any other nation of the world from daring to attack out nation for any reason, sir. Once we have these weapons of mass destruction in our arsenal, we'll make our move again the cursed land of the Jews, and once we have destroyed this miserable country. We'll take over the rest of the Middle East, sir. Colonel Khatami, once we have control of the Middle East, we'll be in command of the oil the world relies so heavily upon. Think Colonel think what this will mean to our country and the peoples of Iran, sir. When we're in control of the oil supplies of the Middle East, we'll control the world entire sir.

"Every cursed nation that relies upon the oil from the Middle East to make their foul machines and cars run, will find themselves locked to the whim of our wants and desires, sir. We, the people of Iran will order them to follow our orders, our true religion, or we'll cut off their precious oil supplies, and that nation will dry up and cease to exist in this world, Colonel. We'll be free to turn the other nations we would control against the hated United States and her people. The United States will soon become known as what she truly is a Pariah nation that prays upon the weaker nations of the world they scare with their military might.

"Always bending the knees of those weaker nations who cower before the United States military might and threats, to force their bidding and control over those nations. Once we have alienated the United States from the world, we can force her to her foul knees, and turn their will to that of our own. Or the United States will find itself hated by every nation on the face of the earth who'll owe their allegiance to Iran, sir. The nations of the world will kneel to the nation of Iran and for Allah, or they'll no longer be a nation, Colonel. Any curse nation that dares defy Iran's will, will find itself being attack by the nations we shall band together against them.

"Yes Colonel Khatami, we're including the once powerful and well feared Russian nation, who is no longer a world power in her own right. The Russian bear has had its fangs and claws removed by the hated United States. China will be included in the nations that we'll control. China's economy is growing at such an alarming pace that the Chinese government will be depleting their own nation's natural resources in no time, and then they'll be forced to depend on us to supply oil and gas they need to the worthless fools. Or their cursed nation would soon be grinding its gears to a stop for lack of oil. Then that once powerful nation would soon dry up and crumble into the dust it was born from, sir.

"Colonel Khatami, there is so much behind what our wise President of Iran is trying to accomplish, and he's planning for the future fate of Iran, sir. With our attack against the United States within the next few weeks, will be the start of what our President has set in mind for the world, sir. But this in not the proper time to get involved in this conversation, Colonel Khatami, I have given you more than enough information of the future plans of Iran to make you want to carry out orders that come directly from your President, or myself sir. Colonel Khatami, I believe it's time we enjoy our lunch, sir. I don't want our soldiers doing something on this cursed Cuban military base without either you or myself watching their every move, sir.

"I don't trust the loathsome government of Cuba, and I trust this hateful Colonel Gonzales even less, Colonel. I cannot wait for the great day to arrive that'll allow me to seek my revenge upon his worthless shoulders, because of the countless insults I was forced to endure at the hands and mouth of this great fool during our training and preparing for our attack against America. Shall we go and eat something for ourselves Colonel Khatami Sir?"

"Yes sir, by all means General Kalantari Sir, I'm hungry sir. General, I want to thank you for taking me into your confidence, by informing me of the future plans of our government and President, sir. I assure you General Kalantari I shall bring nothing less but complete glory for what we're planning to do in the future, General." Colonel Khatami offered as he bowed towards his Commander, showing him he was behind their operation in the United States.

General Kalantari returned the Colonel's slight nod with one of his own, as he allowed a sarcastic smile to cross his lips as he replied. "Colonel Khatami, I expected nothing less from you, or our warriors, sir. If you would've responded in any other fashion but the one you have replied with, I would've killed you on the spot without a thought. In case you're not aware sir, each of the fighters that makes up our terrorist cell, was handpicked personally by myself for this operation, sir. I demanded from my Commander the moment I was placed in command of this operation to hand pick my fighters, because I wanted the soldiers who I knew would follow their orders as received, without the slightest hesitation or questions, Colonel Khatami Sir."

The Vulture stopped speaking to allow everything he said to his second in command, for him to absorb every word he uttered. When enough time passed, the upset General offered. "Colonel Khatami, I believe it's time we eat if we want to be done before our soldiers are finished with their foul meals, and they leave the mess to carry out their next duties. Like I have just informed you Colonel Khatami, I don't want our foolish people walking around on this cursed Cuban military base, without you or I keeping a close eye on the fools, sir.

"I'm concerned if one of the fools might have a change of heart, and they try to get political asylum from Cuba, or worse, from the hated United States. Although I trust them with my life, one cannot be certain until they're activated on our operation, Colonel. There is another reason for concern, Colonel Khatami. I'm worried one of these Cuban fools might try to turn one of our fighter's head before we're on our mission. I hate having the cursed foreign soldiers mingling with our soldiers, Colonel. These fools have not shared life in another country, and they're prone to commit sins as we witness with the lowly whores of this foul land they call Cuba.

"If we lose one of our soldiers to these desires, it'll place our entire mission in jeopardy, sir. Come Colonel Khatami, let's go and eat so we can keep our eyes on this bunch of fools we call soldiers. I'm getting hungry and I want to check on our soldiers. I noticed some of our fools were becoming short with their Cuban counterparts. I don't need a fight breaking out between our soldiers and the worthless Cuban soldiers assigned to assist us in our cause, Colonel.

"Bah, it's hard to be in command of soldiers foaming at the mouth to begin their mission against our enemy. There is so much one must be on the alert for. It seems trouble is lucking behind every tree, behind every box. I believe stress is starting to get me, Colonel Khatami. I thank the Almighty Allah for placing an officer such as yourself, as my second in command. At least I understand you're here to help me through what I must endure, Colonel."

SEVEN THIRTY P.M. ON THURSDAY, APRIL 26th, 2006 ON THE TINY ISLAND OF MARATHON IN THE FLORIDA KEYS

Captain Robert Walker and Sergeant Dorothy Ramirez from the Special Forces Unit known as the Multi-Nation Rapid Response Force from Camp Lejeune, were suffering from exhaustion as they finished eating supper. They worked all day preparing for their fishing trip with the country singer. They wanted to be well prepared for the trip, and made certain they were. The Captain wracked his brains with the preparation, because they wanted everything to be perfect for their time on the water. He was concerned, because he knew he had everything on his boat, but they were using someone else's boat, and he did not know what this Captain was equipped for.

He was prepared if game fish were not biting, he would gear up for bottom fish which he caught something on a paying charter. Although they were going out for tuna and the few dolphins thought to be the leading elements for when the dolphin started to run by the Island, he did not know if the female Captain would be geared up to go after anything else that might be biting, if they did not have any luck with the larger game fish. Many times, the Captain's of other boats went out for one specific kind of fish, and they rarely if ever change in midstream for another type of fish, if the game fish weren't hitting. This was why some local Captains returned to dock skunked catching no fish on the charter.

No one going out fishing on the next day did anything that night, because they wanted to go to sleep early so they would be well rested for tomorrow's fun on the water. The Mutt and his lady never visited Walker and his girlfriend for the day, they stayed at home and when

Regina came home from work, she made supper for the Mutt, and they rested the day and night. Even though she never let on to the Mutt and others, Regina was sad she was not going out with her dear friends on the fishing trip with the country singer. She never mentioned it to the Mutt, but she approached her boss to see if she could wiggle Friday off, but they were too busy for the boss to allow her to miss work. Regina sure made the best of it and she waited on the Mutt hand and foot for the night to make him relax, and not think about her missing their fishing trip with them.

The Mutt was upset Regina was not going, but like his girlfriend he did not do anything that might rub it in she was missing a great day of fishing with the others. He loved it when they were out on the water together, it always ended up in a sexual experience and great fun, and they came in with caught fish. The Mutt relaxed and he allowed his lady to spoil him rotten all night and before they went to bed, they made love nice and easy.

Walker did speak to Toby during the day, and he made certain the singer knew what he had to bring on board the boat for his comforts and needs. The last time he spoke to the singer was after supper, and then he turned his attention to his lady. He was after her all night, trying to get her interested in making love. But she was so worked up about their fishing trip that she was not interested in making love to her man. At nine thirty, he had enough of her putting him off and he walked into the kitchen behind her at the sink. He leaned against her and rested his chin on her shoulder and reached around and cupped her breasts from behind, and whispered.

"C'mon doll, Robert's in bed for the night and I'm horny as hell, lady. How's bout we have us a little fun before we turn in for the stinking night, honey? I wanna be in bed by at least ten tonight, so we get plenty of rest for tomorrow's fun on the water, girl. C'mon baby, the hell with the damn dishes, we have something more important to do than clean the damn things, baby."

He started to attack the buttons on her blouse, and when he had it opened, he began pawing her breasts which caused her to purr at him sexily. "Boy Robert, you sure do know how to get my motor running, mister. You keep doing that and I'm going to rape you right where you stand, buster. Look honey, I want to finish cleaning the dishes though, it's not fair to leave them for Cathy to look after when she comes to take care of Robert Jr. you know, baby. It's bad enough she's spending the night here to look after our son, mister."

"That's what I wanted to hear sister, you wanna rape my ass honey. Fuck the damn dishes and let's have some real fun, honey." He replied with a smirk as he turned her around, and took one of her nipples in his mouth and began sucking and running his tongue over it, until her nipple responded to his manipulation.

"Mmmmmmm, don't you dare stop now mister. You got me wet between the legs already my lover." She mumbled barely over a whisper as she tried to reach around herself and turn off the water. But she was unable to reach the faucet because of the way he was holding her as he attacked her breast with his hands and mouth.

He was leaning so heavily on her that her hair was getting wet from the water in the sink, but it was Walker who turned off the water. Then he picked her up in his arms and carried her into the living room and put her on the couch. Once she was seated, he began working on her pants, he opened and then pulled them off her body. All the while she was purring like a content kitten getting its head scratched. When he had her naked, he kissed her neck and then he worked his way to her shoulders as he headed for her nipples again. He found them waiting and worked them over with his mouth then his tongue and teeth, and hands.

Now, he had her where he wanted her, wiggling all over the couch as he worked his way down the length of her sleek body with his hands and mouth. When he reached her bellybutton, he dipped his tongue into the little pool and wiggled it around gently. This set her off and she was seeing stars zipping around before her tightly shut eyes with anticipation on where he was heading next with his skilled tongue and hands.

He left her bellybutton, and ran his tongue over the lower part of her belly, tickling her as he licked both sides of her hips and kissing and nipping them with his teeth. He was taking his time getting to her favorite spot on his lover's exquisite body. He next slid his tongue down the outsides of her thighs, forcing her to break out in a cold sweat and a moan. When he felt he had her really going, he grabbed her knees and yanked her legs opened so quickly that he took her by surprise, and she complained in a dreamy tone at him. "Oh you animal you, I love it when you take control of me like this, mister. Do your worst to me, do me now big boy."

He looked at her who had her eyes pressed closed as she waited for him to continue making love to her with his mouth and hands. She was smiling that certain smile a woman puts on when she was being pleased by her lover, and then he replied. "If you liked that move honey, you'll love what I'm gonna do to your bod next, sweetheart."

He lowered his head and began to run his tongue over the inner and lower part of her thigh. Slowly, still working his tongue in small circles over her inner thigh, he worked his way up to her love making center. When he ran his tongue lightly over her flowering petals, she moaned aloud as she tried to hold his head there and make him work her over good. But he was not done with driving her crazy just yet. He fought off the slight pressure she was placing on his head, and he slowly started to work his way down the inner thigh of her other leg. Doing what he done to her other thigh with his tongue, and light little nips of her flesh, as he went on pleasing her.

When she realized his tongue left her spot, she mumbled sexily barely over a whisper at him. "You little bastard, you're going to make me beg you again, aren't you mister?"

He ignored her bitch as he continued to run his tongue down the inner thigh of her other leg, and when he reached her knee, he ran his tongue over the hollow of the back of the knee, licking and kissing it gently. Again, setting off shooting stars in her eyes, and she wiggled her rearend up towards his mouth to give him easier access to the back of her knee, as she moaned as he continued working her over like he was doing.

Now, she was moving her hips in conjunction with his revolving tongue, and when he heard her moan again, he left this spot and started to work his way back up towards the center of her fever. He started working his way up her inner thigh and when his tongue found her center, he gave her a quick lick, actually making her jump and moan again from what he was doing to her body. He pulled away and slowly inserted one finger in her, and then he started to turn it, causing her to arch her back to his probe in response and she mumbled "Of my God".

When she arched her back and cried out, he attacked her with his tongue and finger. He licked every inch of her center, and when he found the little pearl he was searching for, he drew it in his mouth and rolled his tongue gently over it and sucked on it. This made her really wiggle around on the couch. She was still arching her back, but now she was wiggling her hips to his motion of his tongue. She held her eyes locked shut tight and was moaning to beat the band. Once again, she locked his head in her hand, and she was trying to guide his actions. Suddenly, she arched her back as tight a she could, and then shuddered and dropped her rearend down on the couch as she came and cried out "Oh my God" again and he continued working on her.

Again, he worked her over until she was back in the blind fever of allowing him to please her. He licked both sides of her center of pleasure, running his tongue over the lips of her pleasures, and when he found the pearl again and he drew it in his mouth, she instantly came a second time while she had his head locked in her hands, and sweat ran down the sides of her face and she cried, "Oh my God, oh God I'm going to cum, oh God.' She began rubbing herself against his lips and tongue as she came a third time, and when she was finished she relaxed and released the hold she had on his head, and she allowed him to breathe.

He removed his head from between her legs and leaned back and rested his rearend on his legs, and he stared at his lady who seemed like she was in another world. The beautiful smile glued to her lips, informed him he done her good and proper, and she was pleased by him and his action. He always tried to please his lady before making love to her. She opened her dreamy eyes that were tearing, and she looked him in the face and mumbled.

"Oh God Robert, that was absolutely wonderful my love, now I know why I keep you hanging around all the time, mister. But it's my turn to please you a little, buster. Get up and sit on the couch my lover, and I'll show you the stars I was looking at." Her voice got a little hard, like she was actually ordering him to do so. She then stood up as he replaced her on the couch, and the moment he was comfortable, she knelt down between his legs and went to work on the belt of his pants. She opened the belt, button, and undid the zipper and when she had them loose. She pulled them down his legs she was going to take control of her pleasing her man, and to do this she left his pants bunched up around his ankles so he could not move on her. She placed her knee right in the crotch of the bunched up pants, actually pinning his feet to the floor so he could not move. And like him, she grabbed his knees and then she yanked his legs apart and placed her chest between them so she could get at his swaying member.

He was sitting with his eyes shut in anticipation of what she was going to do to his body. His wait was not long to suffer through. She kissed the inner thigh of his left leg, and she licked it as she started to work her way up his leg. About mid-way up his leg, she suddenly bit him on his thigh mischievously, making him jump and smile after he opened his eyes and looked down at her. Her forehead was brushing against his rock hard member and it was beginning to drive him nuts from his needs for her to be working him over with her mouth. She felt his desire mounting and she decided she was going to do the same thing he done to her, she was going to make him wait as long as possible before giving him the pleasure he wanted.

Now it was his turn to grab her by the head and hair as he tried to guide her mouth towards his waiting shaft, and it was her turn to resist the pressure he was placing on her. She knew exactly what she was doing, she was making him wait until he could no longer stand it, and he took over for her and forced her to please him like he wanted. She did not have to wait long for that to happen, because the first time her breath brushed over his shaft, he instantly grabbed her by the hair with one hand, and he took hold of his shaft with the other and forced himself in her mouth whether she was ready for it or not.

She moaned and began to hum as she started to slide her mouth up and down on his rock hard member, and when she felt it swell to where it almost no longer fit in her mouth, she increased her up and down motion. He arched his back high as his rearend left the couch, and he erupted in her mouth. She knew how much he liked to see himself cum in her mouth, so she pulled off his shaft and received a stream of cum on her cheek and lips. He came in another heavy stream and she had to move her face from the end of his shaft, or she would have received this stream in her eyes. She could not help herself because of the way he was coming and she started to laugh, but when another stream shot her in the face, she complained at him as if she was upset with him.

"Good God Walker, how much more of this stuff do you have inside you, mister?"

He did not reply, instead he grabbed her by the hair and forced her mouth back on the end of his shaft as he shot another stream in her mouth. He was coming so hard she almost gagged on it, but she continued to slide her mouth on his shaft until she was certain he finished. Again she laughed at her lover as she pulled off his softening shaft, and started to clean the mess he just sprayed over her face and chest, and complained again. "I'm telling you Walker the next time I give you head, I'm not going to allow you to go so long before taking care of you, mister. Dammit to hell, you almost drowned me in this stuff this time, buster."

After she finished bitching at him, she leaned forward and placed a kiss on the end of his shaft, then she nipped him with her teeth, making him jump from the sudden nip, and he smiled as he said. "Hey baby, what can I tell ya? I keep telling you not to wait so long before we have some fun, love. If you don't wanna be drown in it then you betta take care of me more often than you're doing, honey." Again, he flashed one of his famous smiles at her.

"You'll do anything to get a little head off me buster. I must tell you that was a good try, but it's not going to work mister. I keep telling you, you take care of me and I'll take care of you the same way, lover. You know what they say, 'if you don't eat it you don't need it, buster.'" She flashed a smile that would have melted the hardest heart at her lover and soldier.

"Hey honey, what say we hit the sack, we gotta get up early tomorrow morning, and it's getting late?" He asked her as he got off of the couch and stretched his legs.

"You got it big boy, but first I want to check on Robert Jr. and the babysitter. I'm glad she was able to sleep over tonight Robert, or we might have been late getting down to the dock tomorrow morning." She offered as she stood and picked up her shirt from the floor and slipped into it as she headed for the stairs to check on their son and babysitter.

He loved it when his girlfriend wore one of her blouses, or his shirt as the only thing she had on, because she had outstanding legs and a rearend only God could sculpture. She was nearly dancing as she rushed to the stairs. He knew she was not coming back downstairs for the night, so he checked and locked the doors, shut off the lights and went upstairs. By the time he entered their bedroom, she was already under the covers.

The moment she saw him enter their bedroom she announced. "The little one is sleeping like an angel and like his father, this is the only time he's acting like one, mister. You trained him well Bobby. He's a carbon copy of you mister. Cathy was up and she told me not to worry about him, she'd make certain he gets off to school okay. She also told me not to worry about any dishes we leave behind, she offered to clean them before leaving our home. She promised she'll return before Robert Jr. gets out of school, and she's prepared to fix him supper and wait for us if we find ourselves running late from our fishing trip. Every day I thank our lucky stars for finding her, she's a God send, Bobby. I would've been forced to leave the service if I didn't find her and she agreed to take care of our son while we're away. I'm so happy we're on the Island enjoying our son and the close friends we made down here, Bobby."

He got in bed and replied as he shut the last light in the house. "I know what you're saying, honey. Cathy has made our lives a lot easier by taking care of the kid for us, baby. We hafta pay her more money for babysitting for us."

CHAPTER TWENTY ONE

THURSDAY, APRIL 26th, 2006 AT SEVEN TEN P.M. ON THE TINY ISLAND OF CUBA

The Persian General Abdol Karim Kalantari, known as the Vulture to his soldiers, found himself standing on the wood dock with the boat moored to the piling. The dock and boat was a beehive of activity as his soldiers prepared to shove off on their mission within a few hours. This time the Cuban Colonel, Felix Gonzales was not with him, but he was expected to arrive shortly.

General Kalantari was screaming at the Cuban soldiers as well as his own warriors, as the Cuban troopers helped complete any last minute needs and wants for the boat and his Persian soldiers and their mission. Everything was ready and if he wanted, the terrorist cell could shove off this very minute for the shore of the United States to setup their attack against that country. The only reason the Vulture refrained from sailing off on his mission at this point, was because he was informed they would not be allowed to leave Cuba until after ten p.m. It was figured if he left for the United States at that time, he would be landing on Marathon between nine thirty and ten a.m. the following morning.

Arriving at that time would give the General's boat a better cloak of cover. Anyone seeing a boat docking at this time of the day on the Island, would think the Captain and boat was coming in from a good fishing trip, and it was not a terrorist threat to the United States. So he used his time up by constantly yelling at any soldier his eyes fell upon, no matter whose troops they were, as they continued to work on the boat and their equipment.

Standing by the General's side was his second in command, Colonel Heshmotallah Khatami, and he was amused at the way the Vulture was screaming at anyone he laid his eyes on. It was the Iranian Colonel who drew his General's attention to the other end of the dock, as Colonel Gonzales stepped on the wood. Without being told to move off, Colonel Khatami stepped away from his Commander's side, to give him privacy so he could speak to the Cuban in private.

Colonel Gonzales noticed the Persian Colonel quickly move away from the Vulture, and his anger grew in him as he stared at the other officer. The Cuban did not like this Iranian Colonel any better than he liked his Commander. Cautiously eyeing the Persian soldier until he was well away from the General, Colonel Gonzales walked up to the Vulture and he put his hand out and they shook hands. Neither officer bothered to salute the other, because each one of them was constantly trying to upstage and insult the other by this insult.

The wise Cuban Officer turned his attention to everything taking place on the boat and dock area, and he noticed how well and alert the Persian fighters were acting and carrying out their duties. They seemed well rested and charged up with energy, and they were raring to go on their mission to attack the United States. The Cuban Officer smiled, more over the fact that soon he would be ride of these Persian terrorists, than he was with seeing how well they wanted to get started on their mission.

Once he had his fill of watching the soldiers work on the boat, Colonel Gonzales turned to the Persian General and offered him. "General Kalantari, it seems to me your Second in Command has everything under his control at this point, sir. I see no need for us to be standing out here watching them work, sir. If you'd not mind, follow me to your private living quarters so we could speak in seclusion, until it's time for you to start your mission, sir? There are a few last minute things I'd like to go over with you before you leave, General Kalantari Sir."

General Kalantari shrugged at the Cuban, because he was bored to death watching the activity going on board the boat and dock. The Vulture drew in a breath and held it before letting it out in a rush. He did not trust or like this foul smelling Cuban Officer standing before him. But he was tied to him by his duty to his President and their mission. The Persian General turned to his second in command standing some fifty paces from him, and he was busy speaking to one of the Persian terrorists. He snarled at him in a harsh voice. "Colonel Khatami." Then he waited for the Colonel to come over to his side. When he got there, the Iranian Commander ordered him in no uncertain terms.

"Colonel Khatami, I'm going to leave you in Command of our soldiers, sir. I'm leaving the dock to speak with Colonel Gonzales in our office. He has a few things to offer, and I must find out what is on his mind before we can leave this Island and begin our operation. I shall be but a few moments because my duty is with my soldiers, not speaking pleasantries with this Cuban Commander, sir." The Iranian General looked his Colonel in the eyes as he waited for his reply.

"Yes Sir General Kalantari, I shall follow my orders faithfully for you and Allah, sir." Colonel Khatami replied confidently as he snapped to attention, and he saluted his Commander correctly. Every thought locked in the Persian Colonel's mind, was aimed on the attack they were going to carry out against the United States, and he was dying to start on their operation.

With that said General Abdol Karim Kalantari turned to Colonel Felix Gonzales and nodded towards the good looking young Cuban soldier.

That was all Colonel Gonzales was waiting for, when the Persian nodded towards him, he immediately turned on his heels and they started for the Colonel's quarters he was allowing the Persian to use as his personal office, while he and his soldiers were on the Cuban military base. As they walked off the dock, Colonel Gonzales made certain he did not speak a word to any of his lesser soldiers helping the foreign soldiers prepare the boat for travel to the United States. He wanted to display for the Iranian Officer that here in Cuba. The Commanding Officer did not have to check in with his Second in Command, to inform him of what he was doing next on the military base. He also wanted to show this foreigner on Cuba his soldiers were so well trained that they knew what the other was doing at all times. So there was no need to hold one another's hand while preparing for a military operation for any soldiers under his command.

As they entered the office, Colonel Gonzales immediately took the chair resting behind the desk, forcing the Iranian Commander to sit in the chair facing him, and it was commonly used by lesser soldiers speaking to the Commander of the base. Already, the Cuban won another slight victory over the angry Iranian terrorist. Smiling broadly, the Cuban Colonel stared at the Persian and then without a word he reached for the bottom drawer and removed a bottle of Cuban Rum, and happily poured a glass full for them to enjoy. The Cuban soldier slid the General's glass across the desk, and he took his glass and sat back in the chair. He then flipped his feet on the desk as he stared at the Persian soldier. What happened next was up to wise and crafty General Kalantari to carry out.

General Kalantari returned the hard stare from the Cuban Officer, knowing he was going to lose more face before the hated Colonel, by doing what was silently ordered. General Kalantari leaned forward in his chair and took the glass of rum and lifted it in his hand, and then he saluted the Cuban. Colonel Felix Gonzales nodded as an ugly sneer crossed his lips. General Kalantari returned the nod and downed the harsh tasting liquid. Fighting not to display the horrible face rum always caused the General to make when he drank it.

When the dangerous Persian Commander finished the drink in one quick gulp, Colonel Gonzales leaned forward in his chair after taking his feet from the desk, as he said to the Persian General in a booming voice. "Very good General Kalantari, it's good for me to see you have learned the proper way to salute a good Cuban Officer, sir. General, I guess you're wondering why I have asked you to come to this office, sir. Well General Kalantari, I happen to know that we suffered through many of our own little private wars while you and your soldiers were visiting my Island of Cuba, sir. But I believe it's now time for us to set our differences aside, so your mind will be clear to begin your operation in peace within the United States. General Kalantari Sir, allow me to tell you a little about myself, sir.

"My father was one of the soldiers killed with the greatest patriot to our nation, Che. But before my father went to battle with Commander Che, the Officer gave my father this medallion, sir." Colonel Gonzales stopped speaking and reached in his pocket and removed the medal, and fingered the fine silver medal like it was the hair of his wife. Suddenly, the Cuban Officer drew in a breath and reached out his hand and offered the medal to the Persian soldier.

General Kalantari took the medal from the Cuban as if it was a precious item. Then he closely examined the medal, not knowing what it truly represented as he rubbed it with his thumb, cleaning a little tarnish from the corner of it.

"General Kalantari, I can see by your eyes you don't recognize the deity engraved upon the medal. That is Saint Christopher, the patron Saint of all who travel upon the roads of the world to their final destiny. He offers the carrier of his image a safe journey home. I offered it to you as a keepsake, and hopefully General Kalantari, the Saint will help guarantee success to your operation in the United States, and a safe trip back to your country. I carried that medal in my pocket ever since the first day my father placed it in my hand. It has always given me great comfort when I needed it the most, and as you can see General Kalantari, any mission I was sent on by my government, I always returned home safely. I know you're not of the same faith as I, and I'm not trying to insult you by offering you a Christian medal for your protection.

"But I believe you'll need all the help you can have on your side, when you and your soldiers attack America for your country and mine. It'd honor me if you'd see fit to carry that medal on your person for this mission, sir. Later when I visit your nation of Iran, you can always give it back to me if you want, General." Colonel Gonzales offered to the Persian Military Officer.

General Kalantari was no fool and he reacted correctly before the Cuban by offering the medal the reverence it deserved. But under his breath he was cursing the Cuban Officer, and the deity he handed him. He was actually appalled at holding the image of a false religious person in his hand, especially when he had no belief in any religion other than the Islamic fate, the true religion of the world. Besides, he knew if he stepped foot on Iranian soil carrying this false image he felt was another way to show what Satan looked like. He would instantly be put to death by the Basij morality police, or the Iranian Revolutionary Guards who worked and were the henchmen for the Ayatullah who was the true power in all Iran.

General Kalantari looked from the medallion to the Cuban who handed it to him, and then replied in a voice that sounded like he was pleased for the gift. "Colonel Gonzales, you're wise beyond your years I see. Yes, it's time we set aside our differences for the sake of my mission. I thank you for this medal and I hope I can bring it the honor you offered it. Although it does not represent my religious beliefs, I too believe one can never have too much protection when he's heading off to do battle with ones enemies." General Kalantari carefully placed the medallion in his breast pocked, buttoned the button and then patted it gently before the Cuban Officer.

Colonel Gonzales smiled over the response of the medal he gave this Persian fool as he began speaking. "General Kalantari, you honored me greatly by accepting what I offered you. I'm further honored by you carrying the medal with you on this mission. It makes me feel I and Che shall be standing by your side, and taking part of this mission when you attack our common enemy. I thank you for offering me such an honor. Perhaps, I'm forced to change the way I have looked upon you and your fine soldiers, sir. You're true heroes to Iran and Cuba." Colonel Gonzales said as he continued to start into the eyes of the Persian Officer while studying his face.

"I assure you Colonel Gonzalcs, now I know you and this other Officer will accompany me on my mission, if only by spirit it shall add to the confidence I have for a successful mission against the United States. Colonel Gonzales, if there is nothing else you wish to speak with me. I'd like to get back to my soldiers and make certain they have looked after everything to look after for our mission. I don't enjoy being away from my troops at so crucial a time. I like to make certain everything is perfect any time I set off on another operation for my country." General Kalantari remarked with a sort of snap in his tone as he stared at the Cuban Officer.

"Yes General Kalantari, I understand how you feel being away from your troops. I too like to be with my soldiers before setting off on a mission, sir. Thinking about it a little further General Kalantari, I see nothing pressing we must discuss any further. You have the weapons and provisions needed for the success of your mission, so you might as well go and attend to your soldiers. But I shall not be accompanying you back to the dock, sir. Because I have a number of things I must see after for myself. But I'll join you and your soldiers at nine thirty before you leave my island. I want to be with you when you leave my country to attack the United States for us, General." Colonel Gonzales stopped speaking and waited for the Persian General to leave for his soldiers on the dock area of his military base.

As General Kalantari rose to leave he did not know what to do next, he did not know if he should offer the Cuban his hand, or salute him. If he saluted the Cuban, it would be the first time he would since first arriving on this base. And, since they already shook hands when they arrived on the base, he did not see the need to repeat this most useless of acts for the hated Cuban Commander. Finally, General Kalantari decided to turn and leave the office, because he knew he would be seeing this Cuban once more before he was off the Island of Cuba. Then he would no longer have any need to speak to this man in his life. But one thing he did know, if the Cuban fool dared to visit Iran, he would never leave his country alive. Once he was out of the office, General Kalantari started breathing properly as he headed for the dock and his soldiers.

Colonel Gonzales remained seated and he watched the powerful Persian Commander quickly leave his office. He hated this man with such a passion that his entire body was actually shaking from anger. When the door closed behind the Iranian Officer, Colonel Gonzales immediately reached for the phone and dialed the private number of his President. He was ordered to report directly to Castro when it was near time the group of Persian fighters was going to leave his Island. On the third ring, the phone was answered and the voice demanded to know who the speaker wished to speak with, and when Colonel Gonzales identified himself to the voice. It ordered him to remain on the line while he got Presidente Castro.

General Kalantari rushed back for the dock at a quick pace, and he was appalled at what he discovered waiting for him. Many of his soldiers were sitting on crates dotting the dock, or they sat with their feet hanging over the peer above the water. There were only a few soldiers doing anything of worth on the boat or dock. There was a severe lack of discipline that none of his soldiers bothered to snap to attention and salute the General, as he stormed back to the boat. His eyes searched the area looking for his second in command, and when Colonel Khatami came strolling out of the cabin of the boat like there was nothing wrong with what his soldiers were doing. General Kalantari barked savagely at him from the peer, as he glared down at him.

"By the sacred sands of Mecca Colonel Khatami, what in the devil are these cursed fools doing? None of these lowly infidels had the wherewithal to salute their Commander, when I arrived here. How dare these foul camel dung heaps sit around when there is such an important operation to begin, Colonel? I would've expected them to be doing anything in their power to remain busy to maintain their alertness for this mission. Colonel Khatami, I'm greatly displeased by your serious lack of control over our worthless fighters at this divine time, when I'm not present to make certain they're doing what they have to ensure the success of our mission.

"I was under the belief that you knew how to command our foolish soldiers when I was not near the worthless soldiers. Now Colonel, I shall be forced to second guess my decision to make you my replacement after seeing how poorly you have maintained your control over our lowly soldiers carrying out their duties for this operation. You three god forsaken fools who have your feet dangling over the dock waiting to feed the sharks your feet, if you don't get on your foul feet and stand at attention and saluting me, you fools will find yourselves without feet to stand upon! Get on your feet immediately, or I'll leave you behind on this worthless Island of fools" General Kalantari roared at the three young soldiers as he held them in his harsh glare now.

The moment General Kalantari turned his attention on the three soldiers enjoying themselves, Colonel Khatami rushed off the boat and nearly ran to stand at attention before his Commanding Officer. When the Vulture looked back at the Colonel, he instantly saluted him.

The Vulture completely ignored his Colonel's fine salute as he glanced at the soldiers in his terrorist cell. One by one they immediately made themselves look busy, and when the Persian General was satisfied with the troop's reaction and he felt he had reinstalled the fires of hell burning within the souls of his people. He turned his attention back to his Second in Command and addressed him in a much calmer tone of voice as he offered him.

"Colonel Khatami, don't take what I have said to you to heart, sir. I don't expect you to be able to watch all our foolish soldiers at all times while they were under your Command, sir. Especially when you have your own things in which you have to look after, sir. All soldiers are like foolish children, and if you take your eyes off them for one moment. They'll surely do what is wrong for them to be doing sir. You're still my pick for Second in Command, and my pick to replace me when I'm moved to our capital city to serve our President personally, sir." The Vulture shot a quick and rare smile at his Second in Command.

"I must admit General Kalantari Sir, I was fearful you were truly upset with me when you first started to dress me down in front of our foolish soldiers, sir. But I had to check on the storage of the weapons in the boat, before we left for the United States, and that was what I was doing when you returned to the dock area, General Sir." Colonel Khatami replied as he returned the General's smile with one of his own, deeply relieved he was not angry at him.

"I assure you sir you worry over nothing to be concerned with, Colonel Khatami Sir. Look at how busy our worthless fools are, sir. Sometimes it's worth it when you dress down your Second in Command for the sake of the other soldiers who'll soon be under your complete control, as you can see for yourself by the way the foolish jackals are working, sir. When you find yourself in Command of a group of soldiers sir, which you'll be in command soon enough Colonel, Command them and they'll be willing follow you to the very gates of hell when you demand this of the lowly jackals, sir." General Kalantari looked at his watch and was pleased to see it was nearing nine p.m. Now they had a little over an hour before they could start for their assault on the United States, and leave Cuba at the same time.

The cunning and extremely dangerous Vulture began to speak to his Colonel again. "Colonel Khatami Sir, we'll soon be leaving this cursed land of lowly pigs for the United States. It'll not be very long before we have completed our mission, and we'll be sitting safely back in our beloved country again, sir. When it's nine p.m., providing all preparations for our departure from this worthless Island has been completed, you'll release our fighters from any further duties for the rest of the night. Yes, I see from the cursed look on your foul face, you know they were resting Colonel. But being their Commander, these worthless fools will relax when I give them orders to do so, not when they want to take it on themselves to relax. That is one of the many powers you Command when you're in charge of a group of soldiers, sir.

"If I had my way, we'd be leaving this foul Island at this very minute, but my hands are tied sir, and I'm forced to wait until this lowly infidel of a Cuban allows us to leave this filthy Island of lowly dog eaters, sir. He's scheduled to return to the dock at nine thirty and give us a speech, and then we shall leave, sir. It's so dark and I cannot see one star in the Heavens, I cannot understand why we cannot leave this minute. But such is the fate of any Commander when one finds himself relying on someone else for their cursed assistance, Colonel." General Kalantari stopped speaking and looked at his quarters to see if the Cuban was heading for the dock earlier than first suggested. A new wave of anger instantly filled his body, when the Iranian did not see any sign of the Cuban heading for the dock. He spat on the floor and then turned away from the direction that he was looking in for the Cuban soldier.

At nine p.m., Colonel Khatami followed his orders and he suddenly bellowed at his soldiers trying to look like they were working on last minute items for their operation. "Soldiers of Iran, we have everything ready for our sacred mission, so I'm ordering you to stop faking work and relax until it's time for us to leave this Island. But no one is allowed to leave the dock area for any reason. If you find you have forgotten a personal item, it'll remain on this Island forever. Nothing from this point is of further interest to us, except for this boat and our operation.

"Do whatever you please, as long as you remain near the boat. I don't want to be forced to look for anyone who might drift away from this cursed station. If I'm forced to go looking for anyone when we're ready to leave, I assure you, you will regret it by the time I'm finished with you. Follow your orders, there is bottled water by the last piling of the dock, drink plenty of water while we're still on land, eat if you're hungry. Because we'll not eat again until we land in the United States, but I know not when. You have your orders, follow them as issued."

Colonel Khatami stopped speaking and watched as his warriors stopped what they were doing, and they gathered in groups and began talking amongst themselves. In no time, some Iranian soldiers started laughing over an off color joke one told to the other soldiers. The Colonel was pleased because he noticed the female fighters remained together with the males, instead of pairing off and staying to themselves. This showed him his soldiers were comfortable working with each other, and it displayed his fighters were a good unit ready to fight any action side by side, and this would help to ensure the success for their operation in the United States.

General Kalantari allowed his Second in Command to order his soldiers, because he was busy speaking to the Cuban, Major Johan Rodriguez who he liked from the compliment of Cuban troops assisting his soldiers. Over the months he was stationed on Cuba, this officer was the only one the Vulture trusted, or liked. The Persian found the Major forthright with help and a genuine friend. The Cuban was trying to act as a go between the General and Colonel Perez or Colonel Gonzales, whenever there was a problem arising between the three officers that caused friction among them. General Kalantari found this officer to be concerned with the success of his mission, and this forced him to like the Cuban and rely on him at times. The Cuban and Persian Officers were enjoying a cigarette, and they were watching their own group of soldiers to make certain everything was running smoothly between the two groups working so close together.

As the time slowly passed for all concerned with getting the Persian soldiers on their way, no one noticed Colonel Gonzales walking towards the dock. By the time General Kalantari noticed the Cuban Officer, he was already standing on the dock and proudly walking towards him. The moment Colonel Khatami noticed the Cuban Commander, he made his excuses to his Commanding Officer and he left the General's side, and went over to a number of his soldiers speaking together. Major Rodriguez remained by the Persian's side until his Commander reached where they were standing. Colonel Felix Gonzales snapped off a sharp salute at his officer, and then he growled at him at the same time.

"Major Rodriguez Sir, I'm certain you have pressing matters that need your immediate attention, sir? I wish to speak to the General in private if you don't mind, sir."

Colonel Johan Rodriguez bowed slightly to his Commander, and then he turned on his heels and went over to his soldiers who were busy watching their Colonel come onto the dock area. When he was with his soldiers, he ordered them to gather the rest of the Cuban soldiers on the peer, and then they were to leave the dock area immediately as a proud working unit of warriors. He knew there was no further need for any Cuban soldiers to remain by the dock area, not with it being so close to the time for the group of Persian fighters to leave the Island of Cuba to begin their mission in the United States.

When they were alone, Colonel Gonzales offered the Persian leader. "General Kalantari, I took the liberty to order our cooks to prepare a number of sandwiches and other food items for your soldiers to enjoy while you're sailing for the United States. I ordered this, because I didn't know when the next time your soldiers might eat on this operation, sir. General, it's almost time for you and your soldiers to leave my Island. In fact General Kalantari, the moment you can get your soldiers on board the boat, you'll be free to leave my Island of Cuba. By that time, it'll be near enough to your scheduled departure time for it to be okay to leave." With that said Colonel Gonzales reached out and offered his hand to the Persian Officer who was staring at him.

General Kalantari shook the Cuban's hand, and while he was holding onto it, he bellowed out to his soldiers. "All Persian fighters, you're ordered to board the cursed boat. We're leaving to begin our assault against the United States."

The Vulture was proud at the speed his soldiers poured onto the boat, and when they were all on board, he spoke his last words to the Cuban who was much help to him, but yet he was constantly trying to insult him. "Colonel Gonzales, I again thank you and your soldiers for their assistance and training of my worthless soldiers. Without that much needed help, I would've never been able to carry out my mission successfully, sir. Colonel, my troops are on board the boat, and they're waiting me, sir. I shall leave you, Allahu Akhbar." The Iranian General offered as he went to attention before the Cuban Officer, and he saluted him smartly and held it.

Colonel Felix Gonzales ignored the religious comment made by the Persian as he went to attention and returned the Persian's salute with one of his own. Then he added as he held his salute on the foreign soldier. "Good luck on your mission against the United States, General Kalantari. I shall be monitoring the news reports that'll soon be coming from the United States, and when I read about your successful attack against the Americans. I shall report the same to the Presidente of my country that you and your honorable soldiers were successful with their attack on our sworn enemies, General Kalantari Sir."

"I thank you for that statement Colonel Gonzales, and I shall report to my President about the help you and your soldiers offered my soldiers. I'm certain my President will personally thank your President for allowing you to assist us." With that said, General Kalantari saluted a number of Cuban soldiers helping his fighters where they gathered at the end of the dock to wait their Commanding Officer, and he leaned over the peer and jumped on to the waiting boat.

The General's order to his Second in Command was. "Colonel Khatami, start the engines. We leave on our mission against the United States. Major Keshavaz, you'll cast off all mooring lines holding the boat to the foul dock. The rest of my soldiers, you all will do whatever is necessary for you to assist us leaving Cuba. If any of you have no duties to perform, the soldiers without orders will go inside the cursed cabin and wait there until you are need. I want everyone to be armed the moment we enter the break waters of the foul Island. I want to be ready for anything that might come our way."

When the lines were cast off, and Colonel Khatami carefully guided the large fishing boat away from the dock, and then he steered it out into the deeper waters of the inlet at just above idle speed. Once the boat was in the deeper water, the Colonel immediately increased the speed of the boat and headed for the open sea.

General Kalantari kept his eyes glued to the stern of the boat, and watched as the Cuban Commander stared as they left the Island. As his last act of defiance against the Cuban Colonel, General Kalantari reached in his pocket and he removed the small medal he gave him. He stared at the Cuban as he tossed the medal in the water at the stern of his boat. Once he threw the medal away, he barked in the wind created by his boat. "So is the cursed fate of all worthless infidel trinkets that don't come from the one true religion. How dare you give me one of your false emblems to carry on my person to battle? I should've taken time to shove the thing down your foul throat, Colonel Gonzales. I dare you to visit my country and see what waits your arrival there, infidel. Colonel Khatami, let's get this boat out of the waters of Cuba, have our soldiers protect us from any possible attack from the Cubans, sir."

FRIDAY, APRIL 27th, 2006 AT THREE A.M. ON THE ISLAND OF MARATHON IN THE FLORIDA KEYS

Captain Robert Walker's alarm clock started driving him crazy at exactly three a.m. He jumped out of bed with a stark because of the alarm, and when he realized it was time for them to get up, he looked at Sergeant Dorothy Ramirez who obviously did not hear the alarm go off, and she was still sleeping peacefully. He leaned over the bed and placed his hands on her rearend, and then he gave her a good shove as he bitched at her at the same time. "C'mon honey, it's time to get up baby. We gotta get going honey."

"Leave me alone I don't want to wake up to make love to you now, I'm still exhausted mister. If you're horny, take care of yourself in the bathroom and let me sleep until I'm ready to get up. What the devil are you doing up this early in the morning anyway, mister? Go back to sleep and leave me alone will you please. We should have gone to bed earlier than we did, mister, but you had to have your way with me last night before we went to sleep." She griped at him without turning to see him as she complained at him for waking her so early.

"Okay, I'll leave your little ass alone, but when I'm out there fishing with your new boyfriend and you're still sleeping, don't blame me baby. Just remember that I tried to wake you up sister." He smirked at her, knowing those words will get her in action fast enough.

"Oh God that's right, we're going fishing today. What time is it anyway, Bobby? Why didn't you wake me earlier than now mister? If we end up being late getting to the dock, I'll never forgive you for it Robert. You know how important it is for us to go fishing with Toby today." She bitched angrily at him as she threw the covers from her body, and got out of bed. Then she began to run around the room like a chicken with her head cut off, as she quickly got dressed, and then she ran downstairs to prepare their morning meal for her and Walker. There was no way she was going to allow them to start the day without eating first.

He took the time to take a quick shower because they were up so early, and he came walking downstairs like he did not have a care in the world. He walked into the kitchen and seated himself at the table, and waited for Ramirez to finish preparing their morning meal.

She glanced over her shoulder as she scrambled the eggs and snapped at him. "I don't understand how you can be so damn calm this morning, Bobby. We have so much to do, and you're walking around like all you have to do is jump in the car and drive down to the dock and shove off and go fishing. You know how important this fishing trip is to me mister."

"You betta calm down or they're gonna hafta bury your lovely little ass standing up, honey. We have plenty of time to get everything in the car, enjoy breakfast, and then get to the dock."

"You might think we have plenty of time to spare, I still have to fix my face."

"What the hell for for crap sake? We're not going to be in a stinking fashion show you know, we're going fishing, and the damn fish don't give a shit how you look, baby. You don't gotta look good for the damn fish, baby." He mumbled at his lady.

"We're going fishing with the country singer and I want to look good for him, mister."

"Oh yeah, I forgot we're going fishing with your new boyfriend, baby." He smirked at his lady, but he was not prepared for her response as she hit him in the head with a wooden spoon and she growled at him at the same time. "How many damn times do I have to tell you he's not my boyfriend, buster? I just love the way he sings that's all Robert, and I don't want to look like a frump in front of him, mister."

"Hey girl, you're really angry at me huh?" He replied as he rubbed the side of his head where she struck him with the spoon.

"If you call him my boyfriend once more, you'll see how angry I get at you, enough with the joke already mister." She fired at her lover and soldier.

"What joke is that?" The Mutt asked as he walked into the kitchen of his best friends, and he went over to the table and sat down in front of the plate she set aside for him.

"Oh, I see your twin bother from another mother has arrived, mister. Walker's being a wise ass this morning, that's all Frankie. I'm glad you got here so early, you can amuse mister funny pants over there while I fix my face, honey." She said to the Mutt.

"What the hell are you gonna fix your face up for, Raz? We're going fishing and you don't…"

"Am I going to have trouble with you too now, mister?" She growled at the Mutt as she turned away from the stove and placed her hands on her hips and glared at the soldier angrily.

"Me? No way am I gonna give you any trouble this morning, little sister." The Mutt replied with a sort of a laugh as he pointed to his chest with the fork he held in his hand. Then he turned his attention to Walker and mumbled at him barely over a whisper. "What the hell's wrong with your lady today, man? Didn't you take care of her last night buddy? If you were not up to the task, you coulda called me and I woulda satisfied her, man."

He was looking at the crazy shirt the Mutt was wearing for the fishing trip, and this caused his friend to ask Walker, "What." as he returned his stare.

"Nice fucking shirt there stupid, you lose a bet or something with your girl, man?"

"You don't like, my lady brought it for me just for this stinking fishing trip, man." He replied as he pulled the two ends of his shirt apart so Walker and Ramirez could see the wild print on the shirt that went from the front and around to his back.

Ramirez could not help herself and she laughed as she added. "Well Frankie, all you need is to have your face painted and a red rubber nose, and you could get a job in any circus in the world, mister. Are you really going to wear that shirt while we're fishing, stupid? You might scare the fish off it's so loud and embarrassing."

"Yeah what the hell's wrong with it little sister? I like the damn thing honey."

"Holy shirt, I need a pair of stinking sun glasses if I'm gonna look at the jerk dressed in that damn shirt all day while we're fishing, people." The massive No Neck complained as he put his hand over his eyes to shield them from the Mutt's glaring and multicolored shirt, and then he added to his complaint. "Nice shirt pal, didja lose a bet or…"

"Yeah yeah big man, I heard the stinking joke from the uther wiseguy over there, buster." He interrupted the big man and pointed at Walker with his fork.

"Well, I'm damn glad I'm not the only one who is getting blind by your lousy shirt, stupid."

"Ha ha, funny, you shoulda been a stinking comedian or somethin, man. Sit down and fill your fat face will ya man." The Mutt snapped at the massive man as he took his seat by the table.

Ramirez placed scrambled eggs and bacon on the three soldier's plates, and then she took her plate upstairs so she could fix her face and get ready for their fishing trip and eat her breakfast at the same time.

The Neck scooped up some eggs and before he put them in his mouth he asked Walker. "Hey man, where the hell's she going in such a stinking hurry? She shoulda ate with us man."

"She's gonna fix up her face man." The Mutt said as he shoveled the eggs in his mouth.

"For a fucking fishing trip she's dolling herself up, what the hell for man? Besides, she looks good enuf for me the way she was already, man."

"You wanna ask her buddy, we did and we're still suffering from her response, man."

"No, not really, I kinda like the way my balls are swinging between my stinking legs, man. I have no intention of upsetting Raz for any reason you guys. I seen her when she was angry, it wasn't a pretty sight to see, buddy." The Neck replied as he went back to eating.

"Upset Raz with what man?" Buckethead asked as he entered the kitchen of Walker's place.

"It's betta you don't know what we're talking about, man. Sit down and eat big guy." Walker offered as he pointed to the dish Ramirez fixed for him even though he was not there yet.

Buckethead did not comment on the Mutt's shirt, he already busted his horns over it when they were at his place, and he started eating his morning meal in peace and quiet.

Ramirez came downstairs carrying her plate, the guys finished eating and Walker said. "Man honey, you look really hooooooot for just going fishing, baby."

Buckethead offered with a smile to Walker. "She always looks hot no matter where the hell we're going stupid. Even when we're going out on another stinking mission, buddy."

"Oh, you're so sweet this morning Bucket." She replied as she walked across the kitchen and kissed him on the side of his cheek and smiled at the huge and dangerous man.

"Oh you're so sweet Bucket." The Mutt mimicked Ramirez which caused her to bitch at him.

"Well he is, and some of you slobs should take an example from him you know."

"He's only trying to get in your stinking pants, Raz." The Mutt retorted at her.

"Well I got news for you other pigs, he's the only one who might get where he's aiming at with comments like the one he just offered to me, stupid." She fired back hotly at the three other soldiers sitting at the kitchen table.

"Is that all it takes to get in your pants now-a-days, just butter you up a little baby girl?" The Mutt answered while trying to keep this conversation going on for a while longer.

"Well you know what they say dog man, a little bit of butter helps things slide along nice and easy mister." She snapped as she wiggled her hips at him.

"Then I'm gonna buy me a tub of the shit right now, girl. Hey Raz, to get in your pants I'd put you up on a pedestal for the stinking day."

"Hey baby, the only reason the stinking Mutt would ever put you up on a fucking pedestal, is so he could look up your damn dress. Anything that fuck does, always has sex involved with it, baby." Walker warned his lady over what the Mutt just said.

"You're just as bad as your partner in crime is, mister. All you two ever think about is sex. You two must have been born under the same slimy rock." She said to the Mutt.

"What can I tell ya baby girl, when it comes to perversion, I wear the badge of honor, sister." He retorted as he flashed a smile.

"That's not the only thing you wear buster. Dressed in that crazy ass shirt, I don't think anyone is going to allow you in a store to buy anything, mister." She remarked to the Mutt, she was not going to allow him win, and she could not get over the loud shirt he was wearing.

"Ouch, that was colder than the other side of the stinking pillow you know, little sister. You almost hurt my stinking feelings with that last zinger you just fired off at my ass, Raz. I'm sensitive and that statement coulda sent me to the shrink. I'm now a broken man and I need to talk to someone about it, honey."

"Talk to the fucking fish we're gonna catch, dog man." Walker growled as he got up from the table, and made a quick motion for the men to follow him out to the garage.

"You better take the Mutt along with you Robert, and put him to work so he leaves me alone for a change." She offered as she smiled at the four men.

"Yeah honey, the Mutt's a workaholic, any time you mention stinking work, he goes out and gets fucking drunk, baby." Walker remarked as he slapped his lifelong friend on his back, and the four of them headed for the garage.

She laughed as she watched the four elite soldiers leave and pick up the gear Walker wanted to take with them on the trip. She knew they were going to load them in the car and just as soon as it was loaded, they were going to leave for the dock.

She quickly cleaned up the kitchen the best she could, so their babysitter did not get stuck cleaning up after them. Before she started to wash the dishes, Walker called her from the garage. "C'mon girl, we're ready to leave for the stinking dock and you're holding us up, girl. Drop whatever the hell you're doing in there and get out here so we can shove off for the damn boat, baby. We got everything stuffed in the car and we're waiting on you, pretty lady.

She tried to wash the dishes, but Walker was not backing off as he warned her from the garage. "Raz, if you ain't out here in two fucking minutes, you're gonna be here after I'm gone, girl. We gotta get going or we're gonna end up late for getting down to the stinking dock. Your frigging boyfri… err…. Tee K is gonna be real pissed at you if you're the reason why we late, honey."

"I know, I know, I'm coming Bobby. Give me a few more minutes to get this done."

"You ain't got a few minutes to spare Raz." He bitched as he came back in the kitchen to see what she was doing and he added to his bitch at her. "C'mon Raz, the stinking babysitter told you last night to leave the dishes and she'd do them for ya, girl. C'mon, we're gonna be late."

"Hey Raz, don't pay attention to the big slob, we have plenty of time before we're late for the stinking boat. Walker's just pissed off because they useta send his father down in the mines to make sure it was safe for the stinking canaries, before the miners went to work." The Mutt offered as he walked in the kitchen to see what the hold up was with Ramirez

Walker looked at the Mutt with his eyes ablaze, and he snapped angrily at him for overriding him in front of Ramirez. "Fuck you man, keep your fucking nose outta my stinking business."

"Hey man, you're gonna turn my head with all this stinking flattery, man." The Mutt replied.

"I'll turn your fucking head for ya alright, buddy. You wanna know something else mister?"

"Naw, I think I know enuf already pal. Why don't you get offa her ass and leave her alone so she can finish up what she's doing, and then we can leave for the damn dock, man."

"You're really pushing it this fucking morning, stupid." He growled at the Mutt, and then he turned his attention back to Ramirez who was still trying to clean up the dishes as he and the Mutt fired more barbs at one another while they waited for Ramirez to finish up.

"C'mon Raz, you knew we gotta be down at the stinking dock by Zero Six Hundred fucking Hours, and you're still in here screwing around with the damn dishes, dammit."

"What?" The Mutt asked as he stared back at Walker for the moment with a grin on his lips.

"Now don't tell me you don't know we hafta be down at the dock at six fucking a.m. this morning, man." Walker hissed at his lifelong friend as he stared at him.

"Why the hell didn't you say that in the first stinking place man."

"Whatsumatter buddy, did the fucking zero throw ya off stride some, stupid?" Walker said as he smirked at his friend.

"Wow, you're really getting to be a stinking grouch this morning, buster. Hey Raz, you got some raw meat or something we can throw at him so your old man calms down a little, honey?"

"I have the only thing that'll calm him down when he gets like this Mutt." Ramirez turned to Walker and she opened her shirt and she gave him a good flash of her breasts.

"Hey girl that not only helped calmed the dopey bastard down some, but it sure helped me out a helluva lot at the same time, girl. Man, I'm feeling a little sleazy over looking at your Casabas like this Raz, which is really weird for my ass. Because I usually like the stinking sleazy feeling, honey. Man you got some set of tits there Raz." The Mutt offered as he enjoyed the show she was giving him and the others in the kitchen.

The quick flash from Ramirez instantly calmed Walker down, and now he was standing there giving Ramirez all the time she needed to finish cleaning up the dishes. But he did turn to the Mutt and say to him. "And you, since when did you ever do anything that made you feel even a little bit sleazy, asshole? As far as I knew, I didn't think you even understood the definition of the word sleazy, man. I hate to admit this buddy, but you're starting to surprise me a little lately with all the stinking smarts you're starting to display, pal."

"What the hell can I tell ya man? I done some things in my life that I'm not very proud of man, and the few things I'm proud of, were kinda disgusting at that, my old friend." The grinning Mutt offered as he looked Walker dead in the eye while trying to keep a strait face.

Walker turned and looked at Ramirez because he did not know how to reply to the Mutt, and when she looked at Walker, they both started laughing over his comment.

Ramirez had the kitchen cleaned up, so she put the dish towel down and said to the men. "Well you two birds, it looks to me that I'm now waiting for you guys to move so we can get going. Are we ready to head out for the dock, gentlemen?"

"Gentlemen, now you're really trying to insult the both of us, girl. What the hell's with the gentlemen slug you just fired off at us, baby?" The Mutt replied as he looked at Ramirez.

"Pardon me, I didn't mean to insult you two shitbirds. C'mon you slim balls, we have to leave so we can be at the dock before Toby gets there before us." She corrected herself for them.

"That's betta Raz, I'd hate like hell to be known as a stinking gentlemen you know. Not after all the work I done not to be recognized as one, honey." The Mutt said with a laugh in his tone.

"Yes dog man, I understand how hard you work at not trying to be mistaken as a gentlemen mister." She complained as she walked between the two men, and went out the door leading to the garage. Walker followed the Mutt out of his home and he locked the door behind him.

"Hey Walker, do you mind if I ask you a question man?" The Mutt asked him.

"Not in the least man, fire away." He replied as he closed the garage door and locked it.

"Hey man, do you think Raz was trying to hurt our feelings with that last zinger, man?"

"Well you know Raz as well as I do, do you think she was trying to insult you stupid?"

"Abso fucking lutely man." The Mutt replied in a flat tone of voice this time.

"Then you answered your own fucking question, man." Walker said back to him.

CHAPTER TWENTY TWO

FRIDAY, APRIL 27th, 2006. FIVE THIRTY IN THE MORNING ON BOARD THE BOAT CARRYING THE PERSIAN SOLDIERS TO THE UNITED STATES

Persian General Abdol Karim Kalantari, was carefully guiding the forty two foot boat through a shallow area situated just off the north section of Key West. The terrorist commander made good time with the boat heading for the Florida Keys, and he decided to take over command of the boat from the automatic helm system and run the boat for himself for a little while. He was employing the GPS and depth finder systems to know where he was, and how deep the water was below the keel of the boat. He looked to the back of the boat, and noticed two of his female fighters were dressed in bathing suits that left little to the imagination, and they had fishing lines in the water and were actually trying their hand at fishing.

So far, they came across seven small pleasure boats as they headed out to the open Ocean in their search of game fish. Every boat they passed, the other Captains took time to wave at General Kalantari as he navigated the boat around Key West. He was pleased by the pleasant response of anyone they passed on the water. As it was, not one of the other Captains became the least bit concerned by his boat, or the soldiers he allowed to remain outside the cabin. He figured this was because Major Fereshteh Mansouri and Sergeant Azamalaie Shirazi were dressed in the smallest of bathing suits he ever saw in his life.

Both female soldiers were making it look like they were fishing as the boat moved through the water off Key West at ten knots. Two other of his soldiers were at the stern of the boat, and Colonel Keshmotallah Khatami and Major Ghassan Abidal al-Zubedi were dressed in bathing suits, and they were acting like they were trying to help the women fish. General Kalantari picked these two male soldiers to dress in bathing suits, because they were in the best physical shape of all his soldiers. He was also dressed in a bathing suit.

As the boat carrying the cell of terrorists left the waters surrounding Key West, the number of other pleasure boats they came across, were far less. As their boat crossed over a cove outside Key West, the Persian General noticed a number of large sail and other pleasure boats moored in the center of the narrow inlet. Major Mansouri handed her fishing pole to Major al-Zabedi, and she left the stern of the boat and walked up to General Kalantari. She kissed him lovingly on the lips, and then asked him with concern lacing her tone. "General Kalantari Sir, why are there so many boats in the waters in that protective cove like that, sir? Is it because there might be good fishing in that area, and they're catching fish sir?"

The Persian Commander let out with a hardy laugh as he pulled the female Major close to his body and kissed her on the neck. He ordered the soldiers exposed on the boat to act like lovers enjoying fishing as he offered. "My little flower from the desert sands, the boats as resting in that inlet for the same reason you called it a protective cove. Before I left Cuba, the cursed fool Gonzales informed me I'll be coming across a number of protective coves and harbors where many boats visiting the Florida Keys, moored their boats. They do this so they don't have to pay for the privilege of remaining on the Keys without having to pay land taxes and the likes. Even their own people are constantly trying to rip off their foolish government, woman."

General Kalantari loved the feeling of the beautiful female Major being pressed up so close against his body. It thrilled him because he was feeling skin to skin contact, and he had all he could do refraining from pulling Major Mansouri down to the deck and making mad, passionate love to her on the deck of the boat, and it did not matter to him if the other soldiers on the boat watched them making love to each other.

Major Mansouri was also enjoying the close contact of their nearly naked bodies, and she was making the best of it by deviously rubbing her crotch up against the Vulture's rock hard body, and purring as she continued to lean against his body.

When the Vulture had enough of her teasing, he whispered in her ear. "Young evil woman who was born from the armpit of the evil devil, if you continue to tease me like you're doing, I'm going to attack you on the boat, woman. You might think I have to maintain control of this cursed boat, but it's on automatic helm. So I can leave my post any time I so choose woman. I suggest you return to the back of the boat and continue acting like you're fishing, so no one becomes suspicious about our reason for being on the water with this cursed boat, woman."

"Do you know where we are on the water General Kalantari Sir, and if you do, how long before we finally reach this Florida Key called Marathon, sir?" Major Mansouri asked her Commanding Officer with concern in her tone of voice, as she looked out of the boat windshield at the water before her. It was starting to show the first signs of getting light enough for them to actually see where they were going on the water.

"Yes I do know where we are Major Mansouri. We're about five miles away from Key West, and we're on an active heading due north, woman. All those lights we passed were coming from the American Coast Guard station on the worthless Island of Key West, Major. We're now less than forty five miles away from the cursed Island of Marathon. I'm forced to inform you this worthless Island we're heading for, is not called a Key but an Island, woman."

"How long do you think it'll take before we finally arrive at the Island of Marathon, General Kalantari Sir? I'm afraid to offer sir, but I'm getting tired of being on this cursed water for so long a time sir. It's starting to upset my stomach a little, and I'm beginning to feel woozy in my head I fear, General." Major Mansouri complained as she put her hands to her head to show her Commander she was serious about her complaint.

"Let me see." General Kalantari replied as he looked at his watch, it was five minutes to six and he did some quick calculations, and then he replied to the female officer. "I'm afraid we're about three and a half hours away from Marathon, Major. Fereshteh, if you're beginning to feel a little ill, look in the first aide kit of this foul boat. I was informed by Major Rodriguez there are some pills stored in there that'll help fight off the foul effects of sea sickness, woman. Don't allow it to get worse on you, or it might get bad enough for me to be forced to leave you on Marathon, and you'll miss the rest of the operation. I done a little investigation about sea sickness, and it can get bad enough to affect the inner ear, and disable the one inflicted with it to the point he be hospitalized if it becomes bad enough, women."

"I don't want to miss our operation, so I believe I shall do as you suggested, and check the first aide kit and find these pills you just spoke of, General Kalantari Sir." The worried Major replied as she struggled out of his arms, and then she went in the cabin of the boat to search for the first aide kit. She found it mounted in the head and opened it and found the pills. She opened the jar and removed two, and took them with some water. But being in the cabin while the boat was in motion, caused her to get sicker to her stomach, and she rushed out of the cabin for fresh air to try and settle down her stomach down again.

The Vulture noticed how green his Major became and he smiled because she was feeling so ill. He knew he would never leave her behind as he threatens her no matter what kind of physical shape, she was in. If she was in too bad a shape to continue with the mission, he would leave her in a motel room and once the operation was completed he would return and they would leave the United States the same why they entered. It was not because she was needed for the success of their operation; it was because he was in love with the beautiful young female Persian now.

SIX THIRTY A.M. FRIDAY, APRIL 27th, 2006 THE SIX MILE GRIL AND MARINA ON THE ISLAND OF MARATHON

Everyone going on the fishing trip was on the charter boat, and the twin engines were purring as the female Captain looked after a few last minute items, before she pulled away from the dock. Before the group boarded her boat, the Captain took the time to introduce herself to everyone on board. "Good morning lady and gentlemen, I'm Captain Sandi and this is my vessel named The Cherokee Lady. She's a thirty four foot Lurhs, and she's a damn good fishing vessel. I want everyone to get ready to shove off, because I want to be under the old Seven Mile Bridge and heading out for the Sombrero Lighthouse which marks the way to the Ocean side of the Island in a few moments, and we're going to be doing a little yellow tail snapper fishing first.

"The yellow tails have been running heavy just south of the lighthouse, and we'll bang a number of them before we go deep for the bigger game fish. By ten o'clock I'll be heading seven to ten miles out to where there has been reported a tuna run from thirty to one hundred and ten pounds in size. The few dolphin that have been showing up early, usually start their own runs between twelve and two o'clock in the afternoon. So we'll have enough of time to go after some of them while we are out too."

Captain Robert Walker and his lady, Sergeant Dorothy Ramirez, along with Toby, were paying close attention to everything the female Captain was saying to them. Walker was pleased the Captain announced she was prepared to go after a number of fish on this charter, and that meant they would come in with something on the hook. He was concerned, because he did not want to be on the water all day, and not come in with some fish. The Neck and Buckethead were interested in staring at the fabulous shape of the female Captain then they were with paying any attention to what she was telling them.

The soldiers and singer sat in chairs, or hung onto any hand grabs of the boat, as the Captain took over the helm after she had the first mate cast off the mooring lines, and she increased the idle of the motors and the boat slowly pulled away from the dock. The excitement between the fishermen was high, and Walker could see how happy Toby was going fishing with him again.

As the Captain skillfully worked the boat down the canal to the bay side, she called over her shoulder to everyone. "Please forgive me, but I forgot to introduce you all to my First Mate, his name is Carl Williams, and he's in charge of the gear, period. No one on board is allowed to bait or work the rods unless Carl is by your side. While we're trolling, if a fish hits, Carl will work the rod and hook the fish, and then he'll give the rod to the first one who wants to land a fish. I'll not tolerate any problems on my vessel, you can drink all you want, but if you get drunk and become unruly. I'll immediately terminate the charter and return to the dock, and there'll be no refunds. If you get out of hand, I'll stop the vessel and call the Coast Guard and have you removed from my vessel. I'm sorry if this sounds a little harsh, but we had one Captain from the Island out on a charter, and his customers got so drunk they almost took over his vessel. That's why the Captains adopted these stronger policies. These rules are for your protect as well as they are for the Captain and First Mate of the boat."

Captain Sandi finished speaking as the boat broke free of the canal, and it was heading towards the bay, she increased the speed to half throttle and the boat lunched forwards. When the Captain turned into the waterway, she went to full power and the boat increased speed to twenty five knots, cutting a good wake in the water. Within six minutes, the boat was going under the old Seven Mile Bridge, and Walker straightened up because it looked like the bridge was going to take the flying tower off the boat. People walking the old bridge or fishing from it, stopped what they were doing and watched and waved as the boat flew under the bridge. In another hundred feet, the boat charged under the new Seven Mile Bridge, and now the boat was heading towards the Sombrero Lighthouse. They were sailing by Boot Key at five hundred yards from land.

When the boat made its way in from Boot Key, the Captain turned the boat and she cut down on the speed of the vessel at the same time. Once she had the boat about four miles north of Boot Key, she turned the boat and aimed it towards the Sombrero Lighthouse and she dropped the speed of the boat down to between three and four knots.

The first mate went in action and he ran to the back of the boat and dropped four chum blocks into perforated bags and then he hung them over the side as the boat turned again, and it aimed itself east towards Key Colony, and the Captain placed the speed of the vessel at idle and it was slowly drifting towards the east.

Walker looked behind the boat and he could see a good chum slick rapidly developing behind the stern. He knew the Captain was going to draw yellow tails towards her trap. The surface of the water was dotted with a number of buoys from crab traps that had not been brought in by the trappers yet. They were on the grace period, but all crab and lobster traps had to be out of the water by the end of the month, or the owners would be fined by the Coast Guard.

Now, the first mate was running all over the back of the boat as he set up four light tackle poles and rigged them for the smaller fish. But the mate did not drop any lines in the water until the chum slick was about three quarters of a mile long. To increase the chum slick, the mate kept walking from one bag to the other and jiggling it into the water to get more of the slick out.

As the boat drifted east, the Captain kept an eye on the length and width of the slick, and when she noticed the first ripple in the water which meant a yellow tail hit a piece of chum, she called out to the mate. "Carl, get the hooks in the water, we have action out there."

Without looking at the Captain, Carl released the bail on two reels and the twelve pound test line started peeling off the reel. When the line was about fifty to six yards out, he passed the rods to Walker and the singer, and then he went to work on the remaining poles and released line on them. There were only four poles allowed fishing at any time, if they put out more than that, the lines would get tangled with each other. When the line was out far enough, Carl handed the third pole to Ramirez, and the forth one to No Neck. Buckethead stood by and watched as the others fished until one of them caught one. Once someone caught a fish, the open pole was going to be passed to him, and the one not fishing would be handed the pole from the next one who caught a fish. That way everyone on board the charter would get their chances to fish.

The Cherokee Lady was just about sitting dead in the water, and the Captain smiled because she saw how heavy the chum slick was building up, and it extended nearly a mile behind her boat. She was pleased when she saw the other charter boats going out, once the Captains noticed the chum slick, they gave it a wide birth as not to cut the chum slick in half and disrupt the fishing of the charter boat.

Even the smaller boats noticed and gave the slick a wide birth. This was another consideration any Captains offered to another, because no Captain wanted his chum slick cut in half by another vessel on the water.

Walker was staring at the surface of the water, searching for any sign of a fish near his bait. He jumped when Toby's bail snapped shut with a loud click, and the singer set the hook. The mate was allowing the fishermen to set the hooks on the smaller fish, but the game fish was his responsibility. The pole bent almost into a U shape as he fought the fish, he could not just horse the fish in, or the fish would snap the light line, he had to play the fish in. The mate moved to his side to lend a hand when Walker's bail snapped shut, and he was now fighting a fish. Ramirez's bail snapped shut and when the Captain noticed her mate did not pick it up, she called out. "Fish on." She drew her mate's attention to the only other female on board the boat.

The mate turned to Ramirez, but when he saw how well she was fighting the fish, he turned his attention back to the singer. The mate knew this man was the one paying for the charter, so he was going to make certain he brought in fish, especially the first fish caught.

Toby got the fish up along the portside of the boat, and the mate was hanging over the side and he netted the small fish and brought him on board. It was about two and a quarter pounder, and the mate skillfully removed the hook and then he stuffed the fish inside the ice filled fish box and closed the lid. Before he baited the hook and got the line back in the water, Walker's fish was up to the side of the boat on the starboard side, and he had to bring his fish in on his own. His fish was about two pounds and Toby started to bust his horns by telling him his fish was bigger as he grinned at the extremely dangerous specialized soldier.

The first mate dumped the fish in the box and baited Toby's pole and handed it to Buckethead before Ramirez got her fish up to the side of the boat. The mate landed it and baited the two lines. He returned one to Ramirez as he gave the other pole to the singer. Walker was forced to stand by until someone landed the next fish so he could go again.

Action on the boat was brisk, with each fisherman hooking one fish after the other, because they were hitting the lines so quickly, and driving the first mate crazy with trying to keep up with all the action. The female Captain was pleased with the way her first mate was keeping up with the amount of fish being caught by her customers on the charter.

ON BOARD THE BOAT CARRYING THE PERSIAN TERRORISTS HEADING FOR THE UNITED STATES. SEVEN THIRTY A.M., FRIDAY, APRIL 27th, 2006

General Abdol Karim Kalantari remained standing at the helm of the boat, even though the boat was basically steering itself through the shallow waters off the Florida Key known as Cudjoe Key. He looked at his watch and did some quick figuring, and knew his boat was less than two hours away from his final destination of Marathon Island. The boat was chugging along at a steady six knots, and the Persian Officer was fighting desperately not to take over the helm of the boat again, and increasing the speed so he could arrive at Marathon in half the time he figured on. He too was starting to become slightly ill to his stomach, and feeling the first signs of a headache coming on. Feeling the way he was, General Kalantari cast a quick look at the female Major Fereshteh Mansouri making like she and the other officer, Major Ghassan Abidal al-Zubedi were fishing. He noticed she was not showing any signs of becoming ill.

Taking a bit of his own advice that he earlier gave Major Mansouri, he left the helm and went below to the cabin and searched until he found the first aide kit. He opened it and found the pills that would help him with his seasickness, and he swallowed two of the horrible tasting pills that left a terrible aftertaste in his mouth.

After taking the pills, he returned to the helm, even though he was not needed to steer the craft. But standing at the wheel made the foreign officer feel like he was doing something constructive, and it also gave him something to do. He looked over the water before the bow of the vessel that seemed like it stretched out forever, and he was amazed at how calm and flat the water was. When he left Cuba, he was dreading running into a rough sea. But so far the water the entire way was absolutely perfect to be on the water.

Major Fereshteh Mansouri took notice of her Commander leaving the helm, and when he returned to his post, she gave her pole to another soldier and strolled up to the General and she asked him. "General Kalantari Sir, are you alright sir? I was concerned when you left your post for a few moments, sir. Is there any way I could be of assistance for you sir?"

"I'm afraid I might have caught what was bothering you earlier, woman. I'm feeling slightly ill, so I followed my own advice and took some piles that help with the seasickness. You have taken them, how long does it take before they start to have an effect on the sickness, woman?" He asked as he swiped at the sweat building on his forehead.

"I'm sorry to offer General Kalantari Sir, but I have no idea how long it takes for the pills to help, sir. I didn't pay much attention to it sir, all I know was soon I was feeling a lot better sir, although my stomach is still a little upset, sir." Major Mansouri replied with a smile.

"I hope it doesn't take long, for I'm really beginning to feel ill." The Commander snapped as he turned a bright green and he looked back at the female Major and tried to smile at her.

"It's much better if you take your mind off of feeling ill, General Kalantari Sir. Now that we are speaking sir, how much longer before we reach this Island we're searching for, General" The Major asked her Commander, trying to get his mind off of feeling ill.

"It's strange you ask me that question Major Mansouri, because I just checked the time and our position, and I believe we're less than two hours away from Marathon. Soon, we'll be off this cursed water, and have our feet planted on dry land again. This is a terrible way for a true soldier for Allah to be forced to begin his operation, by being out on the water for twelve hours. I'm a land soldier, not a fish who enjoys water. Ahhh, I pray Almighty Allah to again show me the soothing and warm sands of our vast deserts in Iran, woman." General Kalantari complained at the female officer as he again ran his hand over his sweaty face.

"It shall not be very long until we're back on land again sir, and then we'll start to feel much better about ourselves, General. The God of our fathers is calling for us to avenge the wrongs the land of Satan has caused to our beloved country, sir. Soon, we shall enjoy pleasure to hurt the sinful lands we're about to attack, General Kalantari." Major Mansouri tried to keep engaging her Commander in conversation, because she was still trying to get his mind off the sickness turning him green and slightly dizzy.

General Kalantari's hands were shaking as he continued to fight off the effects of the sickness assaulting his body. But he was also trying to will his mind to order his body to get over it before they reached Marathon. Speaking to Major Mansouri was helping him feel a lot better though, because the shaking was lessening, and the sweat was also letting up a little. The longer the Persian Commander spoke with the officer, the more he began to feel better.

General Kalantari ordered Major Mansouri to return to the stern of the boat, because they were starting to come across a number of small boats as they headed out for their day of fishing on the water. Suddenly, Major al-Zubedi called out from the stern of the boat, and pointed towards the sea to what was causing him some concern. "General Kalantari Sir, I believe I see one of those American Coast Guard boats Colonel Gonzales warned us about, before we left Cuba sir. It's far out, but it definitely looks like one of those ships he showed us the pictures of, General."

The Iranian Commander looked in the direction his Major was pointing, and he noticed a ship that looked military in nature. He cursed as he picked up the field glasses and trained them on the larger ship as it cut through the water like a knife at a quick rate of speed. As the Persian Officer focused the glasses, he was able to tell it was indeed a Coast Guard Cutter. But the ship was paralleling his boat and heading in the opposite direction, and the larger ship was at least three miles from his craft. Seeing the Coast Guard ship was not interested in them, or what they were doing on the water, the General let out his breath as he placed the glasses in their holder. But he failed to realize his illness left his body, and he was feeling much better.

General Kalantari realized why Colonel Gonzales had the automatic helm guide his boat so close to any land mass they passed. He knew because they were so close to land, the hunting Coast Guard ships would not easily notice, or challenge them as they headed for Marathon. Again he found himself thanking Allah for placing Colonel Gonzales in his path of fate.

Major Mansouri returned to the stern and retrieved her pole and was standing proudly while making like she was fishing. General Kalantari looked at the officer and smiled as he marveled over her exquisite shape and fine looks, and he thanked his lucky stars she was interested in him romantically. The Persian General forgot all about his illness and faking like he was steering the boat as he continued to stare at the stunning beauty standing on the stern of his craft. And now, for the first time since he agreed to attack the United States, he was having second thoughts about his mission and what might happen to them during the attack.

He started to entertain thoughts of forgetting about assaulting the United States. Now he found himself thinking about putting in to shore and turning himself and the Major over to the American authorities, and asking for political asylum. He found himself wondering how it would be like to live in the United States with the Major. He heard countless stories of how the American authorities gave cash to anyone they allowed into their country under the asylum plead. Living in the United States, having money the fools would give him, and having the Major hanging on his arm everywhere he went in the United States, was a thrilling thought indeed.

The General closed his eyes to better see them living in the United States and enjoying the many wonders this nation had to offer people who lived there in his mind's eye. Then he thought of how wonderful it would be never to see sand unless he and the Major were visiting a beach. He always wanted to see snow, and enjoy walking and playing in it. He also wanted to see the change in seasons, to enjoy the pleasing color changes of the trees he saw pictures of. Then he remembered how plain it was to live in Iran, always seeing vast deserts of sand, suffering through blinding sandstorms, and never seeing trees unless they were palm and date trees. How he wanted to walk on a sea of grass, and smell the grass as it was growing. To visit department stores where one could buy anything his heart wanted, grocery stores stocked to overflowing with food someone wanted to enjoy.

A sudden noise from the stern of the boat broke the trance the powerful Iranian Commander was enjoying. When his mind came back to reality, the officer placed these pleasant thoughts out of his mind as he looked for where the sound came from. What he saw made him smile as he stared at what was happening on the boat. Major al-Zubedi baited his hook, and he was fighting a fish that took his bait. Major Mansouri was yelling orders on how the Major should fight the fish, and they were both laughing as he struggled with the fish.

As the boat continued it steady sail towards Marathon, General Kalantari left the helm and went to the stern to see the fish his Major was fighting. He too found himself giving the Major orders on how to try and land the fish. Whatever type of fish it was, it was a large one and two other fighters came out of the cabin to see the fish. This was the first time in many months General Kalantari heard his soldiers laughing, or enjoying themselves the way these two were enjoying themselves, while trying to drag the fish to the boat.

It was Major Mansouri who was the first to see the fin and she realized it was a shark Major al-Zubedi caught, and she told him so. Once Major al-Zubedi realized he hooked a shark, he lost interest in landing the fish he even wanted to stop fighting it. General Kalantari ended the war between the fish and his soldier when he took a knife, and leaned over and cut the Major's line.

The pole jumped up and almost hit the Major in the face, as the shark turned and dove back into the deepness of the water. Major Mansouri looked at the Vulture with questioning eyes, and her Commander did not like the look as he barked nastily at her over it.

"What is this you offer me cursed daughter of the hot desert sands? How dare you look at me in this ugly a manner? Don't dare look down the end of your nose at me, or I shall order it removed and fed to dogs. We're heading for the United States to destroy the lowly infidels we're not here to enjoy their foul land and what it has to offer. Don't forget this warning, or I shall order your back ripped opened by the sting of the lash. Enough of this foolishness, I don't want you fools trying to catch another cursed fish. The rest of you arses of a camel, get inside the cabin before I have you shot. This is not a game we're entering, and there is no room for any thoughts in our minds but for the success of our mission. I shall not accept anything but those thoughts." With that said General Kalantari turned on his heels and went back to the helm and stared out the windshield to see where the boat was heading.

Major al-Zubedi looked crushed he lost the fish, and Major Mansouri felt bad as she leaned over and rested her hand on his arm, and she smiled as she offered. "Major al-Zubedi Sir, when we return to Iran, I shall rent a boat and the two of us will go into the Persian Gulf, and we shall try our hands at fishing off the shores of our own country, sir. Major, if you hook a fish there, you'll land it and we'll enjoy it as our supper, sir. But our Commanding Officer is correct with his orders, the only thoughts that should be lurking in our minds, is the success of our operation. Soon, we shall be heading home and enjoying our own country and treasures sir."

ON BOARD THE CHEROKEE LADY OFF OF THE COAST OF MARATHON

Captain Robert Walker, Sergeant Dorothy Ramirez, along with the country singer, the Mutt, Lieutenant Frank Hall, No Neck, Sergeant Robert Abbott, and Buckethead, Sergeant Vincent Lambardo were having such a blast catching so many yellow tail snappers, they completely forgot about the time. The first mate of the Cherokee Lady was also having a good time with the group of soldiers and the singer, laughing at their jokes, and putting their fish in the storage area of the boat. This was because the chum line was three hundred feet wide by the stern and working well for them, and it extended well beyond where they could see it, and the yellow tail seem to have taken up residence in the thick cloud of chopped up fish, and other luring baits mix in the frozen five pound blocks of chum.

Captain Sandi was keeping a close eye on the time, because she wanted to pick up the lines soon, and head out to deeper water off Marathon to catch the larger game fish. She looked at her watch, it was three minutes past nine, and she decided to give the customers another hour, maybe a little while longer if the fish were still hitting before she barked out, "Lines in." Then she would move the boat out to the much deeper waters off Marathon for some serious game fishing. The female Captain was all smiles as she watched the group of fishermen laughing and having a good time catching the smaller but good eating fish.

Because of where the charter vessel was fishing, the other boats coming out of Boot Key went around the Sombrero Lighthouse as not to upset the chum line. Walker, as always was on alert and he noticed the crafts charging passed the lighthouse on their way out to deeper water. He looked to the north and he could see many boats starting to go back and forth as they tried to catch fish. He then looked at the Captain, and he drew her attention out to the boats to see if she wanted to move out to the deeper water now.

The Captain was aware he was also a Captain who ran a charter business on the Island, and she smiled as she replied to his alarm. "I see you have a good eye there Captain Walker. I've been listening to the radio and there's a good weed line developing about nine miles north off the lighthouse in about five hundred feet of water. But as of yet, no one's reporting they're catching any fish, sir. I'm going to remain here for another hour or so, and by that time the tuna should be starting to make their run for the east, and we'll go after some of them at that time, sir. I'm keeping my eye on things so don't worry about it sir. I know what I'm doing here."

He smiled at the good looking female Captain as he offered her with a smile. "I'm sure you know what the hell you're doing on the water, Captain. I just wanted to make sure you saw the vessels lining up on the weed line out there, that's all. I could tell from here they musta found a weed line, Captain." But his attention was ripped away from the Captain when a fish suddenly hit his line, and he was forced to pay attention to what he was doing, and not what the other crafts were doing further out to sea.

The Captain smiled, happy the fish took his mind off of what was going on by the weed line. She sort of resented him for watching what she should be worried about. She disliked having another Captain on board her vessel, because her and her mate had to be at their best, or he was going to rip them on the Island and possibly hurt her charter business. As she thought about when she first discovered another Captain was going to be on her boat, she almost told the one chartering her vessel for the day to look for another craft to use.

He was fighting his fish and he was staring at the water. He could tell the fish was not a keeper from the weak fight it was giving him, but he was also using it for practice by playing with it as he pulled it towards the boat. For some reason he looked far out behind the charter boat, and he noticed a flying tower off in the distance, and he felt this vessel must be by the Bahia Honda State Park and beach. The beach was one of two rated the top five because of the pristine waters and sugar like sand. Bahia Honda was eleven miles from Marathon, and if it was not for the tuna tower, he would not have noticed the other craft. But the thing that drew his attention to the tower was the heading it was on. If the approaching boat continued on its present course, it would steam right up their chum line and crash into the stern of their boat.

He shook his head and smiled as he thought he was becoming too cynical about anything that drew his attention to it. Because he knew any Captain out on the water, would never sail his boat up an active chum line and crash into another craft. Besides, it was way too far away to be any way concerned about the other boat. He removed his eyes from the tuna tower and placed his attention on the small fish on his line and fighting.

By the time he landed the fish, even the first mate was laughing at the size. The fish could not have been eight inches long, and when the mate removed it from the line carefully as not to hurt the fish before he released it, he asked Walker if he wanted to take a picture with the monster of the deep. Even Toby was laughing about the small size of the fish, and he ribbed Walker about it. The Mutt wanted to keep the fish and have it mounted for Walker, but the mate informed him it was an illegal size, and they would get in trouble and fined if they kept the fish. The mate smiled again as he released the fish over the side of the boat.

Captain Sandi knew what the small size of the yellow tail meant to their fishing. It meant a shark or another large game fish must be in the area, and it drove the yellow tails out of the chum line. She looked up and down the chum line, and sure enough, she spotted a dorsal fin of a shark and from the size and shape of it, she knew it was a Hammerhead shark. Now, she knew they were no longer going to be enjoying good fishing at this spot.

Even though he was laughing with his friends on the charter, he also knew what the small fish meant to their fishing. Something in the water chased the larger yellow tails out of the chum line, but he never picked up the fin. But as he looked for what game fish scared off the fish they were catching, he again picked up the tuna tower which seemed much larger now. That was because he figured the oncoming boat he was concerned with was off Sunshine Key now, which was passed the seven mile bridge.

He noticed the vessel did not change course and felt this strange, because the boat was coming across the rock pile as the fishermen from the Island liked to call it. It was where the debris from the construction of the old railroad was dumped to make an artificial reef and good fishing in the area, and to get rid of the debris. If the Captain of the boat was interested in fishing, he would have stopped there and tried his luck for grouper and permit, and any bottom dwelling fish. He was training his interest on the boat rather than fishing.

Twice, the female Captain looked to where Walker was staring, but she did not pick up anything that might be spooking him. She was not looking for any trouble, and she did see the other craft that seemed to be coming straight at them, but it was five miles from where she might get concern over what that Captain might be up to.

Although they were still pulling in yellow tail, they were smaller than the ones they were catching moments before. So that meant the shark was still in the area, and if he was, the yellow tail would not return to the chum line. Captain Sandi knew their fishing here was over and her chum line was broken by the shark, and she was about ready to signal her first mate to pull in the lines, when the line on Buckethead's reel started being stripped off by the yard.

"Holy shit, I think I just got a fucking whale on the end of my fucking line, man!" Buckethead cried out as he sat up and took interest in fishing again, as he fought whatever it was caught on his line. He was trying to see the fish as he worked it in the water, but he did not see any sign of it, just the pull on his line.

Ramirez and the Mutt pulled in their lines so as not to interfere with Bucket's fish. Toby had his line out of the water, and the first mate was baiting his hook stripped by one of the yellow tails still hanging around the chum line. The smaller fish were not enough for the shark to bother with. All the others on board the charter vessel were moving around and trying to stay out of Bucket's way. The first mate left the singer's gear, and was standing by Buckethead, and he was trying to tell him how to properly fight the fish he hooks up with the light tackle they were using for the yellow tail.

"C'mon Buckethead, you can't let the damn fish get his head down on you man, or he's going to snap your line on you, or throw the hook back at ya. You're doing it all wrong man, do you want me to takeover and properly work the fish for ya until he tires, and once he's exhausted you can have the pole back and land him. If you keep fighting it the way you're doing, you're going to lose the fish sure as hell, buddy." The first mate offered with concern because he felt Buckethead was not going to get the fish near enough to the boat for them to see what it was, before the fish broke his line.

"Hell no asshole, I'll get the fucking fish to the ever loving frigging boat by myself, man. You be ready to gaff the damn thing when I get him close enuf to the damn boat to do your act with it, man." Buckethead barked angrily at the first mate, as he did not take his attention off the fish. He was dying to see what it was himself.

"Okay Bucket, but if you keep fighting him the way you're doing it, you're not going to see what he is." The first mate complained at Buckethead, and he was using his nickname because everyone else on the boat was calling each other by them, so he also picked up the habit as well.

Walker was standing near Captain Sandi and he mumbled so no one else on board the boat heard what he said, as they watched the big man fighting the fish. "You know the big jerk hooked the damn shark that drove the stinking yellow tails from the chum line."

"I know that, but he's having so much fun fighting it, so we might as well allow him to continue until the fish finally breaks his line on him, Captain Walker sir." The Captain replied with a smile as she looked at Walker.

CHAPTER TWENTY THREE

ON BOARD THE BOAT CARRYING THE LATEST GROUP OF TERRORISTS TO ATTACK THE UNITED STATES

General Abdol Karim Kalantari's boat was almost across the area that covered the open section that paralleled the seven mile bridge leading to the Island of Marathon, so he ordered the three soldiers he had dressed in bathing suits to go below and dress in their regular clothes, and then arm themselves as his soldiers on the boat were. The Commander of the group of Persian terrorists also dressed, and then he tucked the MP5K-PDW under his shirt with the sling controlling it. He returned to the helm but did not button his shirt in case he needed the weapon. He returned to the helm as his boat got about three hundred yards off the edge of Boot Key.

He too was interested in the charter boat he was rapidly closing in on. He did not understand why his boat did not turn automatically, because they were closer to another boat than he would have allowed. One thing that was not explained to him by the Cuban Officer was the automatic helm would not recognize another boat, and if they came across one, he would have to take over the helm and move the boat out of harm's way or the two boats would collide. This was the first boat the Black Fin neared close enough to be concerned with, and he did not know what to do.

Major Mansouri and Major Khatami came out of the cabin and joined their concerned Commander stationed at the helm of their boat. They were armed and ready to engage any problem they came across. Emotions were high on the Black Fin since General Kalantari announced the land mass they were seeing was the Island of Marathon. He had no way of knowing it was only Boot Key that protected Marathon from the full force of a hurricane that might hit the Island. The General's automatic helm was programmed to take his boat down Sister's Creek which was on the far end of Boot Key, and it lead to the main land of Marathon. The boat was going to travel through the channel and dock at the Marina that allowed sailors to get on land just across from the shopping center of Publix's.

Major Mansour noticed their boat closing in on the charter boat, and she brought this up to the Vulture's attention and he replied. "I see the cursed boat before us, and I'm waiting for the automatic helm to move our boat out of this collision course. I was informed this helm would do anything to protect this miserable boat, woman. What is this foul stink I'm smelling, can the waters off this Island be so polluted it smells like the devil's armpit, woman?"

"General Kalantari, the boat we're closing in on is a commercial fishing boat sir, and judging by the number of people I'm seeing on the other boat. The smell we're suffering has to be what the commercial boat does to draw help fish to the boat so they can catch them, sir." Major Mansouri offered in a rush to her Commanding Officer. She was able to see how upset he was, one because they were coming dangerously close to another boat, and the second reason was from the terrible smell coming from the chum line they just entered. The female officer was able to see the fish oil floating on the surface of the water, and she knew this was where the terrible odor was coming from, as it got stronger when they entered the slick.

General Kalantari ripped his eyes way from the other boat they were closing in on, and he glared savagely at the female soldier as he growled at her at the same time. "All of a sudden, you know an awful lot about how the cursed infidels of this evil place fish in their foul lands, Major Mansouri! Is there something you have failed to mention to me woman?"

"What do you mean by that statement, General Kalantari Sir?" Major Mansouri snapped as angrily back at her Commander, as she automatically placed her hands on her hips and stared at him. She did not like what he might have suggested about her.

"I didn't mean a thing by my statement, foul woman. I just wanted to know how you know so much about how these cursed and lowly infidel's fish in their foul country woman that is all." General Kalantari fired back nastily at her as he again turned his attention to the commercial fishing boat that was now less than a mile directly in front of them.

"Oh, well General Kalantari Sir, while we were going through our training back on the Island of Cuba, I made friends with a young Cuban soldier, a Lieutenant Esteban Navarro, and he informed me he visited his family living in the Florida Keys on a number of occasions. And, since we were going to invade the United States through these same Islands he visited, I thought it might be a good idea if I found out all I could about these worthless Islands that make up the Florida Keys, sir. Every time I saw this Cuban soldier, I spoke to him about the Keys, and it was during one of these conversations that he informed me how the hated American's fish in their waters, sir. That is why I know of this strong stink we're picking up at this time sir, and I believe the strong odor is coming from what the worthless American dogs call a chum line I believe, General Kalantari Sir." Major Mansouri replied to her Commanding Officer while maintaining the sharp edge in her tone.

"I don't have the time for this kind of foolishness, woman. I have a boat lying directly in our path, and I don't know if this foul machine is going to crash our boat into the cursed American one. When by the devil's hand is this cursed machine ever going to turn so we don't hit the other foul American craft, woman?" General Kalantari asked his female officer as his forehead broke out in a cold sweat as their boat continued to close in on the charter boat three quarters of a mile ahead of them.

"General Kalantari, if the boat doesn't turn on its own, I suggest you take over control of the boat and turn it yourself, sir. We cannot afford a possible collision with another craft on the water, sir. If that happens, it'd place a quick end to our entire operation, and we'll find ourselves locked in the fight of our lives with the police authorities of this foul Island, who would be carrying out their duties to make certain none of us drown if we hit that other boat and sink, sir. Also General, if we come too close to that other boat, the Captain of that craft might complain to the United States Coast Guard about us, and we're labile to have them challenge us, even if we don't actually collide with the other ship, General Kalantari Sir.

"But either way we look at it General Kalantami Sir, it'd spell the quick end of our mission in the United States sir, even before we had a chance to carry out our mission for Allah and our President, sir. General Kalantari Sir, you have to do something, and you have to do it soon at that, before we end up in serious trouble with the other boat out before us, sir. Think of all we would lose because we didn't control the evil driven boat until we ended up where we were scheduled to land in this god forbidden and cursed Island, General Kalantari Sir." Major Fereshteh Mansouri was begging her Commanding Officer now to take over command of the craft and turn the boat before it was too late, and they hit the other boat, or they came so close it caused the other Captain to alert the Coast Guard on them.

General Kalantari ripped his eyes off his female Major staring at him with pleading eyes, and he focused them on the boat about a mile dead ahead of them. His mind was screaming to do something, and to do it in a hurry. But he was deathly afraid to take command of the boat this close to Marathon. Before he left Cuba, Colonel Gonzales warned him in no uncertain terms, the waters surrounding Marathon were extremely shallow at many points, and warned him to allow the automatic helm to control the boat until he was able to dock at their destination on the Island. There he would place his soldiers on land, and the help he offered him would protect and supply them with the vehicles they needed to get them to Miami and their target.

ON BOARD THE CHEROKEE LADY

When the approaching boat cut into the chum line, Captain Robert Walker and the female Captain got angry. But as the other boat continued traveling directly at the stern of the Cherokee Lady, they grew more concern about the Captain's intentions. Slowly, the large boat coming from Cuba kept creeping its way directly at the stern of the Cherokee Lady. Now, everyone on board the charter boat noticed, and they became concerned at how close the other craft was coming to theirs. All but the massive Buckethead, he was still involved with trying to land the fish he was fighting on his light tackle. Everyone on the stern of the boat moved up towards the cabin, for fear the other boat was going to plow right into them. Toby noticed the other boat and screamed at the female Captain of their charter vessel.

"Captain, doesn't that damn fool see us sitting out here for Christ sake!"

"I don't know what's wrong with the asshole. He has to see us sitting here unless he's totally blind dammit, or he must be running his vessel with his eyes shut for the love of God." Captain Sandi roared back at the singer with fear lacing her tone, as she stared at the other boat rapidly closing in on them. In all her life on the water, she never had a Captain of another charter boat come so close to hers, let alone cut into her chum line like this one just did.

Walker looked at the Captain, and she read the wild look in his eyes. She realized he wanted to do something about the other boat coming down on them from the stern, as she nearly roared at the other Captain on her boat. "What's wrong with that damn Captain, didn't he see our chum line out there? The damn fool he is, I should call the Coast Guard on him, dammit."

"The hell with the fucking chum line Captain, doesn't the other Captain see our vessel sitting here, dammit? He's gonna plow right into the stern of this damn thing if he doesn't veer off soon. God dammit, I wish I had my M-16 on this fucking boat, I'd run a zip in front of his boat, and if that didn't turn the asshole. I'd chew up his stinking helm on the lousy bastard." He growled as he stared at the other boat still coming right at them.

Finally, Buckethead took notice of the other boat so close to them, and he got angry when the other boat crossed his line, and the props of the engines cut his line. His rod snapped back and he turned and yelled at Walker like he was going to be able to do something about the other boat. "Hey Walker, didja see what that uther fucking boat just did to me, man? He cut across my fucking line and cut my fish off my line with his stinking engines, man. If you don't do sumthin about that asshole man, I'm gonna dive in the stinking water and swim after his fricking ass, buddy. Then I'm gonna grab his fucking boat by the damn bow and drag the damn thing under the water on the asshole, man. What the hell is the sonofabitch doing so fricking close to our boat anyway, man? If he doesn't turn fast, he's gonna smash right into our damn ass?"

Everyone standing with the Captain by the helm, ignored the Bucket's complain as the Captain went into action, and she ordered Walker to move. "Captain Walker, I want you to get back at the stern and wave your arms at that asshole, and try and get him to turn off our backside, sir. I'm going to start our engines and prepare to take evasive maneuvers before the damn fool runs his craft right up the stern of this vessel on us, sir. Dammit, I don't have the time to hail the Coast Guard and get them on this asshole before he slams into us, sir. I have to move the boat now dammit. Get going sir and try and get his attention before they hit us, sir."

The concerned female Captain screamed at Walker as she turned for the helm and started her engines and slammed the throttles to the hilts, and she drastically cut the wheel hard to the starboard side, and the deeper waters off to that side of the boat. She did not want to cut the wheel towards portside, because she knew shallower waters rested there and she would run aground, and be trapped and the other Captain would cut her boat in half broadside. She started laying on her air horns as the Cherokee Lady lunged forward, and the boat responded to the harsh turn she demanded from her boat.

ON BOARD GENERAL ABDOL KARIM KALANTARI'S BOAT

The fuming Vulture was glued to the deck before his helm as he continued to stare at the other boat that was less than a quarter of a mile before the bow of his boat now. The General's boat was aimed directly at the stern of the other boat, and he was frozen in place while he waited for the automatic helm to react to the boat dead ahead of his craft. He knew he was too close to the other boat for safety reasons, but what to do about this situation was never properly explained to him by the Cuban when he went over everything he might face on the water while heading for the shores of the United States with his soldiers on board the vessel.

Major Fereshtch Mansouri stood alongside General Kalantari, and she was staring at the other boat as their vessel continued to close in on it at eight knots. She looked at her Commanding Officer and saw in his eyes he did not know what to do next, and she said to him. "General Kalantari Sir." She was trying to snap him out of his trance.

General Kalantari turned and looked at his Major and snapped at her savagely. "Major, what is wrong with this cursed boat sailing under the devil's guiding hand? Does this foul thing not see the other boat lying directly in our fooking path? The automatic helm has to respond to this threat, or the foul thing is going to cause us to crash into the other boat."

"General Kalantari Sir, I don't believe the automatic helm sees that other boat, sir. I believe if we're going to avoid hitting it, you'll have to take command and turn the wheel, so we don't hit the boat. General, you have to turn the boat or we're going to crash into it!" The Major nearly yelled at her Commanding Officer. Her tone was highly elevated because of the fear of crashing into the other boat made her scared, and she wanted her Commander to do something.

"But the lowly dog of the god cursed Cuban fool who informed me that the worthless automatic helm would turn the boat on its own accord, before we got in any trouble with the miserable boat, woman. I don't believe for one second, I should interfere with the course of the evil boat by taking over the helm. If I take over the helm on the god cursed machine guiding it for us, I might turn the boat in the wrong direction and then possibly hit something else that sits in this cursed water off this foul Island that I'm unaware of, woman." He yelled at the soldier while not taking his eyes off the other boat for one second. All he could see was the other boat was getting larger as they closed in on it

"But General Kalantari, if you don't take over the helm and turn the boat, we're going to crash into the other boat, sir. I'd much rather you turn the boat and get in other trouble, than to allow the automatic helm to plow this boat into the other one, sir."

General Kalantari was confused as what to do next with the boat he would not move. But when the vessel less than one hundred yards before his bow he when in action, he jumped over the action of the other Captain. Now, there was someone on the back of the boat, and he was waving his arms frantically, and making the motion for him to veer off with his hands. As the Vulture continued to stare at the other vessel, a cloud of heavy smoke came bellowing from the waterline from the other boat's exhaust, and when the other boat lunged wildly forward and carried out a harsh and erratic turn towards its starboard side. He went in action and the Vulture grabbed the wheel and cut it hard to the portside of his craft. Everyone standing on either boat went suddenly pitching in the direction their boat was harshly turning in.

Walker was hanging onto one of the kleets on the stern, or he would have been flung into the water, when the Captain moved the vessel so violently. When he got his feet back under him, he stared hotly at the other boat as it went into a hard turn in the opposite direction than the Cherokee Lady was carrying out. He knew the other Captain just aimed his boat at the shallow reef line that surrounded Boot Key, and he was going to run aground in the shallow waters. He was worried, if the other boat ran aground at the speed it was traveling, it was going to rip the bottom out of the boat out. But that vessel was not his worry, because he turned his head to check on his friends. The first one he looked for was his girlfriend. He smiled when he saw Ramirez safely hanging onto the tuna tower so she did not fall.

When he knew his lady was okay, he checked on the rest of his party. Everyone else was hanging onto the tuna tower, or anything else they could hold on to stop them from falling or being pitched into the water. The Captain was hanging onto the side of the boat with one hand, and maintaining control of the steering wheel of the vessel with the other.

Slowly, the Cherokee Lady gained control over the turn she was forced into by the excited Captain. The bow of the vessel returned to the water and dug in and helped stabilize the boat, and the Captain turned the wheel to the center to get her on a straight heading. When she felt the craft was okay, she called over her shoulder. "Walker, what's going on with the other vessel?"

General Kalantari grabbed hold of the wheel and spun it, and the boat instantly responded to his commands. The vessel leaned to the portside and one of her props almost came out of the water. The bow of the Black Fin boat sliced through the water, and no sooner did the boat straighten out then it lifted high out of the water from the bow. It seemed like some unforeseen giant hand suddenly grabbed the back of the boat and stopped it dead in its tracks. Terrible loud grinding sounds came from the bow as the craft slammed into the shallow water less than a foot under the surface of the water. The Persian fighter's gathered in the cabin came pouring out when the water started to flood the front of the boat. The craft came to a stop, with the bow sticking out of the water. Chunks of boat floated on the surface as gear, items the General needed, and anything stored on the boat, slid into the water.

"Hey Captain the uther boat just ran aground and she hit real hard and is going down. I see a whole pack of idiots coming out of the damn cabin. It doesn't look like any of the flaming asses know what the fuck they're doing on board the disabled vessel, Captain. I can't locate the Captain in the mess of people, and I see no one taking charge of the others on board the craft. How many fucking people does the asshole have on board that damn thing? He's seriously overloaded for the size of the vessel. You betta inform Coast Guard we have a floundering vessel Captain, and then you betta get in there and help out before the assholes end up drowning. Judging by the way they're acting, I don't think any of them can even swim for fuck sake." He replied as he watched the mayhem taking place on the stern of the other boat.

"I'm on it Captain." The Captain reached for her radio and pressed the button and roared into the mike. "One Nine to United States Coast Guard Command Center Marathon, this is the Captain of the Cherokee Lady, I'm reporting a vessel running hard aground seven thousand yards from the mouth of Sister's Creek on the west side of the Island of Boot Key. The vessel hit ground hard, and is in danger of sinking. So far, there are no Mae West's (people) in the water, sir. But the vessel is definitely sinking. I'm changing course and am heading in to help out any Mae West's who need assistance. I'll remain on position until help arrives from you, sir. Over."

"This is United States Coast Guard Command Center Marathon, Florida. We received your Mayday transmission five by five, and are dispatching two go fast pontoon vessels for immediate assistance to your reported Mae West situation, Captain. We're also notifying the United States Coast Guard Cutter Sea Spray, and ordering her to report to the scene of the accident at this time, Captain. We thank you for your assistance in this matter, and we'll speak to you once we're on site and take your report, Captain. We should be arriving on scene within thirty minutes at the latest, Captain. This is United States Coast Guard Command Center Marathon, standing by on One, Nine for further assistance. Over and out."

"Walker, I have the Coast Guard responding to the accident site sir, and I'm turning towards the floundering vessel to lend assistance to them, sir. Stand by while I turn the craft, and we'll lend them a hand and take them on board our vessel until the Coast Guard gets here and they take them off our hands for us, Captain Walker. We have to go fast pontoon boats coming out of Coast Guard Command, sir." The female Captain of the vessel warned Walker and the others on board the boat with her of her impending turn again.

Sergeant Dorothy Ramirez was standing by the female Captain while Captain Robert Walker was standing by the stern, and he was keeping a close eye on the people he saw on the other boat getting ready to abandon it. The Mutt was with the women and he looked at their concern and offered. "Hey girls, if you put your breasts together, you can think a lot betta you know."

Captain Sandi and Ramirez gave the Mutt such a disgusted look that he turned and went to the back of the boat to get away from the two angry women. Walker heard the comment and he looked at the Mutt when he got by his side and snapped at him. "One of these fucking days you're gonna say something that's important, stupid. You never take anything serious in your wasted life do you, buddy? This ain't no fucking game we're playing here, we got people in trouble out there and we gotta help them, and then we're gonna kick their fucking asses, man."

The Captain skillfully turned her vessel, and it was heading directly at the floundering boat, she was traveling at just idle speed so she could better control her boat in the shallow waters.

General Kalantari struggled to his feet because he was sent flying when his boat hit the reef, and he was taking command of his fighters who were battered and bleeding from numerous nicks and cuts. Major Mansouri was getting to her feet because she was pitched to the deck from the violent collision of the boat and shoreline. She looked at her Commander, and then she informed him. "General, the boat is sinking and it's no longer any further use to us, sir. I suggest we abandon the boat and swim towards that land about a hundred yards from us, sir."

General Kalantari looked in the direction his Major was pointing in, and he snapped at her. "That is a good idea Major, have our foolish soldiers get over the side of this cursed boat and swim towards that land, make certain they take their cursed weapons with them in case we're challenged by any of the local police of this foul Island. We cannot allow anyone to interfere with our mission now we're so near land."

Colonel Khatami rushed to his Commander's side, and he excitedly pointed out the boat they almost collided with, had turned and was heading directly for them.

"The worthless infidels are coming to help us, and we must be prepared to kill any of them who try to help us, sir. We have to make land and locate the ones Colonel Gonzales ordered to help us with our mission, sir. Take three of these worthless soldiers with you to the stern of this foul boat, and if that other boat comes too near us, shoot and kill the fools on the craft, sir. Nothing the hated American fools do must stop us from completing our mission in this cursed land of endless sin and lust, Colonel."

Walker was leaning over the side of the boat watching the wild action taking place on the stern of the rapidly sinking other boat. He cocked his head to the side when he noticed four people on the floundering boat rush to the stern of the vessel. In his mind it registered if he did not know better, he would swear these people were taking up defensive positions against them, and they were preparing to fire on them. As their boat closed in on the disabled craft, he was just about to call out and warn the female Captain of the possible danger, when a short burst of automatic weapon fire racked across the helm of his boat. Two rounds ripped into the shoulder of the Captain, sending her flying and crashing to the deck.

The instant Ramirez heard and recognized the sound of weapon fire, she instantly ducked and it was the only reason she was not hit by any rounds. The Mutt also ducked down and reached up and pulled the staring singer down behind the protection of the bow. The rest of the soldiers on board the vessel likewise took protection behind anything they could hide behind. Walker pulled his head in and dove for the deck for his protection. He looked at the Mutt still trying to help protect the scared country singer, and he grumbled at him in an angry voice.

"Someone around here is being awful damn careless with fucking fire arms, man."

"Yeah, I heard it man. Whatdaya wanna do bout it man? Are we gonna allow them flaming assholes to shoot at us and not do anything about it, Homes?" The Mutt replied as he kept his hand resting on Toby's head to keep it down so it did not get blown off on him.

"I don't know man this isn't our stinking fight to tangle with, buddy. Hey Bucket, check on the stinking Captain's condition and see if she's still alive, man. Neck, get your ass up here on the double quick and help the Mutt out with the damn singer. Ramirez, whatdaya wanna fucking do about this shit we're in, sister? Do we act, or do we keep our stinking heads down and allow the frigging Coast Guard people handle this for us, girl?" Walker asked as he looked at his girlfriend as Buckethead reported to him that the wounded Captain of the boat just brought the long dirt nap, she was dead.

Before Ramirez could reply to his question, the Neck got up to them and she saw he was bleeding in the arm, and offered to Walker. "Robert, I was going to say we stay out of this one, but they have drawn first blood from us. So, I want blood from them. What do you think this is about, Bobby? Why the hell are they shooting at us?"

"One of us is hit, who's hit dammit?" Walker roared at his people on the boat.

"I don't wanna answer that question Walker because you're gonna get on my stinking ass for taking a round, man." No Neck offered as he got up to Walker crawling on his belly.

"You, I shoulda known it was you who took a fucking round, you asshole." Walker roared at the big man as he struck out with his foot and kicked him on the side of his head and then added. "How the fuck many times are you gonna take a stinking round before you finally get your fat head down, so you don't get hit again, buster? How bad you wounded asshole?"

"It's nothing, just a stinking nick that's all, buddy. It ain't gonna stop me from getting revenge on these stinking assholes who grazed my fucking ass, man. Didn't they know we were coming to help them, man?" The Neck complained as he licked the wound so Walker could see that it was not anything to worry about.

"Well people that settles it then for us. These assholes drew first blood, and we'll draw their last before we're done with the fucking idiots. I don't know what the hell's going on, but I'm sure as hell gonna find out in a fast hurry it up. It's a shame they killed that damn Captain, I kinda liked her man. That gives us two reasons to go after them…"

"Why do you think they fired on us Walker? What the hell do you think they're up to man?" Buckethead asked with concern lacing his tone as he stared at Walker and waited for his answer.

"Let me tell you something pal, they ain't here to go on a fucking sightseeing tour, man. What the fuck do you think a group of people heavily armed want in the United States, asshole?" He snapped back at the massive man, and then he shook his head at him.

"I think they're up to no good buddy, do you think they might be another group of fucking terrorists, and they're planning to attack us in our own stinking country, man?" Buckethead replied to Walker, and then he smiled a quick victory smile.

"You won the stinking cigar buddy. Of course they're a bunch of fucking cowards, and they're here to hurt innocent Americans. But this time they made one major stinking mistake, they walked across our fucking path, and we're gonna stop them cold, before they can carry out their rotten plans. Hey Mutt, you got the stinking civilian, we're gonna get these pricks. You take the civilian and get him out of harm's way the moment we're on fucking ground, man."

"Hey wait a minute here Walker, I'm in with the rest of you guys. If this group of people is trying to sneak into the United States to cause another terrorist attack against us, I want to be part of you guys who stop the damn assholes, sir." Toby complained as he looked into Walker's eyes and then waited for the reply to his complaint.

"I really fucking appreciate it man, but you're a fucking civilian, and you're gonna end up getting in our stinking way and getting yourself or someone else killed, because you don't know what the fuck you're doing attacking a bunch of damn terrorists trying to get in our country, man. Let the Mutt get you outta our way safely man, that'll be enuf help from you over this mess, pal." He snapped hotly at the country singer as he held him in his angry gaze.

"No way Walker, I want to be part of your guys. I know how to handle a weapon I've been hunting since I was a kid with my father. Besides, you called me an armature, let me tell you something about armatures. Remember the Ark was built by an armature, and the Titanic was built by professionals, and you know what happened to them ships." He offered in his defense.

"You got a pretty good point there buddy and hunting is all well, good, and a lot of stinking fun, man. But what you were hunting in the fucking woods wasn't trying to kill you back, man. Let the stinking Mutt get you the hell outta our fucking way man, and let it go at that will ya buster." Walker growled angrily at the singer.

"I'm not leaving you people, I want to help you stop these people from attacking us, Captain Walker!" He demanded hotly as he now openly glared back at Walker this time around.

Walker stared at the singer for several moments, and then he laughed as he shook his head and snarled back at him. "Okay man you got it. But if you get in my fucking way, the terrorists are gonna be the least of your stinking problems to deal with, pal. I'll pop a damn cap in your stinking ass and then I'll leave you where you fall…" He stopped speaking when the Cherokee Lady drifted onto the same reef the terrorist boat hit. When it came to a stop, Walker warned the others on the vessel. "Okay people, it looks like it's too late for us to get the stinking civilian the fuck outta harm's way anyhow. We need some fucking weapons if we're gonna put up a defense against these lousy scumbags, people."

"I got us some stinking weapons Walker. Looking for weapons on this tub didn't give us much to pick from man. I found two spear gun and extra spears, two flare guns, and four dive knives. That's all there is man." The Neck reported to Walker with a smirk on his lips.

"It looks like they'll hafta fucking do until we can get back to my place, and then we can arm ourselves for bear and go after these fucks good and proper. I'll take a spear gun and give the uther one to the Mutt. The rest of you people hafta pick and chose from the other weapons we got. We'll make the best of it for the time being. Neck, you and Bucket keep a watch on the damn singer. If he gets in your way, put him to sleep nice and peacefully like, and we'll pick him up later once the fun and games are over with, man. Raz, you stay by me, I'm sure these fucks are gonna try and get on Boot Key so they can disappear on the stinking Island, until they can get transportation and head for their intended target." Walker growled at the Neck and he started handing out the weapons he found.

There's no chance these people might be a bunch of stinking Cuban refugees trying to sneak into our country?"

No chance in hell, not with the way they're fucking armed and firing at us. Regular refugees want nothing more than to disappear real quick like. These scumbags are here to cause us pain and suffering, stupid." Walker fired back at the Neck.

"Stupid, huh buddy? Neck complained under his breath at his Captain

Once everyone on board the Cherokee Lady was armed with a mess of different weapons, Walker took charge and he poked his head just above the gunnels to see what the terrorists were up to. The Cherokee Lady ended up running aground a hundred and fifty feet away from the other boat. Walker took a quick look, and then he ducked his head back down and reported to the rest of his anxious people.

"Okay grunts we have at least six of the lousy turds going over the side of the stinking boat, and they're trudging their way to Boot Key. I saw some of their weapons, and it looks like they're armed with the MPS5K PDW machine guns. The way the few of them I saw being carried, the lousy pukes look like they know how to use the damn things, guys. I want everyone to dip over the starboard side of this damn tub and get on Boot Key as quickly as possible. The water can't be five feet deep here and it gets shallow real quick on us. I wanna get on the damn Island before any of them scumbags do, people. Once we're on the stinking Island, we'll set up and pick a few of the bastards off and take their weapons. Once we're properly armed with the machine guns, we'll level the playing field with the rest of the turds, and then we'll show them the errors in their way of think of trying to attack us in our country.

"Right now we're at the disadvantage, so we gotta change that bullshit in a fast hurry it up. Get over the damn side and make your way for the stinking Island. You two tree trunks keep the civilian between you guys so he doesn't get lost on us, or the lousy turds don't get him before we get them. Mutt, Raz, you're with me and we'll go over the side last and follow the uthers to the Island. When we get on the Boot Key, we'll make our way to the left and intercept the pricks and get their stinking weapons for our use.

"I didn't get a good number on the stinking bad guys, but I placed the number between fifteen and twenty, and I picked up a number of hens with the male pricks. From the looks of them, they look like a pack of fucking A-rabs, but it's obvious they came from the direction of Cuba. So they could be a bunch of stinking Cuban refugees who would rather fight it out with us, than be shipped back to their damn Island. Either way, they drew first blood against us and we gotta pay them back for that one. Besides people, they killed the Captain of the stinking vessel and that makes them fair game for revenge."

"Hey Walker, I got dibs on some of the hens, man. If we take them out, I'm free to check them out my way, man." The Mutt offered with a huge smile on his lips as he stared at Walker.

"Fuck you Mutt we don't have time to play with the damn hens. Get serious, we got a shit filled situation here, and we gotta stop them before they get offa the damn Island and we lose them." Walker stopped speaking and gave the look that forced Buckethead and No Neck to action. The Neck pulled the singer to his feet and shoved him to the starboard side of the vessel, as Buckethead allowed his body to slip over the side, barely upsetting the surface of the water. The Neck helped Toby over the side and when he was standing on the sea floor, the water barely came up to his armpits. The Neck was the next to go over the side. Walker poked his head above the gunnels again to make certain the bad guys did not see his people heading for the Island. Once he was sure they did not pick them up they took off.

Where the soldiers got to Boot Key, the undergrowth was heavy and hid them from the terrorists. When the group was ashore, Walker led the way for the others to their targets. The going was rough for them, and with the soldiers trying to be as silent as possible, it was taking them longer than Walker figured on, for them to set up on the terrorists also coming ashore.

The Vulture, General Kalantari remained on the boat and he was busy pushing his soldiers over the side. He wanted everyone off the vessel before the Coast Guard arrived on site, and they stopped them from getting ashore. The water was deep, but once his soldiers climbed up the reef, the water was barely over their knees. The Persian terrorists moved slowly because they were carrying their extra equipment and weapons.

Walker's people were on Boot Key a while before the first of the Persian fighters made it to shore, and the American soldiers were heading off to intercept the group of terrorists through the bushes and soft mud of the small Island known as Boot Key.

Major Mansouri and Colonel Khatami remained as the last soldiers to leave the sinking boat. They wanted to make certain the Vulture got off safely. When General Kalantari slid his body over the side and ended up in the water, the other officers followed him. When they were in the water and heading for Boot Key, Major Mansouri was the one who spotted the speed boats coming around the end of the Island, and turn and headed directly for the two boats stuck on the submerged reef. She moved up to the General's side and offered him. "General Kalantari, we have to make haste, I see the boats responding to the accident, and they're coming at us fast, sir."

The Vulture glanced at the two boats and replied. "We'll be on shore before those two boats get near us, woman. You go before me and order our people to hide in the woods so the Coast Guard people don't pick them up on the cursed Island, and they summon the police authorities against us. I cannot believe how bad the beginning of this operation is taking off for us."

Major Mansouri left her General and she rushed through the water and barked at the other Persian fighters already on shore. "General Kalantari is coming, but he has ordered you to hide in the bushes and be prepared to defend yourselves."

CHAPTER TWENTY FOUR

Captain Robert Walker was leading the rest of his people towards where the terrorists were landing on Boot Key. He came across a small clearing and looked to the Ocean and saw the two boats aground seventy yards away from shore. He smiled when he saw the Coast Guard pontoon vessels speeding towards the boats, and he figured by the time help came, they would be in control of whoever killed the Captain of his charter boat.

Almost all of General Kalantari's soldiers were now on land and the Vulture, along with his Major and Colonel, were the last ones in the water heading for Boot Key. Walking in the shallow water was almost impossible, with the General's feet constantly getting tangled up in the sea grass and sinking into the soft mud of the bottom. Mud, sand, and crushed sea shells filled his boots and dug into his skin and drove him crazy, and he could not wait to reach shore so he could empty his boots and wash his feet clean. He smiled as he came out of the water with his officers in tow, but his smile quickly left his lips when he saw someone not part of his group, crotch down and line himself up with one of his fighters hiding in the heavy undergrowth in a defensive posture.

Instantly, the Vulture dropped down to a knee, the move forced some of the filth filling his boots to ooze out of them. Major Mansouri and Colonel Khatami also dropped to the ground and whipped their weapons around and prepared to attack whoever caused their Commander alarm. Major Mansouri cautiously moved up to the General's side, and then she looked in his eyes.

Without saying a word to his female Major, General Kalantari pointed towards the person he picked up hiding in the bushes who looked like he was preparing to attack one of their soldiers from ambush. Major Mansouri looked in the direction her Commanding Officer pointed in with the barrel of his weapon, and she stared until she finally noticed the sudden but slight movement from the other person hiding in the underbrush.

When the Major picked up the other person obviously not with their soldiers, she mumbled to the Vulture. "General Kalantari, that has to be one of the people from the other boat that crashed into the reef. From what I can see of the person, it looks like a female. I'd be pleased if you'll allow me the honor to dispatch this lowly woman, and then I shall place the rest of our soldiers on alert for any more of the people from the other boat, sir."

"Yes Major Mansouri, it has to be someone from the other cursed boat that we nearly crashed into. I shall give you the honor to attack the first American fool in his or her own foul country, woman. But I don't want you to dispatch this person because I want you to take her alive. That way we'll have an American hostage when we have to stop the other fools who must also be on this Island by now, and they intend to attack us along with this foul woman we spotted prepared to attack us." The angry Persian General hissed at her while not removing his eyes away from the person he picked up hiding in the woods.

"Yes General Kalantari, your order is my command. I shall take the worthless infidel as my hostage, and we shall see what the other fools from the other boat are going to do next, sir." Major Mansouri replied as she moved out to intercept the other person who skillfully zeroed in on one of their foolish fighters.

As Walker's group came to where most of the Persian invaders came ashore, he picked up three of them hiding in the bushes. He pointed them out to the others with him, and then he aimed Sergeant Ramirez at one of the strangers, and the Mutt at another one, and he planned to take out the third one he spotted. He left Buckethead and No Neck behind to protect the country singer. Walker waited until Ramirez moved after her target, and when he was certain the target did not pick up his girlfriend moving towards him, he went after his target.

What he did not see, was the three Persian Officers who just came ashore, or he would have realized he sent Ramirez directly into a trap she would not be able to get out on her own.

Ramirez was trying to control her breathing as she held the razor sharp dive knife in her hand, and stealthy moved in on her target. She moved her feet like she was walking on ice, and did not make a sound as she closed in on the unsuspecting person hiding behind a bush, and she could see the modified MP-5 machine gun held in his hands as her target stared in the direction opposite from where she was going to hit him from. Sweat rolled in her eyes, but she dared not wipe at it for fear of giving away her position to the one she was about to attack from behind.

Major Mansouri kept a close eye on the skillful female attacker as she moved in on her foolish soldier, and she allowed anger to creep into her mind. She was fuming because Captain Saeed Mahebian did not pick up the person setup in a good position to attack him from his blind side. But as the enemy attacker slowly closed in on the unsuspecting Iranian Captain, Major Mansouri also skillfully closed in on the soon to be attacker.

Sergeant Ramirez was several feet away from the man with the weapon, and she bent down and prepared to pounce on his back. When she was ready to act, she drew in a deep gulp of air and held it as she suddenly leaped forwards and came crashing down on the unsuspecting man's back. When she landed on his back, her full weight forced the Iranian terrorist to the ground, and the weapon flew from his hands. Instantly, she slid the knife under his throat and hissed savagely at him. "If you make a move for your damn weapon or call out, I'll cut your throat and no words will come out. You're my prisoner and I order you to give up, buster."

Major Mansouri went in action at the same instant Ramirez attacker her Captain. In a flash, she was behind Ramirez standing over her with her weapon pointing right at her back, and she then growled at the female American attacker as if her words alone would kill the attacker. "Foolish woman, I don't think you want to cut my foolish Captain's worthless throat. If you kill him I shall be forced to kill you in return, woman. You said my Captain was your prisoner, well lowly infidel, you're my prisoner and I command you to drop that knife, and lock your fingers behind your worthless head, woman."

Ramirez's head was spinning and she cursed herself for not picking up the other person who held her under her weapon. She was angry as hell for allowing herself to be captured so easily. Thinking on whether or not to kill the one, and then try to disarm the other made her hesitate to follow the other person's orders, and it forced the female terrorist to warn her again.

"Go ahead cursed worthless American infidel and kill my foolish Captain, because he's lower than a filthy dog for allowing you to capture him so easily, a god cursed lowly woman. But remember which from the hated United States. If you kill the foolish one I'll kill you just as swiftly. Again I order you drop the knife and put your hands behind your foolish head and then lock your fingers together, or I'll kill you as you breathe, American bitch." To drive her point home, Major Mansouri jammed the barrel of her weapon against her head, to inform her she was not threatening to kill her, she would kill her.

The moment Ramirez felt the barrel of the weapon pressed against the back of her head she instantly realized she did not have a chance of killing the one, and getting the drop on the other one before she killed her. Ever so slowly, she released her grasp on the handle of the knife and allowed the knife to fall free from her hand, and then she moved both her hands to the back of her head and laced her fingers together as ordered.

The moment she released the knife from her hand, the stunned Persian Captain went in action and he flipped Ramirez off his back and then he jumped to his feet. When he was standing, he kicked her in the stomach as hard as he could kick, driving the air out of her lungs. The still fuming Captain then swung his weapon around and aimed it at the woman struggling desperately to catch her breath, and he was about to shoot her when Major Mansouri hissed at him angrily. "Captain Mahebian, don't take the anger you're suffering for allowing yourself to be so foolishly beaten by this worthless American woman.

"You have failed to watch around you as you were taught, fool. Your failure is your failure to live with, and beating her will not remove that failure from your worthless shoulders or memory. Our General wants this lowly woman taken alive, and I'm prepared to shoot you for not only your failure, but to protect her from your unwarranted wrath aimed at this cursed woman, sir. Lower your cursed weapon and prepare your foul self to fend off another attack from her friends who must also be hiding on this worthless Island."

Captain Mahebian glared harshly as he stared directly at the female Major, which caused her to hiss at him again. "Don't you dare to look at me as if I was some kind of filth lying beneath your lowly feet, Captain! You have failed on your mission, and if it was not for my help and protecting your worthless back, you'd already be lying dead and completely useless to our mission. Follow your orders faithfully, fool."

Major Mansouri stared back at the Captain with one eye, while she kept the other on the woman still struggling to breathe properly. When Captain Mahebian returned to protecting his area of responsibility, Major Mansouri knelt down on one knee and she looked deeply and angrily into Ramirez's eyes, and then she warned her in no uncertain terms. "Foolish American woman, you are my prisoner, if you make any foolish moves against me, I'll kill you without hesitation. I shall give you a minute to compose yourself. Then we're going to get up and you are going to call out to the rest of your foul people, and you'll order them to come out of the woods one at a time and give themselves up to me and my friends."

Ramirez brought her knees up to her chest in an effort to get her breathing under control. When she was feeling better, she looked into the burning eyes of the extremely angry looking Iranian woman who had her weapon trained on her face as she waited for Ramirez to move.

The moment she moved her legs up to her chest, Major Mansouri jumped back to her feet. She made up her mind she was dealing with a woman who was not a stranger to military action. She believed this woman was either a police officer, or is or was in the military at one time in her life, and she was taking precautions dealing with a woman she felt was extremely dangerous, and she would kill her if the American female got half a chance.

When Sergeant Ramirez was feeling better and breathing right, she said her first words to the woman aiming her weapon at her. "What is going on? Why are you aiming a gun at me? What have I done to you that has you so angry? Do you mind if I stand up and stretch my legs please?"

"What you have done to cause my anger, is you tried to attack and kill one of my friends. You are lucky I didn't kill you for that foolish attempt on your part, woman. You may stand and stretch your foul legs, but if you try anything against me, I'll kill you that fast foolish woman. Where are the rest of your lowly friends who were on that cursed boat with you hiding? When you are standing, you will call out to the others and tell them to come out of their hiding places with their hands over their cursed heads, and we'll allow you to live. Make us hunt them down, and we'll kill everyone who is with you, woman." Major Mansouri snarled at the American woman as she stepped back to give her room to stand, and she would be out of reach of the American, if she tried something against her.

When Ramirez was standing on shaky legs, she drew in a deep breath and held it. Major Mansouri saw the distress the young woman was in and she asked her. "Are you alright?"

"Yes." Ramirez replied as she straightened up and had her hands laced together behind her head again. Out of the corner of her eye she tried to locate Walker, she wanted him to come gets her, and save her life from this angry woman.

"This is good cursed woman, now you will call out to the other fools with you on that foul boat. You'll tell them to come out of their hiding place at once and if they don't, I will kill you in front of them, woman." Major Mansouri snapped nastily at Ramirez as she again leveled her weapon right at her chest. General Kalantari and Colonel Khatami quickly joined their female Major as she held the American captive.

Walker had no idea what was going on with Ramirez. He lost sight of her when she went in the heavy bush after her target. He had no fear in his mind of her being caught as he closed in on the target, he had his eyes locked on. This guy seemed bored to death and he was smoking, and had his weapon leaning against a skinny tree as he enjoyed his smoke.

He was just about to pounce on his target when he heard his name being called out by Ramirez. She knew Buckethead and the Neck was not in the area, they were protecting the singer, so she called out Walker and the Mutt's name. She was hoping the other two soldiers would go active the moment they heard her calling out for Walker, and they would free them from their captors.

"Robert, you and Frankie have to come out, they have me a prisoner and they say if you two don't come out immediately, they'll kill me and hunt you down."

Walker immediately pulled off his target and ducked down to see what was going on with Ramirez. His blood froze when he saw her standing with her hands held behind her head, and there were three people standing with her, and one of them was aiming a weapon at her chest. He cursed, because he knew there was no way he could possibly free her, not with the weapons the strangers were armed with. He heard a slight noise to his left, and when he looked in that direction, he picked up the Mutt come walking out of the bush with his hands held behind his head. Now he knew he had to come out of hiding as well. As he walked out of the bush he smiled, because he knew why Ramirez only called the two of them out.

The instant No Neck and Buckethead heard Ramirez call out Walker's name they both ducked back into the heavy undergrowth of the Island, and they dragged the singer with them. When they were under cover, the Neck bitched at Buckethead. "What the fuck are we gonna do now man? If we try and hit the lousy pricks, they'll ice Raz and the uthers on us, man."

"We're gonna hang tight and see what the fuck happens next, man. You keep your eye on this stinking prick and I'm gonna move up so I can have a betta look at what the fuck's happen with our people, man." Buckethead growled at the Neck, and then he got on his belly and carefully inched forward towards where his people were stalking the terrorists from the other boat.

Walker walked slowly out of the bush with his hands behind his head like Ramirez's, and he allowed the man he was going to jump to take charge of him. The excited Persian soldier expertly searched his body for any hidden weapons, and then he shoved Walker towards the rest of his group gathering around the dangerous and fuming Commander of the terrorist group, the Vulture. The Mutt joined the group, and he was being guarded by the soldier he was ready to kill a few moments ago.

General Kalantari allowed a slight smile to slowly cross his lips as he watched the two American males being skillfully guarded by his Persian fighters, and they were leading them to him. Suddenly, the officer leaned forward and barked savagely at Ramirez. "Where are the rest of the cursed jackals who were with you on that foul boat? I saw more than these few people on board that foul boat. Where are they hiding woman?"

She had to turn to face the man asking her the question in broken but understandable English, and when her eyes locked on his, she snapped at his face. "The others on board the boat, were killed when you opened fired on us. This is all who still alive from that attack."

"Hmmmmm foolish woman, do I believe your deceiving lies or not?" General Kalantari remarked angrily as he held her locked in his harsh gaze. His mind was going over the story he was told by Colonel Gonzales to use, if he was ever challenged by anyone in authority in the United States when his boat reached its final destination there. The Persian General and Commander of the terrorists diverted his eyes from Ramirez's filthy face, and then aimed them at the two men who just entered the group of his soldiers. He picked out the one he knew had to be in command of the others and snapped at the male. "I take it you are the man who is called Walker? Are you the man in command of these other worthless jackals, mister? I mean you no harm, I only wanted to come to America and be free of Castro's ironfisted rule."

"Yeah, I'm Walker, and I guess you guys are fucking Cubans, huh?" Walker smirked at the man questioning him while displaying no fear of him or the situation he was trapped in.

"I warn you Mr. Walker, don't try and be cute with me fool or you'll live long enough to regret your foolish follies. You don't ask any questions of me, I do the questioning here mister." The Vulture snapped at Walker as he moved a little closer to him, and then he stared him in the eyes.

Walker shrugged back at the angry acting man glaring at him.

"All you worthless and arrogant Americans are always the same, you lowly jackals all think of yourselves as foolish heroes and brave men. Mr. Walker, it depends on you if you and the rest of your cursed friends here will live to see another sunrise come to your worthless eyes. Where are the rest of your loathsome people hiding? You will order the other infidels to come out of the jungle and come to me at once."

"Hey buddy we're all that survived the fucking boat wreck, man." Walker replied hotly to General Kalantari, not believing these people were Cubans as they were pretending to be. He was able to pick up the slight Arab accent and Arab mannerisms from them. He was certain he was speaking to the man in command of a terrorist cell that just landing in the United States.

The Vulture looked long and hard into Walker's fuming eyes, but inside he was smiling, because he believed the others with these three were already dead. This man confirmed it, and he did not have a chance to communicate with the female prisoner before he replied.

"Mr. Walker, what am I to do with you and the other fools who are with you, American dog? I don't want to kill any one. I never did, all we wanted to do was come to the United States and live free like everyone here enjoys. I'm sorry some have died for our want of freedom, but we were desperate to leave Cuba before we died under Castro's rule."

"So you said Mac. Look pal, I have no stinking problem with anyone from Cuba making their damn bird to the United States, so as you said to live free, man. I have helped a good number of you people to make it to America safely myself, buddy. I'll tell you what you can do for ya self man, you can set us free and we'll make like we never saw you fucking people make it to the damn shore, pal. You still have enuf time to disappear, the Coast Guard just got over to the two disabled boats, and they're probably looking for any possible survivors, and they're most likely looking after the dead and wounded they found on my boat.

"So I suggest you make like a fucking ghost and disappear as quickly as you can, buddy. But if you kill us then you're gonna have every mother loving cop on the stinking Island hunting your fucking ass down, man. So far you people made it to the United States, but if you fire that damn weapon now, you're gonna alert the damn Coast

Guard people, and they'll in return alert the local police authorities and you people won't make it offa this stinking Key in one fucking piece, man." Again, Walker smirked at the dangerous looking man questioning him.

General Kalantari was slightly amused over the way this brave young American man spoke to him, but he knew he was correct. He could not take the chance of killing anyone else before he and the rest of his fighters got off this Island, and they made their way for Miami. Suddenly, the Vulture drew in his breath and added. "Look Mr. Walker, I have no intention of killing you or your friends. You are civilians, and as such you're no threat against me or my people. But I'm also having a problem allowing you and your friends to go free. If I freed you, what would stop you from notifying the police authorities and informing them of our presence on this Island?"

"All I can give you is my fucking word man." Walker fired right back at the Vulture that fast.

Major Mansouri moved up to her Commander's side and she rested her hand lightly on his arm. General Kalantari turned to see what his Major wanted of him. She leaned her head closer to his ear and whispered. "General Kalantari, it's getting late and we have to worry about the Coast Guard people, or their cursed police coming to find out what happened with the crash of two boats in their foul waters, sir. We don't have the time to engage this man in further conversation, sir. I suggest we kill the males, and then take the female as our hostage, in case we are stopped by their cursed police officers on this Island, sir."

"Yes, Major Mansouri, you're correct woman. I shall do as you have suggested. We'll kill the two men with our knives so as not to alert the Coast Guard people, and we'll take the woman hostage, and once we reach Miami, we'll kill and be rid of her." General Kalantari straightened his back and glared at Captain Saeed Mahebian who he was fuming at, because he did not realize he was under attack by the female prisoner. He then bellowed at him.

"Captain Mahebian, you'll take control of the two male prisoners and hold them in your custody until we made it to our fellow Cuban brothers and sisters who offered to help us, once we have successfully entered the cursed United States. Once we're safe with them, you'll release the two lowly jackals and follow. You know where we're scheduled to meet and we'll wait for you there. The rest of my people, prepare to get off this worthless Island."

Walker listened to the General's words, and picked up the usual Arab mannerisms and words and knew he was dealing with a bunch of Arabs. He had no idea they were Persian or Iranians, he just lumped them all together in the same pot. He realized the Commander just ordered his soldier to kill them, once the bulk of the invaders got out of the area.

Buckethead skillfully worked his way close enough to the group of people to hear the words from the General, and he too realized the Commander just ordered his Captain to kill both Walker and the Mutt when they left the three. He waved Neck and the singer over to his side, and then he quickly informed them they had to attack the invader holding their friends and fellow soldiers when the others left him behind, or they were going to lose their favorite turds from the Unit. Buckethead and the Neck prepared themselves to attack the lone invader the moment they had the opportunity to go into action against him.

Walker glanced to his side and looked at the Mutt, and he picked up the slight nod that informed him he also knew the Captain just received orders to kill them. Walker breathed a little easier, knowing the Mutt was going to be with his actions when he went after the Captain the other terrorist was leaving behind in charge of them.

Ramirez resisted the soldier holding her arms pinned behind her back, she did not want to become a hostage to these people, and she also understood the Captain was going to kill her lover and her best friend, and she wanted to help them. But Major Mansouri placed a quick end to her struggling and resistance when she aimed her MP-5 at her face and ordered savagely. "Woman, I have no need to keep you alive, so if you give me any reason whatsoever to kill you, I shall do it without the slightest hesitation. Be still and follow our orders or I'll kill you, and leave your worthless body behind to be found by your hated police authorities, woman."

Ramirez glanced at Walker and he snapped his head no and she stopped struggling, and she acted like she submitted to Major Mansouri's orders.

When the Major saw the hostage stop resisting, she snarled angrily at her. "That is much better foolish woman, if you continue to obey my orders, you might live through this and you'll be back with these cursed men before you know it, woman."

"Enough foolishness, we have to leave this area before further help for these two arrive, and we find ourselves being forced to engage the infidels." General Kalantari snapped at his soldiers, and with a fling of his hand. He started his soldiers out of the bush so they could linkup with their help and get off the Island of Marathon. Then he watched as his soldiers followed out his orders, and left Captain Mahebian with his two prisoners.

Ramirez was being controlled by a second Persian female, Major Sayeh Rahimi along with Captain Jahangeer Keshavaz, and they dragged Ramirez with the rest of their fighters. Ramirez offered all the resistance she could as she allowed herself to be dragged along with the others. She kept trying to glance back at Walker and the Mutt, looking for help from them.

Walker was fuming over the fact the terrorist were taking his lady as their hostage as he was forced to kneel before the Captain with the Mutt forced into the same position. He was foaming at the mouth with the want to kill the terrorists who just invaded his Island. But for the moment he was completely helpless to get Ramirez and hit the invaders at the same time. Captain Mahebian, Walker, and the Mutt watched the other invaders quickly disappear in the underbrush.

Once they were out of sight, Captain Mahebian sneered at the two as he slid the hammer of his weapon back and then chambered a round in the weapon. Then he offered to his two prisoners. "I'm sorry it has come down to this, because I don't really want to shoot either of you infidels. I know I can't kill the both of you with a knife as I was ordered to do. But I must follow my orders and leave no witnesses alive to betray us..."

"Why don't you wanna shoot us pal, if I had a weapon in my hands, I'd wanna shoot you buster." Walker snapped at the Captain as he taught up his body and prepared to attack the man.

"Enough, I grow tired of your foolish wit. I shall kill you, and then I'll rejoin my people and carry out the rest of our mission in the United States. Prepare yourselves, because I'm not an uncivilized soldier, and I shall give you a second to make peace with your God."

Walker was about to spring up and attack the Persian Captain, hoping if he was killed at least the Mutt would deal with the foreigner, and then get Ramirez away from the other terrorist. But he was suddenly frozen in place when he suddenly picked up Buckethead coming out of the bushes directly behind the Captain with his arms spread wide as he prepared to grab the smaller man. The way Buckethead was charging at the Iranian Captain made him look larger in life than he truly was. In an instant, he wrapped his powerful arms around the foreign Captain's body, and then he placed him into a breath robbing bear hug. His arms wrapped the weapon up and held it pressed into the chest of the terrorist as he now struggled to try and breathe.

In a flash, Walker was on his feet and he grabbed the Captain around the throat and started to choke the life out of him. The Mutt was by Walker's side and he locked his hands on the weapon as he told Buckethead to release his grasp on the enemy soldier. When Buckethead released the fighter, the Mutt pulled the weapon free from his hands, and Walker dragged the Iranian Officer forward until he fell to his knees. When he fell, Walker pushed him back with the weight of his body, and he fell on top of him and released his hold around the Captain's throat. Once he had him locked up in the submission position, he hissed in his face.

"Okay mutherfucker, you were saying you were gonna kill me, huh pal? Well buster, your stinking life hangs in the balance now man. I wanna know where your fucking friends are taking Ramirez. If you wanna live, you better tell me everything I wanna know from your stinking ass, pal. What's your mission in the States? Where are your fucking friends heading for, and what do they intend to attack while here? What country do you damn pissants come from, and don't tell me you're fucking Cuban? You made too many A-rab remarks for me to believe you people are stinking Cubans, buster. You betta talk and be truthful bout it pal, because I have ways of making you talk fucker, and I assure you that you won't enjoy what I'll do to your stinking body, before I allow you to finally die, mister. Tell me everything before I start on your ass, buster." Walker warned his prisoner as he slammed him hard in the face with his fist.

"Don't threaten me with a death, you're an American, and Americans have not the stomach or heart to extract information from one of your prisoners harshly. Look at what has happened to your worthless soldiers at the jail in Iraq, Abi Ghraib. Even your people hated your soldiers for what they did to our faithful fighters. You have laws in this worthless country of yours, and they shall appoint me a lawyer who'll get me off the crimes you accuse me of. You also have laws on how you have to treat your prisoners, and I am a prisoner of war in your foul hands."

"I got some fucking sad news for your sagging ass, buster." Walker roared in the Persian Captain's face as he pulled his face closer to his by his shirt, and then he continued with his angry words aimed at his prisoner. "You're fast running out of fucking world to live in man. I don't believe in the stinking laws that protect criminals like you from fucking punishment, man. I don't see you as a stinking prisoner of war either, buster. I see standing before me a mass murderer and saboteur, and I'll deal out your punishment as I see fit, Mac."

"Hey man, in case you haven't realized it yet, you're dealing with the meanest mutherfucking rat in the fucking shit house, man. He's nuttier than a stinking squirrel's turd, buddy. You betta tell him what he wants to know if you know what's good for ya stinking ass, man. I saw Walker kill someone in the past for no good reason, and it wasn't a pretty sight to behold, buster. Even the stinking dude's own mother couldn't recognize her son when he finished with his lousy ass." The Mutt offered, trying to help Walker break down his prisoner's will.

Captain Mahebian tried to turn his head to see who was speaking to him, but Walker would not release his hold as he snarled in his face again. "Any fucking time man, I never rush a man who wants to die as much as you do, pal. I fucking asked you a bunch of stinking questions man, and as of yet you have failed to answer any of them, pal. I won't ask you a fucking gain. Talk to me or you'll live long enuf to regret it buster!"

"I don't fear your angry words or foolish threats, Mister. You'll not harm me because you're much too civilized for that, Mr. American. We from the Middle East are not afraid of death, you Americans want life and will do anything to remain alive. So keep your worthless threats to yourself and turn me over to your police authorities."

"You think and I'll prove you way of fucking think wrong in your mixed up crazy ass world, man." Walker warned him as he moved and ripped his shirt from his body, and then he growled at the Mutt. "Hey dog man you got one of those fucking knives from the boat on ya?"

"Right here man." The Mutt replied as he handed Walker the knife and then smiled.

Walker took the razor sharp dive knife and looked at it as he held it hovering over the Persian Captain's stunned eyes, and then he moved it towards his arm and warned the Iranian terrorist in no uncertain terms. "Look here buster, if you don't tell me everything I wanna fucking know right now. I'll skin your fucking ass a live."

"I don't believe you'll harm me in any way, you Americans are too civilized for that."

"We'll see about that man." Walker growled as he slid the knife over the Iranian's upper arm. He dragged the knife until he opened a gash about four inches long, and it made his prisoner squirm under him as he warned the Persian again. "That's only the fucking start of it man. I got all fucking day to enjoy this and cut you up into nice, neat little fucking pieces before I finally allow you to die, and leave your slimy ass laying where it is so the stinking land crabs can make a feast of your stinking body, buddy. Are you sure you don't wanna talk to me yet, pal?"

"You can go to the devil with yourself, because he's waiting for your foul appear before him, you lowly American dog you."

"Buckethead and Neck grab the stinking Captain's arms and stretch the damn things over his head." When the soldiers had the prisoner held the way Walker wanted him, he started to slide the knife on the inner arm from the wrist to his armpit. This caused the Persian to cry out as blood rushed from the long wound and Walker hissed again in his face. "Hey man, I know this shit must hurt like fucking hell pal, so if you want the damn pain to stop and you live, tell me everything I wanna know about you and your scumbag friends, man."

Watching what Walker was doing to his prisoner, forced the country singer to turn his head away and gag so he did not have to witness the ongoing torture of the poor man.

The Mutt was leaning over and watching Walker work on the prisoner and he laughed. "Hey man, that's disgusting but that's going in my fucking act, man. Go postal on his stinking ass."

Walker was about to start another cut on the Iranian's arm when he said. "Please, no more, I'll tell you everything you wanted to know, Mr. American." Captain Mahebian was in fear the angry man called Walker, was going to actually skin him alive like he threatened to do, as he stared at the wild acting and fuming Walker.

"That's betta buddy, fucking beg for it man. It's the only way you're gonna save your stinking life here, man." The Mutt barked at the scared looking Persian prisoner.

Walker stopped cutting the Iranian, but he held the knife so the terrorist could easily see it as he asked the foreign officer and would be terrorist. "Okay pal, you said you were gonna talk man. Where the hell are your fucking friends going? What's their stinking target here and who the fuck are you working for, mister?"

Captain Saeed Mahebian remembered everything he was told to say to anyone who might take him prisoner, and he replied to Walker. "We work for Abo Haru sir."

"What the hell is Abo Haru buster?" Walker hissed as he threatened him with the knife again.

"Abo Haru is the Father of Terror sir." Captain Mahebian replied through trembling lips.

"You mean fucking bin Laden, buster?" Walker growled in his face this time.

"Yes Mr. American, we work for Usama bin Laden, and he has ordered us to come to the United States to destroy a certain target. Our target rests in Miami, and we're ordered to destroy it with the explosives we carry with us."

"What's this fucking target you're after, buster?" He asked angrily as he glared at him.

Captain Mahebian went through great lengths to describe their operation while maintaining the fact he and his soldiers were working for bin Laden, and once he began to speak, Walker could not shut him up for a minute. The Iranian went so far as to tell him of the help they were to receive while in the United States offered from the Cuban government, and the soldiers who helped them train for their mission. By the time the sacred to death Persian Captain finished speaking Walker hated the Cubans as much as he hated the Iranians.

When he was done with the Persian Captain, Walker turned to the Mutt and ordered him. "Hey dog man, get on your horse and follow those uther scumbags offa Boot Key, man. Stick with them until you see where the fuck they go and who helps them on the stinking Island. We'll be right behind you when we finish with this little prick here, man. Get going and remember they have Raz as their fucking hostage and we gotta free her before we go after these uther pricks, man. Move out buddy, and if you get a chance to get Raz away from the dopey bastards, do it and we'll stop them before they can even leave the stinking Keys."

"How the hell do you wanna play this one out, Walker?" The Mutt asked his old friend.

"Face on, no fucking cops. This is our nut to fucking crack because they took Raz, man."

"What about Colonel Leadbetter, Walker? Do you wanna get him involved in this one, man?"

"Fuck him where he breathes from, man. He's getting too use to fighting any action we're involved in from the stinking cheap seats, man. This one is solely on our frigging asses Mutt. We'll treat this one like any other action we're involved in, buddy. We'll kill the stinking terrorists and stop them from destroying their intended target slicker than fucking snot, man." He snapped at the Mutt as he stared at him and then added. "Don't be too stinking cautious on this one while you're out there man, or you're gonna fuck up our actions. Its balls to the fucking wall all the way on this one dog man so stay hot and loose while you're trailing them lousy fucks."

"Is there any other way for us to react against any stinking terrorists who think they can hurt us here in our own country, man? But are we outta your fucking mind Walker? We gotta get the stinking Colonel and the rest of our people involved in this mess. We're gonna need all the fucking help we can muster against these people, Walker." The Mutt said to his friend.

"Hey pal, they got Raz and we gotta get her away from them lousy bastards before they kill her on us, buddy."

"Fuck that bullshit, Raz is expendable Walker. Our main concern is to stop these pricks from carrying out their fucking attack against our country. Think of all the innocent people they'll kill if they pull off their attack. The life of one chick ain't worth all those stinking lives, man. We gotta get at them before we try and save Raz's ass, Walker. I know how you feel about this shit, but there's something more important than Raz in this stinking action, Walker. She ain't worth another stinking terrorist attack where hundreds and maybe even thousands of innocent civilians might be killed on their mission, man."

He looked hard and long at his closest friend for so many years. Walker knew the Mutt was right to worry about the attack against our civilians more than Ramirez's life, but he could not help himself as he snapped back at him. "Hey man, there's nothing more important to me than Raz, buddy. We get her out first, and then we'll deal with the stinking terrorists. Why the fuck do you think I don't wanna inform the damn Colonel of this shit for, because he'll think the same way, and he wouldn't hesitate in the least to throw Raz under a fucking bus to stop this damn attack. We get Raz back first, and then get the pricks."

"You got it Walker." The Mutt replied as he gave in and started to follow Walker's orders.

"Hey stupid, you want the only fucking MP-5 we got from this prick for protection, man?"

"Naw, I work best with my hands Walker." The Mutt smirked as he smiled at him.

When the Mutt was off and trailing the terrorists and Ramirez, Buckethead asked as he held on the arm of the exhausted and scared Iranian prisoner. "Hey Walker, whatdaya wanna do with this lousy little prick here, man? I'm getting kinda tired of holding onto the little dude, man."

Walker looked at the Iranian as he was being held on the ground by his large soldiers, and he snapped at Buckethead. "He wanted to be thought of and treated as a soldier, so be it man. We'll give him a forty five caliber Court Marshal and blow his head offa his stinking shoulders."

"That'd be my pleasure to carry out that order man." Buckethead growled as he let go of the Captain's arm, and the Neck let go of the other and the Iranian reached for his damaged arm with his other hand. Then he started begging for his life to be spared again.

Buckethead stood and picked up the MP-5 in the same motion and carefully aimed it at the Captain's face. But Toby started speaking before he could pull the trigger on the crying man. "Walker, you can't kill him in cold blood. That isn't done in the States, sir."

"I'm not gonna kill him in cold blood, I'm gonna allow him to heat up some first then kill him. What the fuck do you want me to do with the lousy little scumbag? Do ya want me to drag his ass with us as we stop the rest of his fucking buddies from destroying a huge chunk of Miami, man? No friend, he's betta off dead because if we allow him live, some stinking mouthpiece will come along and get him off the charges scott free, and then we'll hafta deal with the little prick again sometime in the damn future, my friend. NO, this is the best way to deal with the motherfucker, kill him Bucket!"

The country singer went to complain again at Walker, but his complain was instantly cut off when a single shot rang out, and it splattered the Persian Captain's head on the ground. He refused to look at what the bullet done to the terrorist's head.

"I hope the Coast Guard people didn't hear that round go off." The Mutt grumbled.

Walker heard the helicopter coming at them even before he located it, and he yelled at the three people with him. "C'mon, that hasta be a stinking Coast Guard helicopter, and by now they musta checked out both boats and found the dead bitch Captain from our boat. We gotta get offa Boot Key before they alert the local cops and they close off the only route offa this damn Key. We gotta stay in the bushes or they'll pick us up and have the cops get us, and we won't be able to stop these damn pukes." No sooner did he saw the words than he spotted the helicopter as it took up position over the two disabled boats.

General Kalantari and his Persian soldiers walked over the only bridge that allowed anyone to walk out to Boot Key. No one was allowed to live on Boot Key, it was wide open land. Major Mansouri was keeping a close eye on Ramirez as were the other Persian soldiers guarding and guided her walking before them through the bushes. Their weapons were well hidden under their clothes, and by the time they were over the bridge, they seemed like just visitors to Marathon.

The Mutt was right behind the group of terrorists and when he saw the group get over the bridge, he crossed it. He was walking nonchalantly behind them at a hundred yards back, and anytime one of the persons he was trailing looked behind them. He acted like he was looking for something on the floor, or he was checking out one of the countless live a board boats dotting the harbor. He saw the Coast Guard helicopter heading over the Island of Boot Key, and knew where it was heading.

Walker pushed his people at a good steady pace even though they were getting beaten up by the low hanging branches from trees. He had to get everyone off Boot Key before the Sheriff department got involved with the search for who killed the Captain of the charter boat. He knew the police were going to jump to the conclusion the people who got off the boat were Cuban refugees trying to sneak into the United States illegally, and they would shut down Boot Key.

Finally, Walker's group was at the foot of the bridge leading to the mainland of Marathon. They had to come out of the undergrowth to get over the bridge. So before they came out of the bush, he warned everyone to look like they were not on the run or hunting. The group split up and crossed the bridge without arousing the bored to death bridge tender. He was reading a book and did not even notice them cross. When they were on the other side of the bridge, Walker heard the sirens and ordered his people to rush to the stores on the road.

Just as his people reached the fish store off the road, the first of the Sheriff cars came screaming around the corner and turn down their road. He and his people walked between parked cars for the store, and he opened the door to one and acted like he had just got out of the car. It was a good move, because as the Sheriff car passed by them, the officer gave Walker's group a hard look before his car shot over the bridge at breakneck speed. Walker had his people enter the store, and he brought a fish before leaving. While they were in the store, five other police cars sped by and they headed over the Boot Key Bridge as fast as they could travel.

Walker's soldiers and civilian gathered outside the store about one hundred yards from Highway One. He knew once they were on that road, they would not draw attention to themselves until they linked up with the Mutt, and he informed them where the group of terrorists disappeared to on the Island.

In the distance he heard more sirens rapidly closing in on them, and they seemed like they were heading right at them. He ordered his people to hustle it up so they could be on Highway One before the rest of the other police cars arrived on the road leading out to Book Key. He was right to move his people along quicker, and when they were on the main road, four Highway Trooper cars cut across the road to Boot Key, and they blocked it off to traffic. Walker and his people looked like they belonged to the Island because of the way they were dressed and acted, so the police drove by them. No Neck was the first one to spot the Mutt walking directly towards them from the other direction.

The massive soldier pointed the Mutt out to Walker, and when he looked at his friend, he noticed him sipping on a soda as he walked towards them like he did not have a care in the world. He slowed his people down and when the Mutt joined them, Walker snapped at the other soldier. "You're starting to damage my good fucking mood, man. Well stupid, I'm glad to see you're taking this shit seriously this time. Don't let what happened upset you in the fricking least pal. I wouldn't want to screw up your stinking mood on ya today man."

"Hey man, don't blame me for this shit, I voted for the green M and Ms. What the hell are you getting so fucking pissed off at me for, man? I'm only doing what you said to do, Homes. I'm trying to act like nuthin's wrong, buddy." The Mutt gripped at Walker with a smirk.

"Yeah, I guess you're right man, its betta not to draw attention to yourself by acting suspicious. Didja see where the fucking terrorists went when they left Boot Key, buddy?" He asked the Mutt.

"Hey Walker, I hate to tell you this shit man, but they out number us three to one man."

"If their stinking numbers scare you then stop counting them, Homes. I asked you if you saw where they headed off for man, and you didn't reply buster. You wanted to be fucking funny instead man. Where the fuck did they go man?" Walker snapped at his friend.

"Yeah sure, I saw where they fucking went friend, but I ain't scared of nuthin, man. I wanted to tell you that shit pal. When they came offa Boot Key, they went east three blocks and walked behind the West Marine store. I followed them the best I could Walker. They had two white Chevy carry all vans parked there with drivers waiting for them to linkup with them. They piled into the stinking vans and pulled into the flow of traffic, they're heading for Miami, man." The Mutt reported to the anxious Walker.

"That fucking rips it, if they got offa the fucking Island before we could stop the lousy pricks. It looks like we're going mobile. We're gonna hafta get to my place so we can get betta arm up, and then we're gonna trail them to their fucking target and stop them slick as snot…"

Another two Sheriff cars came flying by Walker and his people, and they interrupted his words as everyone watched the speeding cars pass by them. Then he went on with his words. "C'mon people, we gotta get the hell offa the stinking road before some buck cop decides to stop us and see why we're so beat up from our fucking walk through the damn bushes. Once we get back to my place, we can dump the civilian off and get him offa our stinking hands. Then we can get after these lousy pricks." Walker glanced at the singer, and the civilian was shaking his head no, and he knew he was going to have some trouble getting rid of him. Even before Toby could raise a complaint at Walker, he snarled at him.

"Look man, now is not the fucking time to give me any stinking lip shit about this crap, buddy. We'll talk about it when we get back to my place. Right now, I'm only interested in getting betta weapons in my fucking hands, and then getting Ramirez out of the damn terrorist's hands, and then stop them from completing their stinking mission." Walker glared at the civilian and shook his head and then turned to the Mutt and said.

"We gotta hot foot it over to my place. I gotta make certain the babysitter can look after my kid while we go after Raz and the stinking terrorists. We gotta arm ourselves and get some transportation so we can follow these pricks and see how we're gonna get Raz outta their damn hands. Are all you guys with me for this one or what? We might get a little bloody on this fucking mess this time, people."

CHAPTER TWENTY FIVE

The three soldiers working with Walker agreed to do whatever they had to do to free Ramirez and then stop the terrorists from carrying out their attack against the United States. Walker looked at the singer and he agreed to allow him to go with them even though he did not want him along. He shook his head at the civilian as he bitched at people. "We gotta get offa this fucking road before we're stopped and get over to my place. We're like sitting ducks out here."

"Hey Walker, I can call this chick I met at the bar, she's got a boat for a car, and she can come here and pick us up and get us over to your place, man." Neck offered to Walker.

"That's great, call her and get her ass over here ten minutes ago, man."

The Neck walked into the store and used their phone. Walker and the rest went in and acted like they were going to buy something. The Neck went out of the store and he waited for his girlfriend to arrive. Walker was looking out of the window when an old Oldsmobile pulled up in front of the Neck, and he turned and waved to Walker in the store.

He looked at the rest of his people with him and gave them a quick head movement, and they quickly followed him out the store. They piled into the car and the girl took off without asking any questions, driving them to Walker's place. The girl knew where Walker lived because she attended one of his famous parties a few weeks back.

The girl pulled the car onto Walker's property and before she came to a full stop, Walker had his door opened and he was dragging his foot on the ground. When he could, he jumped out of the car and ran for his place. The babysitter was still there and she was concerned because they were back from fishing so early. He stopped her from asking any questions as he barked at her. "Cathy, we have an emergency and I need you to take care of my kid for a few days."

Cathy was used to Walker asking her to take care of their child when the service called him for a mission or active duty, and she felt the soldiers were just activated as she replied. "Sure thing Robert, it'll be my pleasure to look after your son while you're away, sir." She knew better than to ask him what the emergency was because he was in the Special Forces, and he was on call by his command any time. This was not the first time he had an emergency.

Walker smiled and then he charged up the stairs like the devil was chasing after him to his and Ramirez's bedroom. He ran over to his walk in closet and moved the clothes from the front of the safe he had stored inside the large closet. He quickly fumbled with the tumbler and had the safe opened in no time flat. Buckethead, the Mutt, No Neck and Toby, followed him to his bedroom and watched as he removed a number of M-16 rifles and handed one each to his friends. Then he pulled out a number of thirty round clips loaded with rounds for the weapons, and threw them on the bed, and the others took four each of them for themselves. He leaned his M-16 against the safe door and pulled out a number of Swig nine mm pistols, and he passed one to each member of his group with a number of extra clips for the pistols.

Walker took the only K-bar knife he had in the safe, and he carefully slid it in his boot. His shirt and pants were dry, and the sand and crushed sea shells stuck in his boots no longer bothered him as he prepared to rescue his girlfriend. That was the only thing locked in his mind. He took two boxes of loose rounds in a five hundred round military ammo box from the safe, and tossed them on the bed. He wanted to be well prepared for the fight of his life against this new batch of terrorists who just snuck into the United States, and he wanted enough rounds as to not run out when the fighting started. When he had everything he wanted out of the safe, he closed the door and spun the tumbler because there were still a number of weapons stored inside it.

He came out of the closet as the others stuffed the extra clips in their pockets, and then they waited for Walker to give them further orders before shoving off after the terrorists. He was breathing heavy because he was so upset the enemy had Ramirez in their hands. When he got his breathing under control he asked the Mutt. "Hey pal, are you gonna be able to pick out these fucking vehicles once we get on the road and we start chasing the lousy pricks down, man?"

"Easy man, I'll be able to pick them out of any traffic we come across, man. Does this mean I'm coming with you Walker?" The Mutt asked, afraid he might get orders to protect his home, or remain on the Island so he could direct the cops when they went after the terrorists.

"Yeah, you might as well come along man, school isn't fucking helping you out much anyway, buddy." Walker smirked at his best friend in life.

"Ha fucking ha, that was a pretty good one there, man. I didn't see that one coming at me, buddy." The Mutt replied, happy he was going along with the rest of them on this action, and then he added. "Hey Walker, you know we have the king, queen, and fucking jack stacked up against us on this stinking move, man. We ain't gonna be able to rely on any of the stinking local cops for any fucking help with these damn slobs, man."

"We gotta get a fucking move on it people, because it's not gonna take the stinking cops long to figure out we were the ones on the fucking charter with the dead Captain. I'd bet the barn the stinking cops are at the damn dock by now, and they musta ran the plates of the vehicles parked in the lot by now. My car is parked where we picked up the friggin boat from at the dock." Walker warned the others with him as he reached into his top drawer and removed a clean undershirt he was going to use as a sweat rag, and then he barked at the others.

"C'mon people, we gotta get fucking moving. We'll use Raz's SUV because we should all be able to fit in her damn car comfortably." Walker rushed out of his bedroom with the others following him as they charged down the stairs as one.

Cathy was standing by the front door and she was shocked to see the small group of soldiers and the one civilian running passed her carrying automatic weapons out in the open. Over the times she was in Walker's home to watch their child, she never once witnessed the soldiers leaving on a mission armed the way they were for this one. She stepped aside and allowed the men to charge out of the home, and she closed the door after them.

Before Walker left the home, he pressed the button for the garage door opener, and by the time the soldiers were out of the house, the garage door was opened. He jumped into the driver's seat after pitching his weapon in the car, and he started the SUV and spun the tires as he drove the vehicle out of the garage. He had to slam on his brakes to stop the car so the others could get in, and before the doors were even closed, he backed up and turned the car and ate deep ruts in his driveway as he tore off his property with the vehicle. When the tires grabbed the asphalt, the tires stopped spinning and dug in and the SUV roared down the narrow road.

Walker did not slow down when the vehicle came to the end of their road, and he spun the wheel hard to the right and cut off another car as his SUV turned onto Highway One. He started going in and out of the flow of traffic while trying to make up time on the terrorists. He was cutting off cars as he went flying by them, and he did not care a lick for the other drivers. The way he was driving, caused one vehicle he cut off to smack into the rearend of another car on the road, but he did not stop to see if anyone in the other cars were hurt.

Once they got off the Island of Marathon and were driving on the one lane zone, the road opened up and Walker floored his car. In seconds he was traveling at ninety five miles an hour and his speed caused the Mutt to complain at him. "Hey man, if we go any fucking faster buddy, we're gonna go back in stinking time man."

Walker did not reply to the Mutt's joke as he kept his eyes glued to the road. On Grassy Key, the traffic slowed down to a crawl and this forced him to get on the shoulder of the road and he flew pass a number of cars stopped on the road, so someone could turn his vehicle into the Dolphin Research Center. Walker cursed in a roar as he passed the cars and his vehicle tore up the side of the road, and the spinning tires sent a bellowing cloud of dust in the air behind him. Once he was back on the road he floored the car and rapidly picked up speed again. Sweat ran in his eyes as he stared at the road. He roared as he flew down the road. "This stinking traffic's fucking killing me dammit! I wish these flaming asses would get the fuck outta my fricking way so I can make up some time on them fucks, dammit."

"How much of a head start do you think they have on us, man?" The Mutt asked Walker.

"We made up some of the fucking time on the lousy turds, and I'm certain they aren't driving like we are for Christ sake. So, I figure the rotten bastards got about a good half an hour start on us, or maybe a little betta than that. But we should be able to catch up to them soon enuf on the eighteen mile stretch." Walker's anger was displayed in his tone and his cursing as he pushed his car further on the road.

The Mutt settled in his seat, and he was forced to grab the handhold above the door, as Walker cut onto the shoulder again to get around another car going the speed limit. The Neck was getting a little concerned over the way Walker was driving and he grumbled at him. "Hey Walker, you betta fucking come back down to earth with your stinking driving man, or you're gonna pick up a damn cop who's gonna wanna stop you for your own good, man."

"I don't give a shit man I'm not in the shit giving business. But if I was to give a shit, the cops would be the first ones I'd give it to, man. I feel sorry for any stinking cop who tries to stop us while we're trying to save Raz's ass and stop these lousy bastards at the same time, man. I got a reason to be driving like this." Walker snapped at his friend in the back seat of the vehicle.

It took Walker forty five minutes to reach Key Largo, a drive that should have taken between an hour, to an hour and fifteen minutes. But the traffic was getting heavy and slower on the last Island of the Florida Keys. That was because the construction workers were widening the entire length of the eighteen mile stretch from one lane, to a double lane road in and out of the Keys. This was so in case a hurricane was coming at the Islands, the authorities could turn all four lanes out of the Keys, and they could get more people out of the Keys faster than with just two lanes out of the chain of small Islands.

Walker had to drop down to forty miles an hour, and he started cursing to beat the band again. "What the fuck's wrong with this damn traffic, man? For the love of God, I can get out and make betta fucking time on my damn feet than the speed we're driving now, dammit."

"You betta calm down some Walker or you might blow a fucking head gasket, man. You gotta remember they're working on the eighteen mile stretch, and if you don't like the speed you're going now buddy. Wait, the speed limit through the construction zone is just thirty five mile an hour." The Mutt offered, trying to calm Walker down before he crashed the car.

"God dammit, I forgot about them fuckers working on the stinking road. That means we're not gonna be able to catch up to them pricks on the strip." Walker bitched as he slowed down.

"What the hell were you gonna do with them if we were able to catch up to them on the damn strip, man?" The Mutt asked.

"I woulda stopped them one way or the uther pal, even if I had to slam the car into them to accomplish it, man." Walker replied to his lifelong friend with a snap in his tone.

"Then I'm glad for the stinking traffic ahead of us, man. I didn't know we were on a stinking suicide mission on this one, Walker. Hey buddy, how the hell are you doing with gas in this fucking thing, man? The way you're driving this thing, you must be sucking the shit up real fast, buddy." The Mutt asked Walker, allowing curses to creep into his words now.

Walker took a quick glance at his gas gauge and cursed again as he answered the Mutt's last question of him. "God dammit, we're on the discouraging side of fucking empty, man."

"What the hell does that shit mean? We're on the discouraging side of fucking empty, pal."

"It means we're almost outta fucking gas and we're gonna hafta stop to fill her up, man." Walker growled at the Mutt as he started to look for a gas station on the left side of the road.

The Mutt realized Walker was looking for a gas station and he started hunting for one as well. He saw the Mobile sign about a mile ahead of them and warned Walker about it. "Hey buddy we got a gas station coming up fast on my side about a mile ahead of us. I suggest you get into the left lane man. This traffic is fucking murder, and if you don't get over now, you might not be able to get over in time when we finally reach the damn thing, man."

Walker started to get his vehicle into the other lane, he snapped his right hand blinker on, but the traffic was so heavy no one was allowing him to get over. The Mutt got so angry he actually stuck his head out the side window, and he started to yell at the other drivers on the side of his car. A lady saw a wild acting man yelling at her from the other car, and she slowed up to get away from the angry man. When she backed off enough, Walker cut his wheel and slid his car into the right lane. It was a good thing he was able to get over, because the gas station was a just hundred yards ahead of him now. Walker zipped into the station and pulled up to one of the pumps. He got out of the car and used his military charge card to pay for the needed fuel.

When the car was filled, he jumped back in it and started up the car and left a patch of rubber as he floored the car. He was so angry he cut a car off so he could get back on the road. The driver of the other car laid on the horn at Walker, but he stuck his hand out of the window and flashed the driver the one finger salute. This move backed the other driver off of his bumper and he paid attention to the road.

Driving through the construction zone was nothing short of sheer mayhem for Walker, five times he was forced to stop his car, and he had to wait for the workers to allow the traffic to move again. Every time he stopped his car, he let out with a new and savage string of curses. The Mutt was getting upset with Walker's black mood, and when he started cursing because the traffic forced him to stop his vehicle again, he snapped angrily at him in an attempt to try and calm him down a little.

"Hey man, you gotta remember every time we're forced to stop for the stinking traffic, so are the terrorists getting stopped, man. That means they're not opening up the fricking gap on us any while we're stuck at this stop, Walker."

Because his car was not moving, Walker glanced at his friend and replied. "That was a good point, man. I'm surprised it came from you buddy. It shows me you're starting to take this thing seriously, and you're using your stinking head at the same time, buster."

"Hey man, I'm as surprised over it as you are." The Mutt replied to Walker with a smile.

"I don't know why the two of you shitbirds are so surprised by the Mutt having a good idea for once in his life, man. The dinosaurs had a brain the size of a walnut, and they ruled the world for sixty million years Walker. And even a clock that's stopped is right twice a day, man." The Neck offered with a laugh, never passing up a chance to dump on one of his fellow soldiers.

"Huh, another fucking country heard from I see, man." The Mutt fired at the big man.

With all the bantering going on between the three soldiers, caused Walker to calm down a little, and he relaxed the death like grip he was holding onto the steering wheel of the vehicle. He let out his breath to help himself calm down more. But when the traffic started to move again, his anger returned to his taught body and mind as he started moving, and again he was trying to get in front of any cars on the road before him in the long line of traffic.

The country singer was sitting in the back seat with Neck and Buckethead, he was scared to death by the anger and way Walker was driving the car. He was suffering from second guessing himself for wanting to be part of the soldiers as they went after this new batch of terrorists and his missing girlfriend. This was the first time in his life he ever held a loaded M-16 assault rifle in his hands, and he was thinking, wondering if he would have the nerve and strength to kill another human being with the weapon, if he needed to do it if the situation arose.

The singer was holding his tongue, but his mind wanted him to tell Walker the next time the car stopped for traffic, he was getting out and allow them to go after Ramirez and the terrorists without him. He was scared to death about getting killed in the action once they caught up with the terrorists. He did not want to die and leave his wife and children alone in the world.

The concerned Neck brought his mind back to reality with his bitch about the Mutt, and the Mutt's reply to his words. Everyone riding in the car was laughing and this served to confuse the civilian singer even more. His mind could not comprehend how these young and extremely dangerous soldiers could laugh before they had to kill some other human beings, as they were planning to do in the very near future.

Before everyone left Walker's place on Marathon, he handed each of them small pocket handheld radios, this was so they could remain in constant communication when they started to stalk the terrorists heading for Miami. Buckethead had his portable radio out, and he was smart enough to check the power of the unit, and then he said to his Commanding Officer. "Hey Walker, it's a damn good fucking thing these damn radios are hot, man. What the hell good would they be to us if the batteries were dead, buddy?"

"I know that stupid, that's why I keep them on the charging standing at all times man. In case you don't know it man, sometimes I'm forced to use the radios for communication while I'm out on a stinking charter." Walker snapped over his shoulder at the big man, not taking his eyes off the road for a second.

Buckethead looked at the radio and then he glanced out of the widow. He thought if he engaged Walker in a further conversation, it might get him in a slightly better mood. It did not work as Walker barked angrily at the massive man, and he went back to driving the car.

The traffic on this section of the eighteen mile stretch was not as bad as it was where the heavy construction work was going on, and he had the speed up to fifty miles an hour. The SUV was about half way through the stretch, but the cars he was chasing after, was less than four miles from getting out of the Keys, and then getting on one of the major highways that would take them to their target on this end of southern Florida.

General Kalantari was as upset over the heavy and slow moving traffic as Walker was further back on the eighteen mile stretch. But where the terrorists were driving, the traffic was starting to open up. The Vulture had no idea Walker and a number of his highly trained friends were chasing after him, and he did not know how much Walker closed the gap between him and their car. The Persian General had Colonel Khatami, the Vulture's second in command, Major Mansouri, the Vulture's lover, along with Colonel Nasser Makaeem Taleqani, Sergeant Bassam Abu Fallahi and Major Sayeh Rahimi and Captain Jahangeer Keshavaz, who were in charge of their hostage, Sergeant Dorothy Ramirez in his lead car being driven by the Cuban helper.

Even though they had one more person inside the Vulture's car, there was still some room left in the vehicle. The second carryall had the Cuban drive, with Major Ghassan Abidal al-Zubedi as the Commander of this second group. Along with Colonel Amir Jopaiporu, Captain Farhad Nobakht, Major Gholamhoussein Mahajerani, Major Hamidroz al-Layluz, Captain Morteza Dastjeedi and Sergeant Azamalaie Shirazi, the third female of the Persian terrorist group.

Ramirez was seated between two Persian terrorists, and her hands were secured behind her back. She was smart enough not to offer any resistance, but she was also keeping her ears and eyes opened, and she listened to every word the terrorists spoke, and watched their every move. She wanted to know everything they were planning to do on this attack against the United States. The terrorists were so well trained for this mission they were speaking English without a trace of an Iranian accent. She was calm because she knew beyond a shadow of a doubt that Walker, the Mutt, Buckethead and No Neck was coming after the terrorists and her.

Every once in a while, the terrorist seated on either side of their hostage would glance over at her to make certain she was not up to something against them. When they noticed her sitting beside them and not making any trouble for them, they would turn their attention back to the outside of the vehicle and look at the flow of traffic.

General Kalantari was seated in the front seat with the Cuban driver, and he was studying the detailed map of the city of downtown Miami. The Vulture found his target printed on the map, and he checked the roadway they should use to make it to their destination. The Vulture looked up from the map and stared at the driver as he asked him with concern in his voice.

"You do know how to get us to our target err…? I'm terribly sorry, but I don't know your name, driver. I want to make certain you know where my intended target is in this god cursed country of lowly infidels." This was the first time the extremely dangerous Persian Officer spoke to the Cuban driver since he first stepped foot in the American made carryall vehicle.

"General Kalantari, I know who you are sir, but I shall not introduce myself to you. As far as you're concerned, you don't know me and I don't know you, sir. It's far better for the both of us this way, sir. I know what roads we need to use to get you to the target you have selected for your attack in Florida, sir. But my orders don't cover my getting you to your target. I have orders to get you to a hotel near your target, and then I'm instructed to leave this vehicle and the other one for your use to attack your aim, sir. I have secondary transportation set up for myself and my other driver when we reach your hotel, sir. Once I have deposited you and your soldiers at the hotel, my responsibility to you and your mission will be completed sir.

"I'm afraid you'll have to find your own way to your intended target, sir. I've been ordered to inform you that you'll receive no further assistance from any Cuban living in the United States, until you have carried out your mission, sir. We'll then offer you further assistance once you and your surviving soldiers make your way back to the Island of Marathon. I have people set up on that Island who'll assist you getting off the Island, and then safely out of United States territorial waters. I have no orders other than these few to follow, sir. I don't know where you'll be brought to once we have you out of the United States sir, nor do I wish to know of where you will end up, sir." The calm Cuban driver replied mater of factly to the surprised Vulture without taking his eyes off the road or the flow of traffic.

General Kalantari wanted nothing more than grabbing this smug acting Cuban infidel by the neck, and choking him to death for the angry words aimed at him. The Vulture was relying on much more help from his Cuban allies in the United States. But after speaking to the driver, he now knew he was basically on his own once the driver dropped them off where he was taking them. After getting his temper under control again, the dangerous Persian General asked the driver calmly as he continued fishing for any information from the driver.

"Since I don't know your name and you refuse to tell me, I shall call you driver. May I ask you where you intend to drop us off, and how close this place will be to our intended target?"

The Cuban nodded over being called the driver by the Iranian as he offered him. "General Kalantari, the hotel I shall drop you and your fellow soldiers off at, is known as the Best Western. The structure is just two miles away from your target, General. It's the only major hotel in the area that you should not arouse interest in when you move in, sir. I had a number of my people check out the area surrounding your target, and this is the only place we have settled on, for you and your warriors to inhabit until you start your mission, sir. I have to inform you that you should park the two vehicles I shall leave with you in a place with easy access out of the area, once you have completed you attack on the target, sir.

"General Kalantari, I have to inform you, a number of my associates will be keeping a close eye on your operation as your soldiers attack the target, sir. If it's at all possible for us assisting you out of the area without compromising ourselves. There is a strong possibility we'll act and help you and your surviving soldiers out of the area safely, sir. But that decision rests solely in my hands, General. But I warn you in no uncertain terms General Kalantari. I shall not place any of my people at risk if your mission goes wrong, sir. My responsibility rests with protecting my operatives working in the United States first, sir.

"My country and a number of her soldiers have gone through great lengths to get our operatives working safely within the United States, for any future operation my President decides to carry out against the hated Americans. We have many problems created for my country by the cowards and traitors who have decided to flee to the safety of the United States, and these traitors are constantly talking the American government into keeping the stifling sanctions set in place against my country. General, I believe if these cowards did not come to the United States, the United States and my country would be at peace with each other. Bah, the dom exiles General Kalantari." The Cuban driver complained, and then let it go when he realized who he was speaking to over the problems facing his country.

General Kalantari was pleased when the driver stopped his complaining about the Cuban exiles living peacefully in the United States. Because he knew every nation in the world was suffering mostly the same sort of problems with people unhappy with the way their government was running their countries. The Vulture felt he was not going to get any further help from this hateful Cuban driver, because he believed once the drivers drove off. They would never see them again until he returned to the Island of Marathon.

The driver pointed out of the windshield and the Vulture looked at what he was pointing at. The General saw the sign stating the Florida Turnpike was six miles ahead, and he understood they were out of the Florida Keys, and it would be only a matter of a few minutes before they went after the road that would take them up to their target. As the Vulture looked out the window, he asked the driver. "Once we're in the area of my target, will you be so kind as to do a quick drive by it, so I can see the place before we attack it, sir?"

"I don't know because that request wasn't part of my orders from my Commander, General Kalantari. But I don't see the harm in our taking a casual drive by the place, so you can see your target first hand, and get a little familiar with it, sir. It'll serve to show you how to reach it when it comes time for you to attack your target, sir. I shall point out all the roads to you while you locate them on the map, you'll need to get you and your warriors to their target. You may wish to highlight them on your map as I show them to you, sir. I'll not inform my control of the drive by, in case it'd upset him if I do it, General Kalantari Sir." The Cuban driver offered without looking at the Vulture.

"I'd really appreciate that, Driver. Because this is the first time, I shall even see this miserable cursed city in the United States. I shall do as you offered me, Drive." The upset Persian General almost snorted his response at the Cuban driver.

The Cuban nodded at the General as he continued to drive the car.

WALKER'S VEHICLE

Again, Captain Robert Walker found himself stuck in the slow moving flow of traffic as a loaded dump truck slowly pulled off the road.

The Mutt grumbled at Walker before he could explode. "This traffic is fucking murder."

"Hey man, I'm fucking drowning here and you're describing the fricking water to me, buddy. I can see for myself the stinking traffic sucks the big one, buddy." He turned this time to the Mutt and glared at him to drive his bitch home. His sharp eyes were darting all over the place as he searched for any way to jump ahead of some of the stalled traffic. But before he could try anything foolish, the traffic started to move again for the soldiers.

Walker jumped his vehicle into the oncoming lane and shot up three cars before he was forced back in his own lane by traffic coming at him. Buckethead did not like the move in the least and he roared at Walker. "Hey man, that was fucking nuts man. Look man, if I'm gonna fucking die, I wanna die fighting the stinking enemy. I don't wanna die in a head on collision on this stinking road. You betta calm down with the damn driving, or I'm getting outta this here tin coffin, man."

The Neck was just as angry and he added to Walker. "Yeah man, that goes for me to Homes."

Walker was hot and he snarled at his two soldiers in the rear seat. "You two fucking clowns call yourselves god damn killers. I'd trade the both of you fucks in for one god damn girl scout that'll follow fucking orders." Walker then turned to the Mutt and snapped at him also. "And, what about you, buster?"

"I don't know about the uther guys, but I was kinda turned on by that last move, man."

Walker had to laugh at the Mutt's response, but he did some quick thinking and realized if he did not start driving a little saner, there was a good possibility they would crash before they were able to overtake the terrorists in the two cars ahead of them. Suddenly, he drew in a huge gulp of air, and then he started to slow down to go along with the flow of traffic. The other soldiers saw he was slowing down some, and they started breathing a little easier. The singer, who was hanging onto the handhold of the door for dear life, also relaxed his death grip on it. He was too scared to get in on dumping on Walker over the way he was driving.

His weapon slid off of his lap, and it rested on the floor by his feet. The Neck turned to the civilian and smiled. This helped to calm him down more, as he returned the smile. The Neck then leaned nearer the singer and grumbled so only he could hear his words.

"Hey man, you betta pick up your stinking weapon from the damn floor man. If Walker sees the damn thing lying on the floor, he's libel to stick it up your ass and pull the fucking trigger on ya. He's a real stickler when it comes to protecting your weapon at all times, buddy. You gotta remember this shit, your weapon's no damn good unless it's in your fucking hands and ready to fucking use to defend yourself with, friend. A soldier without a god damn weapon is just another dumb ass fucking civilian in caught up in war games, man."

The confused singer did not know if the soldier was kidding with him or not, but he reached down and picked up the weapon from the floor and laid it across his lap again. Once he had the weapon he smiled at the huge soldier.

Walker was starting to make good time on the road again, and when they entered the last passing zone on the eighteen mile stretch, he got out in the speed land and in seconds, the car was traveling at a hundred miles an hour. He passed ten cars and when the road narrowed back to one lane, he was forced to slow down to fifty five because of the traffic bunching up in front of him. But now he was less than seven miles away from the highway where he could make up more of the time on the cars with the terrorists and Ramirez. He smiled because they were almost completely out of the Keys and he calmed down further.

GENERAL KALANTARI'S VEHICLE

General Kalantari was also smiling when he noticed the sign for I-95, but the smile quickly faded when he saw the exit was six miles ahead of his vehicle. They got onto the Florida Turnpike and they were traveling at seventy one miles an hour. The driver wanted to stay as close to the legal speed limit as possible, so as not to draw attention to his vehicle.

The Vulture allowed himself to rest his head on the headrest, and he closed his eyes for a few moments of peace. He was enjoying the speed of the car, but the driver started to slow down and the exhausted Persian General opened his eyes, fearing something was wrong on the road. He noticed the slowing traffic ahead of them, and he snapped at his driver in an angry voice. "By the great grey beard of the Holy Prophet Himself, don't dare tell me there's another cursed accident or road construction going to force us to get stuck in this traffic again. I'm tired of riding in this cursed car I fear I'd not be able to endure another traffic jam on this miserable day."

The driver allowed a slight chuckle over the discomfort the Vulture was suffering from as he offered in a pleasant tone to the Iranian Officer. "No General Kalantari, it's not another traffic jam at all, sir. What we're experiencing is a brief slowdown so we can pay a toll for the privilege of driving on this crumbling road. It should take us a few moments to get through the toll, and then we'll be driving at the correct speed again until we come across the second toll before we are off this roadway, General Kalantari Sir."

"Will there be any more of these cursed tolls on the other highway we shall use to get to my target?" General Kalantari asked with concern as he watched the driver throw three quarters in the basket, and the red light went green and they were moving again.

The driver again chuckled over the Iranian's question as he responded calmly. "No General Kalantari, there are no such tolls on the other roadway we shall be using. Once we're on I-95, it'll be clear driving all the way up to our final destination. We'll be before the usual heavy rush hour traffic, so we should be able to make rather good time to the target, sir."

"I thank the Almighty Allah for that much, driver. I can use all the breaks I can receive on this operation. To be honest, I cannot wait for this process to be completed. I miss the warming and friendly sands of my deserts in Iran. I've been away from my country for much too long a time, and I fear what the youth of my country will be trying to do now. The youth of my country are adopting too many of the ways of the infidel West, and their sinful ways are beginning to corrupt and pollute the youth of all Persian and Arab lands of the Middle East. I long for the faithful day when America looks like the vast deserts of my lands. In the past, all the opulent and aggressive countries have been brought down to their cursed knees, when they have outgrown their civilians. The United States' time is waiting on the bloody wingtips of the Vulture, and soon the claws of the deadly Vulture will strangle the leaders of this evil country of sin and lust."

"Yes General Kalantari, we in Cuba also believe the United States days are numbered as a leading and powerful country in the flow of things that take place in the world. We have been doing everything in our power to bring about the collapse of the United States." The Cuban driver grumbled at his passenger without looking at him because of the traffic now.

"That is why we're carrying out this attack against the worthless fools who live in these foul lands, Driver. We must keep the pressure on the hateful civilians of this miserable country. We have to make them afraid to venture out of their cursed homes, and fight against the American government from sending their worthless troops to another Arab land, when their civilians feel so threatened in there own country. Once we have confined the loathsome United States troops within their own foul borders. We'll then be free to attack and destroy the Arab countries of the Middle East like Iraq, Kuwait, and Saudi Arabia and destroy these troublesome nations.

"Once we have control over these mongrel Arab countries, we'll then attack the weak and foolish nations of Jordan, Lebanon and Egypt. My wise government will not be satisfied until we have destroyed all mislead Arab countries who believe in a false religion, and they don't respect us. Bah, this is in the future and as we Persians believe, only the journey is written, not the destination. The fate of Iran and the

Middle East rests in the hands of the Allah." The wise and feared Iranian General mumbled as he turned and looked out of the window of his vehicle.

The Cuban driver shook his head over the Vulture's last remarks, because he knew no matter what Cuba or Iran does against the United States. They could never be able to do enough damage to destroy the power and influence of the United States over any country. He smiled whenever he heard the politicians of his country bragging they will force the United States to her knees, like they had some divine power in their possession that would hurt the United States.

The second pay toll came up and when by, and since the Cuban warned the Vulture to keep his eyes on the signs as they looked for the exit that would bring them onto Highway I-95, they were driving in silence. The exhausted driver moved his car into the last or the slow lane of the roadway, and he brought his speed down to fifty five miles an hour. The driver spotted the road sign before the Persian did, and he slowed down more, and carefully turned off the road.

The Vulture stared at the sign, and when he saw it read Highway One a mile ahead, he asked the driver. "Is this not the same road we used to get out of the Florida Keys?"

"Yes, it is General, but if we took it from the Keys we would've been in heavy traffic all the way up to this part of the roadway. I'm afraid we'll be forced to drive on this road for twenty one miles, before we reach Highway I-95, sir. Err… General Kalantari, I fear you'll be soon upset, because we'll be forced to drive through the center of Miami on this road, and even though we are driving at not the peak driving time or rush hour. We'll find ourselves locked in maddening traffic in the city until we can drive through it, sir." The Cuban offered to the Vulture as he warned him of what they would soon be facing with the oncoming traffic on the new road.

"May Allah curse this miserable land and foul road the fools drive upon to hell. Is there any way for us to avoid this traffic you have warned me of?" The Vulture snarled at the driver, already angry he was going to find himself stuck in heavy traffic in a short while.

"I'm quite certain there are some other roads that'd take us around the traffic, but I'm not briefed on any other roads that'd assist us, sir. I was given the most direct route to your target when I set out to assist you, General. I'd be afraid to venture off the roads I know in search of an easier way to our destination. Besides, I'm certain my control is keeping a close eye on me, and if I was to deviate from the roads he had assigned, I'd feel his wrath falling upon my shoulders." The concerned driver offered to the Persian seated next to him in the car.

"I'll reside myself to make the best of this foul traffic ahead of us then, Driver." General Kalantari snapped as he settled in his seat and glared out the windshield.

WALKER'S VEHICLE

Captain Robert Walker's SUV got off Highway One and he entered the Florida Turnpike, and growled at the people in the car. "Thank God we're finally out of the damn Keys for crap sake. Everyone, I want you to keep your damn eyes opened for any white SUV or carryalls on the damn road. We're gonna check them out as we pass them. Mutt, if you see the lousy pricks let me know and then we'll react from there, man."

"You got it man, but I think they're well ahead of us by now buddy. Hey Walker, we know how they're gonna make it up to their stinking target. Maybe we can make up some time on the scumbags if we don't get offa the highway at Exit 12, buddy…" The Mutt started to offer but was cut off in mid sentence when Walker growled at him.

"What the hell are you driving at man? C'mon, I need any input you can offer me man. If you think you know a way to save us some time, I need to know about it buddy!"

"Calm the fuck down a little for fuck sake and give me a stinking chance to talk to you for Christ sake. The way you're going, you're gonna kill us if you ain't more careful with your damn driving, buddy." The Mutt growled at Walker, and then he explained for his Commanding Officer. "Walker, we know from the dude we iced off back on Boot Key that the fucking assholes planned to turn offa the Turnpike at Exit 12, and take Highway One over to I-95. But if we take the stinking Turnpike up to Exit 25, that's the Tamiami Trail, it'll take us out on I-95 below where these pricks intend to attack us.

"You gotta know the flaming assholes are gonna get tied up in the heavy fucking traffic of downtown Miami where they entered I-95 from. And, they're gonna lose a helluva lot of time because of the damn traffic. I figure we'll come out on 95 maybe an hour before the assholes should be able to get there, man." The Mutt flashed a smile of triumph at Walker, proud he offered a way for him to beat the terrorists to their target.

"That's what I'm fucking talking about guys. If we can beat them fucking pricks to their damn target, we can setup and follow them and wait for our chance to get Raz outta their stinking grasp, and then we can take the lot of them out as slick as snot at our pleasure after that." Walker replied in an excited tone of voice as he turned his attention back to the road ahead of him, and he started darting in and out of the traffic again.

THE TERRORISTS VEHICLES

General Kalantari's car was making good time on Highway One until they entered downtown Miami, and they started to get stopped by red lights and a heavy traffic. The Vulture's temper started getting the best of him, and when they were almost sideswiped by a car that tried to make a red light in front of them, he roared at the driver. "God curse you to the fires of hell for eternity you great fool you. If you were living in my country and driving like that, you'd be suffering the slow death of a thousand cuts upon your worthless body, filthy infidel."

The driver laughed as he offered to the angry acting foreign officer seated to his right. "General Kalantari, if that driver made you angry, I'm afraid that you're in for a long and upsetting drive, sir. We just started feeling the effects of the maddening traffic in this area of the city. We're going to be forced to deal with this heavy traffic for at least five miles, before the lights and traffic ends. The roads in this area of the highway are always like this day and the night, General Kalantari."

"What the devil are we doing driving on this cursed road then, Driver? I'm certain there are other roads we can make use of for you to get me and my fighters to our target. I hope you're not just wasting our time using this road." The Iranian snapped at his driver as he glared at him.

"I informed you once I was ordered by my Commander to take certain roads to your target, General Kalantari. I was further ordered by that same Commanding Officer not to deviate from this ordered course for any reason whatsoever, and I follow my orders faithfully, sir. It'll not be a long time before the traffic opens, and then we shall travel at the designated speed of the roads again, sir." The Cuban snapped at the Persian Officer in a hot tone, he was beginning to get upset with the General and his constant complaining since he first stepped foot in his car, and he started driving him to his target.

"You seem to have an answer for every complaint I aim at you, Driver. Bah, I'm forced to trust you to get us to our target as quickly as possible, and I shall remain quiet until that time has come for me to enjoy."

"I'd appreciate that offer General Kalantari, because the traffic is maddening enough, and when I'm forced to listen to you complaining about the flow of traffic, the weather and the time it's taking us to drive up to your target area, it adds heavily to the many problems I'm having driving in this dom traffic, sir. I don't particularly enjoy driving, especially when the traffic is heavy, sir. I'd rather be at my home enjoying my wife's attention, than to be driving at this time, General." The driver allowed anger to creep into his voice addressing the Persian Officer.

The Vulture decided it was no further use to speak or be angry with this Cuban driver, so he resided himself to sit back and wait for the traffic to open, so they could get to the target and check it and the surrounding area out, so he could make the design of his attack profile on his waiting target. Adding to the discomfort of the Vulture was the temperature. It was in the middle eighties, but it was very humid, and the temperature made the air-conditioning in the vehicle feel like it was not working properly.

The Vulture was trying his best to hide his mounting anger not only to the driver, but he was also trying to hide it from the rest of his fighters at the same time. The last thing he wanted to have happen was to make his soldiers feel he was upset, and having them second guessing him or his orders or their mission.

The longer they were stuck in the heavy traffic of downtown Miami, the more vehicles seemed to enter the roadway, and the more the traffic grew, the angrier the Vulture became. Under his breath, he cursed not only the United States but he also cursed his country for dropping to the low of carrying out a terrorist attack against the United States.

He cursed Cuba and his driver, and he also cursed Captain Mahebian for not linking back up with them before they left the tiny Island of Marathon. He did not deceive himself in the least because in the back of his mind. He was certain his Captain was dead, and the man he knew as Walker must have surely killed him, or he captured his Captain and turned him over to the local police authorities. A fear suddenly engulfed his whole being, and he found himself looking for any sigh of being trailed by the police of America.

CHAPTER TWENTY SIX

Captain Robert Walker was still driving like a wild man on the road as they paid the second toll on the Florida Turnpike, and he was trying to make up for time they lost at the toll booth. The traffic was light and within second he was driving eighty six miles an hour again. He shot passed Exit 12 that read South Dixie Highway or Highway One, and the Mutt reading the exit signs for him announced.

"Hey Walker, this is where our turds hadta turn offa the stinking Turnpike. We're gonna make up good time on the dumb fucks by going this uther way, buddy. I feel we'll be where they're heading and beat them there by a good half an hour or more. Then all we gotta do is stake out their fucking target ourselves, and wait for the lousy pricks to show up on the scene so we can get at them then, man."

"That's great, where do we hafta turn off this stinking road, and where do you think them fucks are by now, man?" Walker asked the Mutt while he paid attention to the road ahead. He was trying to keep an eye out for any possible radar traps while also watching the road. The last thing he wanted to do was tangle with any cops.

"We gotta turn offa the stinking Turnpike at Exit 25, that's the Tamiami Trail. Once we turn off there, we'll be fifteen minutes from the target, man. I think the fucks we're chasing are more than likely stuck in heavy traffic in South Miami somewhere at this time, Homes." The Mutt replied as he checked his map, and then added to his words. "Hey man, they're probably stuck somewhere near the Sunset Drive, buddy. I don't think they entered Coral Gables yet, Homes."

"That's good for us man, we're gonna beat the rotten bastards for sure, if you're fucking right man." He replied without taking his eyes off the road.

"I'm always fucking right man it's just you never believe me when I say something, Homes." The Mutt retorted with a grin.

GENERAL KALANTARI'S VEHICLE

The Vulture, General Abdol Karim Kalantari checked the next road sign and it read Sunset Drive, and under that sign another one read Coral Gables Exit, two miles and he breathed a great sigh of relief, feeling they were only a few miles away from where the traffic would finally open up for them. But he was wrong with his thoughts, because they still have to get through the major part of downtown Miami before the traffic would lighten up to where they could go at least the speed limit, and then make up some time they lost because of the heavy flow of traffic.

CAPTAIN WALKER'S VEHICLE

Buckethead was looking out the side window and was the first one who spotted a cop car pulled on the center grass divider, and he immediately warned Walker about the parked car. "Hey Walker, you got a stinking cop parked on the divider and I think he's running radar, man."

He immediately slowed down to the proper speed and when they passed the cop car, he realized the cop was running radar on the south bound traffic lane, and he stomped on his gas pedal and floored his car. In seconds he was back up to eighty seven miles an hour.

The Neck, still concerned over the way Walker was pushing the car, offered in a concerned voice to him. "Hey man, I'm willing to bet if the stinking cops are running radar on the south bound lane then up ahead they hafta be running it against the north bound lane. Maybe you should think about slowing down to the fricking speed of fucking light, just in case I'm fucking right and there's some cops ahead of us, man."

He did not look into his rear view mirror to see his face as he weighed the Neck's words, and then he let up on the gas and slowed the car down to just short of seventy five miles an hour. He slowed down none too soon, because by the next overpass, a Highway Patrol car was parked in the grass divider, and he was running radar on his lane of traffic. There were three other police cars off the shoulder, waiting to be told which cars to pull over for speeding.

Walker let out his breath in a rush as he said to the Neck. "That was a good call on your fucking part, buddy. If I was going faster, that prick woulda came after my ass sure as shit flows down hill. Since we're so far ahead of them lousy pricks, I'm gonna slow down and do seventy five, the cops won't bug my ass for that speed."

"Thank God for that much Walker." Buckethead and the huge Neck said at the same time.

"What the hell's wrong with the two of you birds? Is my driving scaring you two killers? Damn and you road blocks call yourselves fucking Tier One Soldiers, no fail teams huh? You two should take a fucking example from that damn civilian back there. He's not saying a stinking peep, and you two are crying like a pair of stinking hookers who did not have a trick to turn over for a few hours." Walker fired at the two of them with a wide grin.

"Yeah Walker, you should see the stinking civilian puke back here for yourself, man. If he could get any fucking lower in his fucking seat, he'd be under the damn car, buddy. He's so damn scared he's as white as a stinking ghost, and he's holding on his weapon for dear life, friend." The Neck replied to Walker's barb with a snap.

"Bunch of stinking crybabies I got myself stuck with on this damn mission I see. I'd trade the both of ya in for a stinking girl scout who'd follow orders without complaint." Walker complained more to himself than to the other soldiers in the car.

"Like I told you before man, I don't mind fucking dying, but I don't wanna die crashing into another stinking car. If I gotta die, I wanna go out fighting the friggin enemy, man." Buckethead grumbled at Walker as he looked at his eyes through the rear view mirror.

The Mutt was being quiet because he was still watching the road signs. When they passed Exit 20, the Mutt informed Walker. "Hey man, we got five more exits to go before we gotta turn offa this fucking road. At least we don't hafta get stuck being stopped by another damn toll man, that was the last one before we turn."

"We're making real good time on this fricking highway. It was a good idea to take this road all the up to the uther one, so we can beat the lousy pricks there, buddy. We're gonna pull this fucking thing off slick as shit through a goose. We're gonna get Raz away from the terrorists, and then we're gonna stop the fucking terrorists from pulling off another attack against our land, buddy. We're gonna come out of this stinking mess smelling like a frigging rose." Walker said in an excited voice as their car passed Exit 22.

GENERAL KALANTARI'S VEHICLE

The Vulture, General Abdol Karim Kalantari's vehicle just passed 37th Avenue on the South Dixie Highway, and they were only six miles away from the start of I-95, and twelve miles away from their intended target. But the traffic was still moving at thirty five miles an hour, and this was allowing Walker's vehicle to close the gap on the terrorists rapidly. The Vulture had no idea Walker and the other soldiers with him were heavily armed, and now stalking them on the roads. The Persian General was positive if the two hated Americans were able to kill his Captain that one of the Americans would have talked to the police, and they were the ones who might be looking for them on the road.

General Kalantari had no idea his Captain informed Walker of their target before he was killed by the American soldiers, and how they were going to get there, along with the roads they were going to use. The Iranian Officer was certain the police on Marathon were still looking for them on that Island. At best, he felt by now, the police would have closed down all the traffic coming onto and out of the chain of small Islands that made up the Florida Keys. He believed once he attacked their target, the police stationed on those Islands would relax their security, and they would waste their time helping the police officers from Miami looking for him and his people in that area, while they were heading back to the Florida Keys to escape the United States.

As the two vehicles carrying the group of terrorists was forced to stop for another red light. General Kalantari talked himself into relaxing and he allowed the vehicle go at the speed the traffic would allow. The Iranian Officer realized no matter how upset he got over the slow flow of traffic and his Cuban driver. All his angry would do absolutely nothing to move the traffic along any faster than it was currently moving. So he turned his head and looked out of the side window to try and calm himself down further.

Walker spun the wheel and his car turned off the Florida Turnpike, and he was now traveling on Highway 41. Here, the road was a three and four lane highway at times, but he was being plagued with a flood of stop lights on just about every block. So far, the lights were working with him, and he was speeding at sixty two miles an hour. Two blocks ahead, he saw the light still green so he increased his speed to make the light before it went red on him. When he was half a block from the light it turned to yellow, but he did not get off of the gas. Everyone riding in the car tensed up when they realized he was going through the light. It turned solid red light while his car was a hundred feet from it. But he still did not get off the gas and he hunched up his shoulders as he prepared to dodge through the traffic to get through the light.

"Jesus Christ Almighty Walker, you're gonna fucking kill all of us in this damn thing before we even get at the stinking terrorists for crap sake! You betta cool down some or we're gonna be dead, and then fucks will pull off their attack and kill Raz, man." Buckethead roared as he braced himself for being involved in a crash.

He completely ignored Buckethead's complaint as he yelled and his car charged by a car that crossed in front of him, and he had to spin the wheel to the right in order to avoid hitting a second car, as two other cars coming at him locked their breaks and slid into one another, and then they spun out and stalled. A police officer waiting for the light to change saw what was happening and who caused the accident, and he tried to get across the road. But his cruiser was suddenly hit by two other cars that jumped the light to avoid the accident, stopping him from chasing after Walker's car. By the time it was over, seven cars were involved in crashes along with the one police car.

"Jesus H. Christ Walker, what the fuck are you trying to do, buddy? Are you trying to kill us before we engage the stinking terrorists, man? For your fucking information Walker, I think your brave fucking civilian back here puke here has just went Code Brown and shit his fucking pants. I can't wait to look and see if I'm right. Its sure smells like he just crapped himself over that last fucking move you pulled off man." The Neck grumbled at Walker from the back seat as he checked on the singer's condition to make sure he was alright. The civilian was as green as a saw buck, and he looked like he was going to heave any moment.

"Unless you're a fucking hemorrhoid stay offa my stinking ass will ya man. Take care of the fuck and get offa his fricking ass too, buddy. He's the least of my fucking problems I'm facing right now buster." Walker snarled at the Neck as he did his best to regain control of his car that was caught in a hard slide because of the way he was driving. Finally, he got control and straightened the vehicle out and he stomped on the gas again.

The Mutt was forced to hang onto the handhold on the side of the car, and he was trying to stay in his seat at the same time, and when the car was driving right, he started to look at the road signs ahead of them again. The next sign he saw read 27th Avenue, and he instantly informed Walker where they were. "Hey Evil fucking Kenivel, we just passed by 27th Avenue, and the next one up is 17th Avenue, and that puts us less than four miles away from where these lousy pricks are heading, buddy. And, the fucking way you're driving this damn thing, we should be arriving there in two minutes, well ahead of them lousy bastards, Walker. I told you the traffic on this road would be good to use."

Walker merely nodded in response to the Mutt's brag, and then he snapped at him as he stared at the road ahead of him. "Hey Mutt, where the hell are we gonna link up with these mutherfucking pricks, buddy?"

The Mutt looked at the map and then offered. "Hey Walker, we gotta turn left on 12th Avenue, and take that road north one block, and then we turn right on Flagler Street, and take that road to the I-95 Exit and find a place to park so we can see the exiting traffic from the main highway. We know the rotten bastards will be using 95 to get to the Flagler Exit from that stinking dude we iced off on Marathon, man. I figure the two damn cars will be driving together, and once we pick them up, we can follow them and when we feel its right to act against them, we can jump the pricks and get Raz away from them."

"Where the hell's this fricking 12th Avenue turn coming up man? I don't want you shouting out turn here after it's too late for me to turn this stinking thing safely, man."

"Calm the fuck down will ya man, it's the next road coming up on the left side where you gotta turn. So I suggest you slow the fuck down and stay in the speed lane until we come across the damn cut off for the turn we need." The Mutt warned him as he kept his eyes glued to the road and looked for the exit he wanted.

Walker saw the stop light for 12th Avenue and he started to look for the turning lane. He came up on it and there were two other cars waiting to turn on the road, and he pulled up behind the trailing car and waited for the light to turn green. While he was waiting, he tried his best to get his breathing and anger under control. He was still fuming the terrorists were able to get Ramirez, and he did not stop them before they took off with her as their prisoner.

The traffic was light and when he was able to move, he drove the car up the entrance ramp and cut out in the flow of traffic. He had his right blinker on for the speed lane, but the Mutt reminded him with a snap. "Hey Walker, we ain't gonna stay on this fucking road but for one stinking exit, buddy. So I think you should stay in the slow lane all the way. We got them fucks beat to this friggin exit by a long shot, so lets take it easy man."

He knew the Mutt was correct and he cut back on the gas and slowed down the car, and when he spotted the Flagler road sign, he slowed the vehicle down more. He turned and stayed in the right lane, and then pulled onto Flagler Street. When he turned on the new road, he spotted a gas station and checked his gas. He needed some fuel so he pulled off and fueled his vehicle, but instead of leaving the station, he pulled his SUV over to the side of the station and parked. When the car was parked, he ordered the Neck, Sergeant Robert Abbott out of the vehicle and ordered him to stand in front of the car while they waited for the pair of Chevy carryalls with the terrorists to arrive at their exit.

Captain Walker wanted the Marine Sergeant branded No Neck to stand outside the car so Sergeant Ramirez would easily spot him, and she would know they were there and going to free her from the terrorists. He picked the Neck for another reason, he knew the leader of the terrorists never saw him, and it was safe to leave him standing out in the open.

The Mutt jumped out of the car and he rushed into the Circle K store and picked up some sodas and cakes while they were waiting for the other cars to arrive.

General Kalantari was calm, because he just looked at the road map and realized they were less than six miles away from the exit from the highway. They made better time than expected, and they just passed by the 17th Avenue exit. Without his needing to ask the driver he replied when he noticed the General's look.

"General Kalantari, we should be getting off this endless highway within the next ten minutes at the latest. Then it should take us another ten minutes to reach your target, and maybe another twenty minutes of driving around the area for you to observe and understand your target much better, sir. Then I shall get you and your followers over to the hotel for the night's rest and then you can attack your target at your leisure, sir."

"Yes Driver, I cannot tell you how exhausted I am from this endless drive through this cursed land, sir. I'm longing to destroying my target, and then leaving this land of Satan as quickly as I can get out of here. Although I'm exhausted, I want you to do a drive by the target. So I know how to attack it, and then we'll go to this hotel you called the Best Western and rest for the night." The Vulture grumbled angrily, allowing his sheer exhaustion to creep into his voice.

Finally, the exit they were looking for appeared printed on the next sign, and this perked up the Vulture and the rest of his terrorists. The deadly Persian Officer was sitting upright and paying close attention to the road and traffic ahead of their vehicle. The Iranian soldiers were paying close attention to the last road they were driving on. Sergeant Dorothy Ramirez was also on the alert and committing everything she saw to her memory for future reference, if it was needed for them to stop the terrorists' attack.

The Cuban driver was picking up the renewed energy being emitted from the Persian fighters, and he was likewise getting reenergized. In less time than it took to look at his watch, the driver started to slow down to get off I-95, and turn onto Flagler Street. The traffic was like it never happened, and only a few cars were turning off the highway on this exit. The driver stopped by the exit stop sign with his right blinker on, and found himself waiting for a break in the traffic so he could pull onto Flagler safely. When the road cleared, he pulled out slowly, and he got in the right hand lane on Flagler. Ramirez was trying to pick up the land marks when her blood froze.

Her eyes immediately locked on the massive man the instant she recognized him, while he was standing in front of her SUV with his foot resting on the bumper of the vehicle. Her heart started pounding in her chest as she tried to see if anyone else was sitting in the car the Neck was resting against. For the first time in her life, she found herself cursing the tinted windows she ordered in the car. Although she could not see into her car, she could make out shadows, and she could only believe Walker, the Mutt, and Buckethead were inside the car, and Walker had the Neck standing outside so she would see him, and know he was there to rescue her, and stop the terrorists from carrying out their mission against the United States.

She had no idea Walker dragged the scared to death country singer with him. She never gave it a second thought, because he was a civilian and had no military background or training. Suddenly, she rested her head against the rear seat, and relaxed for the first time since being taken captive by the terrorists. But Major Sayeh Rahimi noticed the actions of their female prisoner, and she looked out the car window to see what was so interesting to her prisoner.

Even though the concerned female terrorist spotted the huge man resting his foot on a car like he had nothing else to do with his life. Major Rahimi did not find anything out of place with this picture, so she continued looking around at what the female prisoner might have picked up and offered her some comfort. When the female terrorist did not find anything out of the ordinary, she wrote it off to the American female spotting something familiar, and she let it go at that. But now, Major Rahimi found herself glancing at Ramirez and keeping a closer eye on her and her actions. Because she was now slightly in fear the young American female might try to alert someone she might have spotted outside the car to their presence in the area, and for their help for her to escape their control of her.

Major Sateh Rahimi felt the relaxation emitting from the prisoner and she found this puzzling. Because she knew if she was being held prisoner, she would be doing everything in her power to try and escape, or at least alert someone to their presence and stop their mission. Now, she started scanning the area of the outside of the vehicle in earnest, thinking their captive had indeed noticed someone who might lend her assistance escaping them. Try as she might, the Iranian soldier did not see anything that might cause her alarm.

The soldier known as No Neck was being coy standing outside of the car. When he spotted the white Chevy carryall turn off the highway, he moved his hand to his forehead, and then he swiped it across it like he was wiping sweat. But Ramirez picked it up as a sort of salute, and she knew it was a signal to inform her they were there, and they were going to get her free.

Major Sayeh Rahimi turned her body in her seat so she could look behind her to see what made her captive secured suddenly. In her look back, she again picked up the huge man in front of the car like he had nothing to do, and she felt if he was a friend of her prisoner, he would have surely have jumped in his car and started following them.

The instant No Neck spotted the Chevy trucks turn off the highway, he glanced in the windshield of Walker's car, and gave him the signal he spotted them. The Neck was dying to jump back in the car and help Walker stop the two vehicles and free Ramirez from the terrorists. One thing he did pick up, was the fact Ramirez was being held prisoner in the lead vehicle, so that was the one they had to hit first, if they wanted to get her away from the terrorists.

Walker also picked up the pair of Chevy trucks as they turned off the highway, and every muscle in his body immediately tensed up and he wanted to spring into action against the terrorists. He wanted nothing more in life than to pull his car on the road and slam it into the lead terrorist vehicle, but his better judgment held him in check. He realized if he stopped the terrorist car on the road, they would immediately kill Ramirez and then he would be involved in a heavy firefight right in the middle of the city of Miami. Countless civilians would be caught up and killed in the heavy cross fire. He understood he had to search out the right position to make his attack against the terrorists to stop their actions, and to save Ramirez.

The Mutt picked up the two vehicles and before he warned Walker, he saw Walker also picked them up. The Mutt rested his hand on his friend's shoulder, reading the thoughts in his mind and he offered. "C'mon man, I know what you're thinking buddy. But if you try anything against the sonofabitches here, they're gonna kill Raz, and we'll have to fight it out with them in the streets of Miami, buddy. We gotta stay cool and wait for our fucking chance to act, so we can get at the lousy bastards. At least we know where they are and where they're heading Walker and that puts us one up on the rotten bastards. We'll get her away from them pricks soon enuf buddy, and then we can have our revenge against them at our leisure, man."

"I know that, I figured that much out for myself, man. But I gotta tell ya pal, I wanna jump out there and stop these fucking pricks more than I want a second son. I hate they have Raz, and they're here to hurt innocent American civilians, man. We gotta fucking stop them and get Raz outta there in one frigging piece if it's the last thing we do." Walker replied like he had no other choice in the matter, and it was destroying him from the inside.

The Mutt was feeling Walker's pain and helplessness, and he wanted to do something to relieve some of the suffering he was going through.

But much like Walker, he was completely helpless to do anything about the situation, but to sit back and wait for the opportunity to react against the terrorists, and get Ramirez away from them.

The Neck remained standing outside the SUV and the moment the two vehicles carrying the terrorists and Ramirez was stopped by another red light on the next block up from them, he reacted. He sprang into action and the huge man ran for the back door of Walker's SUV. He pulled the door opened and yelled at Walker as he sat down. "Hey Walker, Raz is in the first fucking car, and she's sitting in the back seat between two of them mutherfucking terrorists. One of them is a bitch, and she seems like she's on good alert, Homes. She looked at me a coupla times while I was standing out there like a stinking fish outta water, man. I saw a barrel of a weapon in her hands, so they have Raz covered at all times."

"Yeah that's a damn good report Neck. I kinda figured Raz was being held in the lead vehicle buddy, and I thought they would have her covered at all times as well. If not, she woulda freed herself from the stinking bastards on her own, and she woulda taken care of the damn terrorists once she was freed." Walker replied confidently as he started his car, but he did not pull right out on the road. He was staring at the pair of Chevy trucks stopped by the street light, and he decided not to pull out on the road until the light turned green, and they moved out.

He was planning to follow them from a good distance to see if they were going after their target right off, or if the group of terrorists were going to put off the attack until they had time to properly setup against it. He did not think they would go right after the target, he knew he would not if he was running the mission, and if they did not go right in action against their target. It would give them time to get Ramirez away from them, and then stop the terrorists before they could possibly carry out their mission.

The concerned Captain was hoping the terrorists were going to hold up for the night, and that would give him the time they needed to react against them. When the light turned green, Walker pulled out on the road and followed the other cars down the road. The terrorist vehicles were staying almost bumper to bumper with each other as they traveled and turned onto Biscayne Boulevard, and then they started traveling at thirty miles an hour. He allowed two other cars to pull between his vehicle and the terrorist vehicles to help shield him from their view.

As they moved forward, Walker asked the Neck a question. "Hey big man, do you think the friggin terrorist picked up our vehicle when that bitch looked at you, man?"

"I don't know for certain man, she coulda picked up the car I guess. But I think she was more interested in looking at me than our stinking car, man. At least that was the way I saw it, man" The Neck replied to Walker's question.

"I hope you're right buddy, we can't afford to have them pick us up before we go against them." Walker growled as he did his best to keep the large, white Chevy Suburban vehicles in his sight as he trailed them through the traffic as they headed for where Walker knew they were going. He followed the vehicles for about three quarters of a mile, before the Mutt warned him because he had a better view of the two vehicles they were trailing.

"Hey Walker, they just put on their right signal man. You betta drop back a little or you're gonna run right up on their damn asses, before they could turn off the stinking road."

Walker did not reply to the Mutt's warning as he got off the gas and his car slowed down more, and then he looked up at the huge street sign hanging over the roadway. It read in large silvery letters that glowed in the dark, 'The Port of Miami Terminal Exit, one quarter mile ahead'. When he read the sign he cursed, causing the Mutt to ask him with concern.

"What's up with ya man, we knew they were gonna be turning off on this exit, Walker?"

"God dammit Mutt, I was kinda hoping the stinking terrorists wouldn't go right in action when they got here. I was hoping they woulda took a few days hanging around and checking out the area before they tried to hit their fucking target, man. That way it woulda given us some stinking time to get Raz away from the bastards, before we were forced to engage the damn terrorists in armed combat." Walker complained as he watched the two Chevy vehicles slowly turn onto the only road that led to the massive port.

"Calm down man, maybe they're just scoping out the stinking place first, before they crawl into their fucking rat hole for a few days. I don't see them going in action against their target without checking it out first, Walker. I don't think they have their damn equipment with them as yet. I'm certain they're gonna step back for a few days and work out their last minute attack angles, before they go after the stinking target. Hell Walker, we don't know for sure if the ship they're after is sitting in the damn port yet, man." The Mutt fired at Walker as he kept his eyes glued to where the pair of Chevy trucks was heading at about a hundred and fifty yards ahead of them and their vehicle.

"Yeah, I guess you're fucking right with that last suggest, buddy. I gotta get some fucking control over myself or I'm gonna blow this damn thing all to hell and back on us, man. This damn thing got me going by the stinking short hairs, and with these friggin pricks having Raz as their damn prisoner, is making me absolutely fucking crazy. We gotta get these fucks before they can destroy their target, and kill Raz while they're at it, dammit. We gotta be absolutely perfect on this damn mission my friend, or a helluva lot of geeks are gonna pay for our stinking failure, buddy." Walker griped at the Mutt as he waited for his turn to turn onto the only road that led into the port, so he could see what the terrorists were up to.

"Relax man, we'll get Raz away from the bastards easy enuf, and then we'll pick them off as slick as snot, before they can hit their fucking target, Walker. You gotta trust me on this one man." The Mutt replied to Walker and then he flashed him a quick and reassuring smile.

Walker took his eyes off the road for a brief second and he shot a quick smile at his lifelong friend, as he said to him. "I'm fucking glad I have you on my side man."

Buckethead and No Neck offered to Walker as if they were upset. "Hey prick, what about us fucking guys back here man? What the hell do you think we are buddy, chopped fucking liver or sumthin? We're with you guys buster, and we intend to get Raz away from them stinking pricks before they can hurt her."

He smirked as he added for the soldiers riding in the back seat. "Hey guys, I'm sorry I left you two birds out. I know you two tree trunks are with me on any action we do, and that's why I know this mess is gonna work out fine for the lot of us. Neck, I'm warning you, if you get wounded on this one and you ain't killed by the fucking wound. I'm gonna finish your ass off myself, buster. Don't get fucking hurt on this action, you big asshole.

"Yeah, and before I hear from the civilian puke with you uther pukes. I know you're gonna help us and I appreciate it man. When this mess is over with, I'll see you get a fist full of friggin medals for helping us out man, and I'll also draft your skinny little ass into our Unit, pal. If you can hang tough with us on a fucking action then I feel you're wasting your time trying to sing in a fucking mike, when you can be out there fucking helping your country out properly for a stinking change along with the rest of us stinking pukes, man."

Toby was still scared to death to move a muscle let alone speak, but he was able to muster a smile over the words Walker offered. He was hanging onto his weapon for dear life and he was thrilled to death Walker offered to get him into his Special Forces Unit. But the singer had no intention of giving up his singing career for the life of a special operations soldier. But as scared as he was over what was happening, he was extremely charged up to be part of the action. He was being torn apart between troubling thoughts of working with the elite soldiers, or leaving them and saving his life before any trouble really started.

The two Chevy Suburban carryalls slowly entered the Miami Port Authority Terminal area at the proper posted speed of fifteen miles an hour. They followed the signs directing all visitors to the port where to go. General Abdol Karim Kalantari's car pulled up to the main gate security guard and the Cuban driver offered the guard his driver's license for identification, and he informed the guard he was there to pick up his mother and father who were coming in on the Caravel Cruise Ship, and the security guard informed the driver the boat he was there to meet, was not due to dock for another hour and a half now. The security guard stated the boat was fighting heavy seas and it was forced to slow her speed.

Major Sayeh Rahimi leaned over to her side and she produced a small pocket knife and quickly cut through Ramirez's bindings and released her hands. Sergeant Dorothy Ramirez pulled her hands in front of her and she vigorously rubbed her wrists with her hands, trying to get her circulation moving again and stop some of the pain she was suffering from being in the binding for so long. Rahimi allowed her prisoner a second to attend to her discomfort, and then she snarled in no uncertain terms at her.

"Female American pig, you'll straighten your cursed hair with your worthless hands, and then you'll look like you're driving with us to pick up the driver's loathsome family. I warn you woman, if you try in any way to alert this security guard about us. The whites of my eyes will be the last thing you'll ever witness in your life, before you kiss the feet of Allah, hateful woman. Your fate rests in your own hands woman, waste your fate needlessly and you and the foul guard will be dead before you know it, and so will many innocent American civilians if we're forced to defend ourselves in these vehicles. You'll act like we're friends for a long time, woman."

Ramirez turned slightly so she could see the Persian woman's eyes, and what she saw resting in them chilled her to her very soul. She read nothing but sheer hatred and loathing for her emitting from them as she nodded slowly back at the angry looking Iranian female soldier. Her hands immediately when up to her hair, and she tried to smooth it out the best she could with just her hands in the car. Once she was finished fussing around with her hair, she flashed one of her calming smiled at the still extremely angry looking foreign woman.

"That is better woman and that is the way I demand you act while we're stopped by this worthless security guard. Don't be so foolish as to waste your worthless friendship on me woman, it'll be wasted so keep your cursed smile to yourself. Once we're free of this foul man, you'll be allowed to remain without your hands tied behind your worthless back. But I warn you woman, I shall be carrying my knife with me at all times, and if you give me any trouble whatsoever, I'll swiftly slice your throat and allow you to slowly bleed to death, as we kill anyone who tries to help you or interfere with our mission, woman."

The Cuban driver checked the cruise lines schedule in advance, and he was aware one of the boats was due to dock around three thirty that afternoon. The wise foreign driver put on a sour puss like he was suddenly upset he was going to be forced to wait for the boat to finally dock, which prompted the security guard to offer to him in a rather friendly tone of voice and a smile.

"Sir, I'm sorry for the delay, but it won't be that bad for you to endure, sir. The Cruise Lines have a great waiting area setup where they serve hot and cold food, and it's air-conditioned, and you can spend your time watching some of the other boats as they dock at our port facility, sir." The slightly concerned looking security guard smiled at the Cuban driver who nodded and then the guard informed the driver where he was to park his vehicles, while he waited for his parents to arrive at the facility.

The driver did not reply to the security guard as he followed his instructions and parked the vehicle where he was directed to park. Once the vehicles were parked, the terrorists and Ramirez prepared to leave the vehicles. Before they got out, the Vulture turned in his seat and snarled savagely at Ramirez. "Foolish American woman, you'll accompany us to this cursed terminal building. I warn you in advance woman, if you dare to try and alarm the authorities in the building against us, you'll cause a blood bath the likes you have never witnessed before in your worthless life, and many innocent civilians will die because of that alarm.

"We're here to find a person who is missing, and he's scheduled to arrive tomorrow night and we wanted to see where he'll be arriving to meet us, woman. We mean no harm to anyone especially you. All we want to do is be able to live in the United States in peace. Once our friend arrives, we'll release you and you can go on with your life with your cursed friends we left on that Island, and we'll enjoy ours."

The Vulture had no idea he was warning a female soldier from the Marine Special Forces, who was well trained in dealing with any possible terrorists and hostage situations. If General Kalantari realized he was dealing with a profession American soldier, he would have ordered her and the soldiers with her killed, before they left Boot Key on Marathon.

Ramirez was no fool, now she knew Walker and the others were there to free her and stop the terrorists, and she was not going to do anything that might upset their plans. But she understood once she found out the reason for these terrorists to be in the United States, she was honor bound to react against and stop them from carrying out whatever they were up to. So far all she knew was they were after some kind of target, and when their vehicles first pulled onto the Port of Miami Terminal property, she was certain they were after some ship, but she still had no idea what the rest of their plan was about as yet.

Her mind was working in overdrive, trying to figure out what the terrorists were up to and their target. She came to the conclusion something on this ship they were waiting for, was either needed by the terrorists, or the ship was carrying something they could use to create another possible Nine, One, One, attack against her country. As she was concentrating, a hard shove brought her back to reality, and she turned in the direction of the push and she came eye to eye with the angry Major Sayeh Rahimi, and she was glaring at her as she hissed angrily at her. "You heard the words of our Commander, if you fail to obey them properly, I shall kill you first, evil woman. Then we'll kill anyone who challenges us if you call out the alarm to them."

"I have no reason to start trouble, especially since you told me when your friend arrives here, you'll set me free." She replied while trying to sound as convincing as possible.

"That is much better an attitude to adopt over this situation you are mired in worthless American woman, and it shall be my pleasure to dispatch your worthless life of sin and lust if you make any trouble for us while we're visiting this cursed building. Only a few of us are going inside the foul structure, the rest of my friends will remain stationed outside with our vehicles and weapons. So they can offer any assistance needed if anything happens inside the building, woman. Now, you'll follow me out of the car nice and slow, but remember your fate rests within your own worthless hands, woman. If you cause me and my friend's any problems, you'll die that simple. Follow my orders without hesitation, and you will live to see your cursed friends we left on that miserable little Island again. Now follow me and be calm about yourself." As Rahimi finished her words, she flashed the knife to show Ramirez she was armed and ready to kill her.

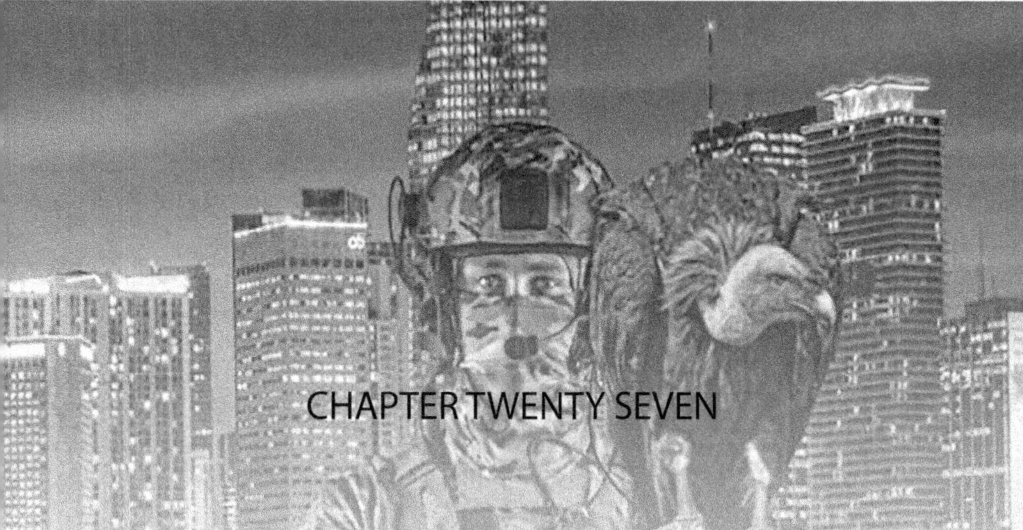

CHAPTER TWENTY SEVEN

Walker got through the security gate and guard by flashing his military identification card and rank in the service. Once he was through the gate security to the facility, he cautiously followed the white Chevy trucks to where they were instructed to park at a good distance between them. He drove past the first four lines of parked civilian cars, and then he parked his SUV well away from the terrorist's vehicles, and he watched everything the terrorists were doing inside the parked trucks. The Mutt broke Walker's concentration by asking him with a slight smirk on his face. "Hey man, what the hell's our fucking plan, oh fearless leader of mine?"

"Well stupid, you know neither of us can go inside the fucking terminal to follow them cocksuckers around. They saw us in fact we're supposed to be dead, buddy. That leaves the two tree trunks and the stinking singer to do the damn act for us, man. They're gonna hafta go inside the damn thing and see what the hell these lousy fucks are up to in there. We're gonna stay out here and keep an eye on them damn cars and the rest of them fucks, and see if we can work out a fricking way to get the drop on them assholes when they come out of the damn building. But we're gonna hafta be patient with this one, man. If there's too many fucking civilian pukes in the way when they come outta the stinking building, we won't be able to react against the bastards, and we'll be stuck following the lousy pricks to where they're gonna stay for the stinking night.

"You assholes got that back there, you guys are gonna hafta follow the bastards into the stinking building and keep a close eye on them while they're in there, and try and see what the fuck they're scoping out in there. Hey Neck, if you see an opportunity to get Raz away from them without placing too many civilians in danger, take the effort and don't get shot. Or I'm gonna finish off what them pricks started with you this time, dammit. If we get Raz away from them pricks then we can go hot any time we want against them, even on the stinking road if we wanna. Take the stinking civilian with you and use him as a sort of fricking buffer between you and them damn terrorists. Out of all of us, he looks like the least fucking threatening to anyone. Just take the damn pistols with you and leave the assault weapons in the car with us.

"We'll try and cover you guys the best we can from out here, but I warn you three. If I hear weapon's fire coming from in there, the stinking Mutt and I are coming in there hunting fucking bear. We'll carry your rifles with us if you three go hot in there, dammit. Shit, they're getting outta the damn vehicles." Walker growled as he sat forward in his seat and he looked out of the windshield of his vehicle as a car door on the first Chevy opened up, and he saw some movement from inside the vehicle.

Major Sayeh Rahimi was the first terrorist to exit the parked car which prompted the Mutt to complain to Walker with a snap in his tone of voice. "Hey man, it's a fucking bitch getting out buddy. Damn, she's a good looker, I got first dibs on her ass when we ice her and I'm gonna fuck her for revenge, man."

"You keep your stinking mind on what we're doing here for a fricking change, and don't fucking worry about the damn bitch will ya buster. When we're done with them pack of assholes, I don't give a flying fuck what you do to her stinking body, man." Walker growled at his lifelong friend as he continued to watch what the terrorists were doing.

Once Major Sayeh Rahimi was on her feet outside the vehicle, she stepped a little further away from the car, and then she waited for Ramirez to get out next. Something about this woman made the short hairs on the back of Major Rahimi's neck stand on edge, but she could not figure out why she was in such fear of this young and pretty American female. She felt the way she moved and walked and stood, made her look more like a military type person than a mere civilian.

But she also felt she might be overreacting a bit, and she decided to keep her prisoner under a tighter surveillance until she received the command to finally kill her from the Vulture and her leader.

Captain Robert Walker saw his long time girlfriend, Sergeant Dorothy Ramirez slowly and extremely cautiously get out of the truck next, just as the passenger door opened at the same time, and a large man got out of the car from the other side of the vehicle. He had to actually force himself to remain seated in his vehicle, because every muscle in his body wanted him to charge out of his vehicle and rush after Ramirez, and get her away from the group of terrorists. He smiled when he noticed Ramirez was so in control of her emotions and actions that she was actually trying to look around the massive and crowded parking lot for him, and the other soldiers he had working with him.

When the Mutt noticed Ramirez getting out of the vehicle, he turned to Walker and warned him in no uncertain terms. "Hey man, you gotta stay fucking cool here buddy. Don't do something stupid my friend. We'll get her away from them safely, man."

Next, the young and concerned Cuban driver got out of the truck and then the driver, General Kalantari, Major Rahimi, and Ramirez headed for the main doors of the huge terminal building. From the way they were walking across the parking lot, it seemed like Ramirez was going along with the terrorists without struggle or resistance.

Walker kept a close eye on the group and the moment they disappeared inside the terminal building entryway, he barked at the other three men sitting in the back seat. "Get out and follow them damn fucks. Neck, try and get Raz away from them bastards. Me and the Mutt will watch the other stinking slobs, and if we see a way to get a jump on them, we'll make our move and take them out, and that'll leave the three with Raz. Get moving you three."

The Neck replied to Walker's order by saying confidently. "You got it man, if we can get her, we will, buddy. If not, we'll see what the sonofabitches are up to in there, Walker."

Walker watched the three men walking and talking as they headed for the terminal entrance. Nothing but their dress was out of place for someone coming to the terminal to pick up a friend or relative from a trip on the sea. He laughed as he saw sand still stuck to their clothes, and there was salt water stains on their clothes, making them look dirty. There hair was a mess and it was matted down to their heads by the salt water they swam through hours before on Marathon. Buckethead seemed like he was having trouble walking, and that was because he was the only one who was stupid enough not to have taken the time to dump the sand and crushed sea shells out of his sneakers while they were driving in the car up to Miami following the terrorists.

When the Neck, Buckethead, and Toby disappeared inside the terminal, Walker turned his attention to the remaining terrorists in and standing by their parked trucks. He let out his breath in a sort of hiss as he saw the way the remaining terrorists decided to protect their cars and themselves. Two each of them got out of the vehicles, and they were just standing by the cars talking together and trying not to draw any extra attention towards themselves or their actions. He quickly realized it was going to be nearly impossible for him and the Mutt to get the jump on the group of terrorists with the guards they posted outside the two vehicles.

The Mutt wanted to get out of the car so he could stretch his legs a bit. But Walker would not allow him to get out of the vehicle for fear the remaining terrorists hanging around in the parking lot, might recognize him if he got out and they fire at him. The Mutt was dying of thirst and he asked if he could get out and buy some more sodas.

Again, Walker would not allow him to leave the car, because he knew the Mutt wanted to get out so he could see if he could get at the two trucks and the drop on the other terrorists milling about the two parked vehicles. He did not want to take any chances at this particular time for fear of endangering Ramirez, or the lives of innocent civilians visiting the massive terminal at the same time. He was forced to give the Mutt a dirty look to try and calm him down and stop him from wanting to get out of the car on him.

The moment the driver, General Abdol Karim Kalantari, Major Sayeh Rahimi, and Sergeant Dorothy Ramirez entered the terminal for the cruse ships, they were met with a wall of mayhem and deafening noise. There was a flood of people speaking different languages running around in all directions. Some of them were obviously upset and they were yelling at anyone who would lend them an ear. Other people were looking after their children, with many kids crying or raising other forms of fuss. Other people were looking for loved ones who wandered away, or were coming in on the next ship. Other excited people were following Port Authority personnel around while they showed them where to assemble for the cruise ship scheduled in soon.

Major Rahimi moved closer to Ramirez and she pressed the tip of her blade against her back as she warned her again in a threatening voice. "I shall warn you once more American pig, if you make any attempt to alarm anyone, or draw any attention to us. I shall kill you, and then we'll kill many of these out of control civilians before we die, woman."

Sergeant Ramirez slightly turned her head to the angry female Persian soldier, and she simply nodded back at her. She had no intention in making trouble for the terrorists, she was too busy scanning the countless faces she saw in the crowd, looking for one of her fellow soldiers to walk by her in an effort to let her know they were there, and they were going to help her.

There were so many people and faces passing her in this section of the terminal that soon, the faces began to blend together to the point where she was worried she might not recognize Walker if he walked by her. She was being shoved back and forth by the maddening crowd, and by Major Rahimi who had a death like hold of her arm, and she was trying to pull her against the crowd. Ramirez resided herself to be pulled in any direction her captive wanted her to go off in. But the deeper the group traveled into the terminal, the crowd lessened until they were standing in an area where few people were gathered, and the ones there, were sitting peacefully in chairs, and some of them were watching a TV, or just talking amongst themselves.

Major Rahimi nearly dragged Ramirez over to some empty chairs and she growled at her to sit. She followed her orders and she sat and folded her arms across her chest. She made like she was comfortable, but she was keeping an eye on every move the terrorists were doing while inside the terminal building. She watched out of the corner of her eye as the one she heard called General Abdol Karim Kalantari and the driver, walked over to a pair of windows and they started looking out in one direction from them. She moved her arms and made like she was trying to scratch an itch by her left ear. This caused her to turn her head to the right to see where the two men were standing and looking out of the large window. Try as she might, she could not see what the two were looking at from her present position in the chairs.

Major Rahimi stood in front of Ramirez and blocked her from making any attempt to escape. When she moved her arm, Major Rahimi tensed up and she prepared her body to kill the female in her custody, if she dared tried anything against her. But when she saw her start to scratch an itch, Rahimi relaxed until she noticed the prisoner was trying to look at the men. Not wanting to create a scene with the young woman, Major Rahimi moved over to Ramirez's side, and she successfully blocked her view of the two men. Anger was building in her chest and Major Rahimi leaned down and hissed in a low voice in Ramirez's ear. "Go ahead foolish woman and try my patience, you'll only discover you're trying my anger, and you'll find yourself dead. I order you to sit back and rest your foul head against the wall, and then you're to close your eyes and you will keep them shut until I tell you to do otherwise, cursed American woman."

She followed her orders from the female terrorists, and when she was sitting with her eyes closed, Major Rahimi turned and looked to the men. She saw them looking to west of where they were standing, and knew they must have found the ship they were looking for, or they found the birth the ship was supposed to occupy. Instantly, she relaxed her shoulders and took some of the pressure off her neck, as she held the knife in her right hand covered by an over shirt she had looped neatly over her arm.

General Kalantari was trying his best to make it look like he was speaking to the other man with him in private. But he was actually trying to locate the unmarked ship carrying five hundred and fifty thousand ton of high explosives in her cargo hold for a special military operation going to be carried out in Iraq within the next few weeks. The extremely dangerous Vulture was informed well in advance that this certain ship was a military transport that was trussed up and disguised and made to look like any normal civilian cargo ship delivering a harmless load of cargo to the massive civilian port terminal. As the wise Vulture made it look like he was speaking to the Cuban driver standing by his side, he was constantly looking over his shoulder and out the window.

The cunning Vulture scanned the five cargo ships docked a hundred yards from where he stood. From his position and the way the ships were docked, he was able to see four of the five bows of the ships, so he could easily read the names of them. The first ship was called the Sea Spray, the second ship was the Night Wind, and the third ship was named the White Dolphin.

General Kalantari shook his head out of anger because the ships were not the one he was looking for. The Vulture was forced to shift his weight and move more to his left to better read the name of the last ship he could see from his position. He was looking for the ship named the Whale Shark. When the General moved, he was able to see the bow of the last ship docked in this area, but as he was about to read the name, two men walked out of the building and stopped right in his field of vision, and their bodies blocked him from reading the name of this last ship. The Vulture placed a disgusted and nasty look on his face as he waited for the two men to move off so he could see the last ship and get the name of that large cargo ship.

One of the men was taking the time to light a cigarette, and it seemed like the second man was waiting for him to get it lit before they continued with their duties. The Iranian terrorist saw the men were dressed in the same uniforms as the men he saw working for the terminal complex. It seemed like a short lifetime General Kalantari was forced to wait until the two men moved off, and he was finally able to see the name of the last ship. Sure enough, it was the Whale Shark, but there was also something else that brought a smile to the Vulture's lips.

Sitting off to the right side of the Whale Shark was the last of the five cargo ships docked in this area, and sitting to the side of the Whale Shark some eighty yards or so away, sat one of the massive and so called super tankers. Just from the way this ship was sitting deep in the water, the Vulture realized it was loaded with raw crude oil. Now he knew if he was able to explode the military cargo ship loaded with many sorts of different and extremely powerful explosives, the explosion that detonation would cause at the terminal port would surely cause the behemoth of a fuel carrying cargo ship to explode, adding dramatically to the cataclysm he was about to release against the United States with his attack against them.

The Vulture smiled sarcastically over this latest discovery, because now he knew for certain he was going to do much more damage to the United States than he first figured on with his attack against the country. General Kalantari leaned a little closer to his young Cuban driver and he announced barely over a whisper to him. "My friend and brother from another country, in this unending war we have declared against this foul country of evil doers, I have very good news for you to share with your fellow countrymen. The ship we're after is resting in its birth, but there is an added pleasure for us to enjoy. There is a massive fuel cargo ship birthed right next to our target, and her fuel will add greatly to the death we shall soon visit on the United States and her foul civilians. We my brother, shall deal a lethal and deadly blow to our enemy for our cause for mine and your countries, and also for the delight of Allah.

"For Allah truly enjoys when we destroy another haven of the evil Satan, and this god cursed country is the breeding grounds for everything Satan wishes to cast upon the faithful followers of Allah. Come my young friend and ally, because I have seen enough of this foul place to last me a lifetime. But I shall inform you here and now, the way these ships are docked will allow my fighters for Allah cause an easy path to destroy them all. From what I have seen of the security of this worthless place, they are not well prepared to defend themselves against my attack. You would have figured the great fools who run this miserable country, would have surely learned an extremely valuable lesson on how to better protect themselves from the successful attack that our divine guiding hand in Afghanistan, Usama bin Laden had taught them with his attack against the lowly dogs and their buildings of evil.

"But the fools of this loathsome country would much rather fight between themselves, because of their party then to protect the civilians of this cursed country who were foolish enough to elect them to their office of power for their guidance and protection. I thank the Almighty Allah for this dream of Democracy, because it allows us to attack these worthless fools who believe they have the freedoms of the world to enjoy, when in fact they have only the freedoms we shall allow them to continue to enjoy. With each successful attack we deliver against the fools, more of their so called freedoms will become a thing of the past. Soon, the foolish civilians of this and other cursed countries that don't follow the true religion of Islam, will only have the freedoms a military state can possibly offer to them, my faithful brother.

"We, the true believers of Islam will force the cursed civilians of this foul country to demand their worthless soldiers return to their own lands to protect them while they sleep in their cursed beds at night. Once we have the United States' military removed from every Arab country of the world, our freedom fighters will replace them and we will then control the countries the once powerful and feared United States controlled. What the hated United States did with her military might, we shall do with the power oil gives to the Arab nations of the world. Any worthless nation that doesn't want to force their civilians to follow the rule of Islam, will have their oil supplies cut off, and if they don't come around to our beliefs, their worthless nations will dry up from the lack of oil to run their cursed cars and machinery.

"Their nation's economy will grind to a halt, and their nation will suffer riots in the streets from their starving civilians, and these fools will force their government to see the errors in their beliefs, and cause them to beg us to become true followers of Islam. Any nation that doesn't bend their knees to our demands will suffer famine, riots, and other forms of civil disorder. Bah, this is for our leaders to set right, we are but the mere soldiers who'll bring forth the dreams of the ones we shall place in control of such matters for our countries." General Kalantari stopped speaking, but something he was reading that was locked in the eyes of the Cuban driver, caused him to add to his words that he had just spouted off for the driver's benefit.

"My Cuban brother, in our fight against the great Satan, I see much concern etched within your eyes. Of course, any nation that sides with my country will be allowed to follow their true path to destiny. We only stride to change the cursed lowly infidels and non-believers of Islam."

Some relief entered the driver's eyes, but he knew Cuba was mostly a Roman Catholic nation, and if this man boasting so much about Islam being the only religion to believe in. He knew his country and Iran was going to be forever at odds with each other. But the Vulture's sharp mind was clear, because he understood if Iran was able to pull off what she was attempting to do, first rule the Middle East and bring about the destruction of Israel. Then Iran's eyes will be cast upon the rest of the nations of the world, and the only nations allowed to exist, will be the ones who bring to their hearts the Islamic beliefs. All other nations would be destroyed.

Feeling he laid to rest the concerns his Cuban was suffering, General Kalantari mumbled to the driver. "Come along my brother, because I have seen enough of this foul place, and I believe it is time for you to take us to this hotel you have spoken about."

The soldiers know as the Neck and Buckethead strolled into the Miami Port Terminal, with the singer walking behind the two large men. The three were walking like they did not have a care in the world, as they looked for Ramirez and the terrorists in the terminal. Just the size of the two men caused many civilians to move out of their way. One security guard took notice of the three men, but because of the way they were walking and smiling, he felt they were there to pick someone up. The Neck wanted to stop and get something to eat, but Buckethead wanted to keep looking for Ramirez. The Neck stopped long enough to pick up three bottles of water and handed them to the other two men. There was less a crowd as when Ramirez and the terrorists entered the building, this was because most of the people causing the mayhem either found their friends, or settled in to wait for the incoming cruse ship to dock at the terminal.

Buckethead was the first to spot Ramirez sitting in a chair, and the woman terrorist hovering over her like she was guarding her. Bucket drew Neck's attention to their Sergeant, and the three of them slowly drifted towards where Ramirez was seated. When they got close enough to her, Buckethead noticed she had her head resting against the wall, and she had her eyes shut. He wanted to get her attention to let her know they were with her, but he did not want to draw the attention of the female terrorist obviously guarding her to their presence. The three men continued to move closer to Ramirez, and when they were close enough to her to let her know they were there, Buckethead suddenly turned to the Neck and growled loud enough to draw Ramirez's attention to them.

"Hey man, if you step on my stinking foot again, I'm gonna knock you three sewers back, man."

The Neck was taken aback over Buckethead's angry warning, because he knew he never stepped on his foot. But his confusion was cleared up when Ramirez's head snapped straight up and she opened her eyes and looked right at the three men. She would know Buckethead's voice anywhere, and she looked and gave him a quick smile.

But she was not the only person who looked at the angry acting and massive man standing ten to fifteen away feet from her. Major Sayeh Rahimi also took notice of the two huge men and she smiled when she saw they might get involved in a fight, because one of them was obviously angry at the other for some reason she did not hear. Never once did it ever enter her mind these two men might be a threat against her and her Persian fighters inside the terminal. A number of people close to the two men heard the warning and they were looking at them.

Ramirez looked up and noticed Major Rahimi was staring at the men and not at her, so she sent Buckethead glancing at her as much as he could without arousing her captor's attention, a quick message with her eyes. She looked hard at him, and moved her eyes to the right, causing Buckethead to look in the direction she was aiming his attention in.

Buckethead picked up the leader of the terrorists, and the man he entered the Miami Terminal with. They were standing by the set of windows, and it seemed like they were turning and going to head back to the female terrorist and their prisoner, Sergeant Dorothy Ramirez.

The moment General Kalantari turned and started walking towards where Ramirez was seated Buckethead moved to a number of empty seats as he bitched at the Neck following him as was the singer. "Hey man, I can't wait for my girlfriend to arrive so we can get the hell outta this here dump. There are too many people hanging around for me to be comfortable with."

Buckethead was also sending a signal to the Neck, warning him not to try anything against the terrorists inside the terminal, because there were too many civilians hanging around the area for them to be successful with an attack. The three men took seats facing out the terminal windows and the empty birth cleared for the incoming cruse ship's use.

General Kalantari picked up the slight commotion caused by Buckethead and the Neck, and he moved quicker towards where Major Rahimi was standing, and when he was by her side he grumbled at her. "What was that about? Are those three men a threat against us woman?"

Major Rahimi replied to her Commanding Officer just above a whisper. "General Kalantari, it seems those men are here to pick someone up from the ship scheduled to arrive momentarily at this Port, sir. It seems they are not fond of each other, one of the fools stepped on the other's foul foot, and it almost came to blows between the two large fools, sir. See, they are seated and looking to where the ship will soon dock. No General Kalantari, I don't believe they are a threat against us, sir. How did you make out? Were you able to locate our target for us sir?"

"That is good to hear woman, I was concerned there was going to be trouble with the foolish men. Yes woman, we found our target and it's far better than I ever dared to believe possible. But now is not the proper time to explain what we have discovered resting at this place. Come woman, take command of your prisoner and we shall leave this foul place. I am exhausted and I want to go to the hotel and rest so I'm ready to make our hit on this god cursed place tomorrow night, and deliver our message to the people of this worthless country, woman. I feel there are too many eyes and they're looking at us and their ears are listening to anything we say.

"We are too venerable in the open like this while only being armed with pistols and knives. We have to get back to our brothers and sisters in the parking lot before they become concerned for our health, and the fools take it on themselves to enter this terminal looking for trouble. Take control of the worthless woman and we shall leave."

Major Rahimi bowed her head towards the Vulture, and then turned from him and looked at Ramirez and hissed in a low voice. "Come American pig, is time for us to leave. Remember, if you make trouble or cause alarm, there are many civilians who will pay for such foolishness."

Major Sayeh Rahimi stepped out and away from in front of Ramirez, and she waited for her to stand. The instant she was on her feet, Major Rahimi stepped behind her and applied pressure to the tip of her knife in Ramirez's back to remind her of what was waiting for her if she made a move against them. But even feeling the tip of the knife threatening her, did not remove the wonderful feeling she was enjoying. Once she saw Buckethead and the other soldier, she knew Walker and the Mutt could not be far, and she realized they were going to rescue her from the terrorists. But she was also confused, because she could not believe Walker allowed the country singer to be part of whatever he was planning to get her away from the terrorists, and then stopping the attackers from completing their mission against the United States.

Major Rahimi did not allow Ramirez to be alone with her thoughts, when she did not follow her General and the Cuban right away, Rahimi gave her an unnoticed shove forward. Drawing in her breath, Ramirez followed the pressure from the female officer. As she moved to follow the terrorists, Ramirez cast a quick glance to where her fellow soldiers were seated. She noticed Buckethead was on his feet, and staring at her as she walked. Again she had to hide a reassuring smile when she saw Buckethead give her the thumbs up signal.

The men waited until the terrorists and Ramirez walked across the waiting area of the terminal, and was heading directly at the doors to the parking area. When Buckethead felt the terrorists were far enough from them to start following, he growled at the other men. "That's it, let's go."

The Neck stood and started to bitch at his fellow soldier. "Hey man, this shit really sucks the big one man. We coulda got the drop on them scumbags' easy enuf, and ripped them a fricking part with our bare hands before they could hurt Raz, or anyone else in this fucking place. What the fuck did we go through this stinking special training crap for, only to sit on our damn thumbs and allow them flaming assholes to disrespect one of our people, man?"

"Keep it cool big man you heard Walker's fucking orders man. If we couldn't get at them damn assholes without getting a mess of stinking civilians involved in any action we might hafta make against these pukes. Then we were to as you just said, sit on our damn thumbs and wait for a betta time to react against the lousy bastards. I don't know about you buddy, but I for one don't want Walker mad at my stinking ass for any reason. I kinda like the way my balls swing between my legs. C'mon man, we gotta catch up to these lousy little bastards and see what the fuck they are doing outside this stinking dump."

Buckethead led the way for the other two men, and they quickly made their way across the large waiting area and headed out the stack of double doors. Buckethead came out of the terminal first, and he immediately looked around until he spotted the terrorists and Ramirez, and they were already standing by their two parked vehicles. The American soldier turned and looked and saw the singer standing behind him and he growled at Toby. "Where the fuck's the uther stinking jerk with us at for crap sake? Walker's gonna kill all of us if we get separated for any stinking reason, man."

Before he could reply to Buckethead's question, the Neck came out of the doors and grinned at the angry looking Buckethead as he offered. "Hey man, I though Walker and the Mutt could use something to fucking drink." No Neck stopped long enough for him to grab a number of free bottles of water. He wanted extra for them, and also wanted to bring some water for Walker and the Mutt, who were waiting while roasting in the heat of the Florida sun baking on the cars.

"Yeah, that was good thinking on your part, fella. It gave the stinking assholes time to get back to their fucking cars. I hope Walker spotted the lousy pricks. I wonder if he's gonna try something against the stinking bastards before they leave the lot. We're gonna hang tight here and wait and if we see Walker and the Mutt make a move on the flaming assholes, and if he does we'll react and attack them bastards from here." Buckethead said as he continued to stare at the terrorists who seemed like they were getting into their cars.

The moment the terrorists and Ramirez came out the front door of the massive building, Walker noticed them and he immediately alerted the Mutt. "Here they come I guess our people couldn't get the stinking drop on the bastards, dammit. Shit, they got Raz walking in the middle of them, and the uther pricks standing by the trucks got them covered from there. We're fucked from getting at them from here for shit sake. It looks like we're gonna hafta wait until we can get a betta opportunity to get at the bastards, buddy. There are the rest of our people, and they're taking up positions in case we go afta the pricks from here, man. They have orders to stand pack unless we move out against them, Mutt."

"Walker, I didn't think we were gonna be able to get the jump on the scumbags around here, there's too many damn civilians hanging around the damn place, man. What's our fucking plan now, man?" The Mutt asked Walker while he held the terrorists in his deadly glare.

"I guess we're gonna follow the pricks around this fucking city until they bed down for the stinking night. I'm hoping they rent a damn room in a hotel we can work with. Once they're in their rooms, they should be easy for us to take out and get Raz away from them, buddy." Walker mumbled as he kept the terrorist in his view while trying to control his anger.

Major Rahimi took Ramirez over to the back door of the Chevy and opened the door for her. She slid in the truck without being ordered to and she sat next to Captain Keshavaz and he glared angrily at her as she got comfortable on the seat. When she was settled in the car, Major Rahimi got in the car next. General Kalantari walked the driver to the car door, and rushed around the truck and got in the front passenger seat. When he was seated, the Vulture said to the driver.

"It's time for us to leave this cursed place. I want you to drive slowly through the installation, so I can observe any security preparations I might not have observed from inside the foul terminal building. I'm quite certain the fools who run this cursed installation have not increased their security operations since the attack on the United States from Usama bin Laden and his soldiers of freedom." The Persian officer stopped speaking to the driver and he turned in his seat and looked at Ramirez, and then snapped at her harshly as he held her in his angry glare.

"Young American pig, you have done well not trying to alert the security guards who work here. Now woman, if you follow the rest of my orders as faithfully, you'll soon be home to the loathsome American infidel you're married to, woman." General Kalantari looked at Ramirez's hand and locked his eyes on her ring, and then continued with his angry words. "I'm certain the fool is worried about you woman, and he must be wondering where we have taken you. Major Rahimi, you'll secure this female pig's hands behind her back that way she'll not try anything foolish until we're out of this cursed place, woman."

Major Rahimi followed her orders from her Commander without the slightest hesitation, as she pushed Ramirez harshly forward, and she again secured her hands behind her back. The female Major roughly pulled her hands in back of her, and when she finished, she gave a hard pull on the rope to make certain it was secured properly. The hard pull on the rope sent searing pain into Ramirez's shoulders and upper back area.

As his Major secured their prisoner, General Kalantari placed a nasty sneer on his lips as he continued to stare at Ramirez. The look was one that informed the receiver he knew something she did not. The Vulture was certain one of the men he ordered Captain Mahebian to kill on Marathon in the Florida Keys, was the one married to this woman in his car.

Ramirez returned the glare from the Vulture with one of her own, and this made Kalantari become concerned over her reaction. He broke off his stare down and turned in his seat. But this time his mind was working, the look she gave him, informed him she must know something that could be a threat against his mission. Right there he decided he was going to interrogate this woman once they secured the hotel rooms. He was going to interrogate her in such a fashion, and if she did not survive his questioning methods, it did not matter a lick to him. He wanted to know what was giving her the steadfast strength to openly defy him like she was doing.

The Vulture suddenly believed this American woman might be a soldier, because any civilian would be shaking in their worthless shoes with being taken prisoner, and being held hostage by what she had to believe were terrorists who had invaded her country. Something she noticed inside the terminal building, gave her this power over him, and he did not like that feeling in the least. The Vulture looked towards the massive terminal building as their truck left its parking spot. All he saw was a mess of people leaving or entering the huge building.

There were quite a number of people hanging around the front of the massive building, but they were mostly smoking which was not allowed inside the building. Nothing he detected seemed out of place, and he even glanced by Buckethead, No Neck, and the country singer, as the three of them walked into the endless parking lot heading for their SUV. Two of the men were smoking, and this did not see out of pace for the Iranian Military Officer.

As the lead Chevy Suburban began to travel down the road taking them out of the huge terminal complex towards the main road they would use to get over to the hotel. General Kalantari allowed himself to relax inside the vehicle, but he was still determined to find out what this woman saw inside the building that gave her this sudden power not to fear him. He checked out any extra security precautions the guards adopted for the safety of the massive complex, and he saw nothing that would stop him from carrying out his mission.

The moment the Chevy trucks pulled out of the lot, Walker started his SUV and pulled out and up to his other three standing by the terminal entrance. He stopped his vehicle long enough for the three to jump in, and then he continued following the other vehicles out the complex.

Buckethead was excited as he reported to Walker over what happened inside the terminal and everything he saw. "Walker, Raz looked great, and when she noticed us she smiled at me. She pointed out the uther two shitbirds not with her when we entered the stinking building, buddy. She was being guarded by the fricking bitch the Mutt wants to rape, man."

"Where were the uther pricks and what the fuck were they up to?" Walker snarled at the huge man while not taking his eyes off of the vehicles ahead of him by four car lengths now.

"I don't know what the hell they were doing in there, Walker. It looked to me like they were just standing by the windows talking. I looked around and tried to see what they might be trying to locate, but all I saw was a number of cargo ships parked by their docks. I didn't see anyone from outside give them any kinda signals or acknowledge their presence by the windows, man. Do you think that prick on the damn Island lied to us about what they were up to, buddy?"

"Hey stupid, remember the bastards are up here and they're trying to locate a certain ship that goes by the name of Whale Shark. Something about that ship means some shit to these bastards. It was the only thing the uther prick wouldn't or couldn't tell us about, man." Walker bitched at the big man as he cast his eyes towards a number of ships docked at the peer, and he tried to locate the ship he was speaking about.

Buckethead put on an ugly puss over being called stupid by Walker, but his anger left his body when the Mutt called out and offered. "Hey Walker, there's the fucking Whale Shark, she's the second ship from the end. She's parked right by that big fucking fuel carrying cargo ship to our left, man. You wanna check out the damn ship, man?"

Walker took a quick look at the ship and was surprised. It was not a military ship it looked like an old cargo ship in need of major repairs. He put his attention back on the road and ordered the Mutt. "Hey dog man, first off, the ship isn't parked, it's moored at the dock. Anyway, take a good look at that ship and see if you can see anything that might make these bastards interested in its cargo, or attack it. I can't get a good look at it and drive at the same fucking time, man."

"You got it Home boy, slow down a little more so I can get a betta look at the damn tub of rust for myself, man." The Mutt replied as he studied the massive ship.

"If I slow down any more, we might as well get out and fucking walk around this dump." Walker complained at his life long friend as he kept the terrorist's vehicles in his stare.

The Mutt ignored Walker's angry bitch as he studied the cargo ship. He picked up three people working on the ship, and they were dressed in naval uniforms and it hit him. The Whale Shark had to be some kind of military ship decked out as a civilian one, so as not to draw any attention to it. The Mutt smiled over this discovery and reported to Walker. "Hey Walker, I'm picking up a number of stinking swabbies hanging around on that rust tub, so that makes it a military ship. I'll tell you this man, if the stinking Navy went through this much trouble to try and hide the fact the Whale Shark is a military ship. It hasta be have something they don't want any fucking civilians around here to know about."

"God dammit, that makes it absolutely necessary for us to get in contact with Colonel Leadbetter. We gotta find out what the fuck that stinking ships carrying, so we know why these lousy pricks want the damn thing, man. He's the only fuck who can find this shit out quick enuf for us to do something about it, before the pricks hit it."

"Do you think we can make contact with the number ten prick with these radios you gave us to use, Homes?" The Mutt asked as he turned and looked at Walker's face for a brief moment.

"Sure you can, just side to band one, three and hit the button. That's a direct link with the stinking Colonel. I had the radios adjusted in case I was on the water and a mission came in."

CHAPTER TWENTY EIGHT

The Mutt smiled as he quickly tuned in the radio to the frequency and hit the button and grumbled into the radio. "This is Lieutenant Frank Hall and I wanna speak to Colonel Leadbetter. This is a Fire Fly communication."

Sergeant John Kirkpatrick was manning the Colonel's desk while Colonel Bruce Leadbetter was out of his office doing something on the massive Camp Lejeune Military Base. When the call from the Mutt came in and the soldier classified it as a Fire Fly communication, it immediately got the Sergeant's attention. He picked up his radio and replied in a sharp voice. "This is Sergeant Kirkpatrick, what's going on and why the hell are you using the emergency code number for this communication, Lieutenant Hall Sir?"

"Never mind that shit Sarge. I gotta speak to the Colonel A-SAP. This is an emergency situation and we need him to do something for us to assist this emergency for us, Sergeant. Just follow your stinking orders as you have received them, and get the god damn Colonel double quick, or I'll have your fricking ass for supper, mister. My classifying this fucking emergency as a Fire Fly communication should be enuf for you to get the damn Colonel for my ass."

"Yes Sir, hang on while I page the Colonel through the intercom for you, Lieutenant Hall Sir. It might take a few moments to get him here because I don't know where the Colonel is on the base at this time, sir." Sergeant Kirkpatrick offered as he flipped on the loud speaker intercom for this section of the base and he barked into it. "Colonel

Leadbetter Sir, you're needed at your office immediately, sir. This is a priority two request, Colonel. I repeat, Colonel Leadbetter, you're needed at your office immediately, sir."

Colonel Leadbetter was having a field day riding one of the new recruits for his recent screw up on the practice field, when he heard he was being paged by his Desk Sergeant. He cursed as he headed for his office at a quick pace. He was wondering who needed him and his specialized troops on the field this time to protect their asses. The fuming Marine Colonel left the new soldier and jogged to his office. He came plowing into the room and snarled at his Sergeant in a heated tone. "Okay buster, who the hell needs our fucking asses this time, mister?"

"Colonel Leadbetter Sir, I have Lieutenant Hall on the radio and he's reporting a Fire Fly communication, sir. He didn't inform me what it is about sir, he said he wanted to speak directly to you sir." The Sergeant reported to his Commander the moment he was in the office.

"The fucking Mutt's reporting a damn Fire Fly alert to my office huh, what the fuck happened to Walker, and why the fuck isn't that sonofabitch reporting this Fire Fly communication instead of this other damn nut job, mister? Give me the damn mike so I can find out what the hell's happening for myself with these damn troopers, mister." The Colonel angrily took the mike from his Sergeant and then snarled into it hotly. "This is Colonel Leadbetter, what the fuck's going on Mutt, and where the hell is your fricking partner in crime at, mister? You better not be busting my damn horns again, because you people got nothing better to do with your damn down time while on leave or you're just lonely and wanted to hear my damn voice again. Or I'm going to skin your damn ass alive for sending this emergency communication to my ass, mister."

"Colonel Leadbetter Sir, we got a shit filled situation on our stinking hands and we need your help with it, sir. This is no joke sir, some stinking terrorists got hold of Sergeant Ramirez and we're hot on their fucking heels, sir. Captain Walker, Sergeant Lombardo, and Sergeant Abbott are with me, and we got Toby with us also, sir." The Mutt reported to his Commanding Officer.

"What the fuck is a Toby mister, and what the hell's the damn situation you're handling and talking about, mister? Arrr… fuck that other shit buster. Based on your report, I'm going to send out a flash alert and get the rest of our people moving on the double quick, sir. You said something about some damn terrorists. Explain yourself immediately or I'll take a giant shit on your fucking face, mister." The Colonel warned his excited soldier over the radio.

The Mutt ignored the Colonel's bitch about the country singer being with them as he explained everything they had so far to his concerned Commander. Then he informed the Colonel of the help he needed. "Colonel Leadbetter, we have information the terrorists are up here to hit a fucking ship called the Whale Shark, sir. The ship's presently docked at the Miami Port Terminal, sir. We actually passed by the damn ship and it looked like a garbage scowl to me, sir. But I picked up a pack of stinking Navy pukes working on it, and that means it's a military ship fixed up to look like a stinking civilian ship for some fucking reason, sir. We gotta know what the ship is carrying so we know how to handle our approach against it and the damn terrorists."

"Hang on while I find out what the damn ships carrying, mister." Colonel Leadbetter growled into the radio, and then he turned his attention to his Sergeant and snapped at the concerned looking soldier. "We got a terrorist situation on our fucking hands, mister. Send out the alert for our people to report back to base ASAP. You also have to get in contact with Navy Command and find out what the fuck they're doing with a ship called the Whale Shark in Miami. These flaming assholes in Florida think they're following a number of terrorists, and an attack on the Miami Port Terminal is possible. The Mutt seems serious, and that's enough for me to react to his warning. Let me know when you find out something about this damn ship, mister."

The concerned Marine Colonel went back to the Mutt on the radio. "Okay Lieutenant Hall, we got the wheels in motion up here, mister. When I get any information on this damn ship you want to know about, I'll let you know buster. Now fill me in on the missing damn pieces to this mess you people are in, so I better know how to setup the rest of my fucking people, sir."

The Mutt did his best to explain everything that happened to his Commanding Officer, and by the time he finished, the Colonel was fuming and angry with Walker for not checking in with him sooner and trying to get at the terrorists himself. He informed the Mutt that Ramirez was not the main reason to carry out this operation against the terrorists. Before the Colonel signed off with the Mutt, he told him not to worry about the cargo ship, that there would be plenty of military assists guarding it by the time the terrorists decided to attack it.

The moment the Colonel was off the radio with the Mutt he went into action, he alerted soldiers from his base and had them heading out for the Miami Port Terminal to protect the ship, and whatever it was carrying in her holds against the possible terrorist attack.

When he got off the phone with his alert, Sergeant Kirkpatrick reported on the contents of the cargo ship, and this information cleared up why the terrorist cell was after this particular ship docked at the Miami Port Terminal. The Colonel informed Naval Command of the present situation, and they informed him they were going to dispatch SEAL Team Six by air, to better protect their ship. The Colonel was pleased over how everything was shaping up and he smirked as he thought, let the terrorists try and hit that damn ship now, and they'll find themselves dying of lead poisoning.

When the Mutt was off the radio with the Colonel, Walker asked him what went on. He went over what he and the Colonel spoke about, and this satisfied him and he turned his attention back to the pair of Chevy trucks as they stopped, and prepared to turn right onto Biscayne Boulevard. Right across the street from where they were waiting to turn was the entrance to the Orange Bowl Arena. When the trucks were on the road, Walker turned onto the same street. He followed the two trucks back to Flagler Street and the Chevy trucks made another right onto that road. Walker was pissed off because he did not know where the terrorists were heading.

The terrorists drove until they came out on the cross road to Flagler and 12th Avenue, and then they turned onto 12th Avenue and made another quick right into the Best Western Hotel. Walker was smart enough to go through the red light and followed Flagler to the next light that was 17th Avenue, and he made a right and took this road to the next light. He then made a right onto 36th Street, and took this road one block until he came across 12th Avenue again, and then he made a right and slowly went down this block until he was able to see the Best Western Hotel again from his car. He stopped in the middle of the street and began to look for a place where he could park his car, or ditch it until he needed it again. He passed the underpass for the Dolphin Expressway and the Neck said to him from the back seat.

"Hey Walker, there's a dirt road by the side of the expressway where you can probably park the damn thing. It looks like a place where people park when they wanna car pool together, I guess. It's got a fence around the damn spot, and there are three cars in it, man."

"That's what I was fucking looking for man." Walker growled as he placed his car in reverse, and then backed up until he was able to make the turn into the small parking area. There was a sign stating no overnight parking was allowed in the small lot. But Walker did not care what the sign said. His thoughts were set to get Ramirez away from the terrorists, and then stop them from carrying out their planned attack on the naval cargo ship. Just as he parked the car, the radio went off and it was Colonel Leadbetter reporting back to him.

"Walker this is Colonel Leadbetter, where the hell are you, mister? You better get on this damn radio double quick, because I want to speak to you buster. Walker, come in mister."

Walker keyed his radio and snapped in it. "Colonel, this is Walker, what do you got sir?"

"Walker, the first thing I want to discuss with you buster. Is why the fuck you took it upon yourself to play God, and be superman and take care of a fucking invading terrorist cell by yourself and those few shitbirds you have operating with you, mister? You know the damn orders pertaining to this type of situation, buster. If you discover a terrorist cell operating within the borders of the United States, you're to inform command immediately, and then you're ordered to wait your next fucking orders from me, mister. You have answers to supply if you want to keep your ass out of the stinking Brig for this lack of following direct orders, buster."

"Colonel Leadbetter, I didn't have the fucking luxury of time to repot in about this damn situation, sir. So you can do whatever the fuck you wanna do to my stinking ass and get it over with, sir. They have Raz, and I wanna get her away from the friggin scumbags before they kill her, sir." Walker snapped back into the radio extremely angrily at the Colonel.

"Look here buster you're entering this mess in the wrong frame of mind, mister. Ramirez is not the problem here buster, the fucking terrorists are, Walker. Ramirez is a soldier, and as a soldier she knows where she stands in this fucking situation, buster. If we can get her from them, that's good for our fucking side, mister. If not, she's a soldier. Our main concern is to stop the damn terrorists from attacking that fucking ship at port, period! If Ramirez goes down in an operation we try against these slobs, she'll be remembered as laying down her life for her country, plain and simple, sir." Colonel Leadbetter snarled angrily at Walker, while trying to get his head straight for what he had to carry off to make this situation work out successfully, and stop the terrorists before they could attack that ship.

"You might think she's gonna be remembered as laying down her fucking life for this country, Colonel Leadbetter. As long as there's a fucking breath left in my damn body, I'll do everything in my power to save her stinking ass, sir." Walker snarled at the Colonel over the radio.

"God dammit, I knew this shit was going to come up sooner or later and bite me on the damn ass, between you and this bitch of yours, mister. I should've never allowed you two shitbirds to start playing house together in the first place. You two fools are soldiers, not some damn civilian puke's in love with each other, dammit. You people are supposed to love the Marine Corps and country and nothing else, buster. Shit, dammit, I guess we'll speak about this shit later on, once you people stopped the terrorists' attack, mister.

"Err… the reason I called you back is to inform you that ship you're so damn concerned with, is loaded down with a cargo of extremely high explosives scheduled to make their way to fucking Iraq two days from today, mister. If those fucking terrorists pop that damn ship off where she's docked, Walker, the explosion will leave a massive creator where half of Miami use to be sitting, mister. I have people from this base heading to Miami as we speak Captain, and the Navy is also dispatching their top notch SEAL Team to protect the damn ship from a possible terrorist attack against the damn thing. So I don't think the fucking terrorists will be able to get within a half god damn mile of that damn thing and live through it.

"Walker, if the damn terrorists are able to get by you and those asses with you, and we think of them as soldiers, the terrorists will never be able to carry out their fucking attack on the damn ship now, I assure you of that much, mister. The defensive troops being dispatched should be arriving at the damn Port within the next three hours, Walker. We alerted the Miami police departments, and they're scrambling their specialized SWAT teams to the terminal as we speak, Captain. Once the damn SWAT teams get on site, they're going to shut down the entire fucking terminal. Lock, stock, and fucking barrel and anyone who gets stuck on the facility will be there until this present situation is over with, Walker." The concerned Marine Colonel bitched at Walker as he stopped speaking to draw in a quick breath.

"That's all well and good to know Colonel. But I'm more concerned getting at the terrorists than I am at hearing this uther shit, sir. They're hold up at the Best Western Hotel situated at the corner of Flagler Street and 12th Avenue, Colonel Leadbetter. And, I figure they're gonna stay here for the night, and try and hit the Port Terminal and ship sometime tomorrow. I'm go…"

The Colonel cut Walker off in mid-sentence and he ordered him. "You're going to stay right the fuck where you are, buster! For the love of God Walker, you don't have any damn weapons with you to stop the damn terrorists with, mister. This has to be a joint fucking operation buster, involving the local Miami fucking police, the FBI, and anyone else who wants to join in on the damn bandwagon along with us, Captain. I'm ordering you to stand pack and wait until we get our damn support forces down to the fucking port and…"

Walker interrupted the Colonel this time, as he snapped over his handheld radio at his Commanding Officer. "Colonel Leadbetter, we're fucking armed and ready to go, sir. We have M-16s for each of us, and we also have Sig 9mm pistols also, sir. We now presently have the friggin terrorists trapped inside the damn hotel, and this is the best place for us to try and hit the lousy little fucks if we really wanna stop them cold, and also stand a stinking chance of getting Raz away from them alive while we're at it sir…"

"Look Walker, I already informed you that Ramirez is expendable on this fucking operation, Captain. I'm not going to take any damn lips shit from you over that order, mister. Your main concern is to stop these damn terrorists from accomplishing their hit on the damn port. Christ sake Walker, you give me a fucking headache no amount of god damn aspirin in the world will relieve. Damn it to hell and back again, okay Walker, I'm pleased you had the smarts to arms yourself, and when this mess is over, I'll be asking where the hell you got your hands on so many automatic weapons, buster." Colonel Leadbetter took some time as he stopped speaking and thought of his next orders he was going to issue to his young and extremely dangerous officer. Once he formulated his thoughts, he offered his Captain.

"Okay Walker, I'm going to stick my dick inside a blender for you and your damn people down there. I'm going to issue you the following orders. If you screw up my orders, you better head for a country we don't have an extradition agreement with, buster. Because if you screw up, you'll not want me to get my fucking hands around your neck for one fricking second, mister. Listen up buster, because this is what you're going to do on this one, Captain. You're given my permission to go after the terrorists and you'll either kill or take them prisoners. I hope you heard me right, and noticed I placed you will kill them first on this order, Captain.

"Walker, you'll do everything in your power to get Ramirez away from the damn terrorists. But if you feel trying to get her free will jeopardize your other orders you'll have to use your best judgment in your actions and act accordingly. I know you'll make the right decisions when it comes to winning Ramirez's freedom from the terrorists, and the mission you're on. Your main objective is to stop the terrorists from achieving their intention above any other concerns in this mess. If you chose to go after Ramirez first Captain, I don't want to know about it, as long as you get the damn terrorists while you're at it, sir.

"I shall notify the Miami Police Department of your presence at this Best Western Hotel, and I'll further inform the police officer I shall be speaking with that you people are in command of any mission to be carried out against these damn terrorists, Captain. I'll further inform the officer this is a military operation, and let me tell you something here and now. I'm putting my neck way out for you fucking pack of screaming squirrels. You know as well as I do that I should be informing General White about this latest situation, sir.

"He's the one who should be running it before the President, the FBI, and his staff, before you go after the damn terrorists, sir. But because time is of the essence on this one mister, I'm taking it upon my own shoulders, and I'm ordering you people into action, sir. If the police want to assist you on this attack, that's good for your ass, but they'll be subject to any and all your fucking commands, Captain. Or I'll order them not to enter the fucking area until you people have completed your damn orders and it turns out to be a mop up situation, sir.

"Okay Walker, you have the green light to begin your attack against this batch of terrorists, sir. Good luck on this mission Walker, and anything I can help you with, ask and you'll have it at your disposal, sir. If the police show up before you go in action, have them evacuate as many non-combatants from the area as possible, sir. I don't want to hear about any large numbers of collateral damage and breakage to the damn civilians of the area. Errr… Walker, good luck with getting Ramirez away from them fucks. I know no matter what I tell you to the contrary, you're going to do whatever you want on this one, so go and get her away from them people, mister."

"Outstanding Colonel Leadbetter, I can't tell you how important it was for me to hear those last orders, sir. I promise Colonel, I'll get Ramirez away from the terrorists, and not one of the terrorists will leave the hotel alive, or be our prisoners. As of this time sir, their mission is done for sir." Walker boasted over the small handheld radio locked in his mitt.

"That's a good brag there Walker. I hope your mouth isn't writing checks your damn ass can't cash, mister. Get a move on it Captain and do what you were trained for, mister. I want this mess done by the time General White finds out about it, and he places his first call to my ass.

I have no intention of speaking to the General while there is an active operation being carried out against a bunch of fucking terrorists who just invaded our country, Captain."

The instant Captain Robert Walker was finished speaking to Colonel Bruce Leadbetter, the Mutt, Lieutenant Frank Hall barked at him. "Well buddy, what the hell did old what's his fucking puss have to say this time man? Is he gonna allow us to get Raz away from these lousy little pricks, and then take out our revenge out on these uther scumbags, man?"

"What the fuck are you asking me for? I'm sure you heard him as he spoke over the damn radio, dog man. But in case you weren't paying attention to the damn conversation, the Colonel gave us the green light to get Raz, and naturalize the stinking terrorists at the same time. He also told me if the local police show up, they're to follow our orders, period. This stinking mess is strictly a fucking military operation, which places us in the driver's seat on how we wanna deal with this situation, dog man. Have any of you people been keeping an eye on what the terrorists are doing out there, and maybe picked up the damn rooms they took over in the stinking dump?" He snapped at the three soldiers and one civilian gathered around him at this moment.

General Abdol Karim Kalantari ordered the pair of Cuban drivers to remain with the two vehicles while he and Major Fereshteh Mansouri went into the hotel and secured the rooms for them. Before the Vulture entered the hotel lobby, he noticed a third vehicle pull into the parking lot, and it stopped near the two parked vehicles he was in control of. Instantly, the terrorist known as the Vulture realized the car scheduled to remove the two Cuban drivers from the area arrived, and it was stopped in the parking lot. Yet the motor was still running on the new vehicle, and the driver did not bother to get out of the machine, he continued to sit in the vehicle and waited for the two Cubans to jump into his waiting vehicle.

The hotel was built like a horseshoe type structure where the visitors could walk to their rooms through the hallways and yet stay inside the building. Or they could get to their rooms by driving to them, and then entering the hallway nearer their rooms.

The Vulture and Major Mansouri decided not to speak to the driver of the other car, as they walked into the lobby like they did not have a care in the world. General Kalantari allowed Major Mansouri to do all the talking to the hotel clerk for the both of them, because she barely had a Persian accent, and she also spoke the best English of all the Iranian terrorists of the group.

Major Mansouri smiled at the clerk, and she asked to rent four double rooms for the night. She added she wanted the rooms separated to each side of the hotel. This was so if they were attacked while at the hotel, at least some of their Persian fighters would be able to escape the attack. The clerk was more than happy to rent four rooms to the pretty stranger, and he had no problem having the rooms separated like she requested. Once the hotel clerk was paid in cash for the four rooms, he got the keys and handed them to the young woman without asking any further questions of her on why they were staying at his hotel.

The moment Major Mansouri was handed the keys, both General Kalantari and Major Mansouri turned and walked out of the building without saying anything more to the manager. When the two terrorists were outside the building, they headed for the parked Chevy's and one sedan car with the Cuban driver waiting inside the car, and when the Vulture was alongside the first truck. The occupants got out and he handed Colonel Nasser Makaeem Taleqani a set of keys to the rooms on the other side of the U shaped type structure of the hotel. Then he snapped at his military officer in a harsh tone of voice.

"Colonel Taleqani, you'll take the fighters in your vehicle and you'll stay at the rooms numbered on your cursed keys. I demand you keep one of our worthless people awake all night, in case we come under attack while resting at this foul cursed establishment. Colonel, if you hear any weapon fire coming from our area of the hotel, you'll not come to our aide. Instead you and your fighters will leave this foul place, and then you'll command the others and make for the Terminal and carry out our orders with the soldiers you will have at your command. I assure you Colonel Taleqani, if we hear weapon fire coming from your area of this cursed structure.

"I or any other fighters with me will not come to your aide, instead I shall leave this place with the soldiers I have, and I'll carry on with our mission. We're in this god forsaken country to attack the foul Terminal and that is all, Colonel Taleqani. Our mission in this country is the only thing we must complete, or our President will curse our souls forever. Take these worthless keys and go to your cursed rooms. I plan to leave this foul establishment at eight a.m., and I believe we shall complete our mission with a simple cast of the mighty sword of justice by ten a.m., and by one o'clock in the afternoon, we shall be back on that miserable Island known as Marathon. Then, the cursed Cuban brothers will get us off the foul Island, and hopefully, if AnshAllah, God wills it so. We'll simply vanish from this country like a mirage, and be back in Cuba in the middle of tomorrow night at the latest, fool.

"By the ten Prophets of Islam I warn you Colonel, Allah is merciful but you will find the exact opposite with me. Any of your soldiers who are not ready to leave this place by the time I stated, will wish their pig mothers had never met their cursed fathers. Once we're back in Cuba, by the great Prophet's will, I'll slice Colonel Gonzales into small pieces for his many insults he had leveled against my person. I pray to Allah for revenge upon all who stood in our way for this mission. By the five sacred prayers of the Holy Qu'ran, good fortune to you Colonel, may Allah grant you a life of a thousand years my faithful brother. Be gone with you and see to your fellow soldiers. I demand they all be well rested for our mission of tomorrow morning."

"Fear not a worry about our upcoming mission, General Kalantari. Everything shall be as you have ordered, sir. My soldiers will be well prepared to begin our worthy mission against this land of lowly infidels and jackals at the time you have ordered it to be so, sir." With that said, the Persian Colonel took the keys from his Commanding Officer, and then he turned to his soldiers and ordered. "My faithful brothers and sisters, you heard what our General has just ordered. We shall follow his instructions, or we'll be cursed by our leaders in Iran." The Colonel led the way for his other soldiers to their rooms on the far side of the hotel.

General Kalantari watched as half his soldiers headed for the other side of the hotel, and then he turned to the rest of the fighters. He looked at Major Mansouri and snapped at her. "Major, you'll be in command of our cursed prisoner all the while we're resting at this foul place, woman. If she gives you any trouble, you'll dispatch her without hesitation. But you shall use a knife on her foul body to make your kill silent, and to cause the prisoner the most pain and suffering before you allow her to die." The angry Vulture kept an eye on his female Major as she walked around the vehicle and she grabbed Sergeant Dorothy Ramirez roughly by the shoulder. She took charge of Ramirez from Captain Jahangeer Keshavaz and Major Sayah Rahimi, who were assigned by the Vulture to guard Ramirez while they were traveling to their target area.

Once Major Mansouri had control of Ramirez, she snarled at her. "Lowly infidel of an American pig, give me any reason, any reason whatsoever to send you on your way to your final judgment kneeling before the feet of Allah. I beg you to make trouble so I can dispatch you and wash my faithful hands with my leader's orders to guard your foul self. Being this close to an American bitch makes me ill to my stomach, woman." With her warning hissed threateningly at her captive, Major Mansouri then gave Ramirez a hard shove forward, almost causing her to lose her footing and tumble to the floor. If it was not for the side of the parked Chevy truck that broke her fall, she would have surely fell to the ground.

Major Mansouri did not stop her from falling. In her mind she wanted her to fall. She knew if the American fell, she would not have had the use of her hands to break her fall, and she would have suffered injuries. The female Persian Major wanted to cause Ramirez pain.

The Vulture smiled over the harsh treatment his female Major was dishing out to their helpless American captive, because he wanted to cause the female captive to suffer before he began his interrogation of her. He intended to interrogate her once they were settled in their hotel room. He was concerned over the American's strange reaction when they drove through the town when they were heading to examine their intended target earlier in the day. That reason, along with his want to just hurt any American wherever he came across one, was the Vulture's main driving force to hurt this helpless woman.

Once the extremely dangerous Vulture was certain his female Major had full control over their captive, he snapped at her. "Major

Mansouri, you'll bring our foolish prisoner to our room on the third floor of this cursed establishment of the lowly infidels of this country. Colonel Khatami, you and Major Rahimi will be sharing the room with us. I shall use Major Rahimi to help controlling this worthless American female prisoner. Captain Keshavaz, you and Captain Dastjeedi, along with Major al-Layluz and Captain Noakht, will share room Three, Seven, and the same orders apply to you fighters. You shall order at least one of our faithful fighters to remain awake all night in case someone decides to try and attack us in our sleep. You can split this order between all the fighters ordered in your room, so not one of our fighters will be deprived of their sleep for the full night.

"I shall be ready to begin our attack in the United States at exactly eight a.m. tomorrow morning, and I shall level the same threat against you as I have just warned the other fools of our group. If anyone from our group is not ready to begin our attack at that time, I assure you you'll rule the day when your fathers produced you within the womb of your mothers. Let's get out of this cursed parking lot and out of the sight. Standing here makes me realize just how venerable we truly are while we're within the land of hated infidels."

With that said the Vulture turned on his heels and stomped his way for the entrance to the hotel. The other fighters followed their leader to their rooms. Major Mansouri was walking behind Ramirez, and she was keeping a close eye on her as she struggled to keep up with the others of the group. Major Mansouri was smart enough to have covered over the rope holding Ramirez's arms behind her back with a sweater she found inside the vehicle. The way she was walking, it made her look like she was holding her sweater behind her back.

When the Vulture and the other terrorists headed for the hallway, the two Cuban drivers got out of the other vehicles. Once they were out, they headed right for the waiting vehicle, and the moment they were seated in it. The third vehicle immediately pulled out of the hotel parking lot, and then quickly disappeared in the light flow of traffic.

Buckethead, Sergeant Vincent Lombardo left the other three soldiers after he was ordered by the Mutt to keep an eye on the terrorists, and to see if he could figure out which room they were taking Ramirez to. When the Vulture headed for the side door leading into this wing of the hotel, Buckethead followed them at a safe distance after he copied down the license plate number of the vehicle that picked up the Cuban drivers and left the parking lot. When the group of terrorists disappeared into the building, Buckethead followed them. There were three elevators at the far end of the corridor, and the large American soldier walked right up to the terrorists. He pushed the button for the elevator and flashed a quick smile and gave a slight nod at the obvious leader of the terrorist group standing in the hallway.

The Vulture gave Buckethead a quick glance and returned the slight nod, and then he pushed the button for the third floor. By luck, Buckethead pushed the same floor number which the Vulture took notice of. He figured this huge man was staying in the hotel on that floor. The Vulture's elevator door opened first and his fighters with Ramirez entered the cab. But Buckethead remained standing in the hallway and he grumbled at the group. "Man, that car's full up, I guess I'll wait for the next elevator."

Again, General Kalantari nodded at the big man. But the Vulture also blocked the way for Buckethead to enter the cab with the other terrorists. He remained in Buckethead's way until the doors closed. When the elevator doors closed before him, Sergeant Lombardo let out a deep sigh. But he did smile when he made direct eye contact with Sergeant Ramirez, and he noticed her shoulders release the tensions she was suffering from. He also noticed the slight smile she flashed him before the elevator doors closed.

Buckethead's elevator door opened and he jumped into the cab and waited to be delivered to the third floor. He came out just as the door to room Three, One Seven closed, and he figured that was the room the one group of terrorists were holding Ramirez in. This decision was based on what he witnessed still going on down the hallway. Half of the terrorists were still walking down the long hallway, and Sergeant Dorothy Ramirez was not with them.

He followed the other group of terrorists down the hallway and when the group stopped before the room numbered Three, Two, Three. Buckethead walked through this group of Iranians as if he was heading for his room on this floor. Just as he turned the corner of the hallway, he stopped and gave a quick look around the side of the wall, and he watched as the last group entered that room without looking to where he disappeared to. When the terrorists were inside the room, he actually ran for the emergency stairwell and took two steps at a time running down them, heading for the outside of the building. The man crashed through the double set of fireproof doors and ended up coming out at the far end of the hotel parking lot. Then he ran across it and jumped over the low row of hedges separating the hotel from the road, and he continued running for where Walker and the other soldiers parked Ramirez's SUV, to make his report to Walker.

The Mutt replied to Walker's last question. "Yeah Walker, I ordered Buckethead to keep a stinking eye on the fucking terrorists as they entered the damn hotel. I sent him because he was the only one of us left that the stinking terrorists didn't see so far, man."

"Out fucking standing stupid, it's good to see you're using your head for more than just a fucking hat rack, man. When the hell didja send the big jerk out to watch these sonofabitches?" He growled hotly at his lifelong friend as he stared at him angrily. He was still flipping over the fact the terrorist was able to grab Ramirez, and he was not going to relax until he had her safely away from them, and the terrorists were dead.

"Hey man, back offa my stinking ass a little will ya, buddy. I know this thing with Raz must have your nuts tied in a fucking knot on ya man. But dumping on my damn ass because I'm trying to get some shit offa your fucking ass isn't gonna help you any, buddy. I feel Bucket should be coming back soon man." The Mutt offered as he looked down the block towards the Best Western Hotel and smiled when he saw the huge man heading back to them. Then he boasted to Walker with a triumphant smile plastered on his lips. "Here he comes now man, so calm the fuck down before you blow a fucking head gasket on your ass, man."

Captain Robert Walker looked down the block after listening to the Mutt, and he immediately picked up the huge Buckethead coming right at him. He placed his hands on his hips and waited not so patiently for the big man to get back to the group. Buckethead jogged his way over to Walker and the rest of the guys with him, and when he was standing before the angry looking Marine Captain while trying to catch his breath. The Captain growled at the huge man. "Stop sucking up all of the fucking oxygen in the damn world, and make your damn report before I hop you in that fat ass of yours, buster."

"Hey man, that's why you're the stinking boss all the damn time Walker. Calm down a little will ya man, I know where half the fucking terrorists are held up inside the damn hotel. Four of the damn assholes brought Raz into room Three, One, Seven, W, in the wing of the hotel that's closest and facing the road, Walker. Two people with Raz were chicks, and one of them was shoving Raz around, and I could tell by the look on her face she was really pissed off about the shoving thing going on, man. Before you ask me Walker, yeah I stood four feet away from her and when she saw me, she smiled at me buddy. Seeing me so near made her relax a little, she knows you gotta be near if I was there, Captain.

"Four other stinking terrorists, all males when in room Three, Two Three, W or West I guess the W stands for Walker, and I walked right through the bunch of lousy little scumbags. That room was some twenty feet away from the other room with the bastards in it. I'm telling ya man, I had all I could do not to attack the damn creeps where they stood, Captain. I woulda killed the lot of the lousy bastards with my bare hands. Anyway Walker, once we get in room Three, One Seven, West and get Raz away from these rotten fucks, we can then set about to finish off the other pukes at our stinking leisure man.

"Two pukes with Raz in the first room, one a female, the other one who I took to be the head cheese of the group seems to be the ones who'll give us the most fucking trouble from the group of lousy scumbags, man. The other dumb shits are just mere target practice for us when we go hot and heavy and we hit them." Buckethead offered to Walker with a smile on his lips as he stared at his commanding officer.

"That was a damn good report there Buckethead, at least we know what we're going up against inside the stinking building, and where Raz is being held. I'm glad you didn't act against the lousy pukes though. If you did, that woulda placed us in a bad and possible no win situation. The only thing we have working in our stinking favor is surprise. As long as we can get inside the building without being detected by any of the terrorists, we're in the driver's seat for this stinking operation,

Bucket. Well people, here's what we're gonna do and the way we're gonna hit the building and the damn terrorists." Walker growled at his people as he cast a glance toward the hotel about a thousand feet away from where Walker's group was gathered.

Once he was done looking at the building like he was trying to see through the walls of the structure. He added to his words for his fellow soldiers. "Okay people, here's what we're gonna do next. We're gonna split up into two separate groups of attackers. One group is gonna hit the stinking terrorists on the uther side of the damn building, while the second group hits the uther group of terrorist who have Raz. We're gonna hit them hard and fast at the same time, so one action won't alert the uther group of scumbags they're under attack by our asses. We're gonna also do this by the…" Walker stopped speaking the moment Buckethead drew his attention towards the other end of the road.

He turned and looked down the end of the road and noticed a Miami police squad car stop at the top of the road, and the two cops riding inside got out of their vehicle and gave Walker and his group a hard look for a few moments, while they checked out the soldiers to see if they were the ones they were instructed to take their orders from.

"Hey Walker, it looks like the stinking Colonel called out the fuzz to help us with this stinking mess, man." The Mutt grumbled as he stared at the officers as they continued to stare back at them. Almost instantly, a second Miami squad car pulled to a stop at the other the end of the road from the other direction, and the driver remained inside the vehicle and nodded towards the small group of American soldiers standing in the middle of the street.

Walker gave the police officer the thumbs up signal to acknowledge their presence, and the driver of the second car then got out and he started to speak to the other officers who pulled up behind his squad car. While Walker and the others kept their eyes glued on the police officers and watching what they were doing, three more squad cars suddenly showed up. The officers got out of the vehicles and they quickly spread out in the surrounding area and started going to some of the local homes and knocking on the doors, and then removing the civilians from the homes and the possible action that might go down.

When the police officer obviously in command of the other policemen had the rest of his officers following his orders, he finally turned and then he started to walk towards Walker and the others who were standing with him.

CHAPTER TWENTY NINE

"Uh oh man, here comes the stinking head cheese of the cops, Walker. Are you gonna put him in his place good and proper right off the friggin bat, or are you gonna dance him around a bit first, man?" The Mutt asked his closest friend and fellow soldier.

"Just watch me man, I ain't gonna allow this little puke screw things up on us and we lose Raz to these bastards in the process." Walker growled at his fellow military officer as he aimed his harsh glare at the police officer walking towards them, while using the shadows and the darkness to blind him in case any of the terrorists were keeping an eye out of their rooms.

Captain Robert Walker shifted his weight on his feet while waiting for the police officer to reach them. Like the officer, he and his soldiers and one civilian were using the darkness closing in to keep their presence from the terrorists. They were crotched behind their vehicle waiting for the cop to reach them. When the officer walked up to their position, Walker immediately introduced himself to the officer by offering.

"Hey man my name's Captain Robert Walker, and I'm a Captain in the Multi National Rapid Response Force that the Chairman of the Joint Chiefs of Staff specially organized. To pit us up against any stinking terrorists who think they can harm our fricking civilians living in the United States and elsewhere, throughout the rest of the stinking world, man."

"Yes Captain Walker and I'm Major William Peterson from the Miami Special Branch of the Police Force in Command of terrorist actions in my county, sir. I'm please to meet ya sir."

"Same here Major Peterson Sir, but I feel we hafta get off on the right foot from the start of this stinking mess, sir. I've been placed in Command of any action we take against this latest batch of stinking terrorists to invade our country, sir. I betta let you know, the lousy scumbags have one of my people as their hostage. So this is why I'm in Command of this damn mess. We gotta see if we can get her away from them and then we'll level the sonofabitches nice and quick, while hopefully doing the least amount of collateral damage to the stinking hotel, and the rest of the area and civilians while we're at it, sir. I mean to tell..."

Walker would have gone on with his bitch if the grinning police officer did not interrupt him and as he offered the commanding soldier. "Yes Captain Walker, we have been informed in advance from your Commanding Officer, a Colonel Bruce Leadbetter that this action was to be controlled by his people operating in the field, and you people were stalking the terrorists. I must offer you this Captain Walker I'm damn pleased you people found these terrorists before they were able to carry out their attack on the Port Terminal, sir. I also want to inform you that we dispatched three separate SWAT teams to the Terminal, and they have the entire area blanketed, sir. There's no way in hell anyone is going to be able to hit that place and live through it, sir. Also Captain, the ship in question has been moved away from the Port, along with the two fuel tankers also ported at the Terminal, sir.

"Furthermore, Captain Walker, there's enough military types who are heavily armed, also showing up at the Terminal, with more soldiers arriving every moment, sir. Someone in Washington has pushed the right buttons, and everyone is hoping on this one, sir. At the moment, I have my officers moving the civilians out of the danger zone, in case there's a shootout with the terrorists, sir. Also Captain Walker, I have two other SWAT teams consisting of twelve officers in each team, currently taking up positions in the surrounding area, sir. We'll position them in the area where they'll..."

This time it was Captain Walker who interrupted the police commander by growling at him. "Hey man, I'm gonna have my fucking people out there in the field, and I don't need your damn cops putting a fricking cap in any of my stinking people by friggin mistake, man. Especially because none of my people are gonna be dressed in their stinking uniforms for this action, sir. How the hell are you gonna be able to tell the damn difference between my people and the stinking terrorists out there, Major Peterson?"

"Well I hate to tell you this Captain Walker. But your Commanding Officer has ordered us to stay out of any action against the terrorists, sir. But he further ordered we're not to allow anyone off the property once your people engaged the terrorists. He gave us direct orders in no uncertain terms absolutely no one was to leave the hotel property, period sir. I guess your Commander gave these orders in case your people were dispatched by the terrorists, and they tried to continue with their operation, sir. So you'll have to inform your people if the terrorists get the upper hand on them, they better sit tight and allow my Officers take out anyone you people might miss, sir."

"Yeah sure Major Peterson that sounds like a fricking order the lousy prick would issue to you people to get you outta the way, sir." Walker remarked as he smirked at the concerned looking young Miami Police Commander.

The police officer returned Walker's smile as he went on with his words without missing a beat. "Captain Walker, my Officers have strict orders to observe your people as they go into action against the building and terrorists, sir. They're to memorize your people so they don't make any errors and take one of your people out by mistake, sir. I have direct orders from your Commander, once you naturalize the terrorists, you as their Commander are to come out of the building by the same door you entered the structure. Once you're outside, you're to wave something white before you. My Officers have orders not to hit anyone with a white flag, sir. Also Captain, once we've established contact with the hotel clerk and you people go in action, sir. We'll order the clerk to send out a message to his clientele, and have him order the civilians to remain locked in their rooms until everything is over with, sir…"

"Who the fuck gave you those stupid ass orders, Major?" Walker snarled at the police officer.

"No one gave me those orders, sir. It was the only idea I was able to come up with to try and keep the civilians out of harm's way, sir." The stunned looking Miami Police Officer replied.

"Look man, you can't allow that dumb ass hotel clerk to notify his stinking clients about our presence in there, sir. He'll only end up alerting the damn terrorists, and that'll take the surprise we have waiting for them away from us. That's the only thing we have working in our favor, Major. Surprise, if the terrorists know we're coming for them. They'll be ready and waiting for us, and they'll kill their hostage, and then give us one helluva battle, sir."

"Hold on a moment there will you please, Captain Walker. I'm not stupid sir. I had the intentions of notifying the hotel clerk, but only after we heard your weapon fire going off inside the structure. Or we got the okay from you to start clearing out the civilians staying at the hotel, sir. We can't possibly allow a live firefight to take place inside the hotel with so many civilians staying at the damn place, sir. Captain Walker, I know if he let out the alarm before you people went after the damn terrorists, he'd also be alerting the terrorists to your pending attack aimed against them, sir."

"Look Major Peterson, I know there are a ton of stinking civilian lives at stake here, sir. But we have to keep the damn terrorists from learning we're coming afta their lousy asses, sir. Here is what you can do sir. We know the damn terrorists are on the third floor of this structure. Half of them are on the east side, so we can have some of your people go into the stinking building on the first and second floors and start moving some of the people out nice and orderly. Once they're out of the building, they're to leave the area on foot so as not to alert the terrorists.

"The people on the third floor of this stinking dump are gonna hafta take their damn chances until we know how we're gonna hit the terrorists. Once we hit them, your people can get the civilian on the third floor out of harm's way as we work over the terrorists, or order them through the phone system to remain locked in their damn rooms, Major. Have them hide in the damn bath tubs of their rooms. It's the safest place to hide when we hafta start shooting the lousy scumbags in there, Major." Walker replied to the police officer.

"You seem quite certain you're going to have to drive the terrorists out of the rooms with weapons, sir." The concerned looking Miami Police Major offered back to Walker.

"Sure, as shit flows down stream we're going hot against the damn terrorists held up in there, sir. I ain't into this damn thing to take any fucking prisoners you know, sir. By the way Major, we don't know where the second batch of stinking terrorists is staying inside that building, sir. It might be a good idea if you get some of your people to speak to the damn clerk and find out where the uther pricks are staying. That way you'll know where you can start moving the uther civilian's outta the stinking building on the uther side of this place, sir. It'll help us to know where they are, I only had one guy checking out the pricks, and he stayed with the group who had one of our own as their prisoner, Major Peterson." Captain Walker grumbled as he cautiously eyes the Miami Police Officer for a brief moment.

"I can handle that easy enough for you, Captain Walker. Do you have any idea how many terrorists we're talking about on this one, sir?" Major Peterson asked the military officer.

"Yeah, we got a good number on the stinking terrorists and we place their number at fifteen, minus the one we iced off back on Marathon, sir. We also lost the two drivers for the group of pricks. They had a third bastard pick them up and they drove offa the damn property before you guys showed up here."

"Yes sir, we heard there was some kind of confrontation that happened down in the Keys, sir. But it was never announced it was a confrontation between a number of soldiers and a group of terrorists, sir. Something else I must inform you about sir, there was an APB put out on you for detainment in a shooting and murder on that Island, sir. But when we were contacted by your Commanding Officer, he informed us about this and a possible terrorist situation, and the warrant was immediately lifted on you, sir. Dammit Captain I wish to hell you would've informed me some of the damn terrorists got off the property before we arrived, sir. We could've picked them up by this time, Captain. You wouldn't have identification on the suspect's vehicle they used to drive off in, do you sir?" Major Peterson asked as he put on a disgusted look.

"Hey Major Peterson, I can help you out good and proper with that problem, sir." The massive Buckethead offered as he suddenly butted into the conversation at this time.

Walker and Peterson turned to look at the huge man, as Walker growled at him. "Go man."

Buckethead replied when ordered to report by Walker. "Hey Major, I copied down the stinking plate number of the fucking car the uther pricks drove off in, sir. It was a late model Buick Regal, dark blue with a rag top. A two door and the plate number was Sam, Foxtrot, One, Seven, Hotel and the vehicle had three occupants in the damn thing, sir. When the car left the parking lot, it turned down Flagler Street, and I took it for granted they were heading right for I-95, to get out of the area as fast as they could drive off, sir."

Major Peterson immediately offered to Buckethead. "That was a good report sir. Will you excuse me for a moment while I take care of the ones who escaped our setup, sir?"

"Yeah sure, knock your stinking socks off man." Bucket replied to the Police Commander.

Major Peterson gave the Bucket a queer look as he keyed the radio receiver resting on his shoulder, and Buckethead and Walker listened in on his conversation. "To all units working on special assignment Seven, Five this is important. We have a vehicle obviously heading southbound on I-95. I'm ordering an APB (All Points Bulletin) to be on the lookout for a late model dark blue two door Buick Regal with a cloth top. The license plate number reads as follows, Sam, Foxtrot, One, Seven Hotel. The wanted vehicle will have three male occupants and they're to be approached as extremely dangerous. It's believed they are armed and desperate. They're suspected terrorists. Command, alert any Highway Patrol cars to be on the lookout for this vehicle. That is all." The Major ended his alert and then he looked at Walker again.

"That's handled now Major, one thing I wanna warn you of sir. If you send any of your people into the zone, they're to be dressed as civilians. I don't want your people dressed in uniforms that might alert the stinking terrorists on us, sir." Walker growled at the officer.

"That places me in the same worry, Captain Walker. If my people are going into what you called the zone, how will your people know the difference between my Officers and the terrorists once you go after them, Captain?" The concerned police officer asked Walker.

"It looks like your people are gonna hafta take their chances in the field just like my people will hafta do, sir. If it's that big a concern to you then have your people get out of the danger zone when we move in for the stinking kill, sir. I'll notify you well in advance of every move we make, before we make it, Major. So you and the rest of your people will know what we're up to at all times in the field, sir. Or you people can just stay the hell outta the fucking way, and let us do our act like we're trained for, sir. It's that simple, Major Peterson Sir." Walker again growled at the officer, upset over having to explain everything he was going to do to the police officer.

"Captain Walker, I'd wish you'd remember we're both on the same side here, sir."

"I understand that Major Peterson, but I wish you'd understand this mess is being handled in a military response, and I'm in Command of this fucking operation, sir. I'm not usta having to explain my actions to any stinking civilian, even though you're a Police Officer I still classify you and your people as civilians, sir. Major, I have a group of flaming assholes who are hell bent on hurting civilians of this country, my country Major. And, I intend to put a stop their stinking actions in any fashion I have to employ, sir. One more point I hafta make and you hafta understand, sir. These assholes in there have one of my people as their fucking hostage, sir. That's enuf reason for me and any uther soldier in the Armed Forces to want these fucking people's asses hanging on their damn door, Major Peterson Sir.

"Look Major, I can only warn you in advance of our actions against the terrorists, and your people are gonna hafta give way so we don't gotta worry about running into another armed person running around in there, sir. I'm warning you in no uncertain terms Major Peterson, and you hafta warn the rest of your people as well, sir. If we come across any armed person in the field, we're not gonna have the time or luxury to find out if that person's a threat or not against us, sir. We're going in there hunting for bear, and anyone outta fucking place or armed will hafta take their stinking chances, if they intend to be part of this damn action, sir. This is the best I can possibly offer you and your people, sir." Captain Walker stopped speaking and he put his famous fuck you look on his face, as he waited to hear the officer's reply to his last words of warning to the officer and the rest of his people.

"Captain Walker, I understand what you're saying sir, and I understand you're in Command of this operation and my people are here to serve as the backup for your troops, sir. I'll have my people work with you on this one, and I'll even allow you to place my people where you want them, and they'll do the best for your orders, sir." The Police Officer Commander offered.

"I'm pleased we understand each uther, Major Peterson. When and if I have any need of your people, I'll make contact with you. At this time Major, I want your Officers offa the hotel property and allow my people to handle the terrorists. I guess you betta follow my Commander's orders, and if anyone gets by us in there, your people will hafta handle them on the outside, sir."

"I have my people fanning out and surrounding the damn hotel as we speak, Captain Walker Sir. I'm scheduled to have over one hundred Officers dispersed out in the field, along with another twenty Officers from the elite SWAT teams we employ, sir. We'll stay off the hotel property and out of your way until advised to do otherwise by you, sir." Major Peterson sort of nodded slightly towards the young military officer.

"Thanks again Major, look sir, I gotta get back to my people and get them hoping, sir. The longer we wait to get at the terrorists, the more chance they might kill their hostage, sir."

"Yes Captain Walker and like you sir, I have to get back to my people and make certain they understand their orders, sir. I'll have a select group of Officers enter the building dressed as civilians, and they'll start getting the renters out of the building in an orderly manner from the first and second floors of the stricture, sir. These Officers will have strict orders to stay off the third floor. That way you won't have to worry about coming across any of my Officers and someone makes a mistake, Captain." With that said, Major Peterson saluted the military officer, and then he walked away from Walker and his people. Even though the Major did not let on, the police officer noticed the one person in Walker's group who looked rather uncomfortable holding his weapon. Major Peterson felt this man was a civilian and for some reason, he was mixed up with the elite soldiers packing up in order to hit the terrorists in the hotel.

When the officer was out of the picture, Walker turned to his people and gave out orders. "Okay, listen up you guys because this is how we're gonna handle this shit. Bucket, I want you to take the Neck and find the rooms the uther shits are held up in. Once you find the pricks you'll keep their rooms under observation, and if they try and come out of the rooms for any reason, waste them on the fucking spot. I don't want you guys playing around with these lousy pricks. They're too dangerous to play any games with. Ice pack (kill) the lot of them, the uther fools don't have Raz so they're dead. I'm gonna take the Mutt and the uther shit and we're gonna get Raz out alive. You people take off the moment you check your weapons. Hey guys, keep an eye out for any cops, you know somewhere we're gonna cross some of them pricks, and I don't need any shootout happening between friends on this one. Take off as soon as possible."

Walker stared at Buckethead until he went into action. Bucket went to where he had his weapon leaning against Ramirez's SUV and he checked the chamber to make certain a round was ready to go, and then he checked his pocket for extra clips for his M-16. When he was satisfied, he turned to Walker and gave him a nod. The Neck also checked his weapon, and then he fell in behind Buckethead, and they both headed for the Best Western Hotel property.

"Great man, now we can be on a stinking episode of cops." Buckethead grumbled as he waited for the Neck to catch up with him, and then they headed off to follow out their orders.

Once the two soldiers left them, Walker, the Mutt and Toby headed for their weapons. The Mutt checked out the singer's weapon for him, and then he handed it over to the civilian with a warning at the same time. "Hey man, the fucking thing's loaded and ready for bear, so don't go shooting yourself in the stinking foot, asshole. And, you betta not go and shoot us either man, or I'm gonna spray ya and leave ya ass right where it falls in there, buddy."

Walker cut in and growled. "Mutt he's fucking helping us so get offa his stinking ass will ya, man. Betta yet, I want you to keep a close eye on his stinking ass. You asses are gonna keep an eye on the terrorists in the room without Raz. I'll cover the room with the uther assholes and Raz. I don't know how the hell we're gonna get her the hell outta the fricking room in one stinking piece though. I guess I'll hafta figure that one out once we go active against this friggin group of assholes in there, man."

"Hey Walker, you know they're gonna out number us four to one, man." The Mutt offered as he turned and looked at the hotel resting a half a block away from where he was standing.

"Hey pal if their numbers make ya fucking nervous, like I told you before, don't count them man. With our training, four to one is good fucking odds for us to go up against if you were to ask me, buddy. The only weak link we have in our chain is this civilian asshole we have working with us, man. That's why I want you to keep a close eye on his stinking ass in there, buddy. The way Raz feels about the dopey asshole, she's labile to throw a stinking conniption fit if anything happens to him when we go against the damn terrorists." Walker gave Lieutenant Frank Hall the look, informing him he was ready to move out and then he turned to the civilian.

"Hey man, are you friggin ready to do this fucking thing with us pal? There's no backing out now for your ass, man."

"I guess I'm ready as I'll ever be, Robert." He replied to the angry looking military officer.

"That's not fucking good enuf for my stinking ass, and never allow good enuf to be good enuf, man. I gotta know if your mind and heart is in this fucking thing, man. If it ain't, you're not gonna be part of this fucking thing when it goes down, buster." Walker's stare sharpened as he openly glared at the country singer now.

Buckethead and the Neck rushed over to the Best Western Hotel, and when they entered the property, the Neck noticed a police officer with an M-16 and waved to him. The officer moved towards the soldiers and nodded towards the Neck. Bucket offered the Miami cop.

"Hey man, we gotta speak to the desk clerk in there, and we want you to follow us in so we don't scare the living crap outta the little dude, sir. We need his fucking help for a few moments, man."

"Sure thing sir, do you want me to lead or do you want to lead the way, sir." The concerned looking officer replied as he immediately returned Bucket's smile with one of his own.

"I'll do the leading here man, its just I don't want the dopey dude to drop fucking dead when we go walking in there armed like we are, buddy." Buckethead flashed one of his quick smiles.

"That sounds like a good idea soldier." The officer allowed Bucket to step before him.

The three men entered the lobby like they were ready to kill everyone they looked at. The stunned clerk looked like he was going to take off in a dead run until the officer spoke to him. "Calm down son, we have an emergency and we need your help, sir. These men to my left are American soldiers, and they're here to ask you a few questions which you're instructed to answer as quickly as they are asked of you, sir. Once they're finished I'll take over, and you'll have to work with me until this situation is over with, sir."

The still stunned desk clerk turned his attention to Buckethead, and then he waited for his to speak so he knew what he wanted from him.

"Hey pal, about an hour and a half ago you checked in a number of fucking people into this stinking dump. Half of them went to rooms on that side of this friggin rat nest, fella." Buckethead pointed towards the side of the building facing the road where Walker parked his SUV, and then he added to his words for the still scared hotel clerk. "I know what rooms them slugs are in man, what I need to know from you is? What are the fucking rooms the uther damn slugs took in here man?"

"It's against hotel policy to give out any room numbers to anyone, especially someone with a rifle in his hands, sir." The clerk offered rather cautiously to the huge man glaring right at him.

The officer spoke again. "Look, this is a national emergency pertaining to the Homeland Defense Order and it supersedes hotel policy, sir. What rooms are the other people renting, sir?"

The clerk looked from Buckethead to the police officer and then back to Buckethead and then he looked at his sign in book and replied. "The other group is renting rooms One, Three, Five, E and One, Three, Nine, E. The rooms are on the east side of the second wing. They're across from the elevator there, sir." The clerk pointed to the stainless-steel set of door for the elevators.

"Thanks, a fucking lot pal, that's all I needed to know from your ass, man. Hey Officer he's all yours to deal with now sir. I take it you're gonna start getting the damn civilians from the first and second floors out of this stinking dump, sir."

"That's the reason why I accompanied you and the other soldier into the hotel, sir. I was ordered to start moving the civilians out of the hotel as quietly and quickly as possible, soldier." The police officer replied and he did not offer his name to the huge soldier, and then he watched him and the second large soldier quickly head over to the bank of elevators.

The Neck was stride for stride with Buckethead, and he asked him as they stopped right before the elevator doors. "Hey Bucket, how the hell do you wanna handle this stinking mess, man?"

"We're gonna take this damn thing up to the third floor, and then we're gonna get out and find a broom closet where we can hide in and keep an eye on the two rooms at the same time, man. If any of the fucking slugs come outta their damn rooms for any reason, we're gonna send them on their way to Paradise, that's how we're gonna handle it man. You heard Walker's orders these, assholes are nothing but shit to us, man. They ain't got Raz so we can take them out at our leisure man." Buckethead replied to his fellow soldier as he pressed the button for the elevator.

Once Buckethead and Neck disappeared inside the hotel, Walker, Mutt and the country singer went in action. Walker led the way as the three of them headed for the west side of the hotel structure. The excited and angry Captain went to the same door Buckethead used when he came out of the building half an hour ago, and the three of them entered the building carrying their weapons held at the ready. When Walker entered the building, he ran into a pretty young woman getting ice for her room. The moment the woman saw Walker and the Mutt, and they were carrying automatic weapons she dropped the ice bucket and ran for her room screaming. The Mutt moved up to Walker's side and offered him.

"You see man, I was right about you. I told you you gotta do something about your fucking puss, Walker. You scared the living shit right outta that pretty poor little chick, man."

Captain Robert Walker stopped moving forward for a brief second to give the Mutt the look that informed him he better stop screwing around or else. The Mutt stared at Walker for a moment then he smiled, forcing Walker to shake his head at him.

The singer noticed the harsh look and he commented. "You look awful pissed off, Robert."

"Pissed off man." Walker nearly roared at the singer, and then continued with his growl. "Look fella, this is gonna be like getting seven shares of shit in a one shit suitcase. So you betta pay strict attention to all my friggin orders, and if you don't happen to hear one of my orders, then you betta be able to read my fucking mind, because I won't repeat an order a second time. If I see you outta place, I'm gonna put a cap in your ass and save the terrorists ammunition. Don't try and be funny around here, you're nuthin but a stinking civilian, buster. Shit man, I shoulda had my stinking head examined for allowing you to tag along on this damn mission with us in the first place, pal. Wait until I get my fricking hands on Raz's purdy little ass for hooking up with you from the start, man."

The singer did not know how to respond to Walker's angry growl at him, and only when Walker flashed him a smile did the singer understand he was only busting his horns on him.

The smile gave the Mutt the courage to pipe up to the singer. "Hey man, in case you don't know this, Walker was born pissed off, and once he shit on his neighbor's lawn because the neighbor's dog crapped on his lawn. He's meaner than a gut shot Grizzly. Pissed off, Walker was so mean as a child his mother was forced to feed him with a stinking sling shot, and his father went down to the zoo and slugged the stork square in the chops for delivering him to his family. Pissed off huh man? You don't know what the fucking word pissed off really means until you see Walker in fucking action against any of his enemy, buster."

"Stop beating your fucking gums and pay attention to what the fuck we're doing here for once in your wasted life, stupid. We got ourselves one helluva stinking mess on our damn hands, and we're gonna hafta be betta than our best if we wanna get Raz the fuck out of this one in one fucking piece, buster. Pay attention and stop screwing around will ya buddy." Walker gave the Mutt another quick smile to show him he was not really pissed off at him.

"We, hey pal can you define we for me a little betta, man? I don't think I like the stinking word we on this one, man." The Mutt replied as he returned Walker's smile with one of his own.

"You just love displaying that damn fifth grade friggin education of yours, don't ya man? Stop screwing around on this one and get fucking read, we hafta stop these damn slugs and get Raz the hell away from them, buddy." Walker growled at his lifelong friend as he held him in his angry glare while waiting for his reply.

When no reply came, he led the way towards the staircase with the Mutt and the singer following him. As they struggled up the stairs, Walker bitched at the Mutt. "Hey birdbrain, before you ask me, we're taking the stinking stairs because I wanna come out on the floor carefully. If we took the damn elevator, we coulda come out on the floor, and in case the head rat stationed one of his stinking people in the hallway and he spotted us with these damn weapons. We coulda found ourselves in one helluva firefight before we were able to set up for it, buddy. This way we'll be setup for anything we happen to plow into up there, man."

"Hey Walker, you ain't gotta explain anything to me man. All you gotta do is point me in the right direction of anyone you want splattered, and then sit back and watch me do my act." The Mutt replied without missing a step as the three of them continued to charge up the stairs.

Walker was the first one to reach the third floor landing, and he pulled up and waited for the Mutt and Toby to catch up with him, while he was standing on the stairwell side of the fire proof metal door leading onto the floor the terrorists were positioned on. Once they were on the landing, the Captain started to issue orders to the others. "Mutt, you take the civilian puke with you and you two stakes out the second fucking room with the uther shits who don't have Raz are hold up. I'll wait until I know you're set by the stinking room, and then I'll go into action against the uther pricks in here, man."

"How the fuck are you gonna be able to handle that group of flaming assholes who got Raz as their prisoner all by your fucking self, man? Look Walker, far be it for me to try and tell you how to setup a stinking hot enter into a compromised room, buddy. But I gotta tell you this man, I think all three of us should stick together and concentrate our efforts against the assholes that have Raz as their stinking hostage, buddy. Before you blow up at me man, hear me out first Walker. I say all three of us should hit the damn room and get Raz outta there safely first, and then we can turn our attention against the uther group of assholes and take them out without so much pressure being placed on our damn shoulders to be perfect on our attack. We can always arm Raz with the singer's stinking weapon, and then she can help us do in the uther pricks. I'm sure she's gonna want some revenge for these assholes manhandling her like they're doing since they got her." The Mutt stopped speaking and waited to hear what he thought of his last words.

He stared at his lifelong friend for a second and then he shook his head as he replied to his Lieutenant. "You know something man, I think you're right on this one, buddy. We betta stick together and free Raz first from these asses. Once we have her, we can then step back and allow the police to handle the uther dumb shits, and if the police wanna take them prisoners, they can for all I care, man. You know if we go in there after them, there ain't gonna be one of the little scumbags left alive to question, buddy."

"Hey man I'm always fucking right, it's just you don't listen to me as much as you really should most of the time, man. I've been in this long enuf to know what the fuck I'm talking bout, buddy." The Mutt remarked smartly along with a smirk plastered on his lips, relieved his Commander was starting to see things the way he wanted him to, and he was not reacting with just anger against the fools who had Raz as their hostage inside the apartment.

"Hey man just because I happened to agree with you on this one buddy, don't let it go to your stinking head on ya, asshole. Let's get a move on it Raz is waiting for our stinking help, friend." He fired at the grinning Mutt, and then he laughed at him.

The Mutt leaned up against the wall and Walker went over to the heavy fire door and cracked it open just enough to see onto the landing and down the hallway where he knew the apartment the terrorists were held up in was. He was pleasantly surprised the leader of the terrorists did not have the smarts and take the precaution to leave one of his people standing guard outside in the hallway to cut off any possible attack aimed against them inside the room. He pulled his head inside the door and then leaned against the wall as he shook out a Marboro cigarette from the pack, and popped it in his mouth and lit it. He blew out the smoke over his head and then he offered to the others with him. "You ain't gonna believe this stinking shit for a stinking second buddy, but the leading dumb shit of these assholes didn't leave a stinking spotter on guard out in the damn hallway to protect his ass inside the room, man."

The Mutt grabbed the cigarette from Walker's mouth and took a good pull from it, before handing it back to him and then he replied to his Captain. "Hey man I guess they don't believe we're on to them yet man. I don't know about you buddy, but I'm taking this as a stinking break for our side, and Heaven knows we can use all the stinking breaks we can possibly get on this one, Walker. I'm betting the fricking head cheese of this group of stinking terrorists with Raz, believes we were killed back on the stinking Island by the asshole ordered to do us in. So he has no fear about us trailing them up to this dump and attacking them and stopping their attack on the Terminal and getting Raz alive from them, Homes."

CHAPTER THIRTY

Even as the Mutt was saying the words, General Kalantari remembered leaving Captain Saeed Mahebian behind to dispatch the two men who were with this hostage he was holding. He turned and looked at the pretty American female and noticed she seemed strangely comfortable like she was no longer in any fear he was going to kill her. With a quick hand signal, the Vulture called Major Fereshteh Mansouri to his side, and then led her away from the other two Persian fighters and the hostage in the room, and then he whispered so only she could hear his words.

"Major Mansouri, I have a feeling all is not right with our operation we plan against the hated American infidels of this evil land. Look at the filthy pig sitting there woman, she seems like she is with knowledge someone is coming to rescue her. I have not heard from that lowly camel's ass I left behind to kill her two male friends on that cursed Island we landed on in the United States. I have an overpowering fear the two men were able to kill our foolish Captain, and they might have been able to follow us all the way here. Looking at this American female pig, I am beginning to believe she is military trained, and that makes the two with her military trained. I don't like the cursed feeling I'm suffering through for one moment, woman."

"What do you suggest we do about this troubling feeling you're experiencing, General Kalantari? We can always kill her and leave this foul room before her cursed friends find and trap us here, sir." Major Mansouri asked the Vulture as she stared him in his eyes.

"I don't know what to do about my troubling concerns, woman. I fear my worries might make me act foolishly, woman. Everything so far with our operation has gone without many problems, except for our stumbling over this foul woman and her two infidel friends on that miserable Island. I don't want to commit a foolish mistake at this stage of our mission, just because I truly don't like the way this cursed American female pig is acting all of a sudden on us, woman."

"If the lowly woman is causing you such concern, why not allow me to kill her, so at least she is off your troubled mind, General Kalantari Sir." Major Mansouri requested of the Vulture.

"No, no woman, I believe that would be a very foolish move on our part to kill that lowly woman for the time being." The Vulture replied as he cast a quick glance at the seated and smug looking Ramirez. Then he added to his words of worry to his female Major. "No, if my fears are founded, I believe we might have need of her as a hostage to bargain with, if her two cursed friends are still alive and they're after us, woman. No, allow things to remain as they are for the moment, Major. I hate the foul way that cursed woman is sitting and staring at us, like she knows something that's going to be most harmful to us."

"Well I shall correct that problem at once for us, General Kalantari Sir." With that uttered, Major Mansouri walked over to the couch where Ramirez was tied and seated, and she looked at the American Sergeant with sheer hatred lacing her eyes. Then Major Mansouri laid a hard slap across her face as she hissed nastily at her in a controlled anger. "Foul and lowly filthy American pig, I don't know what you have to look so smug about. Your worthless life rests entirely in my hands, and if I have my way about it, you'll breathe your last breath on this foul of days." Major Mansouri laid a second hard slap across Ramirez's face as she continued to glare at her.

Ramirez had enough of being threatened by this female soldier and she returned the Persian's angry stare with one of her own, causing the Major to hiss and react against the ugly glare she gave her. Without thinking about it, Major Mansouri drew her knife and ran it against the cheek of Ramirez, opening a two inch gash on the side of her face. But to her surprise, Ramirez did not even cry out, instead she continued to stare the ugly death stare at the female Iranian Officer.

The terrible look Ramirez was still giving her, forced the female Persian Major to hiss at her again. "God cursed lowly infidel of the desert sands, I shall teach you the proper way to respect me." The irate Major raised her hand with the knife and moved against Ramirez, but this time she was stopped in her tracks when General Kalantari roared at his Major.

"Major Mansouri! I just told you I didn't want that American pig harmed in any way, but I see you chose to ignore my orders, woman. I order you to stand away from that lowly infidel, and now you're to go outside and keep an eye on the elevators leading to this foul floor. I should have stationed someone out in the hallway all along. You'll go outside and stand your post until I see fit to have you relieved of this duty, and allow you back inside this worthless room, woman. You'll leave for your duty immediately Major, but you'll arm yourself with a pistol and you will keep it out of sight, unless you're attacked by one of these foul jackals of this evil country. You will also be very pleasant to anyone you happen to see outside this miserable room, unless you deem them to be a threat against you or us, woman. Leave here at once Major!"

Major Mansouri stared at the Vulture while trying to control her raging anger. She hated being yelled at by the General, especially in front of the hostage and the other two male Persian fighter in the room with her. With her shoulders trembling with rage, the Major walked over to the table and laid her knife on it and picked up the Colt nine mm pistol, and slid it under her loose fitting blouse and placed it in her waistband and covered it with her shirt until it was out of sight. She then gave the General one last look then nodded and headed for the door as ordered. Her actions caused the General to say. "Major Mansouri, I'll have you relieved in an hour's time, I trust you'll be able to control yourself when you're allowed back in this cursed room."

Major Mansouri turned to look at her leader and she mumbled at the Vulture cautiously. "I shall wait to be relieved by your order, and then I shall return and carry out all your orders faithfully, General Kalantari Sir."

IN THE HALLWAY OF THE HOTEL

Captain Robert Walker left the metal fire door slightly ajar, and he was standing against the wall in such a way where he could keep an eye on the door to the terrorist's room. He heard and noticed the door to room Thirty, One, Seven, West open, and he shoved himself away from the wall with the power in his shoulders. His action caused the Mutt and singer to react, and they both moved their weapons into a better firing position.

The specially trained Marine Captain immediately adopted a defensive posture as he stared at the young woman who just walked out of the apartment he was watching. He kept the woman locked up in his sight as she started walking down the hallway from where they were hiding. Suddenly, the woman turned and started walking towards where they were at. He allowed the door to close then he and the others took off down the stairs as quietly and quickly as possible. The Mutt and the singer went down to the second floor landing and entered that floor and waited for Walker to catch up to them. The Captain stopped on the stairway and waited to see if the female terrorist was going to enter the stairwell and check it out. He breathed when he waited long enough and realized she was not going to enter the stairwell. He realized she was the spotter for the other terrorists held up with Ramirez in the room.

He nearly jumped down the steps and entered the second floor and found the Mutt and Toby waiting for him. He walked over to them and warned the Mutt in a disgusted tone. "Well man that makes it so much harder for us to get at the fucking room, dammit. They stationed one of the lousy shits in the hallway on the floor. A chick at that man, we hafta think of a way to get her the hell outta the way, so we can get inside the fucking room and free Raz."

Without thinking about it Toby offered. "I can do it for you Robert."

Walker cocked his head to the side and then he stared at the civilian singer before he growled at him. "You can do it for me huh buster? What the fuck can you do for me, man? Look buddy, I admire your sand, but you gotta remember we're dealing with evidently highly trained group of Muslim terrorists, and they're just waiting for someone to try something against them. So they can prove to us how dedicated they are to their fucking cause and want to die for that cause, stupid. That damn bitch out in the fucking hallway will cut you up and eat ya ass for breakfast before you know what the fuck's happening to ya, man."

"No Walker, listen I can do it for you sir. Look Robert, none of the terrorists saw me or even know me, so they don't even know I exist and am working with you. Besides Walker, someone has to approach and get her out of the way so you can do whatever you're going to do to get your girlfriend away from the terrorists safely. Since they never saw me, and I don't look anything like a soldier…"

"You can say that again my friend." The Mutt snarled at the singer as he glared at him.

Toby ignored the Mutt's nasty remark as he continued with his words to the young Marine Captain. "I should be able to walk up to that woman and catch her off guard, Walker."

"What the fuck are you gonna do once you're standing by her stinking side, man? Fucking sing to her stinking ass or something, dopey." Walker snapped at the country singer.

"Funny Walker, you're not giving me a chance here, let me finish with what I want to do before you jump down my throat. Look Robert, I've been hanging around you people long enough to see how you people tick and work together. Besides, I have some hand to hand training in my background, and once I have her off guard I can slug her in the jaw and then drag her over to the stairwell, and you can secure her in any fashion you have to, in order to get her out of the way until we have your girlfriend away from them. Robert, I'm the only one who might stand a good chance of getting anywhere near her before she can alert the rest of the terrorists inside the room. I can do this for you, I swear Robert."

He stared at the singer for a few moments before replying to his offer. "I have to agree with your fucking logic, you're making a helluva lotta sense to my ass, man. Look motherfucker, if you can pull this off,

I'll get you so stinking drunk it'll take you a fucking week to sober up, but if you fail, I'll put a cap in your ass if your actions cost the life of Raz. You got that man?"

"Hey Walker, you're not gonna trust the life of Raz to this stinking civilian puke here are ya man? Look at him he's shaking like a fucking French soldier on the battlefield, Walker. I'll get that bitch outta the stinking way myself, slick as snot. At least we'll be sending a true soldier out to do a soldier's fucking job, instead of sending this fucking civilian to do our job and screw things up on us, buddy. This stinking civilian puke doesn't know what the fuck he's doing or even talking about. He doesn't even know which end of the fucking weapon the frigging bullet comes outta, Walker. He shouldn't be standing wit us while we're discussing a military action, let alone trying to be an active part in it with us, buddy. He's nuthin but warmed over shit in my eyes, man." The Mutt growled as he stepped in front of the singer and stared at Walker.

Walker knew where the Mutt was coming from as he replied at the angry soldier. "Look man, you wouldn't get within fifty feet of that bitch before she's firing at your ass. Remember she saw you and me and knows what we look like. If you step one fricking foot out on that fucking floor, all hell will break loose. Look friend, after thinking about this slug's words, I hafta agree with him. Out of the three of us he's the only turd who might be able to get close enuf to that bitch to get the jump on her." He smiled again at the Mutt.

After seeing the stern but smiling look on Walker's face, the Mutt knew he made up his mind about using the civilian on this operation, and anything he could offer to the Captain would be a waste of time on his part. But he did offer Walker cautiously before he got off the civilian's back. "Okay man, I see your stinking puss and I guess the civilian has the front door for this one, man. But one thing I gotta know before I put in wit this crazy ass fucking deal, man. How the fuck is this civilian puke gonna pull this thing off without alarming the other pukes in the room?"

"That's a good fucking question you just asked Mutt, and I'm gonna find out what the fuck he has on his stinking mind, before I give him the green light to approach this friggin foreign bitch." He replied as he turned his attention back to the singer and nearly barked his words at him this time. "Okay pal, as of this moment you have my full fucking attention. What the fuck do you have in mind to get at that bitch standing guard in the hallway, buddy? I betta warn you pal, if I don't like what you have in mind, you're not gonna go out and fuck this damn thing up on us, man. If you can't hack it, don't step up to the plate and take a swing at the ball, man. If you can't do it then we're gonna make a hot entry on the damn room and Raz will hafta take her fucking chances of making it through the attack alive when we hit them."

Toby started to speak the moment Walker allowed him to. "Robert, I can go up the other staircase and come out on the third floor and make it look like I'm looking for the room I rented in the hotel. The way I look and am dressed, there's no way she can possibly think…"

"Yeah man you look like an unmade fucking bed, stupid." The Mutt snapped at the singer.

"Knock it off will ya, we gotta hear what the dopey fuck has on his mind, stupid!" Walker snarled at the Mutt as he gave him the look that warned him he was working on his nerves.

Toby turned and gave the Mutt a nasty look before he continued his words. "I'll look like I'm confused and I'll walk up to her like I want to ask her a question. I'll start a conversation with her and when I see my chance, I'll punch her in the face and hopefully knock her out cold with one punch. Once she's down I'll drag her over to the stairwell and you can take charge of her. Once she's out of the way, you and Mutt can do whatever you need to do to get inside the room and free Ramirez, and then take out the other terrorists in the room."

"That seems simple enuf and a simple action has a betta chance of success, mister." Walker offered as he started looking for a second stairwell leading up to the third floor. He spotted it on the other end of the floor and he and the other two started walking for it.

As they walked, the singer asked the Mutt for a cigarette.

"What the hell for, you don't fucking smoke buddy. Look pal, I gotta be honest wit you man. I don't like the fact you're working with us, man. Step back and let me do my stinking act like I was trained to do, buddy. At least we'll know we'll get Raz the hell outta there alive, man." The Mutt fired back at the singer while not trying to hide his anger in the least from him over having the civilian working with them on this military mission.

"Because I'm going to use it as a prop so I can get the drop on the woman in the hallway, Mutt. I'll use the excuse I need a light and I'll start a conversation with her until I can get the drop on her and do her in." He offered to the Mutt while trying to calm him down over his offer to help the two soldiers rescue Sergeant Dorothy Ramirez from the terrorists.

"A fucking prop? What the hell do you think you're going out on, buddy? On one of your fucking shows, man? You see what I mean Walker this fucking civilian thinks this stinking action is a damn game, man." The Mutt gave a look that informed the singer he though that was a good idea.

Toby turned to Walker just as they reached the other stairwell and he offered. "Hey Robert, give me the keys to your car please. I don't only want a cigarette in my hand, but I want a key so it looks like I'm looking for my room on the third floor."

"I like the way you're think here man. If I didn't know betta, I'd swear I was speaking to a fellow soldier who knew what the fuck he was doing on a mission. Here's my keys man."

The singer pulled the key to the car off the ring because it looked most like a hotel room key. He had no idea the hotel used a credit card to open the door to the room though. Once he had the key locked in his hand, he turned and went to open the door, but Walker stopped him by saying.

"Hey man don't go yet, you gotta give us some time to get to the uther stairwell and up to the third floor of this dump again. I wanna be set in position to lend you a hand if things go sour on ya ass. Check your watch and give us a minute to get back in position then you head up the stairs. I'll keep a close eye on the lousy bitch and if I see you're heading for any trouble, we'll react and hopefully save your stinking life for ya, man." He gave the singer a quick smile.

"Thanks a lot, I'd really appreciate it if you can keep me from being killed, Robert."

"No sweat man, we're going on zero seconds, remember give us the sixty seconds to get set in place. Then you set off for your part of this damn mission, we'll protect you the best we can from the uther stairwell, buddy. Good luck man. A word of warning though, if this thing breaks down and the Mutt and I are forced to come out of the hallway to help ya, we're coming out firing hot and heavy, and we're gonna continue on and hit the apartment at the same time. So if we hafta act I want you to drop down to the stinking floor and stay there and keep your head low, until we tell you what to do next man. Don't try and be a fucking hero out there, get down and stay outta the fucking way until we finish our stinking act, if we're forced to help you out, Toby." Walker offered his hand to the singer and they shook.

The Mutt also offered the civilian his hand and slapped him on the back and gave him a quick smile. Walker and the Mutt then took off and headed for the other stairwell. Toby watched them until they disappeared and then he stared counting down the seconds until he went in action.

Walker and the Mutt took two steps at a time to be set in position before the civilian country singer started his act. They were out of breath as Walker reached the door leading to the third floor. Cautiously he cracked the fire door open enough so he could look onto the floor, he spotted the female terrorist and he was amazed at what he saw.

Major Fereshtch Mansouri was standing in the hallway about ten feet away from the door leading to the room the terrorists were holding Raz in, and she actually looked like she was bored to death, and also looked like she was not on full alert. He then checked his watch and noticed he still had seven seconds left before the singer started up the other stairwell. He looked at the Mutt and then he ordered him. "Get in touch with Buckethead and let him know what the fuck we're up to here, buddy. Tell him he has the green light to take out his uther fucking targets the moment he wants to act against them, man."

The Mutt nodded at Walker as he keyed his mike. Walker went back to looking at the female terrorist stationed in the hallway just in case the singer started for his mission before he was supposed to move out. "Hey Bucket, this is the Mutt, reply man."

"Go Mutt! Whatdaya got going down man?" The Bucket replied in his mike.

"We're hot and on the move and as of this moment you have the green to splash your fucking targets at will, Bucket. Good luck and do them in for us, man. Be safe buddy."

"I read you loud and clear Mutt, will splash our targets. Consider them out of the picture. Out."

"Out!" The Mutt replied and then he looked at Walker and gave him the thumb's up.

He returned the nod and turned his attention to the hallway and terrorist on station there. He was looking for the first sign of the singer coming out on the floor. He could just see the other stairwell door from his present position. Every muscle in his taught body was on full alert as he waited to go into action against the terrorists.

Right to the second, Toby opened the door to the landing and stepped out on the floor. The instant he was on the floor, the female terrorist went on full alert and she cautiously moved away from the wall and locked her eyes on the stranger, as he checked the number on the first apartment door he looked at. Walker smiled because the singer looked so awkward and out of place and non-threatening as he fumbled around with his key, cigarette and trying to walk at the same time as he checked the second door number and looked at the key in his hand.

The Mutt moved over to Walker's side and he was looking out the crack in the door and he offered to Walker. "Hey man do you really think he knows what the fuck he's doing out there?"

"I know you don't stupid." Walker fired back at his lifelong friend.

"Funny man, with ten thousand fucking comedians outta work, you're trying to be one man."

Major Fereshteh Mansouri went on alert the moment she noticed the fire door leading to the third floor open. When he stepped out of the doorway she kept her eyes glued on the tall stranger, but when she spotted him looking at the numbers printed on the doors to the rooms, she cautiously let down her guard a little. Mainly because she did not want to cause the stranger any undue alarm by looking like she was going to attack him, and also because she deemed he was just another American fool renting one of the rooms at the hotel. Nevertheless, the Persian female Officer kept her eyes locked on the tall and good looking stranger, and when their eyes met, the man gave her a quick smile and a slight nod of his head.

Major Mansoui returned the stranger's smile and she allowed herself to relax even more. Something about the stranger was almost soothing to her. He was young and good looking, and his smile was real and aimed at her. The terrorist watched as the man continued to check the number printed on the door to a room three doors away from hers, and then he checked a key he held in his hand and shook his head no.

The singer was acting like he was a little tipsy as he smiled at the woman in the hallway for a second time. Then he stopped in the hallway and placed the unlit cigarette in his mouth and went fishing around in his pockets like he was looking for his lighter.

Walker smiled as he watched the singer as he was pulling off his act like he was really what he was trying to act like. He jabbed the Mutt in the ribs as he mumbled at him proudly. "Man, Mutt this fucking guy's good, look at the stinking bitch, she's even smiling at the dopey bastard."

Toby moved over to the next door and checked the number, now he was standing less than twenty feet away from the terrorist. He was still acting like he was looking for a match or lighter for his cigarette. He puffed on the unlit smoke to make his act look more convincing.

Major Fereshteh Mansouri checked her pockets for anything that might light the stranger's cigarette. She was certain in her mind the stranger was going to ask her for a light, if and when he finally walked up to her, unless he found his apartment or a match for his cigarette first. Again, she smiled at the young singer when their eyes locked together another time, and she nodded kindly back at him again also.

The friendliness emitting from the terrorist gave him the power and confidence to walk up to her and grumbled. "Ma'am, you wouldn't happen to have a light on you please? I can't seem to find my lighter or my apartment. My friends dropped me off at this hotel and I'm afraid I might have had a little too much to drink, and my girlfriend is angry and told me to go and sleep it off." He padded his pants pockets making like he was still looking for a match and he swayed slightly.

Again Major Mansour smiled at the pleasant looking stranger as she replied. "Sir, I'm afraid there are signs all over the place warning against smoking inside the building. I don't have a cigarette lighter or matches on my person, sir. What room number are you looking for perhaps I can direct you to the room you have rented in this establishment. I myself am a stranger to the area, and I'm sharing a room with my lover. But I wanted a breath of fresh air and came into the hallway for a little private time for myself, sir." Major Mansouri spoke almost perfect English with just a slight trace of an accent, and she was trying her best not to alarm the pleasant looking stranger in any way, shape of form.

This was the break he was looking for and when she asked him what room number, he picked up his arm and dropped the key at the same time as he replied. "The number's on my key."

Toby and Major Mansouri went for the key lying on the floor at the same time, but Toby allowed the female to pick it up and when she was going into a standing position, he violently plowed his fist in her unprotected jaw. He punched the woman with all the might he had in his body, and the blow was delivered with enough force to send the smaller and much lighter woman flying backwards, and landing hard on the floor some five feet from where he was standing.

Walker went to leave the landing, but the Mutt instantly grabbed his arm and stopped him from moving out as he warned him at the same time. "Hey man, we betta stay here in case the assholes inside the damn apartment heard the slight commotion out in the hallway. Let the dopey ass drag the stinking bitch over to us like he said he would, buddy. We can protect him much betta from in here where we're stationed, man."

Toby was on the body of the smallish woman in a flash, landing on her chest with his legs to each side of her body and before he checked on her, he smashed his fist in her face a second time. He was that excited, amped up and he wanted to make certain the female terrorist was out cold, before he tried to move her body out of the hallway. He got off her and then stood up and bent down and grabbed her by both arms and then he dragged the unconscious woman over to the hallway fire door. When he was near enough, Walker flung the door opened and he stepped out and helped the struggling singer drag the terrorist into the stairwell.

When they were behind the door the Mutt took over and he pulled Major Mansouri behind the door and moved her to the stairs leading up to the roof area. Then he proceeded to pad her body down and mumbled to Walker when he discovered the nine millimeter pistol. "Hey man, lookie at what I just found me, and new fucking toy man."

"Is that the only weapon she has on her stinking body, stupid? You betta check her out betta man, she's label to have a weapon stuffed on her anywhere, man." Walker growled at him.

"Dunno know yet, I didn't finish searching her stinking bod, man." The Mutt replied while ignoring Walker calling him stupid as he went back to checking out the Major's person. Once the Mutt was done searching her he announced to Walker. "I'm done searching the crazy bitch and she ain't got no uther stinking weapon on her, man. Whatdaya want me to do wit her?"

"Is that what you were doing to her, searching her buddy? Man stupid, I though you were trying to guess her fucking weight the way your hands were all over her stinking body, man. Too answer your last question for ya, whatdaya think I want you to do with her stinking ass, stupid? We have to secure her so she's no longer a stinking threat against us, while we do in her fucking friends and get Raz the hell away from them, man."

"I ain't got no rope so I can tie her up, Walker." The Mutt offered, knowing what Walker wanted him to do with the terrorist to get her out of the picture.

"And!" Walker snapped back hotly at the Mutt.

"And what man? You want me to do her in so she's no longer a stinking threat against us, man?" The Mutt asked making certain Walker wanted her out of the way that way.

Walker did not reply, instead he merely nodded until his eyes fell upon the face of the downed woman, and then he stared at her and waited for the Mutt to do his act.

"You fucking got it man, she's friggin history." The Mutt snapped as he moved in on the helpless woman and he took her head in both his hands. Even before the stunned singer was able to raise a protest to what the Mutt was doing, all three men heard the ugly snapping of her neck, as the Mutt gave her head a quick turn. Her body jerked violently once and then it came to a rest lying on the steps where the Mutt dropped her unconscious body. He turned the terrorist's head once more to make certain he broke her neck cleanly, and the terrible sound of bones grinding together informed them the woman was surely dead.

Walker did not react to the Mutt's action as he turned his attention back to the apartment door where the terrorists were holding his girlfriend hostage. He saw death so many times in his life that it did not affect him any longer. He was still looking out the door when the Mutt went to his side and asked him with some concern lacing his tone.

"Hey man, now that we got the chick the fuck outta the way, what are we gonna do now, man? We gotta find a way to get the door to that apartment opened, so we can get at the damn terrorists, my friend. You know if we attack the door, they'll kill Raz before we can help her."

"I know that stupid, and I think I'm gonna use the civilian once more to get the door opened for us. Look Mutt, before we jump off on this stinking thing, why don't you find out how the fuck Buckethead's working out with neutralizing the uther stinking terrorists, man."

"Sure thing Walker." The Mutt picked up his handheld radio and keyed it and barked in it. "Bucket, Mutt here, how the hell are you making out man?"

Buckethead, Sergeant Vincent Lambardo and No Neck, Sergeant Robert Abbott was too busy attacking the room with the other terrorists held up to reply to the Mutt's call. Buckethead hit the door and drove it into the apartment with his weight and power of his body, following it to the floor as No Neck followed him into the apartment while firing his weapon at anyone he picked up inside the room. Buckethead fired at a terrorist while lying on the destroy door under him. In less than a heartbeat, the action was over with four Persian terrorists lying dead on the floor, their bodies riddle with bullets.

The moment the police stationed on the other floors heard the weapons fire they immediately went in action, and they charged up the stairs leading to the third floor landing. The Neck and Buckethead walked out of the destroyed apartment, and they headed for the second room with the surviving terrorists still hiding in it. But this time they were not so lucky, because the terrorists in this room were alerted by the weapon fire, and they were armed and waiting to be attacked. Neither of the American soldiers was stupid enough to stand in front of the door, knowing the terrorists had to be alerted by now.

Buckethead stood on the right side of the door, and the Neck stood to the left side. Buckethead reached out and rammed his fist against the apartment door, and the terrorist's response was to send fifteen rounds ripping into the metal door. The Neck smiled at Buckethead and he gave him a foul look. It was at this point they heard the Mutt trying to raise them. The Neck looked at Buckethead and warned him. "Hey man, we're kinda tied up at the moment, so you might as well reply to the dopey slug and report what we're up to over here, man. You know how the fucking Mutt is and if you don't reply to his call, the fuck is gonna come here and eat the both of us a fucking live, man."

"You got that right man." Buckethead replied as he fished the small radio out of his pocket and keyed the mike and replied in it. "Yeah Mutt, Bucket here man. What's up?"

"It's about fucking time you replied, what the fuck took you so long to get back to me man?"

"We took out four terrorists in the first room slick as goose crap, and we're waiting to hit the second room and finish off the rest of the dumb shits in this section of the hotel, man."

"Did either of you shitbirds get clipped on the first attack, man? We didn't hear anything from where we're stationed, so our part of this operation is still a go for us here."

"No way Mutt, we took the fucks out before they even had a stinking chance to get their damn weapons. But the second room's gonna give us some problems, because the rotten pricks hiding in this room are alert and waiting for us. They just tried to place a round in the middle of my stinking forehead on me, Homes." Bucket reported as he looked at the holes drilled into the door by the rounds passing through it.

"Listen up stupid, take your fucking time with the dopey pricks, time's on our side over there. We just cleared the hallway of the stinking bitch guard, and we're gonna hit the apartment with Raz in it as soon as I'm finished jaw jacking wit your ass, buddy. Walker wanted you two birds to be careful with these people, and he also wants…"

Buckethead turned just as a flood of excited police officers heavily armed came charging through the door leading to the third floor near where they were waiting to attack the second apartment. Some civilians renting rooms on this floor came out of their rooms to see what was happening. A number of officers peeled off from the others and charged down the hallway, ordering any civilians to get back inside their rooms and ordered them away from the doors.

"Hey Mutt, we have an ocean of stinking blue coming at us man. Whatdaya want me to do now man?" Bucker growled into the radio as he cut the Mutt's words off in mid-sentence.

The Mutt turned and looked at Walker and the Captain grumbled back at him. "Tell the assholes to let the police handle the uther fucking terrorists for them, dammit. Then order the two asses to get their cans over to us on the double quick, so they can keep the terrorist in the uther apartment under surveillance while we hit the apartment with Raz in it, man."

The Mutt nodded at Walker, and then he relayed his orders to the other two specialized soldiers. When the Mutt finished with Buckethead and the Neck, he broke off the connection and looked at Walker again.

"Those two assholes did a helluva job Mutt. We didn't hear a fucking thing over here, so the damn terrorists in these apartments still have no idea they're under attack. Mark up another break for our side on this stinking mess. Look Mutt, I guess you betta raise Major Peterson on the damn radio, and inform the cop we're active and he betta get his people working on securing the uther side of the stinking third floor. Warn the dopey fuck we didn't move out yet, so he betta keep his people offa this area of the floor until we advise him otherwise." He growled as he now turned his attention to the scared looking civilian with him.

The Mutt worked the radio and followed Walker's last orders as the Marine Captain started to speak with the country singer standing tall and staring at the two soldiers.

"Hey buddy calm down a little man, you look like you're gonna fucking wet yourself, man. You're doing great so far and I need you to work for me again, man."

He had to swallow and then he asked Walker. "What do you want me to do this time Robert, and with my looking like I'm going to wet myself, forget it, it's too late, I did."

Walker laughed over his response, and then he began to tell him what he wanted him to do next. "Look Toby, I want you to walk up to the damn apartment door and knock on it and announce you have the hotel complimentary snacks for the assholes hold up inside the damn apartment. I'm banking on the fact they stationed the bitch in the hallway, hoping they believe the bitch gave you permission to deliver the food to them."

The Mutt was busy speaking to Major Peterson, and when he started to inform him they were about to move out against the terrorists. The Miami Police Officer replied he was aware of the last action, and his people were taking over for the soldiers on the other side of the hotel. He told the Mutt he had a number of police officers gathered on the second floor below where he and Walker were waiting, and they was foaming at the mouth to lend the two elite soldiers and one civilian a hand with the now trapped terrorists. It was clear to the Mutt that the Miami Officers were taking this possible attack on their city personally.

Toby was stunned at the orders Walker was laying on him, he did not want to get that near the armed terrorists inside the apartment. He did not know what to do, on one hand he wanted to help his friend rescue his pretty girlfriend, but on the other hand he was scared to death over what might be waiting for them on the other side of the door to the apartment, and he was not looking forward to killing someone.

"Look stupid, I can see by the stinking expression on your damn puss you're scared to death over this shit. That's good fear will stop you from doing something stupid, pal. I want you to walk over to the door and bang on it and then tell the assholes inside the room you have some fucking food for them. They're so sound asleep at the switch I'm betting the assholes will think the bitch gave you clearance to knock on the damn door. You do what I fucking tell you. But in case they might be on to us, once you knock on the door, step to the side if they decide to shoot through the door at ya, man." Walker snarled at the civilian, trying to make him find his backbone for this part of their operation.

"What happens when the terrorist opens the door? What am I to do then Walker?"

"Look man, the Mutt and myself will be standing along side ya, and when the door starts to open, I'm gonna shove you the fuck outta my way, and me and the stinking Mutt will take care of the fucking terrorists good and proper. You hit the floor and you stay there until I tell you to do utherwise, buddy."

"God Walker, I never dreamed you'd place me in a deadly situation like this man."

"Look stupid, you're the one who wanted to come along with me on this one, pal. Besides, you country people are always waving the flag around and bragging how fucking patriotic you people are. Don't tell me the first time someone pats you on the stinking back, and then asks you to place your fucking dick in a damn blender for the sake of your country, you're gonna friggin crap out on me, mister." Walker's stare sharpened harshly as he looked the singer dead in the eyes as he waited for his response.

"Okay Walker I'm going to help you, but please try and keep me alive when you attack them." He mumbled as he returned Walker's stare and then swallowed his guts and asked him a question. "Say Walker, do you have any idea how many terrorists are inside this room? I want to know what we're going up against, before I step up and help you Robert."

"Don't step up if you can't keep up, buddy. I know you never did something like this before in your wasted fucking life, pal. So I'm telling ya you got some guts, and guts are enuf man. There are three jerks hiding inside the damn room, two males and a female, but they're heavily armed and they know what the fuck they're doing with the damn weapons. Toby, you get outta my way the moment the stinking door starts to open, and hit the fucking floor and you'll be okay, man." He gave the singer a reassuring smile.

Pulling in a deep breath and holding it for a brief moment, the country singer asked his next question of the angry sounding Marine Captain. "Okay, okay I'm in with you, when do you want me to go to the door, Robert?"

Walker turned to the Mutt and asked him. "Hey stupid, are you ready to go hot against these dopey slugs in there man?"

"I was born fucking ready for any stinking action dealing wit a group of stinking terrorists, my friend. One of these days you're gonna dump the stupid and respect me the way you should, man." The Mutt replied and complained at the same time.

"That'll be the fucking day, stupid. You ready, I'm sending the jerk out there to knock on the stinking door for us, man." Walker grinned at his lifelong friend and then waited for his reply.

The Mutt cocked his head and nodded, and then he hitched his weapon up to the firing position and checked the chamber, to make certain he had a round chambered in it. This action informed Walker he was ready to begin his work and free Ramirez, or die trying.

"Hey man, I wanna thank you for doing this shit with me Mutt, you too Toby. It's my girlfriend who has her tits stuck on the damn wire, and you people are the wire cutters on this one. Once this mess is over with, I'm gonna get you all blind stinking drunk for your help on this one. I knew I could count on you for your help any time Mutt, but you Toby, you don't own me shit and here you are, standing tall with me with a weapon locked in your damn hands, and you're ready to kill someone for me and my lady. Thanks for sticking with me I couldn't fucking do this shit without you two birds helping my ass." Walker offered honestly to the two people standing alongside him and waiting to go to the gates of hell with him.

He turned his attention back to the civilian and he warned him in no uncertain words. "Okay man, it's time for you to start you stinking act for us, man. Remember pal, once the friggin door starts to open, get the fuck outta the way as fast as you can move, and then drop down to the fucking floor so you'll remain safe until we're done with these stinking fucks, buddy."

"Okay Walker, I'm heading out."

"Don't sweat it man, we're right behind you." Walker added as he opened the fire proof door and held it open so the singer, and then the Mutt could enter the floor. All three headed for the apartment with the terrorists inside, and when he stopped right before the door, the Mutt and Walker stopped and then stood up against the wall on the doorknob side. Then Walker gave him a quick nod and the singer raised his hand and knocked on the closed door.

CHAPTER ONE

Inside Apartment Three, One, Seven West, the remaining three terrorists stopped dead in their tracks and they stared at the door after hearing the knock. Major Sayah Rahimi turned and she looked the deadly Vulture in the eyes, her own eyes displayed the fear she was suffering.

The Vulture raised his finger to his lips to silence the other two terrorists and then he whispered. "Colonel Khatami, arm yourself and stay deep inside the apartment, Major Rahimi, arm yourself and stand ready to kill the person on the other side of the door. Stand ready for attack until we know if it is the cursed woman and she knocked to ask permission to go to the bathroom. I'll answer the foul door, if it's our enemy I'll immediately step aside and you'll kill them, and then we'll fight our way out of this cursed structure housing these lowly jackals. Major, if it is our hated enemy, once we killed the lowly infidels you'll kill this American pig and then we'll leave this establishment instantly."

The Vulture casually walked over to the coffee table and he picked up his nine millimeter pistol and carried it with him to the front door of the apartment, and he carefully laid it down on the side table within easy reach of his hand, and then he stood by the door and waited.

When the door did not open right away, the surprised singer turned and looked at Walker standing to his left side. Walker put a disgusted look on his face as he shook his head angrily, and then he raised his hand and made a fist and made like he was knocking on the door.

Toby nodded because he knew Walker wanted him to knock again, and he did.

Instantly from within the apartment, a voice that sounded angry at the world hissed. "Yes, what is it you want at my door?"

"Sir, I was sent from the front desk with a complimentary meal for you and your friends to enjoy. We do this for all our cliental staying at the hotel, sir. I spoke to your girlfriend out here and she took what she wanted to eat from the tray, and then she told me to knock on the door, sir." The shaking singer offered in a shaky voice.

The deeply relieved Vulture looked at Colonel Khatami and smiled at his officer, thinking it was his angry female Major trying to get a rise out of them by allowing this fool to knock on the apartment door, and scaring them half to death. The Vulture vowed he was going to take this infraction out on the hide of his Major with the lash when they returned to Iran, after they successfully destroyed their target in the United States. Letting out his breath he did not even know he was holding, General Abdol Karim Kalantari turned back to the door and reached for the doorknob and gave it a quick turn.

The Captain was staring at the doorknob and the instant he noticed it start to turn, he moved in and roughly shoved Toby out of his way, sending the singer sprawling to the floor, and the Mutt grinned when he saw him curl up in a ball and cover his head with his hands.

When Walker heard the click from the striker, informing him the latch cleared the holder, he sent his full weight against the door. The door flung opened with such force it smashed into the Vulture's face, sending him tumbling into the side table, and sent him and his weapon falling to the floor. The Mutt was right behind him as he fell into the room.

The Mutt remained standing in the doorway and when he spotted Colonel Khatami move his weapon to his shoulder to get a bead on him, he fired a short burst of five rounds smashing into the Iranian terrorist's body. Killing him instantly before the Persian Officer was able to bring his weapon up in its firing position on his body.

Walker, lying on the floor scanned the rest of the room. He spotted Ramirez sitting on the couch and when he came crashing into the room, she immediately rolled off the couch and laid out on the floor. He continued to search the room and when he picked up the female terrorists and she removed her weapon from his direction and was trying to get Ramirez locked up in her sights, he leveled his weapon at her chest and pumped six rounds ripping into her body.

Major Rahimi's body was pitched back a few feet as the tiny harbingers of death ripped into her body. The terrorist was dead before her body came to rest lying on the floor.

Walker was aware of the third person inside the room, and the instant he fired at the female terrorist, he immediately rolled over on his side in time to see the Vulture trying to right himself, and he was also struggling to reach for his pistol just out of his reach on the floor at the same time. He hissed at the Persian General in a terrifying voice. "Go for it man, but take your fucking time while reaching for that damn weapon, man. I never rush a man who wants to fucking die as bad as you obviously do, stupid."

The chilling tone the American addressed him in, froze the Vulture's hand and he turned and looked at the man warning him. His eyes registered the surprise in his eyes when he instantly recognized Walker who was up on one knee now, and he was aiming a weapon right at his chest. General Kalantari drew in a breath to settle himself down some, and then he offered to the wild looking young man who held his life in his hand. "I don't want to shoot you."

"Why the hell not motherfucker, I wanna shoot you man." Walker replied nastily as he got up on his feet and stepped out of the way, and the Mutt ran in the room and checked on the bodies of the two downed terrorists, before making his way to Ramirez who was still lying on the floor. All the while, Walker held his weapon trained on the Vulture's chest, he was ready to kill him.

The Mutt offered to Walker. "Hey man, the two idiots are deada than a fucking doorknob,"

The Vulture allowed his body to relax as he tried speaking to the enraged Walker, but all the while he was speaking to the American soldier, he was allowing his hand to slowly inch ever so slightly towards his weapon lying on the floor. "I don't know who you are and why you have chosen to stick your cursed nose into my business. But since you have disrupted my plan, all I want to do is now leave this cursed room and get out of your foul country, mister."

"Whatever you and the rest of your lousy scumbags do in my country is my stinking business, motherfucker. I'm tired of you camel jockeys trying to hurt my people all over the world." Walker snarled at the Vulture as he watched the fool reaching for his weapon on the floor. He was going to allow the man to just reach his weapon, and then he planned to cut him in half.

The Vulture tried a smile that was more a sneer at the young American, but it did nothing to soften his deadly stance against him.

The Mutt was busy untying Ramirez and when he removed the gag from her mouth, she immediately yelled at Walker in an excited tone of voice. "Kill the rotten sonofabitch because he's the damn leader of the damn terrorists. If you don't kill him, give me a weapon and get out of the way and I'll kill him myself Walker."

"So you are the boyfriend of this filthy American bitch who was enjoying our presence in this foul land. She speaks words of hatred from her heart and she would make a very good and well respected Persian woman. How did you and the one with you get away from Captain Mahebian, he was well trained and obviously you have killed him?"

"Obviously I fucking killed him, asshole." Walker snapped as he watched the jerk still reaching for his weapon.

"How did you know of my destination within your foul country, soldier? You don't mind me calling you a soldier, because that is what I believe you are soldier." The Vulture remarked just as his index finger felt the first sign of his pistol.

"I'm a fucking soldier and I easily got the drop on the asshole you left behind to kill me and my friend, asshole. How I knew where you were going and your target, your asshole crapped out on you the moment I threatened to kill his ass. He told me all about your damn plan and stinking target. He was no fun at all buster just a simple threat on his god damn life, and he talked like a fucking baby and told me everything I wanted to know. So much for fucking training, Mac."

"Don't talk to that sonofabitch, kill him Walker. He's fucking dangerous." Ramirez yelled at Walker as the Mutt held her down on the floor by placing his knee in the middle of her back, and pressing down with his full weight. The Mutt could not allow her to get up and get in Walker's way and the terrorist getting the drop on Walker and him.

"Your girlfriend is allowing her want for revenge to cloud her better judgment, Mr. Walker. Since I'm no longer a threat against the target I was sent here to destroy, why do you not allow me to walk away and leave your foul country in peace? I swear Mr. Walker if you allow me to leave in peace, I shall never place another foot within your country." The Vulture was trying to force him to lower his guard so he could reach his weapon and kill the wild looking American soldier. General Kalantari wanted nothing more in life than to kill the one who destroyed his plans. If he was the only one he killed in the United States, he would go to Paradise and kiss the feet of Allah for seeking his revenge upon the head of the man who stopped his mission.

"I don't know you so I don't fucking owe you, buster. You use my name again and I'll kill you on general principles. Motherfucker, you're like a god damn cockroach, and if you're not stepped on and destroyed good and proper, you'll come back sometime in the future and find another way to crawl into my country, and try again to kill my people." He hissed savagely at the Vulture over the barrel of his weapon while still holding it dead on his chest.

"Arrr, I'm beginning to think further words will be a waste of time on our parts, soldier. What are you going to do now American soldier? Kill an unarmed man like you're threatening to do and as your girlfriend is suggesting you do against me." The Vulture growled, displaying his anger at Walker as his fingers started to work their way around the grip of his weapon still just out of his reach, and it was stopping the Vulture from attacking Walker, as he stared at the soldier with hatred glowing in his eyes.

"Hey man, you don't hafta fucking die unarmed you know, you're friggin reaching for your fucking weapon, so go for it man and see how far you fucking get with the stinking move, pal. Come on and make your damn move man. I gotta take me a fucking leak, pal." He warned the terrorist as he continued to glare at him over the barrel of his weapon, daring the Vulture to make his move against him.

For a fleeting moment, Walkers' words made the Vulture hesitate, now he understood Walker was aware he was trying to get his weapon so he could kill him if he was only able to kill one of the American soldiers before he was killed by the other soldier in the room. Drawing in a breath, General Abdol Karim Kalantami threw caution aside, and he made a quick grab for his weapon.

Walker allowed the terrorists to wrap his fingers around his weapon and even lift it off the floor, before he let got with a nine round burst, running the barrel of his weapon along the Vulture's body, and hitting him with all nine rounds.

The Vulture's body jumped while lying on the floor as the bullets continued ripped into his body and robbed him of life. They hit him with such savagery it made his hand send his weapon flying in the air, bouncing on the floor and ended up five feet away from his body.

The Mutt, Lieutenant Frank Hall and Sergeant Dorothy Ramirez saw the Vulture grab for his weapon and Ramirez yelled at her lover. "Walkerrrrr!!!!" But her scream was drowned out from the roar as he fired his weapon and killed the threat lying on the floor by his feet.

Ramirez struggled so much that the Mutt was forced to remove his knee from the middle of her back, and she was on her feet in a flash, and she ran across the room to her lover. She crashed so hard into Walker she actually knocked him to the floor as she hugged him and she cried and kissed him at the same time. "Oh God Walker, I was so afraid I was never going to see you again this side of hell. Why the hell didn't you just kill the sonofabitch outright, and not allow him to talk to you. You don't understand how dangerous that man was, Bobby. Anything could have happened when he was talking with you."

The Mutt walked over to the Vulture and checked on him, then announced proudly to Walker and Ramirez. "Man Walker, you did him in good and proper, that's one less cockroach that's not gonna come back and haunt us later on, man. Good job my friend, but I'm afraid we're not done with our mission just yet, man. We still got another room full of stinking terrorists we hafta deal with, before we can hang it up for the fucking day man."

Walker pulled his face from Ramirez and he grumbled at his friend. "Hey man, as far as I'm fucking concerned, I got what I came for. The police can handle the uther slugs. I'm done in, and besides, I'm not letting go of this here chick for a stinking second, man."

"I can respect that man I'm sick and tired of putting my family's jewels on the line. I wonder where the two tree trunks are hiding at, Walker. They shoulda got here by now man." The Mutt complained at his lifelong friend with a smirk on his lips.

"At this moment I don't give a flying shit where they might be, man. Buckethead and the stinking Neck can take care of themselves easy enuf. Hey stupid, where the fuck is the damn singer at anyhow? I haven't seen hide nor hair of the dopey bastard since we first entered this room." Walker offered as he struggled up to his feet, and then he helped Ramirez up to hers.

"The last time I saw the little prick he was sprawled out on the stinking floor in the hallway like a scared girl. I bet he shit himself when you shoved him outta our way. I can't wait to check and see if he did, man." The Mutt mumbled happily as he walked past Walker and Ramirez and he went out of the room to check on the country western singer.

He was struggling to his feet when the Mutt got to him and gave him a hand. He was shaking like a leaf and was afraid to look inside the room for fear of what he might see. The Mutt slammed his hand down on his back as announced to the civilian with a wide grin. "Hey man we did it pal, all the stinking terrorists inside this fucking room are dead and Raz is safe and sound man. And, it's all because of the guts you displayed working with us, man. You did real good for a stinking civilian puke who didn't know what the fuck he was doing, man."

Outside, the Miami Police Officers took matters into their own hands, and the moment Walker and his group went after the terrorists in room Three, One Seven, they assaulted room Three, Two, Three. But here the police got lucky, because this group of terrorists were not so willing to die for their cause, and when the police challenged them, all four would be Persian terrorists gave up to the police without firing a shot, and they were in their custody.

Ramirez and Walker came walking out of the all but destroyed hotel room, and they smiled at the disheveled looking country western singer, then Ramirez bitched at Walker. "I can't believe you dragged that poor man on an operation like this, mister. I'm warning you Walker, if you broke him on me, you're going to go months without sex, buster."

The Mutt laughed as he bitched at Ramirez. "It's Malice in Wonderland and it's great to have you back with us where you belong, baby. But the next time don't allow yourself to get captured by any stinking slugs. You missed out on all the stinking fun we had getting them, honey."

Walker slapped sticks (forearms) with the Mutt then he turned to the singer and said to him. "Thanks man, but I'm afraid the Mutt's right, we still got some stinking terrorists alive, and we hafta deal with them before we're done. Do you still want to tag alone with us, man?"

"After what I've been through so far, you couldn't drive me away with a stick, Walker." He replied with a grin.

"Cool, then I'm gonna take Bonnie and Clod and get after the other pukes." The Mutt offered, but his words were cut off by Major Peterson as he informed the exhausted soldiers.

"Captain Walker, you don't have to worry about the other terrorists, sir. We already got them sir, we went after them the moment you people hit this room, sir. They didn't have the stomach to fight and they gave up the moment we challenged them, Captain. As of this moment sir, the building is secured and all the terrorists are accounted for one way or the other, sir. The eight terrorists on the other side of the building are dead Captain Walker. It looks like your job is done here sir. Oh, by the way Captain, we stopped the Buick on I-95 sir, and we took the three Cuban occupants in custody, that's everyone working with these terrorists sir, until we start an investigation and find out if anyone else was involved in this action, sir. The three occupants were definitely Cuban sir, and once our people find out who was fronting them from Cuba, there's going to be hell to pay for their support teams, sir."

"Who the fuck do you think were fronting them, Major?" Walker grumbled hotly as he rested his arm on Ramirez's shoulder, and then he started to lead her and the rest of his people towards the stairwell he used to attack the terrorists moments ago. All he wanted to do now was head home and see his kid, have a cold beer, and make love to his lady. Then report in to Colonel Bruce Leadbetter and inform him of how the mission went. All four young and battered people were thoroughly exhausted as they headed for Ramirez's car. The Neck and Buckethead caught up with their group in the stairwell, and they all left the hotel still carrying their weapons, and walking past a flood of police officers still wildly charging into the building.